"In its day (1953-1967), *Manhunt* magazine was highly regarded by the crime-fiction community, and drew contributions from most of its era's best-remembered authors."

—*Rap Sheet*

"Some of the best hardboiled crime fiction of the 1950s."

—Mike Ashley, "Collecting Crime"

"I'd like to stick my neck out and suggest that issue-for-issue and pound-for-pound, *Manhunt* was the best and most consistent crime mag around."

—Kevin Burton Smith, *Thrilling Detective Web Site*

"One of the finest mystery magazines ever published."

—Clark Howard, *Collected Short Stories: 1960s*

D0555676

THE BEST OF
MANHUNT

A COLLECTION OF THE BEST STORIES FROM MANHUNT MAGAZINE

Foreword by Lawrence Block

Afterword by Barry N. Malzberg

Edited and Introduction by Jeff Vorzimmer

STARK
HOUSE

Stark House Press • Eureka California
www.starkhousepress.com

THE BEST OF MANHUNT
Published by Stark House Press
1315 H Street
Eureka, CA 95501
griffinskye3@sbcglobal.net
www.starkhousepress.com

ISBN: 978-1-944520-68-7

Book design by ¡caliente!design, Austin, Texas

First Stark House Press Edition: July 2019

This book is dedicated to the incredible team that helped make it happen. That team includes Barry Malzberg, Lawrence Block, Bill Pronzini, Henry Morrison, Greg Shepard, David Rachels, Max Allan Collins, James Traylor and Rick Ollerman.

I also want to give special thanks to Ann Hoadley, who is always my first proofreader, and has put up with my working 24/7 for the last four months on this project. I also want to thank my children Zoë and Kai for bearing with me.

Table of Contents

Foreword

Lawrence Block

It was early in 1957 when I first bought a copy of *Manhunt.* I'd never seen the magazine before, but I figured I really ought to have a look at it, because the editor had just suggested I find a better ending for the story I'd sent him.

I was in my sophomore year at Antioch College, and had recently returned to the campus in Yellow Springs, Ohio, after three months as a mailroom attendant at Pines Publications in New York. I'd shared a Barrow Street apartment with two fellow students, and one Sunday afternoon in October I set up my typewriter in the kitchen and wrote a story about a young criminal who was making a living via mail fraud. *Anyone who starves in this country deserves it,* it began. I called it "You Can't Lose" and didn't even think about sending it anywhere.

Back at Antioch, I remembered the story. I also remembered a collection of short stories by Evan Hunter; I'd liked and admired them, and had noted at the time that many of them had been originally published in a magazine called *Manhunt.* I looked up the magazine in *Writer's Market,* mailed off the story, and figured it'd get me another rejection slip for my burgeoning collection.

Instead what it got me was a brief note from *Manhunt'*s editor, one Francis X. Lewis. He liked it, but wondered if I could work up a better ending for it. I don't know that he used the word *twist* or *zinger,* but that was the gist of it.

So I walked into town, and somewhere—the drugstore, I suppose—I found that month's issue of *Manhunt.* I read it cover to cover, and liked what I read. By the time I was finished I had an idea for a new ending for my story. If I remember correctly, I had my narrator invest all his ill-gotten gains in an enterprise run by someone who was clearly a cleverer con man than our hero. That worked nicely when O. Henry pulled it off in "The Man at the Top," but, well, he got there first, didn't he? By half a century or so . . .

Never mind. I sent the revised story off to Mr. Lewis, and he sent it back and said it seemed a little obvious, or predictable. He was kind enough not to mention O. Henry. I shrugged and put the story away, and that was that.

And then at the end of the spring semester I thought of another way to end the story, and when school was out I drove to Cape Cod and took a room in an attic above a barber shop in Hyannis and wrote a story a day for about two weeks. The first one was a rewrite of "You Can't Lose," with that new ending, and I sent it off to New York, and the note I got back was from an assistant, who was confident Mr. Lewis would buy the story when he returned from vacation. (There was no assistant. Scott Meredith, who was Francis X. Lewis, wrote the note. *Manhunt* had cash-flow problems that month, so this was a way to accept the story without having to pay for it right away. Welcome to the world of publishing, young fellow . . .)

A month later, I'd ditched the Cape and found a furnished room in New York and, remarkably enough, hired on as an assistant editor at Scott Meredith Literary Agency. It was my job to read manuscripts submitted by hopeful writers who paid

Foreword   3 fees to have Scott read and critique their work, and what they got for their five bucks was me. I read dozens of stories every week, almost all of them terrible, and I can't imagine a better learning experience for someone who wanted to be a writer.

A week or so in, my fellow workers began discussing *Manhunt,* which of course was secretly edited in-house. They wanted to bait me into saying something snotty about the magazine, but what I told them was that it looked as though the editor was in the process of buying a story of mine.

They thought I was full of crap, but went and checked, and there was "You Can't Lose" in the magazine's inventory. Next thing I knew, Scott's brother Sidney was standing next to my desk. Scott was out of town that week, but Sid was on hand to offer me a contract.

"Now *Manhunt* pays two cents a word," he said, "and your story's two thousand words long, so you'd get forty dollars for it. But our clients get better rates, and we can pay a hundred dollars for the story if you're our client. You can sign right here."

I signed right there.

"Now you're our client," Sid told me.

"That's great," I said. "And I'll be getting a hundred dollars for the story?"

He shook his head. "You get ninety," he said. "We get ten."

Welcome to the world of publishing, young fellow.

Was it that sale that made me a crime writer?

It certainly gave me a boost in that direction. One thing it definitely made me was a reader of *Manhunt*—and its several imitators. At the time there was a back-date magazine store on Eighth Avenue between 42nd and 43rd Streets, a big room lined with shelves and bookcases. They had a whole section of crime fiction magazines, *Manhunt* and *Trapped* and *Guilty* and *Keyhole* and *Sure-Fire* and *Two-Fisted* and, oh, I can't even remember the titles. *Manhunt* was the unquestioned leader, but the others drew the same writers and filled their pages with stories that hadn't made the cut at *Manhunt.*

I bought every issue I could get my hands on. My discretionary income was minimal, I must say. My base pay from Scott Meredith was $65 a week before taxes. (I could add a dollar for every story I read and critiqued beyond the weekly quota of forty, and I was fast, so I probably averaged $75-$85 a week in gross income.) My rent was low and I wasn't living high, and as I recall those magazines were two-for-a-quarter. I bought them, I lugged them home, and I read them.

Now you might think of this as a busman's holiday, and an unlikely choice for someone who'd spent the whole day having to read garbage. But I liked the stories in the magazines, and saturating myself in them instilled in me a deep, basic sense of what did and didn't work in a short story. On some unconscious level I suppose I synthesized what I read, and when ideas came to me, I was better equipped to work out what to do with them.

I spent the better part of a year at Scott Meredith. I'd started in August, and intended to quit when it was time to return to Antioch at the end of October. But two weeks into the job I knew I wanted to drop out of school; what I was learning in that office at 580 Fifth Avenue was of far more interest to me than what was being offered in Yellow Springs.

By the time I did give up the job, in May or June of 1958, I had sold another couple of stories to *Manhunt,* maybe eight or ten to W. W. Scott for *Trapped* and *Guilty*, and perhaps as many to the penny-a-word magazines from Pontiac Publications. I'd fielded other assignments as well—a couple of confession stories, articles for male-interest *True* and *Argosy* imitators, and whatever else came my way. (One piece for a medical story magazine began "My name is Brad Havilland. I'm forty-two years old, and I'm the best bowel surgeon in the state." I have a lot to answer for.)

Ah, *Manhunt.* Some outstanding writers got their start in its pages, and some giants in mainstream fiction—Nelson Algren, Erskine Caldwell—were persuaded to supply original stories for the publication. I was surprised, making my way through these stories again, to note how many of them I actually remembered. I read them sixty years ago, and somehow they stayed with me.

And if I had to single out one story, it would be Evan Hunter's "The Last Spin." It is, to my mind, a master class in the short story.

I think you'll enjoy it. Indeed, I think you'll enjoy what you read in the following pages.

The Story Selection
Jeff Vorzimmer

There is always a dilemma when creating an anthology of the best stories from a single source, such as by a specific author or, in this case, magazine. You quickly realize that, by the very fact of their being the best stories, they've already made appearances in other—often, numerous—anthologies, but yet must be included in any "best of" collection. That is certainly true of some of the stories we have included, especially the stories by Evan Hunter and Fletcher Flora's "The Collector Comes After Payday," which are probably the most anthologized stories in this collection. But many of the stories included here are making their first appearance in print in sixty years. Even stories the reader might have encountered previously, are worth reading again, especially in the context of other stories from *Manhunt* of the same period to get a clear historical perspective on the era and the nourish quality of the magazine itself.

We tried to be as objective as possible in the selection of the stories. Aside from the popularity of stories as measured by inclusion in previous collections, we also considered reviews, awards, input from mystery writers and appearances as the basis for television series episodes, such as Alfred Hitchcock Presents and M. Squad.

Manhunt stories have been the basis for 23 episodes of *Alfred Hitchcock Presents/Alfred Hitchcock Hour*, three episodes of *Mike Hammer*, three episodes of *M-Squad*, episodes of *Schlitz Playhouse 90*, *Celebrity Playhouse*, *Studio 57*, *State Trooper* and, more recently, three episodes of ShowTime's *Fallen Angels* series from the mid-'90s. Seven such stories are included here.

Although stories from *Manhunt* have appeared in over a hundred anthologies, there have been only two collections of stories specifically from *Manhunt*, published in 1958 and '59, edited by Scott & Sidney Meredith. The first of these anthologies, *The Best From Manhunt*, was the starting point for this collection. The first 13 stories duplicate the content and order of that book.

There was also a collection of stories from the British version of *Manhunt* magazine, *Bloodhound Detective Story Magazine*. The book, *The Bloodhound Anthology*, published a year later in 1959, was also edited by Scott & Sidney Meredith. It duplicated the contents of *The Best From Manhunt*, with exception of replacing Erskine Caldwell's "In Memory of Judith Courtright" with Henry Kane's "I'm No Hero", which appeared in the British version of *Suspense* magazine, and added three new *Manhunt/Bloodhound* stories, "Return Engagement" by Frank Kane, "Bad Word" by David Alexander and "Self-Defense" by Harold Q. Masur.

The three additional *Manhunt/Bloodhound* stories from *The Bloodhound Anthology* are included in this collection and follow the 13 from *The Best From Manhunt* collection, so that the first 19 stories make up the content of *The Bloodhound Anthology*, minus, of course, the Henry Kane *Suspense* story.

Introduction: The Tortured History of Manhunt

Jeff Vorzimmer

February 2019

The first issue of *Manhunt* appeared on newsstands in late 1952 and within two years became the widely acknowledged successor to *Black Mask*, which had ceased publication the year before. The stories in *Manhunt* captured the noir of Cold War angst like no other fiction magazine of its time and paved the way for television anthology shows such as *Alfred Hitchcock Presents* and *The Twilight Zone*.

Manhunt can best be described as a joint venture between publisher Archer St. John and literary agent Scott Meredith, both based in New York. In 1952, St. John published comic books and had recently ventured into and, in fact, developed 3D comics and graphic novels. His company, St. John Publishing, produced what is considered the first graphic novel, *It Rhymes with Lust*, in 1950, which was part crime, part romance, and followed that up later the same year with *The Case of the Winking Buddha*. Neither book sold very well and the line, dubbed "Pictures Novels," was discontinued after the second title.

Archer St. John, always an admirer of *Black Mask*, the premier pulp magazine from the 1920s through the 40s, felt that since that magazine's demise there was a void in the world of crime-fiction magazines and an opportunity. Of course, comic book publishers don't usually have big editorial staffs nor do they solicit manuscript submissions. For that, St. John approached Scott Meredith, a literary agent who was beginning to turn the publishing world on its ear with practices such as charging would-be writers reading fees and submitting manuscripts to publishers simultaneously, creating an auction system of competing bids.

For Scott Meredith it was an opportunity to get his stable of writers in print and create another stream of income. St. John served as the front man to avoid any ethical questions or conflict of interest charges that Meredith might otherwise face. St. John would manage the production of the magazine from layout and illustration to the printing and distribution of the magazine while Meredith's office would supply a steady supply of fiction and editing.

Of course, it was not a very well-kept secret within the publishing business. Those in the business, with even a passing familiarity with the roster of the Scott Meredith Literary Agency, would notice a preponderance of his clients on the pages of *Manhunt*. In fact, all ten of the most prolific contributors to the magazine were Meredith authors who, between them, contributed over one-fifth of all stories that appeared in *Manhunt* over the course of its fourteen-year run.

Manhunt has often been referred to, then and now, as a closed shop, only available to the Meredith stable of authors, but that's not entirely true. As often as not, writers not represented by an agent would submit stories directly to *Manhunt*. These were forwarded to the Meredith office and occasionally published in the magazine, though the authors were not usually signed to a publishing contract on the strength of a single story. This would at times create awkward moments when a producer from a television studio such as Screen Gems or Revue—producers of *Alfred Hitchcock Presents* and *M Squad*—would call up the agency looking to secure the rights to a story they read in *Manhunt*. The Meredith agent would stall the producer, scramble to locate and sign the author, then make the deal.

Archer St. John originally wanted to call the magazine *Mickey Spillane's Mystery Magazine* to compete with *Ellery Queen's Mystery Magazine*, albeit with grittier, more hard-boiled stories. Having Spillane's name on the masthead would have been appealing to both St. John and Meredith in that, by 1952, Spillane's first six books had combined sales of 20 million copies. His first book, *I, The Jury* had sold 3.5 million copies by 1953, when it was adapted for the screen.

When Scott Meredith checked Spillane's contract with his publisher, Dutton, he found a clause that gave the publisher total control of Mickey Spillane's name in conjunction with any books *or periodicals*. If they were to use Spillane's name on the magazine they had to get Dutton's permission. However, Dutton balked at the idea.

Dutton felt that short stories were a distraction for Spillane, and they wanted him to get back to the business of writing novels. At that point, it had been over a year since Spillane had delivered his last novel to them (and it would be ten years before he delivered his next one). The name of the magazine was changed to *Manhunt*, a named borrowed from a then-defunct crime comic book.

St. John intended to kick off the magazine with a Mickey Spillane story. He had heard that *Collier's Magazine* had turned down a novella Spillane had written, "Everybody's Watching Me," and offered to serialize the novella in the first four issues of the new magazine and pay Spillane $25,000 (equivalent to $237,000 today). If Spillane's name could not be on the masthead, it would at least be on the cover of the first four issues.

The print run of the first issue, dated January 1953, was 600,000 copies and sold out in five days. It was digest size (5½"x7½"), 144 pages and priced at 35¢ and $4 for a year's subscription. In addition to the lead story by Spillane, the issue also included stories by Cornell Woolrich under the name of William Irish; Ross Macdonald, under his real name, Kenneth Millar; and Evan Hunter, later known by the pen name Ed McBain. It also included a story featuring Richard Prather's detective Shell Scott, featured in six novels of his own over the previous three years, and, who rivaled Spillane's Mike Hammer in popularity, and another featuring Frank Kane's Johnny Liddell. Stories by Floyd Mahannah, Charles Beckman, Jr. and Sam Cobb (Stanley L. Colbert) rounded out the issue.

St. John had his favorite artist, Matt Baker, a black man in the predominantly white world of comic book illustration, do the artwork for *Manhunt*. Baker was the artist who had drawn the panels for the first of the two graphic novels St. John had published, but brought an entirely new look to the *Manhunt* illustrations, heavy ink and each highlighted with a different spot color. Each story had one illustration on the first page in a style not unlike *Black Mask*.

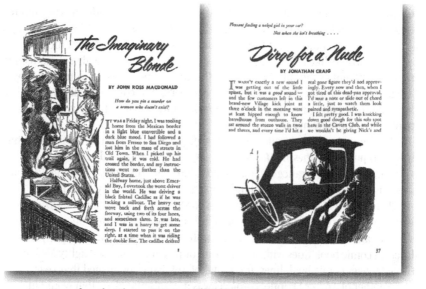

Pages from the February 1953 issue of *Manhunt* with illustrations by Matt Baker

Baker himself would do most of the illustrations for the first nine issues thereby setting the style used for the entire 15-year run. Up-and-coming young artists such as Robert McGinnis, Walter Popp and Robert Maguire, as well as older, more established artists, such as Frank Uppwall and Willard Downes, painted the covers.

The editorial note on the contents page of the second issue stated that the press run of the first issue probably should have been closer to a million copies. St. John apparently split the difference and ran 800,000 copies of the second issue. In addition to the second installment of "Everybody's Watching Me," the lead story was another by Kenneth Millar, a Lew Archer story titled "The Imaginary Blonde" under his new pseudonym John Ross Macdonald. There were also two more stories by Evan Hunter under the pseudonyms Richard Marsten and Hunt Collins, a Paul Pine story by John Evans, as well as stories by Jonathan Craig (Frank E. Smith), Fletcher Flora, Richard Deming, Eleazar Lipsky and Michael Fessier.

In addition to the contributors of the first two issues, the third issue was notable in that it included stories by older, more established writers such as Leslie Charteris with a Saint story, Craig Rice (Georgiana Craig) with a John J. Malone story, as well as stories by William Lindsay Gresham and Bruno Fischer.

The third issue also contained another two stories by Evan Hunter, one under the pseudonym Richard Marsten. In fact, Evan Hunter contributed 16 stories to the first 9 issues of *Manhunt* under his own name and various pseudonyms and 48 stories over the entire life of the magazine, making him the most prolific contributor by far. For a magazine that was supposed to be all about Mickey Spillane, it was turning out to be about Evan Hunter.

By mid-1953, St. John, with Meredith's help, started a campaign to lure big name authors to *Manhunt*. They approached James M. Cain, Raymond Chandler,

Rex Stout, Erle Stanley Gardner, Nelson Algren and Erskine Caldwell. They offered as much as $5,000 (about $47,000 today) for a 5,000-word story. This was the kind of money writers could expect from the slick magazines, but not from the pulps.

Many writers like Erle Stanley Gardner initially balked at the idea of publishing in *Manhunt*, but eventually succumbed. Gardner's first response to his agent was, "I hate to turn down an offer of $5000 for a story, but, confidentially, I don't like this magazine concept with which *Manhunt* started out. I think it is a definite menace to legitimate mystery fiction."

By the end of the decade all the big-name writers, including Gardner, had agreed to publish stories in *Manhunt*, though many appeared only once, the last being the only appearance by Raymond Chandler. His story, "Wrong Pigeon," previously published only in England, appeared in the February 1960 issue.

The year 1953 would be the peak year for St. John Publications. *Manhunt* was turning out to be one of its biggest-selling titles, spawning spin-off titles *Verdict* and *Menace*, and its 3D comics were selling millions of copies. The company had 35 different comic book titles with several lines of romance comics, Mighty Mouse and Three Stooges comic book lines, for a total of 169 issues published that year.

Another of Archer St. John's projects was a man's magazine that would include articles of interest to men, photos of women in various stages of undress and quality fiction. However, he was concerned about the post office not allowing the mailing of what they would certainly deem pornographic material to subscribers. After *Playboy* appeared in December 1953, he was emboldened to move ahead with the project.

In 1954, Archer brought in his 24-year-old son Michael to help run the business, while he focused on the new men's magazine, *Nugget*. Again, he turned to his favorite artist, Matt Baker, to do the illustrations in the magazine. Although that year would turn out to be another good year for St. John Publications, there was trouble on the horizon.

In the spring of 1954, there was a backlash against violence in comic books that were clearly aimed at children. The crusade was led by New York psychiatrist Fredric Wertham who published the now-infamous *Seduction of the Innocent*, a book-length study of the adverse effects of violent comic books on young minds, and led to a Senate investigation, which issued its own *Comic Books and Juvenile Delinquency Interim Report* that included a list of comic book titles it deemed inappropriate for children. There were, of course, some St. John titles on the list.

It was also apparent in early 1954 that 3D comics were just a passing fad. Sales of 3D comics plummeted to the point that, by March of 1954, 3D titles had all but disappeared. The sales of comic books in general were in a slump, brought on in large part by the scare created by politicians and PTA groups after the Wertham study.

Other forces were coming to bear that would have a personal effect on Archer St. John and the fate of St. John Publications. In August of 1954, President Eisenhower signed *The Communist Control Act*, which outlawed the Communist Party in the United States. Anyone who had ever been a member of the Communist Party could face imprisonment or even the revocation of citizenship. Archer's brother, the famous journalist Robert St. John, living a self-imposed exile in Switzerland and doing research for books on South Africa and Israel, was determined by the FBI to have been a member of the Communist Party. On September 24, 1954, Robert St. John was summoned to the American Consulate in Geneva and stripped of his passport. When Robert asked why his passport was being taken from him, the reply from the Consul-General was that it was because of his Communist Party activity.

Robert turned to his brother Archer back in the States for help to get his passport reinstated and the necessary affidavits for the appeal. Over the following months Archer, who was very close to his brother Robert, became increasingly frustrated by the stonewalling he got from the U. S. government on his brother's case.

Adding to his personal turmoil was the fact Archer was separated from his wife and living at the New York Athletic Club. His employees at St. John Publications also suspected he was addicted to amphetamines, in addition to being an alcoholic. By mid-1955 Robert's case had still not been decided, though he had submitted numerous affidavits from noted citizens that affirmed that he was never a member of the Communist Party.

In August, Archer told family members that he was being blackmailed, but didn't give anyone any details. His son Michael told him not to give in to the blackmailers. Archer told his son that he was staying at the apartment of a friend but wouldn't tell him where.

On Friday night August 12, 1955, Robert St. John got a call in Switzerland from Archer in New York who told him, "Never in my life have I felt so frustrated. I feel like I'm banging my head against a stone wall. I see no possibility of my getting your passport back. I've done everything in my power to help you, but I've failed. I'm sick over this." The next morning Robert got a call telling him that his brother had overdosed on sleeping pills, an apparent suicide. He was 54 years old.

At times, Archer St. John's life resembled a story from the pages of *Manhunt*— Al Capone's gang once kidnapped him, in 1925, when he was young newspaper publisher—and his death was no different. The apartment where Archer had been staying was a duplex penthouse owned by an attractive, redheaded former model and divorcee named Frances Stratford. She had been sleeping in an upstairs bedroom and had found Archer downstairs lying next to the couch, unresponsive, at 11:30 a.m. that Saturday morning.

A couple had been seen leaving the apartment the night before, and the police were investigating. The following Monday, the *New York Daily News* reported, "A couple of shadowy West Side characters, a man and a woman, suspected of feeding dope pills to magazine publisher Archer St. John, were being hunted . . . by detectives investigating St. John's mysterious death in the penthouse apartment of a former Powers model."

After St. John's death, his wife, Gertrude-Faye, known as "G-F" or "Geff," showed up at the offices of St. John Publications and promptly fired the entire staff, including Matt Baker. Apparently, she hadn't wanted anyone around who knew about her husband's affairs. The irony was that none of the staff knew anything about St. John's private love life, not even Baker who was probably as close to him as anybody.

Despite the failure of the previous *Manhunt* clones, *Verdict*, which lasted only four issues in late 1953 and *Menace*, which lasted two issues, the following year, Michael St. John decided to expand his own editorial staff and to introduce yet two more titles, *Mantrap* and *Murder!* in 1956. Unfortunately, the new titles suffered from the same lackluster sales of the first two spin-off titles and were discontinued just as quickly.

Undaunted by the failure of four new titles in as many years, Michael kept searching for a formula that would repeat the success of *Manhunt*. What Michael and his business manager, Richard Decker, came up with was an opposite, more genteel, direction. They approached Alfred Hitchcock with an offer to license his name and image for a mystery digest.

Alfred Hitchcock's Mystery Magazine was an immediate success and, in fact, sales would steadily increase throughout the rest of the decade while those of *Manhunt* were in steady decline, down to 169,000 by 1957. Its digest size, with two-column layout and heavily inked spot color illustrations, were identical to *Manhunt*'s.

In an effort to boost sales of both *Manhunt* and *Alfred Hitchcock's Mystery Magazine*, St. John and Decker decided to increase the size of both magazines from their current digest size to regular magazine size to get, what they hoped would be, more attention on newsstands. What it got *Manhunt* was the unwanted attention of the Federal District Attorney.

After only the second issue at the bigger magazine size, Michael St. John, Richard E. Decker, Charles W. Adams (the Art Director) and Flying Eagle Publications (a subsidiary of St. John's Publications and holding company of *Manhunt*) were indicted on March 14, 1957, for "mailing or delivery copies of the April, 1957, issue of a publication entitled *Manhunt* containing obscene, lewd, lascivious, filthy or indecent matter" in violation of United States Penal Code 18 U. S. C. §1461.

In District Court in Concord, New Hampshire, St. John's lawyers moved to have the charges dismissed on the grounds that the complaint didn't identify what article was specifically being charged in the issue as "obscene, lewd, filthy or indecent." They argued that "the indictment is so loosely drawn that it would not afford them protection from further prosecution." District Court Judge Aloysius J. Connor agreed and threw out the indictments on August 7, 1957.

Federal prosecutors promptly refiled charges with specific complaints: "All six of the stories have definitely weird overtones and can certainly be characterized as crude, course, vulgar, and on the whole disgusting. But tested by the reaction of the community as a whole—the average member of society—it seems to us that only the feature novelette, 'Body on a White Carpet,' and the illustration appearing on page 25 accompanying the story entitled 'Object of Desire,' could be found to fall within the ban of the statute as limited in its application by the important public interest in a free press protected in the First Amendment." The defendants faced a fine of $5,000 ($43,000 in today's dollars) and up to five years in prison.

The offending illustration by Jack Coughlin accompanying the story
"Object of Desire" on page 25 of the April 1957 issue.

In March of 1957, Jack Coughlin, the freelancer who did the illustration for "Object of Desire," was called into Art Director Charles Adams' office. Adams handed Coughlin a copy of the latest issue of *Manhunt* and asked him to turn to page 25, saying there was a problem with the illustration there and asked him to explain. Coughlin looked at it, focused on the woman in the illustration, and said he couldn't see a problem. Adams told him to look at the man's crotch. It was then that what appeared to be a penis seemed to almost leap off the page. "Once you see it, you can't *not* see it, Coughlin said.

Apparently an employee of the printing company in Concord, New Hampshire had called Adams attention to it. Adams eventually brought Coughlin to a New York City courtroom where Coughlin gave a deposition before a judge claiming that the illustration wasn't intentionally obscene, but rather a fluke of the scratchboard engraving process used in *Manhunt* illustrations. Coughlin, who was paid $35 for the illustration was never asked to do another for the magazine. He was told sometime later that the judge had believed him and the case was never tried in the State of New York.

However, on December 1, 1958, the final verdict of the District Court jury was that Flying Eagle Publications and Michael St. John were guilty and fined $3,000 ($26,000 today). Judge Connor gave St. John a separate fine of $1000, a suspended sentence of six months in jail and two-year probation. Richard E. Decker and Charles W. Adams were acquitted. Michael St. John immediately appealed the verdict and the case went to Federal Appeals Court.

On January 21, 1960, the Federal Appeals Court in Boston set aside the verdict of the District Court and ordered a new trial. Chief Judge Peter Woodbury found that the prosecutors had erred in their instructions to the jury by telling them that two defendants, Decker and Adams, originally listed on the indictment had "been separated from this action" rather than that they were acquitted.

The new trial was scheduled to begin March 28, 1960, but Michael St. John's lawyers requested that the case delayed until the next court term later that year.

Early the next year the Court of Appeals concurred with the decision of the Circuit Court. On January 10, 1961, Judge Bailey Aldrich upheld the original conviction and fine of $5,000. After three years and nine months of litigation, St. John Publishing was financially drained. The circulation of *Manhunt* had dropped to 100,000, and Richard Decker had split with St. John in the summer of 1960, taking *Alfred Hitchcock's Mystery Magazine* with him to Palm Beach, Florida.

Scott Meredith had always been annoyed with what seemed to be chronic cash-flow problems at St. John, and it only got worse. The magazine limped along for the next six years, and fewer of Meredith's writers appeared in the magazine. Only 33 stories by the top ten Meredith contributors appeared in the 1960s.

Only three Evan Hunter stories appeared in *Manhunt* in the 60s, the last story, fittingly, in the last issue of April/May 1967. By then the circulation had dropped to a little over 74,000 copies. Michael St. John decided to get out of the publishing business entirely and sold off all the assets of St John Publishing, including *Nugget*.

Sources:
Aldrich, Baily, Circuit Judge, United States Court of Appeals, *Flying Eagle Publications v. United States, 285 F.2d 307*, January 10, 1961
Ashley, Michael, author, Kemp, Earl and Ortiz, Luiz editors, *Cult Magazines A-Z: A Curious Compendium of Culturally Obsessive & Curiously Expressive Publications*, 2009, Nonstop Press
Benson, John, *Confessions, Romances, Secrets, and Temptations: Archer St. John and the St. John Romance Comics*, 2007, Fantagraphics Books
Benson, John, *Romance Without Tears*, 2003, Fantagraphics Books
Fugate, Francis L. and Roberta B., Secrets of the World's Best-Selling Writer, 1980, William Morrow and Company, Inc.
Carlson, Michael, Interview with Mickey Spillane, *Crime Time* website, June 29, 2002
Chicago Tribune, Chicago, IL, July 8, 1925, pg. 16
Collins, Max Allan and Traylor, James L, *Spillane* (to be published in 2020)
Contento, William G. with Greenberg, Martin H., *Index to Crime and Mystery Anthologies*, 1991

Cook, Michael L., *Monthly Murders: A Checklist and Chronological Listing of Fiction in the Digest-Size Mystery Magazines in the United States and England*, 1982

Coughlin, Jack, Artist (Freelancer for St. John Publications), Interview, February 14, 2019

Horowitz, Terry Fred, *Merchant of Words The Life of Robert St. John*, 2014, Rowman & Littlefield

Meredith, Scott and Meredith, Sidney, *The Best From Manhunt*, 1958, Perma-Books

Morgan, Hal and Symmes, Dan, *Amazing 3-D*, 1982, Little, Brown and Company

Morrison, Henry, Literary Agent and former Scott Meredith Literary Agency employee (1957-1964), Interview, January 29, 2019

Nashua Telegraph, Nashua, NH, January 22, 1960, pg. 2

Nashua Telegraph, Nashua, NH, March 24, 1960, pg. 16

Nashua Telegraph, Nashua, NH, January 11, 1961, pg. 2

New York Daily News, New York, NY, August 15, 1955, pg. C5

N. W. Ayers & Sons Directory of Newspapers and Periodicals, 1954-1967

The Ottawa Citizen, Ottawa, Canada, March 2, 1957, pg. 2

The Portsmouth Herald, Portsmouth, NH, March 15, 1957, pg. 7

The Portsmouth Herald, Portsmouth, NH, December 2, 1958, pg. 8

Quattro, Ken, *Archer St. John & The Little Company That Could*, 2006, www.comicartville.com

Waller, Drake, *It Rhymes with Lust*, 1950, 2007, Dark Horse Books

Woodbury, Peter, Chief Judge, United States Court of Appeals, First Circuit, *Flying Eagle Publications v. United States, 273 F.2d 799*, January 21, 1960

Introduction from The Best From Manhunt
Scott and Sidney Meredith

March 1958

About thirty years ago a young oil-company executive named Raymond Chandler and a young private detective named Dashiell Hammett began to pick up a few bucks on the side by writing a new and entirely different kind of crime fiction. Their stories, which revolutionized the genre, were based on a simple premise which is elementary to any working cop: the fact that murder is sordid.

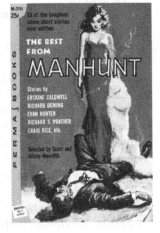

Chandler and Hammett were the first writers to abandon what might be called the genteel-puzzle school of mystery fiction and write about crime the way it really happens; they were the first to write crime stories the way a couple of hardened harness bulls might discuss real cases which had just been wrapped up in the precinct.

They knew, for one thing, that real-life murder is rarely a mystery, that the average killing is a husband-wife or known-enemies case, with the arrest just a routine pick-up. They knew that a real-life killer who got fancy and tried an elaborate murder of the puzzle-story type would run up against modem criminology and be nabbed in ten minutes, and that most real murders which remain temporarily or permanently in the Open File as unsolved are those in which an unknown thug belts a stranger in an alley to get his wallet—and just happens to hit too hard. They knew that there probably hasn't been a case in history which has been solved by a gifted, eccentric amateur, that murders are solved by homicide detectives—hard, tough guys in a hard, tough job.

And they knew that murder and other crime is several hundred times more likely to occur in the slums, the backwaters, the tough sections of town, than in the mansions of the rich and other upper-crust locales favored by the genteel-puzzle writers; and that detectives are bound to have considerably more traffic with prostitutes and pimps than with presidents of banks, considerably more dealings with stoolies and snowbirds than with society matrons, and considerably more contact with the mugging, the rape, and knife-in-the-gut-in-a-barroom-brawl than with the Well-Dressed-Body-in-the-Library.

And so Chandler and Hammett, and the others who followed close behind them, began to write about the *real* crimes and the *real* locales and the *real* crime-solvers and investigation methods, and in so doing created an entirely new field of fiction: the grim, realistic, unsugared, and honest crime story. Their stories were rarely pretty, but always plausible; sometimes frightening, but never merely foolish.

When you read the early Chandler and Hammett, you realize that, like most pioneering projects that have since been improved upon, the stuff was pretty crude and imperfect. But this no more diminishes the significance of their invention than going to Europe on the S. S. *United States* lessens the importance of Fulton's invention of the steamboat. The simple fact is that the tough realistic crime story has been brought a long way in thirty years by many writers—including Hammett and Chandler themselves in their later work. [In this anthology we've selected sixteen stories that we believe are among the very best of this type. Some of these authors, like Richard Deming, Harold Q. Masur, Henry Kane, Frank Kane and David Alexander, are well known for their full-length novels published in the Bloodhound series.][1] And much of this progress has been the result of a little magazine called *Manhunt*.

Manhunt, created and published by the late Archer St. John and subsequently carried on by his son Michael, came along after *Black Mask* (which had published the earliest efforts in the tough-crime field) had worn itself out and ceased publication[2]; and the new magazine was noticeable from the start as the deep-sea swim of tough-crime fiction as compared to Black Mask's first tentative steps in the murky water. It was created to give readers in short form the same hard, unsentimental, bitterly realistic kind of crime story usually available only in booklengths, particularly paperback books, and the editors made it clear from the start that the magazine was for neither the sensitive nor the romantic.

"We don't want the kind of story which *might* happen," said an early editorial bulletin to authors. "We want the kind of story which *does* happen—in Harlem, on Times Square at 4 A.M., on the country's skid rows, in the isolated and struggling areas of the Deep South, places like that. We don't want sentiment and we don't want prettifying; we want the same kind of realism a New York detective employs when he tells you there are so many muggings, criminal assaults, and even murders in certain parts of the city that the metropolitan newspapers don't even bother to run a two-line story on a crime there. We're as much interested in the whydunit and the howdunit as the whodunit, and we want out stuff to be tough as hell. . . ."

From the start, *Manhunt* has been a showcase for the best in realistic crime fiction, and for the best writers in the field and those writers who occasionally do tough stories, among them Evan Hunter, Richard S. Prather, Mickey Spillane, Henry Kane, Frank Kane, Richard Deming, Bruno Fischer, Fredric Brown, Hal Ellson, John Ross Macdonald, Wade Miller, Erskine Caldwell, James M. Cain, Nelson Algren, W. R. Burnett, James T. Farrell, Meyer Levin, Erle Stanley Gardner, Rex Stout, Craig Rice, William Irish and a great many others.

In this anthology, selected from the seven-hundred-plus stories[3] published in *Manhunt* thus far, we've included the very best published by the magazine to date. There are so many really first-rate stories in Manhunt that this is a mere scratching of the surface. We hope to bring you many more in later collections, including some that we'd have liked to use in the present collection if we'd had more space.

In any case, we think these stories illustrate tough-crime writing at its best. And we think that, if you like 'em tough, you're going to enjoy the fiction that follows.

Notes:

1. The Bloodhound Anthology (©1959, T. V. Boardman & Co., Ltd.) adds these lines and then skips to the last paragraph.

2. *Black Mask* ceased publication in 1951, a year and a half before the advent of *Manhunt*.

3. This number would have to include non-fiction articles as well. The total number of stories published through 1957 was actually 630.

On The Sidewalk, Bleeding

Evan Hunter

July 1957

The boy lay bleeding in the rain.

He was sixteen years old, and he wore a bright purple silk jacket, and the lettering across the back of the jacket read THE ROYALS. The boy's name was Andy, and the name was delicately scripted in black thread on the front of the jacket, just over the heart. *Andy.*

He had been stabbed ten minutes ago.

The knife had entered just below his rib cage and had been drawn across his body violently, tearing a wide gap in his flesh. He lay on the sidewalk with the March rain drilling his jacket and drilling his body and washing away the blood that poured from his open wound. He had known excruciating pain when the knife ripped across his body, and then sudden comparative relief when the blade was pulled away. He had heard the voice saying, "That's for you, Royal!" and then the sound of footsteps hurrying into the rain, and then he had fallen to the sidewalk, clutching his stomach, trying to stop the flow of blood.

He tried to yell for help, but he had no voice. He did not know why his voice had deserted him, or why the rain had become so suddenly fierce, or why there was an open hole in his body from which his life ran redly, steadily. It was 11:30 P.M., but he did not know the time.

There was another thing he did not know.

He did not know he was dying.

He lay on the sidewalk, bleeding, and he thought only, *That was a fierce rumble, they got me good that time,* but he did not know he was dying. He would have been frightened had he known. In his ignorance, he lay bleeding and wishing he could cry out for help, but there was no voice in his throat. There was only the bubbling of blood from between his lips whenever he opened his mouth to speak. He lay silent in his pain, waiting, waiting for someone to find him. He could hear the sound of automobile tires hushed on the muzzle of rain-swept streets, far away at the other end of the long alley. He lay with his face pressed to the sidewalk, and he could see the splash of neon far away at the other end of the alley, tinting the pavement red and green, slickly brilliant in the rain.

He wondered if Laura would be angry.

He had left the jump to get a package of cigarettes. He had told her he would be back in a few minutes, and then he had gone downstairs and found the candy store closed. He knew that Alfredo's on the next block would be open until at least two, and he had started through the alley, and that was when he'd been ambushed. He could hear the faint sound of music now, coming from a long, long way off, and he wondered if Laura was dancing, wondered if she had missed him yet. Maybe she thought he wasn't coming back. Maybe she thought he'd cut out for good. Maybe she'd already left the jump and gone home. He thought of her face, the brown eyes and the jet-black hair, and thinking of her he forgot his pain a little, forgot that blood was rushing from his body. Someday he would marry Laura. Someday he would marry her, and they would have a lot of kids, and then they would get out of the neighborhood. They would move to a clean project in the Bronx, or maybe they would move to Staten Island. When they were married, when they had kids . . .

He heard footsteps at the other end of the alley, and he lifted his cheek from the sidewalk and looked into the darkness and tried to cry out, but again there was only a soft hissing bubble of blood on his mouth. The man came down the alley. He had not seen Andy yet. He walked, and then stopped to lean against the brick of the building, and then walked again. He saw Andy then and came toward him, and he stood over him for a long time, the minutes ticking, ticking, watching him and not speaking. Then he said, "What's a matter, buddy?"

Andy could not speak, and he could barely move. He lifted his face slightly and looked up at the man, and in the rain-swept alley he smelled the sickening odor of alcohol and realized the man was drunk. He did not feel any particular panic. He did not know he was dying, and so he felt only mild disappointment that the man who had found him was drunk. The man was smiling.

"Did you fall down, buddy?" he asked. "You mus' be as drunk as I am." He grinned, seemed to remember why he had entered the alley in the first place, and said, "Don' go way. I'll be ri' back."

The man lurched away. Andy heard his footsteps, and then the sound of the man colliding with a garbage can, and some mild swearing, and then the sound of the man urinating, lost in the steady wash of the rain. He waited for the man to come back.

It was 11:39.

When the man returned, he squatted alongside Andy. He studied him with drunken dignity. "You gonna catch cold here," he said. "What's a matter? You like layin' in the wet?"

Andy could not answer. The man tried to focus his eyes on Andy's face. The rain spattered around them.

"You like a drink?"

Andy shook his head. "I gotta bottle. Here," the man said.

He pulled a pint bottle from his inside jacket pocket. He uncapped it and extended it to Andy. Andy tried to move, but pain wrenched him back flat against the sidewalk.

"Take it," the man said. He kept watching Andy. "Take it." When Andy did not move, he said, "Nev' mind, I'll have one m'self." He tilted the bottle to his lips, and then wiped the back of his hand across his mouth. "You too young to be drinkin', anyway. Should be 'shamed of yourself, drunk an' layin' in a alley, all wet. Shame on you. I gotta good minda calla cop."

Andy nodded. Yes, he tried to say. Yes, call a cop. Please. Call one.

"Oh, you don' like that, huh?" the drunk said. "You don' wanna cop to fin' you all drunk an' wet in a alley, huh? Okay, buddy. This time you get off easy." He got to his feet. "This time you lucky," he said. He waved broadly at Andy, and then almost lost his footing. "S'long, buddy," he said.

Wait, Andy thought. *Wait, please, I'm bleeding.*

The Best of *Manhunt*

"S'long," the drunk said again, "I see you around," and then he staggered off up the alley.

Andy lay and thought, *Laura, Laura. Are you dancing?*

The couple came into the alley suddenly. They ran into the alley together, running from the rain, the boy holding the girl's elbow, the girl spreading a newspaper over her head to protect her hair. Andy lay crumpled against the pavement, and he watched them run into the alley laughing, and then duck into the doorway not ten feet from him.

"Man, what rain!" the boy said. "You could drown out there."

"I have to get home," the girl said. "It's late, Freddie. I have to get home."

"We got time," Freddie said. "Your people won't raise a fuss if you're a little late. Not with this kind of weather."

"It's dark," the girl said, and she giggled.

"Yeah," the boy answered, his voice very low.

"Freddie . . .?"

"Um?"

"You're . . . you're standing very close to me."

"Um."

There was a long silence. Then the girl said, "Oh," only that single word, and Andy knew she'd been kissed, and he suddenly hungered for Laura's mouth. It was then that he wondered if he would ever kiss Laura again. It was then that he wondered if he was dying.

No, he thought, I *can't be dying, not from a little street rumble, not from just getting cut. Guys get cut all the time in rumbles. I can't be dying. No, that's stupid. That don't make any sense at all.*

"You shouldn't," the girl said.

"Why not?"

"I don't know."

"Do you like it?"

"Yes."

"So?"

"I don't know."

"I love you, Angela," the boy said.

"I love you, too, Freddie," the girl said, and Andy listened and thought, *I love you, Laura. Laura, I think maybe I'm dying. Laura, this is stupid but I think maybe I'm dying. Laura, I think I'm dying!* He tried to speak. He tried to move. He tried to crawl toward the doorway where he could see the two figures in embrace. He tried to make a noise, a sound, and a grunt came from his lips, and then he tried again, and another grunt came, a low animal grunt of pain.

"What was that?" the girl said, suddenly alarmed, breaking away from the boy.

"I don't know," he answered.

"Go look, Freddie."

"No. Wait."

Andy moved his lips again. Again the sound came from him.

"Freddie!"

"What?"

"I'm scared."

"I'll go see," the boy said.

He stepped into the alley. He walked over to where Andy lay on the ground. He stood over him, watching him.

"You all right?" he asked.

"What is it?" Angela said from the doorway.

"Somebody's hurt," Freddie said.

"Let's get out of here," Angela said.

"No. Wait a minute."

He knelt down beside Andy. "You cut?" he asked.

Andy nodded.

The boy kept looking at him. He saw the lettering on the jacket then, THE ROYALS. He turned to Angela.

"He's a Royal," he said.

"Let's . . . what . . . what do you want to do, Freddie?"

"I don't know. I don't want to get mixed up in this. He's a Royal. We help him, and the Guardians'll be down on our necks. I don't want to get mixed up in this, Angela."

"Is he . . . is he hurt bad?"

"Yeah, it looks that way."

"What shall we do?"

"I don't know."

"We can't leave him here in the rain." Angela hesitated. "Can we?"

"If we get a cop, the Guardians'll find out who." Freddie said. "I don't know, Angela. I don't know."

Angela hesitated a long time before answering. Then she said, "I have to get home, Freddie. My people will begin to worry."

"Yeah," Freddie said. He looked at Andy again. "You all right?" he asked. Andy lifted his face from the sidewalk, and his eyes said, Please, please help me, and maybe Freddie read what his eyes were saying, and maybe he didn't.

Behind him, Angela said, "Freddie, let's get out of here! Please!"

There was urgency in her voice, urgency bordering on the edge of panic. Freddie stood up. He looked at Andy again, and then mumbled, "I'm sorry," and then he took Angela's arm and together they ran toward the neon splash at the other end of the alley.

Why, they're afraid of the Guardians, Andy thought in amazement. *But why should they be? I wasn't afraid of the Guardians. I never turkeyed out of a rumble with the Guardians. I got heart. But I'm bleeding.*

The rain was soothing somehow. It was a cold rain, but his body was hot all over, and the rain helped to cool him. He had always liked rain. He could remember sitting in Laura's house one time, the rain running down the windows, and just looking out over the street, watching the people running from the rain. That was when he'd first joined the Royals. He could remember how happy he was the Royals had taken him. The Royals and the Guardians, two of the biggest. He was a Royal. There had been meaning to the title.

Now, in the alley, with the cold rain washing his hot body, he wondered about the meaning. If he died, he was Andy. He was not a Royal. He was simply Andy, and he was dead. And he wondered suddenly if the Guardians who had ambushed him and knifed him had ever once realized he was Andy. Had they known that he was Andy, or had they simply known that he was a Royal wearing a purple silk jacket? Had they stabbed *him,* Andy, or had they only stabbed the jacket and the title, and what good was the title if you were dying?

I'm Andy, he screamed wordlessly. *For Christ's sake, I'm Andy!*

An old lady stopped at the other end of the alley. The garbage cans were stacked there, beating noisily in the rain. The old lady carried an umbrella with broken ribs, carried it with all the dignity of a queen. She stepped into the mouth of the alley, a shopping bag over one arm. She lifted the lids of the garbage cans delicately, and she did not hear Andy grunt because she was a little deaf and because the rain was beating a steady relentless tattoo on the cans. She had been searching and foraging for the better part of the night. She collected her string and her newspapers, and an old hat with a feather on it from one of the garbage cans, and a broken footstool from another of the cans. And then she delicately replaced the lids and lifted her umbrella high and walked out of the alley mouth with queenly dignity. She had worked swiftly and soundlessly, and now she was gone.

The alley looked very long now. He could see people passing at the other end of it, and he wondered who the people were, and he wondered if he would ever get to know them, wondered who it was on the Guardians who had stabbed him, who had plunged the knife into his body. "That's for you, Royal!" the voice had said, and then the footsteps, his arms being released by the others, the fall to the pavement. "That's for you, Royal!" Even in his pain, even as he collapsed, there had been some sort of pride in knowing he was a Royal. Now there was no pride at all. With the rain beginning to chill him, with the blood pouring steadily between his fingers, he knew only a sort of dizziness, and within the giddy dizziness, he could only think, *I want to be Andy.*

It was not very much to ask of the world.

He watched the world passing at the other end of the alley. The world didn't know he was Andy. The world didn't know he was alive. He wanted to say, "Hey, I'm alive! Hey, look at me! I'm alive! Don't you know I'm alive? Don't you know I exist?"

He felt weak and very tired. He felt alone and wet and feverish and chilled, and he knew he was going to die now, and the knowledge made him suddenly sad. He was not frightened. For some reason, he was not frightened. He was only filled with an overwhelming sadness that his life would be over at sixteen. He felt all at once as if he had never done anything, never seen anything, never been anywhere. There were so many things to do, and he wondered why he'd never thought of them before, wondered why the rumbles and the jumps and the purple jacket had always seemed so important to him before, and now they seemed like such small things in a world he was missing, a world that was rushing past at the other end of the alley.

I don't want to die, he thought. *I haven't lived yet*

It seemed very important to him that he take off the purple jacket. He was very close to dying, and when they found him, he did not want them to say, "Oh, it's a Royal." With great effort, he rolled over onto his back. He felt the pain tearing at his stomach when he moved, a pain he did not think was possible. But he wanted to take off the jacket. If he never did another thing, he wanted to take off the jacket. The jacket had only one meaning now, and that was a very simple meaning.

If he had not been wearing the jacket, he would not have been stabbed. The knife had not been plunged in hatred of Andy. The knife hated only the purple jacket. The jacket was a stupid meaningless thing that was robbing him of his life. He wanted the jacket off his back. With an enormous loathing, he wanted the jacket off his back.

He lay struggling with the shiny wet material. His arms were heavy, and pain ripped fire across his body whenever he moved. But he squirmed and fought and twisted until one arm was free and then the other, and then he rolled away from the jacket and lay quite still, breathing heavily, listening to the sound of his breathing and the sound of the rain and thinking, *Rain is sweet, I'm Andy.*

She found him in the alleyway a minute past midnight. She left the dance to look for him, and when she found him she knelt beside him and said, "Andy, it's me, Laura." He did not answer her. She backed away from him, tears springing into her eyes, and then she ran from the alley hysterically and did not stop running until she found the cop. And now, standing with the cop, she looked down at him, and the cop rose and said, "He's dead," and all the crying was out of her now. She stood in the rain and said nothing, looking at the dead boy on the pavement, and looking at the purple jacket that rested a foot away from his body. The cop picked up the jacket and turned it over in his hands.

"A Royal, huh?" he said.

The rain seemed to beat more steadily now, more fiercely.

She looked at the cop and, very quietly, she said, "His name is Andy."

The cop slung the jacket over his arm. He took out his black pad, and he flipped it open to a blank page.

"A Royal," he said.

Then he began writing.

Mugger Murder
Richard Deming

April 1953

I was surprised to see Sergeant Nels Parker in the Coroner's Court audience, for homicide detectives spend too much of their time there on official business to develop any morbid curiosity about cases not assigned to them. I was in the audience myself, of course, but as a police reporter this was my regular beat on Friday mornings, and after five years of similar Friday mornings, nothing but the continued necessity of making a living could have gotten me within miles of the place.

When I spotted him two rows ahead of me, I moved up and slid into the vacant seat next to him.

"Busman's holiday, Sergeant?" I asked.

His long face turned and he cocked one dull eye at me. For so many years Nels had practiced looking dull in order to throw homicide witnesses off guard, the expression had become habitual.

"How are you, Sam?" he said.

"You haven't got a case today, have you?" I persisted.

His head gave a small shake and he turned his eyes front again. Since he seemed to have no desire to explain his presence, I let the matter drop. But as the only inquest scheduled was on the body of a Joseph Garcia, age twenty-one and of no known address, I at least knew what case interested him.

The first witness was a patrolman named Donald Lutz, a thick bodied and round faced young fellow who looked as though he, like the dead man, was no more than twenty-one.

In response to the deputy coroner's request to describe the circumstances of Joseph Garcia's death as he knew them, the youthful patrolman said, "Well, it was Wednesday . . . night before last . . . about eleven thirty, and I was walking my beat along Broadway just south of Market. As I passed this alley mouth, I heard a scuffling sound in the alley and flashed my light down it. I saw these two guys struggling, one with a hammerlock on the other guy's head, and just as my light touched them, the guy with the hammerlock gave a hard twist, the other guy went sort of limp, and the first guy let him drop to the alley floor. I moved in with my night stick ready, but the guy stood still and made no move either to run or come at me. He just stood there with his hands at his sides and said, 'Officer, this man tried to rob me.'

"I told him to stand back, and knelt to look at the man lying down. Near as I could tell, he was dead, but in the dark with just a flashlight I couldn't be sure, and I didn't want to take a chance on him waking up and running away while I went to the nearest call box. So I stayed right there and used my stick on the concrete to bring the cop from the next beat. That was Patrolman George Mason.

"Mason went to call for a patrol car and a doctor while I stayed with the two guys. That's about all I know about things except when the doctor got there, he said the guy lying down was dead."

The deputy coroner said, "And the dead man was later identified as Joseph Garcia?"

Patrolman Lutz nodded. "Yes, sir."

"And the man Garcia was struggling with. Will you identify him, please?"

The policeman pointed his finger at a short, plump man of about fifty seated in a chair apart from the audience and within a few feet of where the jury was lined up along the left wall. He was a quietly dressed man with a bland, faintly vacuous smile and an appearance of softness about him until you examined him closely. Then you suspected that a good deal of his plumpness was muscle rather than fat, and you noticed his shoulders were unnaturally wide.

"That's him there," the young patrolman said. "Robert Hummel."

Just in front of the platform containing the deputy coroner's bench was a long table, one end pointing toward the platform and the other end toward the audience. On the right side of this table, seated side-wise to it with his back to the audience, sat the assistant circuit attorney in charge of the case. On its left side sat Marcus Prout, one of St. Louis's most prominent criminal lawyers.

Now the assistant C. A. said, "Patrolman Lutz, I understand Robert Hummel had in his possession a .38 caliber pistol at the time of the incident you just described. Is that right?"

"Well, not exactly in his possession, sir. It was lying in the alley nearby, where he'd dropped it. It turned out he had a permit to carry it."

Marcus Prout put in, "Officer, was there any other weapon in sight?"

"Yes, sir. An open clasp knife lay in the alley. This was later established as belonging to the deceased. Robert Hummel claimed Garcia drew it on him, he in turn drew his gun to defend himself, and ordered the deceased to drop the knife. However, the deceased continued to come at him. Hummel said he didn't want to shoot the man, so he used the gun to knock the knife from Garcia's hand, then dropped the gun and grappled with him."

The lawyer asked, "Was there any mark on the deceased's wrist to support that statement?"

"The post mortem report notes a bruise," the deputy coroner interrupted, and glanced over at the jury.

Marcus Prout rose from his chair and strolled toward the patrolman. "Officer, did the deceased . . . this Joseph Garcia . . . have a police record?"

"Yes, sir. One arrest and a suspended sentence for mugging."

"Mugging is a slang term for robbery with force, isn't it?"

"Yes, sir. Generally without a weapon. You get a guy around the neck from behind and go through his pockets with your free hand. There's other methods classified as mugging, but that's the way Garcia did it the time he was convicted."

The lawyer said, "Did you draw any inference from the fact that Robert Hummel, with a gun against a knife, used the gun merely to disarm his opponent and then grappled with him with his bare hands?"

The policeman said, "I don't exactly know what you mean."

"I mean, did it not occur to you as obvious Robert Hummel's statement that he did not wish to shoot his opponent was true, and that he went out of his way to avoid seriously injuring Garcia, when under the circumstances he would have been fully justified in shooting the man through the heart? And that Garcia's subsequent death in spite of Mr. Hummel's precaution must have been an accident resulting from Robert Hummel exerting more strength than he intended in the excitement of the moment?"

This leading question would have been stricken from the record in a regular court, of course, for not only was it deliberately slanted at the jury rather than to the witness, it asked for an opinion on a matter of which the witness could not possibly have had actual knowledge. But in Coroner's Court the legal formalities of a court of law are almost entirely lacking inasmuch as no one is on trial for anything, the jury's sole duty being to determine how the deceased met death. I was therefore not surprised when neither the assistant circuit attorney nor the deputy coroner made any objection to the question.

Patrolman Lutz said he had not thought about the matter, which seemed to satisfy Marcus Prout, as he had asked the question only to implant it in the jury's mind anyway. The lawyer went back to his seat.

When the deputy coroner asked if there were any more questions, both Prout and the assistant C. A. shook their heads. The patrolman was dismissed and Norman Paisley was called as a witness.

Norman Paisley was a thin, dried up man of middle age who looked like a school janitor. To the deputy coroner's first question he gave his address as a rooming house on South Broadway two blocks south of Market.

"Were you a customer at Stoyle's Tavern on Sixth near Olive this past Wednesday night?" the deputy coroner asked.

"Yes, sir. All evening from seven till they closed at one thirty."

"Did you know the deceased Joseph Garcia?"

"To talk to, yes, sir. I used to run into him at Stoyle's Tavern off and on. I didn't know where he lived or what he did, or nothing like that, though."

"I see. Was the deceased a customer at Stoyle's that night?"

"Yes, sir. He come in several times during the evening. I guess he was bar cruising all up and down Sixth Street."

"Was he alone?"

"Yes, sir."

The deputy coroner said, "Do you recognize any other person now present as a customer at Stoyle's the night before last?"

Norman Paisley pointed at Robert Hummel. "Him. He come in about a quarter of eleven and left at eleven fifteen. I noticed him particular because he bought the house a couple of drinks."

The assistant C. A. cut in. "Was Joseph Garcia present during this period?"

"Yes, sir. He even remarked about it. When Mr. Hummel bought a drink, Joe said to me, 'That damn fool must be made of money. He just bought the house a drink at a place I was in up the street.'"

Marcus Prout asked, "Did you get the impression Garcia was following Hummel?"

"No, sir. Joe come in first, as a matter of fact, and Mr. Hummel come in right after him."

The lawyer looked surprised. He started to ask another question, changed his mind and waved his hand dismissingly. The assistant C. A. stepped into the breach.

"Mr. Paisley, did you get the impression the deceased was particularly interested in Robert Hummel?"

"Not right at first. But when Hummel bought the second drink, he happened to be standing close to Joe at the bar, and when he opened his wallet to pay, Joe looked kind of startled. I was standing the other side of Joe, but even from there I could see there was a lot of bills in it. After that Joe couldn't seem to keep his eyes off Hummel."

Marcus Prout spoke again. "When Hummel finally left the bar, did Garcia follow him?"

"Yes, sir. He went right out after him."

The assistant C. A. said, "Did you get the impression Garcia left because Hummel did? That is, that the deceased was actually following Mr. Hummel? Or that he just happened to leave about the same time?"

"Why, I don't know," Paisley said. "I never thought about it at the time. I guess Joe must of followed him out figuring to roll him."

Marcus Prout smiled at this answer and the assistant C. A. grunted. When both indicated they had no further questions, the witness was dismissed.

Shuffling the papers in front of him, the deputy coroner located the post mortem report, cleared his throat and said, "The autopsy shows death by suffocation due to a crushed larynx."

Following this announcement, he rose from his bench, advanced to the edge of the platform and asked in a loud voice, "Are any relatives of the deceased present?"

When there was no reply to this routine question, he turned to the jury and signified they were to go out.

While the six man jury was out, I tried to figure what Nels Parker's interest in the case could be. On the surface it was simply a case of a mugger being killed in self-defense by his intended victim, and the inquest was obviously a routine affair designed to clear the intended victim of any blame. The slant of the questions, not only of Robert Mummer's lawyer, but those of the assistant circuit attorney and the deputy coroner as well, indicated no one expected or wanted any verdict other than justifiable homicide.

I had no time to question Nels about it though, for the jury was out only thirty seconds. When it filed back in, the foreman read the verdict I expected: justifiable homicide.

Ordinarily, beyond noting down his name, age and address for my news item, I would have paid no further attention to the man who had just been cleared of homicide, for he was not a particularly impressive person. Nels Parker's unexplained interest in the case intrigued me though, and noting the sergeant

The Best of *Manhunt*

continued to linger in the courtroom until Robert Hummel finished shaking hands with his lawyer and finally moved toward the door, I lingered beside him.

When Robert Hummel was erect, you were less conscious of his unusually broad shoulders and the muscle underlying his fat than you were when he was seated. He looked like a well fed businessman who had reached the age when he ought to start watching his blood pressure. He also looked like the last person in the world you would expect to resist a professional mugger so successfully and so violently that the mugger ended up dead.

As the man passed from the courtroom, Nels continued to watch his back through the open door until he reached the stairs at the end of the hall and started down. Then the sergeant gave his head a slight shake and moved toward the stairs himself.

Falling in beside him, I said, "Buy you a drink, Sergeant?"

His dull eyes flicked at me. "One beer maybe. I got to get back to Homicide."

The nearest tavern to the Coroner's Court Building was a half block west. I waited until we were standing at the bar with a pair of draft beers in front of us before I asked any questions.

Then I said, "A story hidden here somewhere, Sergeant?"

He shook his head, tapped his glass once on the bar to indicate luck and sipped at his beer. "No story, Sam."

"Not even off the record?"

"Just a pipe dream I had, Sam. You couldn't print it without risking a libel suit."

"Then I won't print it. But I got curiosity. Whose case was this Garcia's? On Homicide, I mean."

"Corporal Brady," Nels said. "He wasn't there because the thing was so routine, all they needed was the beat cop's testimony. Probably I ought to have my head examined for wasting my time on a case I wasn't even assigned to."

When he lapsed into silence I asked, "What's the story?"

He drank half his beer before he answered. Then he said, "I was just interested because this guy Hummel killed a guy once before."

I raised my eyebrows.

"Almost the same circumstances too," the sergeant said. "A mugger down along Commercial Alley. Only that time the guy's larynx wasn't crushed. Hummel just choked him to death."

"Judas Priest!" I said. "Was there an inquest?"

Nels nodded. "Routine. Happened about twelve years ago. There's no doubt it was on the up and up. The mugger had a record as long as your arm and it was pretty well established Hummel never saw the guy before he was suddenly waylaid by him. Apparently the mugger had been loitering in a doorway for some time waiting for a likely victim to pass, for they turned up a witness placing him there a full hour before he tangled with Hummel. Picking Hummel was pure accident, and the mugger was just unlucky to jump a guy who looked soft, but turned out to have the strength of a gorilla." The sergeant paused, then added reflectively, "There wasn't any of this flashing a roll in dives then." His tone as he made the last statement struck me as odd.

"What do you mean by that?" I asked.

But the sergeant ignored my question. "Hummel didn't carry a gun then either. Matter of fact, it was as a result of the incident that he applied for a permit. He didn't have trouble getting one because he's an antique and rare coin buyer and carries large amounts of cash."

"You've been doing some detailed checking on the man." I remarked.

"Yeah. But it doesn't add up."

I eyed him narrowly for a moment, then signaled the bartender for two more beers. I said, "Now give me the pipe dream."

"Pipe dream?" he asked.

"You mentioned your interest in the case was a kind of pipe dream. You think there's some connection between the two cases?"

Nels took a sip of his fresh beer and shook his head. "I'm sure there isn't. Not between the two muggers anyway. Maybe a kind of psychological connection."

"What does that mean?"

"Well," the sergeant said slowly, "I figure the case twelve years ago was just what it seemed to be. A guy unexpectedly jumped Hummel, and Hummel killed him defending himself. So was the case today, I guess. With a slight difference. Maybe this time Hummel killed deliberately when he was jumped."

"You mean he deliberately lured Garcia into attacking him?"

"Think back over the testimony," Nels said. "Remember how surprised the great lawyer looked when the witness said Hummel had followed *Joe* in?"

"There was even something about Garcia remarking he had run into Hummel in another tavern. But why? What would be Hummel's motive?"

Nels was silent for a moment. Finally he said, "I checked back over unsolved homicides for the past twelve years, and seven of them were guys with records as muggers. They were found dead in alleys, some strangled, some broken necks."

"My God!" I said.

"That makes nine he could have killed."

For a moment I couldn't speak. "But why, for God's sake?"

Without inflection Nels said, "Twelve years ago I imagine Robert Hummel was just a normal guy. Or at least I imagine any abnormal urges he had were merely latent. Then he killed in self-defense. My pipe dream is that maybe he discovered he enjoyed it. You've heard of psychopathic killers."

"But . . . but . . ." I stuttered.

"But what? A guy flashes a roll in dives. There any law to stop him? A mugger tails him for an easy roll. The guy kills the mugger, and if nobody sees it, he just walks away. If he gets caught in the act, he merely tells the truth and the law gives him a pat on the back for defending himself against attack by a criminal. It's a psychopath's dream. He's figured a way to kill legally."

"But . . ." I whispered. "But . . . he couldn't possibly again . . ."

"The law says you can use whatever force is necessary to resist attack on your person or property. If you use more than necessary, theoretically you're guilty of manslaughter. In the case of a farmer shooting a kid stealing watermelons, we can prove unnecessary force, but how do you prove it in a case like today's? And even if we established beyond reasonable doubt that Hummel deliberately enticed a robbery attempt . . . which we couldn't do without a confession, no matter what we suspect . . . he still has a legal right to defend himself."

"You mean you intend to do nothing about a homicidal maniac?"

"Sure," Nels said calmly. "Next time we'll put a white light in his face and hammer questions at him until Marcus Prout walks in with a writ of habeas corpus. But unless we get a confession that he used more force than necessary to protect himself, he's safe even if he kills a man every week."

He laughed without any humor whatever, "Beyond picking him up and questioning him every time he kills, there isn't one damned thing in the world we can do to stop him."

Decision
Helen Nielsen

June 1957

Ruth had never been in a courtroom before. It was exciting—like something from a movie or the television. She paused just inside the doorway, the matron at her side, and as she did so the flashbulbs began to explode, and all the people in the room turned to stare at her. For just a moment she was startled and embarrassed. One hand automatically tugged at the front of her blue wool suit jacket—it had a way of riding up since she'd put on weight. Not that Ruth was plump. Her figure was good—too good for comfort, because Ruth, although she'd trained herself to conceal it, was excessively shy. But she was also feminine. She tugged at the jacket, and then she brushed a wisp of blonde hair from her forehead—and all of this with such a well-practiced concealment of emotion that the caption writers would be dusting off such phrases as "stony-faced tigress" and "iceberg killer" to fit under those pictures in the afternoon editions. By this time the flashbulbs had stopped exploding, and a policeman was clearing the way.

Ruth walked forward to the table where Mr. Jennings was waiting for her. He pulled out her chair and smiled.

"Good morning, Miss Kramer. You're looking well this morning"

Ruth didn't answer. She sat down, and then Mr. Jennings sat down beside her and began to fuss with some papers in his briefcase. Mr. Jennings was rather shy himself—and nervous. Ruth had heard it remarked that this was his first capital case, which accounted for the nervousness. Public Defender. She ran the words over in her mind. They had a good sound. This man was going to defend her from the public. No, that wasn't what the words really meant, Ruth knew. She'd learned a great many in her thirty-odd years, and she knew what just about all the words meant; but that's the way they sounded to her when she ran them over in her mind. She liked Mr. Jennings. He reminded her of Allan. Younger and more serious, but just as neat. That was the important thing. His white shirt was freshly laundered, his narrow tie was clipped in place, and his suit must have just come from the pressers. He was clean shaven and smelled of one of those lotions the ad writers call brisk and masculine.

But staring at Mr. Jennings would only make him more nervous. Ruth looked about the courtroom. The jury was in the box, their assorted faces wearing different degrees of strain. Ruth's bland face concealed an inner smile. The jury seemed even more nervous than Mr. Jennings. It might have been on trial instead of her. Then she turned and looked at the spectators. No trial since the Romans fed live dinners to the lions had been complete without them. The public—society. That was a word that amused her even more than the faces of the jury—society. There it was in its assembled might, neither frightening nor particularly offended. Curious was a better word. Curious society awaiting its cue to acquit or condemn, because society never knew until it was told what to do. It was like a huge mirror in which one saw not one reflection, but that of a crowd.

If I smiled, Ruth thought, they would smile back. If I waved my hand, they would wave their hands. They never do anything of themselves. They never act; they only re-act.

That was society, and she was outside of it now because she'd broken the first rule. She'd made a decision . . .

Everybody in the neighborhood could tell you how devoted Ruth Kramer was to her parents. Such a good girl. Such a hard worker. Such a good provider since poor old Mr. Kramer had to stop working. There wasn't a mother on the block who didn't envy Mrs. Kramer's relationship with her daughter. Not many young people were so thoughtful. Not many cared so much. Everybody in the neighborhood could tell you everything they knew about Ruth Kramer—which was nothing.

Ruth couldn't remember when she'd started hating her father. It might have been the time when she was five and caught him killing the puppies. They were new-born and hardly aware of life, and maybe it was the only thing to do with times so hard and food so short; but it was horrible to watch him toss their bodies, still warm and wriggling, into the post-holes he'd been digging for the back fence. It was even more horrible to hear him boast about it later.

"Six-post-holes, six puppies at the bottom. I saved myself all that work of digging graves."

"Otto, don't talk about it. Not in front of the child," Anna Kramer would say.

"Why not talk about it? She has to learn to save—work, money. Nobody can waste anything in life."

Otto Kramer had a simple philosophy. He never questioned life; he never argued with it. "A bed to sleep on, a table to eat on, a stove to cook on—what more do you need?" A very simple philosophy. Worry and fear belonged in a woman's world, and he had no sympathy for either. If Ruth had tears she could shed them in her mother's thin, tight arms. There was no other warmth in the world.

And there was no money to be wasted on the foolishness of pain.

"A woman is supposed to have babies. That's what she's made for. I ain't got money to throw away on hospital bills. It's all foolishness anyway. It's all in a woman's mind."

Otto Kramer spoke and that was law. Anna never argued with her husband. She just grew thin and pale and cried a great deal when he was away, and when her time came it wasn't all in her mind after all. Hidden behind the pantry door, a child heard everything.

"You thick-skulled old-country men ought to be horsewhipped!" the doctor said. "You lost a son for your stinginess, and you damned near lost a wife! Leave her alone now until she gets her strength back—understand? Leave her alone or I'll take care of you myself!"

Crouched in the darkness behind the pantry door, Ruth didn't understand—except that in some way her mother was in danger from this man she was growing to hate and needed protection. She never forgot.

There were a great many things the neighbors didn't know about Ruth Kramer. They didn't know, for instance, that when she was fourteen she slept with a knife hidden under her pillow. Nobody knew that. Not even her mother. But Ruth had watched and guarded for a long time, and by that time the quarreling and night noises beyond the paper-thin walls had taken on a strange and ominous significance. The knife was for her fear—a nameless fear that was doomed to silence.

Anna Kramer didn't like to talk about such things.

"Forget the silly things you hear, child. It's not for you to worry about."

But Ruth wasn't a child. She was fourteen. At fourteen it seems there should be an end to misery.

"Why don't you get a divorce?" she, asked.

Divorce! A shocking word. Where had she gotten such an idea? Divorce was a sin! It seemed to Ruth that perpetual unhappiness was an even greater sin; but she didn't have a chance to argue the point. The tight, thin arms were about her again, closing out the world. She mustn't think of such things. She had her school-work to think about, and that scholarship—

Ruth didn't win the scholarship. She suffered a breakdown and couldn't even finish the semester; but in a way, her sickness was a good thing. It gave her time to think things out. There had to be a reason for all this unhappiness, and there had to be a way out. If only they weren't so poor. If only there was a little extra money to fix up the house and have friends and live the way other people lived. Ruth thought it all out and then put the knife back in the knife drawer because it was foolishness, even if it was a sign of rebellion. She knew a better way.

There was no trouble about going back to school. School was an extravagance and a waste on a female. Work was good. Work kept young people out of trouble.

"I went to work when I was twelve years old," Otto Kramer said. "Fifteen hours a day and a straw pallet in the back of the shop. I had no time for racing around in old cars and playing jazz records all night like young people do nowadays. Hoodlums! Nothing but hoodlums!"

Ruth didn't argue. The old cars and the jazz records weren't to be a part of her life anyway. There was no time. Work was for days and study was for evenings, because her father was wrong about education. He was wrong about a lot of things, but she didn't argue about any of them. Arguments and quarreling were a waste of time. She learned to withdraw from them—to tune out the voices behind the wall at night, just as she tuned up the music on her bedside radio. But she always listened with half an ear, and she never forgot to watch. And she never forgot her plan. Every problem had to have a solution, and she was going to find the solution for happiness. Otto Kramer's house remained a fortress from without; but within, it began to change. The floors were carpeted, the windows curtained, a plumber installed a new sink, and the ice-man didn't have to stop by after the refrigerator was delivered. The plan began to work. Anna Kramer's face learned how to smile; but Otto's remained grim.

"Foolishness! Damn foolishness! Throw money around like that and you'll be sorry!"

And just to prove his point, he lost his job and never did get around to finding another one.

It might have been then that Ruth Kramer began to hate her father; but for the next few years she was too busy to think about it. Every problem had to have a solution. She did her positive thinking and took another course at night school. After that, she got a better job with longer hours. The problem was still there, but there wasn't so much time to think about it. What was happiness anyway? How many people ever knew? When the quarrelling was especially bad, and the tears too heavy—Ruth could never bear to hear her mother cry—she could set a balance again with flowers sent as a surprise, or some new piece for the shelf of china miniatures Anna Kramer so loved. And there was always the music to be turned up louder so the neighbors wouldn't hear. From the outside, everything was lovely. Nobody ever went into the house but the three people who lived inside, enduring one another while the years piled up behind them like a stack of unpaid bills. And everything in life had to be paid for sooner or later. Far back in her mind, crowded now with more knowledge than she could ever use, Ruth knew that.

The bills began coming due when she met Allan.

She'd never thought about men. They were in her world; but they were only names on the doors of offices, or voices answering the telephone. They sat behind desks that always held a photograph of the wife and children, and they sometimes paid compliments and gave raises.

"I wish we had more employees like you, Miss Kramer. I never have to worry about how you're going to do your work."

That kind of compliment—never anything about her hair-do, which was severe and neat, or her suits, which were tailored to conceal her thinness and build up her bustline. Men were hands on desktops, voices on the telephone, and signatures on the paycheck. They were the office wolf to be ignored, the out of town customer to be kidded, and the serious young man who missed his mother to be gently brushed aside. And a dour old man who now sat at home in his chair in the corner like a pile of dirty rags.

But Allan Roberts wasn't any of these things. Allan was that old bill coming due. If she'd known, she wouldn't have been so pleased when he called her into his office that first day.

"I like the way you work, Miss Kramer. You must have been with the company a long time."

A new engineer with top rating, and he'd noticed her out of the whole office staff. Ruth was flattered.

"Twelve years," she admitted, wishing, for some reason, that it didn't sound so long.

"Good. You know more about procedure than I do. You're just the assistant I need on this hotel job."

That's how it started—strictly business. But it was a big job—an important job. It meant long hours with late dinners in some hole-in-the-wall restaurant, with a juke box wailing and a lot of talk and laughter to ease the strain of a hard, tense job. It meant work on Sunday, with Allan's convertible honking at the curb, and Ruth hurrying out before he had time to come to the door. And, eventually, it meant talk at home.

"You're with this man an awful lot," Anna Kramer said.

"He's nice," Ruth admitted. "And smart. I'm learning a lot on this job."

"He looks nice. He dresses nice."

"He's got a responsible job. He has to dress nice."

"Your father used to dress nice. I'll never forget when I met him—silk shirts, derby hat, walking stick."

"My father?"

"Handsome, too. I remember thinking that I'd never seen such a handsome man—and such big ideas for the future."

They'd never talked like this before. Anna Kramer's eyes were far away; then they met Ruth's and changed the subject.

"I suppose you'll be working Sunday."

"I suppose I will," Ruth said.

"We'll miss church again."

"I keep telling you, you should make friends with the neighbors and go with them."

Anna sighed. Her eyes found the miniatures on the shelf.

"You know how your father feels about neighbors. I don't like to start a fuss and get you upset when we have such a nice home now."

Ruth worked Sunday. She worked many Sundays, and then, as much as she dreaded it, the job ended.

"But we're invited to the opening," Allan said. "When shall I pick you up?"

She hadn't counted on that. Working with Allan was fun. Dinner in those small cafés was fun. But a hotel opening wasn't like a concert, or a lecture, or a class at evening school.

"I suppose it's formal," she hedged.

"I hope so. You'll be a knockout in an evening gown."

He was kidding her, of course. Allan was a great kidder. Still, she didn't like to refuse. It might even jeopardize her job. She took a lunch hour for shopping, because she'd never owned an evening dress. That was when she became the last person to be aware of what had been going on under those tailored suits all the years. Allan wasn't kidding.

Cinderella went to the ball. Poor Cinderella, who was always losing things. A dance floor wasn't much good to a collector of Bach, but Allan was gallant.

"I might as well be honest," he said. "It doesn't show because I have my shoes made to order, but I've got two left feet. Let's see how the terrace looks in the moonlight."

The terrace looked the way all terraces look in the moonlight. Ruth was trembling when she pulled away from him. They hadn't taught her anything like that in night school. But she was embarrassed, too. He must have known. He could go back to the office and tell stories in the washroom about how he'd frightened that straight-laced Miss Kramer who was so efficient in so many other things.

"You live with your parents, don't you?"

She expected that. She didn't have to answer. She already felt alone.

"I mean, you don't have any other ties to hold you here?" She didn't expect that.

"To hold me?"

"There's a new contract coming up in Mexico City. A big one—six months, maybe a year. I'm getting the assignment, and I'd like to have you come along. I think we work well together."

She didn't expect that at all. Mexico City. A Latin beat from the dance floor came up behind them, a deep, throbbing rhythm, and Ruth began to hear it for the first time. To hear it, and feel it, with a stirring and churning starting inside her as if something were being born.

And she could feel Allan's eyes smiling in the darkness.

"I think you'd like Mexico," he said. "I think the change will do you good. Anyway, you've got a couple of weeks to decide."

It was much after midnight when Cinderella came home from the ball. She stopped humming at the doorway and let herself in quietly; but she needn't have been so cautious. As soon as she switched on the lights, she saw her mother huddled in the wing-chair.

"You didn't have to wait up—" she began, and then she saw her mother's face. "What is it? What's wrong?"

The face of a martyr taking up the cross.

"Nothing," Anna answered. "Nothing for you to worry about."

"Nothing? Then why aren't you in bed?"

Haunted eyes looked at her. A thin hand tugged at the throat of a worn robe, and the sleeve fell back to show an ugly bruise.

"Mother—!"

"Go to bed," Anna said. "You had a nice time, didn't you? Go to bed and don't worry about me."

"But you've been hurt!"

"It doesn't matter. It's happened before."

"*He* did it!"

An anger flared up as old as a knife tucked away under a pillow.

"Don't—don't talk so loud! He's asleep now."

"But you don't have to put up with this! You don't have to live with him!"

Anna's eyes swept the room. A beautiful room—perfect, like the miniatures on the shelf. The home she'd always wanted. Some plans did work.

"Maybe he's sick," Ruth said. "Maybe if he saw a doctor—"

"You know what your father thinks of doctors."

"But if he's violent—"

Anna wore a sad smile.

"I told you—it's nothing. It's happened before. You would have noticed if you weren't always so busy. He's an old man, that's all. An old man gets angry when—when he can't do what he used to do."

Anna fell silent. There was shame in her eyes for having almost spoken of the forbidden subject. She got up out of the chair and started toward the hall.

"You're not going back there?"

The sad smile came back.

"I told you—it's nothing. I shouldn't have said anything and ruined your good time. Go to bed now. It's all right. As long as I have you, everything is all right."

The arms closed about Ruth's shoulders in a goodnight embrace. Nothing . . . nothing . . . Ruth turned out the lamp when she was gone and sat alone in the darkness. Nothing . . . She began to tremble.

Ruth didn't go to Mexico City. At the office, her breakdown was written off to overwork on the hotel job. When she returned, Allan was gone. He never came back. For a time there was an empty place where he had been, a kind of misty pitfall with a mental sign in front of it: "Keep Away—Danger," and then the emptiness began to fill up with odds and ends of more work, more books, a course in clay modelling, and a season's ticket to the symphony. At home she played the music louder to drown out the endless quarrelling, and learned not to mention separation, or a doctor, or doing anything at all.

On her thirtieth birthday, Ruth bought her first bottle of whiskey. She kept it in a closet where her mother wouldn't find it. Good people, who didn't do sinful things—such as not facing problems—didn't drink. The bottle helped on the long nights when sleep wouldn't come. A little later, she dropped the modelling class because she'd lost interest in it, and the homework was cluttering up her room, and she had to stop going to the concerts because they made her nervous. But she couldn't sit around the house watching the slow death come. She drove out nights, and in time found a hole-in-the-wall bar where a three piece combo wandered deep into the wild nowhere, and a sad singer sobbed out the woes of the shadow people, who feel no pain and dream old dreams that never come true because they live in the land of no decision.

There were objections, of course.

"I wish you wouldn't go out so much alone," Anna Kramer said, "especially at nights."

Ruth laughed. She laughed a lot lately.

"Alone? How else could I go?"

The hurt look, and then—

"We used to take such nice rides on Sunday."

"I'll take you for a ride on Sunday."

"But every night—out. Honestly, I don't know what to make of you anymore. You'd think I had enough trouble with your father!"

"Oh, God—!"

Then a door would slam, the music go loud, and she'd dig the bottle out of the closet.

The trouble at the office was a long time coming. It wasn't her fault. Everything cluttered, everything a mess. The youngsters were coming in—fresh and eager and green. No use trying to teach them anything. They knew it all. It got so that Ruth hardly talked to anyone except the clown in the sales department who told ribald jokes and made her laugh without knowing why. The trouble was a long time coming, but it came suddenly when it arrived. With gloves, of course. Working too hard. Too much responsibility. Not a demotion, understand, but the hours will be shorter and, of course, the pay. Ruth understood. The strange thing was how little she cared.

She didn't go home after work. She drove around for a few hours, and then drifted back to that hole in the wall where the shadows moaned, and crouched, and waited. Now it seemed that they were waiting for her—that this was the destiny she'd been bound for all these years. This was what came of hiding behind pantry doors and trembling in the darkness with a knife under her pillow. She knew what was wrong. She couldn't bury it in the books or try to hide it in the bottom of an empty bottle anymore. It crawled inside her like a worm of dread, and there was only one way to get rid of it. She ordered a double whiskey to steel her nerve.

The shadow people moved about her with hungry faces. At first she'd come only to watch them; now she belonged. She had only to give the sign. They were waiting. One, in particular, a dark, dirty, unshaven man.

They went out together. They drove to a dark street—dead end. It seemed appropriate.

No preliminaries. This wasn't a high school prom. He knew what she wanted. His mouth closed over hers, and his hands began tearing at her blouse. Ruth shuddered. The stirring that had started with Allan's kiss was churning up like an angry sea. A wall was crumbling. A high wall, a high tower—

But her hands were pushing him away.

He clawed at her, swearing softly. She pushed him back against the door.

"You crazy bitch!"

He came at her again, ugly and cruel. She saw his face dimly—unshaven, leering, smelling of liquor and filth. All of her strength went into her lunge. He fell backward against the door handle. It opened, spilling him out in the street. She had the motor started by the time he'd scrambled to his feet. The headlights caught him for one wild moment as she backed away—an angry and bewildered man, muttering curses and fumbling at his trousers.

She drove blindly, half sobbing. When it was far enough behind, she parked and sat alone in the darkness. The wall had started to crumble, and when a thing started it had to go on until it was done. She smashed the "Danger" sign in her mind and stared deep into the emptiness that was Allan's. Allan was gone. Allan would never come back. She'd never hear his laughter, or see the way his eyes crinkled, or feel that second kiss that had made all the difference. But the world wasn't over. There was other laughter and other eyes, and there was a difference! There had to be!

But before she could find it, there was one thing she must do. One thing for certain.

She drove home, noticing for the first time how the hedges had become shaggy and how the lawn had turned brown. There were so many things to do, and never enough time. She went into the house. Her father sat in his chair in the corner like a heap of dirty rags. Her mother looked up with anxious eyes. She hurried past them to her room. One thing she *must* do . . .

"Ruth! What are you doing? Where are you going?"

One suitcase was enough. The furniture, the lamps, the books didn't matter. Let the dead bury the dead. One suitcase and tomorrow was enough.

"Why are you packing? What's happened? What's wrong?"

No answers. No explanations. No trouble. Ruth closed the suitcase and started toward the door. They were there, both of them. The woman and the old man. Bewildered, frightened. She tried to get through the door without speaking, but they blocked the way.

"I'm leaving," she said.

"Leaving? For a trip? On business?"

"Forever," Ruth said.

"But why? What have I done?"

Tears were welling up in the woman's eyes. Ruth couldn't bear tears. She tried to push past. Her father was in the way.

"Who do you think you are?" he demanded. "You answer your mother!"

"There is no answer."

"You be careful now! You ain't so damn smart as you think. You ain't no better than us! You'll end up in the gutter like I always said!"

He shouldn't have said it—not ever, but especially not then. An ugly, dirty, unshaven old man. She looked at him and trembled, and then it started again—the shuddering, the churning inside.

"Let me go!" she gasped.

He tried to push her back into the room. He slapped her across the face, and the wall was crumbling again. She had the suitcase in her hand. She swung with all her might. She heard him go down, and then the ugly, evil face was gone . . .

"Ruth—what have you done?"

He was on the floor—quiet and bleeding.

"Your own father! You've struck down your own father!"

Anna knelt beside him, cradling his bleeding head in her arms.

"Otto! Otto, are you alive? *Liebchen*—"

Ruth stared at them. The woman sobbing, her head bowed and her tight, thin arms, cradling him closer and closer to her breast. Her child. Her broken child caught up in the great-mother-lust, that subtle rape from which there is no escape save one . . .

And the wall was crumbling so that Ruth's breath came in great, silent sobs. When a thing started it had to be finished, one way or another. She moved slowly toward her mother.

The murmur of voices in the courtroom silenced and everybody rose as the judge came to the bench. A handsome, dignified man graving at the temples. Stern and fatherly. He sat down, and everybody sat down. It was about to begin. Exciting. Just like in the movies.

And then a man came across the room and bent down to whisper in Mr. Jennings' ear. Mr. Jennings looked happy. He turned to Ruth.

"Good news!" he said. "Your father has regained consciousness. He's ready to testify that he struck you first—that you retaliated in self-defense."

Of course, Ruth thought. Somebody has to look after him.

"That gives you a good chance of getting off completely. We should have little trouble proving that your mother's death was accidental. Everybody knows how devoted you were."

For just a moment Ruth felt the quick stab of panic; and then her poise returned and she sat back quietly. The jury—only faces in a mirror. She'd never let them acquit her. Nobody was going to send her back to that house now that she'd made her decision.

The Collector Comes After Payday
Fletcher Flora

August 1953

Frankie looked through a lot of bars before he found the old man. He was sitting in a booth in a joint on lower Market Street with a dame Frankie didn't know. They were both sitting on the same side of the booth, and Frankie could see that their thighs were plastered together like a couple of strips of Scotch tape.

"Come on home, Pop," Frankie said. "You come on home."

The woman looked up at him, and her lips twisted in a scarlet sneer. The scarlet was smeared on the lips, as if she'd been doing a lot of kissing, and the lips had a kind of bruised and swollen look, as if the kisses had been pretty enthusiastic.

"Go to hell away, sonny," she said.

She lifted her martini glass by its thin stem and tilted it against her mouth. Frankie reached across the booth in front of the old man and slapped the glass out of her hand. It shivered with a thin, musical sound against the wall, and gin and vermouth splashed down between the full, alert breasts that were half out of her low-cut dress. The olive bounced on the table and rolled off.

The woman raised up as far as she could in the cramped booth, her eyes hot and smoky with gin and rage.

"You little son of a bitch," she said softly.

Frankie grabbed her by a wrist and twisted the skin around on the bone.

"Leave Pop alone," he said. "You quit acting like a tramp and leave him alone."

Then the old man hacked down on Frankie's arm with the horny edge of his hand. It was like getting hit with a dull hatchet. Frankie's fingers went numb, dropping away from the woman's wrist, and he swung sideways with his left hand at the old man's face. The old man caught the fist in a big palm and gave Frankie a hard shove backward.

"Blow, sonny," he said.

For a guy not young at all, he was plenty tough. His eyes were like two yellow agates, and his mouth was a thin, cruel trap under a bold nose. From the way his body behaved, it was obvious that he still had good muscular coordination. He was poised, balanced like a trained fighter.

Frankie saw everything in a kind of pink, billowing mist. He moved back up to the booth with his fists clenched, and in spite of everything he could do, tears of fury and frustration spilled out of his eyes and streaked his cheeks.

"You get the hell out of this," he said. "You ought to be ashamed, drinking and playing around this way."

The old man slipped out of the booth, quick as a snake, and chopped Frankie in the mouth with a short right that traveled straight as a piston. Frankie hit the floor and rolled over, spitting a tooth and blood. He was crazy. Getting up, he staggered back at the old man, cursing and sobbing and swinging like a girl. This time the old man set him up with a left jab and threw a bomb. Frankie went over backward like a post, his head smacking with a wet rotten sound.

No one bothered about him. Except to laugh, that is. Lying there on the floor, he could hear the laughter rise and diminish and rise again. It was the final and utter degradation of a guy who'd never had much dignity to start with. Rolling over and struggling up to his hands and knees, he was violently sick, his stomach contracting and expanding in harsh spasms. After a long time, he got the rest of the way to his feet in slow, agonizing stages. His chin and shirt front were foul with blood and spittle.

In the booth, ignoring him, the old man and the woman were in a hot clinch, their mouths adhering in mutual suction. The lecherous old man's right hand was busy, and Frankie saw through his private red fog the quivering reaction of the woman's straining body. Turning away, Frankie went out. The floor kept tilting up under his feet and then dropping suddenly away. All around him, he could hear the ribald laughter.

2.

It was six blocks to the place where he'd parked his old Plymouth. He walked slowly along the littered, narrow street, hugging the dark buildings, the night air a knife in his lungs. Now and then he stopped to lean against solid brick until the erratic pavement leveled off and held still. Once, at the mouth of an alley, he was sick again, bringing up a thin, bitter fluid into his mouth.

It took him almost an hour to get back to the shabby walkup apartment that was the best a guy with no luck could manage. In the bathroom, he splashed cold water on his face, gasping with pain. The smoky mirror above the lavatory distorted his face, exaggerating the ugliness of smashed, swollen lips drawn back from bloody gums. He patted his face dry with a towel and poured himself a double shot in the living room. He tossed the whiskey far back into his mouth beyond his raw lips, gagging and choking from the sudden fiery wash in his throat.

Dropping into a chair, he began to think. Not with any conscious direction. His mind functioned, with everything coming now to a bad end, in a kind of numb and lucid detachment. Suddenly, he was strangely indifferent. Nothing had happened, after all, that couldn't have been anticipated by a guy with no luck whatever.

It was funny, the way he was no longer very concerned about anything. Sitting there in the drab living room in the dull immunity to shame that comes from the ultimate humiliation, he found his mind working itself back at random to the early days at home with the old man. Back to the days when his mother, a beaten nonentity, had been alive. Not a lovable character, the old man. Not easy on wife or kid. A harsh meter of stern discipline for all delinquencies but his own. A master of the deferred payment technique. In the old days, when Frankie was a kid at home, wrongdoing had never been met with swift and unconsidered punishment that would have been as quickly forgotten. The old man had remarked and remembered. Later, often after Frankie had completely forgotten the adolescent evil he'd committed, there was sure to be something that he wanted very much to do. Then the old man would look at him with skimmed milk eyes and say, "No. Have you forgotten the offense for which you haven't paid? For that, you cannot do this thing."

Wait till it really hurts. That had been the old man's way.

Remembering, Frankie laughed softly, air hissing with no inflection of humor through the hole where his lost tooth had been. No luck. Never any luck. He'd even been a loser in drawing an old man—a bastard with a memory like an elephant and a perverted set of values.

The laughter hurt Frankie's mangled lips, and he cut it off, sitting slumped in the chair with his eyes in a dead focus on the floor. It was really very strange, the way he felt. Not tired. Not sleepy. Not much of anything. Just sort of released and out of it, like a religious queer staring at his belly button.

He was still sitting there at three o'clock in the morning when the old man came in. He was sloppy drunk, and the lines of his face had blurred, letting his features run together in a kind of soft smear. His eyes were rheumy infections in the smear, and his mouth still wore enough of the cheap lipstick to give him the appearance of wearing a grotesque clown's mask. He stood, swaying, almost helpless, with his legs spread wide and his hands on his hips in a posture of defiance, and Frankie looked back at him from his chair. It made him sick to see the old man so ugly, satiety in his flaccid face and the nauseous perfume of juniper berries like a fog around him.

The old man spit and laughed hoarsely. The saliva landed on the toe of Frankie's shoe, a milky blob. Without moving, Frankie watched the old man weave into the bedroom with erratic manipulation of legs and hips.

Frankie kept on sitting in the chair for perhaps five minutes longer, then he sighed and got up and walked into the bedroom after the old man. The old man was standing in the middle of the room in his underwear. His legs were corded with swollen blue veins that bulged the fish-belly skin. On the right thigh there was an angry red spot that would probably blacken. When he saw Frankie watching him, his rheumy eyes went hot with scorn.

"My son," he said. "My precious son, Frankie."

Frankie didn't answer. As he moved toward the old man slowly, smiling faintly, the pain of the smile on his mangled lips was a pale reflection of the dull pain in his heart. He had almost closed the distance between them before the old man's gin-soaked brain understood that Frankie was going to kill him. And he was too drunk now to defend himself, even against Frankie. The scorn faded from his eyes and terror flooded in, cold and incredulous.

"No, Frankie," he whispered. "For God's sake, no."

Frankie still didn't say anything, and the old man tried to back away, but by that time it was too late, and Frankie's thumbs were buried in his throat. His tongue came out, his legs beat in a hellish threshing, and his fists battered wildly at Frankie's face. But it did no good, for Frankie was feeling very strong. He was feeling stronger than he had ever felt in his life before. And good, too. A powerful, surging sense of well-being. A wild, singing exhilaration that increased in ratio to the pressure of his grip.

The old man had been dead for minutes when Frankie finally let him go. He slipped down to the floor in a limp huddle of old flesh and fabric, and Frankie stood looking down at him, the narcotic-like pleasure draining out of him and leaving him again with that odd, incongruous feeling of detachment.

He realized, of course, that the end was his as much as the old man's. It was the end for both of them. Recalling the .38 revolver on a shelf in the closet, he considered for a moment the idea of suicide, but not very seriously. Not that he was repelled by the thought of death. It was just that he didn't quite have the guts.

He supposed that he should call the police, and he went so far as to turn away toward the living room and the telephone. Then he stopped, struck by an idea that captured his fancy. He saw himself walking into the precinct station with the old man's dead body in his arms. He heard himself saying quietly, "This is my father. I've just killed him." Drab little Frankie, no-luck Frankie, having in the end his moment of dramatic ascendancy. It was a prospect that fed an old and functional hunger of his soul, and he turned back, looking at the body on the floor. Smiling dreamily with his thick lips, he felt within himself a rebirth of that singing exhilaration.

At the last moment, he found in himself a sick horror that made it impossible for him to bear excessive contact with the dead flesh, so he dressed the body, struggling with uncooperative arms and legs. After that, it was so easy. It was so crazy easy. If he'd given a damn, if he'd really been trying to get away with it, he could never have pulled it off in a million years.

With the old man dead in his arms, he walked out of the apartment and down the stairs and across the walk to the Plymouth at the curb. He opened the front door and put him in the seat and closed the door again. Then, standing there beside the car, he looked around and saw that there was no one in sight. So far as he knew, not a soul had seen him.

It was then that the enormity of the thing struck him, and he began to laugh softly, hysteria threading the laughter. No-luck Frankie doing a thing like that. No-luck Frankie himself just walking out of an apartment house with a corpse in his arms and not a damned soul the wiser. You couldn't get life any crazier than that. He kept on laughing, clutching the handle of the car door with one hand, his body shaking and his lips cracking open again to let a thin red line trace its way down his chin.

After a while, he choked off the laughter on a series of throaty little gasps that tore painfully at his throat. Lighting a cigarette, he went around the car and got in beside the old man on the driver's side.

He drove at a moderate rate of speed, savoring morbidly the approach to his big scene. Now, in the process of execution, the drama of it gained even more in its appeal to him. It gave him a kind of satisfaction he had never known.

He was driving east on Mason Street. The side streets on the south descended to their intersections on forty-five-degree grades. Possessing the right-of-way, he crossed the intersections without looking, absorbed in his thoughts. For that reason, he neither saw nor heard the transport van until it was too late. At the last instant, he heard the shrill screaming of rubber on concrete and looked up and right to see the tremendous steel monster roaring down upon him.

His own scream cut across the complaint of giant tires, and he hurled himself away reflexively, striking the door with a shoulder and clawing at the handle. The door burst open at the precise instant of impact, and he was catapulted through the air like a flapping doll. Striking the pavement, he rolled over and over, protecting his head with his arms instinctively. The overwhelming crash of the Plymouth crumpling under the van was modified in his ears by the fading of consciousness.

On his back, he lay quietly and was aware of smaller sounds—distant screams, pounding feet, horrified voices, and, after a bit, the far away whine of sirens growing steadily nearer and louder.

Someone knelt beside him, felt his pulse, said in manifest incredulity, "This guy's hardly scratched. It's a God-damned miracle."

A voice, more distant, rising on the threat of hysteria, "Christ! This one's hamburger. Nothing but hamburger."

And he continued to lie there in the screaming night with the laughter coming back and the wild wonder growing. What was it? What in God's name was it? A guy who'd started and ended with a sour bastard of an old man and never any luck between. A guy who'd had it all, and most of it bad. A guy like that getting, all of a sudden, two fantastic breaks you wouldn't have believed could happen. Walking out of a house with a body in his arms, scot-free and away. Surviving with no more than a few bruises a smash-up that should have smeared him for keeps. Maybe it was because he'd quit caring. Maybe the tide turns when you no longer give a damn.

Then, in a sudden comprehensive flash, the full significance of the situation struck him. Hamburger, someone had said. Nothing but hamburger. Thanks to the cock-eyed collaboration of the gods and a truck driver, *he had disposed of the old man in a manner above suspicion.* He lay on the pavement with the wonder of it still growing and growing, and his insides shook with delirious internal laughter.

4.

In time, he rode a litter to an ambulance, and the ambulance to a hospital. He slept like a child in antiseptic cleanliness between cool sheets, and in the morning he had pictures taken of his head. Twenty-four hours later he was told that there was no concussion, and released. With the most sympathetic cooperation of officials, he collected the old man at the morgue and transferred him to a crematory.

When he left the crematory, he took the old man with him in an urn. In the apartment, he set the urn on a table in the living room and stood looking at it. He had developed for the old man, since the smash-up, a feeling of warm affection. In his heart there was no hard feeling, no lingering animosity. He found his parent in his present state, a handful of ashes, considerably more lovable than he had ever found him before. Besides, he had brought Frankie luck. In the end, in shame and violence and blood, he had brought him the luck he had never had.

Putting the old man away on a shelf in the closet, Frankie checked his finances and found that he could assemble forty dollars. He fingered the green stuff and considered possibilities. Eagerness to ride his luck had assumed the force of compulsion. In the saddle, he left the apartment and went over to Nick Loemke's bar on Market Street.

He found Nick in a lull, polishing glass behind the mahogany. Nick examined him sleepily and made a swipe at the bar with his towel.

"What's on your mind, Frankie?"

"Double shot of rye," Frankie said.

His lips and gums were still a little raw, so he took it easy with the rye, tossing it in short swallows on the back of his tongue.

"Where's Joe Tonty anchored this week?" he asked.

"What the hell do you care, Frankie? You can't afford to operate in that class."

"You never know. You never know until you try."

Frankie finished his rye and spun the glass off his fingertips across the bar. It hit the trough on the inside edge and hopped up into the air. Nick had to grab it in a hurry to keep it from going off onto the floor. He glared at Frankie and doused the glass in the antiseptic solution under the bar.

"What the hell's the matter with you, Frankie? You lost your marbles?"

"Okay, okay," Frankie said. "I ask for information and you give me lip. You going to tell me where Tonty's anchored, or aren't you?"

Nick shrugged. "All right, sucker. It's your lettuce. Over on Third Street. Upstairs over the old Bonfile garage."

Frankie dropped a skin on the bar and went out. Between Third and Fourth, he navigated a narrow, cluttered alley to the rear of the Bonfile garage and climbed a flight of iron, exterior stairs to a plank door that was locked. He pounded on the door with the meaty heel of his fist and got the response of a crack with an eye and a voice behind it.

The voice said, "Hello, Frankie. What the hell you doing here?"

"This where Tonty's anchored?"

"That's right."

"Then what the hell you think I'm doing here? You want me to spell it out for you?"

The crack widened to reveal a flat face split in a grin between thick ears. "My, my. We're riding high tonight, ain't we?"

"You want my money or not?"

The crack spread still wider, and the grinning gorilla shuffled back out of it. "Sure, Frankie, sure. Every little bit helps."

Frankie went in past the gorilla and down the long cement-floored room to the craps table. It was still early, and the big stuff wasn't moving yet. Just right for forty bucks. Or thirty-nine, deducting a double shot.

Frankie got his belly against the edge of the table and laid a fast side bet that the point would come.

It came.

He laid three more in a hurry, betting the accumulation and mixing them pro and con without thinking much about it.

The points came or not, just as Frankie bet them.

When the dice came around to him, he was fat, and he laid the bundle. He tossed a seven, made his point twice, and tossed another seven, letting the bundle grow. Then, playing a hunch without benefit of thought, he drew most of the bundle off the table.

He crapped out and passed the dice.

Across the table, Joe Tonty's face was a slab of gray rock. His eyes flicked over Frankie, and his shoulders twitched in a shrug.

"Your luck's running, Frankie. You better ride it."

"Sure," Frankie said. "I'll ride."

It kept running for two hours, and Frankie rode it all the way. When he finally had a sudden flat feeling, a kind of interior collapse, he pulled out. Not that he felt his luck had quit running for keeps. Just resting. Just taking a breather. He descended the iron steps into the alley and crossed over to Market for a nightcap at Nick's. A little later, in the living room of the apartment, he counted eight grand. It was hard to believe, little Frankie with eight big grand all at once and all his own. Not even any withholding tax.

He was shaken again by the silent delirium that was becoming an integral element of his chronic mood, and he went over to the closet and opened the door, looking up at the old man in his urn.

"Thanks, Pop," he said. "Thanks."

5.

He slept soundly and got up about noon. After a hearty lunch, he went to the track with the eight grand in his pocket. He was in time for the second race, and he checked the entries. But he didn't feel anything, so he let it go.

Checking the entries in the third, he still didn't get any nudge. Something seemed to be getting in the way, coming between him and his luck. Maybe, he realized suddenly, it was the warm pressure of a long flank against his.

He turned, looking into brown eyes that were as warm and the touch of flank. Under the eyes there was a flash of white in a margin of red, and above them, a heavy sheen of pale yellow with streaks of off-white running through it. At first, Frankie thought she'd just been sloppy with a dye job, but then he saw that the two-toned effect was natural.

"Crowded, isn't it?" she said.

Frankie grinned. "I like crowds."

He was trying to think of what the hair reminded him of when he got the nudge. His eyes popped down to the program in his hands and back up to the dame. Inside, he'd gone breathless and tense, the way a guy does when he's on the verge of something big.

"What's your name, baby?"

The red and white smile flashed again. "Call me Taffy. Because of my hair, you see."

He saw, all right. He saw a hell of a lot more than she thought he did. He saw number four in the third, and the name was Taffy Candy. One would bring ten if

Taffy won, and even Frankie, who was no mental giant, could add another cipher to eight thousand and read the result.

Don't give yourself time to think, that was the trick. If you start thinking, you start figuring odds and consequences, and you're a dead duck. He stood up and slapped the program against his leg.

"Hold a spot for me, baby. If I'm on the beam, it'll be a big day for you and me and a horse."

He hit the window just before closing time and laid the eight grand on Taffy's nose. At the rail of the track, he watched the horses run, and he wasn't surprised, not even excited, when Taffy came in by the nose that had his eight grand on it. It was astonishing how quickly he was becoming accustomed to good fortune. He was already anticipating the breaks as if he'd had them forever. As if they were a natural right.

Like that girl in the stands, for instance. The girl who called herself Taffy. Standing there by the rail, he thought with glandular stirrings of the warm pressure of flank, the strangely alluring two-toned pastel hair, the brown eyes and scarlet smile. A few days ago, he wouldn't have given himself a chance with a dame like that. He'd have taken it out in thinking. But now it was different. Luck and a few grand made a hell of a difference. The difference between thinking and acting.

With eight times ten in his pocket, he went back to the stands. Climbing up to her level with his eyes full of nylon, he grinned and said, "We all came in, baby, you and me and the horse. Let's move out of here."

She strained a mocking look through incredible lashes. "I've already got a date, honey. I'm supposed to meet a guy here."

"To hell with him."

Her eyebrows arched their plucked backs, and a practiced tease showed through the lashes. "What makes you think I'd just walk off with you, mister?"

Frankie dug into his pocket for enough green to make an impression. The bills were crisp. They made small ticking sounds when he flipped them with a thumb nail.

"This, maybe," he said.

She eyed the persuasion and stood up. "That's good thinking, honey," she said.

6.

A long time and a lot of places later, Frankie awoke to the gray light that filtered into his shabby apartment. It was depressing, he thought, to awake in a dump like this. It was something that had to be changed.

"Look, baby," he said. "Today we shop for another place. A big place uptown. Carpets up to your knees, foam rubber stuff, the works. How about it, baby?"

Beside him, Taffy pressed closer, her lips moving against his naked shoulder with a sleepy animal purr of contentment.

So that day they rented the uptown place, and moved in, and a couple months later Frankie bought the Circle Club.

The club was a nice little spot tucked into a so-so block just outside the perimeter of the big-time glitter area. It was a good location for a brisk trade with the right guy handling it. The current owner was being pressed for the payment of debts by parties who didn't like waiting, and Frankie bought him out for a song.

It was a swell break. Just one more in a long line. Frankie shot a wad on fancy trimmings, and booked a combination that could really jump. With the combo there was a sleek canary who had something for the eyes as well as the ears. The food and the liquor were fair, which is all anyone expects in a night spot, and up to the time of Linda Lee, business was good.

After Linda Lee, business was more than good. It was booming. The word always goes out on a gal like Linda. The guys come in with their dames, and after they've had the quota of looking that the tariff buys, they go someplace and turn off the lights and pretend that the dames are Linda.

Linda Lee wasn't her real name, of course, but it suited her looks and her business. Ostensibly, the business was dancing. Actually, it was taking off her clothes. In Linda's case, that was sufficient. As for the looks, they were Linda's, and they were something. Dusky skin and eyes on the slant. Black hair with blue highlights, soft and shining, brushing her shoulders and slashing across her forehead in bangs above perfect unplucked brows. A lithe, vibrant body with an upswept effect that a guy couldn't believe from seeing and so had to keep coming back for another look to convince himself.

She sent Frankie. At first, the day she came into his office at the Circle Club looking for a job, he didn't see anything but a looker in a town that was littered with them. That was when she still had her clothes on.

He rocked back in his swivel and stared across his desk at her through the thin, lifting smoke from his cigarette.

"You a dancer, you say?"

"Yes."

"A good one."

"Not very."

That surprised Frankie. He took his cigarette out of his mouth and let his eyes make a brief tour of her points of interest.

"No? What else you got that a guy would pay to see?"

She showed him what she had. Frankie sat there watching her emerge slowly from her clothes, and the small office got steadily smaller, so hot that it was almost suffocating. Frankie's knitted tie was hemp instead of silk, and the knot was a hangman's knot, cutting deeply into his throat until he was breathing in labored gasps. The palms of his hands dripped salty water. His whole body was wet with sweat.

When he was able to speak, he said, "Who the hell's going to care about the dancing? Can you start tonight?"

She could and did. And so did Frankie. For a guy with a temperature as high as his, he played it pretty cool. He kept the pressure on her, all right, but he didn't force it. Not that he was too good for it. It just wasn't practical. The threat of being fired doesn't mean much to a gal with a dozen other places to go. By the time Frankie was desperate enough for threats, he was having to raise her pay every second week to hang on to her.

She liked him, though. He knew damned well she liked him. He could tell by the way the heat came up in her slanted eyes when she looked at him. He could tell by the way her hands sometimes reached out for him, touching him lightly, straying with brief abandon. But she was like mercury. He couldn't hold her when he reached back.

7.

The night he decided to try mink, he came into the club late, just as Linda was moving onto the small circular floor in a blue spot. He stood for a minute against the wall, holding the long cardboard box under his arm, watching the emerging dusky body, his pulse matching the tropical tempo of drums in the darkness. Before the act was over, he moved on around the edge of the floor and back to the door of Linda's room.

Inside, he lay the box on the dressing table and sat down. Waiting, he could hear faintly the crescendo of drums and muted brass that indicated Linda's exit. The sound of her footsteps in the hall was lost in the surge of applause that continued long after she had left the floor.

She closed the door behind her and stood leaning against it, head back and eyes shining, her breasts rising and falling in deep, rhythmic breathing. Light and shadow stressed the convexities and hollows of her body.

"Hello, Frankie," she said. "Nice surprise."

He stood up, pulses hammering. "Nicer than you think, baby. I've brought you something."

She saw the box behind him on the dressing table and moved toward it, flat muscles rippling with silken smoothness beneath dusky skin. Her exclamation was like a delighted child's.

"Tell me what it is."

"Open it, baby."

Her fingers worked deftly at the knot of the cord, lifted the top of the box away. Without speaking, she shook out the luxurious fur coat, slipped into it and hugged it around her body. She stood entranced, her back to Frankie, looking at her reflection in the dim depths of the mirror.

Closing in behind her, he took her shoulders in his hands. Capturing the hands in hers, she pulled them around her body and under the coat. Her head fell back onto his shoulder. Her breath sighed through parted lips. He could feel in his hands the vibrations of her shivering flesh.

She said sleepily, "You're a sweet guy, Frankie. A lucky guy, too. You're going places. Too bad I can't go along."

"Why not, baby? Why not go along?"

Her head rolled on his shoulder, her lips burning his neck. "Look, Frankie. When I go for a ride, I go first-class. No cheap tourist accommodations for Linda."

"I don't get you, baby. You call mink cheap?"

"It's not the mink. It's being second. It's the idea of taking what's left over."

"You mean Taffy?"

She closed her eyes and said nothing, and Frankie laughed softly. "Taffy's expendable, baby. Strictly expendable."

"Just like that? Maybe she won't let go."

"How the hell can she help it?"

"She's legal. That always helps."

"Married? You think Taffy and I are married?" He laughed again, his shoulders shaking with it. "Taffy and I are temporary, baby. I never figure it any other way. Nothing on paper. All off the record. We last just as long as I want us to."

She twisted against him, her arms coming up around his neck. Her breath was in his mouth.

"How long, Frankie? How long do you want?"

His hand moved down the soft curve of her spine, drawing her in. He said hoarsely, "As far as Taffy's concerned, I quit wanting when I saw you. Tonight I'll make it official."

She put her mouth over his, and he felt the hot flicking of her tongue. Then she pushed away violently, staggering back against the dressing table. The mink hung open from her shoulders.

"Afterward, Frankie," she whispered. "Afterward."

He stood there blind, everything dissolved in shimmering waves of heat. At last, sight returning, he laughed shakily and moved to the door. Hand on the knob, he looked back at her.

"Like you say, baby—afterward."

8.

He went out into the hall and through the rear door into the alley. There was a small area back there in which he kept his convertible Caddy tucked away. Long, sleek, ice-blue and glittering chrome. A long way from the old Plymouth.

Behind the wheel, sending the big machine singing through the streets, he felt the tremendous uplift that comes to a man who approaches a crisis with assurance of triumph. His emotional drive was in harmony with the leashed power of the Caddy's throbbing engine. Wearing his new personality, he could hardly remember the old Frankie. It was impossible to believe that he had once, not long ago, been driven by shame to a longing for death. Life was good. All it required was luck and guts. With luck and guts, a guy could do anything. A guy could live forever.

At the uptown apartment house, he ascended in the swift, whispering elevator and let himself into his living room with the key he carried. The living room itself was dark, but light sliced into the darkness from the partially open door of the bedroom. Silently, he crossed the carpet that wasn't actually quite up to his knees and pushed the bedroom door all the way open.

Taffy was reading in bed. Her sheer nylon gown kept nothing hidden, but what it showed was nothing Frankie hadn't seen before, and he was tired of it. He stood for a moment looking at her, wondering what would be the best way to do it. The direct way, he decided. The tough way. Get it over with, and to hell with it.

From the bed, Taffy said, "Hi, honey. You're early tonight."

Without answering, Frankie walked over to the closet and slammed back one of the sliding panels. He dragged a cowhide overnight bag off a shelf and carried it to the bed. Snapping the locks, he spread the bag open.

Taffy sat up straighter against her silk pillows, two small spots of color burning suddenly over her cheek bones. "What's up, Frankie? You going someplace?"

He went to a chest of drawers, returned with pajamas and a clean shirt. "That ought to be obvious. As a matter of fact, I'm going to a hotel."

"Why, Frankie? What's the idea?"

He looked down at her, feeling the strong emotional drive. "The idea is that we're through, baby. Finished. I'm moving out."

Her breath whistled in a sharp sucking inhalation, and she swung out of bed in a fragile nylon mist. Her hands clutched at him.

"No, Frankie! Not like this. Not after all the luck I've brought you."

He laughed brutally, remembering the old man. "It wasn't you who brought me luck, baby. It was someone else. That's something you'll never know anything about."

He turned, heading for the chest again, and she grabbed his arm, jerking. He spun with the force of the jerk, smashing his backhand across her mouth. She staggered off until the underside of her knees caught on the bed and held her steady. A bright drop of blood formed on her lower lip and dropped onto her chin. A whimper of pain crawled out of her throat.

"Why, Frankie? Just tell me why."

He shrugged. "A guy grows. A guy goes on to something better. That's just the way it is, baby."

"It's more than that. It's a lot bigger than that. You think I've been two-timing you, Frankie?"

He repeated his brutal laugh. "Two-timing me? I'll tell you something, baby. I wouldn't give a damn if you were sleeping with every punk in town. That's how much I care." He paused, savoring sadism, finding it pleasant. "You want it straight, baby? It's just that I'm sick of you. I'm sick to my guts with the sight of you. That clear enough?"

She came back to him, slowly, lifting her arms like a supplicant. He waited until she was close enough, then he hit her across the mouth again.

Turning his back, he returned to the chest and got the rest of the articles he needed. Just a few things. Enough for the night and tomorrow. In the morning he'd send someone around to clean things out.

At the bed, he tossed the stuff into the overnight bag and snapped it shut.

Over his shoulder, he said, "The rent's paid to the end of the month. After that, you better look for another place to live."

She didn't respond, and remembering his tooth brush, he went into the bathroom for it. When he came out, she was standing there with a .38 in her hand. It was the same .38 he'd once considered killing himself with. That had been the old Frankie, of course.

Not the new Frankie. Death was no consideration in the life of the new Frankie.

"You rotten son of a bitch," she said.

He laughed aloud and started for her, and he just couldn't believe it when the slug slammed into his shoulder.

He looked down in amazement at the place where the crimson began to seep, and his incredulous eyes raised just in time to receive the second slug squarely between them.

And, like the night the old man died, it was funny. In the last split second of sight, it wasn't Taffy standing there with the gun at all. It was the old man again.

The old man with a memory like an elephant.

The old man who always waited until it really hurt.

Try It My Way
Jack Ritchie

August 1955

A t four o'clock they thought of shutting off the water. I took the half-filled saucepan out of the sink and poured it into one of the big cookpots lined up on the floor.

Keegan stopped fooling with the automatic long enough to pour me a glass of vanilla extract from the quart bottle.

I took a couple of swallows and wiped my mouth on my sleeve. Then I pulled the bill of the guard cap lower and walked to the other end of the kitchen.

They were both in their underwear. Brock sat cross-legged, staring at the back of his big hands without interest, and Stevens hugged his legs tight to his chest, his eyes trying not to look up at me.

I grinned. "Here we got two types," I said. "Notice the nice gray hair, the clear healthy skin, and them baby-blue eyes on Stevens."

Turk was at the big window keeping an eye on the exercise yard. He turned his head. "A real nice grandpop. I remember the twinkle in his eye when he used his stick on my kidneys."

"Watch this, Turk," I said. I reached down and put my hand on Stevens' shoulder. He shrank away and began trembling.

Turk laughed. "That's good to see. I'm glad I lived so long."

"Stevens is remembering all the little things he used to do to make life interesting for us," I said. "And now he's scared silly that we got better imaginations."

I shifted my smile to Brock. "Now, this here boy's got no imagination at all. He's got free hand, but he can't think of the clever things like Stevens can."

Brock met my eyes. "I'm thinking of some now, Gomez."

I grinned at him a long time, and then I went to the window.

The guards were in a straggling arc around the three sides of the mess-hall wing. Some of them were standing, but most were taking it easy, hunkered on their heels and waiting for the warden to think of something.

I went back to my chair. "Keegan," I said, "I'll tell you about Davis. You're too young in here to remember him."

I lit a cigarette and exhaled smoke. "Davis was afraid of cats. Crazy afraid about them, and everybody knew it. And one day he made the mistake of using unrespectful words to Stevens, and he got tossed into the hole."

I put my feet on the table. "Davis had one peaceful day, and then he began screaming. Real interesting screaming, and it was all about how there was a cat in the hole with him."

Keegan took the clip out of the automatic and examined it.

"After a couple of hours Davis suddenly didn't make any more noise. When somebody bothered to wonder about that and take a look, he found Davis had beat his brains out against the wall."

I looked at Stevens. "In one of the corners was a black-as-spades cat licking his paws. Now, I wonder how he could of got in there."

Turk turned away from the window. "The warden's waving a hanky, and he's coming around to the main door."

Keegan got up and went into the dining hall, and I could hear his footsteps as he made his way through the emptiness of it. He began moving some of the tables and benches away from the double doors.

There would be guards in the corridor, but they wouldn't try to force their way in as long as we had Brock and Stevens with us.

In five minutes Keegan returned with Warden Cramer.

Cramer's eyes went to Brock and Stevens.

"They're doing just fine, Warden," I said. "But they might be a little chilly."

His eyes moved to the uniform I was wearing, and his mouth tightened. "This isn't going to get you anywhere, Gomez," he said.

"Tell us what we got to lose, Warden," I said. "I'm the short-timer here, and I got ninety years to wait."

He shifted his attention to Keegan. "For one thing, you got your lives to lose if anything happens to Brock or Stevens."

Keegan sipped his glass of extract and smiled at him.

"All right," Cramer snapped. "Let's have what you expect from me."

"A nice fast car and an open gate," Keegan said.

The warden's eyes were hard. "It wouldn't do you much good. You couldn't get far."

"We'll have Brock and Stevens along to show us the way," Keegan said. "Something clever should come to us when it gets dark."

Cramer walked over to Stevens and Brock. "They haven't tried anything rough on you, have they?"

"Just words," Brock said.

Cramer came back to us. "You have one hour to give this up."

I smiled. "And if we don't, Warden? Are you going to try what you haven't got nerve enough to do now?"

Cramer's face colored angrily.

"Remember," I said. "Keep it quiet and orderly out there. If you come for us, start thinking of words to use for Stevens' widow."

Keegan took the warden back out, and while he was gone I searched through the kitchen drawers until I found a whetstone. I began sharpening the nine-inch meat knife I carried.

When Keegan came back, he refilled our glasses.

Brock uncrossed his legs and rubbed circulation back into them. "Before that stuff goes to your head, Keegan, do some thinking. If Cramer lets you three get away with this, there won't be a guard safe in the country. He's not going to let that happen."

"Start hoping you're wrong," Turk said. "Work on it real hard."

I got to my feet and went over to Stevens. "Maybe I should cut off a few ears and toss them out into the yard for Cramer to admire. It might impress him that we mean business."

I got down on one knee in front of him. "Whose ears should it be, Stevens? Yours or Brock's?"

Stevens licked his lips and tried to look away, but his eyes came back to the knife in my hand.

I grabbed a handful of his hair and jerked his head back. I put the tip of my knife under his jaw. "You got two seconds to make up your mind."

His voice was the strangled whisper of terror. "Brock. Make it Brock."

I let go of him and stood up. "See, Brock," I said. "He wants his ears real bad. He don't love you at all when it comes to that"

Keegan was watching me. "Did you get your thrill, Gomez?"

"Sure," I said. "I got a mean streak in me, and it has to be fed."

Keegan lighted one of the cigars we'd found in Brock's uniform and took Turk's place at the window.

I went back to the table and sat down. "With Davis it was cats," I said. "With some people it's the dark or maybe high places."

I watched Turk pouring himself a drink. "I'm thinking of the time the drier in the laundry flared up," I said. "Just a short in the wiring and nothing to get excited about. Remember the size of Stevens' eyes when he thought he might get burned?" I picked up a pack of book matches and lit one. I let it burn low, and Turk watched it. When I blew it out, Turk took the pack and went over to Stevens.

Turk stood there grinning, and then he tore one of the matches out of the pack and lit it.

Stevens' eyes got wide, and he backed away as he watched it burn.

"Let him alone, Turk," Keegan said from the window.

"All I want is a little fun," Turk said. "I got it coming."

Keegan came away from the window. "I just told you something, Turk."

Turk met his eyes for a few moments, and then he shrugged and walked away.

"Gomez, the idea man, and Turk, the pupil," Brock said. "You got nice company, Keegan."

"Stevens is with you," Keegan said. "Want to brag about him?"

Five o'clock passed and nothing happened. I relieved Keegan at the window and waved to the photographers who were behind the line of guards taking pictures.

The warden finished talking to a knot of reporters, and then he started through the guards.

"Cramer's coming back," I said. "And he hasn't got a car under his arm."

Keegan left to let him in. When he came back with the warden, they took seats at the table.

"Well?" Keegan asked.

"You might as well quit this before somebody gets hurt," Cramer said. "You're not getting out of here and that's that."

"We're stubborn and we think different," Keegan said. He glanced at the wrist watch he'd taken from Brock. "We're not going to drag this out until there's snow in hell. It's ten after five right now. We'll give you until seven."

"It's out of my hands," Cramer said. "I talked to the governor, and he says positively nothing doing."

"You got almost two hours to change his mind," I said.

"You know what will happen if you let anything happen to Brock or Stevens. You'll all be held equally responsible." Cramer's eyes went around the three of us and settled on Keegan. "You got sense enough to know that this won't work."

Keegan smiled thinly. "I'm the outdoor type, and I been in here six years. Don't count on me being able to think clear."

The warden got up. "Seven o'clock is going to come and go. It's not any special time on my clock."

He looked at the pots of water. "We can wait a long time out there. Longer than that will last."

When he was gone, Keegan sat at the table slowly smoking his cigar. It was quiet except for the sounds the guards made as they talked to each other in the yard.

At six Turk took my place at the window. I refilled my glass and lit a cigarette. "Cramer's got the notion that we don't have the guts to do like we say. I vote to build a fire under Stevens. He should get loud enough for even the governor to hear."

I let a whole book of matches flare up and tossed it at Stevens.

He shrieked as he skittered away from it. His face got pasty white and twitched with fright as be crouched in the corner watching me.

Keegan got up. "I thought I said words about doing things like that."

I glanced up. "Not to me."

"You're getting told now."

I looked at the bigness of his shoulders and the way his hands hung, ready to use.

I picked up the knife and smiled. "We'll leave it at your way for now. When it gets past seven we can argue about it."

At six thirty the dusk began pushing into the room. Keegan went to the light switch and tried it. Nothing happened.

It was quarter to seven when the floodlights in the yard were turned on. Inside the kitchen pillars of light leaned against the windows.

Seven o'clock came and passed.

At ten after, I finished the last of the vanilla extract and threw the glass at the sink. "Now let's do it my way," I said. "Let them listen to Stevens die and they'll find us a car real fast."

Cellophane crackled as Keegan unwrapped another cigar. "Stop smacking your lips over Stevens and start thinking."

I sat on the edge of the table and began flipping the knife at the piece of light that lay over one corner of it and waited.

"Let's look at this thing with brains," Keegan said. "The party's over. We've had it."

I kept playing with the knife, and neither Turk nor I said anything.

Keegan went on. "Like Brock said, if we get away with it here, the same thing will be tried in every pen in the country. That's why Cramer's not going to let it happen."

"He'll have to," I said. "If we do it my way. We give them one body. That makes them know we got nothing more to lose. We can burn only once, and it'll be no cost to us to give them another corpse if they don't do like we say."

Keegan reached for his glass and then saw that it was empty. He pushed it away. "Use that beautiful imagination of yours now, Gomez. Suppose even that doesn't work. Start thinking about the hot seat."

Brock spoke from the darkness. "I watched a dozen of them take the walk. Ask me how scared they were."

I looked toward Brock and Stevens. They were in the shadows, but I knew they were watching and hoping.

Turk broke the silence. "It's not going to be a happy time for us when Brock and Stevens put on their uniforms again."

"I'm not looking forward to it either," Keegan said. "But it's better than frying."

There was another long quiet, and then Turk sighed. "That part about being alive persuades me."

Keegan's face came into the light as he leaned forward.

"Make it unanimous, Gomez."

Brock spoke again. "It's something to see when they turn on the juice. They jump against the straps like the devil was burning inside of them. They're supposed to be dead in a second, but it don't look like that to me, Gomez. Not when they fight it like that."

I stuck the knife into the table. "I'm finished," I said. "Just like you are."

Keegan relaxed back into his chair. "First I finish this cigar. It'll be a long time before I taste another one."

And then I saw it.

I whirled toward the window, and it was there on the sill, a small silhouette against the light.

I whipped off my cap and smashed at it again and again until it was a broken stain on the stone.

"Jesus!" Turk said sharply. "You scared the hell out of me, jumping up like that. It wasn't nothing but a little cockroach."

Another floodlight flashed on outside, and a slant of light cut across the room and fell on Stevens.

Iciness gripped at my insides. Stevens knew about them now, and I knew what he was thinking about. He knew what I was afraid of. When we were back in our cells he'd know what to do to me.

I jerked the knife out of the table and went after him.

Keegan shouted and moved forward, but he was too late to stop me.

Keegan pulled at me, but I didn't let go of Stevens until I was through. Keegan looked down at the body, and then his eyes met mine.

"All right, Gomez," he said quietly. "Now we got no choice. We try it your way."

Movie Night
Robert Turner

July 1957

The house next door to ours is empty now. The Baylors have gone to another city where Mrs. Baylor's folks live and can help out. The people who bought the Baylor house won't be moving in for another week. We'll be glad when they do. It may help a little to have someone in that empty house next door. Not much, though. Nothing will help much, not even the loaded gun I keep in the house all the time now. The only thing that would have helped the night the whole thing started, we wouldn't let Fred Baylor do.

Fred wasn't really a bad guy. Sure, he could be a little boorish with that low boiling point of his and he sometimes had some slipshod views about life, but then, who hasn't? But he was a good man on his job and he surely was a good family man who never boozed it up or stepped out on his wife, and his kids were all well behaved. He was a pretty good neighbor.

Anyhow, Thursday nights at the drive-in movie near our neighborhood were family nights, which meant that a carful of people were admitted for a dollar. The Baylors and my wife and I had gotten into the habit of going every Thursday night. It was something to do, you know, a way to get out of the house for a change.

Our older daughter, Marie, took care of her little sister as well as the two Baylor kids, over at our house. We each gave Marie a dollar for baby-sitting, and the thing was fine with everybody.

The night of the trouble, the picture at the drive-in dealt with juvenile delinquency. It was a vicious story that pulled no punches. Before it was half over, Baylor, who takes his movies as excitably as a ten-year-old boy, anyway, was boiling over. He seemed to take every hoodlum act portrayed on the screen as a personal affront.

At first the two women and myself laughed and tried to kid him out of it. This only enraged him more. Finally, disgusted, I said:

"Fred, relax, take it easy! It's only a movie. It's not real. You're spoiling the thing for the rest of us. Calm down before you blow a fuse."

"You don't understand, Gene," he said. "It's not just this movie; it's the whole lousy deal with these kids. It's just that this picture is the payoff for me; it sums everything up. For years all I hear is juvenile delinquency, juvenile delinquency, and what should and shouldn't be done about it. Preaching, preaching. And all of it bull. There's only one thing should be done."

"All right, brain-boy," his wife, Dot, butted in. "You know the answer to a big problem that's got everybody else stumped, okay, okay!"

"You're damn right!" Baylor pounded his knee. "People have got to start standing up to these punks for a change. What are they, for God's sake? They're not real criminals. They're not even grown men; just a bunch of little rats, wet behind the ears yet and too full of animal spirits, and yet they've got all grownups scared stiff of them."

"They may be kids," I told him. "But a lot of them are grown up physically. I've seen some *I* wouldn't want to tangle with."

"You see?" he said. "There you are. People are afraid of them now, by sheer reputation alone. A few of them get really vicious, and thousands of them ride along on that rep, getting away with anything they try. What these punks need is a few grown men to stand up to them, teach them a little respect, slap them down, knock the stuffing out of them the first time they start anything, the very first time. Then they'll learn their lesson before they get too far out of hand. That kind of discipline they understand."

"Okay, okay," Dot Baylor said. "Very shrewd, very scientific. Now, how about hushing your large mouth for a while and letting the rest of us enjoy the picture? Please, huh, Fred, huh?"

Baylor quieted a little but kept erupting and grumbling through the rest of the picture. When it was over he said:

"Man, oh, man, what an ending! That ties it up. The punks turn over a new leaf, are sorry for what they've done, all because some social worker saves one of their lives and everybody lives happily ever after. . . . Can you imagine the way the *real* jaydees are laughing at that one? That's just the kind of thing makes 'em so damn cocky—nobody *does* anything to 'em. Nobody gives 'em a dose of their own medicine, like maybe breaking a few of their heads or something."

"*Arf, arf, arf!*" Dot said now, a little embarrassed. "Listen to Tiger Boy Baylor. Only his bark is worse than his bite. . . . Now, let's drop the subject and all head for the snack bar for hotdogs and Cokes. Okay?"

I breathed a sigh of relief, hoping Baylor's harangue was over for the evening, and hastily opened the door to get out and follow Dot's suggestion.

It was intermission time, with nothing on the screen but local advertisements, and crowds from the cars were all heading toward the rest rooms and the big snack bar, at the rear of the movie lot. As we walked along, Baylor said:

"You think I'm wrong about these young punks, watch the way they'll be acting at the snack bar. They'll be swaggering all over the place, trying to look tough, ready to start trouble because they know damn well nobody'll have guts enough to try to stop them."

Baylor and his wife were walking in front of us as he said that, and I saw Dot grab his arm and hug it to her. I heard her whisper, "Hold it, Buster. We don't want any demonstrations of your methods, understand? Please, Fred, for my sake, don't start any trouble."

"Sure," he said, somewhat less surly. "*I* won't start anything. I promise you that."

The snack bar was already pretty crowded when we got there, and I saw that Baylor had been partly right; there was an unusually large showing of boys between the ages of fifteen and twenty, probably because of the type of film playing, and some of them were plenty tough-looking. And they *were* swaggering around and trying to look sinister.

A feeling of foreboding suddenly took hold of me then. I had an almost uncontrollable urge to wheel around and get out of there fast, to take Anne back to the car and forget about refreshments until we got home. But then Anne said, "Mmmmmm, I'm dying for one of those good franks they make here. Maybe I'll even have two. Can I, honey?"

She looked up at me and her eyes were dancing and she was smiling and she looked twenty years old, at the most, that moment. I couldn't spoil her fun for some silly hunch. I told her:

"Doll, you can have all the hotdogs in the place and a whole barrel of root beer to wash 'em down. Y'know why? Because you're de most beautiful chick in de dive, see?" I leered at her.

She laughed and lightly dug her elbow into my ribs. Then we were right in the middle of the big jam around the hotdog and soft drink counters, fighting our way in and further conversation was impossible.

A few minutes later we all had our dogs and drinks and moved back away from the counters, but it was still pretty crowded there in the enclosure, where everybody was standing around eating, loath to go back to their cars until just before the second feature was set to start.

Right behind Fred and Dot Baylor were four or five real young thug types, horsing around. They were overly loud and their language wasn't any too gentle, and people were staring at them disapprovingly but it didn't seem to bother them. If anything, they seemed to enjoy the attention; their voices grew louder, their horseplay—trying to spill each other's drinks, shoving each other, stuff like that— grew rougher.

All this time Dot Baylor and my wife, Anne, were jabbering about something, but I wasn't paying them any attention. I kept an eye on the bunch behind Baylor and his wife. Soon I found myself nervously gulping my hot dog and forcing down the last of my drink too fast and encouraging the others to do the same.

"Come on," I said. "Let's finish up and get out of this crazy mob and back to the car."

Baylor saw me glance at the bunch behind him. "What for?" he demanded. "Take it easy; enjoy yourself. Don't let those guys make you nervous. We got as much right here as they have. What's the big hurry?"

It was almost as though it had been timed, the way he got his answer.

Behind Baylor, one youth playfully pushed another a little too hard. He lost his balance and stumbled awkwardly against Baylor. Baylor's arm was jogged, and some of his drink slopped onto his shirt. Hot color flooded his face as the boy who had bumped him, a kid about seventeen, stocky and bull-shouldered, with bushy black hair and side burns, merely glanced around casually and said, "Whoops!" and then laughingly rejoined the rest of the bunch.

His voice achingly tight, Baylor said, "How do you like that? The dirty little punk doesn't even have sense enough to apologize."

He turned suddenly and approached the group behind him. He grabbed the kid who'd bumped him by the shoulder and spun him about.

"Hey, you," he said. "Didn't anybody ever teach you any manners? Where were you brought up, in a gutter or something?"

The laughter slipped from the gang's faces. The one Baylor was speaking to knit his thick black brows. He shrugged Baylor's hand from his shoulder. He said, "What's the matter with *you?*"

"You know," Baylor told him. "You knock me off my feet and slop soda all over my shirt without even bothering to apologize, and then ask what's the matter. Maybe I ought to *teach* you a few manners."

The bushy-haired kid gave a self-conscious laugh and turned to the others. "Hey, listen to this cat," he said. "Dig this here hardcase, huh? He's got a couple spots on his shirt, he wants to make a Supreme Court case."

"All right, wise guy," Baylor said. "How do *you* like it?"

He tossed the rest of his soft drink full into the kid's face. The kid gasped and smeared his eyes with the back of a hand. "Why, you dirty creep!" he said. He threw a haymaker at Baylor's jaw, but he was slow and clumsy. Baylor blocked the punch with the palm of his left hand. He brought his right I up in a short arc, and it caught the bushy-haired kid on the point of the jaw. His legs buckled, and he dropped.

Then one of the others rushed Baylor. He resembled the bushy-haired kid, except that he was smaller and thinner. He said, "You can't do that to my brother. I'm going to cut you. I'll cut your damn heart out for that."

He had a switchblade, sprung open, in his hand. He held it with the cutting edge up, thumb bracing it, like an experienced knife fighter.

I moved in fast, not even thinking about it, not doing the hero bit, just acting on instinct. I punted the knife from the kid's hand.

When he grabbed his wrist and turned to me in surprise, Fred Baylor went for *him* then. He grabbed a handful of the kid's shirt front. "Pull a knife on me, will you?" he said. With his free hand he whip-slapped the kid back and forth, back and forth. The kid's nose and lips were bleeding by the time a special officer employed by the theater pushed through the crowd and helped me pull Baylor away.

It was over then. When the officer demanded to know what had happened, the kids were sullen, uncommunicative, but Baylor came right out with the whole story. Then the officer, a beefy, quiet, but capable-looking man, bent and picked up the dropped knife. He studied it for a moment and then looked up at Baylor.

"We've had trouble with this bunch before, mister. But it looks like we got 'em cold, this time, with this kind of evidence. It'll be assault and possession. We might even get an assault with intent to kill on one of them. You'll have to prefer charges, of course."

Baylor was calmed down a little, but his face was still somewhat flushed and his temper still wasn't in full control. "That suits me fine," he said, glaring at the kids. "Maybe some time in the poky'll teach these young punks some respect for decent citizens. The sooner they're stopped cold, the better, for my money. What do I have to do to prefer charges?"

The bushy-haired kid who had started the trouble, still rubbing his swollen jaw, said, "That's right, mac, go right on bein' a wise guy. Give us some more trouble now. Go right ahead. You push any charges against me and my brother, you'll never forget it. We got plenty friends who won't let you."

Baylor looked at Bushy Hair, ducked his head toward him in a disparaging gesture, and then turned to the officer. "Listen to this young squirt. Now he's trying to scare me off. He *still* thinks he can tough-talk his way out of trouble. Let's go, officer, and do whatever has to be done to lock these punks up."

Then Dot, Baylor's wife, stepped toward him. She grabbed at his arm. She was very pale, and her eyes were big and frightened. "No, Fred!" she gasped. "Wait a minute. What's the sense in getting further involved? Haven't you done enough? What do you want to do now, get our names in the newspaper, lose a lot of time from your job going to court to testify? It isn't worth it, Fred. It isn't *our* job to try and fight a thing like this. Come on now, let's get out of here."

Baylor looked down at her in surprise and indecision. "But, honey." he said. "We can't just let these guys get away with a ruckus like this in a public place, pulling a knife, trying to kill me, stuff like that. You let 'em get away with it once and—"

"I don't care," she broke in. "That's none of our business. We've had all the trouble we need already. You want to get a reputation in town as a common brawler, a man who goes around hitting kids, and—"

"Hey, wait a minute," he stopped her. "This *kid* is almost as big as me and he was *armed,* honey!"

"Please, Fred!" She kept plucking at his arm, her face working desperately. "I tell you it's not *up* to us. At least think of *me* a little. *I* don't want to become involved, have to leave the kids to spend days in court, testifying and all. Please, Fred, use some sense, some good judgment."

I could see he was beginning to weaken. I could see Dot's point, too. Frankly, I began to think of what a nuisance it might be for all of us. I could be called as a witness, too. I said:

"Fred, maybe Dot's got something there. I think we've done all that's necessary. These kids have had a scare; that's probably enough punishment. They won't bother anybody else. Maybe you'd better skip it, Fred."

The cop stepped in then. "I can't *make* you prefer charges, mister, but I *can* tell you what I think. If you let these young thugs off, it'll be a big mistake. If they're not *really* stopped now that the law has a chance to step in, God knows what they'll be up to next. It's up to you, mister."

"That's fine for you to say," Dot Baylor told him. "It's only part of your job, things like this. But my husband's got other things to think about—his family, his own job. We don't want to get involved any further and that's it."

For a long moment Baylor looked at his wife, and then he turned to the cop, said with a wry grin, "I guess she's the boss, officer." He shrugged. "Maybe she's right, so to hell with it. Sorry."

There was a little more talk but the issue seemed to be settled, and in another few minutes the cop ordered the gang of kids off the lot and we returned to the car. The Baylors walked ahead of us, and we couldn't hear all of what they were saying but they were arguing, and it seemed to be because Fred Baylor still wasn't sure he'd done the right thing.

Back at the car we decided that since the second picture didn't look like much, anyhow, and none of us was now in the mood to sit here and stare at the screen, there was no sense in staying.

None of us spoke much the rest of the way home. At the house they picked up their kids and paid Marie for baby-sitting. There were some slightly cool or at least unenthusiastic good nights and they went home.

Anne and I sat up for a while reading and talking. It was well after midnight before we went to bed. How long we'd been asleep I didn't know at the time, when we were awakened by the most shrilly piercing, frightening scream I'd ever heard.

We both jumped out of bed, and I put on the light and ran to the window. I looked out and saw that the outside front door light of the Baylor's house was on. A few feet down the front walk, Dot Baylor, in her nightgown, was standing in the wash of light from the door, and her mouth was gaped for that God-awful screaming. Then it stopped, and Dot Baylor collapsed on the walk.

We ran downstairs, and I made Anne stay in the house until I saw what this was all about. Outside, I soon found out. On their lawn, behind shrubbery that had obscured the sight from our bedroom window, was the body of a man, clad in pajamas, sprawled on his back. It was Fred Baylor, although I didn't recognize him right off.

I went and squatted down beside him. His face was a mask of blood; some of it still spurting from what seemed to be thousands of pinholes and tiny cuts all over his face.

When he weakly mumbled something, I realized that he wasn't dead or even unconscious. I tried to help him to his feet, but he protested, screaming, "No, no! My legs, oh, my God-damn legs!"

Through big rents at the knees of his pajamas, I saw that his kneecaps were swollen twice their normal size.

It was much, much later, after we'd taken Fred Baylor and his wife, Dot, who was suffering from shock, to the hospital, that we learned what had happened.

The Baylors were awakened by the sound of someone knocking on their front door. Fred went down to investigate. There was nobody there, but in the moonlight he saw, halfway down the walk, a figure sprawled face down on the sidewalk, moaning. Naturally, he went to investigate.

As he bent over the figure, something hit him in the face. When he straightened, the figure on the ground sprang up and started swinging some object at him. Then he was hit a number of times across the knees with what the police surmised to be pick-ax handles. At the same time he was being hit in the face repeatedly with what the police said, again surmising, must have been socks filled with broken glass.

Well, we all knew who had done it, of course. But a police lieutenant said, "You're probably right, but we'll have a hell of a time doing anything about it unless some neighbor saw them, or at least their car. We'll somehow learn who those kids at the drive-in were and pick 'em up for questioning, of course. But they'll all stick together; they'll all have alibis and we won't be able to get anything on 'em."

That was the way it was, too. No neighbor had seen them (or at least none would admit to it). No real arrest was made.

Fred Baylor wasn't too horribly scarred; it would only look as though he were badly pock-marked. By some miracle, neither of his eyes was damaged. But both kneecaps were badly smashed. He's had three operations on them already but he'll never walk right again, they say. And Fred had been a steel worker.

When I went to see Fred Baylor in the hospital, he was not only a physically beaten man; he was whipped, period. All the old familiar fight and fire was gone out of him. Except for one moment, when he looked up at me, with something pretty close to disgust in his eyes.

"You and Dot," he said. "The peace-lovers, who didn't want any more trouble, who didn't want to get involved!" He pointed down to his leg. "How about this kind of involvement? This was the easy way, hah? The right way?"

I felt color flushing up from my neck, but I didn't say anything. I couldn't meet Baylor's eyes, either. I wondered briefly how his wife, Dot, must feel now, about shooting her mouth off and interfering that night. And then I mumbled some kind of goodbye and left.

I didn't let what Baylor said or what had happened to him, get me down, though. Not right away. Not until a couple of nights later when a rock the size of a grapefruit crashed through our living-room window, just skimming the head of our daughter, sitting watching TV. Attached to the rock was a note made up from words cut out of a newspaper. It said, *When the cops stop watching this neighborhood so close you're next wise guy.*

In Memory of Judith Courtright

Erskine Caldwell

October 1955

It was a long time before anyone in Lancaster was able to discover the reason why
Merle Randolph killed himself with his father's shot-gun that Monday morning
in early spring just as the bell was ringing for classes to begin at the consolidated
school.

For one thing, it was an almost unheard-of tragedy for any boy of eighteen to
commit suicide, and, besides, nobody in Lancaster could think of the slightest
motive that would induce a boy like Merle Randolph to take his own life.

Merle's mother, Sarah Randolph, heard the blast of the shotgun a few minutes
after Merle finished eating breakfast and left for school, but she paid little or no
attention to it at the time, because several of the neighbors had recently become
interested in marksmanship and were frequently firing shotguns, rifles, and pistols
at tin cans and other targets.

However, as it happened, when Merle's father, George Randolph, as he had
been in the habit of doing for many years, came home from the hardware store at
noon to eat lunch, Sarah remembered having heard the sound of the shot and she
told George that the more she thought about it the stranger it seemed that anybody
would be target-practicing so early in the morning. When George finished eating,
he left the house and walked across the backyard to the rear of the garage. That
was when it was first known that Merle Randolph had killed himself.

It was Merle's senior year in high school and, besides having satisfactory grades
in all of his studies, he had been the leading scorer and star player on the basketball
team for the past two years. The basketball season had closed on Saturday night of
the previous week when Lancaster High played a winning game—the score was 72
to 64—against one of the high school teams in New Orleans.

Naturally, everybody in Lancaster had been highly elated by the result, and
even the New Orleans newspapers had praised the Lancaster team for being
successful against a high school that had an enrollment ten times larger than
Lancaster's. Lancaster was a small town of about four thousand population in an
agricultural and lumbering community and was situated in the piney-woods region
of the coastal plain about sixty-five miles northeast of New Orleans. The
consolidated school in Lancaster had an enrollment of approximately three
hundred boys and girls in the primary and grammar school grades and about a
hundred and fifty students in the high school.

When the Lancaster school opened during the first week of the previous
September, there were two new teachers on the faculty. One of the new teachers was
Eve Grayson, who taught the first grade, and the other one was Judith Courtright,
who was in charge of the kindergarten.

Eve and Judith had graduated from the state teachers' college, where they had
been roommates for two years, and it had long been their ambition to begin their

teaching careers in the same school. They had been very pleased and happy when they were notified shortly after graduation that their applications had been approved and accepted by the Lancaster school board and that arrangements would be made for them to share a small apartment in a private home during the school year. The letter each of them received was signed by George Randolph, who was president of the school board.

Unlike Judith, who was a reserved, soft-spoken, dark-haired girl, Eve Grayson was vivacious, carefree, impulsive, and brightly blonde-haired. She was twenty-one at that time, a year younger than Judith, and she had been very popular with numerous young men, as well as with several of the unmarried instructors, throughout her four years in college. It was not unusual, then, for Eve to be upset and exceedingly unhappy when she came to Lancaster and was confronted by the fact that it was a policy of the school board to make a pointed request of all unmarried teachers that they have dates only on weekends and not during the school week.

Eve rebelled at once by going out in public on a Tuesday night with a young bank clerk, and two days later she received a firmly-worded reminder from the school board-that her services would not be required in the future if she did not respect the board's request. The final paragraph of the letter explained that the board felt that teachers would not set a good example to the students if they engaged in frivolous activities during the evening hours of the school week. That was how it happened that Eve Grayson resigned from her teaching position at the end of the first week of the term. She left immediately on a bus for New Orleans.

Judith was unhappy about what had happened, because she and Eve had been such close friends for the past two years, but she knew it was useless to argue with anyone as headstrong and impetuous as Eve Grayson. Eve had tried to persuade Judith to resign and go to New Orleans with her, but Judith looked forward to a career of teaching and she wanted to be successful from the beginning, especially since she was not engaged to be married and fully expected to teach school for many years.

However, she wanted to keep Eve Grayson's friendship, and she promised to visit Eve in New Orleans on many weekends during the remainder of the school year. When Judith questioned her about the kind of job she could get in New Orleans in order to support herself, Eve laughed and told her not to worry about that. She reminded Judith that she had been to New Orleans several times during summer vacations and that she knew her way around.

During the fall term of school, Judith met several young men of the town, and she had an occasional date on weekends with some of them. However, none of the men she met in Lancaster impressed her seriously and she had no thoughts of marriage. She spent the Christmas holidays with her parents in the northern part of the state, where her father owned a drug store, even though in letter after letter Eve Grayson had urged and begged her to come to New Orleans for the holidays, promising that she would meet many interesting men while she was there.

Each time Judith answered one of Eve's letters, she always promised that she would come to New Orleans soon for a weekend visit. Eve wrote to her in detail about the comfortable apartment she had rented, describing the furnishings of the two bedrooms and the large parlor, and always ended her letters by begging Judith to share it with her. She still had not told Judith what kind of job she had or about the work she was doing, even though Judith continued to ask her about it nearly every time she wrote.

When Judith came back to Lancaster at the end of the Christmas holidays, she was met at the train by Merle Randolph.

With a shy boyish grin, and trying manfully to hide the blush on his cheeks, Merle came up to her at the railroad station and said that he had his father's automobile and that he had come to take her to the house where she had her small apartment. As she got into the sedan, she was thinking that Merle's father had sent him—and probably after much protest on Merle's part—to meet her and help her with her baggage, and that it was merely a courtesy to her from the president of the school board.

While they were driving through town, Judith tried several times to get Merle to talk to her, but he was noticeably shy and embarrassed in her presence and he answered all of her questions by nervously nodding or shaking his head.

Finally, though, when they reached the house where she lived, and with an abrupt and unexpected boldness, Merle stopped the car and gripped her hands before she could open the door and get out. Catching her breath, Judith looked at him in surprise.

"Miss Courtright—" Merle said excitedly, his voice quavering. "Miss Courtright—"

His whole face was flushed by that time and she could feel the violent trembling of his hands.

"What is it, Merle?" Judith asked as calmly as she could. She had seen him glance shyly at her a number of times at school, and somehow she had been aware that frequently he was watching her from a distance while she was on the playground with her kindergarten class. There was the time, too, when she was walking home late one afternoon and suddenly had the feeling that Merle Randolph was following her, but when she looked back over her shoulder, there was no one within sight. "Tell me what it is, Merle," she said after that, looking directly at him.

"Miss Courtright—I want to ask you something—" he said hesitantly.

"What is it you want to ask me, Merle?"

"Miss Courtright—I want to see you—" he said, quickly averting his eyes. "Will you let me—Miss Courtright—will you?"

"Of course, Merle," she said, smiling a little. "You're seeing me right now."

"I don't mean like this—I mean the other way—"

"What other way, Merle?"

"Well—a different way—"

He was gazing at her pleadingly, as though begging for understanding. She wanted to tell him that she did understand, and she wondered what she could say or what gesture she could make that would put him at ease, but at the same time she hesitated to let herself encourage him. She could feel a slight trembling of her body.

"Will you—Miss Courtright?" she heard him say.

"What other way do you mean, Merle?" she asked then.

"I want to see you tonight—"

"Why do you want to do that?" she asked, turning and looking away from him. She was certain she realized what he meant, but just the same some impulse drove her to want to hear him say it. "Tell me why, Merle."

"Because it's—because I like you—Miss Courtright—and I want—"

"No, Merle," she spoke up quickly, looking into his face and shaking her head firmly. She realized the time had come when she must discourage him. "You can't do that."

"Why not?" he asked dejectedly. "Don't you like me?"

"It's not that, Merle. Of course, I like you. You are a very fine boy. I admire you very much. But—but I'm a teacher, and it just wouldn't do for a teacher to see one of the students—not the way you're talking about. Now you understand, don't you?"

"Nobody would know about it—Miss Courtright," he persisted, squeezing her hands more tightly. "I could come here to see you after dark tonight—and nobody would ever know about it."

He moved closer as he spoke and she could feel the tenseness of his muscular body as he pressed against her. Judith closed her eyes momentarily, telling herself that she must not let him kiss her, because she was afraid if that happen she would no longer have control over herself.

"You're so beautiful—Miss Courtright," he was saying in a husky voice. "Everything about you is beautiful—you're the prettiest girl I've ever seen. I've watched you every day since you came here to teach—and you're prettier all the time." He squeezed her hands in his powerful grip. "Let me come to see you tonight! Please let me! Please, Miss Courtright!"

Taking a deep breath, Judith smiled at him tenderly as she slowly shook her head.

"No, Merle," she spoke to him in a low voice, trying to be as kind as she could. "You must remember that I'm twenty-two years old, and you're only eighteen. Even if I weren't a teacher, and you weren't one of the students, there would still be that difference. You understand now, don't you?"

"That doesn't make any difference," he protested. "That doesn't matter at all. I don't care about that."

"But I do, Merle," she told him steadfastly, trying to withdraw her hands from his. "It makes a great deal of difference to me."

"I don't see why," he said, sad with disappointment.

She smiled at him kindly. "Someday you'll understand, Merle."

With a sudden movement, he put his arms around her and pulled her tightly against him, and she realized that he would surely kiss her if she did not get away from him at once. Pushing against him with all her might, she managed to open the door of the car and get out before he could stop her.

Presently, subdued and silent, and not looking at her, Merle took her two suitcases from the car and carried them to the front door of the house. Putting down the suitcases, and with only a hasty glance at her, Merle turned and hurried back to the car. While her eyes slowly filled with tears, she stood at the door until the sedan had passed out of sight up the street.

Judith took the bus to New Orleans as soon as school was dismissed on Friday afternoon.

Several days before that she had written to Eve Grayson and said that at last she was coming to spend the week-end, and Eve had promptly sent her a joyous telegram. She arrived in New Orleans at dusk and took a taxi to Eve's apartment.

It had been four months since they had last seen each other, and for two hours they talked and laughed about everything they could think of, the only exception being that in the beginning Judith was careful not to mention Merle Randolph. Several times while they were talking, Eve would try to make Judith promise to come to visit her every week-end during the remainder of the school year. Judith would say that she would try to come as often as she could from that week onward. Each time that happened, Eve would pour some more whisky into their glasses and they would drink a toast to the week-ends to come.

After they had had several drinks, Judith finally told Eve about Merle Randolph and how he continued to try to persuade her to let him come to see her by writing pleading notes and putting them on her desk at school or under her apartment door.

"The boy is infatuated with you, Judith," Eve said knowingly. "Why don't you let him come to see you just once, anyway?"

"Oh, I couldn't do that," she protested. "It's too much of a risk. Somebody would find out about it, and then I'd have to resign and leave Lancaster. Besides, I don't know what might happen if we were alone together like that."

Eve laughed. "It's my guess that it would be the most spectacular kissing-date in the history of Lancaster."

"That's what I'd be afraid of," Judith said frankly.

Later in the evening, after they had eaten dinner, the phone rang several times. Each time Eve answered the call, she would say that she was engaged for the evening and then ask the caller to phone again the next night. During the evening, and until they finally went to bed at midnight, Judith attempted several times to get Eve to tell her what kind of job she had and about the kind of work she did, but Eve always laughed and said it was too unimportant to talk about at a time like that when they had not seen each other for so long a time and had so many interesting things to talk about.

Late the next afternoon, which was Saturday, and the day before Judith was going to return to Lancaster, the phone rang. After Eve had talked to someone for awhile, she told Judith that one of her friends would be there in a few minutes. Then just before the doorbell rang, Eve asked her if she would mind waiting in the other bedroom for a little while.

Judith had just gone into her room and closed the door when she heard a man's voice in the parlor, and in a few minutes she heard the closing of Eve's bedroom door. During the next half-hour she could hear voices and sounds in the room next to hers, although she was unable to understand anything that was said, and then later there was a knock on her door. When she opened it, Eve came into the room and sat down on the bed.

"Where is your friend?" she asked Eve.

"Oh, he's gone."

"So soon?"

Eve answered with a nod of her head.

"Does he always leave so quickly?" Judith asked.

Eve smiled at her. "What you mean, Judith, is do they always leave so soon—not just he."

"I don't understand," Judith told her.

Eve got up from the bed. "Let's go make ourselves a drink, Judith," she said as she walked from the room.

They went into the kitchenette and filled two glasses with ice cubes and whisky. Nothing was said until they went into the parlor and sat down on the sofa.

"I hope you're coming back next week-end," Eve said presently. "Please do, Judith."

"I don't think I can come that soon," Judith said. "But I will come back again—if you want me to."

"Then promise to come back two weeks from now," Eve begged. "I want to introduce you to some friends of mine. I'm sure you'll like them."

"All right," Judith agreed. "It's a promise."

The phone rang and Eve got up to answer it.

It was Saturday again, and another warm night in early spring. Judith had come to spend the week-end with Eve once more. Every week during the past two months she had left Lancaster on the bus as soon as school was dismissed on Friday afternoon, returning there from New Orleans late Sunday night.

The phone had rung several times already that evening, and, as they were in the habit of doing now, she and Eve took turns answering the calls. Shortly after eleven o'clock the phone rang once more, and it was Judith's turn to answer it. Somebody who would not give his name asked if he could come to the apartment right away.

Eve was in her room when the doorbell rang, and Judith opened the door. Startled, she stepped backward, putting her hand over her mouth. Even in the dimly lighted room, Judith had recognized him at once. Merle Randolph's tall muscular figure and stubby light hair and shy expression were more conspicuously his than ever before. He still had not looked directly at her. He had gone to the middle of the parlor and was standing there glancing at the strange surroundings.'

Judith slowly closed the door and stood with her back against it as thoughts raced in confusion through her mind. The next thing she was aware of, Merle had turned around and was staring open-mouthed at her.

"Miss Courtright—" he said almost indistinctly. "Miss Courtright—what are you doing here—"

Judith could find no way to answer him. She continued to stand there with her back pressed tightly against the door, gripping her hands and holding her breath for moment after moment. The room seemed to have suddenly been filled with sultry, stifling heat.

"But—Miss Courtright—you're not—" Merle said, shaking his head in disbelief.

"What are you doing here, Merle?" she asked weakly.

"We played a basketball game in New Orleans tonight—and we won it, too— the score was 72 to 64. It was the last game of the season for us and the coach said we could walk around town for a while or go to a movie and not have to get back to the hotel till midnight. While I was walking around, somebody told me to call a certain phone number—if I wanted to—but I didn't know you—"

Judith managed to smile slightly. "I'm glad Lancaster won the game," she said.

There was a brief interval of silence in the room after that.

"What are you going to do—Merle?" Judith asked finally.

Merle shook his head. "I don't know—Miss Courtright—but I can't stay here! I've got to go!"

"But, Merle—"

As he came across the room in long strides, Judith moved away from the door. When he reached it, he flung open the door, and, without looking at her again, ran toward the street. After he had gone, Judith closed the door and locked it securely.

By the time she reached the sofa and fell upon it, her eyes were filled with tears. Sometime later she was aware that Eve was shaking her and begging her to tell what had happened, but Judith closed her eyes more tightly and cried out with all the despair of her heart.

Day's Work
Jonathan Lord

July 1953

They were walking toward the waterfront area, walking quietly, when they heard the car hit the kid. They stopped short at the sound of the kid's scream, and then they began to run toward the accident.

They were quietly dressed, conservative-looking men, lean and hard-muscled and in perfect condition, and they didn't puff or get out of breath. As they ran, the taller man said, "It sounded like a bad one." He had blond hair, blue eyes, and thin, sensitive features, and there was a look of shock on his face as he stared ahead through the darkness.

The other man was very short, just a shade over five feet, and his hair and eyes were dark. "Yeah," he said. "That car was going plenty fast." He added softly, "Hell of a thing, street accidents."

They turned a corner, and the accident was right there before them. The kid was about ten or eleven, lying stiff and unmoving, his body thrown a full foot ahead of the front wheels of the car. The driver stood alongside the car, his face chalk-white and his lips twitching, staring at the kid and at the gathering crowd, and then back at the kid. "I didn't even see him," he said. "He come running out from between two parked cars. . . . "

The blond man stepped forward, looking at the crowd. "Anybody send for an ambulance?" he asked.

A woman in the crowd answered him. "Man went to call one," she said. "Ain't no use, though—the kid's gone. I saw the whole thing. I—"

"You never can tell," the blond man said. "Doctors can do wonderful things sometimes. You never can tell." He stared down at the kid. "I wonder if we ought to move him, cover him or something."

"Better not," the short man said. "If he *is* still alive, you can harm him by moving him." He looked down at the kid, and then turned his face away. "Hell of a thing, huh, Joe? A little kid like that . . ."'

The blond man's eyes caught the driver's, and the driver took a blind step forward, toward him. "I didn't even see him," the driver said. "He come out suddenly—" He stopped short as the blond man turned away.

Then a police car arrived, with the ambulance right behind it, and the two men stepped away into the crowd. They stood watching sadly as an interne examined the boy briefly and placed a sheet over his body.

"We better go," the short man said. "We don't want to be late."

The blond man glanced at his watch, a thin-gold, expensive timepiece. "We won't be late," he said. "We've got an hour. Mr. Conners said he won't be there until eleven."

They stood watching a few minutes longer. Then they walked away, headed again for the waterfront area, walking silently for almost two blocks. Finally the short man said, "Things like that break your heart."

The blond man nodded. "Kid was just about the same age as my oldest," he said.

"Mine, too," the short man said. "Scares the hell out of a father, seeing something like that."

The blond man nodded again. "Worst thing is," he said, "there isn't a damn thing you can do about it. You can't expect a ten-year-old kid to hang around the house all day, and you can't expect the kid to hang around his mother all day, either. You've just got to pound it into his head about being careful when he crosses the streets—and then you keep your fingers crossed."

"That's the rub, all right," the short man said. "I ever catch one of my kids crossing in the middle of the street, I'll pound his can so he won't sit down for a month."

They were deep in the waterfront area now, and the streets were shabby and rundown and completely deserted. They continued walking, talking softly, until they reached the water's edge.

"This is the spot, right here," the blond man said. "The boat's supposed to come in over there, near that painted line."

"We better get in the shadows," the short man said.

There was darkness just a few feet to the left of them, off where the street light did not penetrate, and they walked over until the shadows enclosed them, waiting for the third man to show up. He came after they'd waited fifteen minutes.

He was extremely tall, much taller than the other two, and dressed in the same quiet, conservative way, but his clothes were a bit shabbier than theirs, and he was very nervous. He stopped at the water's edge, looked at his watch, and then stood staring out at the water.

The men in shadows stood watching him for a moment, and then the blond man stepped forward. "Better forget the boat, Marty," he said.

The man at the water's edge turned and stared at him, sick fear on his face.

"Better forget the boat," the blond man said. "You won't be on it tonight."

The tall man's lips were trembling now, and he pressed them together to steady them. He said, finally, "Give me a break, Joe. . . . "

"No breaks," the blond man said.

"For God's sake, Joe," the tall man said, "act like a human being—let me get on that boat. Who the hell will ever know? I'll spend the rest of my life out of the country. Jesus, Joe, we grew up together—we been friends twenty years."

The blond man shook his head. "You shouldn't have done it," he said. "We stopped being friends when Mr. Conners gave us the order on you this afternoon. No breaks, Marty."

The tall man stared at him for a moment, and then, hopelessly, he shrugged his shoulders.

"Maybe you better turn around, Marty," the blond man said softly.

The tall man turned his back and then, abruptly, began to run. He had taken four steps when a bullet cut him down, onto his knees. There were three more shots, and he cried out once softly and fell forward on his face.

The two men walked up to the body, and the blond man turned the dead one over with the toe of his shoe and studied him for a moment. "All right," he said. "Let's get the guns into the drink, and move." The guns made gentle splashes as they hit.

The men waited a moment longer to make sure there were no footsteps approaching, and then they left. They did not run; they walked away slowly and in silence.

They were silent again for almost two blocks, and then the short man said, "I just can't get that accident out of my mind. Awful thing to see."

"Awful," the blond man said. "I hope they give that driver twenty years. Imagine the bastard—driving fast on a dark night like this." He shook his head. "I better have another talk with my kids first thing tomorrow morning."

The Scrapbook
Jonathan Craig (Frank E. Smith)

September 1953

Old Charlie Stevens had just finished trucking the last of the big cartons out to the loading platform, and now he sat on his shipping table, turning a stub of black marking crayon over and over in his short, spatulate fingers and watching Lois Anderson adjust the seams of her stockings.

A girl should wear a garter belt instead of round garters, he reflected, and then her seams wouldn't always be twisting around. Still . . . round garters, if a girl wore them up as high on her legs as Lois wore them, looked a damn sight prettier; you had to give them that.

Lois glanced up at him through her lashes, and smiled. "Shame, Charlie." She laughed. "A man your age."

He grinned at her and looked away, and felt the crayon break between his fingers. She didn't think of him as a man at all, he knew. She made the same mistake all the rest of them did, the mistake he wanted them to make; she thought he was too old to notice a girl's legs. Or anything else. Too old to notice, and too old to do anything about it even if he did.

He stared hard at the calendar over the zoning chart, trying to keep the amusement out of his eyes. She wouldn't have her skirt hiked up like that if she knew about the scrapbook, he thought. He took out his handkerchief and wiped his silver-rimmed glasses, and then ran the handkerchief back across his bald head and mopped at the wrinkled, sagging flesh back of his neck.

Lois smoothed her skirt down and came over to lean against the edge of the shipping table. "You got a cigarette, Charlie?" she asked.

He gave her a cigarette and lit it for her, watching the way she sucked the smoke deep into her lungs.

"I don't know how you do it," Lois said.

"Do what?"

"All those heavy boxes." She shook her head. "I mean . . . well, a man your age, and all."

"Sixty-one isn't so old," Charlie said. "And besides, handling weight is more knowing how than muscle. You sort of let the weight work for you."

"Well," she said, "anyhow, your vacation starts tomorrow, doesn't it?"

He nodded. She didn't believe he was only sixty-one, he knew.

"We'll miss you while you're gone," she said. "Everyone around here likes you a lot, Charlie."

He didn't say anything. He knew they liked him at Morton's. Everybody from Mr. Morton himself right on down the line liked him. Next to Mr. Morton, he'd been here longer, and worked harder, than anybody else. And each year at vacation time Mr. Morton had come back to the shipping department to tell him to enjoy himself, and to give him an envelope with a fifty-dollar vacation bonus.

Lois dropped her cigarette to the floor and ground it out with her heel. "Got to get back," she said. "The ladies' room is always jammed up at quitting time, and that's why I had to come back here to—"

"Sure," Charlie said. He wondered what Lois' pretty face would look like if he were to take her to his furnished room on West Seventy-third Street and show her the scrapbook. She looked a little like that girl in St. Louis. Let's see . . . that was back in '47. Her name had been Diane Benton, and he could remember exactly how she had looked when he killed her, and how the picture on the front page of the St. Louis *Post-Dispatch* had been blown up from an amateur snapshot so that you couldn't really tell how pretty she was. But there'd been a better picture of her the next day, and that was the one he'd put in his scrapbook.

"Have fun on your vacation, Charlie," Lois said. She smiled at him. "And don't give the girls too had a time." She moved off toward the door that led to the front office.

He watched the lithe swing of her hips until the door closed behind her. Then he slid off the shipping table and went over to his locker to change into his street clothes. A real pretty girl, he thought. She did look like that girl in St. Louis, all right, but she walked like the one in Baltimore. A girl didn't have to roll her hips that way, and if she did she was really asking for it. But with Lois it was force of habit; she wouldn't waste the motion on him.

He'd just finished knotting his tie when Jack Morton came through the door and strode toward him. He nodded and said, "Hello, Mr. Morton."

"*Mr.* Morton, hell! It's *Jack,* goddam it! Can't you ever remember, you old—" He broke off and laughed, and slapped Charlie on the shoulder. "Well, you are ready?"

"Just about," Charlie said.

"Good," Morton said. He reached into his inside coat pocket and handed Charlie an envelope. "Just got a minute, Charlie, to tell you to have fun." He winked. "I figured you could use a little extra liquor money."

"Thanks," Charlie said.

Morton glanced at his watch. "Forget about this place," he said. "Just concentrate on having a good time. Okay?"

"All right," Charlie said.

Morton slapped him on the shoulder again and hurried back the way he had come.

Charlie turned and picked up his lunch bucket and walked the length of the shipping room to punch the time clock that was reserved for himself and the porter.

Forty-five minutes later, Charlie closed the door of his third-floor room behind him and locked it, and went directly to the closet where he kept his heavy, brassbound trunk. He dragged the trunk to the middle of the floor, found his key, and knelt down beside it. The padlock in the hasp was nearly as large as his palm, and it was the most expensive he had been able to find. He unlocked it, lifted the tray from the top of the trunk, and reached down beneath a layer of smaller books for his scrapbook.

It was an unusually large book, large enough to hold entire newspaper pages without folding them. He sat cross-legged on the floor, opened the book, and stared at the beautiful girl looking back at him from the front page of the Buffalo *Courier-Express*.

Elaine Bishop had been the first, and one of the youngest. Seventeen. The newspaper had yellowed in the eight years since he'd killed Elaine, but he needed no newspaper photo graph to remember how lovely she had been. And the words in the long account of what the *Courier-Express* called "the most brutal sex murder in the history of New England" were as clearly imprinted on his mind as they were in the newspaper columns.

He could remember every detail of Elaine Bishop's murder, and of the seven others that had followed it, as vividly as he could remember his trip home on the Seventh Avenue subway this evening.

He thumbed through the scrapbook slowly and lovingly. Eight of them, he thought. And every one of them a real beauty. One of them for every vacation he'd taken in the last eight years, and no two of them from the same city. He'd spent that first real vacation in Boston, and in the years that followed he had gone to St. Louis and Baltimore and Richmond and Philadelphia and Cleveland and Pittsburgh and Miami. Eight beautiful young girls in eight years, and never a single hitch. Two of the girls had succeeded in clawing him a little before he killed them, and that girl in Richmond—that Gloria Roberts—had kneed him pretty bad; but that was all.

He'd always been able to come back to New York feeling like another man, ready to start planning and saving for the vacation next year. And along with his savings and plans, his anticipation had always mounted steadily until when vacation time finally came, the urgent need to rape and kill had become the only thing in his mind. Between vacations he talked to only the girls at Morton's.

It had been wonderful to come back to his job and listen to what everybody said about the horrible out-of-town sex crimes. He'd always gotten such a kick out of shaking his head sadly with the best of them, and muttering about what he'd like to do with such a fiend—if he were a younger man, of course.

He glanced at the alarm clock on the dresser. He'd better get started, he thought. He didn't want to get to Washington, D. C., too late. . . .

Charlie turned the rented Plymouth into Massachusetts Avenue and drove slowly along beneath the high-vaulted arch of the overhanging tree. At three o'clock in the morning Washington, D. C., was more like a country town than a city. And after the surge and thrust and pace of Manhattan, Charlie found the quiet, deserted streets irritating. He remembered that someone had told him Washington after midnight was like a cemetery with lights.

He turned the corner at Sixteenth Street and pulled to the curb. He lit a cigarette and smoked it down, and had almost decided to give up for the night when a Buick convertible passed him and pulled to a stop a few yards ahead. He watched while a girl jumped from the car, slammed the door behind her angrily, and started up the walk to an apartment house. The man behind the wheel of the Buick called something after her in a bitter voice, raced the motor, and jerked the car away from the curb. It careened around the next corner.

Charlie could see the girl plainly in the light from the medieval lanterns at either side of the apartment-house entrance. She was young and she was pretty, and the body beneath her tight-waisted summer dress brought a taut, dry feeling to his throat. He slid across the front seat and opened the door and walked toward the apartment house. He didn't hurry, and the look he cast both ways along the street was casual.

The girl was standing in front of the elevator doors. Her finger was still on the self-service button, and she was even younger and prettier than Charlie had thought. She glanced at him with wide-set, angry blue eyes, and then jabbed at the button again. Her face was flushed, and her sharp, high breasts quivered a little with the movement of her body as she stepped back suddenly to look up at the floor indicator.

After that first glance she paid no further attention to Charlie. Why should she? he thought. An old man . . . too old for anything.

He was close enough to her to smell the clean, soapy scent of her hair before she noticed him again. And then it was too late.

There was no sound. He stood back and looked down at her, and gently massaged his right thumb with the fingers of his left hand. It took a lot of pressure to keep your thumb in a girl's throat long enough to kill her. But it was the best way, he'd discovered. He didn't like to mark a pretty girl any more than he had to—anyhow, not till later. Right now, and for the next hour or so, he wanted his blue-eyed teenager exactly the way she was.

He picked her up and carried her to the door. When he was certain the street was clear he walked rapidly to the Plymouth and put the girl on the back seat. Midway between Washington and Baltimore there was an abandoned side road he knew about. It would be as good a place as any.

On his first morning back at work, Charlie punched the time clock and walked out into the main office in search of Lois Anderson. He could always depend on Lois for a highly emotional reaction to his murders, and he liked the way she had of inventing little details of her own to make the story even more sensational. He found her near the water cooler, talking to two of the other girls. There was a folded newspaper under her arm.

"Welcome back, Charlie," Lois said, and then, in almost the same breath, "Isn't it horrible?"

Charlie nodded and drew a paper cup of water. "What kind of a man would do a thing like that?" he said, and shook his head. "Inhuman, that's what it is."

Lois glanced at him quickly. "I mean about the fire, Charlie. The one in the tenement over in Brooklyn."

"Fire?" Charlie said.

"You know. Last night. Two people dead, and three more of them not expected to live."

"Oh," Charlie said. He dropped the paper cup in the receptacle and cleared his throat. "I thought you meant about that girl in Washington. If you ask me, a fiend like that should . . ." He let his voice trail off, glowering at the floor.

"That was pretty bad, all right," Lois said. "But they'll get him sooner or later." She unfolded the newspaper and pointed to a photograph on the first page. "Those firemen take some terrible chances, don't they? Look at this one here, on the top of the ladder."

One of the other girls said, "Just think of it. Those poor people. Like rats in a trap."

Charlie drew another cup of water and drank it slowly. "They said that maniac in Washington killed her one place and . . . well, you know . . . he did that someplace else. I didn't get a chance to read much about it." He looked at Lois expectantly.

"They'll get him," Lois said. She folded the newspaper again. "The city ought to do something about all those firetraps. They ought to make the landlords put in fire escapes for every room." The other girls nodded, and walked back toward their desks.

Charlie crumpled his paper cup into a small ball and rolled it around in his clenched fist. "I read that girl's name, but I can't remember it."

"Who?" Lois said.

"The one in Washington," Charlie said. "The one—"

"Oh," Lois said. "Well, it doesn't make much difference now. Look, Charlie, Mr. Morton told me he wanted to see you as soon as you got in this morning. I forgot till just now."

Charlie stared at the newspaper beneath Lois' arm, and nodded. "All right," he said.

"It's nice having you back, Charlie," Lois said, and walked over toward the bank of bookkeeping machines.

Charlie stared after her a moment, feeling a strange sort of emptiness inside him. He let his breath out slowly and started toward Mr. Morton's office. That Lois wouldn't be so interested in fires if she knew who she'd just been talking to, he thought. And those other girls, too. Getting all worked up over a little fire. If they knew they'd been standing just two feet from . . . He remembered he was still holding the paper cup, and tossed it toward the nearest wastebasket.

He opened the door to Mr. Morton's office and stepped inside.

Morton looked up and smiled. "Good to see you back, Charlie," he said. "Things really got fouled up while you were gone. The guy we got to take your place didn't know his backside from a hole in the ground." He picked up a handful of bills of lading. "See what you can do to straighten these out, eh?"

Charlie took the bills of lading. There was a newspaper on Morton's desk, he saw. And it was the right one. It was the one with the girl's picture on the first page.

He gestured toward the newspaper with his free hand. "An awful thing."

"What's that?" Morton asked. "And Charlie, about those—"

"That girl getting it that way in Washington," Charlie said. "An awful thing." He fixed his eyes on the knot in Morton's tie. "You've got a daughter about the same age, haven't you, Mr. Morton? About eighteen?"

"Sixteen," Morton said. "There's a couple of back orders in that stack, Charlie. See if the stuff's come through yet."

Charlie moistened his lips. "If I was that girl's dad, I'd spend the rest of my life hunting the guy that did it. And when I found him . . ." He looked at Morton and smiled grimly. "You say your girl's sixteen, Mr. Morton?"

Morton lifted a sheet of paper from his desk and extended it to Charlie. "Here's one more, Charlie. Got loose from the others, somehow."

Charlie took the bill of lading. The palms of his hands were moist now; the air in here was too close and warm.

Morton looked at him questioningly. "Everything okay, Charlie?"

Charlie tucked the bills of lading beneath his arm and dried his palms against his trouser legs. "Sure," he said. "Everything's fine, Mr. Morton."

Morton rattled some papers on his desk. "I guess that's it, then, Charlie."

Charlie nodded and left the office. On his way back to the shipping department he stopped at the water cooler for another cup of water. For the first time in years he was not in the mood to work. Everything seemed wrong, somehow. It had never been this way before when he'd come back from his vacation.

He went to his shipping table and tried to work on the bills of lading. But it was no good. He couldn't concentrate, and half the time the figures blurred before his eyes so that he couldn't see them at all. He put the bills of lading aside and began shifting the heavy cartons from one end of the room to the other. They didn't need shifting, but it gave him something to do with his hands, an excuse to bring his muscles into play. He worked savagely, building up a sweat. After an hour of it he felt no better than he had before.

They'd cheated him, by God. Lois, and Mr. Morton, and the rest of them. A fire in a tenement and a bunch of fouled up bills of lading, and they forgot all about what had happened in Washington. What was the good in doing what he'd done if they didn't even want to talk about it? Hell, they'd talked it all out before he got back. That was it. They'd talked it all out of their systems Friday, and here it was Monday—and now all the hell they cared about was a couple of burned up bastards in a tenement and a bunch of screwed up bills of lading. By God, they'd talk out of the other side of their face if he ever spread that scrapbook out in front of them!

And those girls. Nine of them now. They'd had their pictures in the papers. Every one of them. But he had not. He was responsible for all the attention they'd had. Millions of people had looked at their pictures, read about them. And what had it got him? Nothing. If other people didn't know you were responsible, it didn't mean a thing.

He took off his glasses and wiped them, and then he went back out to the main office. He went over to Lois, breathing heavily, conscious of the sweat that crawled along his ribs and the insides of his arms.

Lois glanced up at him and smiled. "I'm real busy, Charlie. . . . "

Charlie nodded. "I know. But I got to thinking." The inside of his mouth felt drawn and dry. "What kind of a guy do you figure he was?"

She frowned. "Who, Charlie?"

"That guy in Washington," he said tightly. "The one that killed that little girl. What kind of a guy do you figure he was?"

"How would I know?" she said. "For heaven's sake, Charlie. . . . Can't you see I'm busy?"

"But not too busy to talk about that fire," Charlie said. "You weren't too busy to talk about that, Lois."

Her eyes widened. "Charlie! What's wrong with you?" He turned his back on her and strode toward the street door. There was only one thing to do now, he knew.

He hailed the first taxi that cruised past him and gave the driver the number of his rooming house.

When Charlie got back to Morton's, he was more excited than he had ever been before. Everything was going to be different now. No one in the history of the country had ever done what he had. He had read hundreds of cases, but nobody before had even come close to him. His name would go down for all time. And not after he was dead, either, by God. Not after he couldn't enjoy it.

He went straight to Lois Anderson's desk and slammed the big scrapbook down in front of her. She glanced at it, and then looked up at him, puzzled. "Charlie, what—"

"It was me," Charlie said. "I killed them. I killed every goddam one of them!" He knew he was shouting now, and didn't care.

He looked about him. Every face in the room was turned toward him.

"Come here, you bastards!" Charlie yelled. "Come here and look at this!"

Quiet Day in the County Jail
Craig Rice (Georgiana Craig)

July 1953

"Cut that singing out, Artie," the girl's voice called.

Artie, the head trusty, put down his guitar and walked into the cell that was half of what had been named the Presidential Suite. It was unlocked, because its tenant was only being held in protective custody as a material witness.

"What's the matter, Red?" he asked gently. "You nervous?"

She was beautiful, and she was pale, and she did seem too young and too fair to die. She was sitting on the edge of her bunk, wrapped in a green chenille bathrobe. The hair that had given her her nickname was loose over her shoulders. A cigarette blazed between her trembling fingers.

"Shadow fell over my tombstone, I guess," she said. "Forget it."

He patted her awkwardly on the shoulder and said, "You'd better get some sleep while you can." Right away he knew that had been the wrong thing to say, but it was too late to do anything about it now.

She looked at him with eyes that for a moment were bright with fear. "You don't need to remind me. They can't let me get back to Detroit alive."

"Shut up, Red," he said, even more gently. "That isn't what I meant." His voice managed to get back to normal. "I mean they're bringing in Aggie."

"Hot damn!" A smile and a little color came back to her face. "Well," she said thoughtfully, "the jail does need a good cleaning." She crushed out her cigarette in the fruit-jar top that served as an ash tray. "Artie, is there a drink anywhere in the house?"

"Need one?" He looked at her, a mixture of admiration, brotherly affection, sympathy, and a touch of fear. "We confiscated a pint of gin off a guy. Most of it's left. I'll get it."

Her lower lip was trembling almost as much as her pale fingers.

"Red, kid," he said softly, "you're in the safest place in the world. Jail, that is. Everything is going to be all right."

He grinned at her reassuringly, paused at the door, and burst into song again.

> "The sheriff spoke in a quiet tone,
> She seemed so beautiful and so young,
> As he said, 'tonight you're all alone,
> And tomorrow you must be hung—'"

He ducked the folded magazine she threw at him and said, "Take it easy, Red. Even the President doesn't have a better bodyguard. I'll be right back."

The Santa Maria County Jail was as informal as a Sunday-school picnic, and on weekends and holidays, twice as noisy. Small and fitted with only the essentials, it filled the second floor of the police station. The Presidential Suite consisted of two cells in a far corner reserved for women, juveniles, and special prisoners. Right now Red had it to herself.

Because she wasn't, strictly speaking, a prisoner and because she had her bankroll with her, the cell had sheets, a pillow, and pillow case. Her expensive clothes were carefully placed on hangers. And because Red was a friendly person, a bunch of blue flowers smiled from a jelly glass on an improvised table that had been made of two suitcases and a length of board.

Artie came back, his hand under his tan jacket. The cell was in semidarkness; Red was still sitting on the edge of the bunk. He picked up the white enameled cup from the washstand, poured in a generous drink, added a little water, and handed it to her.

"Dirty trick," Red said. "Toss a guy in the can and then take his gin away."

"He won't miss it," Artie assured her. "He's the mayor's second cousin, and he's got eighteen dollars on deposit downstairs." He added, "You'd better keep the bottle."

"I may need it," she said. She looked up at him, six foot if he was half an inch, crew-cut blond hair, a deeply lined face. She slid the bottle between the mattresses of the bunk across from her, downed the contents of the cup fast, choked, and gasped, "*Water!*"

Artie rushed it to her. "Next time, hold your breath." He paused. "Red, you aren't really scared, are you?"

"Who, me?" she said, turning her eyes away. Her hands shook as she gulped the water, and half of it spilled on the floor.

"Red, kid," he said, taking the cup from her hands. "All you got to do is wait till they take you back to Detroit, just for you to testify. Then you're in the clear."

"They'll never let me get to that courtroom," she said, very quietly.

"Don't talk silly," Artie said. "You'll be protected. You'll be safe."

Their eyes met. They were both lying, and they both knew it.

She turned away first, punched up her pillow, lit a cigarette, and said, "Let's talk about you. What happens? I saw your lawyer come up here yesterday."

"The case comes up week after next," Artie said. "If the judge gets well, that is. The county's only got two judges, and one of 'em's sick. Two thousand cases were ahead of me, but they got it down to one thousand nine hundred and forty-four. When this other judge gets over his tonsillitis, or ulcers, or beri beri, or whatever it is, I'm first on the calendar. It'll be a short trial. They reduced the charge to manslaughter, and my lawyer's charging self-defense."

He blew his nose, lit a cigarette. "Red," he said, "I love my wife. She wrote me every day I was in the South Pacific. I love my kids. She brings them to see me every Sunday. I have a nice little ranch, I'm building up a trucking business. I met this guy, he came over to my house, the wife and kids were up visiting her mother, we had a few beers. He went wild and pulled a gun on me. I tried to take it away from him, and it went off."

Red reached between the mattresses for the bottle, poured a generous two inches into the cup, and handed it to Artie. She had a hunch it was he who needed moral support now.

"You'll get off," she told him. "They may even give you a bounty."

That got a laugh out of him, which was what she wanted. He flicked the ash from his cigarette and said, "Hell, it hasn't been too bad here, these eleven months. Since I been a trusty, I got the run of the place. I go out and do marketing, run errands, eat good and sleep good. Could be worse."

She said with a tired quietness, "I'd rather be here than dead in the streets."

"Red, you quit that kind of talk."

"They got to get me before I can testify," she said.

"I told you before, you're in the safest place in the world." Suddenly the jail seemed to shake. There were sounds from downstairs just a little louder than the Bronx Zoo at feeding time, and about the same pitch.

"That would be Aggie," Red said.

"Couldn't be anyone else." Artie grinned. He rose, locked her cell door, and said, "Sorry I have to do this, but it's only for a few minutes." He called, "Hey, Pablo!"

Red settled down on her bunk and listened to the rumpus. Aggie was resisting arrest in two languages, and from the sounds, it was taking both trusties and Fred, the night jailer to hold her.

Aggie was probably the best cleaning woman in Santa Maria. She was also probably the loudest drunk. She was happy with a bottle, she was just as happy with a pail of soap and water and a mop. Periodically when the jail needed a thorough scrubbing, the word went down the line, "Tour the bars and pick up Aggie."

Aggie always was brought into the jail sounding like a combination of a major riot and a bomb landing in the next block. Next morning the judge invariably sentenced her to six days, which could be worked out in three, and Aggie, cheerful if slightly hung over, filled a pail with soap and hot water and reached for the nearest mop.

Red put her fingers in her ears as Aggie was shoved into the next-door cell and locked in. Aggie went right on shouting.

Artie unlocked the metal grill door to Red's room and said, "You asleep?"

"Slept right through it," Red said cheerfully.

The other trusty, the small, sad-eyed Pablo, came in with Artie. "This we take from Aggie," he said gravely.

The bottle was passed around solemnly. Red shuddered. "Can't these cops ever arrest anybody with champagne?"

"Me, I like Scotch," Artie said.

She passed the bottle to him. "Shut your eyes and pretend that it's Scotch."

There was more noise from the cell next door.

"That Aggie, she makes with the yell," Pablo said.

"I make with the yell myself," Red said grimly. She raised her voice. "Shut up!"

There was a moment's silence, and then an answering yell. "You're who, and what'cha here for?"

"I'm the ax killer you been reading about in the papers," Red called. "And I've got the ax right here, the one I chopped up seven people with. The police let me keep it because I know the mayor. And my cell door is unlocked, and I've got a key to yours, and I like it quiet when I sleep."

There was a long and what promised to be a nightlong silence.

Artie and Pablo waved good night and went away. That was at four A.M.

By eight o'clock in the morning, the sun had been turning the heat on for an hour and a half. Red stirred restlessly, felt a hand pat her shoulder gently, turned over and opened her eyes.

It was Fred, the night jailer. "Going off duty now, Red. Just came by to say goodbye and wish you luck."

Suddenly wide awake, she sat up, pulling the blankets around her shoulders. "What do you mean, goodbye?"

Fred looked embarrassed. "I thought they were moving you out today."

"Nobody's told me yet," she said. She didn't need to look in a mirror; she could feel her face turning pale.

"Well," he said, "well, in case they do. Good luck. Don't worry, Red. Come back and visit us when it's all over."

"Sure will," she said heartily. "I'll do just that little thing."

He knew she'd never be back in Santa Maria, and so did she.

They shook hands. She said, "Fred, please thank your wife for sending me the flowers." Flowers for a corpse that was still walking around and talking. "Wait a minute, will you?"

She reached for her robe, wrapping it around her, slid off the bunk, and rummaged through the suitcase that was under the bed, until she pulled out what looked like a handful of tissue paper. She sat on the edge of the bunk, untangled the tissue paper, and pulled out a brooch. It blazed green, yellow, and white fire in the early-morning sunlight.

"Please give this to her. It's a phony, just a hunk of costume jewelry, but I think it's pretty. The one thing that isn't phony is the thanks to her that go with it."

"Gosh, Red," Fred said. He choked for a minute, rewrapped the brooch in the tissue paper, and stuck in his pocket. "Gosh." He paused again. "She wanted to send you some more flowers."

"Tell her to save them for my wake," Red said, managing to keep her voice light. She walked over to the window and stood looking out.

Fred stood for a moment, uncertainty drawn on his broad red face. Finally he walked over and put a hand on her arm. "Red," he said, feeling for words, "if—I mean, if something happens to you—I mean, well, I got friends, we'll find out who did it—"

She turned around, smiling. "Thanks. Now beat it, bum. I've got to get some sleep."

There was something she vaguely remembered from high school. She fished for it in her mind, and all that came to her was "There is a time to sleep, and a time to stay awake." She knew that wasn't right, but it didn't matter now.

She paced up and down the cell. She scrubbed her face and put on fresh make-up. She combed her lovely red hair until it was smooth and shining. She brushed on lipstick and tended to her eyebrows. She put on a pair of dove-gray slacks, a pale-green sweater, and darker-green sandals.

Eight thirty. She remembered Aggie with a sudden sense of guilt. She raced into the main room and yelled for Artie.

"Honey, open up Aggie's door. She's got to be in court by nine, and I've got to wash her face."

"Will do," he said, reaching for the keys. He looked appreciatively. "You're going to be missed, Red."

Again she could feel the color drain out of her face. "Who says?"

Artie avoided her eyes as he unlocked the door to Aggie's cell. After a moment of inspection and thought, Red went next door and collected a comb, make-up, powder, a lipstick, a big fluffy towel, mouthwash, and the remains of the gin. Five vigorous shakes woke Aggie.

"Come on, kid," Red said. "You've got to be in court in half an hour."

Aggie began moaning. An inch of gin in the enameled cup took care of that. She got her eyes open enough to stay that way on the fourth blink, and said, "Red! You still here?"

"Haven't thrown me out yet," Red said, with false cheerfulness. "Babe, do yourself proud in court. Wash your face, and I'll put your make-up on for you and fix your hair." She looked at Aggie's dress and shook her head sadly.

Well, there was one of her own that just might fit. She was as tall as Aggie, and the dress would stretch sideways.

At two minutes to nine, Aggie was on her way downstairs, hair combed, face made up, smelling slightly of mouthwash and Daphne cologne, and wearing a blue jersey dress that would never shrink back into shape again.

At ten minutes after nine Aggie came back up the stairs, beaming. "Six or three," she shouted. "Artie, where's the mop?"

Red called from her cell, "Artie! Pablo! Somebody!"

It was Artie who came to the door. "A mouse?" he asked.

"I want breakfast," Red said.

"Breakfast is served in this jail at six thirty," Artie said. "But since you slipped Frank a buck yesterday to buy eggs, I think we can oblige you." He winked at her. "He got a dozen eggs stashed away in the refrigerator. And the coffee's good this morning."

It was Pablo who brought in the tin tray. The eggs were cooked just right, the toast was the right color of tan, and the coffee was as good as advertised.

She smiled at Pablo. She always smiled at Pablo. Today she had an extra one.

Pablo was short and slender and black-haired, and he was almost a permanent prisoner. Frank, the day jailer, had confided in Red that Pablo had been serving a thirty-day drunk charge for almost two years. It had become a regular routine. Sentenced to thirty days. Made a trusty the next day. Released. Arrested the next day, or even sooner.

Artie swore, and Red believed him, that Pablo had once made the round trip from the jail and back in exactly three hours.

And it was Artie who'd told her how Pablo's wife had run away with another man, how he'd lost his job and seen the bank take away his home, all in one month.

"Señorita Red," Pablo said, "would you like I should go and buy you cigarettes?"

She looked at him with pretended sternness. "The last time I gave you a quarter to buy me cigarettes you were gone for two days, and the judge tacked an extra thirty days on you when they did find you."

"It was a mistake," Pablo said with great dignity. "Perhaps you could lend me twenty-five cents. Believe me, it is for a good purpose."

She looked at him, and her eyes softened. After all, Pablo had only two homes. The jail, and the Frisco Bar and Grill. She pulled her change purse from under her pillow, took out a fifty-cent piece, and said, "I hope you have a lot of fun with the good purpose."

That was at ten o'clock in the morning.

The routine daily cleaning was going on, plus Aggie throwing a mop around in the kitchen. Red stood looking out the window at the roof of the bowling alley next door. She lifted her eyes to the mountains that ringed the little city and saw a tiny speck of silver racing across the blue. Would they take her out by plane or train, she wondered.

She could hear Artie going through the big cabinet in the main room, sorting out files. She could hear a prisoner rattling tin trays in the kitchen sink. This will be going on long after I'm gone, she thought. Artie will go on sorting files, then his case will come up in court and chances are he'll be freed; the guy in the kitchen will go on washing dishes and serve his sentence and be on his way. But she would be gone before that, far away from here.

A voice said, "Hey, Red."

She turned around. It was Frank, the day jailer. He was a deceptively gentle-looking man with a friendly face, white hair, and a deadly right when he had to use it. He was one more person in the world she would have trusted with her life.

"Chiefs on his way up to see you. Thought I'd tell you, case you want to powder your face."

"Bless you, Frank." At that moment she heard the buzzer that announced someone was coming up the stairs.

She was sitting on the edge of her bunk, face powdered, when Chief of Police Sankey came in, Frank close behind him. "Red," he said. "I mean, Miss—"

"That's all right," she said.

He sat down on the bunk across from her, a worried, fretful little man with reddish hair and rimless glasses.

"Well," he said, "we finally got the word. They're taking you on a plane this afternoon. Papers all signed, everything set."

She opened her mouth to speak, shut it again, and finally managed to say, "I'll be ready."

He looked embarrassed. He said, "You'll be well protected, naturally. So there's nothing for you to worry about." He paused and added, "Well, good luck."

After he'd gone, Frank patted her shoulder and said, "Everything's going to be all right, Red."

"Oh, sure." She forced a smile to her face. "It's just that I like your jail so well that I hate to leave it. Besides, I feel safe here."

He cleared his throat, started to speak, and changed his mind. He patted her shoulder a second time.

"Frank, I saw the whole thing. I was standing right in the doorway of the Blue Casino. Louie did the job himself, and I was right there. All I could think of was to beat it, fast. Threw some stuff in a couple of suitcases, got the first plane to Kansas City. That's where I bought the car and headed south. I could have made it across the border into Mexico easy, but you guys picked me up."

"Maybe it's just as well," Frank told her reassuringly. "This guy would have had you followed. This way he'll get convicted, and then you won't have a thing to worry about."

"Oh, sure," she said again. She sighed. "It's just luck that some goon was coming down the sidewalk and saw what was going on. He didn't get close enough to recognize Louie, but I was standing there with a light smack on my face, and he spotted me. The Detroit cops picked up Louie on general principles and started looking for me."

She ran a hand through her shining red hair. "I'm their only witness. 'Course, I could get on the stand and swear I didn't see a thing, or I could swear it wasn't Louie."

"You could," Frank said. "But—"

"But I wouldn't," she finished for him. "That is, assuming I ever get to the witness stand."

Artie came in, lit a cigarette, and lounged against the wall.

"This Louie," Frank asked, "was he your boyfriend?"

That brought a laugh from her, the first one that day. "I didn't have a boyfriend. I ran the Blue Casino. A gambling joint. I ran that end of it, and my partner ran the nightclub end." She grinned at them. "I came by these diamonds honestly, pals."

"So that's why you've been able to take us at blackjack," Artie said lazily.

"Well," Frank said, getting up, "you'll be protected on the way to the plane, and you'll be protected on the plane, and you'll probably be taken off it in an armored car."

Artie pinched out his cigarette, dropped it on the floor. "Pablo'll clean up in here when he gets back. He's got the car out now, getting potatoes."

At that moment all hell broke loose in the yard outside. Red and Artie were tied getting to the window. Artie gave a loud whoop and raced for the stairs, yelling for Frank to work the buzzer.

Outside, Pablo was having troubles. The car used by the jail for general errands was parked directly under Red's window, and the trunk compartment was open. What appeared to be about a hundred white chickens, but were actually only six, were creating the disturbance. Pablo was trying to move them from the trunk compartment to a burlap bag, and the chickens were resisting arrest. The scene was beginning to draw a fair-sized audience when reinforcements, in the person of Artie, arrived.

Between them, the chickens were shoved unceremoniously into the bag and tossed, still protesting loudly, into the car. Artie and Pablo got in and drove off.

Frank, who had watched the last act from Red's window, sighed deeply and said, "Sometimes I think they give these trusties too many liberties."

"None of them give you any trouble, though," Red reminded him.

"That's right," he said, "except sometimes Pablo." He looked at her searchingly. "Did you give him any money?"

"I gave him fifty cents," Red confessed. She added, as though in defense, "After all, Frank, it's my last day here."

Frank shook his head sadly. "Another thirty days. Well, he's got to sleep somewhere."

That was at eleven o'clock.

It was some time later when Artie and Pablo came in triumphantly, Pablo carrying a large paper-wrapped bundle. The chickens were not only silent now, but in addition to losing their voices they had lost their feathers and a few other odds and ends, and were candidates for the frying pan.

"Farewell party!" Artie called happily, heading for the kitchen.

Red looked at her suitcases, at the clothes hanging against the walls, at the make-up carefully arranged on the improvised table, and started a half-hearted effort toward packing. But there was plenty of time for that later. She flopped down on the bunk, picked up a magazine, and tried to read. The words seemed to run together and made no sense at all.

Pablo came in the door. He was completely sober, and walking with great dignity. He carried a package, which he presented to Red with even greater dignity.

"For you," he said. "For a going-far-away present."

She unwrapped it. It was a bottle of what was probably the worst wine in the world. This was the important purpose for which Pablo had needed money. She felt tears hot in her eyes.

"Pablo, I thank you," she said with dignity that matched his. She put the package under the bunk, reached between the mattresses for the last of the gin. "For farewell, will you have a drink with me?"

Pablo's dark eyes brightened. "Since you insist upon it."

She rinsed out the enameled cups and divided the gin equally into them. They saluted each other solemnly and silently.

"We will miss you," Pablo said simply.

That was at twelve o'clock.

It was Artie who brought in her lunch, some time later.

"No stew?" she said, looking up and sniffing. "No pinto beans?"

Artie grinned at her as he set the tray down. "Fried chicken." He shook his head thoughtfully. "That Pablo. It isn't enough that he goes out and steals chickens. But he has to steal the chickens from the chief of police."

He went on. "He was going to bring them up here and clean them, but I had an idea. We took them to a restaurant where I know the kitchen help. Result, no evidence."

It was one o'clock when he came to take the tray away and lock Aggie's door. She was, after all, a prisoner, and even in the Santa Maria County Jail, rules were rules. He paused in Red's cell.

"I'll help you pack, after siesta."

She turned her face away. "I can manage, thanks, Artie."

He sat down on the other bunk. "Red, listen. You'll be protected. There's nothing to it. When you get to Detroit they'll put you up in some expensive hotel, with a bodyguard. You testify, and it's all over. There's nothing for you to be scared of."

"Who's scared?" she scoffed, managing to keep her voice steady.

"Red," he said slowly, "Red. Will you let me kiss you, once?"

She stared at him.

"I been here eleven months, Red. I'd just like to kiss a girl again."

She smiled, and lifted her face to him. He kissed her very gently, almost a little-boy kiss.

"It won't seem like the same place without you, Red."

The county jail became silent. Frank had gone out to lunch, and everyone else was asleep. Everybody except Red. She lay on her bunk, her eyes closed, wondering if she would ever sleep again. Finally she gave up. Might as well pack and get it over with.

Midafternoon sunlight was streaming in the windows of the trusties' room when the sound of the big door clanging shut and footsteps on the stairs woke Artie. He swung his long legs off the bed, and walked into the main room.

That was at three o'clock.

Frank and a stranger had just reached the top of the stairs. "Detective Connelly, Detroit police," Frank said, puffing, and nodding toward the stranger. "Red all packed and set to leave?"

"I'll see," Artie said.

Red was sitting on the bunk, her suitcase beside her. She had on a light-beige suit and a small green hat. Her face was very pale. Artie picked up the suitcase. She rose and followed him into the main room.

Pablo had come out of the trusties' room. Aggie, mop in hand, was watching. Everyone was silent.

Red managed a wan smile at the Detroit detective.

"All set?" He tried to smile but didn't look as though he relished this job. She nodded.

Frank said heartily, "Now remember, Red, don't you worry about a thing. He'll take you back, you testify, this Louie will go to jail or the chair, and that's that."

"Sure," Connelly said, with false confidence. "That's the way."

"And you will come back to visit us," Pablo said. "I will still be here."

That eased the tension a little.

There was nothing left to say but goodbye. Then Red went down the stairs without looking back, Connelly and Frank on either side. The two trusties stood looking after her.

At last they walked to her cell and looked in. There was a faint odor of cigarette smoke, gin, and expensive perfume. Artie straightened a wrinkle in the blankets.

"It seems so quiet," he said.

Pablo looked under the bed, pulled out the package. "She forgets and leaves it behind," he said sadly, unwrapping it. "I buy it for her, a going-away present." There were tears in his eyes.

"You're a bad boy, Pablo," Aggie said from the doorway.

Pablo looked wistful.

"I think she'd have wanted you to open it," Artie said very gently.

Pablo ripped off the cap. The bottle of the worst wine in the world was passed around in silence.

The Set-Up
Sam Cobb (Stanley L. Colbert)

January 1953

It was late at night, and I sat around the station house, idly thinking that my newspaper needed me here like it needed a hole in its columns, when the homicide call came in.

Perkins, from the *Globe-Press,* jumped up and grabbed the address from the desk sergeant, and said, "C'mon, I got my car outside. The company pays for the gas and the burned rubber."

I nodded, and we headed for the car. Perkins revved it, made a sharp left turn out of the police lot, and we were off.

"Ain't we got fun?" he asked, driving with one hand and buttoning his shirt collar with the other.

"Drop dead," I said. Mechanically, I watched him fumble with the button and then the tie, but my mind was a million and a half miles away.

"A ten says we get a front-page story this time. I've got a hunch." Perkins was young, and he chattered the way he always did when there was the scent of excitement.

"Just think about driving the car and we'll be all right," I told him.

I would have taken the punk's money easy enough if I'd had ten bucks to cover the bet, but I didn't have a sou to my name. My paycheck was sliced up more ways than a restaurant pie, and between the bookies, bartenders, and a chick named Francie, who knew how to drive me half-crazy, I was in hock up to my elbows.

"You ain't listening," Perkins said, as we slowed down behind a bus driver who acted like he had an inside tip that his company owned Eighth Avenue from curb to curb. "I asked you if you thought it might be a perfect crime. I never covered one of those."

"Naw, you've been reading too many mysteries. Why don't you try comic books for a change; they're educational, help you in your job." He looked grumpy, and maybe for a few minutes he'd let me alone. I hoped so. I had been thinking about Francie all evening, and I couldn't stop. I had to figure out something to tell her tonight.

She was a nice kid when you had the old mazuma, but when your pockets dried up, so did she. When the horses were hitting she couldn't get close enough. Now that nothing was hitting she was going to cut me off. I couldn't let her go. Never mind what was wrong with her. I had to come up with some awful good promises tonight when I saw her, or some awfully good dough.

Perkins turned to me. "I read comic books, too. So what?" he said.

"Keep it up," I said. "That's how guys become managing editors, just reading comic books, that's all. Now get off my back, Junior."

He didn't open his mouth for the next five minutes, and I didn't say anything, either. I just sat there trying to think of something, but nothing came up that sounded like quick money in the bank.

We pulled up sharply in front of a brownstone house in a neighborhood that couldn't make up its mind about whether or not it was respectable. We were about twenty seconds behind the prowl car. Half-heartedly I stepped out and acted like a reporter. We didn't have to get past the vestibule to find out what happened and who did it. Standing by the hall pay phone was a mangy character, sobbing, surrounded by a bunch of people who didn't seem to speak English. He did, though, and you couldn't stop him from talking once he saw Kozlewski, the cop, a few steps ahead of us.

"Me! I did it!" he screamed. "I killed her like this—" He shot his hands out in the air and clenched an imaginary throat, shaking as if he had the chills.

Perkins turned to me and grabbed my arm. "He must have strangled her," he said. Sometimes this Perkins acts like he's brilliant.

Kozlewski knew me from before, and he nodded, which meant I'd better get his name spelled right. Then he turned to the crowd bunched in around us. "Vamoose. Scram. Get lost," he said. He held his man firmly. "Now, speak slow, Buster, so I can understand you, and start from the beginning." Perkins and I reached for notebooks. This character started talking.

"I came home tonight from work," he said. "It was a little earlier than usual, but still it was late. I work a funny shift.

"I started up the stairs to our apartment. Halfway up I saw a man just leaving our door. I thought maybe he was selling something, so I didn't think too much of it. When I walked in my wife looked surprised. She was just putting away a bottle and carrying two glasses into the kitchen. She was only wearing a housecoat. It was open all the way. She had nothing under it."

He had to stop to compose himself. The poor slob. In a second he was ready to continue.

"I asked her who the guy was and what was happening. She shrugged her shoulders and said something about me not bringing home enough money to give her what she wanted and she knew how to make it. All of a sudden like that she said it to me. I don't remember what I said. I grabbed her neck and squeezed until she turned blue and fell to the floor. I couldn't run away. I came downstairs and called the police."

He had to lean against the wall. The small hallway was smoky and booming with chatter. Kozlewski motioned to a fat old lady who was clucking away.

"Which apartment is his?" he asked. She pointed upstairs and said, "Number Two."

Kozlewski grabbed this character by the arm, and we all headed upstairs. He probably figured when the detectives came they'd ask about the place and he'd better look it over. Very thorough, I thought, especially on an open-and-shut case.

He took a quick look at the not-so-pretty body on the floor and let his eyes wander over the room. It was sloppy, but nothing unusual.

"Okay," Kozlewski said. "Let's head back downstairs so I can call in." The character was still whimpering. I turned to Perkins and muttered, "You head down and see if you can get some quotes from the guy. I'll stay here for a minute and see if I can pick up notes on the room and maybe find a picture of the babe. We can swap later."

It sounded all right to Perkins, and Kozlewski didn't argue because he still wanted his name spelled right.

When they left I looked around. There was a bureau in the far corner with a drawer slightly open. I walked over to it and started to leaf through the drawer.

Halfway down, under some sweaters and slips, my hand touched something and suddenly turned to ice. It was a roll of bills. We're back in business, Francie, I thought to myself. Instinctively I looked to the door, but no one was there. I started to edge the money toward my pocket. Then, as I turned my head back, I glanced into the mirror over the dresser.

My back grew prickly, and the short hairs on my spine played pingpong with the balls of sweat that suddenly appeared there. She was moving. Sitting up and rubbing her throat. Watching me, staring at the green bundle in my hand. In another second she'd be composed enough to scream, "Thief!"

I shoved the money in my pocket and took three quick steps toward her, cursing the weak joker downstairs who didn't know he was crying over nothing. Then I found my hands were clutching her bluemarked throat until my fingers were like white pieces of steel twined around her neck. I smiled as I thought for a second about Perkins and his perfect crime. "You aren't gonna holler, sister," I heard myself muttering. "No cheap tramp is gonna make me lose my girl."

The Double Take
Richard S. Prather

July 1953

This was a morning for weeping at funerals, for sticking pins in your own wax image, for leaping into empty graves and pulling the sod in after you. Last night I had been at a party with some friends here in Los Angeles, and I had drunk bourbon and Scotch and martinis and maybe even swamp water from highball glasses, and now my brain was a bomb that went off twice a second.

I thought thirstily of Pete's Bar downstairs on Broadway, right next door to this building, the Hamilton, where I have my detective agency, then got out of my chair, left the office and locked the door behind me. I was Shell Scott, The Bloodshot Eye, and I needed a hair of the horse that bit me.

Before I went downstairs I stopped by the PBX switchboard at the end of the hall. Cute little Hazel glanced up.

"You look terrible," she said.

"I know. I think I'm decomposing. Listen, a client just phoned me and I have to rush out to the Hollywood Roosevelt. I'll be back in an hour or so, but for the next five minutes I'll be in Pete's. Hold down the fort, huh?"

"Sure, Shell. Pete's?" She shook her head.

I tried to grin at her, whereupon she shrank back and covered her eyes, and I left. Hazel is a sweet kid, tiny, and curvy, and since mine is a one-man agency with no receptionist or secretary, the good gal tries to keep informed of my whereabouts.

I tottered down the one flight of stairs into bright June sunshine on Broadway, thinking that my client would have to wait an extra five minutes even though he'd been in a hell of a hurry. But he'd been in a hurry the last time, too, and nothing had come of it. This Frank Harrison had first called me on Monday morning, three days ago, and insisted I come right out to his hotel in Hollywood. When I got there he explained that he was having marital troubles and wanted me to tail his wife and see if I could catch her in any indiscretions. When I told him I seldom handled that kind of job, he'd said to forget it, so I had. The deal had seemed screwy; he'd not only been vague, but hadn't pressed me much to take the case. It had added up to an hour wasted, and no fee.

But this morning when I'd opened the office at nine sharp the phone had been ringing and it was Harrison again. He wanted me right away this time, too, but he had a real case for me, he said, not like last time, and it wasn't tailing his wife. He was in a sweat to get me out to the Roosevelt's bar, the Cinegrill where we were to meet, and was willing to pay me fifty bucks just to listen to his story. I still didn't know what was up, but it sounded like a big one. I hoped it was bigger than the last "job," and, anyway, it couldn't be as big as my head. I went into Pete's.

Pete knew what I wanted as soon as I perched on a stool and he got a good look at my eyeballs, so he immediately mixed the ghastly concoction he gives me for hangovers. I was halfway through it when his phone rang.

He listened a moment, said, "I'll tell him," then turned to me. "That was Hazel," he said. "Some dame was up there looking for you. A wild woman—"

That was as far as he got. I heard somebody come inside the front door, and high heels clicked rapidly over the floor and stopped alongside me. A woman's voice, tight and angry, said, "There you are, you, you—you crook!" and I turned on my stool to look at the wild woman.

I had never seen her before, but that was obviously one of the most unfortunate omissions of my life, because one look at her and I forgot my hangover. She was an absolutely gorgeous little doll, about five feet two inches tall, and any half-dozen of her sixty-two delightful inches would make any man stare, and all of her at once was enough to knock a man's eyes out through the back of his head.

"Oh!" she said. "You ought to be tarred and feathered."

I kept looking. Coal black hair was fluffed around her oval face, and though she couldn't have been more than twenty-four or twenty-five years old, a thin streak of gray ran back from her forehead through that thick, glossy hair. She was dressed in light blue clam-diggers and a man's white shirt which her chest filled out better than any man's ever did, and her eyes were an incredibly light electric blue—shooting sparks at me.

She was angry. She was so hot she looked ready to melt. It seemed, for some strange reason, she was angry with me. This lovely was not one I wanted angry with me; I wanted her happy, and patting my cheek, or perhaps even chewing on my ear.

She looked me up and down and said, "Yes. Yes, you're Shell Scott."

"That's right. Certainly. But—"

"I want that twenty-four thousand dollars and I'm going to get it if I—if I have to *kill* you! I mean it!"

"Huh?"

"It's just money to you, you crook! But it's all he had, all my father's saved in years and years. Folsom's Market, indeed! I'll kill you, I *will!* So give me that money. I know you're in with them."

My head was in very bad shape to begin with, but now I was beginning to think maybe I had mush up there. She hadn't yet said a single word that made sense.

"Take it easy," I said. "You must have the wrong guy."

If anything, that remark made her angrier. She pressed white teeth together, and made noises in her throat, then she said, "I suppose you're not Shell Scott."

"Sure I am, but I don't know what you're babbling about."

"Babbling! *Babbling!* Ho, that's the way you're going to play it, are you? Going to deny everything, pretend it never happened! I knew you would! Well—"

She backed away from me, fumbling with the clasp of a big handbag. I looked at her thinking that one of us was completely mad. Then she dug into her bag and pulled out a chromed pistol, probably a .22 target pistol, and pointed it at me. She was crying now, her face twisted up and tears running down her cheeks, but she still appeared to be getting angrier every second, and slowly the thought seeped into my brain: this tomato is aiming a real gun at me.

She backed away toward the rear of Pete's, but she was still too close to suit me, and close enough so I could see her eyes squeeze shut and her finger tighten on the trigger. I heard the crack of the little gun and I heard a guy who had just come in the door, let out a yelp behind me, and I heard a little tinkle of glass. And then I heard a great clattering and crashing of glass because by this time I was clear over behind the bar with Pete, banging into bottles and glasses on my way down to the floor. I heard the gun crack twice more and then high heels clattered away from me and I peeked over the bar just in time to see the gal disappearing into the ladies' room.

A man on my left yelled, "Janet! *Jan!*" I looked at him just as he got up off the floor, and I remembered the guy who had yelped right after that first shot. He didn't seem to be hurt, though, because he got to his feet and started after the beautiful crazy gal.

He was a husky man, about five-ten, wearing brown slacks and a T-shirt which showed off his impressive chest. Even so, it wasn't as impressive as the last chest I'd seen, and although less than a minute had elapsed since I'd first seen the gal who'd been behind it, I was already understandably curious about her. I vaulted over the bar and yelled at the man, "Hey, you! Hold it!"

He stopped and jerked his head around as I stepped up in front of him. His slightly effeminate face didn't quite go with the masculine build, but many women would probably have called him "handsome" or even "darling." A thick mass of black curly hair came down in a sharp widow's peak on his white forehead. His mouth was full, chin square and dimpled, and large black-lashed brown eyes blinked at me.

"Who the hell was that tomato?" I asked him. "And what's happening?"

"You tell me," he said. And then an odd thing happened. He hadn't yet had time to take a good look at me, but he took it now. He gawked at my white hair, my face, blinked, and his mouth dropped open. "Oh, *Christ!*" he said, and then he took off. Naturally he ran into the ladies' rest room. It just wouldn't have seemed right at that point if he'd gone anyplace else.

I looked over my shoulder at Pete, whose mouth was hanging completely ajar, then I went to the ladies' room and inside. Nobody was there. A wall window was open and I looked out through it at the empty alley, then looked all around the rest room again, but it was still empty.

I went back to the bar and said, "Pete, what the hell did you put in that drink?"

He stared at me, shaking his head. Finally he said, "I never seen nothing like that in my life. Thirteen years I've run this place, but—" He didn't finish it.

My hand was stinging and so was a spot on my chin. Going over the bar I had broken a few bottles and cut my left hand slightly, and one of those little slugs had apparently come close enough to nick my chin. I had also soaked up a considerable amount of spilled whiskey in my clothes and I didn't smell good at all. My head hadn't been helped, either, by the activity.

Pete nodded when I told him to figure up the damage and I'd pay him later, then I went back into the Hamilton Building. It appeared Frank Harrison would have to wait. Also, the way things were going, I wanted to get the .38 Colt Special and harness out of my desk.

At the top of the stairs I walked down to the PBX again. Hazel, busy at the switchboard, didn't see me come up but when I spoke she swung around. "What's with that gal you called Pete's about?" I asked her.

"She find you? Wasn't she a beautiful little thing?"

"Yeah. And she found me."

Hazel's nose was wrinkling. "You *are* decomposing," she said. "Into bourbon. How many shots did you have?"

"Three, I think. But they all missed me."

"Missed you, ha—"

"Shots that beautiful little thing took at me, I mean. With a gun."

Hazel blinked. "You're kidding." I shook my head and she said, "Well, I—she did seem upset, a little on edge."

"She was clear the hell over the edge. What did she say?"

"She asked for you. As a matter of fact, she said, 'Where's that dirty Shell Scott?' I told her you'd gone to Pete's downstairs—" Hazel smiled sweetly— "for some medicine, and she ran away like mad. She seemed very excited."

"She was."

"And a man came rushing up here a minute or two after the girl and asked about her. I said I'd sent her to Pete's—and *he* ran off." She shook her head. "I don't know. I'm a little confused."

That I could understand. Maybe it was something in the L. A. air this morning. I thanked Hazel and walked down to the office, fishing out my keys, but when I got there I noticed the door was already cracked. I shoved it open and walked inside. For the second or third time this morning my jaw dropped open. A guy was seated behind my desk, fussing with some papers on its top, looking businesslike as all hell. He was a big guy, husky, around thirty years old, with white hair sticking up into the air about an inch.

Without looking up, he said, "Be right with you."

I walked to the desk and sank into one of the leather chairs in front of it, a chair I bought for clients to sit in. If the chair had raised up and floated me out of the window while violins played in the distance, my stunned expression would not have changed one iota. In a not very strong voice I said, "Who are you?"

"I'm Shell Scott," he said briskly, glancing up at me.

Ah, yes. That explained it. He was Shell Scott. Now I knew what was wrong. I had gone crazy. My mind had snapped. For a while there I'd thought *I* was Shell Scott.

But slowly reason filtered into my throbbing head again. I'd had all the mad episodes I cared for this morning, and here was a guy I could get my hands on. He was looking squarely at me now, and if ever a man suddenly appeared scared green, this one did. Except for the short white hair and the fact that he was about my size, he didn't resemble me much, and right now he looked sick. I got up and leaned on the desk and shoved my face at him.

"That's interesting," I said pleasantly. "I, too, am Shell Scott."

He let out a grunt and started to get up fast, but I reached out and grabbed a bunch of shirt and tie and throat in my right fist and I yanked him halfway across the desk.

"O. K., you smart sonofabitch," I said. "Let's have a lot of words. Fast, mister, before I break some bones for you."

He squawked and sputtered and tried to jerk away, so I latched onto him with the other hand and started to haul him over the desk where I could get at him good. I only started to though, because I heard somebody behind me. I twisted my head around just in time to see the pretty boy from Pete's, the guy who'd left the ladies' room by the window. Just time to see him, and the leather-wrapped sap in his hand, swinging down at me. Then another bomb, a larger one this time, went off in my head and I could feel myself falling, for miles and miles, through deepening blackness.

I came to in front of my desk, and I stayed there for a couple of minutes, got up, made it to the desk chair and sat down in it. If I had thought my head hurt before, it was nothing to the way it felt now. It took me about ten seconds to go from angry to mad to furious to raging, then I grabbed the phone and got Hazel.

"Where'd those two guys go?"

"What guys?"

"You see anybody leave my office?"

"No, Shell. What's the matter?"

"Plenty." I glanced at my watch. Nine-twenty. Just twenty minutes since I'd first opened the office door this morning and answered the ringing phone. I couldn't have been sprawled on the floor more than a minute or two, but even so my two pals would be far away by now. Well, Harrison was going to have a long wait because I was taking no cases but my own for a while. What with people shooting at me, impersonating me, and batting me on the head, this was a mess I had to find out about fast.

"Hazel," I said, "get me the Hollywood Roosevelt."

While I waited I calmed down a little and, though the throbbing in my head made it difficult, my thoughts got a little clearer. It seemed a big white-haired ape was passing himself off as me, but I didn't have the faintest idea why. He must have been down below on Broadway somewhere, waited till he saw me leave, then come up. What I couldn't figure was how the hell he'd known I'd be leaving my office. He certainly couldn't have intended hanging around all day just in case I left, and he couldn't have known I'd be at Pete's —

I stopped as a thought hit me. "Hazel," I said. "Forget that call." I hung up, thinking. Whitey couldn't have known I'd show up with a hangover, but he might have known I'd be out of here soon after I arrived. All it takes to get a private detective out of his office is—a phone call. An urgent appointment to meet somebody somewhere, say, maybe somebody like Frank Harrison. Could be I was reaching for that one, but I didn't think so. I'd had only the one call this morning, an urgent call that would get me out of the office—and from the very guy who'd pulled the same deal last Monday. And all I'd done Monday was waste an hour. The more I thought about it the more positive I became.

Harrison might still be waiting in the Cinegrill—and he might not. If Harrison were in whatever this caper was with Whitey and Pretty Boy, they'd almost surely phone him soon to let him know I hadn't followed the script; perhaps were even phoning him right now. He'd know, too, that unless I was pretty stupid, I'd sooner or later figure out his part in this.

Excitement started building in me as I grabbed my gun and holster and strapped them on; I was getting an inkling of what might have been wrong with that black-haired lovely. Maybe I'd lost Whitey and Pretty Boy, but with luck I could still get my hands on Harrison. Around his throat, say. I charged out of the office. My head hurt all the way but I made it to the lot where I park my convertible Cadillac, leaped in and roared out onto Broadway. From L. A. to downtown Hollywood I broke hell out of the speed limit, and at the hotel I found a parking spot at the side entrance, hurried through the big lobby and into the Cinegrill.

I remembered Harrison was a very tall diplomat-type with hair graying at the temples and bushy eyebrows over dark eyes. Nobody even remotely like him was in the bar. I asked the bartender, "You know a Frank Harrison?"

"Yes, sir."

"He been in here?"

"Yes, sir. He left just a few minutes ago."

"Left the hotel?"

"No, he went into the lobby."

"Thanks." I hustled back into the lobby and up to the desk. A tall, thin clerk in his middle thirties, wearing rimless glasses looked at me when I stopped.

"I've got an appointment with Mr. Frank Harrison," I said. "What room is he in?"

"Seven-fourteen, sir." The clerk looked a little bewildered. "But Mr. Harrison just left."

"Where'd he go? How long ago?"

The clerk shook his head. "He was checking out. I got his card, and when I turned around I saw him going out the door. Just now. It hasn't been a minute. I don't—"

I turned around and ran for the door swearing under my breath. The bastard would have been at the desk when I came in through the side entrance and headed for the Cinegrill. He must have seen me, and that had been all; he'd powdered. He was well powdered, too, because there wasn't a trace of him when I got out onto Hollywood Boulevard.

Inside the hotel again I checked some more with the bartender and desk clerk, plus two bellboys and a dining-room waitress. After a lot of questions I knew Harrison had often been seen in the bar and dining room with two other men. One was stocky, with curly black hair, white skin, cleft chin, quite handsome—Pretty Boy; the other was bigger and huskier and almost always wore a hat. A bellhop said he looked a bit like me. I told him it *was* me, and left him looking bewildered. Two bellboys and the bartender also told me that Harrison was seen every day, almost *all* of every day, with a blonde woman a few years under thirty whom they all described as "stacked." The three men and the blonde were often a foursome. From the bartender I learned that Harrison had gotten a phone call in the Cinegrill about five minutes before I showed up. That would have been from the other two guys on my list, and fit with Harrison's checking out fast—or starting to. I went back to the desk and chatted some more with the thin clerk after showing him the photostat of my license. Pretty Boy—Bob Foster—was in room 624; Whitey—James Flagg—was in 410; Frank Harrison was in 714.

I asked the clerk, "Harrison married to a blonde?"

"I don't believe he is married, sir."

"He's registered alone?" He nodded, and I said, "I understand he's here a lot with a young woman. Right?"

"Yes, sir. That's Miss Willis."

"A blonde?"

"Yes. Quite, ah, curvaceous."

"What room is she in?"

He had to check. He came back with the card in his hand and said, "Isn't this odd? I had never noticed. She's in seven-sixteen."

It wasn't at all odd. I looked behind him to the slots where room keys were kept. There wasn't any key in the slot for 714. Nor was there any key in the 716 slot. I thanked the clerk, took an elevator to the seventh floor and walked to Harrison's room. There were two things I wanted to do. One was look around inside here to see if maybe my ex-client had left something behind which might help me find him; and the other was to talk with the blonde. As it turned out, I killed two birds with one stone.

The door to 714 was locked, and if I had to I was going to bribe a bellboy to let me in. But, first, I knocked.

It took quite a while, and I had almost decided I'd have to bribe the bellhop, but then there was the sound of movement inside, a muffled voice called something I couldn't understand, and I heard the soft thud of feet coming toward the door. A key clicked in the lock and the door swung open. A girl stood there, yawning, her eyes nearly closed, her head drooping as she stared at approximately the top button of my coat.

She was stark naked. Stark. I had seldom seen *anything* so stark. She had obviously just gotten out of bed, and just as obviously had been sound asleep. She still wasn't awake, because blinking at my chest she mumbled, "Oh, dammit to hell, John."

Then she turned around and walked back into the room. I followed her, as if hypnotized, automatically swinging the door shut behind me. She was about five-six and close to 130 pounds, and she was shaped like what I sometimes muse about after the third highball. Everybody who had described the blonde, and she was a blonde, had been correct: she was not only "stacked" but "ah, curvaceous." There was no mistaking it, either; the one time a man can be positive that a woman's shape is her own is when she is wearing nothing but her shape, and this gal was really in *dandy* shape. She walked away from me toward a bedroom next to this room, like a gal moving in her sleep. She walked to the bed and flopped onto it, pulling a sheet up over her, and I followed her clear to the bed, still coming out of shock, my mind not yet working quite like a well-oiled machine. I managed to figure out that my Frank Harrison was actually named John something. Then she yawned, blinked up at me and said, "Well, dammit to hell, John, stop staring."

And then she stopped suddenly with her mouth stretching wider and wider and her eyes growing enormous as she stared at me. Then she screamed. Man, she screamed like a gal who had just crawled into bed with seventeen tarantulas. I was certainly affecting people in peculiar fashion this morning. She threw off the sheet, leaped to the floor and lit out for an open door in the far wall, leading into the bathroom, and by now that didn't surprise me a bit.

She didn't make it, though. She was only a yard from me at the start, and I took one step toward her, grabbed her wrist and hung on. She stopped screaming and slashed long red fingernails at my face, but I grabbed her hand and shoved her back onto the bed, then said, "Relax, sister. Stop clawing at me and keep your yap closed and I'll let go of you."

She was tense, jerking her arms and trying to get free, but suddenly she relaxed. Her face didn't relax, though; she still glared at me, a mixture of hate, anger, and maybe fright, staining her face. She didn't have makeup on, but her face had a hard, tough-kid attractiveness.

I let go of her and she grabbed the sheet, pulled it up in front of her body. "Get the hell out of here," she said nastily. There was a phone on a bedside stand and her eyes fell on it. She grabbed it, pulled it off the hook. "I'm calling the cops."

I pulled a chair over beside the bed and sat down. Finally she let go of the phone and glared some more at me.

"I didn't think you'd call any cops, sweetheart," I said. "Maybe I will, but you won't. Quite a shock seeing me here, isn't it? I was supposed to meet Frank—I mean, John—in the Cinegrill, not up here. You're in trouble, baby."

"I don't know what you're talking about."

"Not much. You know who I am—"

"You're crazy."

"Shut up. Miss Willis. I got a call from your boy friend at nine sharp this morning. I was supposed to rush out here for an important job; only there isn't any important job. Your John, the guy I know as Frank Harrison, just wanted me out of my office for an hour or so. Right?"

She didn't say anything.

"So another guy could play Shell Scott for a while. Now you tell me why."

Her lips curled and she swore at me.

I said, "Something you don't know. You must have guessed the caper's gone sour, but you probably don't know John has powdered. Left you flat, honey."

She frowned momentarily, then her face smoothed and got blank. It stayed blank.

She was clammed good. Finally I said, "Look, I know enough of it already. There's John, and Bob Foster, and a big white-haired slob named Flagg who probably got his peroxide from you. And don't play innocent because I know you're thick with all of them, especially John. Hell, this is his room. So get smart and—"

The phone rang. She reached for it, then stopped.

I yanked the .38 out from under my coat and said, "Don't get wise; say hello." I took the phone off the hook and held it for her. She said, "Hello," and I put the phone to my ear just in time to hear a man's voice say, "John, baby. I had to blow fast, that bastard was in the hotel. Pack and meet me at Apex." He stopped.

I covered the mouthpiece and told the blonde, "Tell him O.K. Just that, nothing else."

I stuck the phone up in front of her and she said, "The panic's on. Fade out." I got the phone back to my ear just in time to hear the click as he hung up.

The blonde was smiling at me. But she stopped smiling when I stuck my gun back in its holster, then juggled the receiver and said, "Get me the Hollywood Detective Division."

"Hey, wait a minute," the blonde said. "What you calling the cops for?"

"You can't be that stupid. Tehachapi for you, sweetheart. You probably have a lot of friends there. It won't be so bad. Just horrible."

She licked her lips. When the phone was answered I said, "Put Lieutenant Bronson on, will you?"

The gal said, "Wait a minute. Hold off on that call. Let's ... talk about it."

I grinned. "Now you want to talk. No soap. You can talk to the cops. And don't tell me there isn't enough to hold you on."

"Please. I—call him later if you have to." She let go of the sheet and it fell to her waist. I told myself to be strong and look away, but I was weak.

"You got it all wrong," she said softly. "Let's—talk." She tried to smile, but it didn't quite come off. I shook my head.

She threw the sheet all the way back on the bed then, stood up, holding her body erect, and stepped close to me. "Please, honey. We can have fun. Don't you like me, honey?"

"What's with that white-haired ape in my office? And what's Apex?"

"I don't know. I told you before. Honest, Honey, look at me."

That was a pretty silly thing to say, because I sure wasn't looking at the wallpaper. Just then Lieutenant Bronson came on and I said, "Shell Scott here, Bron. Hollywood Roosevelt, room seven-fourteen."

The blonde stepped closer, almost touching me, then picked up my free right hand and passed it around her waist "Hang up," she said. "You won't be sorry." Her voice dropped lower, became a husky murmur as she pressed my fingers into the warm flesh. "Forget it honey. I can be awfully nice."

Bronson was asking me what was up. I said, "Just a second, Bron," then to the girl, "Sounds like a great kick. Just tell me the story, spill your guts—"

She threw my hand away from her, face getting almost ugly, and then she took a wild swing at me. I blocked the blow with my right hand, put my hand flat on her chest and shoved her back against the bed. She sprawled on it, saying some very nasty things.

I said into the phone, "I've got a brassy blonde here for you,"

"What's the score?"

"Frankly, I'm not sure. But I'll sign a complaint. Using foul language, maybe."

"That her? I can hear her."

"Or maybe attempted rape." I grinned at the blonde as she yanked the sheet over her and used some more foul language. I said to Bronson, "Actually, it looks like some kind of confidence game—with me a sucker. I don't know the gal, but you guys might make her. Probably she's got a record." I saw the girl's face change as she winced. "Yeah," I added, "she's got a record. Probably as long as her face is right now."

"I'll send a man up."

"Make it fast, will you? I've got to get out of here, and this beautiful blonde hasn't a stitch of clothes on."

"Huh? She—I'll be right there."

It didn't take him long. By ten-forty-five Bronson, who had arrived grinning—and the three husky sergeants who came with him—had taken the blonde away and I was back in the hotel's lobby. I had given Bronson a rundown on the morning's events, and he'd said they'd keep after the blonde. Neither of us expected any chatter from her, though. After that soft, "I can be awfully nice," she hadn't said anything except swear words and: "I want a lawyer, I know my rights, I want a lawyer." She'd get a lawyer. Tomorrow, maybe.

I went into the Cinegrill and had a bourbon and water while I tried to figure my next move. Bron and I had checked the phone book and city directory for an "Apex" and found almost fifty of them, from Apex Diaper Service to an Apex Junk Yard, which was no help at all, though the cops would check. That lead was undoubtedly no good now that the blonde had warned Harrison. I was getting more and more anxious to find out what the score was, because this was sure shaping up like some kind of con, and I wasn't a bit happy about it.

The confidence man is, in many ways, the elite of the criminal world. Usually intelligent, personable, and more persuasive than Svengali, con-men would be the nicest guys in the world except for one thing: they have no conscience at all. I've run up against con-men before, and they're tricky and treacherous. One of my first clients was an Englishman who had been taken on the rag, a stock swindle, for $140,000. He'd tried to find the man, with no luck, then came to me; I didn't have any luck, either. But when he'd finally given up hope of ever seeing his money again, he'd said to me, of the grifter who had taken him, "I shall always remember him as an extrah-dn'rly chahming chap. He was a pleasant bahstahd." Then he'd paused, thought a bit, and added, "But, by God, he *was* a bahstahd!"

The Englishman was right. Confidence men are psychologists with diplomas from sad people: the suckers, the marks, that the con-boys have taken; and there's not a con-man worthy of the name who wouldn't take a starving widow's last penny or a bishop's last C-note, with never a twinge of remorse. They are the pleasant bastards, the con-men, and they thrive because they can make other men believe that opportunity is not only knocking but chopping the door down—and because of men's desire for a fast, even if dishonest, buck, or else the normal greed that's in most of us. They are the spellbinders, and ordinarily don't resort to violence, or go around shooting holes in people.

And it looked as if three of them, or at least two, were up against me. The other one. Pretty Boy Foster, was a bit violent, I remembered, and swung a mean sap. My head still throbbed. All three men, now that the blonde had told Harrison there was big trouble, would probably be making themselves scarce.

But there was still the girl. The gorgeous little gal with black hair and light blue eyes and the chrome-plated pistol. I thought back over what she'd said to me. There'd been a lot of gibberish about $24,000 and my being a crook and—something else. Something about Folsom's Market. It was worth a check. I looked the place up in the phone book, found it listed on Van Ness Avenue, finished my drink and headed for Folsom's Market.

It was on Van Ness near Washington. I parked, went inside and looked around. Just an ordinary small store; the usual groceries and a glass-faced meat counter extending the length of the left wall. The place was doing a good business. I walked to the single counter where a young red-haired girl about twenty was ringing up a customer's sales on the cash register, and when she'd finished I told her I wanted to speak with the manager. She smiled, then leaned forward to a small mike and said, "Mr. Gordon. Mr. Gordon, please."

In a few seconds a short man in a business suit, with a fleshy pink face and a slight potbelly walked up to me. I told him my name and business, showed him my credentials, then said, "Actually, Mr. Gordon, I don't know if you can help me or not. This morning I talked briefly with a young lady who seemed quite angry with me. She thought I was some kind of crook and mentioned this place, Folsom's Market. Perhaps you know her." I described the little doll, and she was easy enough to describe, particularly with the odd gray streak in her dark hair. That gal was burned into my memory and I remembered every lovely thing about her, but when I finished the manager shook his head.

"Don't remember anything like her around here," he said.

"She mentioned something about her father, and twenty-four thousand dollars. I don't—"

I stopped, because Mr. Gordon suddenly started chuckling. The cashier said, "Oh, it must be that poor old man."

The manager laughed. "This'll kill you," he said. "Some old foreigner about sixty years old came in here this morning, right at eight when we opened up. Said he just wanted to look his store over. *His* store, get that, Mr. Scott. Claimed he'd bought the place, and—this'll kill you—for twenty-four thousand dollars. Oh, boy, a hundred grand wouldn't half buy this spot."

He was laughing about every third word. It had been very funny, he thought. Only it wasn't a bit funny to me, and I felt sick already. The way this deal was starting to figure, I didn't blame the little cutey for taking a few shots at me.

I said slowly, "Exactly what happened? What else did this ... this foreigner do?"

The manager's potbelly shook a little. "Ah, he gawked around for a while, then I talked to the guy. I guess it must of taken me half an hour to convince him Mr. Borrage owns this place—you know Borrage, maybe, owns a dozen independent places like this, real rich fellow—anyway this stupid old guy swore he'd bought the place. For the money and his little grocery store. You imagine that? Finally I gave him Borrage's address and told him to beat it. Hell, I called Borrage, naturally. He got a chuckle out of it, too, when I told him."

The Best of *Manhunt*

Anger was beginning to flicker in me. "Who was this stupid old man?" I asked him.

He shrugged. "Hell, I don't know. I just told him finally to beat it. I couldn't have him hanging around here."

"No." I said. "Of course not. He was a foreigner, huh? You mean he wasn't an Indian?"

Mr. Gordon blinked at me, said, "Hey?" then described the man as well as he could. He told me he'd never seen the guy before, and walked away.

The cashier said softly, "It wasn't like that at all, Mr. Scott. And he left his name with me."

"Swell, honey. Can you give it to me?"

Her face was sober, unsmiling as she nodded. "I just hate that Mr. Gordon," she said. "The way it was, this little man came in early and just stood around, looking pleased and happy, kind of smiling all the time. I noticed he was watching me for a while, when I checked out the customers, then he came over to me and smiled. 'You're a fast worker,' he said to me. 'Very good worker, I'm watching you.' Then he told me I was going to be working for him, that he'd bought this place and was going to move in tomorrow." She frowned. "I didn't know any better. For all I knew, he might have bought the store. I wish he had." She glanced toward the back of the store where Mr. Gordon had gone. "He was a sweet little man."

"What finally happened?"

"Well, he kept standing around, then Mr. Gordon came up here and I asked him if the store had been sold. He went over and talked to the old man a while, started laughing, and talked some more. The old man got all excited and waved his arms around and started shouting. Finally Mr. Gordon got a little sharp—he's like that—and pointed to the door. In a minute the little guy came over to me and wrote his name and address down. He said there was some kind of mistake, but it would be straightened out. Then he left." She paused. "He looked like he was going to cry."

"I see. You got that name handy?"

"Uh-huh." She opened the cash register and took a slip of paper out of it. "He wanted us to be able to get in touch with him; he acted sort of dazed."

"He would have," I said. She handed me the note. On it, in a shaky, laboriously scrawled script, was written an address and: *Emil Elmlund, Elmlund's Neighborhood Grocery. Phone WI2-1258.*

"Use your phone?" I asked.

"Sure."

I dialed WI2-1258. The phone rang several times, then a girl's voice answered, "Hello."

"Hello. Who is this, please?"

"This is Janet Elmlund."

That was what Pretty-Boy had called the girl in Pete's; Janet, and Jan. I said, "Is Mrs. McCurdy there?"

"McCurdy? I—you must have the wrong number."

I told her I wanted WI2-1259, apologized, and hung up. I didn't want her to know I was coming out there. This time she might have a rifle. Then I thanked the cashier, went out to the Cad and headed for Elmlund's Neighborhood Grocery.

It was a small store on a tree-lined street, the kind of "Neighborhood Grocery" you used to see a lot of in the days before supermarkets sprang up on every other corner. A sign on the door said, "Closed Today." A path had been worn in the grass alongside the store's right wall, leading to a small house in the rear. I walked along the path and paused momentarily before the house. It was white, neat, with green trim around the windows, a porch along its front. A man sat on the porch in a wooden chair, leaning forward, elbows on his knees, hands clasped. He was looking right at me as I walked toward him, but he didn't give any sign that he'd noticed me, and his face didn't change expression.

I walked up onto the porch. "Mr. Elmlund?"

He slowly raised his head and looked at me. He was a small man, with a lined brown face and very light blue eyes. Wisps of gray hair still clung to his head. He looked at me and blinked, then said, "Yes."

He looked away from me then, out into the yard again. It was as if I weren't there at all. And, actually, my presence probably didn't mean a thing to him. It was obvious that he had been taken in a confidence game, taken for $24,000 and maybe a dream. I couldn't know all of it yet, but I new enough about how he must feel now, still shocked, dazed, probably not yet thinking at all.

I squatted beside him and said, "Mr. Elmlund, my name is Shell Scott."

For a minute nothing happened, then his eyebrows twitched, pulled down. Frowning, he looked at me. "What?" he said.

I heard the click of high heels, the front door was pushed open and a girl stood there, holding a tray before her with two sandwiches on it. It was the same little lovely, black hair pulled back now and tied with a blue ribbon. She still wore the blue clam-diggers and the man's shirt.

I stood up fast. "Hold everything," I said to her. "Get this through your head—there's a guy in town about my size, with hair the same color as mine, and he's pretending to be me. He's taken my name, and he's used my office. But I never heard of you, or Mr. Elmlund, or Folson's Market until this morning. Now don't throw any sandwiches at me and for Pete's sake don't start shooting."

She had been staring at me open-mouthed ever since she opened the door and spotted me. Finally her mouth came shut with a click and her hands dropped. The tray fell clattering to the porch and the sandwiches rolled almost to my feet. She stared at me for another half-minute without speaking, comprehension growing on her face, then she said, "Oh, no. Oh, no."

"Oh, yes," I said. "Now suppose we all sit down and get to the bottom of this mess."

She said, "Really? Please—you wouldn't—"

"I wouldn't." I showed her several different kinds of identification from my wallet, license, picture, even a fingerprint, and when I finished she was convinced. She blinked those startling blue eyes at me and said, "How awful. I'm so sorry. Can you ever forgive me?"

"Yes. Yes, indeed. Right now, I forgive you."

"You don't. You can't." For the first time since I'd seen her, she wasn't looking furious or shocked, and for the moment at least she seemed even to have forgotten about the money they'd lost. I had, I suppose, spoken with almost frantic eagerness, and now she lowered her head slightly and blinked dark lashes once, and her red lips curved ever so slightly in a soft smile. At that moment I could have forgiven her if she'd been cutting my throat with a hack saw. She said again, "You can't."

"Oh, yes I can. Forget it. Could have happened to anybody."

She laughed softly, then her face sobered as she apparently remembered why I was here. I remembered, too, and started asking questions. Ten minutes later we were all sitting on the porch eating picnic sandwiches and drinking beer, and I had most of the story. Mr. Elmlund—a widower, and Janet's father—had run the store here for more than ten years, paid for it, saved $24,000. He was looking for a larger place and had been talking about this to a customer one day, a well-dressed man, smooth-talking, very tall, graying at the temples. The guy's name was William Klein, but he was also apparently my own Frank Harrison. It seemed Harrison was a real-estate broker and had casually mentioned that he'd let Mr. Elmlund know if he ran across anything that looked good.

Mr. Elmlund sipped his beer and kept talking. Elmlund said to me, "He seemed like a very nice man, friendly. Then when he come in and told me about this place it sounded good. He said this woman was selling the store because her husband had died not long ago. She was selling the store and everything and going back East, wasn't really much interested in making a lot of money out of it. She was rich, had a million dollars or more. She just wanted to get away fast, he said, and would sell for sixty thousand cash. Well, I told him that was too much, but he asked me to look at it—that was Folsom's Market—maybe we could work a deal, he said. So the next Sunday we went there; I didn't think it would hurt none to look."

"Sunday? Was the store open?"

"No, it was closed, but he had a key. That seemed right because he was—he said he was agent for it. Well, it was just like I'd always wanted, a nice store. Nice market there, and plenty room, good location—" He let the words trail off.

The rest of it was more of the same. The old con play; give the mark a glimpse of something he wants bad, then make him think he can have it for little or nothing, tighten the screws. A good con-man can tie up a mark so tight that normal reasoning powers go out the window. And getting a key which would open the store wouldn't have been any more trouble than getting the one which opened my office.

Last Sunday, a week after they'd looked over the store, Harrison had come to Elmlund all excited, saying the widow was anxious to sell and was going to advertise the store for sale in the local papers. If Elmlund wanted the place at a bargain price he'd have to act fast. Thursday—today, now—the ads would appear and the news would be all over town; right then only the widow, Harrison, and Elmlund himself knew about it. So went Harrison's story. After some more talk Harrison had asked how much cash Elmlund could scrape together. When Harrison learned $24,000 was tops, why naturally that was just enough cash—plus the deed to Elmlund's old store—to maybe swing a fast deal. All con-men are actors, expert at making their lines up as they go along, and Harrison must have made up the bit about throwing the deed in merely to make Elmlund think he was paying a more legitimate price; no well-played mark would think of wondering why a widow getting rid of one store so she could blow would take another as part payment.

Janet broke in, looking at me. "That was when Dad thought about having the transaction investigated. He talked to me about it and decided to see you, have you look into it. You see, he thought the sale was still secret, and you could check on it before the ads came out in the papers. And—he just couldn't believe it. He intended originally to invest only about ten thousand above what we'd get out of our store, but, well, it seemed like such a wonderful chance for him, for us. We were both a little suspicious, though."

"Uh-huh." I could see why Elmlund might want the deal checked, and I could even understand why he'd decided to see me instead of somebody else. The last six months I'd been mixed up in a couple cases that got splashed all over the newspapers, and my name was familiar to most of Los Angeles. But another bit puzzled me.

I said, "Janet, this morning in Pete's—" she made a face— "who was the man who charged in and yelled at you? Just as you were—leaving."

"Man? I didn't see any man. I—lost my head." She smiled slightly. "I guess you know. And after—afterwards, I got scared and ran, just wanted to get away. I thought maybe I'd killed somebody."

"I thought maybe you had, myself."

She said, "I was almost crazy. Dad had just told me what had happened, and I was furious. And you'd told Dad everything was fine, that the transaction was on the level—I mean *he* had, that other Shell Scott—you know."

"Yeah. What about that?" I turned to Mr. Elmlund. "When did you see this egg in my office?" I already knew, but I wanted to be sure.

"At nine-thirty on Monday morning, this last Monday. I went in right at nine-thirty, there in the Hamilton Building, and talked to him. He said he'd investigate it for me. Then yesterday morning he came out to the store here and said it was all right. It cost me fifty dollars."

"Sure. That made the con more realistic. You'd have thought it was funny if you weren't soaked a little for the job."

He shrugged and said, "Then, right after I talked yesterday to the detective—that one—he drove me and Janet from here to the real-estate office, the Angelus Realty. Said he was going by there. Well, I stopped at the bank—those ads were supposed to come out in the papers today, you know—and got the money. Then at that office I gave them the money and signed all the papers and things and—that was all. I wasn't supposed to go to the store till tomorrow, but I couldn't wait."

Janet told me where the "real-estate office" was, on Twelfth Street, but I knew that info was no help now. She said that this morning, before she'd come charging in at me, she'd first gone to the Angelus Realtors—probably planning to shoot holes in Harrison, though she didn't say so. But the place had been locked and she'd then come to the Hamilton Building. She remembered the sign "Angelus Realtors" had still been painted on the door, but I knew, sign or no sign, that office would be empty.

I looked at Janet. "This guy I was talking about, the one in Pete's Bar this A.M., was about five-ten, stocky, I suppose you'd say he was damned good-looking. Black hair, even features."

"That sounds like Bob Foster. Cleft chin and brown eyes?"

"That's him. Did you meet him before or after this deal came up?"

"Bob? Why, you can't think he—"

"I can and do. I'm just wondering which way it was; did he set up the con, or did he come in afterwards."

"Why, I met Bob a month before the realtor showed up. Bob and I went out several times."

"Then dear Bob told him to come around, I imagine. I suppose Bob knew your father was thinking about a new store."

"Yes, but—"

"And after you and your father talked about hiring me to make sure the deal was square, did Bob happen to learn about it?"

"Why—he was here when we discussed it. He—" she stopped, eyes widening. "I'd forgotten it until now, but *Bob* suggested that Dad engage an investigator. When we told him we couldn't believe it, that there just had to be something wrong or dishonest about the sale for the price to be so low, *he* suggested we hire a detective to investigate the man and all the rest of it." She paused again. "He even suggested your name, asked us if we'd heard of you or met you. We hadn't met you, but of course we'd read about you in the papers, and told Bob so. He said he knew you, that you were capable and thoroughly honest—and he—made the appointment with you for nine-thirty Monday."

"Good old Bob," I said. "That made it perfect. That would get rid of the last of your doubts. Janet, Bob Foster is probably no more his right name than Harrison is a real-estate dealer. The guy I know as Harrison, you know as Klein; his girl friend calls him John, and his real name is probably Willie Zilch. And I'm not getting these answers by voodoo. Harrison, Foster, and the guy who said he was Shell Scott all stay at the same hotel. They're a team, with so many fake names they sound like a community."

"But Bob—I thought he was interested in me. He was always nice."

"Yeah, pleasant. So you saw him a few times, and then he learned your dad was ripe for a swindle. He tipped Harrison, the inside-man, and they set up the play. The detective angle just tied it tighter. It was easy enough. A phone call to me to get me out of the office, another guy bleaches his hair, walks in and waits for your dad to show, then kills a couple days and reports all's well."

It was quiet for a minute, then I said, "The thing I don't get is how he happened to show up at Pete's right after you did?"

Mr. Elmlund answered that one. "He and Jan were going on a picnic today. When I told her about—about losing my money she ran to the car and drove away. Right after, Bob come in and asked for Janet. I told him what happened. Said she mentioned going to see that Klein and you. Now I think of it, he got a funny look and run off to his car."

"I hate to say it, Janet," I said, "but Bob was probably less interested in the picnic—under the circumstances—than in finding out if everything was still under control."

I thought a minute. The white-haired egg had probably been planted outside waiting for me to leave; when I did, he went up to the office. Bob must have showed up and checked with Hazel, reached Pete's just as Janet started spraying bullets around, chased her but couldn't find her or else knew he'd better tip Whitey fast. So he'd charged to the office just in time to sap me. Something jarred my thoughts there. It bothered me but I couldn't figure out what it was.

I said, "Have you been to the police yet?"

Janet said, "No. We've been so—upset. We haven't done anything since I got back home."

"I'll take care of it, then." I got up. "That's about it, I guess. I'll try running the men down, but it's not likely they'll be easily found. I'll do what I can."

Janet had been sitting quietly, looking at me. Now she got up, took my hand, and pulled me after her into the front room of the house. Inside, she put a hand on my arm and said softly, "You know how sorry I am about this morning. I was a little crazy for a while there. But I want to thank you for coming out, saying you'll help."

"I'll be helping myself, too, Janet."

"I get sick when I think I might actually have shot you." She looked at the raw spot on my chin. "Did I—shoot you there?"

I grinned at her. "It might have been a piece of glass. I landed in some."

"Just a minute." She went away and came back with a bit of gauze and a piece of tape. She pressed it gently against the "wound," as she called it, her fingers cool and soft against my cheek. Her touch sent a tingle over my skin, a slight shiver between my shoulder blades. Then she stretched up and gently pressed her lips against my cheek.

"That better?"

It's funny; some women can leap into your lap, practically strangle you, mash their mouth all over you, kiss you with their lips and tongues and bodies, and leave you cold—I'm talking about *you,* of course. But just the gentle touch of this gal's lips on my cheek turned my spine to spaghetti. That was the fastest fever I ever got; a thermometer in my mouth would have popped open and spouted mercury every which way.

I said, "Get your .22. I'm about to shoot myself full of holes."

She laughed softly, her arms going around my neck, then she started to pull herself up but my head was already on its way down, and when her lips met mine it was a new kind of shock. The blonde back there in the hotel room had been fairly enjoyable, but Janet had more sex and fire and hunger in just her lips than the blonde had in her entire stark body. When Jan's hands slid from my neck and she stepped back I automatically moved toward her, but she put a hand on my chest, smiling, glanced toward the porch, then took my arm and led me outside again.

When my breathing was reasonably normal I said, "Mr. Elmlund, I'm leaving now but if I get any news at all, I'll hurry back—I mean, ha, come back."

Janet chuckled. "Hurry's all right," she said.

Mr. Elmlund said, "Mr. Scott, if you can get our money again I'll pay you anything—half of it—"

"Forget that part. I don't want any money. If I should miraculously get it back, it's all yours."

He looked puzzled. "Why? Why should you help me?"

I said, "Actually, Mr. Elmlund, this is just as important to me. I don't like guys using my name to swindle people; I could get a very nasty reputation that way. Not to mention my dislike for being conned myself and getting hit over the head. For all I know there are guys named Shell Scott all over town, conning people, maybe shooting people. The con worked so well for these guys once, they'll probably try the same angles again—or would have if I hadn't walked in—on—" I stopped. That same idea jarred my thoughts as it had before when I'd been thinking about the guy in my office. It was so simple I should have had it long ago. But now a chill ran down my spine and I leaned toward Mr. Elmlund.

"You weren't supposed to see me—the detective—this morning were you?"

"Why, no. Everything was finished, he already give me his report."

I didn't hear the rest of what he said. I was wondering why the hell Harrison had called me again, why Whitey had needed my office again, if not for Mr. Elmlund.

I swung toward Janet. "Where's your phone? Quick."

She blinked at me, then turned and went into the house. I followed, right on her heels.

"Show me. Hurry."

She pointed out the phone on a table and I grabbed it, dialed the Hamilton Building. There was just a chance—but it was already after noon.

Hazel came on. "This is Shell. Anyone looking for me?"

"Hi, Shell. How's your hangover—"

"This is important, hell with the hangover. Anybody there right after I took off?"

Her voice got brisk. "One man, about fifty, named Carl Strossmin. Said he had an appointment for nine-thirty."

"He say what about?"

"No. I took his name and address. Thirty-six, twenty-two Gramercy. Said he'd phone back; he hasn't called."

"Anything else?"

"That's all."

"Thanks." I hung up. I said aloud, "I'll be damned. They've got another mark."

Jan said, "What?" but I was running for the door. I leaped into the Cad, gunned the motor and swung around in a U-turn. It was clear enough. Somewhere the boys had landed another sucker, and the "investigation" by Shell Scott had worked so well once that they must have used the gimmick again. They would still be around, but if they made this score they'd almost surely be off for Chicago, or Buenos Aires, or no telling where.

Carl Strossmin—I remembered hearing about him. He'd made a lot of money, most of it in deals barely this side of the law; he'd be the perfect mark because he was always looking for the best of it. Where Elmlund had thought he was merely getting an amazing piece of good fortune, Strossmin might well think he was throwing the blocks to somebody else. I didn't much like what I'd heard about Strossmin, but I liked not at all what I knew of Foster and Whitey and Harrison.

When I spotted the number I wanted on Gramercy I slammed on the brakes, jumped out and ran up to the front door of 3622. I rang the bell and banged on the door until a middle-aged woman looked out at me, frowning.

"Say," she said. "What is the matter with you?"

"Mrs. Strossmin?"

"Yes."

"Your husband here?"

Her eyes narrowed. "No. Why? What do you want him for?"

I groaned. "He isn't closing any business deal, is he?"

Her eyes were slits now. "What are you interested for?" She looked me up and down. "They told us there were other people interested. You—"

"Lady, listen. He isn't buying a store, or an old locomotive or anything, is he?"

She pressed her lips together. "I don't think I'd better say anything till he gets back."

"That's fine," I said. "That's great. Because the nice businessmen are crooks. They're confidence men, thieves, they're wanted by police of seventy counties. Kiss your cabbage goodbye, lady—or else start telling me about it fast."

Her lips weren't pressed together any more. They peeled apart like a couple of liver chunks. "Crooks?" she groaned. "*Crooks?*"

"Crooks, gyps, robbers, murderers. Lady, they're dishonest."

She let out a wavering scream and threw her hands in the air. "Crooks!" she wailed. "I told him they were crooks. Oh, I told the old fool, you can bet—!" She fainted.

I swore nastily, jerked the screen door open and picked her up, then carried her to a couch. Finally she came out of it and blinked at me. She opened her mouth.

I said, "If you say 'crooks' once again I'll bat you. Now where the hell did your husband go?"

She started babbling, not one word understandable. But finally she got to her feet and started tottering around. "I wrote it down," she said. "I wrote it down. I wrote—"

"What did you write down?"

"Where he was going. The address." She threw up her hands. "Forty-one thousand dollars! Crooks! Forty-one—"

"Listen," I said. "He have that much money on him?"

"No. He had to go to the bank."

"What bank?" By the time she answered I'd already spotted the phone and was dialing. A bank clerk told me that Carl Strossmin had drawn $41,000 out of his account only half an hour ago. He'd been very excited, but he'd made no mention of what he wanted the money for. I hung up. I knew why Carl hadn't mentioned anything about it: it was a secret.

Mrs. Strossmin was still puttering around, pulling out drawers and occasionally throwing her hands up into the air and screeching. Gradually I got her story and, with what I already knew, put the pieces together. Her husband's appointment with "Shell Scott" had been made two days ago by real-estate dealer "Harrison" himself, here in Strossmin's home. After suggesting that since Strossmin seemed a bit undecided he might feel safer if he engaged a "completely honest" detective, Harrison had dialed a number, chatted a bit, and handed Strossmin the phone. Finally an appointment had been made for nine-thirty this A.M. Strossmin had been talking, of course, to Whitey who most likely was in a phone booth or bar.

Harrison probably wouldn't have suggested me *by name* to Strossmin, expecting the mark to accept his, the realtor's, suggestion, except for one thing, which was itself important to the con: my reputation in L. A. A lot of people here believe I'm crazy, others think I'm stupid, and many, particularly old maids, are sure I'm a fiendish lecher; but there's never been any question about my being honest. This phase of the con was based on making Strossmin—and Elmlund before him—think he was really talking to me when he met Whitey, the Shell Scott of the con, in my office. However when I popped back into the office and messed up that play this morning, the boys had to change their plans fast.

At eleven-thirty, about the time I was driving to Elmlund's, Whitey had come here to Strossmin's home, apologized for not being in his office when Strossmin had arrived this A.M., and said he'd come here to spare Strossmin another trip downtown. After learning what Strossmin wanted investigated, Whitey had pretended surprise and declared solemnly that this was a strange coincidence indeed, because Strossmin was the second man to ask for the identical investigation. Oh, yes, he'd already investigated—for this other eager buyer—and told him that the deal was on the level. No doubt about it, this was the opportunity of the century—and time, sad to say, was terribly short. Apparently, said Whitey, negotiations were going on with dozens of other people—and so on until Strossmin had been in a frenzy of impatience.

Finally Mrs. Strossmin found her slip of paper and thrust it at me. An address was scribbled on it: Apex Realtors, 4870 Normandie Avenue. I grabbed the paper and ran to the Cad.

Apex Realtors was, logically enough, no more than an ordinary house with a sign in the window: Apex Realtors. When I reached it and parked, a small, well-dressed man with a thick mustache was just climbing into a new Buick at the curb. I ran from the Cad to his Buick and stopped him just as he started the engine.

"Mr. Strossmin?"

He was just like his wife. His eyes narrowed. "Yes."

I took a deep breath and blurted it out, "Did you just buy Folsom's Market?"

He grinned. "Beat you, didn't I? You're too late—"

"Shut up. You bought nothing but a headache. How many men inside there?"

He chuckled. "They told me I'd have to hurry. Sorry my good man, but—"

About ready to flip, I yanked out my gun and pointed it at him. *"How many men in there?"*

I thought for a minute he was going to faint, too, but he managed to gasp, "Three."

I said, "You wait here," then turned and ran up to the house. The door was partly ajar, and I hit it and charged inside, the gun in my right hand. There wasn't anybody in sight, but another door straight ahead of me had a sign, "Office," on it. As I went through the door a car motor growled into life behind the house. I ran for the back, found a door standing wide open and jumped through it just as a sky-blue Oldsmobile sedan parked in the alley took off fast. I barely got a glimpse of it, but I knew who was in it. The three con-men were powdering now that they had all the dough they were after. There was a chance they'd seen me, but it wasn't likely. Probably they'd grabbed the dough and left by the back way as soon as Strossmin stepped through the front door.

I raced out front again and sprinted for the Cad, yelling to Strossmin, "Call the police!" He sat there, probably feeling pleased at the coup he'd just put over. He'd call the cops, next week, maybe. I ripped the Cad into gear and roared to the corner, took a right and stepped on the gas. I had to slow at the next intersection, looked both directions and caught a flash of blue two blocks away on my right, swung in after them and pushed the accelerator to the floorboards. I was gaining on them rapidly, and now I had a few seconds to try figuring out how to stop them. Up close I could see the Olds sedan, and the figures of three men inside it, two in the front seat and one in back. Con-men don't usually carry guns, but these guys operated a little differently from most con-men. In the first place they usually make the mark think he's in on a crooked deal, and in the second they almost always try to cool the mark out, allay his suspicions so he doesn't know, at least for a long time, that he's been taken. The boys ahead of me had broken both those rules, and there was a good chance they'd also broken the rule about guns.

But I was less than half a block behind them now and they apparently hadn't tumbled. They must figure they were in the clear, so I had surprise on my side. Well, I'd surprise them.

We were a long way from downtown here, but still in the residential section. I caught up with their car, pulled out on their left and slightly ahead, then as we reached an intersection I swung to my right, cutting them off just as I heard one of the men in the blue Olds yell loudly.

The driver did the instinctive thing, jerked his steering wheel to the right and they went clear up over the curb and stalled on a green lawn before a small house. I was out of my Cad and running toward them, the Colt in my fist, before their car stopped moving twenty feet from me. And one of them *did* have a gun.

They sure as hell knew who I was by now, and I heard the gun crack. A slug snapped past me as I dived for the lawn, skidded a yard. Doors swung open on both sides of the blue Olds. Black-haired Pretty Boy jumped from the back and started running away from me, lugging a briefcase.

I got to my knees, and yelled, "Stop! Hold it or you get it, Foster."

He swung around, crouching, and light gleamed on the metal of a gun in his hand. He fired once at me and missed, and I didn't hold back any longer. I snapped the first shot from my .38 but I aimed the next two times, and he sagged slowly to his knees, then fell forward on his face.

Gray-haired Harrison was a few steps from the car, standing frozen, staring at Foster's body, but Whitey was fifty feet beyond him running like mad. I took out after him, but as I went by Harrison I let him have the full weight of my .38 on the back of his skull. I didn't even look back; he'd keep for a while.

I jammed my gun into its holster and sprinted down the sidewalk, Whitey half a block ahead but losing ground. He wasn't in very good shape, apparently, and after a single block he was damn near staggering. He heard my feet splatting on the pavement behind him and for a moment he held his few yards' advantage, then he slowed again. He must have known I had him, because he stopped and whirled around to face me, ready to go down fighting.

He went down, all right, but not fighting. When he stopped I had been less than ten feet from him, travelling like a fiend, and he spun around just in time to connect his face with my right fist. I must have started the blow from six feet away, just as he began turning, and what with my speed from running, and the force of the blow itself, my fist must have been travelling fifty miles an hour.

It was awful what it did to him. I caught only a flashing glimpse of his face as he swung around, lips peeled back and hands coming up, and then my knuckles landed squarely on his mouth and his lips really peeled back and he started going the same direction I was going and almost as fast. I ran several steps past him before I could stop, but when I turned around he was practically behind me and there was a thin streak of blood for two yards on the sidewalk. He was all crumpled up, out cold, and for a minute I thought he was out for good. But I felt for his heartbeat and found it.

So I squatted by him and waited. Before he came out of it, a little crowd gathered: half a dozen kids and some housewives, one young guy about thirty who came running from half a block away. I told him to call the cops and he phoned. Whitey was still out when the guy came back and said a car was on its way.

Finally Whitey stirred, moaned. I looked around and said to the women, "Get the kids out of here. And maybe you better not stick around yourselves."

The women frowned, shifted uneasily, but they shooed the kids away. Whitey shook his head. Finally he was able to sit up. His face wasn't pretty at all. I grabbed his coat and pulled him close to me.

I said, "Shell Scott, huh? I hear you're a tough baby. Get up, friend."

I stood up and watched him while he got his feet under him. It took him a while, and all the time he didn't say a word. I suppose the decent thing would have been to let him get all the way up, but I didn't wait. When he was halfway up I balled my left fist and slammed it under his chin. It straightened him just enough so I could set myself solidly, and get him good with my right fist. It landed where I wanted it to, on his nose, and he left us for a while longer. He fell onto the grass on his back, and perhaps he had looked a bit like me at one time, but he didn't any more.

The guy who had called the cops helped me carry Whitey back to the blue Oldsmobile. We dumped him and Harrison inside and I climbed in back with them—and with the briefcase—while he went out to the curb and waited for a prowl car. I got busy. When I finished, these three boys had very little money in their wallets and none was in the briefcase. It added up to $67,500. There was Elmlund's $24,000, I figured, plus Strossmin's $41,000, plus my $2500. I lit a cigarette and waited for the cops.

It was two P.M. before I got away. Both cops in the patrol car were men I knew well; Borden and Lane. Lane and I especially were good friends. I gave my story and my angles to Lane, and finally he went along with what I wanted.

I finished it with, "This Strossmin is still so wound up by these guys he'll probably figure it out about next week, but when he does, he should be a good witness. No reason why Elmlund can't be left out of it."

Lane shook his head and rubbed a heavy chin where bristles were already sprouting. "Well ... if this Strossmin doesn't come through in court, we'll need Elmlund."

"You'll get him. Besides, I'll be in court, remember. Enjoying myself."

He nodded. "O. K., Shell."

I handed him the briefcase with $41,000 inside it, told him I'd come to headquarters later, and took off. I'd given Lane the address where I'd left Strossmin, as well as his home address, but Strossmin hadn't waited. I drove to his house.

I could hear them going at it hammer and tongs. Mrs. Strossmin didn't even stop when I rang the bell, but finally her husband opened the door. He just stood there glowering at me. "Well?" he said.

"I just wanted to let you know, Mr. Strossmin, that the police have caught the men who tricked you."

I was going on, but he said, "Trick me? Nobody tricked me. You're trying to trick me."

"Look, mister, I just want you to know your money's safe. The cops have it. My name is Shell Scott—"

"Ha!" he said. "It is, hey? No, it's not, that's not your name, can't fool me. You're a crook, that's what you are."

His wife was in the door.

She screeched in his ear, "What did I say? Old fool, I warned you."

"Mattie," he said. "If you don't sit down and shut up—"

I tried some more, but he just wouldn't believe me. A glowing vision could have appeared in the sky crying, "You been tricked, Strossmin!" and the guy wouldn't have believed it. There are marks like him, who beg to be taken.

So finally I said, "Well, you win."

"What?"

"You win. Nothing I can do about it now. Store's yours." I put on a hangdog look. He cackled.

I said, "You can take over the place today, you know. Well, goodbye—and the better man won."

"Today?"

"Yep. Folsom's Markets, isn't it?"

"Yes, yes."

"Well, you go right down there. Ask for Mr. Gordon."

"Mr. Gordon?"

"Yep." I shook his hand. He cackled, and Mrs. Strossmin screeched at him, and he told her to shut up and I left. They were still going at it as I drove away to the Elmlunds.

Mr. Elmlund didn't quite know what to do when I dropped the big packet of bills on his table and said the hoods were in the clink. He stared at the money for a long time. When finally he did speak it was just, "I don't know what to say."

Jan came out onto the porch and I told them what happened and I thought they were going to crack up for a while, and then I thought they were going to float off over the trees, but finally Mr. Elmlund said, "I must pay you, Mr. Scott. I must."

I said, "No. Besides, I got paid."

Jan was leaning against the side of the door, smiling at me. She'd changed clothes and was wearing a smooth, clinging print dress now, and the way she looked I really should have had on dark glasses. She looked happy, wonderful, and her light blue eyes were half-lidded, her gaze on my mouth.

"No," she said. "You haven't been paid."

Her tongue traced a smooth, gleaming line over her lower lip, and I remembered her fingers on my cheek, her lips against my skin.

"You haven't been paid, Shell."

I had a hunch she was right.

The Man Who Found the Money
James E. Cronin

February 1954

H e was not afraid. There was nothing about the editor's quiet remark to be afraid of. But the skin at the back of his neck had pricked for a second, as if the short hair there had bristled.

That was after he had hunted out the bank, signed for a deposit box, and locked the ninety-two thousand dollars safely into it. Ninety-two thousand dollars in new bills, held together with a gold clip initialed *C. N.*

The ad he wrote out was brief:

Found, early Tuesday morning, a sum of money. Owner may have same by suitable identification and payment for this ad. Box—.

The editor of the Las Vegas *Times* read the ad slowly, eyes following the point of his pencil. "Seventy cents," he said.

Benson pushed the coins across the counter and started out. He felt enormously virtuous but at the same time just a bit annoyed at his own honesty.

"It's none of my business," the editor's flat Western voice caught him at the door, "but was it a *large* sum of money?"

Surprised, Benson turned. "Well—yes."

The editor nodded. "You know," he said, "if I were you, I'd just go on over to the police station and let them know there. Money's important in this town. People are concerned about it."

"Name me a town where they aren't."

"I think you'll find they're more concerned here," the editor said.

That was all. But Benson felt the hair on the back of his neck rise in fear.

He shook off the feeling before he walked into the police station around the corner. Quickly he explained the matter to the sergeant at the desk.

"Just a minute." The sergeant disappeared into an office behind the railing, and almost at once returned. "Captain wants to see you," he said.

A big man, with the moonface and shiny dome of a politician, the captain had blank blue eyes set deep in flabby folds of skin. His blue shirt was open at the neck, dark with sweat under the arms. He motioned Benson to a seat and looked him over.

"You found some money," he began. "How much?"

Benson said, "I don't think I ought to mention the amount. At the proper time—"

"Was it in a gold clip marked *C. N.*?"

"You know about it!"

The captain held up a tanned hand. "Was it a hundred and two thousand dollars?"

Benson felt as if he had been slugged over the heart. Of all the possibilities he'd thought of, this had never occurred to him. With an effort he pulled air into his lungs. "Why-no," he said. "It was ninety-two thousand."

The captain didn't move.

"That's all there was!" Benson said loudly. "Ninety-two thousand! I can't imagine—"

"What's your name?" the captain said. He leaned forward and picked up a pencil.

"Benson. William Benson."

"Address?"

"Two-four-two Wesley, St. Louis."

"Occupation?"

"I'm a teacher—that is, a professor. Are you positive the amount was a hundred and two thousand?"

"Uh-huh. Yeah. When did you get into town?"

"Yesterday morning."

The captain opened a folder on the desk. "Registered at the Mirador?" Benson nodded. "And why did you come to Las Vegas, Professor?"

"To play roulette. But I think that's my own business. What is this, anyhow? Am I being booked? All I did was find some money and report it. If it's short, that's too bad. But I'm not going to stand for—"

"Okay," the captain interrupted heavily. "I just want to get things straight. You didn't win last night? You went broke?" There was only a slight question in the captain's voice.

Benson nodded. He'd scarcely thought about it since he'd awakened. Three years to save four hundred dollars-and one night to see it disappear, like water into the dry Las Vegas sand.

"I went broke," he said.

"Where did you find the money?"

"On Seventh Street, near the hotel. It was lying on the sidewalk in plain sight. Exactly ninety-two thousand!"

"Where were you coming from?"

"The Mesa Inn. It was about three thirty."

"Walk all the way?"

"Yes."

"So then you took the money and went back to the crap table at the Mesa—"

"The hell I did!" Benson slammed his fist on the desk. "Now look, Captain, I'm not accustomed—"

"Relax," said the captain. "What did you do between then and now?"

"I went to my room and counted the money. I didn't know what to do with it at that hour."

"You could have brought it here."

"I didn't think of it," Benson lied. "I thought I'd have to wait until morning to do anything. I finally hid it in my sock and pulled the sock half on. I braced a chair against the door and slept, off and on. It was a hell of a night."

There was no point, Benson realized, in saying anything more than that to the captain. The temptation to stuff the money in his suitcase, leave town at once, had been overpowering. Then he'd thought of something he'd read once: that banks keep a record of big bills.

If the roll had been in tens instead of thousand-dollar bills —*No!* he told himself. *I wouldn't have taken it, anyway. I don't think I would—*

Hell, what was honesty, after all? What was it worth? But he was there, in the police station; it didn't do any good to think about it now.

Benson stood up, feeling suddenly very tired and determined. "Well," he said, "you obviously know who lost the money. Do you want to call him up or shall I?"

"You've got the money with you?"

"It's in a box. At the bank."

The captain waited a second, then reached for the phone. "You're sure there's only ninety-two thousand?"

"I'm sure," Benson said.

The captain shrugged. "Okay. You'll stick around outside for a while. Close the door when you go out." He picked up the receiver.

Benson had been waiting only a few minutes when the flashy green convertible pulled up outside the station. A stocky, well-dressed man in gray flannel climbed out and came briskly in. Benson noticed the cornflower in the buttonhole, the immaculate white Stetson with a medium brim, the tanned face and the determinedly benevolent expression. He had a curious feeling that the face was a mask.

The desk sergeant said, "Good morning, Mr. Newsome!" The gray-clothed man lifted his hand in greeting and went into the captain's office. The door shut. Ten minutes passed.

The desk sergeant said, "You can go in now." Benson walked to the door and opened it. Standing in the door, he had the impression that there had been an argument, though it might have been only a projection of his own uneasiness. He closed the door and stepped inside.

The captain ignored him. His face was redder, and he was methodically tapping his pencil on the desk, concentrating on it. Newsome, squinting to keep the smoke of his cigarette from his eyes, finished jotting something on a piece of paper, looked up and smiled.

"Mr. Benson!" he said, rising and extending his hand. "I'm certainly glad to meet you. I owe you a great debt."

Relief, like cool water, flowed down Benson's throat and into his knotted stomach. He could feel his body go limp. "I was glad to do it," he said. "Though— as the captain's told you—I found only ninety-two thousand of your money."

"Of course," Newsome said. "You checked your count?"

"Oh yes, sure."

Newsome nodded. He didn't seem in the least disturbed. "We'll find it," he said. "That much money doesn't stay lost in this town." For a second he appeared preoccupied, then became brisk again. "I've jotted down a list of denominations which I think will agree—minus the ten thousand—"

"Of course," Benson said. He looked at the list, moved his gaze to Newsome's. He didn't bother to compare them. "Okay, let's go get it," he said. "I'll be glad to get rid of it."

"I'll bet," Newsome said cheerfully. "Then we'll have to think about you. The captain here"—he slapped the hunched figure on the shoulder— "wanted to put you on the eleven o'clock train!"

"And it's still a good idea," the captain said, looking up.

"Hell!" Newsome slapped at the thought with the back of his hand. "Let's go, Benson."

The captain rose, hitching at his pants. "Wait a minute," he said. There was a long pause; he was obviously searching his mind for just the right words. "You— sure you're—uh—satisfied? Both of you?" He was looking at Benson.

Newsome cut in. "Sure, we're satisfied! Just forget the whole thing. Everything's under control—come on, Benson."

He turned and started out of the office. Benson stood for a second looking at the captain; then he followed Newsome helplessly through the front area and out of the station, into the convertible. The seat was hot from the sun; the expensive scent of warm new leather filled his nostrils. He leaned back, fully relaxed, realizing slowly that the whole affair had taken on a *past* air, as if it had long ago been finished.

He'd take that eleven o'clock train, he thought—and maybe he'd have more than the bare carfare home. Newsome's attitude strongly suggested some kind of reward. . . .

But even that wasn't important. All he wanted now was to get home; home to Joyce and the baby; home, even, to the pleasant, shabby monotony of his teaching life. He couldn't expect—didn't want—anything more than that.

At the bank Newsome counted the money with surprising speed, flicking down the corner of the wad with his left thumb. "Ninety-two," he said slowly, went to deposit the money, and returned.

"Now," he said, smiling, "we take care of you. I'll have to talk things over with my partners first—but that'll be all right. First thing, anyhow, we're going out to the Pinto Inn. That's mine, you know."

Then there *would* be a reward, Benson thought, dazzled.

On the drive to the Pinto, Newsome enlarged on his plans. "I tell you you're going to call up your wife and get her to fly out here for a week. Stay at the Pinto, the two of you. Best of everything. On me."

And suddenly, for no reason at all, Benson wanted desperately to get away. Joyce, at the Pinto—it didn't seem right, somehow. Again he told himself angrily that he wasn't making sense. It would be the experience of a lifetime for Joyce: an all-expense Hollywood-type vacation, riding, swimming, golf, entertainment . . . yet he only said reluctantly, "Well—you're more than kind. I'll call her. See what she says."

"That's it," Newsome said. He swung the great car around the drive and stopped before the broad low sandstone steps of the hotel. "Give me an hour, though—to arrange things, check plane schedules, so on—before you call the lady. Right?" Without waiting for an answer he took Benson's arm and started in.

"My bag—"

"Forget it. That's the least of your worries! Come on in here." He steered Benson into the cold gloom of the gambling casino that was the Pinto lobby. From somewhere out of the darkness a man appeared silently, and Newsome left Benson for a second, talked with his lieutenant, and then returned, chattering busily. "This is Mr. Lent, Mr. Benson. He'll take care of you. Make yourself a million—I'll be seeing you in a while, about that call . . ." and still talking, he turned and walked rapidly away into the dark.

Mr. Lent bowed. He explained that Mr. Benson was to have the courtesy of the house. And that meant, precisely? That meant that Mr. Benson simply called for such chips as he wanted, which the croupier would be glad to supply.

"For—nothing, you mean?"

Certainly. And what was Mr. Benson's game?

Crouched over the roulette table, grinning broadly and, he knew, idiotically, Benson felt a hand on his shoulder and spun around. His elbow knocked over a stack of chips, and he heard them clatter to the floor.

"The boss wants to see you," said a dim white coat in the darkness behind him.

"Fine," Benson said, trying to put the chips in his pockets.

"Let me help." Mr. Lent was suddenly, silently, beside him. "I'll cash in for you and bring the money in."

"Good," Benson said carelessly. Mr. Lent, he thought, was a fine fellow. Handy to have around. And the coming week would really be something! Joyce would probably think he was drunk when he told her. What a thrill she'd get out of the Pinto!

Still grinning, he followed the man through the cashier's office. The door was locked behind them. He walked down the narrow aisle between the filing cases and through another door, the guide stepping aside to let him go ahead. He heard the lock click behind him.

Behind a desk in the large office, Newsome stood, holding a phone. He looked up and nodded. "Put her on," he said, and handed the phone to Benson.

High, shrill, full of terror, her voice came through. "Bill!" The receiver shrieked tinnily. "Bill, are you there? Bill!"

He heard his voice saying, remotely, "What is it? Is the baby—what's the matter?"

"Bill. There are two awful men here—they—"

The receiver was ripped from his hand. In a haze he saw Newsome cradle the phone. He reached for it, but Newsome's hands remained on the receiver.

"Sit down." Newsome put one square palm on his chest and shoved him into a chair.

"My wife is in trouble! You cut me off! Why—"

"Your wife isn't in trouble."

"But I heard her—"

"Sit down and listen." Newsome's face, without the beam of benevolence, was the emptiest face Benson had ever seen. "You thought you were getting away with something," he continued evenly. "You fooled the captain. You didn't fool me. If you play straight now, everything will be okay. I don't bother holding grudges. But you get tough, and sometime tonight they're going to find your wife and kid at the bottom of a hill in a burning car."

It was so horrible, so impossible, that Benson felt his mouth pull back into a grin, idiotically, and he stared at Newsome's hand without seeing it for a second. The hand was extended toward him, palm up, waiting.

Newsome said, "And now, you bastard, let's have my ten thousand dollars."

Self-Defense
Harold Q. Masur

February 1955

George Richardson was no assembly line product. He had a long straight body, compelling eyes, a precise mouth, a crisp voice, and the confident assurance of wealth. His hair was silver-gray, though he couldn't have been more than forty-five years of age. He wore his clothes like a college boy and carried himself like a Senator.

He had emerged from his private office to give me a personal convoy. His handshake was quick, firm, and nervous. "Mr. Jordan," he said. "Glad you came. I suppose you're wondering why I wanted to see you."

I nodded. I was not only wondering. I was damned curious, because the outfit that usually handled his law business was a firm of attorneys five names long, with two whole floors in a Wall Street skyscraper. Compared to them, my operation was peanuts.

"Sit down, Mr. Jordan."

I sat in a wide leather chair and took in the surroundings. His office was paneled in Philippine mahogany, with an original Gauguin on the wall and a priceless Sarouk on the floor. Anyone who thought the layout a little too fancy for a crass business enterprise would be right. George Richardson was not in business. His ancestors had saved him the bother. He maintained this office for the sole purpose of keeping an eye on his investments.

He planted his feet in front of me and I could see that he was under pressure. "Are you free to handle something for me, Jordan?" His voice was tight and so were his jaws.

"Why me?" I asked. "Why not your own lawyers?"

He shook his head impatiently. "Because they're specialists; corporation law, probate, contracts. This is way out of their league."

I sat back. "Tell me about it."

"Here. Read this. It's self-explanatory."

He handed me a piece of paper. I unfolded it and read the message. The writer had used a pencil, printing in block letters.

Mr. Richardson, sir,

Your wife will need a black dress unless you play ball. Andy is too young to die. You can prevent it by coughing up a hundred grand. You can accelerate it by talking to the cops.

Use your head and follow instructions. Tonight, six o'clock. Stay near the telephone.

I looked up at George Richardson. He was biting the bottom corner of his lip. "Andy is the son of your second wife?"

"Yes. I adopted him legally when I married Irene."

"How old is he?"

"Four."

"Where did you find this note?"

"In the morning mail."

"May I see the envelope?"

He found it in the center drawer of his desk. The address was printed in pencil, same as the letter. It carried yesterday's postmark and had been mailed somewhere in the Grand Central area. I wondered about the postmark. It was a new switch since Andy was, apparently, still safe.

"What am I supposed to do, Jordan?"

"You're supposed to notify the FBI."

"I know—I know . . ." He was rubbing the creases in his forehead. "Can we afford to risk it? A boy's life is at stake."

I had no words for a moment, thinking it over. I didn't like the responsibility of making a decision. Kidnappers are mean, vindictive, and inhuman. When a life is gone, nobody can bring it back. Resurrection is only a word in the Bible, unrecognized by the medical profession. George Richardson was watching me anxiously.

"Suppose we wait for the telephone call," I said. "We can make our decision then."

He nodded quickly. "I hope you don't think I did wrong. I became a little panicky when I received the letter this morning and I gave in to my first impulse. I went to the bank."

"For the money?"

"Yes. I withdrew it in small denominations. Mixed serial numbers."

"Where is it?"

He pointed to a bulging briefcase leaning against a corner of his desk.

"May I see it?"

"Certainly."

One glance was enough. All that currency, neatly arranged and squared away, gave me an odd sensation. Pieces of engraved paper, that's all, but what they represented was something else, a catalytic agent for most of the crimes committed on God's green footstool.

I put it down. "I'm a lawyer, Mr. Richardson, not a private detective. Why did you pick on me?"

"Because of the way you handled the divorce for my first wife." He managed a smile, half bitter, half wry. "Five hundred dollars a week alimony. That's quite a bite, counselor. My own lawyers couldn't cope with you. All right. I paid but I checked. I know your background, the kind of work you do. You have a talent for situations of this kind. I need your help."

It sounded logical enough. I had nicked him plenty for Lydia, the beautiful, restless, petulant creature he had plucked out of the Copa line and married. Why he married her, I don't know. She must have played her cards right. Probably it was the only way he could get her. The episode was brief but tempestuous, lasting six months. I got her the divorce and five hundred a week. Enough to maintain a penthouse, a convertible, and a boy friend.

The boy friend was Neil Corbin, a far more suitable mate. Lydia was out with him the night she died. Corbin had just brought her home after an extensive tour of the bistros along Fifty-second Street. He let her out at the front door and drove her car to the basement garage. Once upstairs, Lydia apparently went out to the terrace and lost her balance. It was fourteen stories down to the rear courtyard, paved in concrete. It seems she had misgauged her alcoholic capacity. The medical examiner found enough bourbon in her brain to float a ferry-boat.

The cops raked Neil Corbin over the coals. He had a very shady record and no visible means of support, except Lydia. But he stuck to his story. He didn't know about the accident until after he reached the apartment.

It was water under the bridge now, almost a year old.

George Richardson broke into my thoughts. "Will you handle the money part of it for me, Jordan?"

"If you like. But I'm against paying off on the basis of threats alone. Make it that easy and he's liable to try again, on you or someone else."

"I can't help it." His jaw was out, bulldog stubborn. "I'll worry about that when it happens. Right now, Andy's safety comes first."

"Have you thought of sending him away?"

"What good would it do? His home is here. I can't keep him away forever."

"Have you spoken to your wife about this?"

He gave me a startled look. "Of course not. She'd go to pieces." He searched my face anxiously. "Do you think I should?"

"Let's see what happens. In the meantime I've got some work to do. I'll be at my office. Phone me as soon as you get your call. If it—"

He jumped as the phone rang. He was staring at it with his jaw loose. A muscle twitched under his left eye.

"It's only three o'clock," I said. "Answer it."

He unbent an elbow at the handset and got it to his ear. There was an obstruction in his throat and he cleared it out before saying, "Hello."

I could hear the diaphragm rattling in the receiver The unintelligible words were squeak-edged and feverish, like a wire recorder running backwards at high speed. The blood dropped out of George Richardson's face and he spoke in a hoarse, urgent voice.

"Listen, Irene. Do as I say. Sit tight. Don't call a soul. Say nothing. I'll be right home. Understand? Sit tight."

He hung up slowly, automatically, and lifted his eyes. They were stunned.

I said sharply, "What is it?"

His fist landed hard on the desk. "They've done it. They've taken Andy."

"How?"

"Nursery school." He swallowed painfully. "They claim I phoned and said I was sending my car and chauffeur. I haven't got a chauffeur. The man picked him up an hour ago. When my wife got there, Andy was gone." He surged upright. "I must go to her."

"It's time for the FBI," I said.

130   The Best of *Manhunt*

"No." His voice was flat and emphatic. "I'll pay first. We'll call the FBI after Andy comes home."

"It's your decision," I said. "Only make sure you're at the telephone by six o'clock. Which nursery school did Andy attend?"

He told me the name and gave me the address. He had a tight grip on the briefcase and was buttoning his coat when I left.

A spinster named Matilda Kane was the school supervisor. There was nothing wrong with her that twenty-five pounds, properly distributed, and the companionship of an enthusiastic male couldn't cure. Irene Richardson had instructed her to say nothing about the incident, so she phoned the Richardson apartment for a green light before talking. Then she looked at me, her eyes gravely troubled, waiting.

"Did you see the man who called for Andy?"

"Yes. He wore a thin black mustache, horn-rimmed glasses, and a chauffeur's cap."

"And the car he was driving?"

"A Chrysler convertible, light green, the same car Mrs. Richardson usually drove. He must have stolen it."

"Could you identify the man if you saw him again?"

"Yes, I—think so."

"How about Andy? He must have known his father didn't have a chauffeur. Wasn't he reluctant to go along?"

"Andy is a very trusting child."

"Intelligent?"

"No more so than other four-year-olds."

I started to leave. "Thank you, Miss Kane."

"Will you let me know what happens as soon as possible?"

"Of course. But don't blame yourself for lack of omniscience. You had no way of knowing."

She shook her head, looking helpless. "I had spoken to Mr. Richardson several times on the phone. The kidnapper must have been someone who knew him well. He did a wonderful job of imitating Mr. Richardson's voice."

"The whole operation was neatly planned."

But was it? Was it really planned as neatly as it looked? There seemed to be a flaw in the caper, but I couldn't put my finger on it. The letter I'd read kept bothering me.

I scouted the neighborhood, trying to find someone who might have seen a light green Chrysler convertible, chauffeur-driven. But cars are a familiar commodity and it had gone unnoticed.

Shortly after six, I phoned George Richardson and got through to him at once. He sounded grim. "I had my call, Jordan. The kidnapper demands action. Holding Andy is too much of a problem. He wants the money tonight."

"What are your instructions?"

"He told me to walk slowly through Riverside Park at three A.M., carrying the money in a paper parcel. I'm to use the outer path between 72nd and 86th Street. His accomplice has the area under surveillance now, watching for anything suspicious. He'll keep his eye on me all the time. If nobody is staked out along the route, if I'm not being followed, if no cars are around, he'll make contact. If anything goes haywire, his partner will take care of Andy and blow. If the plan runs smoothly, we can expect Andy to be released within the hour somewhere in Manhattan." He paused while static crackled over the wire. "Well, Jordan, what do you think?"

"I think you'd better follow instructions to the letter."

"Of course." There was no doubt in his mind that it was the only course.

"In the meantime," I told him, "I suggest that you stay at your apartment and wait for my call."

"What are you going to do?"

"Nothing. There isn't anything we can do, except sit tight and see what happens."

"I agree. Andy's safety is paramount."

"How is your wife?"

"Frightened. She wants me to thank you for any help you may render."

"I'll do my best."

After we broke the connection, I decided to go home. The next shift might run till dawn or later and I needed rest. I wanted to feel fresh and alert. But closing my eyes failed to erase the picture from my brain. The picture of a four-year-old boy, violently snatched out of safe and familiar surroundings, petrified with fear, held by ruthless men.

They must have evaluated risks and consequences. The enormity of their crime was clear to them. Could they really be trusted to return Andy safe? Andy, an intelligent lad who might some day be in a position to identify them. How simple it would be to eliminate this danger! How easy to wipe away their tracks by killing the boy!

I sat up and abandoned the sofa. I walked stiff-legged around the apartment, feeling impotent, angry with frustration. I thought of the FBI. They had the men, the facilities, the organization. I almost reached for the telephone, but swallowed the impulse, because the scales here were too delicately balanced. We were dealing with jittery and desperate men, their nerves honed to a fine edge, and a single misstep might tip the weights. Kidnapping, a Federal offense, is punishable by death. They had nothing more to lose. Anything might blow the cork, cause them to dump the boy and haul freight.

It was shortly after midnight when I presented myself at the Richardson apartment, on Beekman Place overlooking the East River. I found Irene Richardson to be a tall slender patrician woman with anguished eyes in a drawn face lacking color, fighting to keep herself under control. The muscles in her neck pulled taut, like the strings of a badly tuned cello. She leaned heavily on her husband's arm, not trusting her own voice. Then it came, in a broken appeal, pleading for help and assurance.

"Do you think Andy is safe?"

I caught a warning glint from the man at her side. An hysterical woman on our hands at this time would be a needless handicap.

"Yes," I said.

"He must be so terribly frightened."

"Children are very resilient, Mrs. Richardson. He'll forget all this fast enough once he's home safe."

She closed her eyes as if in prayer. "Dear Lord, I hope so."

She permitted her husband to lead her out of the room. He reappeared a moment later, his jaw set. "All right, Jordan," he rumbled. "Let's go."

I shook my head. "It's too early. If your apartment is being watched, it may make them suspicious."

He nodded and began wearing out the rug, pacing restlessly, champing at the bit, a man driven to the limits of his endurance. He paused at a mirror-covered bar, poured a stiff brandy, and tossed it off, not offering me any. Because of the strain he was under, I forgave his lapse of manners. I would have refused anyway, since alcohol and emergencies don't mix well.

A pack of cigarettes later, I glanced at my strap watch and said, "It's almost time. I don't think we should be seen leaving together. I'll go out first. Follow me in about twenty minutes."

"Where will you be?"

"At the midway mark. I'll take up a position at West End and 79th, the northeast corner. Don't come near me until it's all over. Got that straight?"

"Yes."

I said, "Good luck," and left him chewing the inside of his cheek.

At three A.M., in that neighborhood, the streets were deserted. Overhead, the moon hung like an open porthole in the sky. Against it, the solid mass of buildings was a black silhouette, stretching endlessly. Each intersection was an island bathed in lemon-yellow light, with colored overtones from the traffic signals. An occasional car hissed past, tires humming.

A forgotten cigarette smoked itself between my lips. The luminous hands on my watch continued their slow arc. It was four A.M. and no sign yet of George Richardson.

I pictured him walking slowly and painfully along the outer path of Riverside Park, eyes piercing the darkness, nerves attuned to any interruption, while a boy's life hung in the balance.

A car roared through the night. Twin headlamps came hurtling up the street. Tires screamed as the brakes were suddenly clamped near where I stood and a taxi ground to a jolting halt in front of me. The door opened and George Richardson beckoned.

I climbed in and settled beside him. He was wound up tighter than a dollar watch.

"Where to, Mac?" the driver said.

"Head downtown." Richardson's fingers curled around my arm. His eyes were burning and he spoke in a hoarse, barely controlled whisper. "The man came. He picked me up near 81st Street."

"Was he alone?"

"I think so, yes. He pulled alongside in a car and called my name. I went over and he said, 'Give me the package.' I handed it to him and he stepped on the gas." The fingers tightened on my sleeve, nails digging in. "I got his license number, Jordan. 6Y 46-07. Can you find out who he is?"

"Yes, when the license bureau opens, providing the car isn't stolen."

"We must get Andy back first."

"That goes without saying."

"What do we do now?"

"We wait and see if they keep their promise."

He shook his head. "On the telephone, the man said they'd let Andy go somewhere in Manhattan. How do we know where to find him?"

"We don't. Most probably some cop will pick the boy up and call your apartment."

"Then let's go back." He leaned forward and gave the driver his address.

Irene Richardson was waiting for us. She got the answer from her husband's eyes, took a shuddering breath, and went to prepare a pot of coffee. We commenced the vigil in silence. George sat with his eyes straight ahead, fixed and unblinking. The woman kept working her fingers together, jumping nervously at every sound, watching the telephone, as if willing it to ring.

By five-thirty the clutch was slipping. Suddenly she broke training and was on her feet, chin out of control. "I-I can't stand it . . . Why don't they call? Where is he? Oh, Andy—Andy—"

Her husband got her down on the sofa again, stroking her hands.

I said, "These things take time, Mrs. Richardson."

But the delay bothered me. I didn't like it. There was no reason for it, unless the kidnappers had decided on a double-cross. The same thought must have entered Richardson's mind, for he threw me an angry look, bleak and cold.

Another hour and dawn crept through the window in a soiled gray smudge. Traffic noises began rumbling in the street below. The woman had her face in her hands now, sobbing quietly, shoulders convulsed.

At nine-thirty I went to the telephone and put a call through to a man I knew in the license bureau. I gave him the number and waited while he checked. He got the information and I thanked him.

George Richardson was beside me, gripping my sleeve. "Well?"

"A man named Steve Ballou owns the car. He lives on the west side, near Tenth Avenue. I don't know whether the car was stolen or not."

"Can you find out?"

"Yes." I dialed Homicide West and got through to Detective-Lieutenant John Nola.

"Well, counselor," he said, genuinely pleased. "A pleasure. Haven't heard from you in several months. What cooks on the legal front?"

"The usual," I said. "Will you do me a favor, John?"

"What?"

"I'd like to know if a certain car was stolen."

"That's not my department, but I'll find out for you. Give me the registration number."

"6Y 46-07."

It didn't take long and a moment later his voice was back in my ear. "Got it, counselor. No larceny reported."

"One thing more, Lieutenant. Will you have someone check the files on a character named Steve Ballou? I'd like to know if he has a record."

"Can do. Will call you back."

George Richardson literally bit his fingernails in the interim.

When the phone rang, he grasped the handset and said hoarsely, "Yes?" His face fell and he handed me the instrument.

It was Nola. "Here it is, Scott. Steve Ballou, four times arrested, one conviction, served a term at Sing Sing, released three years ago."

"Known associates?" I asked.

"Seems to be a lone operator. His cellmate up the river was Neil Corbin. They roomed together for a brief time after Corbin was paroled. And that's about it."

"Thank you, John."

"Good luck, counselor." He broke the connection.

George Richardson said, "Did he—what is it, man? For heaven's sake, what's wrong?"

"A lead," I said. "Ballou and Neil Corbin are friends."

"Corbin?" His gaping eyes were bright with conjecture. "Your first wife's boy friend. The man who brought her home the night she was killed."

"He took Andy?"

"One of them did."

A nerve bulged and twitched in his temple. He swung decisively on his heel and stalked from the room. He came back jamming a loaded clip into the heel of an automatic. He handled it well, with a neat economy of motion.

"Took this from a dead German colonel," he said. "Know how to use it, too."

"Oh, no," his wife wailed, "please, George . . ."

He ignored her. "All right, Jordan, let's roll."

"We ought to have some help on this."

"No time for explanations. Let's go."

I followed him down and we took a cab to Ballou's address. It was an ancient brownstone in a seedy neighborhood. Ballou's apartment was on the third floor.

"All right," George said, "here's the program." His voice was incisive, no longer irresolute, and I sensed a subtle change in our relationship. He was leading now, the bloodhound on a scent. "You stand back and to one side, Jordan. I'll ring the bell. If he turns the latch, hit the door hard. We'll take these goons by surprise."

I nodded and we went up. There was a tiny peephole in Ballou's door. I had a feeling the place was deserted, but I braced myself nevertheless. Richardson stood close and rang the bell. There was a long pause. No sound from within, no sound at all.

His finger depressed the button again. Then I heard the latch slide back. The door started to open and I hit it hard. I caught it squarely with my shoulder, almost tearing the hinges off. It struck the man behind it, slamming him back. He caught his balance with a frantic shuffle, eyes staring wildly in his head and I recognized him then, Neil Corbin. His angular face was white and desperate. Panic flooded his eyes.

I saw his hand flash under his lapel and heard Richardson's shout, "Duck, Jordan, duck!"

But I wasn't fast enough and the gun jumped into Corbin's hand. It was a Smith & Wesson, caliber .38, and the gaping barrel looked like an open doorway to hell. I threw myself flat as it thundered and my ears were ringing instantly from the concussion.

I heard a nasty slap that wrung a bleat of pain from Richardson's throat, and Neil Corbin ducked out of the foyer into the living room.

I snaked along the floor to the archway. Neil Corbin had taken to his heels and was racing toward the kitchen. I went after him and when I got there his head was out of the window and he was pulling his leg through to the fire escape.

"Corbin!" I yelled. "Hold it!"

He swiveled and pumped out two blind shots. The slugs bit viciously into the plaster behind me. I saw the searing venom in his eyes as he sighted more carefully and heard Richardson shout behind me. I turned to see him point the gun at Corbin. The shot caught Corbin in the chest and he tumbled over backward, legs flying awkwardly.

I knew he was finished and I didn't bother with him. I went back through the living room and found another door and opened it. A small boy was on the bed, trussed hand and foot, a strip of adhesive tape covering his mouth. From the numb, inanimate look in his eyes I knew that he'd been drugged. I untied him and gently removed the tape from his lips.

George Richardson staggered into the room behind me. His gun was in his hand. "Andy!" he said. "Andy, boy!"

We caught hell, both of us, from the Police Department and from the FBI. Lieutenant Nola, especially, went after my hide. It took all morning and most of the afternoon to get the story told and everything cleaned up. George Richardson's wound was not serious and he was able to navigate under his own power.

When he finally had me alone, the Lieutenant said dourly, "We bust cops from the force for going it alone. You know better than that, Scott. And another thing, you and Richardson left Neil Corbin out on that fire escape wedged between a couple of rungs. Innocent pedestrians can get hurt that way. Don't ever do it again."

"How about Steve Ballou?" I said. "Any chance of nailing him?"

"Ballou is out of it. He had permission from his parole officer to leave the state. He works for a plumbing outfit and he's in Ohio, driving around to see their midwest accounts. Corbin worked this out alone. He must have gotten a lot of information from Lydia Richardson before she was killed."

"That ties it up then."

"Just about, except for two items; a Sullivan Law violation against Mr. Richardson for possession of that Mauser automatic he used—although I doubt if the D. A. will press the charge."

"And the second item?"

"The money. One hundred grand. Corbin hid it somewhere. We took the place apart and couldn't find it."

"That's something to look for. Maybe Richardson can still use my services."

"Yeah." Nola shuffled some papers on his desk. "Sorry, lad. Reports to make out. Keep your nose clean."

My muscles ached with exhaustion. I was saturated with weariness, but I walked anyway, because the past twenty-four hours kept whirling through my brain in brief kaleidoscopic flashes.

The ransom money kept hounding me. And then, quite suddenly, I had a pretty good idea where it was, and I stopped off at a drug store and patronized the phone booth, and put a call through to George Richardson's apartment. His wife answered, sounding exultant, and she thanked me effusively. Her husband was at his office, working late.

I quit the store and flagged a cab.

A light was burning behind the frosted glass door of Richardson's office. He glanced up as I entered and flashed me a gleaming white smile, extending his left hand because his right arm was in a sling. This time he remembered his manners and offered me a drink.

I took it, since I did not expect to get any fee for handling the case.

"You did a fine job of work, Jordan. Fine. I'm delighted."

"How's Andy?"

"Coming along fine. He was under drugs most of the time and hardly remembers a thing." Richardson opened a desk drawer and pulled out a check book. He flipped it open and uncapped a fountain pen. "I'd like to show my appreciation, Jordan, by doubling your usual fee."

"The case isn't closed yet. I'd like to find the ransom money first."

"But where can you look?"

"Right here," I said. "Somewhere in this office."

The smile slid off his face and he sat up sharply, staring at me with a queer puckered look in his eyes. "I—what do you mean?"

"I mean that you never gave it to Corbin, that he never appeared at the park, that the package you carried last night was a phoney stuffed with worthless paper which you tossed into the bushes somewhere."

"You must be crazy!"

"Yeah. Like a fox. That whole kidnapping was a sham, conceived and staged by you, a dodge, dust in the eyes, to conceal your true motive."

"Which was?"

"To murder Neil Corbin. To kill him in front of a witness, apparently in self-defense."

He bent forward stiffly, the muscles in his face rigid. "That's ridiculous."

"Is it? Then let me spell it out. Neil Corbin was blackmailing you. He probably saw you leaving your first wife's apartment the night she was killed and he guessed that she hadn't fallen, that you must have pushed her. He may even have found some evidence to prove it, something you struck her over the head with, bearing your finger-prints, which he hid. He never told the cops, oh, no, not Corbin, there'd be no profit in that. But he told you. He told you and made it pay off."

A strained laugh, short and mirthless. "I don't understand. Why would I kill Lydia?"

"Because of five hundred dollars a week alimony. Twenty-six grand a year. Add it up over a ten year period. Over a quarter of a million. She had no intention of marrying Corbin and relinquishing her income. There was no way of getting off the nut. You'd have to pay and pay and pay. So you decided to have it out with Lydia and waited at her apartment that night. Maybe you tried to make a cash settlement and she laughed in your face. Maybe you lost your head and struck her with a bookend and then had to cover up by dropping her over the ledge.

"You gained nothing, however, because Corbin saw you as he left the garage, and you started paying again. Then you had a bright idea. You dreamed up a scheme. You offered Corbin a lump sum, and probably told him you'd have to get the money from your wife, and that the only way to work it would be through her son Andy. You said you would lend him your car and call the school. You promised to get the money and deliver it to him and bring Andy back. You told him no one else would be involved, the cops would not be notified. And he believed you because you were personally involved.

"You wrote the ransom note yourself, mailed it yourself, and called me in. You arranged for us to find Corbin with the boy and you shot him when we broke into the apartment. There was a peephole in the door and he would have opened it for no one but you. He was expecting you to bring the money."

Beads of moisture had formed along Richardson's upper lip. "Guesswork," he said hoarsely. "All guesswork; you said so yourself."

"Up to that point, yes," I said. "But the rest of it we can prove."

The inner edges of his eyebrows drew together questioningly. "How?"

"You gave me the license number of Ballou's car. But that car is somewhere in Ohio with its owner and couldn't possibly be in New York. The woman at Andy's school thought she recognized your voice. She certainly did, because it actually was your voice. And no professional kidnapper would have written a letter first and then taken the boy. But it made no difference to you because you were in control of the situation at all times. You had no intention of calling the FBI or letting anyone else interfere."

"Look. Jordan. If I wanted to kill Neil Corbin, why didn't I just do it when nobody was around?"

"Because you didn't want to start a homicide investigation. You were afraid the police would find his bank deposits and start looking for their source. They might tie him up to you through Lydia. His deposits would coincide with your withdrawals. No, sir, it was better this way. Involve him in a kidnapping and shoot him in cold blood. You'd be a hero."

Richardson's tongue coiled slowly over his lips. "It's a flimsy case. They can't convict me."

"Not so flimsy," I said. "There's plenty of corroboration, especially when they find the ransom money hidden right here in your office."

He swallowed hugely and his eyes kindled with desperate hope. He was grasping at straws. "Corbin is dead. Nobody can place me near Lydia's apartment the night she fell." But he didn't believe it himself. I waited, watching.

I don't know what he was trying to prove, but suddenly he snatched a letter opener off his desk, and lunged at me. I had to twist him plenty before he subsided.

The way he looked now. I wasn't sure he'd ever live long enough for the State of New York to strap him down and deliver the proper voltage.

I figured he was due for a heart attack any minute, maybe before the boys arrived.

Bad Word
David Alexander

December 1957

O h, I knew where it was all right. It was within a couple of feet of me.
I wanted the thing so bad I was shaking all over and sweating like a plow horse
that's just worked the forty-acre. All I had to do was reach out and open the drawer
and pick it up, but I was afraid to. I couldn't tell if it was the True Spirit or the Evil
Spirit that was inside of me. I had to be sure, you understand. Preacher Bates used
to say that the Devil could get the Evil Spirit inside of you and make you think it
was the True Spirit and when that happened you did something that made you burn
in hellfire forever and a day.

The thing was right there in the bottom drawer of the chest, behind a pile of
socks that needed washing. It had been there since the last time it happened. I'd
meant to throw it away, but somehow I couldn't. I kept thinking that the True Spirit
might move me and if it did I'd have to have it. So I hid it behind the pile of socks
that needed washing. I hadn't washed the socks because I was afraid if I moved
them I'd see it and if I saw it, something would happen again.

So I sat there on the edge of the cot in my room at the Y and I kept staring at
the drawer where I'd hidden it. I didn't have anything on but my shorts. I'd been
getting ready to go down to the shower room and take a bath when the shaking and
the sweating hit me and I knew I had to have the thing in the drawer. It was my
day off and this time of afternoon there wouldn't be anybody in the showers. I didn't
like to take a shower in front of the other fellows because they kidded me. I'm
almost old enough to vote but I'm just a few little inches over five feet tall and I'm
so skinny you could play guitar music on my ribs. I dropped my shorts off and I
walked over naked toward the closet where my old flannel bathrobe with the moth
holes in it was hanging up. On the way I looked at myself in the mirror. I don't
know why I always did that when I didn't have my clothes on. It made me ashamed
to see myself. It hurt so bad it made me want to cry. But I kept on doing it all the
time. It was like when I was a little kid. I'd stick my finger up against a red hot stove
and burn it. I knew it was going to hurt but I kept right on doing it.

Maybe it was a good thing to do. I don't know. Preacher Bates always used to
say that sinners had to flay their flesh and humble their spirits.

I was such a skinny little runt because I never did have enough to eat when I
was growing up, I guess. I couldn't remember a single time when I was a kid that I
wasn't hungry. Pop was a tenant farmer down South and be died before I could
remember and Mom worked the farm but the soil was rocky and she tired out easy
and the chickens weren't good layers. Mostly we lived on poke salad and hominy
grits and cornbread. It wasn't once a month we had a little hog jowl. I was so scared
of being hungry again that every time I got paid off for my dishwashing job I bought
a lot of candy bars and took them up to my room. I didn't smoke or drink, except a
little beer now and then, and I washed my own clothes and didn't have bad habits,

so I could afford to buy the candy bars. I had them hid in a drawer, a different drawer from the one where I'd hid the thing I wanted so bad.

I thought maybe if I took a shower and finished it off with ice-cold water it would stop me shaking and sweating and wanting the thing. Anyway it might make me think clear so I'd know if it was the True Spirit or the Evil Spirit that was pestering me to get it out from behind the pile of socks. I quit looking in the mirror at myself and got my old bathrobe and put it on.

The shower didn't help me any. As soon as I got back in my room I started wanting the thing again and the sweating and the shaking started all over. I still couldn't be sure if it was the True Spirit or the Evil Spirit that possessed me and was tearing me apart like that. I guess maybe Preacher Bates might have known the difference, but he was dead and there weren't any Revelationists around this part of the country. The Revelationists were all in the South, you understand.

Preacher Bates had come to Clayville, the nearest town to our place, when I was a little kid around twelve years old. He had a new religion he called Revealed Prophecy. He set up a Tabernacle made out of tin and canvas and scrap lumber on a vacant lot near the town dump and he held revival meetings and he called his converts Revelationists. Mom was one of his first converts.

I guess the preacher was around forty when he first came to Clayville. He was a big hulk of a man, over six feet in his socks. He was rawbone-built with wide, stooped shoulders and arms so long it made you think of a big ape. He had a mane of black hair that he let grow long on his neck. The scariest thing about him was his eyes. They were big and black and it seemed like they popped right out of his head and flashed with lightning when the True Spirit was inside of him and he got excited. He drank corn squeezings out of a Mason jar any time he felt like it and he didn't make any bones about his drinking, either. He said if a man had the True Spirit in him and knew how to handle liquor it sharpened his wits and helped him shout his praise of the Lord. That's one reason I never felt bad about taking a beer now and then. I'd tried taking hard liquor a time or two but it gagged me. I didn't even like beer much, either, tell the truth, but I'd get lonesome sometimes and go into a saloon and sip at a glass just so there'd be people around me and I could hear them talking.

A lot of folks in Clayville, most of them the people we called "Quality," were dead-set against Preacher Bates. They wanted to tear down his Tabernacle and run him out of town. It wasn't just his drinking and ranting that they objected to. He handled live rattlesnakes to prove that a man with the True Spirit inside of him couldn't come to harm and he made his followers handle rattlers, too. I guess some of his followers didn't have the True Spirit, because they got bit and almost died. Maybe I should tell you here that Preacher Bates got bit a few years later and died. He was trying to handle a big bull rattler that was too slippery for him and it sank its fangs right into his bare arm. The Preacher wouldn't go to a doctor. He just tried to cure himself with corn squeezings and prayer and his arm swelled up as big as a middle-sized tree trunk and he died. But that was a long time later.

Some of the people in Clayville also objected to the fact that Preacher Bates let Lenny Foster come to his revival meetings. Lenny was what they call an epileptic and he had conniption fits. The Preacher's ranting and raving would always get him so excited he'd get into a fit and roll on the floor and foam at the mouth. Preacher Bates said Lenny didn't have a disease at all. He said it was because the Awful Truth of the Lord was revealed to him that he had the spells in meeting.

There were so many rednecks like us that got to be followers of the Preacher that the folks in town couldn't do anything about running him out, unless they wanted to risk causing a knock-down-and-drag-out riot.

Preacher Bates used to give some of his converts what he called a Private Revelation. So far as I could tell, he didn't give his Private Revelation to anybody but ladies in the congregation. Mom would invite him out to supper whenever she had hog jowl on the table. He'd come riding out from town in his secondhand Ford that must have been at least ten years old. After supper, he and Mom would go into the bedroom and shut the door and bolt it and my sister Clarissa and I used to be scared to death because we'd hear groaning and moaning from behind the door. But Mom said that was all part of getting the True Spirit that a Revelationist had to have.

Once when Mom was in town trying to trade a little stuff we'd grown for flour and salt and matches and other things we needed, the Preacher came to the house in the afternoon. My sister Clarissa was just fourteen then. The Preacher said the time had come for Clarissa to have a Private Revelation. He warned her and me that if we ever breathed a word to Mom or anybody about her Revelation we'd be struck down dead and burn in hellfire. He ran me out of the house and took Clarissa into Mom's bedroom. I was scared to death, but I sneaked around back of the house and listened at the window and Clarissa was screaming and sobbing like she was being murdered. After that Preacher Bates came to give Clarissa a Private Revelation every time Mom went to town.

I don't think the Private Revelation could have done Clarissa any good, though. She wasn't even sixteen when she ran away from home and later on Mom heard she was living a life of sin in Memphis. My own sister had become what Preacher Bates said was the worst thing in all the world—a Lewd Woman.

Preacher Bates was around Clayville for about three years before the bull rattler bit him and he died. His convents kept the Tabernacle going but it wasn't the same at all without the Preacher there ranting and raving when the True Spirit was inside of him. The Preacher had only been dead about three months when Mom came down with the ague and passed away. They put me in a county home for a while, but I ran away and headed North and I've been up here in the city ever since, working any kind of job I could to keep the skin and bones together. This dishwashing job has lasted more than three months now and that's the longest I've ever worked at anything.

Sometimes I get these spells. At first I'm sure it's the True Spirit that's moving me and I take the thing that's in the drawer and I go out and I do what I've got to do and then afterward I'm not sure if it was the True Spirit or the Evil Spirit that was speaking to me and I get tormented. I wish there was some real way of knowing, the way Preacher Bates always knew for sure.

I was thinking about Clayville and Mom and Clarissa and Preacher Bates while I sat there in my little room at the Y staring at the drawer where the thing was hidden and wanting it so bad I was about to bust.

I didn't get it right away, though. I got up and put my clothes on first. I put on the only good suit I had. It was a blue serge I'd bought almost new at a second-hand store. It was a little big for me, of course, but it didn't look too bad after I'd had the pants and sleeves cut down. I put on my peaked cap and I started to run out of the room so I wouldn't be tempted to get the thing out of the drawer before I was sure. I had my hand on the doorknob when something happened, something that had really never happened before.

All of a sudden I was *sure.*

I knew that it was the True Spirit I had inside of me this time and that it was urging me to get the thing.

I could see Preacher Bates' big staring eyes blazing at me from a dark corner of the room and I could hear his big bass voice as plain as anything saying, "Get it, boy! Get it!" There couldn't be a mite of doubt about it this time.

I opened the drawer and I pushed aside the pile of socks that needed washing and I got the thing I wanted and I put it in my pocket. I kept my hand in my pocket clasped around it. I was so excited about having it that the palm of my hand was wet and slippery with sweat. I caught a glimpse of myself in the mirror. I wasn't a skinny little runt any more. With the thing in my pocket I was twelve feet tall with a halo 'round my head and my eyes were shining as bright and fierce as Preacher Bates' used to shine.

I was wearing rubber-soled sneakers because they're about the cheapest kind of shoes that you can buy, but when I went downstairs and out to the street I was walking on clouds. I was surprised to find that the world outside was dark and rainy. It had been a bright, sunshiny afternoon when I first started thinking about the thing and wanting it. I must have been sitting on that little cot for hours just staring at the drawer where it was hidden, and wanting it, and thinking about Mom and Clarissa and Preacher Bates. Now it was night. That was kind of a Sign, too. It had always been night when it had happened before.

The rain was a fine, steady mist. It soaked through my clothes by the time I'd walked a few blocks, but I didn't even notice it. To me the rain was like Holy Water the Angels were spraying down on me because I'd had the Revelation and the True Spirit was inside of me.

I walked and walked and I didn't know where I was going. I didn't care. Sometimes I'd hear a teeny Voice, like an echo from a long way off, and it would tell me to turn a corner or cross a street, and I'd obey. I knew I was being led. I was sure I'd know when I reached the right place. It was the very first time that I'd been absolutely sure it was the True Spirit inside of me and I rejoiced. I wanted to sing and shout and jump up and down the way we used to do at the revival meetings. I hadn't eaten anything for hours but I wasn't hungry.

My hand could feel the thing there in my pocket and that was all that mattered.

I don't know how long or how far I walked. I walked through streets with houses and streets with stores. I walked through streets that were dark as pitch and streets that shone with light. The Voice kept saying "Farther! Farther!" and I kept walking and never grew tired and never cared a bit how wet I was.

Once or twice I thought I might have come to the place I was meant to seek. There was a young girl, about my age, I guess, standing under an awning. She had a silk dress on and it was so wet it was plastered to her body and it made her look like a Lewd Woman. But the Voice was just a whisper and I couldn't understand the words, so I just stopped for a minute in the shadows near to her and then I went on again. When I did, I heard the Voice again and I knew I had been right.

Another time I was on a dark street and it smelled of a fish market that was on the corner and the buildings were the kind that real poor people live in. I saw a woman sitting in a lighted window. She was wearing a kimono and it was open so you could see part of her bosom and she was smoking a cigarette and I waited for the Voice to tell me if this was the place, but I didn't hear it, so I went on again. Once I heard something like a whispering or hissing and I stopped and listened and then I realized it was my own breath coming fast because I'd walked so far.

Then I was on a real dark street and it was near the docks. There was a fog now and the foghorns were tooting out on the river and it was a real sad and mournful sound like the chanting the Revelationists set up when they lowered Mom into her grave. It was so dark down here you couldn't see your hand in front of you. Once I stumbled off a curbing and almost fell.

Then I saw the light. It was gleaming there in the darkness and it was as bright as Preacher Bates' eyes used to get when he was preaching one of his hellfire-damnation sermons. All of a sudden the foghorns and the wash of water and the splash of rain blended into one big sound and it was the Voice and it wasn't whispering any more. It was shouting at me that this was the place I'd been sent to find.

The light was an electric sign outside a bar. I hurried toward it and when I got there I had to stand for a minute because I was so out of breath. And all of a sudden I was weak, too, and I was afraid I might faint, so I took a chocolate bar out of my pocket and gobbled it. Then I went into the bar.

It was a dismal-looking place with sawdust on the floor. The bartender was a fat man in a dirty apron. There were three or four men in work clothes drinking at the bar. And there was a woman. As soon as I saw the woman, I knew I had come to the right place.

She was about thirty, I guess, with dyed yellow hair. She was plump and she had a dress that fit her like the skin on a sausage and it was cut real low so you could see the upper part of her bosom. I didn't think she had a thing on under it.

Oh, she was a Lewd Woman. I knew that for sure.

She was a little bit drunk and she was talking and screeching and laughing too loud. I went up and sat down on a stool next to her and told the bartender to give me a beer.

This woman turned and looked at me and she let out a shriek of laughter and she said to the bartender, "Hey, Harry! You order shrimps for dinner? The fishmarket sent us a shrimp. Look at it, Harry. It must be fresh-caught, because it's still dripping wet."

I didn't say anything. I just sat and waited for the beer the bartender was drawing from the tap.

The woman yelled, "Hey, Harry! You ain't going to serve Shrimpie a beer, are you? He ain't big enough to drink. Why, my kid brother was bigger than Shrimpie when he was ten years old."

The guys at the bar laughed, like it was a big joke. I squeezed the thing in my pocket so hard it hurt my hand. The bartender walked toward me with a beer glass in his hand. The foam was slopping down the sides of the glass. He said, "In this joint anybody that can pay gets served."

I put a dollar bill on the bar.

Before the bartender had a chance to take it, the woman grabbed it. She stuffed it down the neck of her dress and let out a shriek of laughter.

Harry stood in front of me holding the beer. He said, "You gonna fish for your buck or pay me out of your pocket?"

The woman said, "You dare reach for that dollar, Shrimpie, and I'll holler copper!"

I looked at her. I was so mad I was about to bust. I kept squeezing the thing in my pocket. I guess the look on my face must have scared her. She took the bill out and she said, "Tell you what, Shrimpie. You buy me a Scotch and I'll put your buck on the bar."

Harry looked at me and I nodded. There wasn't anything else to do. After all, this was the Lewd Woman I was meant to meet.

She drank down her Scotch before I had taken two sips of beer. The bartender gave me thirty cents change.

A big guy wearing khaki work clothes and a windbreaker walked down the bar. He grabbed hold of the woman and spun her around on the stool.

"How's about a little fun for free, Gert?" he said.

The woman slapped him hard in the face and wrenched free of the hold be had on her.

"Take your dirty paws off me!" she yelled. "If you want to see Gertie, come around on payday!"

The big guy laughed and went out the door.

The woman said a dirty word that made me blush. I'd always been taught that saying bad words was one of the worst sins there is. You burn in hellfire forever and a day if you say bad words.

The woman said, "Drink it up, Shrimpie. Haven't you got another buck? Gertie needs another drink. A bird can't fly on one wing, you know."

I gulped down my beer and it made my stomach feel queasy. I put another dollar on the bar.

Gert said, "You ain't so bad, Shrimpie, even if you're knee-high to a flea. You got some more money in your pocket, honey? You buy Gertie a few drinks and maybe we can have some fun."

I told her I had a little more money. I had to stay with her, you understand. If she'd walked down the bar and started drinking with one of the big guys, it would have spoiled everything.

The woman kind of snuggled up against me. I could feel her knee against mine, and her plump hip. Her hip was so warm I could feel the heat even through my wet clothes.

Being close to her like that made me dizzy. I'd never felt like that the other times it had happened. That proved the True Spirit was in me, I guess. She had a real strong perfume on her and the smell of that made me feel dizzy, too. I began to shake so bad I had to clamp my teeth together to keep them from chattering.

I drank more beer than I'd ever drunk all at once before and the woman kept drinking Scotches and pretty soon nearly every bit of the pay I had left was gone. I was getting desperate. The woman was real drunk now. There wasn't anybody left in the bar except the woman and me and the bartender and a real old man down at the other end who had gone off to sleep.

I said to the woman, "Let's get out of here."

She said, "Have you got some money, honey? It'll cost five bucks if you want to come up to my room."

I told her I had five bucks. I did have. I had held it out to pay for my room. The rent was due the next day. The woman made me show her the five. She laughed when I had to undo a safety pin that was holding it to my underwear shirt.

There was still some change on the bar and she made me buy her another Scotch with that. Then she went over to a hat-rack and got a rain cape and an umbrella and we left.

It was still raining hard.

She said we couldn't get a taxi down here in this neighborhood. She took hold of my arm and kind of leaned against me. She was staggering. We must have walked about six blocks, I guess, and turned a couple of corners. I didn't have any idea where we were, but I didn't care. Everything was working out just perfect this time. I didn't need to find an alley, the way I'd had to do the other times it happened.

She came to a beat-up brownstone house with a sign in the window that said *Rooms*. She put a key in the front door and we went inside. The hall stank. Somebody had been frying onions. There was an open garbage pail just inside the hall and that stank, too. And there was another smell that reminded me of the little frame shack where Mom and Clarissa and I had lived together down South. It's the smell old wood gets when the dry rot sets in.

We didn't see anybody in the house. We went up three flights of squeaky stairs. Once or twice the woman staggered and almost fell backward on me.

Finally she unlocked another door.

We went into a little room that was just about big enough for a brass bed and a bureau and a chair. Dirty white curtains and a green blind covered the window. There was wallpaper, but it was so smudged you could hardly tell what the design had been. The woman had pictures of movie actors pinned to the wallpaper. They'd been cut out of magazines.

I stood just inside the door, with my back up against it. I was dizzy and I was winded and breathing hard. I had my hand clutched tight around the thing in my pocket. I think that was all that kept me from falling down in a dead faint. I hadn't ever been alone in a room with a woman like this before. The room had a funny smell. It was a woman-smell, I guess.

The woman took off her wet cape and stood her umbrella in a corner and sat down on the edge of the brass bed. She sat there panting for a minute, then she held out her hand and rubbed two fingers against her thumb.

"Dig out the money, honey," she said. Then she laughed. "Business before pleasure," she said.

I took a step toward her. It was going to happen any minute now. I forgot how tired and dizzy I was. This was what I'd been waiting for all my life. This was going to be better than all the other times, because I was alone with her in a room, with a shade pulled over the window and a locked door behind me.

The woman's eyes narrowed when I took the step toward her. She said, "Hey, I don't like that look in your eyes. You ain't a psycho, are you?"

I took another step. She yelled, "Get out! Get out of here! I don't want any part of you!"

I took the thing out of my pocket.

When she saw it, she tried to scream, but the scream choked in her throat. Then she began to talk to me fast, but her voice was kind of a croak.

"Wait! Don't come any closer! Put that thing away! You won't have to pay, understand? It's for free. Wait, now! Wait just a second!"

She was pulling her dress over her head. Like I'd thought, there wasn't a thing under it. It was the first time in all my life I'd ever seen a woman like that.

"See?" she said. Her eyes were wild and she was scared to death. "You don't need that thing. You don't need money. Just put that thing away and come here, honey!"

I held the thing in my hand and took another step. I was so close now I could feel the heat of her body and smell the perfume on her naked flesh.

Her face was crazy with fear now. When she spoke, her voice wasn't much more than a whisper.

"What—what are you going to do to me?" she asked.

I don't know why, but I went crazy when she asked me that. She never should have asked me that.

"By God, I'll tell you what I'm going to do!" I said. "By God, I'm going to . . ."

And I told her what I was going to do.

And then I was doing it.

It was like the other times it had happened. Once it started I blacked out and didn't come to until it was all over.

When I came to, I was standing on my feet, but I was swaying and the room was spinning around me. I had to balance myself against the bed. I was panting like a winded horse. I was sweating and shaking again, too.

The woman was on the floor at my feet. There was blood all over her.

There was blood on the thing—the switch knife—in my hand, too. There was blood on my hand and blood on my good suit and blood on my sneakers.

I felt terrible. I was scared, because I knew I'd committed a mortal sin and there'd be no forgiveness. I was sure to burn in hellfire forever and a day.

Oh, I didn't mind about the woman. She was a Lewd Woman and it was the True Spirit inside of me that had sent me out to find her. I'd only done what the Voice had told me to do.

But the woman had made me sin before I purified her. She had made me say a bad word.

It was all her fault.

"What are you going to do to me?" Why did she have to ask me that?

I'd told her what I was going to do. I'd said a bad word.

By God, I'd said.

I'd taken the name of the Lord in vain.

Mom never would have liked that. She wouldn't have liked it a little bit.

My Mom was a real religious woman.

Return Engagement
Frank Kane

February 1955

The man in the client's chair was old, tired. White bristles glinted on his chin. His eyes were dull, colorless, almost hidden by heavy, discolored pouches. A thin film of perspiration glistened on his forehead. He watched Johnny Liddell study the torn newspaper clipping.

"I killed him, Liddell. He ruined me. I had to kill him." He tugged a balled-up handkerchief from his hip pocket, swabbed at his forehead.

Liddell scowled at the clipping, tossed it on his desk. "When was this, Terrell?"

The old man licked at his lips. "That's the crazy part about it. It was six months ago. Last September."

Liddell grunted. "He sure took his time about dying. This is Monday's paper. Says he was just killed."

Terrell nodded jerkily. "It's a trap. They're trying to trap me, Liddell." He plucked at his lower lip with a shaking hand. "Don't you understand? That story's a plant."

Liddell considered it. "Why bait a trap six months later, Terrell? Why not right after it happened?"

"How do I know?" The old man pulled himself out of the chair, paced the room. Abel Terrell had been a big man. Now his clothes hung in pathetic folds on his gaunt frame, and his expensive suit was shabby and worn. He stopped next to Liddell. "I just know it's got to be a frame." He jabbed at the clipping with a bony finger. "They say he was killed in a hit and run accident. I should know how he died. I pulled the trigger. I saw him die."

"The paper says he was unidentified. What name did you know him by?"

Terrell walked back to his chair, dropped into it. "Lee. Dennis Lee." He rubbed the palm of his hand across his eyes. "And don't try to tell me it's a case of mistaken identity, Liddell. I'd know his face anywhere. I've seen it often enough in my dreams these past six months."

"And you're sure it's the same?"

"Positive."

"Well, there's one way to find out if it's a trap." The private detective reached down into his bottom drawer, pulled out a bottle and some paper cups. "You get yourself some rest and I'll amble down to see if the John Doe they've got on ice is an old client of mine." He motioned to the bottle. "A drink help?"

Terrell nodded, gnawed nervously at his thumb nail. "You don't think they'll suspect something? Follow you, maybe?"

Liddell grinned. "It's been tried." He picked up a cup, walked across the room to where a water cooler stood against the wall, humming to itself. He filled the cup, brought it back, set it on the corner of the desk. "I wouldn't worry too much about it." He pushed an empty cup and the bottle to the edge of the desk, watched while the older man poured himself a stiff drink and softened it with a touch of water.

"Was there any identifying mark on Dennis Lee that would make the identification positive? In my mind, at any rate."

"He won't be there, I tell you. He couldn't be. He's been dead six months!"

"That's just the point," the private detective nodded. "I don't want them to be able to palm off a phony on me. How about it? Anything I can look for?"

Terrell took a deep swallow from the cup, wiped a vagrant drop from his chin with the side of his hand. "There was a scar. Right under the right ear. You wouldn't notice it until he got mad. Then it turned red." He finished his drink, crumpled the paper in his fist. "About three inches long, ran along the jawbone."

Liddell nodded. "That ought to do it. You got a place to stay?"

The old man shook his head. "I've been afraid to stay in one place more than one night. I've been running ever since it happened."

"Well, maybe now you can stop running." He walked around the desk, scribbled a note on a sheet of paper. "You take this note to Ed Blesch at the Hotel Carson. He'll know what to do."

Terrell took the note, read it incuriously. "Hotel Carson? Where's that?"

"47th off Sixth. It's a fleabag, but you'll be safe there. Stay in your room until I call you."

"How do I register?"

"Any name but your own. Try George Tefft."

The old man nodded, pulled himself laboriously from his chair. "You won't be too long?" Liddell shook his head, watched the man shuffle to the door, where he stopped with his hand on the knob. "You think somebody spotted me and tipped them off? You think that's why they set the trap?"

"If it is a trap."

The old man thought about it, nodded his head. "It's a trap. Lee's been dead six months. He couldn't have died Monday." He opened the door, walked through to the outer office, and closed the door behind him.

Liddell picked up the clipping again, scowled at the face that stared back at him. The caption read: "Know this man? Police have announced that John Doe, victim of a hit and run accident at the corner of Fifth Avenue and 58th Street early this morning has still been unidentified at press time. He carried no identification when the body was found."

2.

The morgue was at the end of a long, silent corridor in the basement of City Hospital. There were two doors at the far end, one lettered *Medical Examiner* on frosted glass, the other opening into a brightly lighted room, painted a sterile white. A tall, thin bald man sat at a white enameled desk, biting on the almost invisible nail of his left thumb while making entries in a ledger. The unshaded bulb in the ceiling caused the attendant's bald pate to gleam shinily.

He looked up as Liddell crossed the room to where he sat, and seemed glad of an excuse to put his pen down. He fished a handkerchief from his pocket, polished the bald spot with a circular swabbing motion. "Looking for someone?" His voice was rusty, as though he didn't get much chance to use it.

"Understand you've got a John Doe you're trying to get a make on." Liddell flipped his credentials in front of the man's eyes.

The thin man shook his head. "Not us, mister. We got a make on all our guests." He continued to gnaw on the macerated cuticle.

Liddell pulled the clipping from his pocket, flipped it on the man's desk. "How about this one? Says here he was John Doe."

The attendant took his thumb from his mouth, leaned over the picture, studied it. "Oh, him. Identification came up with a make on him this morning. Prints on file in Washington." He stared up at Liddell with washed-out blue eyes. "Friend of yours?"

Liddell shrugged. "Could be. The picture wasn't too good. Any chance of seeing him?"

The thin man nodded. "Ain't much to look at. Bounced his head off the curb, looks like." He got up, limped around the desk. "Come with me."

He led the way to a heavy door set in the far wall and tugged it open. Beyond was a high-ceilinged, stone-floored, unheated room with double tiers of metal lockers. Each locker had its own stenciled number.

Liddell wrinkled his nose as the blast of carbolic-laden air enveloped them. There was no word spoken as he followed the thin man across the floor to the rear of the windowless room. The attendant stopped in front of one row of drawers, tugged on a handle. The drawer pulled out with a screech. A piece of canvas that bulged slightly covered its contents.

The attendant reached up and pulled on a high-powered light in an enamel reflector. He grabbed the corner of the canvas, pulled it back, exposing the body of a man.

The face was oyster-white, the hair dank and damp. Despite the misshapen head, it was obviously the body of the man pictured in the clipping.

"That's your boy," the attendant grunted. He pursed his lips, studied the dead man objectively. "Never knew what hit him. Like I said, looks like he bounced his head off the curb."

Liddell nodded. He placed one finger against the dead man's right cheek, rolled the head to the side. The skin was clammy and cold to his touch. He bent closer to the body, detected the three-inch scar that ran along the side of the jaw bone, grunted under his breath.

The attendant watched the performance curiously, swore when the phone in his office started pealing. "Damn thing always rings when you're nowhere near it." He nodded at the body. "Got enough?"

"You go ahead and answer your phone. I'll wait."

The thin man seemed undecided, then shrugged his shoulders. "Guess you can't walk off with him." He showed the yellowed stumps of his teeth in a grin. "Got one babe stashed away I wouldn't trust nobody with, but this one ain't that pretty."

His bad leg clip-clopped across the floor as he hurried to answer the phone. As soon as he had disappeared through the door leading to the outer office, Liddell whipped back the canvas. There were no signs of bullet wounds or any scars of any nature with the exception of an old appendix scar. Liddell scowled at the unmarred expanse of abdomen, pulled the canvas back into place.

He was standing with his hands in his jacket pocket when the attendant limped back across the room.

"Make him?" the thin man wanted to know. He re-covered the dead man's face, slammed the drawer back into place with a clang that reverberated through the entire room.

"I'm not sure. What was the make on him?"

The attendant shook his head. "You'll have to get that from the medical examiner's office." He watched with interest while Liddell's hand disappeared into his pocket, re-appeared with a folded bill. "Although I may have it in my records," he amended hastily.

He fell into step beside Liddell as they re-crossed the room to the office. Outside, he walked around the desk, pulled open a drawer in a small card file, flipped through it. "His name was Dennis Leeman. Mean anything to you?"

Liddell ignored the question, stuck a cigarette in the corner of his mouth. He lit it, filled his lungs with smoke and expelled it in twin streams through his nostrils in an effort to clean out the morgue smell. "Nobody claim him yet?"

The attendant dropped the card back into the file, pushed the drawer shut. "Not yet." He sank into his chair, stared up at Liddell. "My guess is nobody's going to claim him. Unless he's got relatives out of state."

Liddell nodded. "Where's your phone?"

The thin man motioned to the instrument on his desk. "Be my guest."

Liddell dialed the number of the Hotel Carson, asked the operator for George Tefft. "One moment, please," the receiver rattled back.

He could hear the buzz as the switchboard rang, then, "Mr. Tefft doesn't answer. Would you care to leave a message?"

Liddell glowered at the mouthpiece, shook his head. "No message."

3.

The Hotel Carson was an old, weather-beaten stone building that nestled anonymously in a row of similarly weather-beaten stone buildings that line the north side of 47th Street. A small plaque to the right of the door dispelled any doubts as to its identity.

A threadbare and faded carpet that ran the length of the lobby had long ago given up any pretense of serving any useful purpose. The chairs were rickety and unsafe, the artificial rubber plants grimed with dust.

Johnny Liddell waved to the watery-eyed man behind the registration desk, who raised his eyes from the scratch sheet only long enough to return the salutation. The private detective headed for the lone elevator cage in the rear. A pimpled youth with slack lips and discolored bags under his eyes nodded to him as he got in.

"Blesch take care of the old guy I sent over for cold storage?" he asked as the operator followed him into the cage, slammed the door after him.

"Yeah, but the old guy ain't there now." He checked the watch on his wrist. "He checks in about three and about fifteen minutes later he goes tearing out. Kind of surprised me. When he went up, he was carrying an armful of papers. I figured he was holing up for the winter."

Liddell cursed softly. "I sent him over here to stay put."

The pimple faced operator shrugged. "Nobody tell me he's not supposed to go." He eyed Liddell curiously. "Guy hot or something, you're burying him?"

"No, I just wanted him where I could lay my hands on him for some information. He'll be back. I'll wait in his room."

The elevator stopped at the fourth floor with a spine-jarring jerk. The operator slammed open the grill doors, propped them open. "I got a pass key here. I'll let you in." He led the way down the corridor to 412, pushed the door open. He stuck his head in, looked around curiously. "Gone all right."

Liddell slipped him a folded bill, walked into the room, closed the door behind him. Both the bedroom and bathroom were empty. A light had been left burning in a bridge lamp next to the room's only chair. Dumped alongside the chair was a stack of rumpled newspapers.

Liddell walked over, picked up a sheet that had been crumpled into a ball, smoothed it out. The item was a small one at the bottom of a column. It merely stated that the victim of Monday night's hit and run accident had been identified as Dennis Leeman, address unknown.

He stared at the item for a moment, crumpled the paper back into a ball, threw it in the direction of the waste basket. The telephone was on a cigarette-scarred night table next to the bed. He picked up the instrument, asked for the manager's office.

"Blesch speaking," a tired, gruff voice informed him.

"Ed, this is Liddell. I'm in 412. My boy's gone. Any idea where or when?"

Blesch sighed audibly. "You just asked me to check him in, pally. You didn't say anything about watchdogging him. All I know's he made a couple of calls just before he went out. I had the operator keep an eye on the room." A worried note crept into his voice. "No trouble?"

"No trouble," Liddell assured him. "I've got some good news for the guy and I want to pass it along."

"One of the calls was to your office, the other to Stanton 7-6770. He didn't get an answer on the Stanton number and went tearing out."

"Got any idea who has that Stanton number?"

"Look, pally. You're the detective. Me, I got other things on my mind. Running a riding academy like this ain't the best way to grow old gracefully." There was a click as he dropped the receiver back on its hook.

Liddell hung up his receiver, stared at it for a moment. He debated the advisability of waiting until Terrell returned, voted it down. He dropped by the front desk on his way out, left word for the old man to call him as soon as he came in.

4.

Johnny Liddell sat with his desk chair tilted back, staring out the window at Bryant Park twelve stories below. He helped himself to a slug of bourbon from the bottle in the bottom drawer, emptied the paper cup, tossed it at the waste basket.

He consulted his watch, frowned at the time. Almost seven! He reached for the telephone, dialed the Hotel Carson, verified the fact that his client hadn't returned.

He had just hung up the receiver when the phone started to shrill. He let it ring twice, picked up the receiver.

"Liddell?" The voice was familiar, but not the old man's.

"Yeah."

"This is Mike Flannery, Inspector Herlehy's driver. He wants to see you. Can you get down to Perry and Ninth in the Village?"

Liddell frowned at the receiver. "I guess so, but—"

"The inspector says to hurry." The line went dead.

The cab made the distance from midtown to the Village in a record time. Liddell pushed a bill through the front window to the driver, walked across the street to where Inspector Herlehy's black limousine stood against the curb in front of a large excavation.

The driver nodded to him. "He's down in the ditch with a friend of yours," Flannery told him. "He thought you might want in on this."

Abel Terrell was sprawled out on his back, staring up at the small circle of men around him unblinkingly. His heavily knuckled hands were clasped across his midsection as though in a last desperate effort to stem the red tide that had seeped through the laced fingers and had spread in an ugly dark stain on his jacket.

He was dead.

Johnny Liddell looked from the body to Inspector Herlehy. "When did it happen, inspector?"

The inspector pushed his sheriff-style fedora on the back of his head, chomped heavily on the ever-present wad of gum. "Can't tell for sure until the medical examiner gets here. We got the report twenty minutes ago." He took a leather notebook from the man next to him, flipped through the pages. "Couple of kids discovered the body, phoned it in." He snapped the notebook shut, handed it back to his aide. "My guess is he hasn't been dead much over an hour. Ninety minutes at the outside."

Liddell pulled out a pack of cigarettes, held it up for approval, drew a nod. He hung one in his mouth where it waggled when he talked. "How come you called me?" He touched a match to the cigarette, drew a deep drag.

"You tell me what your connection with him was." Herlehy clasped his hands behind his back, rocked on the balls of his feet.

"You're sure there is a connection?"

"Your name and address were written on a slip of paper in his pocket." The inspector reached into his jacket pocket, brought out a folded note. "You gave him a note to Ed Blesch at the Carson telling him to sign the guy in. Why?"

Liddell shrugged. "He was a client. I wanted him on ice until I could get some information he needed."

Someplace in the distance a siren wailed shrilly.

"Come on, Liddell. Don't make me pick it out of you. Who is this guy and what was the beef?" He squinted at a penciled memo. "He registered into the hotel as Tefft. That his name?"

"No. His name's Terrell. He came into my office this morning. Said he killed a man six months ago."

Herlehy scowled. "So you buried him instead of turning him in?"

"It wasn't that simple," Liddell argued. "The man he thought he killed six months ago, turns up dead in a hit and run accident on Monday. He thought it was a trap to bring him into the open. It wasn't."

The inspector spit out a wad of gum, pulled a fresh stick from his pocket, started to denude it. "Guy pulled through, eh?"

Liddell grinned glumly. "That's the funny part of it, inspector. I looked the body over very carefully. There wasn't a sign of a bullet wound on it."

Outside a siren reached for a high note, faded away as the ambulance skidded to a stop at the curb. Two men from the medical examiner's office walked into the excavation, tossed an incurious glance at the body.

"Too bad we've got to move him. After he made it so nice and convenient. Just cover him with dirt and he's set," one of them grinned. "Your boys through with him?"

The inspector nodded. "Where you fellows been?"

"You're not the only division giving us business, you know," the newcomer grinned. He waited until his companion had finished a cursory examination of the body. "Okay to take him?"

"Be my guest," the inspector nodded. He initialed a form, handed it back to the m.e.'s man, watched while a stretcher was brought in and the body loaded onto it. "Let's have a report as soon as you can."

The man in white thought about it for a moment, nodded. "Maybe this will hold you over for awhile. From the looks of the hole in his belly, I'd say it was a pretty safe bet he didn't die of high blood pressure." He followed the covered stretcher out to the ambulance at the curb.

"Very funny fellow," Liddell opined.

"No funnier than the story you're telling, Liddell." The inspector caught him by the arm, led him out to the sidewalk where his limousine sat waiting. "This guy shot a guy, only the guy dies six months later from an auto accident. He knows he pumped the bullets into him, only there's no signs of gunshot scars." He stopped on the sidewalk, oblivious to the crowd of morbidly curious that had gathered. "That's supposed to make sense?" he growled. "Did he at least tell you why he was supposed to have killed this character?"

Liddell considered it for a moment, shook his head. "Not exactly. He just said Lee had ruined him. That he had to kill him."

"Now I suppose you're going to tell me this character he was supposed to have killed but didn't isn't really dead and got up off the slab in the morgue to kill him?"

"That would be a switch," Liddell conceded, "but the last I saw of Lee, he wasn't in any condition to do any traveling. Look, Inspector, I'd like a crack at breaking this one. I can, too, if you'll give me a break."

"Meaning?"

"Don't mention the fact that Terrell took me on. Just give out the story that a vagrant was found shot to death in a foundation excavation in the Village. Let me take it from there."

Herlehy scowled at him. "On one condition. I'm checking the files on this murder he's supposed to have committed. If there's one on the books, no deal. If he was just dreaming the whole thing, you're welcome to it."

"It's a deal. He was supposed to have knocked off this Lee character six months ago. In September. If there's an open file, I keep hands off and let the department handle it. If there isn't, I get first crack at it."

5.

Stanton 7-6770 turned out to be the telephone number of a little night club called the Club Canopy on Perry Street, two blocks south of where Abel Terrell's body had been found. It was 10:30 by the time Johnny Liddell arrived there. He stood across the street, studied the outside of the club.

A neon sign that sputtered fitfully and dyed the facade a dull red spelled out the name *Club Canopy*. The door was three steps up from the sidewalk, and opened into a small vestibule.

Liddell crossed the street, entered the club. The vestibule had been converted into a check room. Beyond lay the main dining room and bar, a huge room that had been constructed by knocking out all the walls on the floor.

He stood at the door and peered into the smoky opaqueness of the interior. Small tables, jammed with parties of four, were packed side by side in a small space bordering on the tiny square reserved for dancing. A thick pall of smoke hung over the entire room, swirling slowly and lazily in the draft from the opened door. The bar itself was long, well-filled. Liddell elbowed himself a place at the bar, turned to survey the room.

The bartender shuffled up, wiped the bar with a damp cloth that left oily circles.

"Bourbon and water," Liddell told him.

The bartender made a pretense of selecting a bottle from the back-bar, reaching under the bar for a glass and some ice. He poured about an ounce of the brown liquid into the glass, reached for the water.

"Better hit that again," Liddell told him.

He made the drink a double, softened it with a touch of water.

Liddell shoved a five at him. "Keep the change."

The bartender took a look at the corner of the bill, raised his eyebrows. "If you figure this buys you anything, but liquor in this joint, you're making a mistake."

Liddell tasted the bourbon, approved. "I'm looking for a friend of mine." Quickly he described Abel Terrell, waited while the bartender screwed his mouth up in concentration. "Have you seen him or his friend lately?"

The bartender blew out his lips, shook his head. "He don't register. He's no regular around here." He squinted into the dimness of the room. "Maybe Ed Carter can help you. He's the maître d'. He gets to know a lot of people I don't ever see." He looked longingly at the bill. "Still go?"

Liddell nodded, watched the bartender shuffle off to the cash register. He happily dumped some silver and a few bills into the glass on the back bar, nodded his thanks to Liddell.

After a moment, a heavy man in a blue suit stopped alongside Liddell. "Can I help you, sir? Mike tells me you're waiting for someone."

Liddell swung around, studied the newcomer. His face was heavy, his lips wet and pouting. His hair was almost white, combed in a three-quarter part. His eyes were expressionless black discs almost hidden in the shadow of fierce white eyebrows. In his lapel he wore a carnation.

"I expected to meet a friend of mine here. His name's Abel Terrell." Liddell fancied he caught a flicker in the eyes, but there was no other change of expression in the fat man's face. "Do you know him?"

The fat man pursed his lips. Little bubbles formed in the middle of them. He shook his head, waggling the heavy jowls that hung over his collar. "I can't say I do. Could you describe him for me?"

Liddell tried to paint a word picture of the dead man as he might have appeared before he lost weight.

The fat man nodded slowly as Liddell finished his description. "I believe I do know your friend by sight." His head continued to bob in agreement. "He was a great admirer of our Miss Patti. You've heard Miss Patti, of course?"

Liddell shook his head. "I don't get around much."

The fat lips were wreathed in a smile that did nothing to change the expression in the man's eyes. "Then you have a treat in store. Miss Patti comes on in a few minutes. I'm sure she'll be glad to see you in her dressing room after the show." He nodded to Liddell, moved down the bar. Several times he stopped for a brief visit with one of his older customers. Finally, he reached the end of the bar, disappeared into the dimness beyond.

Liddell was on his second double bourbon when the floor lights went down. The band struggled hopelessly with a fanfare, a spotlight cut the gloom of the room, picked out the waspwaisted figure of the master of ceremonies as he fluttered across the floor to the microphone. He told a few off-color jokes, sang two choruses of an old song in a nasal whine, held his hands up to stem the non-existent applause.

"And now what you've all been waiting for—the sweetheart of Greenwich Village, Miss Patti!"

The bartender shuffled down to where Liddell sat, took up his station behind him. "This gal is all woman. An awful waste in a joint like this, but she really packs a message," he whispered.

On the floor two men were wheeling out a baby grand. A pasty-faced man with aggressively curly hair and a wet smear for a mouth materialized from nowhere and took his place at the piano. His fingers jumped from key to key until the first bars of a torchy tune became recognizable. The backdrop curtains parted and a blonde stepped out into the spotlight.

She was tall. Thick, metallic golden hair cascaded down over her shoulders in shimmering waves. Her body was ripe, lush. A small waist hinted at the full rounded hips and long shapely legs concealed by the fullness of the gown.

The rumble of conversation died down to a whisper, glasses stopped jangling and waiters froze as she leaned back against the piano. Her voice was husky, the kind that raised the small hairs on the back of Liddell's neck.

The lyrics of her song were blue and off color, but she managed to retain an expression of untroubled innocence. At the end of two numbers, she bowed to a burst of applause, permitted herself to be coaxed into one encore. At the end of that number she refused to be persuaded to do more, turned and went to the backstage door.

Liddell drained his glass, set it back on the bar. An adagio team was just making its appearance on the floor when he reached the end of the bar. He reached the backstage door, started to pull it open when a hand caught him by the arm.

"You're going in the wrong direction, mister," a heavy voice told him. "The men's room's at the other end." The owner of the hand and voice was heavy-shouldered, and the twisted nose and scar tissue over the eyes identified him as a bouncer.

"That's all right, Stanley." The fat figure of Carter, the manager, materialized in the gloom. "The gentleman's a friend of Miss Patti."

"You told me nobody gets in there," the big man grumbled.

"I don't like nobody bothering Patti." He glowered at Liddell. "I'm looking after her. Nobody gets fresh with her. You follow me, friend?"

"Nobody's going to bother Miss Patti, Stanley," the fat man told him firmly. "This gentleman is a friend. Miss Patti will be glad to see him."

The bouncer shuffled his feet uncertainly for a moment, then turned and shuffled off.

"A very difficult man, Stanley." Carter smelled at the carnation in his buttonhole. "Entirely devoted to Miss Patti. A dog-like devotion, you might say." The flat eyes studied Liddell over the carnation.

Stepping through the door to backstage was like stepping into a new world. The tinsel and glamor of the Club Canopy frontside wasn't duplicated backstage. There was nothing but a long, bare, semi-dark corridor with a row of closed doors, and an odor compounded of equal parts of perspiration and perfume.

He stopped in front of a door on which had been stenciled *Miss Patti* and knocked. A throaty voice invited him in.

The blonde sat on a straight-backed chair in front of a littered make-up table. Her thick blonde hair had been pushed back from her face, caught with blue ribbon and allowed to cascade down her back. She wore a matching light blue dressing gown.

She looked up as Liddell walked in. Her eyes were the bluest he had ever seen, her mouth soft and moist. She looked him over, made no attempt to disguise her approval of the heavyset shoulders, the thick hair spiked with grey and the humorous half-grin.

"Well, who are you?" Her speaking voice was husky, intimate.

"A friend of Abel Terrell's. He asked me to meet him here tonight." He checked the watch on his wrist. "He's late. I thought maybe you might know where he was."

The blonde pursed her lips, shook her head. "I haven't seen Abel in months." She lowered her voice. "He had some kind of trouble and had to go away." She turned the full impact of her eyes on him. "Is it safe for him to show his face around? I wouldn't want anything to happen to him."

Liddell found two cigarettes, lighted both, passed one to her. "When he called me, he said he had everything straightened out. He wanted me to bring him some money."

The blonde took a deep drag of the cigarette, let the smoke drift from between half-parted lips. "I'm glad for him if everything is all right." She studied Liddell's face through the eddying smoke. "Didn't he say what he wanted the money for?"

"I didn't ask." He rolled his cigarette between his thumb and forefinger. "He did mention it had something to do with a man named Lee. Do you know anybody named Lee that was connected with Abel?"

The soft lips framed the name, after a moment the girl shook her head. "I don't think so. I've never heard Abel mention the name to the best of my recollection."

Liddell nodded, raked his fingers through his hair. "I had the feeling the money was for Lee. Abel was very secretive about it, wouldn't even tell me where he'd been for the past few months."

The girl held her finger against her lips, cocked her head prettily. Then she got up, opened the dressing room door a crack. There was no one in the corridor. "We can't talk here. These walls are like paper." She walked back, stood close to Liddell. "Maybe Abel saw someone or something that frightened him away."

"Well, how am I going to contact him to let him know I have the money?" He studied the girl's face. "Do you know where to reach him?"

She turned, walked to the dressing table, picked up a comb, ran it through her hair. "I wouldn't do anything that might hurt Abel."

"But you do know how to contact him?"

She dropped the comb, swung around, leaned back on the table. "How do I know that Abel really wants to see you? How do I know that you're not the man he's hiding from?"

Liddell grinned. "A good question. Ask him."

"And who are you?"

"He'll know. Just tell him Johnny."

"Just Johnny?" The blonde pursed her lips humorously. "Don't I get to know the full name?"

"After you've checked with Abel and satisfied yourself I'm a right guy, maybe we'll get to know each other well enough that the only name you'll need will be Johnny."

The blue eyes swept him from head to feet and back. "Could be."

"How long will it take you to reach him?"

"I don't know. But I'm through here at 2:30. I'm sure I'll be able to reach him by then. Why can't we meet then."

Liddell nodded. "I'll pick you up here at 2:30."

"We can't talk here. Make it at my place at three. Apartment 2A, 28 Dyson Street—just about four blocks from here. Do you know where it is?"

Liddell shook his head. "I'll find it. I'll be there at three on the dot."

6.

The clerk in the outside office at headquarters told Johnny Liddell that Inspector Herlehy couldn't be disturbed. He let himself be talked into checking with the inspector himself, plugged in the inter-office phone, muttered into it. He nodded, flipped off the switch.

"I guess he'll see you." He sounded impressed.

Herlehy was sitting on the side of the leather couch in his office, running his fingers through his hair. He was yawning when Liddell walked in.

"You keep the damnedest hours," he complained. "I thought you'd be home in bed by now." He got up, walked over to the sink in the corner, slapped cold water into his face.

"How about it? Find a homicide for September in the name of Lee?"

The inspector dried his face on a towel, hung it on a nail next to the sink. "Nope. But we did find that Terrell did a runout just about that time. Dug up his old secretary. He gave her three months' salary, told her to close the office. She hasn't heard from him since."

Liddell dropped into a chair. "The only way she's likely to now is if she uses an ouija board." He watched the inspector run a comb through his thick white hair. "How about the guy in the morgue?"

Herlehy grunted, stamped back to his desk. "Dennis Leeman. Did time in Chicago for extortion, wanted in L. A. on the same charge." He punched the button on the base of his phone.

"Coffee?"

"Black," Liddell nodded.

A uniformed cop stuck his head in the doorway.

"Two coffees, one black, Ray," Herlehy told him. He waited until the cop had withdrawn his head. "Makes it screwier than ever. Suppose this Lee or Leeman was shaking Terrell for something. Okay, so Terrell knocks him off. That fits. Only trouble is Terrell didn't knock him off."

"Terrell thought he did. He held the rod right against Lee's chest. Saw the blood running from his mouth, he says."

Herlehy drummed on the edge of his desk with his fingers. "You saw the body. Not a mark of a bullet wound." He explored the stubble along his chin with the tips of his fingers. "You don't think this Terrell guy was off his rocker?"

Liddell shrugged. "It could be."

The door opened, the uniformed cop walked in with two containers of coffee, deposited them on the desk. "The black's got a penciled X on the cap," he told them.

Liddell snagged the container, waited until the cop had closed the door after him. "One thing's for sure. Terrell got an awful jolt when he saw Lee's picture in the paper. He got another one when he read the item about the body being identified." He gouged the top out of the container, tested the coffee, burned his tongue and swore at it. "He made two calls. One was to me, the other to a night club in the Village called the Canopy."

An ugly red flush started up from the inspector's collar. "Then you were holding out on me—"

Liddell shook his head. "He didn't reach anybody there. He called about three and the joint doesn't open until eight. I caught the early show in there tonight. Terrell was mixed up in some way with a girl singer named Patti. I've got a date with her at three at her place."

Herlehy carefully removed the top from his coffee, stirred it with his finger. "What do you expect to find out?"

Liddell rolled the warm container between his palms. "I don't know. But it's a cinch the solution to Terrell's murder is down there someplace. He was killed on Perry Street. The Club Canopy's on Perry Street and the girl has an apartment right across from the north end of the excavation where he was killed."

A tight look creased a V between the inspector's brows. He sipped at his coffee, made concentric circles on his blotter with the wet bottom of the container. "I don't know if I have the right to let you go this alone, Liddell," he said finally. "This is homicide and it's a matter for the department. Suppose you turn in everything you have on it—"

"That ain't cricket, inspector. We made a deal."

Herlehy nodded. "I know. But what you said sounded so screwy I never figured it would stand up." .

He took another deep swallow out of the container. "I'm going to have to go back on my word, Liddell. I never had the authority to make any deal like that."

"Give me until morning," Liddell urged. "You can't get the ball rolling until then, anyway. Just give me until morning, then throw the whole thing into the homicide hopper."

Herlehy hesitated, nodded. "Okay. You've got until Lt. Gleason comes on at eight. After that, you'd better keep out of his way. He doesn't like amateurs messing around on his preserves."

7.

Dyson Court was a square block away from Perry Street in the Village. 28 fronted on the back end of the excavation where Terrell's body had been found. The cab dropped Liddell in front of a brownstone building, he ran up the short flight of steps from the street and pushed his way through the vestibule door. A row of mail boxes in the vestibule contributed the information that Patti Marks occupied Apartment 2A.

The hallway was dark, smelled of ancient cooking and old age. He felt his way along the wall to the stairs, climbed slowly to the second floor. Apartment 2A was second floor front. He knocked softly, waited for some sound from within. He checked his watch, noticed it was only 2:45, knocked again. There was still no answer. He tried the doorknob, found the door locked. The lock yielded with a minimum of struggle to the strip of celluloid he carried in his pocket. He stepped in, closed the door behind him. The room was in darkness. He stood still, waited until his eyes were accustomed to the dark. There was no sound in the apartment other than his own breathing.

He felt his way across the room, lit the lamp on the table next to the couch, sank onto it. His watch said 2:48.

It was almost three when he heard the sound of a key in the lock. The door swung open, the blonde stood framed in the doorway. Behind her loomed the broad shoulders of the ex-pug bodyguard, Stanley.

Stanley pushed the girl aside. His eyes were small, mean.

"What are you doing here?" he growled deep in his chest. "I told you I wouldn't let anyone bother Miss Patti."

He shuffled toward Liddell flat-footedly. When he reached the chair, he caught the detective by the lapels, pulled him to his feet. Liddell broke the hold with an upward and outward swing of his arms and smashed his toe into the big man's instep. The bodyguard grunted with pain, dropped his guard. Liddell sunk his right into the big man's middle, chopped down against the side of his neck with his right. The bodyguard hit the floor face first and didn't move.

The blonde stood frozen, tried to swallow her fist. She looked from Liddell to the unconscious man and back. She closed the door, leaned against it. "You were wonderful. I've never seen anybody take Stanley before." She walked over, knelt next to the prizefighter. "He means well. He's the most devoted friend I've ever had." She looked up at Liddell. "I didn't know you were here or I wouldn't have brought him up. He feels better when he brings me right to the door, and since it looked as though you hadn't arrived—"

Liddell nodded. "I understand." He looked down at the unconscious man. "He's gotten soft from tossing helpless drunks out of the club, I guess."

Patti was staring at him with a puzzled frown. "By the way, how did you get in here?"

"The door was open. I thought you left it that way for me, so I came in and got comfortable."

The blonde walked over to the door, pulled it open, examined the latch. "Funny. I guess it didn't catch." Her eyes went down to the man on the floor. "What do we do about him?"

"He'll be all right in a minute. I'll take care of him." He caught the big man under the arms, dragged him to an armchair, dumped him into it. "It might help if you had some smelling salts."

Patti nodded, headed for the bedroom. As soon as the door had closed behind her, Liddell fanned the unconscious man, found him unarmed. He wiped the perspiration from his upper lip with the back of his hand, waited for the girl's return.

After minutes, the door to the bedroom opened. The blonde had changed from her street dress to a pale blue negligee. The blonde hair had been loosened, permitted to cascade down over her shoulders. "I made myself more comfortable," she said. "I hope you don't mind."

Stanley started to cough and gag his way back to consciousness. At first his head rolled uncontrollably, he seemed to have difficulty in focusing his eyes. After a moment, he was able to hold his head up, fix Liddell with a malevolent glare. A thin stream of saliva glistened from the corner of his mouth down his chin.

The Best of *Manhunt*

"He hit me when I wasn't ready." His voice was thick, strangled. He tried weakly to struggle to his feet, let the blonde push him back into the chair.

"You don't understand, Stanley. He's a friend of mine. He isn't bothering me. I asked him to meet me here." She explained it patiently, as though to a child. "He's my friend. He won't hurt me. Do you understand?"

The big man tried to nod. He struggled to his feet with the help of the blonde. She led him to the door, through to the stairway.

When she came back, Liddell was on the couch, a cigarette between his lips. "You're quite a man, mister." She leaned against the door, studied him speculatively. "Who are you, really?"

"A friend of Abel's. Didn't he tell you?"

The blonde walked over to where he sat, lifted the cigarette from between his fingers, took a deep drag. "I couldn't reach him. You don't mind waiting?"

Liddell grinned at her. "I'll struggle through it."

The blonde returned his cigarette, walked over to a curtained alcove that hid the kitchenette, brought back a bottle and some ice. "We may as well be comfortable." She set the ice and brandy down on a small end table, dropped onto the couch beside him. "I'm surprised I haven't heard from Abel by now," she pouted. "It must be that he's afraid of Lou."

Liddell reached past her, dropped ice into each of the glasses, drenched it down with brandy. "Who's Lou?"

The girl accepted a glass, swirled the liquid around the side. "My husband." She made a face, took a swallow of the brandy. "He's crazy. That's one of the reasons I have Stanley with me all the time. Lou would kill me, if he could lay his hands on me." She turned the full power of her eyes on Liddell over the rim of her glass. "Aren't you worried?"

"Why should I be? In the first place, I didn't know you were married. I'm here on business."

The girl stiffened, her eyes grew wide at the sound of a key in the lock. The door pushed open and a tall, thin man stood in the doorway, his hand sunk deep in his jacket pocket. When he grinned, it consisted merely of the peeling of his lips back from his discolored teeth. "I told you I'd catch you at it some night, baby," his voice was low, lethal. "I saw that punchdrunk bodyguard of yours leave. I've been waiting for you."

The blonde seemed to shrink back against the cushions. "Get out of here. You have no right in here, Lou."

The cold grin was back. "No right in my wife's apartment?"

The eyes hop-scotched from the girl to Liddell and back. "No jury would blame me for what I'm going to do."

The blonde licked at her lips. "You're crazy, Lou. You couldn't get away with it." She watched wide-eyed as the man shuffled closer.

"Before I do, I've got something for you." He stopped in front of the girl, slashed the back of his left hand across her cheek.

She moved with lightning speed. Her hand darted under a cushion, reappeared with an ugly short-snouted .38. Lou swung his hand in an arc, knocked her head to her right shoulder, back handed it into position.

The gun bounced out of her hand, fell to the floor at Liddell's feet.

"Stop him, Johnny, stop him. I can't take any more beatings. Kill him!"

Lou moved clumsily toward the gun, stopped as the private detective scooped it up, held it in his fist.

"Quick! Before he kills us both," the girl screamed.

"Anything to accommodate a lady." Liddell squeezed the trigger five times. The gun jumped in his hands as it belched flame. The other man seemed to stagger under the impact of the slugs. His mouth fell open, blood spurted from between his teeth, ran down his chin onto his shirt. He grabbed at his mid-section with bloodstained hands, fell forward.

8.

The blonde got up, tried to turn him over. She sank her hand into his pocket, looked up with stunned eyes. "He had no gun, Johnny. He was unarmed. It—it was murder."

Liddell stepped toward her. The blonde straightened up, backed away. "No, no, don't touch me." She buried her face in her hands, her shoulders shook.

"You wanted him dead, didn't you?"

The girl dropped her hands from her face. "But don't you understand? It's murder." She kept her eyes averted from the man on the floor. "The shots! The police will be here." She ran to the window, pulled back the curtain, looked out. "You'd better get out. Get out of town someplace where I can meet you." When he didn't move, she ran to him, caught his lapels, shook him. "Didn't you hear me? You've got to get out of here."

"What about him?"

The girl caught her lower lip between her teeth. "Stanley will take care of him. He's devoted to me, he'll do anything I say. But he hates you after what you did to him. You'd better not be here." She started pushing him to the door, stopped as if in an afterthought. "But I don't have any money—"

Liddell stuck his hand into his breast pocket, pulled out some bills. "Here. Here's a thousand. There's lots more where that came from."

The blonde wadded it, stuck it down the neck of her negligee. "Hurry. The police will be here!"

Liddell grinned at her. "You're psychic, baby. The police *are* here." He pulled open the door. Inspector Herlehy walked in. "Pretty good, eh, inspector?"

The color drained slowly from the girl's face. "What is this?"

Liddell ceremoniously turned over the gun to the inspector. "I shot that character on the floor five times at close range." He walked over to where the man lay, stirred him with his foot. "On your feet, Buster. It's time for the curtain call."

Lou struggled to his feet, glared at the girl. "I knew you'd pull it once too often," he growled. He was a macabre sight, his face and shirt stained blood-red.

"You'd better sit down," the inspector told him. "You've lost a lot of blood." He looked at Liddell, nodded. "You had the gimmick pegged. I haven't seen it used in years."

"Okay, so you made a fair pinch," the blonde turned her back, walked over to the end table, poured herself a drink, downed it neat. "I suppose the money was marked so you've got an attempted extortion rap." She looked at Liddell. "You still haven't told me who you are, mister."

"Johnny. Johnny Liddell. I'm the private eye Terrell hired this morning to help him out of this mess."

"A lot of good you did him," she snapped.

"Whose idea was the cackle bladder for shakedowns? Yours or Leeman's?"

"Come again?"

Liddell grinned at her. "That gimmick was old when you were in rompers, baby. The old-time con men used it to cool down a mark who started to yell copper. The inside man would provide a gun loaded with blanks, the con man would have the thin rubber bladder filled with chicken blood between his teeth. When he bit the bladder it gave the effect of hemorrhaging from the mouth."

"Okay, so you're real smart. It still only adds up to a year if you get the conviction."

"That's right. A year, and then they electrocute you, baby."

The blonde started. "What are you pulling?"

"How'd you know Terrell was dead?"

"I—the radio. You ought to listen to it once in a while. The midnight news, wise guy."

Liddell shook his head. "Terrell's identity wasn't given out to the papers. Only the killer could have known who he was." He looked to Herlehy. "Right, inspector?"

Herlehy nodded.

"No. You got it wrong. I didn't kill him. Stanley did. He—"

"Stanley might have strangled him or beaten him to death.

He would never have used a gun. Besides, it had to be someone Terrell trusted to get him to go down into that dark foundation. He was too scared to go down there with anyone but you."

"Why me?"

"He thought you had been taken in by Leeman, too. He was going to tell you about how Leeman hadn't died six months ago. Then he got wise, didn't he, that Leeman was only your stooge, that you were head of the shake racket."

The blonde sneered at him. "Okay, Rover boy, let's go. I want to find out whether it was a fit of temporary insanity or whether I was defending my honor."

Graveyard Shift
Steve Frazee

May 1953

Dozing in front of the microphone in the radio dispatcher's office, Joe Crestone blinked groggily when one of the heavy side doors downstairs whushed open and then started rocking back to center. Since midnight the building had been dead still.

The footsteps swung out briskly on the tiles of the lobby. They made quick taps on the steel steps leading up towards the dispatcher's room. Crestone was wide awake. The clock on the radio reeled up another minute. It was 2:17. He swung his chair to face the counter.

She was close to six feet. Her hair was dark, her eyes soft brown. She wore a fur jacket and under that a green woolen dress caught high at her neck with a silver clasp. Her smile was timid. "I—I thought Mr. Walters would be here again." She studied the work schedule of the Midway police department on the board.

"He's got the flu. It was my day off so I'm sitting in for him."

"I see." She stared at the maps on the wall. "I—I just don't know exactly how to start it."

She was white and scared. Crestone let her make up her mind. On the model side, he thought, the kind who pose in two thousand dollar dresses. Plenty of neck above the silver clasp, more gauntness in her face than he had observed at first.

"Hit and run deal?" he asked, eyeing her sharply.

Before she could answer, state patrol car 55 checked in from Middleton, eighteen miles north on Highway 315. A woman dispatcher in Steel City read a CAA flight plan to Bristol for relay to Cosslett. Webster came in with a pickup-and-hold on a 1949 blue Chev with three men. Crestone sent out the information on the pickup-and-hold.

When he swung to the log sheet in the typewriter at his left, she asked, "Do the state cars patrol the old highway from the boarded-up brick works east toward Steel City?"

"State 7? No, not unless there's a crash out there." He wrote a line on the log. "Did you have a wreck?"

She hesitated. "In a way."

He turned back to the desk and pulled a pad to him. "Name?"

"Judith Barrows."

"Address?"

When she did not answer he twisted his head to look at her. He looked into a snub-nosed .38. For one fractured moment the bore was big enough to shoot a golf ball. Crestone sucked in his breath.

"Give me the log sheet," she said. "Don't even brush your arm near the mike or you'll get it in the liver."

He stripped the log sheet from the machine and put it up on the counter. She drew it to her with long, thin fingers that bent into carmine-tipped hooks. "Now, a copy of the code sheet, and not the old one with blanks behind some of the numbers."

Crestone took a code sheet from a folder. When he put it on the counter he saw that she had shrugged out of her fur jacket. He heard the power hum and then Bud Moore said in his bored after-midnight voice, "Seven fifty." Crestone started to reach toward the microphone and then he stopped.

"Acknowledge it," she said softly.

He stared at the .38. She was resting her hand on the counter. The gun looked down at his midsection. He gripped the long bar of the mike switch on the stem of the instrument. Under *Transmit* on the face of the radio a purple button lit up like an evil eye glaring at him. "Seven fifty," he said, then automatically released his grip on the switch.

"Going 10-10 at Circle 7365," Moore said, which meant that he and Jerry Windoff were going out of service temporarily to get a cup of coffee at the Mowhawk Diner out on Sterling Pike.

Crestone's mind froze on 10-10: *report back to this office*. But then she would read it on the code sheet and—His head rocked sidewise. His left elbow jammed against the typewriter. There was a thin crack of tension in her voice when she said, "Answer the car, Buster."

He was still half stunned from the crack on his head when he said, "Seven fifty, 10-4." *Okay, 750*.

"Give me the local code sheet now, Crestone."

He gave that to her. It held sixteen messages for local use, and then there were four blanks. She said, "Don't get any ideas about using Code 17 or any other blank."

Code 17 was unlisted, strictly a private deal between Bill Walters and all cruiser cops: *bring me a hamburger and a jug of coffee*. She had found out plenty from old Bill, a friendly, trusting guy who liked to talk about his work.

"Face the radio, Crestone. Don't worry about me."

He turned around, staring at a transmitter which controlled all law enforcement in the area. It was worthless unless he had the brains and guts to figure out something.

"Where's state patrol 54?" she asked.

"After a 10-47 on State 219." It was on the log; there was no use to lie. He heard papers rustle.

"That's right," she said. "Chasing a possible drunk. Keep everything you say right, Crestone, especially when you talk into that microphone."

The right-hand reel of the clock put up three more minutes. Now it was 2:25. She made no sound behind him. After another minute he could not stand it any longer. He had to look around. She was still there. The gun was still there too, slanted over the edge of the counter.

"Face the radio."

He hesitated, and then while he was turning, the gun bounced off his head again. He sucked air between his teeth and cursed. For a tick of time his anger was almost enough to make him try to lunge up and reach her; but his sanity was greater. She struck him again, sweeping the barrel of the gun on the slope of his skull.

"Don't curse me!" she said.

After a foggy interval Crestone was aware of the messages coming from both channels. Two stolen cars from Bristol. He added them to a list of twenty others stolen that day. Steel City sent a car to investigate a prowler complaint. Seventy miles away state patrol car 86 stopped to pull a dead pig off the highway. The dispatcher in Shannon sent a car to a disturbance at Puddler's Casino. York asked Webster for a weather report on Highway 27.

Then there was just the hum of the radio and the silence at his back. Where was it, one of the banks? No, blowing vaults was a worn-out racket. A payroll at one of the mills or at the automobile assembling plant? Wrong time of week. Besides, that stuff went from the banks by armored cars in daytime.

At the other end of the narrow slot where he was trapped there was a desk, a big steel filing cabinet, and a rack with four sawed-off shotguns. The shells were in a drawer in the bottom of the rack. In another steel cabinet that he could almost reach with his right hand were five pistols and enough ammunition to last a year.

The whole works was as useless now as the radio.

Car 54 asked Shannon for an ambulance at the cloverleaf on State 219. "Two dead, two injured. Didn't catch up with the *dk* soon enough."

"What's *dk?*" Judith Barrows asked quickly.

"Drunk." Crestone's head was aching. "Car 54 will be back here in about an hour. He'll come in to write a report." That was not so, but Crestone wanted to judge her reaction to the time. He leaned toward the radio and twisted his neck to look at her. The one-hour statement had not bothered her.

When he straightened up, he ducked quickly. She laughed. When he raised his head again the gun banged against it. He rolled his head, grinding curses under his breath.

Car 751 came in. Sam Kurowski said, "Any traffic? We've been out of the car a few minutes."

"Where are they?" the woman asked.

Crestone pressed the mike switch.

"10-20, 751?"

"Alley between Franklin and Madison on Tenth Avenue."

When the transmitting light was off she said, "Code 6 them to the corner—the southeast corner—of River and Pitt."

Code 6 was boy trouble, kids yelling, throwing rocks—any of a hundred things. They could spot a cruiser a mile away. When Kurowski and Corky Gunselman got way out north on River and Pitt and found nothing, they would think nothing of it. Crestone followed the woman's orders.

Car 752 came alive. Dewey Purcell said, "Going east on Washington at Sixth Street after *dk*. Give me a 10-28 on K6532."

That does it, Crestone thought. Purcell was hell on drunken drivers. He and Old McGlone would be coming in with a prisoner in about five minutes.

"Give him the registration he asked for, Crestone."

He pulled the vehicle registration book to him. *K6532, 1953 Cadillac cpe., maroon, J. J. Britton, 60 Parkway.* Jimmy Britton, the Hill itself. Damnation! You didn't dump guys like him in the tank overnight; but he took hope from knowing that Purcell was in 752 tonight.

"Give him the 10-28, Buster."

"When they stop. Old McGlone can hardly write, let alone in a car doing eighty after a stinking *dk.*"

Purcell called again from Washington and Trinity. "We got him." A woman's shrill voice came from the background before the car mike was closed. Crestone gave Purcell the registration information.

Crestone stared at the radio. Jimmy Britton would be drunk, affable, mildly surprised at being picked up. Among other things, when he fumbled out his driver's license, he would show his honorary membership in the Midway Police Department. Old McGlone would say, "Ah now, Dewey, let's take the lad home, shall we? No harm's been done, has it?"

But Purcell was tough and he did not give a damn for the social register and he hated drunken drivers. Crestone had been the same way too, and now he was working for a year as a dispatcher.

It was Old McGlone who spoke the next time. "We'll be going up the hill now to 60 Parkway."

No lucky breaks tonight, Crestone thought. Tomorrow he would think of a dozen things he could have done, and every man out there in the cars would do the same. That was tomorrow. The gun was behind him now. She could reach him when he swung, and she could not miss if she shot.

There was a drawer in the desk full of stories of tough private-eyes who took bushels of guns away from dames clad in almost nothing, and then slapped them all over the joint or made love to them. Joe Crestone sighed. His head was aching brutally. He did not feel like taking any guns away from any dames.

Car 750 came back into service. Moore and Windoff had drunk their coffee. Then 752 went out of service temporarily at the Sunset Drive Inn. Crestone knew how Purcell was feeling now, the to-hell-with-it attitude. Old McGlone would be telling him, "There's some things, Dewey boy, that you've got to learn about being a cop." Old McGlone knew them all.

Car 751 signalled arrival at River and Pitt. A few minutes later Kurowski said, "10-98." *Assignment completed.* There was no use to elaborate on nothing.

Judith Barrows said, "Send 751 to the Silver Moon on Oldtown Pike to look for a '49 green Ford sedan with front-end damage."

Crestone obeyed. He studied the map. She wanted 751 north and east all the time. Then where in the southern or southeastern part of Midway was any heavy money? There was a brawl at the Riverview country club tonight, maybe a few thousand loose in pockets and a handful of jewelry, but—

The phone at Crestone's elbow and the extension on the desk near the big filing cabinet spilled sound all over the room.

"Don't touch it until I say so!" the woman said.

She went around the counter and backed into the chair at the other desk. She crossed her legs and steadied the .38 on her knee. She raised the phone and nodded.

"Police station, radio dispatcher," Crestone said.

"Ten cents, please," the operator said.

Crestone heard the pay phone clear. A man asked, "You got a report on State 312?"

"Just a minute." Crestone had never heard of 312.

"Just tell him it's all clear, Buster." Judith Barrows was holding the mouthpiece against her thigh.

"All clear." Crestone held on to hear a jukebox, the clatter of a café—anything to help position the call. The man hung up. A booth, Crestone thought. He put his phone down, staring at the woman's legs. They were beautiful. He did not give a damn. She got up carefully, standing for a moment in a hip-out-of-joint posture. A model, he thought. It was in her walk too when she went around the counter again.

So they knew this end of it was set now. Where was the other end? Somewhere in the southern part of the district covered in normal patrol by Car 751. Anybody could read the red outlines on the map. It struck him then: the Wampum Club. Big business, cold and sure, with a fine patina of politeness, free drinks, free buffet and other incidentals for the regular suckers. The green-and-crackly on the line at Sonny Belmont's Wampum Club. Let the cops take Jimmy Britton home and tuck him in, but Belmont never took his check, drunk or otherwise.

The job would take at least four fast, tough men. Making Sonny's boys hold still for a deal like that was not for amateurs. There was a lot of dough around the Wampum; the income tax lads had been wondering how much for a long time.

So I think I've got it doped, and what good does it do? Belmont could stand the jolt. Why should men like Corky Gunselman and Sam Kurowski risk catching lead to protect money in a joint like the Wampum?

That was not the answer and Crestone knew it.

He looked at the last two stolen cars on the list. A '52 blue Mercury and a '53 green Hornet. That Hudson would go like hell and the Mercury was not so slow either. Both cars stolen around midnight in Bristol. He wondered which one was outside right now. He could be way off, but he had to figure he was right.

Since the Hornet and the Merc were already aired as hot, they would probably be used only to make the run to another car stashed close. East was the natural route. Old State 7 was narrow and twisting, but the farmers who used it would all be sleeping now. Say a half hour to reach the web of highways around Steel City, and then road blocks would be no more than something to annoy whiz kids on their way home with the old man's crate. She had asked about State 7.

Car 751 came in. Kurowski said, "Nothing at the Silver Moon with front-end damage. What's the dope on it?"

"Code 4," Judith Barrows said. "The Ford was last seen going north on Pennsylvania at Third Avenue."

Code 4, *hit and run.* Crestone obeyed the .38.

Kurowski said, "10-4. We'll swing up that way."

She was keeping 751 north, sure enough. The phone exploded. Judith Barrows went around the counter again to the extension. She nodded.

From the background of a noisy party a man said, "Somebody swiped my car." A woman shouted. "Tell 'em it's even paid for!"

Crestone wrote down the information. A '52 cream Cadillac sedan, R607, taken sometime between 12:30 A.M. and 1:30 A.M. "It was right in the damned driveway," the owner complained. "We're having a little party here and—"

"Keys in it?" Crestone asked.

"Sure! It was in my own driveway."

"We'll get on it right away." Crestone hung up.

The woman said, "You won't put *that* one out, Buster."

So he was guessing right. They had a cream Cad waiting. If they planned to use State 7, the quick run for the crew at the Wampum was up the county road past the country club and then on out Canal to where it intersected across the river with State 7 near the old brick plant. Barrows could shoot straight north on Meredith to Glencoe, turn east—Why hell, she would strike State 7 just a hundred yards from the old brick works. The Cad was waiting out there now!

She was behind him once more. As if she had read his thoughts she asked, "What's in your little round head now, Buster?"

"I'm wishing you'd beat it."

She laughed but there were little knots of tension in the sound. The deal must be on at the Wampum now. Before she left she would have to level him. She would swing lower and harder then. The thought made Crestone's headache worse. He hoped she knew the bones on the side of a man's skull couldn't take it like the thick sloping top. She might stretch him so he never got up. He could smell his own sweat.

Before the clincher came he would have to run a test on her. The next time she was in the chair.

One of the side doors made a whushing sound and then a voice boomed across the lobby. "Hey there, Bill, how's the peace and dignity of the community?" It was old Fritz Hood on his way home from the power company's substation. He always stopped to bellow at Bill Walters.

"Hello, Fritz!"

"You, Joey! Where's Bill tonight?"

"Sick."

"The old bastard! I'll go see him before he dies." The door rocked back to center. Hood was gone.

Judith Barrows was in the chair, with her jacket across her lap and the code sheets on the desk. Crestone rose slowly. The fur jacket slid away and showed the .38. Something dropped out of one of the jacket sleeves. He made another step. She tilted the muzzle, resting the edge of her hand on her knee. She cocked the gun then. Her face was white.

Crestone tried to talk himself into it; but he knew she was too scared. An excited or scared dame with a gun. Murder. He backed up and sat down. His head was pounding. On the floor at her feet lay a piece of doubled wire, the raw ends covered with white tape.

The phone sang like a rattlesnake. The woman made a nervous stab at it before she gained control and nodded at Crestone. Mrs. John Slenko, 3648 Locust, had just seen a man in her back yard. She wanted the police.

Judith Barrows' vigilance wavered while she was fumbling her phone back into the cradle. Crestone used his phone to push the *Gain* dial of the radio down to *One* while he was putting the instrument away. He dispatched 750 to Mrs. Slenko's home.

The big dame was in a knot now and Crestone was coming out of it. She had grabbed at the phone because she was expecting a call to tell her that the job at the Wampum was done. She was staying in the chair to be near the phone.

When York and Shannon began to talk about a revoked driver's license, the sounds came faintly.

"What did you do to the radio!"

"Nothing."

The .38 was on his stomach. "What did you do?"

"Nothing, damn it! We get a split-phase power lag on the standby tower every night." He hoped she knew as little of radio as he did. "The reception fades, that's all."

"You're lying! You did something, didn't you?"

"No! You've been watching me every second."

"You're going to get it, Crestone, if anything goes wrong." She was wound-up but the gun was easy.

Car 752 came in, so faint that only "seven-fift'" was audible, but Crestone knew Purcell's voice and he could guess the message. Purcell had sulked in the Sunset Drive Inn, dwelling on the inequalities of traffic code enforcement, but now he and Old McGlone were on their way again.

The woman's voice was a whip crack. "What was it?"

"I'll have to get it on the other mike."

"What other mike?"

Crestone kept his finger close to his chest when he pointed. "On a hook around at the side of the radio."

The faint call came again.

"All right," Judith Barrows said.

There was dust on the curled lead of the hand mike. Crestone said, "Car 750, I read you 10-1. The standby trouble again, as usual." 10-1 meant: *receiving poorly.* From the corner of his eye he saw the woman grab the code sheet to check on him.

Car 750, which had not called, now tried to answer at the same time 752 came in. Crestone said, "Standby, 751. 10-6." *Busy.* Now he had them all confused. He called for a repeat from Car 750 to make it more confused. During the instant Judith Barrows was checking the code number he had used, he turned transmitting power to almost nothing.

Faint murmurs came from the radio as the three local cars asked questions Crestone could not hear. The woman did not like her loss of contact. She got out of her chair. "Where's 751?" she demanded.

Into a dead mike Crestone asked the location of the car. He pretended to hear the answer from the receiver against his ear. "He's trailing a green Ford toward the Wampum Club."

"Get him away from there!" She was panicked for a moment and then she got hold of herself. She grabbed the local code sheet. "Code 9 him to the Silver Moon."

Code 9 was a disturbance. Crestone went through the pretense of calling 751. There was still enough flow of power to light the purple eye.

"Tell him to disregard the Ford," she ordered.

"10-22 previous assignment, 751. Code 9 at the Silver Moon."

When the next small scratch of sound came from the speaker, he said, "Midway, Car 55. Go ahead." He began to write as if he were taking a message: *'52 cream Cadillac sedan, R607, State 7 near old brick plant. Driver resisted arrest.*

She came out of her chair. "What's that message?"

"Car 55 just picked up a guy in a stolen car near the brick works."

It struck her like death. "Give me that paper!"

He tossed it toward her. She raked it in with her heel, and picked it up without taking her eyes off him. She read it at a glance and cursed.

The phone rang. She had it without making her signal to Crestone. He lifted his receiver. A tense voice said, "All set here."

"No!" she cried. "The state patrol just got Brownie and the car!"

"You sure?"

"It just came in on the radio."

"The other way then. You're on your own, kid, till you know where." The man hung up.

Crestone said into the hand mike, "10-4, Car 750." He swung to face the woman when she went around the counter. "Car 750 is four blocks away, coming in."

She raised the gun. "They're coming in," he said. A man might have done it. She broke. It was her own safety now. Her heels made quick taps on the steel steps, a hard scurrying on the lobby tiles.

Crestone loaded the shotgun as he ran. The blue Mercury was at the first meter south of the police parking zone. She spun her wheels on the gutter ice and then the sedan lurched into the street. He put the muzzle on the right front window. Her face was a white blur turned toward him. He could not do it. He shot, instead, at the right rear tire and heard the shot rattle on the bumper.

He raced back to the radio and put the dials where they belonged. He poured it out then in crisp code. All cars, all stations. First, a '53 green Hudson sedan, K2066, possibly four men in car. Left Wampum Club, Midway, two minutes ago. Armed robbery. Dangerous. Second, a '52 blue Mercury sedan, K3109, last seen going north on Meredith one minute ago, possibly shotgun marks on right rear fender.

The phone blasted. "This is Sonny Belmont, Bill. We've had some trouble down here. Four men in a late Hudson tudor, a light color. They cut toward town on Market. The license was a K2—something."

"K2066, a green '53 Hornet, Belmont."

"Who is this?"

"Crestone. What'd they look like?"

Belmont's descriptions were sharp. "I slipped, Joey. They nailed me opening the safe."

"How much?"

"About eighty grand." Belmont said the amount reluctantly. It would be in the papers and he knew it. "How'd you boys get hot so quick, Joey?"

"Luck." Crestone hung up. Car 750 reported that a speeding Hornet sedan had outrun the cruiser and was headed north on 315. Crestone sent that information to all cars north of Midway.

Car 752 came in. "We're on the blue Mercury with the woman," Purcell said. "She's got a flat rear tire."

"She's got a .38 too," Crestone said.

Three minutes later Purcell called from Glencoe and Pitt. "We got her. Car 751 is here with us."

Crestone dispatched Car 751 to the old brick works with the dope on a cream Cadillac sedan. Car 55 came in from Highway 315. "The green Hudson got past me, Midway. I'm turning now to go north. Tell Shannon."

The Shannon dispatcher said, "10-4 on that message, Midway." A moment later he was talking to a sheriff, and then state patrol 54 came in.

When the channels were clear again Crestone called Steel City to cover State 7 from the east, just in case. He called the police chief and the sheriff by telephone. The chief said he would be down at once. Crestone was still talking to the sheriff when Car 751 reported. "We got the cream Cadillac sedan at the brick plant," Kurowski said. "The guy scrammed into the weeds and took the keys with him."

The message went into the mouthpiece of the telephone. The sheriff said, "I'll be down there with a couple of boys in ten minutes." Crestone hung the phone up. He told Car 751 to stand by at the brick works.

Everything was set now. There would be a tough road block at the Y on State 20 and Highway 315. If the Hudson got around that, there would be trouble on ahead, piling up higher as more cars converged.

Crestone lit a cigarette. The phone rang. A man asked, "You got my car yet?"

"What car?"

"My Cadillac! My God, man! I just called you."

"The only stolen car in the world," Crestone said. "Yeah, we got it. You can pick it up at the police garage in the morning. Bring your registration and title and five bucks for towing charges."

"Towing! Is it hurt?"

"No keys."

"Oh," the man said. The party was still going on around him. "Look, officer, I've got an extra set of keys. If you'll send a car around—"

"Get it here in the morning."

"Okay then." The man hung up.

Crestone decided that his skull was breaking. He punched his cigarette out and tried to swallow the bad taste it had left in his mouth.

They brought her in, Purcell and Old McGlone. The tension was gone from her now; she looked beaten down and helpless.

"Cute kid." Purcell held up the .38. "She put a couple of spots on 752 by way of greeting us. Is the chief on his way?"

Crestone nodded. The woman looked at him and said, "I'm sorry I kept hitting you."

"Yeah."

"She was here?" Purcell asked. "She slugged you?"

"She did."

Old McGlone needed a shave as usual. He was staring at Judith Barrows. All at once he asked, "When did you leave Pulaski Avenue, Zelda Tuwin?"

Her eyes jerked up to Old McGlone's face. "Five years ago. It was raining."

"I remember you. You were a chubby kid, Zelda. You—"

"I was a big fat slob!"

"You been a dress model?" Crestone asked.

"Yeah! Big stuff! I got tired of parading in front of bitches and their men. I couldn't eat what I wanted to. I had to walk like I was made of glass. I got tired of it."

Old McGlone nodded. "Sure, sure. So you wanted to have the money like them you pranced in front of. You were doubtless making plenty yourself—for a kid from the Polish section of Midway. You'd have been better off staying on Pulaski and marrying a good boy from the mill, Zelda Tuwin."

Old McGlone looked sad and wistful. He never did want to believe the things he had been seeing for twenty-five years. He was tough but not hard. He understood and he deplored but he never could condemn. Zelda Tuwin watched him for several moments and seemed to recognize those things about him.

And then she stared at the floor.

The chief tramped in. Crestone gave him the story. The chief nodded, watching Zelda Tuwin. He tilted his head toward his office and clumped down the steps. Old McGlone and Purcell took her out, Purcell walking ahead. Old McGlone said, "Watch them steel steps there, Zelda."

After a while the sheriff's car came in. He had Brownie, who had tried to jump a canal and nearly drowned. Car 54 was on the air a moment later.

"We got the Hornet, Midway. Four men. What's the authority?"

"Midway PD. Bring 'em back, and everything they have with them."

"They got it too. Cars 55 and 86 are coming in with me."

Crestone sent out a cancellation on the two stolen cars. He could hear the chief talking to Zelda Tuwin downstairs. He knew how Old McGlone felt about some things there seemed to be no help for. It was 3:41 A.M.

Joe Crestone had a hell of a headache.

The Little Lamb
Fredric Brown

She didn't come home for supper, and by eight o'clock I found some ham in the refrigerator and made myself a sandwich. I wasn't worried, but I was getting restless. I kept walking to the window and looking down the hill toward town, but I couldn't see her coming. It was a moonlit evening, very bright and clear. The lights of the town were nice and the curve of the hills beyond, black against blue under a yellow gibbous moon. I thought I'd like to paint it, but not the moon; you put a moon in a picture and it looks corny, it looks pretty. Van Gogh did it in his picture "The Starry Sky," and it didn't look pretty; it looked frightening, but then again he was crazy when he did it; a sane man couldn't have done many of the things Van Gogh did.

I hadn't cleaned my palette so I picked it up and tried to work a little more on the painting I'd started the day before. It was just blocked in thus far, and I started to mix a green to fill in an area, but it wouldn't come right, and I realized I'd have to wait till daylight to get it right. Evenings, without natural light, I can work on line or I can mold in finishing strokes, but when color's the thing, you've got to have daylight. I cleaned my messed-up palette for a fresh start in the morning, and I cleaned my brushes, and it was getting close to nine o'clock, and still she hadn't come.

No, there wasn't anything to worry about. She was with friends somewhere, and she was all right. My studio is almost a mile from town, up in the hills; and there wasn't any way she could let me know because there's no phone. Probably she was having a drink with the gang at the Waverly Inn, and there was no reason she'd think I'd worry about her. Neither of us lived by the clock; that was understood between us. She'd be home soon.

There was half of a jug of wine left; and I poured myself a drink and sipped it, looking out the window toward town. I turned off the light behind me so I could better watch out the window at the bright night. A mile away, in the valley, I could see the lights of the Waverly Inn. Garish bright, like the loud jukebox that kept me from going there often. Strangely, Lamb never minded the jukebox, although she liked good music, too.

Other lights dotted here and there. Small farms, a few other studios. Hans Wagner's place a quarter of a mile down the slope from mine. Big, with a skylight; I envied him that skylight. But not his strictly academic style. He'd never paint anything quite as good as a color photograph; in fact, he saw things as a camera sees them and painted them without filtering them through the catalyst of the mind. A wonderful draftsman, never more. But his stuff sold; he could afford a skylight.

I sipped the last of my glass of wine, and there was a tight knot in the middle of my stomach. I didn't know why. Often Lamb had been later than this, much later. There wasn't any real reason to worry.

176   The Best of *Manhunt*

I put my glass down on the windowsill and opened the door. But before I went out, I turned the lights back on. A beacon for Lamb, if I should miss her. And if she should look up the hill toward home and the lights were out, she might think I wasn't there and stay longer, wherever she was. She'd know I wouldn't turn in before she got home, no matter how late it was.

Quit being a fool, I told myself; it isn't late yet. It's early, just past nine o'clock. I walked down the hill toward town and the knot in my stomach got tighter and I swore at myself because there was no reason for it. The line of the hills beyond town rose higher as I descended, pointing up the stars. It's difficult to make stars that look like stars. You'd have to make pinholes in the canvas and put a light behind it. I laughed at the idea—but why not? Except that it isn't done, and what did I care about that. But I thought awhile, and I saw why it wasn't done. It would be childish, immature.

I was about to pass Hans Wagner's place, and I slowed my steps thinking that just possibly Lamb might be there. Hans lived alone there and Lamb wouldn't, of course, be there unless a crowd had gone to Hans's from the inn or somewhere. I stopped to listen and there wasn't a sound, so the crowd wasn't there. I went on.

The road branched; there were several ways from here and I might miss her. I took the shortest route, the one she'd be most likely to take if she came directly home from town. It went past Carter Brent's place, but that was dark. There was a light on at Sylvia's place, though, and guitar music. I knocked on the door, and while I was waiting I realized that it was the phonograph and not a live guitarist. It was Segovia playing Bach, the Chaconne from the D-Minor Partita, one of my favorites. Very beautiful, very fine-boned and delicate, like Lamb.

Sylvia came to the door and answered my question. No, she hadn't seen Lamb. And no, she hadn't been at the inn, or anywhere. She'd been home all afternoon and evening, but did I want to drop in for a drink? I was tempted—more by Segovia than by the drink—but I thanked her and went on.

I should have turned around and gone back home instead, because for no reason I was getting into one of my black moods. I was illogically annoyed because I didn't know where Lamb was; if I found her now I'd probably quarrel with her, and I hate quarreling. Not that we do, often. We're each pretty tolerant and understanding—of little things, at least. And Lamb's not having come home yet was still a little thing.

But I could hear the blaring jukebox when I was still a long way from the inn, and it didn't lighten my mood any. I could see in the window now and Lamb wasn't there, not at the bar. But there were still the booths, and besides, someone might know where she was. There were two couples at the bar. I knew them: Charlie and Eve Chandler, and Dick Bristow with a girl from Los Angeles whom I'd met but whose name I couldn't remember. And one fellow, stag, who looked as though he was trying to look like a movie scout from Hollywood. Maybe he really was one.

I went in and, thank God, the jukebox stopped just as I went through the door. I went over to the bar, glancing at the line of booths; Lamb wasn't there.

I said, "Hi," to the four of them that I knew, and to the stag if he wanted to take it to cover him, and to Harry, behind the bar. "Has Lamb been here?" I asked Harry.

"Nope, haven't seen her, Wayne. Not since six; that's when I came on. Want a drink?"

I didn't, particularly; but I didn't want it to look as though I'd come solely for Lamb, so I ordered one.

"How's the painting coming?" Charlie Chandler asked me.

He didn't mean any particular painting and he wouldn't have known anything about it if he had. Charlie runs the local bookstore and—amazingly—he can tell the difference between Thomas Wolfe and a comic book, but he couldn't tell the difference between an El Greco and an Al Capp. Don't misunderstand me on that; I like Al Capp.

So I said, "Fine," as one always says to a meaningless question, and took a swallow of the drink that Harry had put in front of me. I paid for it and wondered how long I'd have to stay in order to make it not too obvious that I'd come only to look for Lamb.

For some reason, conversation died. If anybody had been talking to anybody before I came in, he wasn't now. I glanced at Eve and she was making wet circles on the mahogany of the bar with the bottom of a martini goblet. The olive stirred restlessly in the bottom and I knew suddenly that was the color, the exact color I'd wanted to mix an hour or two ago just before I'd decided not to try to paint. The color of an olive moist with gin and vermouth. Just right for the main sweep of the biggest hill, shading darker to the right, lighter to the left. I stared at the color and memorized it so I'd have it tomorrow. Maybe I'd even try it tonight when I got back home; I had it now, daylight or no. It was right; it was the color that had to be there. I felt good; the black mood that had threatened to come on was gone.

But where was Lamb? If she wasn't home yet when I got back, would I be able to paint? Or would I start worrying about her, without reason? Would I get that tightness in the pit of my stomach?

I saw that my glass was empty. I'd drunk too fast. Now I might as well have another one, or it would be too obvious why I'd come. And I didn't want people— not even people like these—to think I was jealous of Lamb and worried about her. Lamb and I trusted each other implicitly. I was curious as to where she was and I wanted her back, but that was all. I wasn't suspicious of where she might be. They wouldn't realize that.

I said, "Harry, give me a martini." I'd had so few drinks that it wouldn't hurt me to mix them, and I wanted to study that color, intimately and at close hand. It was going to be the central color motif; everything would revolve around it.

Harry handed me the martini. It tasted good. I swished around the olive and it wasn't quite the color I wanted, a little too much in the brown, but I still had the idea. And I still wanted to work on it tonight, if I could find Lamb. If she was there, I could work; I could get the planes of color in, and tomorrow I could mode them, shade them.

But unless I'd missed her, unless she was already home or on her way there, it wasn't too good a chance. We knew dozens of people; I couldn't try every place she might possibly be. But there was one other fairly good chance, Mike's Club, a mile down the road, out of town on the other side. She'd hardly have gone there unless she was with someone who had a car, but that could have happened. I could phone there and find out.

I finished my martini and nibbled the olive and then turned around to walk over to the phone booth. The wavy-haired man who looked as though he might be from Hollywood was just walking back toward the bar from the jukebox, and it was making preliminary scratching noises. He'd dropped a coin into it, and it started to play something loud and brassy. A polka, and a particularly noisy and obnoxious one. I felt like hitting him one in the nose, but I couldn't even catch his eye as he strolled back and took his stool again at the bar. And anyway, he wouldn't have known what I was hitting him for. But the phone booth was just past the jukebox and I wouldn't hear a word, or be heard, if I phoned Mike's.

A record takes about three minutes, and I stood one minute of it and that was enough. I wanted to make that call and get out of there, so I walked toward the booth and I reached around the jukebox and pulled the plug out of the wall. Quietly, not violently at all. But the sudden silence was violent, so violent that I could hear, as though she'd screamed them, the last few words of what Eve Chandler had been saying to Charlie Chandler. Her voice pitched barely to carry above the din of brass—but she might as well have used a public address system once I'd pulled the jukebox's plug.

"—may be at Hans's." Bitten off suddenly, as if she'd intended to say more.

Her eyes met mine and hers looked frightened.

I looked back at Eve Chandler. I didn't pay any attention to Golden Boy from Hollywood; if he wanted to make anything of the fact that I'd ruined his dime, that was his business and he could start it. I went into the phone booth and pulled the door shut. If that jukebox started again before I'd finished my call, it would be my business, and I could start it. The jukebox didn't start again.

I gave the number of Mike's, and when someone answered, I asked, "Is Lamb there?"

"Who did you say?"

"This is Wayne Gray," I said patiently. "Is Lambeth Gray there?"

"Oh." I recognized it now as Mike's voice. "Didn't get you at first. No, Mr. Gray, your wife hasn't been here."

I thanked him and hung up. When I went out of the booth, the Chandlers were gone. I heard a car starting outside.

I waved to Harry and went outside. The taillight of the Chandlers' car was heading up the hill. In the direction they'd have gone if they were heading for Hans Wagner's studio—to warn Lamb that I'd heard something I shouldn't have heard, and that I might come there.

But it was too ridiculous to consider. Whatever gave Eve Chandler the wild idea that Lamb might be with Hans, it was wrong. Lamb wouldn't do anything like that. Eve had probably seen her having a drink or so with Hans somewhere, sometime, and had got the thing wrong. Dead wrong. If nothing else, Lamb would have better taste than that. Hans was handsome, and he was a ladies' man, which I'm not, but he's stupid and he can't paint. Lamb wouldn't fall for a stuffed shirt like Hans Wagner.

But I might as well go home now, I decided. Unless I wanted to give people the impression that I was canvassing the town for my wife, I couldn't very well look any farther or ask any more people if they'd seen her. And although I don't care what people think about me either personally or as a painter, I wouldn't want them to think I had any wrong ideas about Lamb.

I walked off in the wake of the Chandlers' car, through the bright moonlight. I came in sight of Hans's place again, and the Chandlers' car wasn't parked there; if they'd stopped, they'd gone right on. But, of course, they would have, under those circumstances. They wouldn't have wanted me to see that they were parked there; it would have looked bad.

The lights were on there, but I walked on past, up the hill toward my own place. Maybe Lamb was home by now; I hoped so. At any rate, I wasn't going to stop at Hans's. Whether the Chandlers had or not.

Lamb wasn't in sight along the road between Hans's place and mine. But she could have made it before I got that far, even if—well, even if she had been there. If the Chandlers had stopped to warn her.

Three quarters of a mile from the inn to Hans's. Only one quarter of a mile from Hans's place to mine. And Lamb could have run; I had only walked.

Past Hans's place, a beautiful studio with that skylight I envied him. Not the place, not the fancy furnishings, just that wonderful skylight. Oh, yes, you can get wonderful light outdoors, but there's wind and dust just at the wrong time. And when, mostly, you paint out of your head instead of something you're looking at, there's no advantage to being outdoors at all. I don't have to look at a hill while I'm painting it. I've seen a hill.

The light was on at my place, up ahead. But I'd left it on, so that didn't prove Lamb was home. I plodded toward it, getting a little winded by the uphill climb, and I realized I'd been walking too fast. I turned around to look back and there was that composition again, with the gibbous moon a little higher, a little brighter. It had lightened the black of the near hills and the far ones were blacker. I thought, *I can do that.* Gray on black and black on gray. And, so it wouldn't be a monochrome, the yellow lights. Like the lights at Hans's place. Yellow lights like Hans's yellow hair. Tall, Nordic-Teutonic type, handsome. Nice planes in his face. Yes, I could see why women liked him. Women, but not Lamb.

I had my breath back and started climbing again. I called out Lamb's name when I got near the door, but she didn't answer. I went inside, but she wasn't there.

The place was very empty. I poured myself a glass of wine and went over to look at the picture I'd blocked out. It was all wrong; it didn't mean anything. The lines were nice but they didn't mean anything at all. I'd have to scrape the canvas and start over. Well, I'd done that before. It's the only way you get anything, to be ruthless when something's wrong. But I couldn't start it tonight.

The tin clock said it was a quarter to eleven; still, that wasn't late. But I didn't want to think so I decided to read a while. Some poetry, possibly. I went over to the bookcase. I saw Blake, and that made me think of one of his simplest and best poems, "The Lamb." It had always made me think of Lamb— "Little lamb, who made thee?" It had always given me, personally, a funny twist to the line, a connotation that Blake, of course, hadn't intended. But I didn't want to read Blake tonight. T. S. Eliot: "Midnight shakes the memory as a madman shakes a dead geranium." But it wasn't midnight yet, and I wasn't in the mood for Eliot. Not even Prufrock: "Let us go then, you and I, when the evening is spread out against the sky like a patient etherized upon a table—" He could do things with words that I'd have liked to do with pigments, but they aren't the same things, the same medium. Painting and poetry are as different as eating and sleeping. But both fields can be, and are, so wide. Painters can differ as greatly as Bonnard and Braque, yet both be great. Poets as great as Eliot and Blake. "Little lamb, who—" I didn't want to read.

And enough of thinking. I opened the trunk and got my forty-five caliber automatic. The clip was full; I jacked a cartridge into the chamber and put the safety catch on. I put it into my pocket and went outside. I closed the door behind me and started down the hill toward Hans Wagner's studio.

I wondered, had the Chandlers stopped there to warn them? Then either Lamb would have hurried home—or, possibly, she might have gone on with the Chandlers, to their place. She could have figured that to be less obvious than rushing home. So, even if she wasn't there, it would prove nothing. If she was, it would show that the Chandlers hadn't stopped there.

I walked down the road, and I tried to look at the crouching black beast of the hills, the yellow of the lights. But they added up to nothing; they meant nothing. Unfeeling, ungiving-to-feel, like a patient etherized upon a table. Damn Eliot, I thought; the man saw too deeply. The useless striving of the wasteland for something a man can touch but never have, the shaking of a dead geranium. As a madman. Little Lamb. Her dark hair and her darker eyes in the whiteness of her face. And the slender, beautiful whiteness of her body. The softness of her voice and the touch of her hands running through my hair. And Hans Wagner's hair, yellow as that mocking moon.

I knocked on the door. Not loudly, not softly, just a knock.

Was it too long before Hans came?

Did he look frightened? I didn't know. The planes of his face were nice, but what was in them I didn't know. I can see the lines and the planes of faces, but I can't read them. Nor voices.

"Hi, Wayne. Come in," Hans said.

I went inside. Lamb wasn't there, not in the big room, the studio. There were other rooms, of course; a bedroom, a kitchen, a bathroom. I wanted to go look in all of them right away, but that would have been crude. I wouldn't leave until I'd looked in each.

"Getting a little worried about Lamb: she's seldom out alone this late. Have you seen her?" I asked.

Hans shook his blond, handsome head.

"Thought she might have dropped in on her way home," I said casually. I smiled at him. "Maybe I was just getting lonesome and restless. How about dropping back with me for a drink? I've got only wine, but there's plenty of that."

Of course he had to say, "Why not have a drink here?" He said it. He even asked me what I wanted, and I said a martini because he'd have to go out into the kitchen to make that and it would give me a chance to look around.

"Okay, Wayne, I'll have one too," Hans said. "Excuse me a moment."

He went out into the kitchen. I took a quick look into the bathroom and then went into the bedroom and took a good look, even under the bed. Lamb wasn't there. Then I went into the kitchen and said, "Forgot to tell you, make mine light. I might want to paint a bit after I get home."

"Sure," he said.

Lamb wasn't in the kitchen. Nor had she left after I'd knocked or come in; I remember Hans's kitchen door; it's pretty noisy and I hadn't heard it. And it's the only door aside from the front one.

I'd been foolish.

Unless, of course, Lamb had been here and had gone away with the Chandlers when they'd dropped by to warn them, if they had dropped by.

I went back into the big studio with the skylight and wandered around for a minute looking at the things on the walls. They made me want to puke, so I sat down and waited. I'd stay at least a few minutes to make it look all right. Hans came back.

He gave me my drink and I thanked him. I sipped it while he waited patronizingly. Not that I minded that. He made money and I didn't. But I thought worse of him than he could possibly think of me.

"How's your work going, Wayne?"

"Fine," I said. I sipped my drink. He'd taken me at my word and made it weak, mostly vermouth. It tasted lousy that way. But the olive in it looked darker, more the color I'd had in mind. Maybe, just maybe, with the picture built around that color, it would work out.

"Nice place, Hans," I said. "That skylight. I wish I had one."

He shrugged. "You don't work from models anyway, do you? And outdoors is outdoors."

"Outdoors is in your mind," I said. "There isn't any difference." And then I wondered why I was talking to somebody who wouldn't know what I was talking about. I wandered over to the window—the one that faced toward my studio—and looked out of it. I hoped I'd see Lamb on the way there, but I didn't. She wasn't here. Where was she? Even if she'd been here and left when I'd knocked, she'd have been on the way now. I'd have seen her.

I turned. "Were the Chandlers here tonight?" I asked him.

"The Chandlers? No; haven't seen them for a couple of days." He'd finished his drink. "Have another?" he asked.

I started to say no. I didn't. My eyes happened, just happened, to light on a closet door. I'd seen inside it once; it wasn't deep, but it was deep enough for a man to stand inside it. Or a woman.

"Thanks, Hans. Yes."

I walked over and handed him my glass. He went out into the kitchen with the glasses. I walked quietly over to the closet door and tried it.

It was locked.

And there wasn't a key in the door. That didn't make sense. Why would anyone keep a closet locked when he always locked all the outer doors and windows when he left?

Little lamb, who made thee?

Hans came out of the kitchen, a martini in each hand. He saw my hand on the knob of the closet door.

For a moment he stood very still and then his hands began to tremble; the martinis, his and mine, slopped over the rims and made little droplets falling to the floor.

I asked him, pleasantly, "Hans, do you keep your closet locked?"

"Is it locked? No, I don't, ordinarily." And then he realized he hadn't quite said it right, and he said, more fearlessly. "What's the matter with you, Wayne?"

"Nothing," I said. "Nothing at all." I took the forty-five out of my pocket. He was far enough away so that, big as he was, he couldn't think about trying to jump me.

I smiled at him instead. "How's about letting me have the key?"

More martini glistened on the tiles. These tall, big, handsome blonds, they haven't guts; he was scared stiff. He tried to make his voice normal. "I don't know where it is. What's wrong?"

"Nothing," I said. "But stay where you are. Don't move, Hans."

He didn't. The glasses shook, but the olives stayed in them. Barely. I watched him, but I put the muzzle of the big forty-five against the keyhole. I slanted it away from the center of the door so I wouldn't kill anybody who was hiding inside. I did that out of the corner of my eye, watching Hans Wagner.

I pulled the trigger. The sound of the shot, even in that big studio, was deafening, but I didn't take my eyes off Hans. I may have blinked.

I stepped back as the closet door swung slowly open. I lined the muzzle of the forty-five against Hans's heart. I kept it there as the door of the closet swung slowly toward me.

An olive hit the tiles with a sound that wouldn't have been audible, ordinarily. I watched Hans while I looked into the closet as the door swung fully open.

Lamb was there. Naked.

I shot Hans and my hand was steady, so one shot was enough. He fell with his hand moving toward his heart but not having time to get there. His head hit the tiles with a crushing sound. The sound was the sound of death.

I put the gun back into my pocket and my hand was trembling now.

Hans's easel was near me, his palette knife lying on the ledge.

I took the palette knife in my hand and cut my Lamb, my naked Lamb, out of her frame. I rolled her up and held her tightly; no one would ever see her thus. We left together and, hand in hand, started up the hill toward home. I looked at her in the bright moonlight. I laughed, and she laughed, but her laughter was like silver cymbals, and my laughter was like dead petals shaken from a madman's geranium.

Her hand slipped out of mine; and she danced, a white slim wraith.

Back over her shoulder her laughter tinkled and she said, "Remember, darling? Remember that you killed me when I told you about Hans and me? Don't you remember killing me this afternoon? Don't you, darling? Don't you remember?"

The Girl Behind the Hedge
Mickey Spillane

October 1953

The stocky man handed his coat and hat to the attendant and went through the foyer to the main lounge of the club. He stood in the doorway for a scant second, but in that time his eyes had seen all that was to be seen; the chess game beside the windows, the foursome at cards and the lone man at the rear of the room sipping a drink.

He crossed between the tables, nodding briefly to the card players, and went directly to the back of the room. The other man looked up from his drink with a smile. "Afternoon, Inspector. Sit down. Drink?"

"Hello, Dunc. Same as you're drinking."

Almost languidly, the fellow made a motion with his hand. The waiter nodded and left. The inspector settled himself in his chair with a sigh. He was a big man, heavy without being given to fat. Only his high shoes proclaimed him for what he was. When he looked at Chester Duncan he grimaced inwardly, envying him his poise and manner, yet not willing to trade him for anything.

Here, he thought smugly, *is a man who should have everything yet has nothing. True, he has money and position, but the finest of all things, a family life, was denied him.* And with a brood of five in all stages of growth at home, the inspector felt that he had achieved his purpose in life.

The drink came and the inspector took his, sipping it gratefully. When he put it down he said, "I came to thank you for that, er . . . tip. You know, that was the first time I've ever played the market."

"Glad to do it," Duncan said. His hands played with the glass, rolling it around in his palms. He eyebrows shot up suddenly, as though he was amused at something. "I suppose you heard all the ugly rumors."

A flush reddened the inspector's face. "In an offhand way, yes. Some of them were downright ugly." He sipped his drink again and tapped a cigarette on the side table. "You know," he said. "If Walter Harrison's death hadn't been so definitely a suicide, you might be standing an investigation right now."

Duncan smiled slowly. "Come now, Inspector. The market didn't budge until after his death, you know."

"True enough. But rumor has it that you engineered it in some manner." He paused long enough to study Duncan's face. "Tell me, did you?"

"Why should I incriminate myself?"

"It's over and done with. Harrison leaped to his death from the window of a hotel room. The door was locked and there was no possible way anyone could have gotten in that room to give him a push. No, we're quite satisfied that it was suicide, and everybody that ever came in contact with Harrison agrees that he did the world a favor when he died. However, there's still some speculation about you having a hand in things."

"Tell me, Inspector, do you really think I had the courage or the brains to oppose a man like Harrison, and force him to kill himself?"

The inspector frowned, then nodded. "As a matter of fact, yes. You *did* profit by his death."

"So did *you*," Duncan laughed.

"Ummmm."

"Though it's nothing to be ashamed about," Duncan added. "When Harrison died the financial world naturally expected that the stocks he financed were no good and tried to unload. It so happened that I was one of the few who knew they were as good as gold and bought while I could. And, of course, I passed the word on to my friends. Somebody had might as well profit by the death of a . . . a rat."

Through the haze of the smoke Inspector Early saw his face tighten around the mouth. He scowled again, leaning forward in his chair. "Duncan, we've been friends quite a while. I'm just cop enough to be curious and I'm thinking that our late Walter Harrison was cursing you just before he died."

Duncan twirled his glass around. "I've no doubt of it," he said. His eyes met the inspector's. "Would you really like to hear about it?"

"Not if it means your confessing to murder. If that has to happen I'd much rather you spoke directly to the DA."

"Oh, it's nothing like that at all. No, not a bit, Inspector. No matter how hard they tried, they couldn't do a thing that would impair either my honor or reputation. You see, Walter Harrison went to his death through his own greediness."

The inspector settled back in his chair. The waiter came with drinks to replace the empties and the two men toasted each other silently.

"Some of this you probably know already, Inspector," Duncan said . . .

Nevertheless, I'll start at the beginning and tell you everything that happened. Walter Harrison and I met in law school. We were both young and not too studious. We had one thing in common and only one. Both of us were the products of wealthy parents who tried their best to spoil their children. Since we were the only ones who could afford certain—er—pleasures, we naturally gravitated to each other, though when I think back, even at that time, there was little true friendship involved.

It so happened that I had a flair for my studies whereas Walter didn't give a damn. At examination time, I had to carry him. It seemed like a big joke at the time, but actually I was doing all the work while he was having his fling around town. Nor was I the only one he imposed upon in such a way. Many students, impressed with having his friendship, gladly took over his papers. Walter could charm the devil himself if he had to.

And quite often he had to. Many's the time he's talked his way out of spending a weekend in jail for some minor offense—and I've even seen him twist the dean around his little finger, so to speak. Oh, but I remained his loyal friend. I shared everything I had with him, including my women, and even thought it amusing when I went out on a date and met him, only to have him take my girl home.

In the last year of school the crash came. It meant little to me because my father had seen it coming and got out with his fortune increased. Walter's father tried to stick it out and went under. He was one of the ones who killed himself that day.

Walter was quite stricken, of course. He was in a blue funk and got stinking drunk. We had quite a talk and he was for quitting school at once, but I talked him into accepting the money from me and graduating. Come to think of it, he never did pay me back that money. However, it really doesn't matter.

After we left school I went into business with my father and took over the firm when he died. It was that same month that Walter showed up. He stopped in for a visit, and wound up with a position, though at no time did he deceive me as to the real intent of his visit. He got what he came after and in a way it was a good thing for me. Walter was a shrewd businessman.

His rise in the financial world was slightly less than meteoric. He was much too astute to remain in anyone's employ for long, and with the Street talking about Harrison, the Boy Wonder of Wall Street, in every other breath, it was inevitable that he open up his own office. In a sense, we became competitors after that, but always friends.

Pardon me, Inspector, let's say that I was his friend, he never was mine. His ruthlessness was appalling at times, but even then he managed to charm his victims into accepting their lot with a smile. I for one know that he managed the market to make himself a cool million on a deal that left me gasping. More than once he almost cut the bottom out of my business, yet he was always in with a grin and a big hello the next day as if it had been only a tennis match he had won.

If you've followed his rise then you're familiar with the social side of his life. Walter cut quite a swath for himself. Twice, he was almost killed by irate husbands, and if he had been, no jury on earth would have convicted his murderer. There was the time a young girl killed herself rather than let her parents know that she had been having an affair with Walter and had been trapped. He was very generous about it. He offered her money to travel, her choice of doctors and anything she wanted . . . except his name for her child. No, he wasn't ready to give his name away then. That came a few weeks later.

I was engaged to be married at the time. Adrianne was a girl I had loved from the moment I saw her and there aren't words enough to tell how happy I was when she said she'd marry me. We spent most of our waking hours poring over plans for the future. We even selected a site for our house out on the Island and began construction. We were timing the wedding to coincide with the completion of the house and if ever I was a man living in a dream world, it was then. My happiness was complete, as was Adrianne's, or so I thought. Fortune seemed to favor me with more than one smile at the time. For some reason my own career took a sudden spurt and whatever I touched turned to gold, and in no time the Street had taken to following me rather than Walter Harrison. Without realizing it, I turned several deals that had him on his knees, though I doubt if many ever realized it. Walter would never give up the amazing front he affected."

At this point Duncan paused to study his glass, his eyes narrowing. Inspector Early remained motionless, waiting for him to go on . . .

Walter came to see me," Duncan said. "It was a day I shall never forget. I had a dinner engagement with Adrianne and invited him along. Now I know that what he did was done out of sheer spite, nothing else. At first I believed that it was my fault, or hers, never giving Walter a thought . . .

Forgive me if I pass over the details lightly, Inspector. They aren't very pleasant to recall. I had to sit there and watch Adrianne captivated by this charming rat to the point where I was merely a decoration in the chair opposite her. I had to see him join us day after day, night after night, then hear the rumors that they were seeing each other without me, then discover for myself that she was in love with him.

Yes, it was quite an experience. I had the idea of killing them both, then killing myself. When I saw that that could never solve the problem I gave it up.

Adrianne came to me one night. She sat and told me how much she hated to hurt me, but she had fallen in love with Walter Harrison and wanted to marry him. What else was there to do? Naturally, I acted the part of a good loser and called off the engagement. They didn't wait long. A week later they were married and I was the laughing stock of the Street.

Perhaps time might have cured everything if things hadn't turned out the way they did. It wasn't very long afterwards that I learned of a break in their marriage. Word came that Adrianne had changed and I knew for a fact that Walter was far from being true to her.

You see, now I realized the truth. Walter never loved her. He never loved anybody but himself. He married Adrianne because he wanted to hurt me more than anything else in the world. He hated me because I had something he lacked . . . happiness. It was something he searched after desperately himself and always found just out of reach.

In December of that year Adrianne took sick. She wasted away for a month and died. In the final moments she called for me, asking me to forgive her; this much I learned from a servant of hers. Walter, by the way, was enjoying himself at a party when she died. He came home for the funeral and took off immediately for a sojourn in Florida with some attractive showgirl.

God, how I hated that man! I used to dream of killing him! Do you know, if ever my mind drifted from the work I was doing I always pictured myself standing over his corpse with a knife in my hand, laughing my head off.

Every so often I would get word of Walter's various escapades, and they seemed to follow a definite pattern. I made it my business to learn more about him and before long I realized that Walter was almost frenzied in his search to find a woman he could really love. Since he was a fabulously wealthy man he was always suspicious of a woman wanting him more than his wealth, and this very suspicion always was the thing that drove a woman away from him.

It may seem strange to you, but regardless of my attitude, I saw him quite regularly. And equally strange, he never realized that I hated him so. He realized, of course, that he was far from popular in any quarter, but he never suspected me of anything else save a stupid idea of friendship. But as I had learned my lesson the hard way, he never got the chance to impose upon me again, though he never really had need to.

It was a curious thing, the solution I saw to my problem. It had been there all the time, I was aware of it being there, yet using the circumstances never occurred to me until the day I was sitting on my veranda reading a memo from my office manager. The note stated that Walter had pulled another coup in the market and had the Street rocking on its heels. It was one of those times when any variation in Wall Street reflected the economy of the country, and what he did was undermine the entire economic structure of the United States. It was with the greatest effort that we got back to normal without toppling, but in doing so a lot of places had to close up. Walter Harrison, however, had doubled the wealth he could never hope to spend, anyway.

As I said, I was sitting there reading the note when I saw her behind the window in the house across the way. The sun was streaming in, reflecting the gold in her hair, making a picture of beauty so exquisite as to be unbelievable. A servant came and brought her a tray, and as she sat down to lunch, I lost sight of her behind the hedges and the thought came to me of how simple it would all be.

I met Walter for lunch the next day. He was quite exuberant over his latest adventure, treating it like a joke.

I said, "Say, you've never been out to my place on the Island, have you?"

He laughed, and I noticed a little guilt in his eyes. "To tell you the truth," he said, "I would have dropped in if you hadn't built the place for Adrianne. After all . . ."

"Don't be ridiculous, Walter. What's done is done. Look, until things get back to normal, how about staying with me a few days. You need a rest after your little deal."

"Fine, Duncan, fine! Anytime you say."

"All right, I'll pick you up tonight."

We had quite a ride out, stopping at a few places for drinks and hashing over the old days at school. At any other time I might have laughed, but all those reminiscences had taken on an unpleasant air. When we reached the house I had a few friends in to meet the fabulous Walter Harrison, left him accepting their plaudits and went to bed.

We had breakfast on the veranda. Walter ate with relish, breathing deeply of the sea air with animal-like pleasure. At exactly nine o'clock the sunlight flashed off the windows of the house behind mine as the servant threw them open to the morning breeze.

Then she was there. I waved and she waved back. Walter's head turned to look and I heard his breath catch in his throat. She was lovely, her hair a golden cascade that tumbled around her shoulders. Her blouse was a radiant white that enhanced the swell of her breasts, a gleaming contrast to the smooth tanned flesh of her shoulders.

Walter looked like a man in a dream. "Lord, she's lovely!" he said. "Who is she, Dunc?"

I sipped my coffee. "A neighbor," I said lightly.

"Do you . . . do you think I could get to meet her?"

"Perhaps. She's quite young and just a little bit shy and it would be better to have her see me with you a few times before introductions are in order."

He sounded hoarse. His face had taken on an avid, hungry look. "Anything you say, but I have to meet her." He turned around with a grin. "By golly, I'll stay here until I do, too!"

We laughed over that and went back to our cigarettes, but every so often I caught him glancing back toward the hedge with that desperate expression creasing his face.

Being familiar with her schedule, I knew that we wouldn't see her again that day, but Walter knew nothing of this. He tried to keep away from the subject, yet it persisted in coming back. Finally he said, "Incidentally, just who is she?"

"Her name is Evelyn Vaughn. Comes from quite a well-to-do-family."

"She here alone?"

"No, besides the servants she has a nurse and a doctor in attendance. She hasn't been quite well."

"Hell, she looks the picture of health."

"Oh, she is now," I agreed. I walked over and turned on the television and we watched the fights. For the sixth time a call came in for Walter, but his reply was the same. He wasn't going back to New York. I felt the anticipation in his voice, knowing why he was staying, and had to concentrate on the screen to keep from smiling.

Evelyn was there the next day and the next. Walter had taken to waving when I did and when she waved back his face seemed to light up until it looked almost boyish. The sun had tanned him nicely and he pranced around like a colt, especially when she could see him. He pestered me with questions and received evasive answers. Somehow he got the idea that his importance warranted a visit from the house across the way. When I told him that to Evelyn neither wealth nor position meant a thing he looked at me sharply to see if I was telling the truth. To have become what he was he had to be a good reader of faces and he knew that it *was* the truth beyond the shadow of a doubt.

So I sat there day after day watching Walter Harrison fall helplessly in love with a woman he hadn't met yet. He fell in love with the way she waved until each movement of her hand seemed to be for him alone. He fell in love with the luxuriant beauty of her body, letting his eyes follow her as she walked to the water from the house, aching to be close to her. She would turn sometimes and see us watching, and wave.

At night he would stand by the window not hearing what I said because he was watching her windows, hoping for just one glimpse of her, and often I would hear him repeating her name slowly, letting it roll off his tongue like a precious thing.

It couldn't go on that way. I knew it and he knew it. She had just come up from the beach and the water glistened on her skin. She laughed at something the woman said who was with her and shook her head so that her hair flowed down her back.

Walter shouted and waved and she laughed again, waving back. The wind brought her voice to him and Walter stood there, his breath hot in my face. "Look here, Duncan, I'm going to go over and meet her. I can't stand this waiting. Good Lord, what does a guy have to go through to meet a woman?"

"You've never had any trouble before, have you?"

"Never like this!" he said. "Usually they're dropping at my feet. I haven't changed, have I? There's nothing repulsive about me, is there?"

I wanted to tell the truth, but I laughed instead. "You're the same as ever. It wouldn't surprise me if she was dying to meet you, too. I can tell you this . . . she's never been outside as much as since you've been here."

His eyes lit up boyishly. "Really, Dunc. Do you think so?"

"I think so. I can assure you of this, too. If she does seem to like you it's certainly for yourself alone."

As crudely as the barb was placed, it went home. Walter never so much as glanced at me. He was lost in thought for a long time, then: "I'm going over there now, Duncan. I'm crazy about that girl. By God, I'll marry her if it's the last thing I do."

"Don't spoil it, Walter. Tomorrow, I promise you. I'll go over with you."

His eagerness was pathetic. I don't think he slept a wink that night. Long before breakfast he was waiting for me on the veranda. We ate in silence, each minute an eternity for him. He turned repeatedly to look over the hedge and I caught a flash of worry when she didn't appear.

Tight little lines had appeared at the corner of his eyes and he said, "Where is she, Dunc? She should be there by now, shouldn't she?"

"I don't know," I said. "It does seem strange. Just a moment." I rang the bell on the table and my housekeeper came to the door. "Have you seen the Vaughns, Martha?" I asked her.

She nodded sagely. "Oh, yes, sir. They left very early this morning to go back to the city."

Walter turned to me. "Hell!"

"Well, she'll be back," I assured him.

"Damn it, Dunc, that isn't the point!" He stood up and threw his napkin on the seat. "Can't you realize that I'm in love with the girl? I can't wait for her to get back!"

His face flushed with frustration. There was no anger, only the crazy hunger for the woman. I held back my smile. It happened. It happened the way I planned for it to happen. Walter Harrison had fallen so deeply in love, so truly in love that he couldn't control himself. I might have felt sorry for him at that moment if I hadn't asked him, "Walter, as I told you, I know very little about her. Supposing she is already married."

He answered my question with a nasty grimace. "Then she'll get a divorce if I have to break the guy in pieces. I'll break anything that stands in my way, Duncan. I'm going to have her if it's the last thing I do!"

He stalked off to his room. Later I heard the car roar down the road. I let myself laugh then.

I went back to New York and was there a week when my contacts told me of Walter's fruitless search. He used every means at his disposal, but he couldn't locate the girl. I gave him seven days, exactly seven days. You see, that seventh day was the anniversary of the date I introduced him to Adrianne. I'll never forget it. Wherever Walter is now, neither will he.

When I called him I was amazed at the change in his voice. He sounded weak and lost. We exchanged the usual formalities; then I said, "Walter, have you found Evelyn yet?"

He took a long time to answer. "No, she's disappeared completely."

"Oh, I wouldn't say that," I said.

He didn't get it at first. It was almost too much to hope for. "You . . . mean you know where she is?"

"Exactly."

"Where? Please, Dunc . . . where is she?" In a split second he became a vital being again. He was bursting with life and energy, demanding that I tell him.

I laughed and told him to let me get a word in and I would. The silence was ominous then. "She's not very far from here, Walter, in a small hotel right off Fifth Avenue." I gave him the address and had hardly finished when I heard his phone slam against the desk. He was in such a hurry he hadn't bothered to hang up . . .

Duncan stopped and drained his glass, then stared at it remorsefully. The Inspector coughed lightly to attract his attention, his curiosity prompting him to speak. "He found her?" he asked eagerly.

"Oh yes, he found her. He burst right in over all protests, expecting to sweep her off her feet."

This time the inspector fidgeted nervously. "Well, go on."

Duncan motioned for the waiter and lifted a fresh glass in a toast. The inspector did the same. Duncan smiled gently. "When she saw him she laughed and waved. Walter Harrison died an hour later . . . from a window in the same hotel."

It was too much for the inspector. He leaned forward in his chair, his forehead knotted in a frown. "But what happened? Who was she? Damn it, Duncan . . ."

Duncan took a deep breath, then gulped the drink down.

"Evelyn Vaughn was a hopeless imbecile," he said.

"She had the beauty of a goddess and the mentality of a two-year-old. They kept her well tended and dressed so she wouldn't be an object of curiosity. But the only habit she ever learned was to wave bye-bye . . ."

The Best of *Manhunt*

Professional Man
David Goodis

October 1953

At five past five, the elevator operated by Freddy Lamb came to a stop on the street floor. Freddy smiled courteously to the departing passengers. As he said goodnight to the office-weary faces of secretaries and bookkeepers and executives, his voice was soothing and cool-sweet, almost like a caress for the women and a pat on the shoulder for the men. People were very fond of Freddy. He was always so pleasant, so polite and quietly cheerful. Of the five elevator-men in the Chambers Trust Building, Freddy Lamb was the favorite.

His appearance blended with his voice and manner. He was neat and clean and his hair was nicely trimmed. He had light brown hair parted on the side and brushed flat across his head. His eyes were the same color, focused level when he addressed you, but never too intent, never probing. He looked at you as though he liked and trusted you, no matter who you were. When you looked at him you felt mildly stimulated. He seemed much younger than his thirty-three years. There were no lines on his face, no sign of worry or sluggishness or dissipation. The trait that made him an ideal elevator-man was the fact that he never asked questions and never talked about himself At twenty past five, Freddy got the go-home sign from the starter, changed places with the night man, and walked down the corridor to the locker room. Taking off the uniform and putting on his street clothes, he yawned a few times. And while he was sitting on the bench and tying his shoelaces, he closed his eyes for a long moment, as though trying to catch a quick nap. His fingers fell away from the shoelaces and his shoulders drooped and he was in that position when the starter came in.

"Tired?" the starter asked.

"Just a little." Freddy looked up.

"Long day," the starter said. He was always saying that. As though each day was longer than any other.

Freddy finished with the shoelaces. He stood up and said, "You got the dollar-fifty?"

"What dollar-fifty?"

"The loan," Freddy said. He smiled off-handedly. "From last week. You ran short and needed dinner money. Remember?"

The starter's face was blank for a moment. Then he snapped his finger and nodded emphatically. "You're absolutely right," he declared. "I'm glad you reminded me."

He handed Freddy a dollar bill and two quarters. Freddy thanked him and said good-night and walked out. The starter stood there, lighting a cigarette and nodding to himself and thinking, *Nice guy, he waited a week before he asked me, and then he asked me so nice, he's really a nice guy.*

At precisely eight-ten, Freddy Lamb climbed out of the bathtub on the third floor of the uptown rooming house in which he lived. In his room, he opened a dresser drawer, took out silk underwear, silk socks, and a silk handkerchief. When he was fully dressed, he wore a pale grey roll-collar shirt that had cost fourteen dollars, a grey silk gabardine suit costing ninety-seven fifty, and dark grey suede shoes that had set him back twenty-three ninety-five. He broke open a fresh pack of cigarettes and slipped them into a wafer-thin sterling silver case, and then he changed wrist watches. The one he had been wearing was of mediocre quality and had a steel case. The one he wore now was fourteen karat white-gold. But both kept perfect time. He was very particular about the watches he bought. He wouldn't wear a watch that didn't keep absolutely perfect time.

The white-gold watch showed eight-twenty when Freddy walked out of the rooming house. He walked down Sixteenth to Ontario, then over to Broad and caught a cab. He gave the driver an address downtown. The cab's headlights merged with the flooded glare of southbound traffic. Freddy leaned back and lit a cigarette.

"Nice weather," the driver commented.

"Yes, it certainly is," Freddy said.

"I like it this time of year," the driver said, "it ain't too hot and it ain't too cold. It's just right." He glanced at the rear-view mirror and saw that his passenger was putting on a pair of dark glasses. He said, "You in show business?"

"No," Freddy said.

"What's the glasses for?"

Freddy didn't say anything.

"What's the glasses for?" the driver asked.

"The headlights hurt my eyes," Freddy said. He said it somewhat slowly, his tone indicating that he was rather tired and didn't feel like talking.

The driver shrugged and remained quiet for the rest of the ride. He brought the cab to a stop at the corner of Eleventh and Locust. The fare was a dollar twenty. Freddy gave him two dollars and told him to keep the change. As the cab drove away, Freddy walked west on Locust to Twelfth, walked south on Twelfth, then turned west again, moving through a narrow alley. There were no lights in the alley except for a rectangle of green neon far down toward the other end. The rectangle was a glowing frame for the neon wording, *Billy's Hut.* It was also a beckoning finger for that special type of citizen who was never happy unless he was being taken over in a clip joint. They'd soon be flocking through the front entrance on Locust Street. But Freddy Lamb, moving toward the back entrance, had it checked in his mind that the place was empty now. The dial of his wrist watch showed eight-fifty-seven, and he knew it was too early for customers. He also knew that Billy Donofrio was sound asleep on a sofa in the back room, used as a private office. He knew it because he'd been watching Donofrio for more than two weeks and he was well acquainted with Donofrio's nightly habits.

When Freddy was fifteen yards away from *Billy's Hut,* he reached into his inner jacket pocket and took out a pair of white cotton gloves. When he was five yards away, he came to a stop and stood motionless, listening. There was the sound of a record-player from some upstairs flat on the other side of the alley. From another upstairs flat there was the noise of lesbian voices saying, "You did," and "I didn't," and "You did, you did—"

He listened for other sounds and there were none. He let the tip of his tongue come out just a little to moisten the center of his lower lip. Then he took a few forward steps that brought him to a section of brick wall where the bricks were loose. He counted up from the bottom, the light from the green neon showing him the fourth brick, the fifth, the sixth and the seventh. The eighth brick was the one he wanted. He got a grip on its edges jutting away from the wall, pulled at it very slowly and carefully. Then he held it in one hand and his other hand reached into the empty space and made contact with the bone handle of a switchblade. It was a six-inch blade and he'd planted it there two nights ago.

He put the brick back in place and walked to the back door of *Billy's Hut.* Bending to the side to see through the window, he caught sight of Billy Donofrio on the sofa. Billy was flat on his back, one short leg dangling over the side of the sofa, one arm also dangling with fat fingers holding the stub of an unlit cigar. Billy was very short and very fat, and in his sleep he breathed as though it were a great effort. Billy was almost completely bald and what hair he had was more white than black. Billy was fifty-three years old and would never get to be fifty-four.

Freddy Lamb used a skeleton key to open the back door. He did it without sound. And then, without sound, he moved toward the sofa, his eyes focused on the crease of flesh between Billy's third chin and Billy's shirt collar. His arm went up and came down and the blade went into the crease, went in deep to cut the jugular vein, moved left, moved right, to widen the cut so that it was almost from ear to ear. Billy opened his eyes and tried to open his mouth but that was as far as he could take it. He tried to breathe and he couldn't breathe. He heard the voice of Freddy Lamb saying very softly, almost gently, "Good night, Billy." Then he heard Freddy's footsteps moving toward the door, and the door opening, and the footsteps walking out.

Billy didn't hear the door as it closed. By that time he was far away from hearing anything.

On Freddy's wrist, the hands of the white-gold watch pointed to nine twenty-six. He stood on the sidewalk near the entrance of a nightclub called "Yellow Cat." The place was located in a low-rent area of South Philadelphia, and the neighboring structures were mostly tenements and garages and vacant lots heaped with rubbish. The club's exterior complied with the general trend; it was dingy and there was no paint on the wooden walls. But inside it was a different proposition. It was glittering and lavish, the drinks were expensive, and the floorshow featured a first-rate orchestra and singers and dancers. It also featured a unique type of strip-tease entertainment, a quintet of young females who took off their clothes while they sat at your table. For a reasonable bonus they'd let you keep the brassiere or garter or what-not for a souvenir.

The white-gold watch showed nine twenty-eight. Freddy decided to wait another two minutes. His appointment with the owner of "Yellow Cat" had been arranged for nine-thirty. He knew that Herman Charn was waiting anxiously for his arrival, but his personal theory of punctuality stipulated split-second precision, and since they'd made it for nine-thirty he'd see Herman at nine-thirty, not a moment earlier or later.

A taxi pulled up and a blonde stepped out. She paid the driver and walked toward Freddy and he said,

"Hello, Pearl."

Pearl smiled at him. "Kiss me hello."

"Not here," he said.

"Later?"

He nodded. He looked her up and down. She was five-five and weighed one-ten and Nature had given her a body that caused men's eyes to bulge. Freddy's eyes didn't bulge, although he told himself she was something to see. He always enjoyed looking at her. He wondered if he still enjoyed the nights with her. He'd been sharing the nights with her for the past several months and it had reached the point where he wasn't seeing any other women and maybe he was missing out on something. For just a moment he gazed past Pearl, telling himself that she needed him more than he needed her, and knowing it wouldn't be easy to get off the hook.

Well, there wasn't any hurry. He hadn't seen anything else around that interested him. But he wished Pearl would let up on the clinging routine. Maybe he'd really go for her if she wasn't so hungry for him all the time.

Pearl stepped closer to him. The hunger showed in her eyes. She said, "Know what I did today? I took a walk in the park."

"You did?"

"Yeah," she said. "I went to Fairmount Park and took a long walk. All by myself."

"That's nice," he said. He wondered what she was getting at.

She said, "Let's do it together sometimes. Let's go for a walk in the park. It's something we ain't never done. All we do is drink and listen to jazz and find all sorts of ways to knock ourselves out."

He gave her a closer look. This was a former call-girl who'd done a stretch for prostitution, a longer stretch for selling cocaine, and had finally decided she'd done enough time and she might as well go legitimate. She'd learned the art of stripping off her clothes before an audience, and now at twenty-six she was earning a hundred-and-a-half a week. It was clean money, as far as the law was concerned, but maybe in her mind it wasn't clean enough. Maybe she was getting funny ideas, like this walk-in-the-park-routine. Maybe she'd soon be thinking in terms of a cottage for two and a little lawn in the front and shopping for a baby carriage.

He wondered what she'd look like, wearing an apron and standing at a sink and washing dishes.

For some reason the thought disturbed him. He couldn't understand why it should disturb him. He heard her saying, "Can we do it, Freddy? Let's do it on Sunday. We'll go to Fairmount Park."

"We'll talk about it," he cut in quickly. He glanced at his wrist watch. "See you after the show."

He hurried through the club entrance, went past the hat-check counter, past the tables and across the dancefloor and toward a door marked "Private." There was a button adjoining the door and he pressed the button one short, two longs, another short and then there was a buzzing sound. He opened the door and walked into the office. It was a large room and the color motif was yellow-and-gray. The walls and ceiling were gray and the thick carpet was pale yellow. The furniture was bright yellow. There was a short skinny man standing near the desk and his face was gray. Seated at the desk was a large man whose face was a mixture of yellow and gray.

Freddy closed the door behind him. He walked toward the desk. He nodded to the short skinny man and then he looked at the large man and said, "Hello, Herman."

Herman glanced at a clock on the desk. He said, "You're right on time."

"He's always on time," said the short skinny man.

Herman looked at Freddy Lamb and said, "You do it?"

Before Freddy could answer, the short skinny man said, "Sure he did it."

"Shut up, Ziggy," Herman said. He had a soft, sort of gooey voice, as though he spoke with a lot of marshmallow in his mouth. He wore a suit of very soft fabric, thick and fleecy, and his thick hands pressed softly on the desktop. On the little finger of his left hand he wore a large star emerald that radiated a soft green light. Everything about him was soft, except for his eyes. His eyes were iron.

"You do it?" he repeated softly.

Freddy nodded.

"Any trouble?" Herman asked.

"He never has trouble," Ziggy said.

Herman looked at Ziggy. "I told you to shut up." Then, very softly, "Come here, Ziggy."

Ziggy hesitated. He had a ferret face that always looked sort of worried and now it looked very worried.

"Come here," Herman purred.

Ziggy approached the large man. Ziggy was blinking and swallowing hard. Herman reached out and slowly took hold of Ziggy's hand. Herman's thick fingers closed tightly on Ziggy's bony fingers, gave a yank. Ziggy moaned.

"When I tell you to shut up," Herman said, "you'll shut up." He smiled softly and paternally at Ziggy. "Right?"

"Right," Ziggy said. Then he moaned again. His fingers were free now and he looked down at them as an animal gazes sadly at its own crushed paws. He said, "They're all busted."

"They're not all busted," Herman said. "They're damaged just enough to let you know your place. That's one thing you must never forget. Every man who works for me has to know his place." He was still smiling at Ziggy. "Right?"

"Right," Ziggy moaned.

Then Herman looked at Freddy Lamb and said, "Right?"

Freddy didn't say anything. He was looking at Ziggy's fingers. Then his gaze climbed to Ziggy's face. The lips quivered, as though Ziggy was trying to hold back sobs. Freddy remembered the time when nothing could hurt Ziggy, when Ziggy and himself were their own bosses and did their engineering on the waterfront. There were a lot of people on the waterfront who were willing to pay good money to have other people placed on stretchers or in caskets. In those days the rates had been fifteen dollars for a broken jaw, thirty for a fractured pelvis, and a hundred for the complete job. Ziggy handled the black-jack work and the bullet work and Freddy took care of such special functions as switchblade slicing, lye-in-the-eyes, and various powders and pills slipped into a glass of beer or wine or a cup of coffee. There were orders for all sorts of jobs in those days.

Fifteen months ago, he was thinking. And times had sure changed. The independent operator was swallowed up by the big combines. It was especially true in this line of business, which followed the theory that competition, no matter how small, was not good for the overall picture. So the moment had come when he and Ziggy had been approached with an offer, and they knew they had to accept, there wasn't any choice, if they didn't accept they'd be erased. They didn't need to be told about that. They just knew. As much as they hated to do it, they had to do it. The proposition was handed to them on a Wednesday afternoon and that same night they went to work for Herman Charn.

He heard Herman saying, "I'm talking to you, Freddy."

"I hear you," he said.

"You sure?" Herman asked softly. "You sure you hear me?"

Freddy looked at Herman. He said quietly, "I'm on your payroll. I do what you tell me to do. I've done every job exactly the way you wanted it done. Can I do any more than that?"

"Yes," Herman said. His tone was matter-of-fact. He glanced at Ziggy and said, "From here on it's a private discussion. Me and Freddy. Take a walk."

Ziggy's mouth opened just a little. He didn't seem to understand the command. He'd always been included in all the business conferences, and now the look in his eyes was a mixture of puzzlement and injury.

Herman smiled at Ziggy. He pointed to the door. Ziggy bit hard on his lip and moved toward the door and opened it and walked out of the room.

For some moments it was quiet in the room and Freddy had a feeling it was too quiet. He sensed that Herman Charn was aiming something at him, something that had nothing to do with the ordinary run of business.

There was the creaking sound of leather as Herman leaned back in the desk-chair. He folded his big soft fingers across his big soft belly and said, "Sit down, Freddy. Sit down and make yourself comfortable."

Freddy pulled a chair toward the desk. He sat down. He looked at the face of Herman and for just a moment the face became a wall that moved toward him. He winced, his insides quivered. It was a strange sensation, he'd never had it before and he couldn't understand it. But then the moment was gone and he sat there relaxed, his features expressionless, as he waited for Herman to speak.

Herman said, "Want a drink?"

Freddy shook his head.

"Smoke?" Herman lifted the lid of an enameled cigarette-box.

"I got my own," Freddy murmured. He reached into his pocket and took out the flat silver case.

"Smoke one of mine," Herman said. He paused to signify it wasn't a suggestion, it was an order. And then, as though Freddy was a guest rather than an employee, "These smokes are special-made. Come from Egypt. Cost a dime apiece."

Freddy took one. Herman flicked a table-lighter, applied the flame to Freddy's cigarette, lit one for himself, took a slow, soft drag, and let the smoke come out of his nose. Herman waited until all of the smoke was out and then said, "You didn't like what I did to Ziggy."

It was a flat statement that didn't ask for an answer. Freddy sipped at the cigarette, not looking at Herman.

"You didn't like it," Herman persisted softly. "You never like it when I let Ziggy know who's boss."

Freddy shrugged. "That's between you and Ziggy."

"No," Herman said. And he spoke very slowly, with a pause between each word. "It isn't that way at all, I don't do it for Ziggy's benefit. He already knows who's top man around here."

Freddy didn't say anything. But he almost winced. And again his insides quivered.

Herman leaned forward. "Do you know who the top man is?"

"You," Freddy said.

Herman smiled. "Thanks, Freddy. Thanks for saying it." Then the smile vanished and Herman's eyes were hammerheads. "But I'm not sure you mean it."

Freddy took another sip from the Egyptian cigarette. It was strongly flavored tobacco but somehow he wasn't getting any taste from it.

Herman kept leaning forward. "I gotta be sure, Freddy," he said. "You been working for me more than a year. And just like you said, you do all the jobs exactly the way I want them done. You plan them perfect, it's always clean and neat from start to finish. I don't mind saying you're one of the best. I don't think I've ever seen a cooler head. You're as cool as they come, an icicle on wheels."

"That's plenty cool," Freddy murmured.

"It sure is," Herman said. He let the pause drift in again. Then, his lips scarcely moving, "Maybe it's too cool."

Freddy looked at the hammerhead eyes. He wondered what showed in his own eyes. He wondered what thoughts were burning under the cool surface of his own brain.

He heard Herman saying, "I've done a lot of thinking about you. A lot more than you'd ever imagine. You're a puzzler, and one thing I always like to do is play stud poker with a puzzler."

Freddy smiled dimly. "Want to play stud poker?"

"We're playing it now. Without cards." Herman gazed down at the desk-top. His right hand was on the desk-top and he flicked his wrist as though he was turning over the hole-card. His voice was very soft as he said, "I want you to break it up with Pearl."

Freddy heard himself saying, "All right, Herman."

It was as though Freddy hadn't spoken. Herman said, "I'm waiting, Freddy."

"Waiting for what?" He told the dim smile to stay on his lips. It stayed there. He murmured, "You tell me to give her up and I say all right. What more do you want me to say."

"I want you to ask me why. Don't you want to know why?"

Freddy didn't reply. He still wore the dim smile and he was gazing past Herman's head.

"Come on, Freddy. I'm waiting to see your hole-card."

Freddy remained quiet.

"All right," Herman said. "I'll keep on showing you mine. I go for Pearl. I went for her the first time I laid eyes on her. That same night I took her home with me and she stayed over. She did what I wanted her to do but it didn't mean a thing to her, it was just like turning a trick. I thought it wouldn't bother me, once I have them in bed I can put them out of my mind. But this thing with Pearl, it's different. I've had her on my mind and it gets worse all the time and now it's gotten to the point where I have to do something about it. First thing I gotta do is clear the road."

"It's cleared," Freddy said. "I'll tell her tonight I'm not seeing her anymore."

"Just like that?" And Herman snapped his fingers.

"Yes," Freddy said. His fingers made the same sound. "Just like that."

Herman leaned back in the soft leather chair. He looked at the face of Freddy Lamb as though he was trying to solve a cryptogram. Finally he shook his head slowly, and then he gave a heavy sigh and he said, "All right, Freddy. That's all for now."

Freddy stood up. He started toward the door. Half-way across the room he stopped and turned and said, "You promised me a bonus for the Donofrio job."

"This is Monday," Herman said. "I hand out the pay on Friday."

"You said I'd be paid right off."

"Did I?" Herman smiled softly.

"Yes," Freddy said. "You said the deal on Donofrio was something special and the customer was paying fifteen hundred. You told me there was five hundred in it for me and I'd get the bonus the same night I did the job."

Herman opened a desk-drawer and took out a thick roll of bills.

"Can I have it in tens and twenties?" Freddy asked.

Herman lifted his eyebrows. "Why the small change?"

"I'm an elevator man," Freddy said. "The bank would wonder what I was doing with fifties."

"You're right," Herman said. He counted off the five hundred in tens and twenties, and handed the money to Freddy. He leaned back in the chair and watched Freddy folding the bills and pocketing them and walking out of the room. When the door was closed Herman said aloud to himself, "Don't try to figure him out, he's all ice and no soul, strictly a professional."

The white-gold watch showed eleven thirty-five. Freddy sat at a table watching the floor show and drinking from a tall glass of gin and ginger ale. The Yellow Cat was crowded now and Freddy wore the dark glasses and his table was in a darkly shadowed section of the room. He sat there with Ziggy and some other men who worked for Herman. There was Dino, who did his jobs at long range and always used a rifle. There was Shikey, six foot six and weighing three hundred pounds, an expert at bone cracking, gouging, and the removing of teeth. There was Riley, another bone-cracker and strangling specialist.

A tall pretty boy stood in front of the orchestra, clutching the mike as though it was the only support he had in the world. He sang with an ache in his voice, begging someone to "—please understand." The audience liked it and he sang it again. Then two colored lap-dancers came out and worked themselves into a sweat and were gasping for breath as they finished the act. The M. C. walked on and motioned the orchestra to quiet down and grinned at ringside faces as he said, "Ready for dessert?"

"Yeah," a man shouted from ringside. "Let's have the dessert."

"All right," the M. C. said. He cupped his hands to his mouth and called off-stage, "Bring it out, we're all starved for that sweetmeat."

The orchestra went into medium tempo, the lights changed from glaring yellow to a soft violet. And then they came out, seven girls wearing horn-rimmed glasses and ultra-conservative costumes. They walked primly, and all together they resembled the stiff-necked females in a cartoon lampooning the W. C. T. U. It got a big laugh from the audience, and there was some appreciative applause. The young ladies formed a line and slowly waved black parasols as they sang, "—Father, oh father, come home with me now." But then it became, "—Daddy, oh daddy, come home with me now." And as they emphasized the daddy angle, they broke up the line and discarded the parasols and took off their ankle-length dark-blue coats. Then, their fingers loosening the buttons of dark-blue dresses, they moved separately toward the ringside tables. The patrons in the back stood up to get a better look and in the balcony the lenses of seven lamps were focused on seven young women getting undressed.

Dino, who had a footwear fetish, said loudly, "I'll pay forty for a high-heeled shoe."

One of the girls took off her shoe and flung it toward Freddy's table. Shikey caught it and handed it to Dino. A waiter came over and Dino handed him four tens and he took the money to the girl. Riley looked puzzledly at Dino and said, "Whatcha gonna do with a high-heeled shoe?" And Shikey said, "He boils 'em and eats 'em." But Ziggy had another theory. "He bangs the heel against his head," Ziggy said. "That's the way he gets his kicks." Dino sat there gazing lovingly at the shoe in his hand while his other hand caressed the kidskin surface. Then gradually his eyes closed and he murmured, "This is nice, this is so nice."

Riley was watching Dino and saying, "I don't get it."

Ziggy shrugged philosophically. "Some things," he said, "just can't be understood."

"You're so right." It was Freddy talking. He didn't know his lips were making sound. He was looking across the tables at Pearl. She sat with some ringsiders and already she'd taken off considerable clothing, she was half-naked. On her face there was a detached look and her hands moved mechanically as she unbuttoned the buttons and unzipped the zippers. There were three men sitting with her and their eyes feasted on her, they had their mouths open in a sort of mingled fascination and worship. At nearby tables the other strippers were performing but they weren't getting undivided attention. Most of the men were watching Pearl. One of them offered a hundred dollars for her stocking. She took off the stocking and let it dangle from her fingers. In a semi-whisper she asked if there were any higher bids. Freddy told himself that she wasn't happy doing what she was doing. Again he could hear her plaintive voice as she asked him to take her for a walk in the park. Suddenly he knew that he'd like that very much. He wanted to see the sun shining on her hair, instead of the night-club lights. He heard himself saying aloud, "Five hundred."

He didn't shout it, but at the ringside tables they all heard it, and for a moment there was stunned silence. At his own table the silence was very thick. He could feel the pressure of it, and the moment seemed to have substance, something on the order of iron wheels going around and around, making no sound and getting nowhere.

Some things just can't be understood, he thought. He was taking the tens and twenties from his jacket pocket. The five hundred seemed to prove the truth of Ziggy's vague philosophy. Freddy got up from his chair and moved toward an empty table behind some potted ferns adjacent to the orchestra stand. He sat down and placed green money on a yellow tablecloth. He wasn't looking at Pearl as she approached the table. From ringside an awed voice was saying, "For one silk stocking she gets half a grand—"

She seated herself at the table. He shoved the money toward her. He said, "There's your cash. Let's have the stocking."

"This a gag?" she asked quietly. Her eyes were somewhat sullen. There was some laughter from the table where Ziggy and some of the others were seated; they now had the notion it was some sort of joke.

Freddy said, "Take off the stocking."

She looked at the pile of tens and twenties. She said, "Whatcha want the stocking for?"

"Souvenir," he said.

It was the tone of his voice that did it. Her face paled. She started to shake her head very slowly, as though she couldn't believe him.

"Yes," he said, with just the trace of a sigh. "It's all over, Pearl. It's the end of the line."

She went on shaking her head. She couldn't talk.

He said, "I'll hang the stocking in my bedroom."

She was biting her lip, "It's a long time till Christmas."

"For some people it's never Christmas."

"Freddy—" She leaned toward him. "What's it all about? Why're you doing this?"

He shrugged. He didn't say anything.

Her eyes were getting wet. "You won't even give me a reason?"

All he gave her was a cool smile. Then his head was turned and he saw the faces at Ziggy's table and then he focused on the face of the large man who stood behind the table. He saw the iron in the eyes of Herman Charn. He told himself he was doing what Herman had told him to do. And just then he felt the quiver in his insides. It was mostly in the spine as though his spine was gradually turning to jelly.

He spoke to himself without sound. He said, *No, it isn't that, it can't be that.*

Pearl was saying, "All right, Freddy, if that's the way it is."

He nodded very slowly.

Pearl bent over and took the stocking off her leg. She placed the stocking on the table. She picked up the five hundred, counted it off to make sure it was all there.

Then she stood up and said, "No charge, mister. I'd rather keep the memories."

She put the tens and twenties on the tablecloth and walked away. Freddy glanced off to the side and saw a soft smile on the face of Herman Charn.

The floor-show was ended and Freddy was still sitting there at the table. There was a bottle of bourbon in front of him. It had been there for less than twenty minutes and already it was half-empty. There was also a pitcher of ice-water and the pitcher was full. He didn't need a chaser because he couldn't taste the whiskey. He was drinking the whiskey from the water-glass.

A voice said, "Freddy—"

And then a hand tugged at his arm. He looked up and saw Ziggy sitting beside him.

He smiled at Ziggy. He motioned toward the bottle and shot-glass and said, "Have a drink."

Ziggy shrugged. "I might as well while I got the chance. At the rate you're going, that bottle'll soon be empty."

"It's very good bourbon," Freddy said.

"Yeah?" Ziggy was pouring a glass for himself. He swished the liquor into his mouth. Then, looking closely at Freddy, "You don't care whether it's good or not. You'd be gulping it if it was shoe-polish."

Freddy was staring at the tablecloth. "Let's go somewhere and drink some shoe-polish."

Ziggy tugged again at Freddy's arm. He said, "Come out of it."

"Come out of what?"

"The clouds," Ziggy said. "You're in the clouds."

"It's nice in the clouds." Freddy said. "I'm up here having a dandy time. I'm floating."

"Floating? You're drowning." Ziggy pulled urgently at his arm, to get his hand away from a water-glass filled with whiskey. "You're not a drinker, Freddy. What do you want to do, drink yourself into a hospital?"

Freddy grinned. He aimed the grin at nothing in particular. For some moments he sat there motionless. Then he reached into his jacket pocket and took out the silk stocking. He showed it to Ziggy and said, "Look what I got."

"Yeah," Ziggy said. "I seen her give it to you. What's the score on that routine?"

"No score," Freddy said. He went on grinning. "It's a funny way to end a game. Nothing on the scoreboard. Nothing at all."

Ziggy frowned. "You trying to tell me something?"

Freddy looked at the whiskey in the water-glass. He said, "I packed her in."

"No," Ziggy said. His tone was incredulous. "Not Pearl. Not that pigeon. That ain't no ordinary merchandise. You wouldn't walk out on Pearl unless you had a very special reason."

"It was special, all right."

"Tell me about it, Freddy." There was something plaintive in Ziggy's voice, a certain feeling for Freddy that he couldn't put into words. The closest he could get to it was: "After all, I'm on your side, ain't I?"

"No," Freddy said. The grin was slowly fading. "You're on Herman's side." He gazed past Ziggy's head. "We're all on Herman's side."

"Herman? What's he got to do with it?"

"Everything," Freddy said. "Herman's the boss, remember?" He looked at the swollen fingers of Ziggy's right hand. "Herman wants something done, it's got to be done. He gave me orders to break with Pearl. He's the employer and I'm the hired man, so I did what I had to do. I carried out his orders."

Ziggy was quiet for some moments. Then, very quietly, "Well, it figures he wants her for himself. But it don't seem right. It just ain't fair."

"Don't make me laugh," Freddy said. "Who the hell are we to say what's fair?"

"We're human, aren't we?"

"No," Freddy said. He gazed past Ziggy's head. "I don't know what we are. But I know one thing, we're not human. We can't afford to be human, not in this line of business."

Ziggy didn't get it. It was just a little too deep for him.

All he could say was, "You getting funny ideas?"

"I'm not reaching for them, they're just coming to me."

"Take another drink," Ziggy said.

"I'd rather have the laughs." Freddy showed the grin again. "It's really comical, you know? Especially this thing with Pearl. I was thinking of calling it quits anyway. You know how it is with me, Ziggy. I never like to be tied down to one skirt. But tonight Pearl said something that spun me around. We were talking outside the club and she brought it in out of left field. She asked me to take her for a walk in the park."

Ziggy blinked a few times. "What?"

"A walk in the park," Freddy said.

"What for?" Ziggy wanted to know. "She gettin' square all of a sudden? She wanna go around picking flowers?"

"I don't know," Freddy said. "All she said was, it's very nice in Fairmount Park. She asked me to take her there and we'd be together in the park, just taking a walk."

Ziggy pointed to the glass. "You better take that drink."

Freddy reached for the glass. But someone else's hand was there first. He saw the thick soft fingers, the soft green glow of the star-emerald. As the glass of whiskey was shoved out of his reach, he looked up and saw the soft smile on the face of Herman Charn.

"Too much liquor is bad for the kidneys," Herman said. He bent down lower to peer at Freddy's eyes. "You look knocked-out, Freddy. There's a soft couch in the office. Go in there and lie down for awhile."

Freddy got up from the chair. He was somewhat unsteady on his feet. Herman took his arm and helped him make it down the aisle past the tables to the door of the office. He could feel the pressure of Herman's hand on his arm. It was very soft pressure but somehow it felt like a clamp of iron biting into his flesh.

Herman opened the office-door and guided him toward the couch. He fell onto the couch, sent an idiotic grin toward the ceiling, then closed his eyes and went to sleep.

He slept until four-forty in the morning. The sound that woke him up was a scream.

At first it was all blurred, there was too much whiskey-fog in his brain, he had no idea where he was or what was happening. He pushed his knuckles against his eyes. Then, sitting up, he focused on the faces in the room. He saw Shikey and Riley and they had girls sitting in their laps. They were on the other couch at the opposite side of the room. He saw Dino standing near the couch with his arm around the waist of a slim brunette. Then he glanced toward the door and he saw Ziggy. That made seven faces for him to look at. He told himself to keep looking at them. If he concentrated on that, maybe he wouldn't hear the screaming.

But he heard it. The scream was an animal sound and yet he recognized the voice. It came from near the desk and he turned his head very slowly, telling himself he didn't want to look but knowing he had to look.

He saw Pearl kneeling on the floor. Herman stood behind her. With one hand he was twisting her arm up high between her shoulder blades. His other hand was on her head and he was pulling her hair so that her face was drawn back, her throat stretched.

Herman spoke very softly. "You make me very unhappy, Pearl. I don't like to be unhappy."

Then Herman gave her arm another upward twist and pulled tighter on her hair and she screamed again.

The girl in Shikey's lap gave Pearl a scornful look and said, "You're a damn fool."

"In spades." It came from the stripper who nestled against Riley. "All he wants her to do is kiss him like she means it."

Freddy told himself to get up and walk out of the room. He lifted himself from the couch and took a few steps toward the door and heard Herman saying, "Not yet, Freddy. I'll tell you when to go."

He went back to the couch and sat down.

Herman said, "Be sensible, Pearl. Why can't you be sensible?"

Pearl opened her mouth to scream again. But no sound came out. There was too much pain and it was choking her.

The brunette who stood with Dino was saying, "It's a waste of time, Herman, she can't give you what she hasn't got. She just don't have it for you, Herman."

"She'll have it for him," Dino said. "Before he's finished, he'll have her crawling on her belly."

Herman looked at Dino. "No," he said. "She won't do that. I wouldn't let her do that." He cast a downward glance at Pearl. His lips shaped a soft smile. There was something tender in the smile and in his voice. "Pearl, tell me something, why don't you want me?"

He gave her a chance to reply, his fingers slackening the grip on her wrist and her hair. She groaned a few times and then she said, "You got my body, Herman. You can have my body anytime you want it."

"That isn't enough," Herman said. "I want you all the way, a hundred percent. It's got to be like that, Pearl. You're in me so deep it just can't take any other route. It's got to be you and me from here on in, you gotta need me just as much as I need you."

"But Herman—" She gave a dry sob. "I can't lie to you. I just don't feel that way."

"You're gonna feel that way," Herman said.

"No." Pearl sobbed again. "No. No."

"Why not?" He was pulling her hair again, twisting her arm. But it seemed he was suffering more than Pearl. The pain racked his pleading voice. "Why can't you feel something for me?"

Her reply was made without sound. She managed to turn her head just a little, toward the couch. And everyone in the room saw her looking at Freddy.

Herman's face became very pale. His features tightened and twisted and it seemed he was about to burst into tears. He stared up at the ceiling.

Herman shivered. His body shook spasmodically, as though he stood on a vibrating platform. Then all at once the tormented look faded from his eyes, the iron came into his eyes, and the soft smile came onto his lips. He released Pearl, turned away from her, went to the desk and opened the cigarette-box. It was very quiet in the room while Herman stood there lighting the cigarette. He took a slow, easy drag and then he said quietly, "All right, Pearl, you can go home now."

She started to get up from the floor. The brunette came over and helped her up.

"I'll call a cab for you," Herman said. He reached for the telephone and put in the call. As he lowered the phone, he was looking at Pearl and saying, "You want to go home alone?"

Pearl didn't say anything. Her head was lowered and she was leaning against the shoulder of the brunette.

Herman said, "You want Freddy to take you home?"

Pearl raised her head just a little and looked at the face of Freddy Lamb.

Herman laughed softly. "All right," he said. "Freddy'll take you home."

Freddy winced. He sat there staring at the carpet.

Herman told the brunette to fix a drink for Pearl. He said, "Take her to the bar and give her anything she wants." He motioned to the other girls and they got up from the laps of Shikey and Riley. Then all the girls walked out of the room. Herman was quiet for some moments, taking slow drags at the cigarette and looking at the door. Then gradually his head turned and he looked at Freddy. He said, "You're slated, Freddy."

Freddy went on staring at the carpet.

"You're gonna bump her," Herman said.

Freddy closed his eyes.

"Take her somewhere and bump her and bury her," Herman said.

Shikey and Riley looked at each other. Dino had his mouth open and he was staring at Herman. Standing next to the door, Ziggy had his eyes glued to Freddy's face.

"She goes," Herman said. And then, speaking aloud to himself, "She goes because she gives me grief." He hit his hand against his chest. "She hits me here, where I live. Hits me too hard. Hurts me. I don't appreciate getting hurt. Especially here." Again his hand thumped his chest. He said, "You'll do it, Freddy. You'll see to it that I get rid of the hurt."

"Let me do it," Ziggy said. Herman shook his head. He pointed a finger at Freddy. His finger jabbed empty air, and he said, "Freddy does it. Freddy."

Ziggy opened his mouth, tried to close it, couldn't close it, and blurted, "Why take it out on him?"

"That's a stupid question," Herman said mildly. "I'm not taking it out on anybody. I'm giving the job to Freddy because I know he's dependable. I can always depend on Freddy."

Ziggy made a final frantic try. "Please, Herman," he said. "Please don't make him do it."

Herman didn't bother to reply. All he did was give Ziggy a slow appraising look up and down. It was like a soundless warning to Ziggy, letting him know he was walking on thin ice and the ice would crack if he opened his mouth again.

Then Herman turned to Freddy and said, "Where's your blade?"

"Stashed," Freddy said. He was still staring at the carpet.

Herman opened a desk-drawer. He took out a black-handled switch-blade. "Use this," he said, coming toward the couch. He handed the knife to Freddy. "Give it a try," he said.

Freddy pressed the button. The blade flicked out. It glimmered blue-white. He pushed the blade into the handle and tried the button again. He went on trying the button and watching the flash of the blade. It was quiet in the room as the blade went in and out, in and out. Then from the street there was the sound of a horn. Herman said, "That's the taxi." Freddy nodded and got up from the sofa and walked out of the room. As he moved toward the girls who stood at the cocktail bar, he could feel the weight of the knife in the inner pocket of his jacket. He was looking at Pearl and saying, "Come on, let's go," and as he said it, the blade seemed to come out of the knife and slice into his own flesh.

The taxi was cruising north on Sixteenth Street. On Freddy's wrist the white-gold watch said five-twenty. He was watching the parade of unlit windows along the dark street. Pearl was saying something but he didn't hear her. She spoke just a bit louder and he turned and looked at her. He smiled and murmured, "Sorry, I wasn't listening."

"Can't you sit closer?"

He moved closer to her. A mixture of moonlight and streetlamp glow came pouring into the back seat of the taxi and illuminated her face. He saw something in her eyes that caused him to blink several times.

She noticed the way he was blinking and said, "What's the matter?"

He didn't answer. He tried to stop blinking and he couldn't stop.

"Hangover?" Pearl asked.

"No," he said. "I feel alright now, I feel fine."

For some moments she didn't say anything. She was rubbing her sore arm. She tried to stretch it, winced and gasped with pain, and said, "Oh Jesus, it hurts. It really hurts. Maybe it's broken."

"Let me feel it," he said. He put his hand on her arm. He ran his fingers down from above her elbow to her wrist. "It isn't broken," he murmured. "Just a little swollen, that's all. Sprained some ligaments."

She smiled at him. "The hurt goes away when you touch it."

He tried not to look at her, but something fastened his eyes to her face. He kept his hand on her arm. He heard himself saying, "I feel sorry for Herman. If he could see you now, I mean if you'd look at him like you're looking at me—"

"Freddy," she said. "Freddy." Then she leaned toward him. She rested her head on his shoulder.

Then somehow everything was quiet and still and he didn't hear the noise of the taxi's engine, he didn't feel the bumps as the wheels hit the ruts in the cobblestoned surface of Sixteenth Street. But suddenly there was a deep rut and the taxi gave a lurch. He looked up and heard the driver cursing the city engineers. "Goddamit," the driver said. "They got a deal with the tire companies."

Freddy stared past the driver's head, his eyes aimed through the windshield to see the wide intersection where Sixteenth Street met the Parkway. The Parkway was a six-laned drive slanting to the left of the downtown area, going away from the concrete of Philadelphia skyscrapers and pointing toward the green of Fairmount Park.

"Turn left," Freddy said.

They were approaching the intersection, and the driver gave a backward glance. "Left?" the driver asked. "That takes us outta the way. You gave me an address on Seventeenth near Lehigh. We gotta hit it from Sixteenth—"

"I know," Freddy said quietly. "But turn left anyway."

The driver shrugged. "You're the captain." He beat the yellow of a traffic light and the taxi made a left turn onto the Parkway.

Pearl said, "What's this, Freddy? Where're we going?"

"In the park." He wasn't looking at her. "We're gonna do what you said we should do. We're gonna take a walk in the park."

"For real?" Her eyes were lit up. She shook her head, as though she could scarcely believe what he'd just said.

"We'll take a nice walk," he murmured. "Just the two of us. The way you wanted it."

"Oh," she breathed. "Oh, Freddy—"

The driver shrugged again. The taxi went past the big monuments and fountains of Logan Circle, past the Rodin Museum and the Art Museum and onto River Drive. For a mile or so they stayed on the highway, bordering the moonlit water of the river, and then without being told the driver made a turn off the highway, made a series of turns that took them deep into the park. They came to a section where there were no lights, no movement, no sound except the autumn wind drifting through the trees and bushes and tall grass and flowers.

"Stop here," Freddy said.

The taxi came to a stop. They got out and he paid the driver. The driver gave him a queer look and said, "You sure picked a lonely spot."

Freddy looked at the cabman. He didn't say anything.

The driver said, "You're at least three miles off the highway. It's gonna be a problem getting a ride home."

"Is it your problem?" Freddy asked gently.

"Well, no—"

"Then don't worry about it," Freddy said. He smiled amiably. The driver threw a glance at the blonde, smiled, and told himself that the man might have the right idea, after all. With an item like that, any man would want complete privacy. He thought of the bony, buck-toothed woman who waited for him at home, crinkled his face in a distasteful grimace, put the car in gear and drove away.

"Ain't it nice?" Pearl said. "Ain't it wonderful?"

They were walking through a glade where the moonlight showed the autumn colors of fallen leaves. The night air was fragrant with the blended aromas of wild flowers. He had his arm around her shoulder and was leading her toward a narrow lane slopping downward through the trees.

She laughed lightly, happily. "It's like as if you know the place. As if you've been here before."

"No," he said. "I've never been here before."

There was the tinkling sound of a nearby brook. A bird chirped in the bushes. Another bird sang a tender reply.

"Listen," Pearl murmured. "Listen to them."

He listened to the singing of the birds. Now he was guiding Pearl down along the slope and seeing the way it levelled at the bottom and then went up again on all sides. It was a tiny valley down there with the brook running along the edge. He told himself it would happen when they reached the bottom.

He heard Pearl saying, "Wouldn't it be nice if we could stay here?"

He looked at her. "Stay here?"

"Yes," she said. "If we could live here for the rest of our lives. Just be here, away from everything—"

"We'd get lonesome."

"No we wouldn't," she said. "We'd always have company. I'd have you and you'd have me."

They were nearing the bottom of the slope. It was sort of steep now and they had to move slowly. All at once she stumbled and pitched forward and he caught her before she could fall on her face. He steadied her, smiled at her and said, "Okay?"

She nodded. She stood very close to him and gazed into his eyes and said, "You wouldn't let me fall, would you?"

The smile faded. He stared past her. "Not if I could help it."

"I know," she said. "You don't have to tell me."

He went on staring past her. "Tell you what?"

"The situation." She spoke softly, almost in a whisper. "I got it figured, Freddy. It's so easy to figure."

He wanted to close his eyes, he didn't know why he wanted to close his eyes.

He heard her saying, "I know why you packed me in tonight. Orders from Herman."

"That's right." He said it automatically, as though the mention of the name was the shifting of a gear.

"And another thing," she said. "I know why you brought me here." There was a pause, and then, very softly, "Herman."

He nodded.

She started to cry. It was quiet weeping and contained no fear, no hysteria. It was the weeping of farewell. She was crying because she was sad. Then, very slowly, she took the few remaining steps going down to the bottom of the slope. He stood there and watched her as she faced about to look up at him.

He walked down to where she stood, smiling at her and. . . . trying to pretend his hand was not on the switchblade in his pocket. He tried to make himself believe he wasn't going to do it, but he knew that wasn't true. He'd been slated for this job. The combine had him listed as a top-rated operator, one of the best in the business. He'd expended a lot of effort to attain that reputation, to be known as the grade-A expert who'd never muffed an assignment.

He begged himself to stop. He couldn't stop. The knife was open in his hand and his arm flashed out and sideways with the blade sliding in neatly and precisely, cutting the flesh of her throat. She went down very slowly, tried to cough, made a few gurgling sounds, and then rolled over on her back and died looking up at him.

For a long time he stared at her face. There was no expression on her features now. At first he didn't feel anything, and then he realized she was dead, and he had killed her.

He tried to tell himself there was nothing else he could have done, but even though that was true it didn't do any good. He took his glance away from her face and looked down at the white-gold watch to check the hour and the minute, automatically. But somehow the dial was blurred, as though the hands were spinning like tiny propellers. He had the weird feeling that the watch was showing Time traveling backward, so that he found himself checking it in terms of years and decades. He went all the way back to the day when he was eleven years old and they took him to reform school.

In reform school he was taught a lot of things. The thing he learned best was the way to use a knife. The knife became his profession. But somewhere along the line he caught onto the idea of holding a daytime job to cover his night-time activities. He worked in stockrooms and he did some window-cleaning and drove a truck for a fruit-dealer. And finally he became an elevator operator and that was the job he liked best. He'd never realized why he liked it so much but he realized now. He knew that the elevator was nothing more than a moving cell, that the only place for him was a cell. The passengers were just a lot of friendly visitors walking in and out, saying "Good morning, Freddy," and "Good night, Freddy," and they were such nice people. Just the thought of them brought a tender smile to his lips.

Then he realized he was smiling down at her. He sensed a faint glow coming from somewhere, lighting her face. For an instant he had no idea what it was. Then he realized it came from the sky. It was the first signal of approaching sunrise.

The white-gold watch showed five fifty-three. Freddy Lamb told himself to get moving. For some reason he couldn't move. He was looking down at the dead girl. His hand was still clenched about the switchblade, and as he tried to relax it he almost dropped the knife. He looked down at it.

The combine was a cell, too, he told himself. The combine was an elevator from which he could never escape. It was going steadily downwards and there were no stops until the end. There was no way to get out.

Herman had made him kill the girl. Herman would make him do other things. And there was no getting away from that. If he killed Herman there would be someone else.

The elevator was carrying Freddy steadily downward. Already, he had left Pearl somewhere far above him. He realized it all at once, and an unreasonable terror filled him.

Freddy looked at the white-gold watch again. A minute had passed and he knew suddenly that he was slated to do a job on someone in exactly three minutes now. The minutes passed and he stood there alone.

At precisely five fifty-seven he said goodbye to his profession and plunged the blade into his heart.

The Quiet Room
Jonathan Craig (Frank E. Smith)

December 1953

Detective Sergeant Carl Streeter's home on Ashland Avenue was modest. So were the dark gray suits he always wore, and the four-year-old Plymouth he drove. But in various lock boxes around the city he had accumulated nearly fifty thousand dollars.

He was thinking about the money now as he watched his daughter Jeannie clear away the dinner dishes. He never tired of watching her. She had just turned sixteen, but she was already beautiful, and lately she had begun to develop the infinitely feminine movements and mannerisms he had once found so irresistible in her mother.

The thought of his wife soured the moment, and he frowned. It had been wonderful, having Barbara away for a few weeks. But she'd be back from the seashore next Monday, and then the nagging and bickering and general unpleasantness would start up again . . . It didn't seem possible, he reminded himself for probably the ten thousandth time, that anyone who had once been almost as slim and lovely as Jeannie could have grown into two hundred pounds of shapeless, complaining blubber.

"More coffee, Dad?" Jeannie asked.

He pushed his chair back from the table and got up. "No," he said. "I guess I'd better get going if I want to get down to the precinct by seven."

"Seven? But I thought your shift didn't start till eight."

"It doesn't. There are a couple things I want to take care of down there, though."

"When will you be home?"

"Depends. Not until three or four, anyhow. We're a little short-handed."

"You put in too many hours, Dad."

"Maybe," he said. He grinned at her and walked out to the front hall to get his hat. Just another few months, he thought. Six months at the outside, and I'll have enough to put Jeannie in a damned good college, ditch Barbara and her lard, and tell the Chief to go to hell.

Sally Creighton was waiting for him in the Inferno Bar. She pushed a folded piece of paper across the table as he sat down facing her.

"How's the Eighteenth Precinct's one and only policewoman?" Streeter asked.

Sally looked at him narrowly.

"Never mind the amenities. Here's the list we got off that girl last night."

He put the list into his pocket without looking at it. "Did you check them?"

"Don't I always? Only two of them might be good for any money. I marked them. One's a dentist, and the other guy runs a bar and grill over on Summit." She lifted her beer and sipped at it, studying him over the rim of the glass. "There've been a few changes made, Carl." Her bony, angular face was set in hard lines.

"Like what?"

"From now on I'm getting fifty per cent."

"We've been over that before."

"And this is the last time. Fifty per cent, Carl. Starting as of now."

He laughed shortly. "I do the dirty work, and take the chances—and you come in for half, eh?"

"Either that, or I cut out." She put a quarter next to her glass and stood up. "Think it over, Sergeant. You aren't the only bruiser around the Eighteenth that can shake a guy down. Start making with the fifty per cent, or I'll find another partner." She moved toward the door with a long, almost mannish stride.

Streeter spread his fingers flat against the table top, fighting back the anger that he knew would get him nowhere. For almost a full minute he stared at the broken, scarred knuckles of his hands. By God, he thought, if it's the last thing I ever do I'll knock about ten of that woman's yellow teeth down into her belly.

Hell, he'd taught her the racket in the first place. He'd shown her how to scare hell out of those under-age chippies until they thought they were going to spend the rest of their lives in jail if they didn't play ball. Why, he'd even had to educate Sally in the ways of keeping those girls away from the juvenile authorities until she'd had a chance to drain them.

He closed his right fist and clenched it until the knuckles stood up like serrated knobs of solid white bone. Damn that Sally, anyhow; she was getting too greedy. Fifty per cent!

He got up slowly and moved toward the door.

Twenty minutes later, after he had checked in at the precinct and been assigned a cruiser, he pulled up in a No Parking zone and took out the list Sally had given him. His anger had subsided a little now. Actually, he realized, no cop had ever been in a better spot. His first real break with the Department had been when they had organized the Morals Squad and assigned him to it as a roving detective. The second break had occurred when Sally Creighton was transferred to the Eighteenth. He hadn't talked to her more than ten minutes that first day before he'd realized that he had found the right person to work into his ideas.

In three years, working alone every night as he did, he had loaded his safe deposit boxes with almost fifty thousand dollars.

He lit a cigarette and glanced at the list. Of the two names Sally had marked, the man who owned the bar and grill was the best bet. The other, the dentist, lived on the far side of town; and besides, Streeter had found it was always best to brace a man at his place of business. There was a tremendous psychological factor working on his side when he did that, and especially if the guy happened to be a professional man. He memorized the address of the bar and grill and eased the cruiser away from the curb.

It was too late for the short-order dinner crowd and too early for the beer drinkers, and Streeter had the long bar entirely to himself.

The bartender came up, a thin, blond man in his middle thirties.

Streeter ordered beer, and when the blond man brought it to him he said, "I'm looking for Johnny Cabe."

The bartender smiled. "That's me. What can I do for you?"

"Quite a bit, maybe," Streeter said. "It all depends."

Some of the bartender's smile went away. "I don't follow you."

"You will," Streeter said. He took out his wallet and showed the other man his gold badge.

"What's the trouble?" Cabe asked.

"Well, now," Streeter said, "there really doesn't have to be any." He took a swallow of beer and leaned a little closer to Cabe. "You had quite a time for yourself last night, they tell me."

Cabe's eyes grew thoughtful. "Last night? You kidding? All I did was have a few beers over at Ed Riley's place, and—"

"Yeah," Streeter said. "And then you picked up somebody."

"What if I did?"

"Then you took her over to your room."

"So what? They don't put guys in jail for—"

"The hell they don't," Streeter said. "Raping a girl can put you away damned near forever, boy."

"Rape? You're crazy! Hell, she wanted to go. She suggested it."

"Next you're going to tell me she charged you for it."

"Sure, she did. Twenty bucks."

"That's a damn shame," Streeter said. "Because it's still rape, and you're in one hell of a jam."

Cabe moved his lips as if to speak, but there was no sound.

"That girl you took home with you was only fifteen years old," Streeter said. "She—"

"Fifteen! She told me she was nineteen! She *looked* nineteen!"

"You should have looked twice. She's fifteen. That makes it statutory rape, and it doesn't make one damn bit of difference what you thought, or whether she was willing, or if she charged you for it, or anything else." He smiled. "It's statutory rape, brother, and that means you've had it."

Cabe moistened his lips. "I can't believe it."

"Get your hat," Streeter said.

"You're arresting me?"

"I didn't come in here just for the beer. Hurry it up."

"God," the blond man said. "God, officer, I—"

"Kind of hard to get used to the idea, isn't it?" Streeter asked softly.

Cabe's forehead glistened with sweat. "Listen, officer, I got a wife. Best kid on earth, see. I don't know what came over me last night. I just got tight, I guess, and . . . God, I—"

Streeter shook his head slowly. "Good thing you haven't got any children," he said.

The Best of *Manhunt*

"But I have! Two of them. Seven and nine. And my wife, she's—she's going to have another baby pretty soon. That's why—I mean that's how come I was kind of anxious for a woman last night. I—" He broke off, biting at his lower lip.

"Tough," Streeter said. "Real tough. But it's that kind of world, friend. I've got a kid myself, so I know how it is. But—" he shrugged— "there isn't a hell of a lot I can do about it." He shook his head sadly. "When little guys—guys like you and me—get in a jam, it's just plain tough. But guys with dough . . . well, sometimes they can buy their way out."

Cabe looked at him a long moment. "How much dough?"

"Quite a bit," Streeter said. "More than you've got, Johnny. Better get your hat."

"Let's cut out this crap," Cabe said. "I asked you how much dough?"

"We got to think of your wife and kids," Streeter said. "So we'll have to go easy. Let's say a grand."

"I ain't got it."

"You can get it. A little at a time, maybe, but you can get it." He took another swallow of his beer. "How much you got in the cash register?"

"About three hundred. I got to pay the help tonight, or there wouldn't be that much."

"Too bad about the help," Streeter said. "Let's have the three hundred. In a couple weeks I'll be back, By that time you'll have the other seven hundred, eh, Johnny-boy?"

Cabe went to the cash register, took out the money, and came back. "Here," he said. Then, softly beneath his breath he added: "You bastard!"

Streeter put the money in his pocket and stood up. "Thanks, Johnny," he said. "Thanks a lot. You reckon I ought to give you a receipt? A little reminder to get up that other seven hundred bucks?"

"I'll remember," Cabe said.

"I'm afraid you might not,"

Streeter said, smiling. "So here's your receipt." He leaned across the bar and slammed his fist flush against the blond man's mouth.

Johnny Cabe crashed into the back-bar, blood trickling from the corners of his mouth.

"Thanks again, Johnny," Streeter said. "You serve a good glass of beer." He turned and went outside to the cruiser.

He spent the next four hours making routine check-ups and trying to think of improvements in the system he had worked out with Sally Creighton. The system had been working nicely, but it was a long way from foolproof. Most of the cops on the force were honest, and for them Streeter had nothing but contempt. But there were a few like himself, and those were the ones who worried him. He'd had reason lately to suspect that a couple of them were getting on to him. If they did, then his racket was over. They could politic around until they got him busted off the Morals Squad. Then they'd take over themselves. And, he reflected, they wouldn't even have to go that far. They could simply cut themselves in on a good thing.

And that Sally . . . He'd have to start splitting down the middle with her, he knew. Maybe she was even worth it. One thing was sure, she'd learned how to terrify young girls better than anyone else he could have teamed up with. He'd seen her work on just one girl, but it had been enough to convince him. Sally had wrapped her arm around a fourteen-year-old girl's throat in such a way that the girl was helpless. Then, with a hand towel soaked with water, she had beaten the girl across the stomach until she was almost dead. When the girl had recovered slightly, she had been only too willing to tell Sally every man she'd picked up during the last six months.

That particular list of names, Streeter recalled, had been worth a little over ten thousand in shakedown money.

He came to a drug store and braked the cruiser at the curb.

In the phone booth, he dialed Sally's number, humming tunelessly to himself. He felt much better now, with Johnny Cabe's three hundred dollars in his pocket.

When Sally answered, he said, "Streeter. Anything doing?"

"I got one in here now," Sally said. "A real tough baby. I picked her up at Andy's trying to promote a drunk at the bar."

"She talking?" he asked.

"Not a damn word. I got her back in the Quiet room."

"What's her name?"

"Don't know. All she had in her bag was a lipstick and a few bucks." She paused. "Like I said, she's tough. She won't even give us the time of day."

"Listen," Streeter said. "Things are slow tonight. See if you can get her talking. Maybe I can collect a bill here and there."

"That's an idea."

"You haven't lost your technique, have you?"

"No."

"All right. So turn it on. Give her that towel across the belly. That ought to make her talkative."

For the first time he could remember, he heard Sally laugh.

"You know," she said, "I'm just in the mood for something like that. Maybe I will."

"Sure," Streeter said. "The sooner you get me some names, the sooner I get us some dough."

"Don't forget, Carl—it's fifty per cent now."

"Sure."

He hung up and went back out to the cruiser.

After another slow hour of routine checks, he decided to see how Sally was making out with the tough pick-up. He stopped at a diner and called her.

"God," she said, as soon as he had identified himself, "we're really in it now, Carl." Her voice was ragged, and there was panic in it.

"What do you mean?"

"I mean I went too far. I was doing what you said, and—"

"For God's sake, Sally! What's happened?"

"I—I think I broke her neck . . ."

"You think! Don't you know?"

There was a pause. "Yes. I broke her neck, Carl. I didn't mean to, but she was fighting, and all at once I heard something snap and . . ."

The thin film of perspiration along his back and shoulders was suddenly like a sheathe of ice.

"When, Sally? When did it happen?"

"J-just now. Just a minute ago."

"You sure she's dead?"

"Dead or dying. There was a pulse a few seconds ago, but—"

"But her neck! You're positive it's broken? That it just isn't dislocated; or something?"

"It's broken. This is it, Carl. For both of us. God . . ."

"Listen, damn it!" he said. "Was she wearing stockings? Long ones?"

"Yes. What—"

"Take one of them off her and hang her up with it."

She seemed to have trouble breathing. "But I—I can't do that. I—"

"You've got to! Do you hear? It's the only way out. Tie one end of the stocking around her neck. Then put a chair beneath that steam pipe that runs across the ceiling. Haul her up on the chair with you and tie the other end around the pipe. Leave her hanging and kick the chair away, just like she'd done it herself."

He waited, breathing heavily.

"All right," Sally said. "I'll try."

"You'd better. And hurry. Get her up there and then leave the room for a few minutes. When you go back to see your prisoner, she's hanged herself. See? They'll give you hell for leaving her alone with stockings on, but that's all they can do. She panicked and hanged herself; that's all."

"But, Carl, I—"

"No buts! Get busy!"

He opened up the siren and kept it open all the way back to the Eighteenth. He ran up the station steps, through the corridors. He was breathing quickly. When he arrived at the second floor he was soaked with perspiration.

He forced himself to walk leisurely through the large room that housed the detective headquarters, back toward the short corridor that led to the Quiet room. The Quiet room was a small, soundproof detention cell where they sometimes put the screamers and howlers until they calmed down enough for questioning. It had been designed to provide some degree of quiet for the men out in the headquarters room, and not as a torture chamber.

But it had served Streeter and Sally Creighton well and often.

Streeter paused at the door to the corridor and drew a paper cup of water from the cooler. Where in hell was Sally? he wondered. She should be out here by now, killing time before she went back to discover that her prisoner had hanged herself.

He glanced about him. There were only two other detectives in the room, and both were busy with paper work. A man in a T-shirt and blue jeans sat dozing in a chair, one wrist handcuffed to a chair arm.

Then he heard footsteps behind him, and Sally's voice said, "Thank God you're here."

He turned to look at her. Her face was gray and her forehead was sheened with sweat.

"Where've you been?" he asked.

"To the john. I don't know . . . something about this made me sick in the stomach."

"Yeah. Well, let's go down there and get it over with."

He led the way down the corridor to the Quiet room and threw the heavy bolt. The goddamned little chippie, he thought; So she'd thought she was tough . . . Well, she'd asked for it, hadn't she? She'd asked for it, and she'd damn well got it.

He jerked the door open and looked up at the girl hanging from the steam pipe. Her body was moving, very slowly, a few inches to the right and then back again. He stared at her while the floor seemed to tilt beneath his feet and something raw and sickening filled his stomach.

He took a faltering step forward, and then another, his eyes straining and misted. It was difficult for him to see clearly. Absently, he brushed at his eyes with his sleeve. The hanging figure before him sprang into sudden, terrifying focus.

The girl's body was as slim and graceful looking in death as it had been a few hours ago when he had watched her clearing away the dinner dishes. But not the face, not the horribly swollen face.

"Jeannie," he whispered. "Jeannie, Jeannie . . ."

Pistol
Hal Ellson

November 1954

Moms was in a bad mood because the old man didn't show again with the pay-check. He was out hitting up like a real wino and maybe carrying on with that she-hag that hangs in the bar around the corner. Maybe thinks I don't and maybe that's business but what Moms have to take out on me for?

Yeah, she tried to keep me in for her back-lip but I cut out soon as she ain't looking. Had to hit down the fire-escape, but that's not new in my life. Half the time I cut out that way, and nine out of ten that's the route back at night.

Soon as I hit the street I ran into Blubber. He's a big easy-moving guy, darker-skinned than me. I come up out of the cellar like a rocket and start licking for the corner when he calls me and I turn and see him leaning in the doorway.

"Hi, boy, where's the raid?" he says.

I'm standing still by then and I don't want him to know nothing so I say, "What's doing?"

"Things is quiet."

"Maybe too quiet."

"Yeah, Dusty." He stretched and yawned. "It's like things are creeping underneath—if you know what I mean."

"I can guess."

"Next thing you know, fireworks'll be busting out all over the neighborhood."

"Somebody's like to be killed."

Blubber opens his sleepy-looking eyes and stares at me funny-like when I say that. "You sound like a real bad cat," he says.

"Maybe I am," I say.

He laughs then. "Real bad cats don't talk about it," he says. "They do it."

"Do what?"

"Do anything."

We was staring at each other now and I'm angry, but then I know he doesn't mean nothing. Only he don't like talk. Maybe he's easy-going and all that but he's got a strong arm and he carries a switchblade. I ought to know. I mugged with him one night and if it hadn't been for him . . . Anyway, I wasn't mad at him. I didn't know what I was mad at.

"You coming to the meeting?" he finally says.

Then I know why he was waiting and I nod my head. "The way I was heading," I tell him.

"You sure?" he says.

"Yeah, I'm sure."

"It's good you are, cause we wasn't so sure." He meant the Golden Warriors—the club we're both in, only I'm new.

"Because you wasn't around last night," he says. "That's why we wasn't sure."

I know what he meant and what's in his head and didn't feel like answering, but I got no other excuse so I tell him, "I was shining last night." I didn't tell him there was nothing to eat in the house, so he just laughs and says, "That's Little Boy Blue stuff, strictly for the midgets."

"Maybe it is but I needed the money."

"Me, that's the last thing I'd do, shine shoes."

It was the last thing I wanted to do, too, but when there's a knife in your back you crawl on your belly like a snake. I told him that and he only laughed and said, "You coming? It's getting late."

2.

A few minutes later we hit the meeting place. It's down a cellar, a big room that stinks like a rathole. A cat named Skunky rents it. He's a real gone wino; we throw him a bottle and he lets us in. Most everybody's there when we walk in. Clouds of smoke and that special-sweet marijuana smell; somebody coming in in back of us like the flatfoots is chasing him and a carton in his arms, sweat rolling off him. He dumps the loot on the table and there's a scramble till Jess starts. Jess is President of the Golden Warriors, a real nasty type but he can straighten things.

He did, and fast. Then he tossed the cans around, first to the bigshots. I'm new, I'm like nothing at all, so I don't get nothing cause there's not enough to go around. Anyhow, the beer is warm. It just came off a truck. I'm for marijuana but nobody's offering. In fact, I got an uneasy feeling that my company ain't too welcome. Nobody sort of knows me now.

Finally Jess says, "All right, let's get down to business," and I see him glance at me with red in his eye.

Everything gets quiet real fast. I'm watching Jess and I see him grin. He likes to play bigshot. Suddenly he looks at me and says, "We had a meeting last night. Not everybody was here."

My eyes ain't leaving his and he goes on, saying, "This ain't no Crumb A. C. where any old cat can come and go like the King of Egypt."

He's meaning me now, I know he is and everybody else knows. A big-mouth flunky laughed and I felt myself getting hot. Finally Jess comes out with it and says, "Maybe you don't know who I'm talking about," and he nods at me.

"Yeah, I wasn't here last night," I say.

"Yeah, why not?"

"I was shining."

"That's kid stuff, it ain't no excuse."

"I needed the money," I said, hearing someone laugh in back of me. Then someone else said, "Only a punk would dust shoes."

"Yeah, let anybody try taking this punk's spot," I say. "Anybody."

Somebody's moving behind me then and I turn fast and this guy Axe is about to jump me but that old Blubber got him, got a fistful of his jacket and busted it up.

"We got plenty of Cobras to fight," Blubber says. "Ain't no sense fighting among ourselves."

That was sensible-like but I didn't care who messed with me then, didn't care if it was Jess or Blubber or the whole mob. But things quieted down and finally Jess says, "We got more important stuff to discuss. Like I say, it's been too quiet too long. Things is set to bust and what are we doing?"

"Sitting tight," someone said from the crowd.

"Yeah, with nothing to fight with. Nobody's hustling. We got three pistols and then we ain't got nothing. We ain't nowhere now cause three stupid flunkies got picked up by the cops."

"What about your pistol?" Blubber asked. "That ain't available?"

"Any time I want it."

"Yeah, Big Brother don't carry it around. But that's only one piece of pistol."

"It's going to be a piece of your brain if he ever catches you borrowing it at the wrong time."

"Yeah, Big Brother don't bother me. It's some of these new cats, and somebody named Axe."

"What are you getting on my back for?" Axe says.

"You know why."

"I told you what happened. I traded my pistol for another and five bucks. The guy gave me the money, clipped my pistol, and never showed with the other."

"That's not the way I heard it," Jess says.

"Yeah, how did you hear it?"

"You been smoking too much marijuana and playing around. That's how your pistol went down the river. Anyhow," Jess says, looking right at me now, "we need artillery. What about you?"

"I got a zip-gun and a switchblade."

"A zip ain't from nothing."

"No?"

"That's right, man, my baby brother got one of them. We're talking about real stuff, bad stuff."

"Talking is all I hear tonight," I say to Jess. "I don't see nobody else with anything."

Naturally, Jess didn't take to that. Nobody did. They're all looking at me funny-like now, like they're going to stomp me. It got real quiet.

Jess says, "Yeah, you a real bad cat."

"Bad enough."

"You sounding on me, boy?"

"I'm not saying."

"Yeah, you sound like you're sounding. Maybe you want to have it out?"

It was like he's grandstanding for the boys, but I guess he has to cause he's the President and I'm new and he's got to show it. Not that I'm scared of him but I got nothing real against him, either, so I say, "What's the issue? We got no argument, we was talking about guns."

"Okay, man, so we was talking. Just talking, you say, but what are you going to do, being as everybody else is just words?"

"What do you want me to do?"

"You could get a pistol."

"What for?"

"So you won't be just talking. You say so big but that's all. You ain't nothing."

"You got your pistol?" I say to him.

"Anytime I need it I got it to match yours, punk."

Them other cats laughed. I guess it was that more than him. Anyway, I'm mad. Maybe they planned it that way so I say, "You're going to eat them words."

"That's fabulous."

"That's a promise," I say, crazy like, because it is crazy. Because I got no gun and no way of getting one, no money, no connections.

Jess is grinning now. "Break that promise," he says, "and you and us part company. Which'll make you a sad cat around this neighborhood. You can go jump off a cliff then."

I seen them other cats grinning when he says that, cause he's right. You got to be in or you're a dead kitty around here. It ain't safe to walk without friends. I got to get me a pistol. Yeah, how?

The meeting broke up then. Anyway, the business stuff, and Jess says, "I feel like some more beer."

Me, I don't want nothing so I get up and move toward the door. Things are on my mind. Fuzz in my brain. I'm mad coming out of the house tonight and worse now.

"You leaving our company?" Jess says, and before I can answer I hear Axe. He says out loud, "Let that boy go along. He's got shoes to shine."

3.

I went out, hearing them all laughing. It was good to hit that air. That place naturally stinks. It was real dark outside. Nice. Nice sky. People on the stoops. I hear laughing. Radios. Everybody happy. I'm all mixed up inside. Can't go home. Don't want to see my girl. Don't want to talk to nobody. I got to get that pistol. Show Jess, show them all. Yeah.

I hit the corner, mad as a mother lover, and then I hear footsteps behind. I naturally jump. It's only Blubber.

"Man, you're flying. Slow down, it's a hot night. Keep it cool," he says. He puts his hand on my shoulder, I knock it off.

"You're hot," he says. "Let it pass. You just naturally let that Jess fix you."

Which was what I wouldn't admit. "I'm going to get that pistol and shove it down his throat," I say.

"You know where to get one?"

"No."

Blubber lit a butt; he offered me one first but I didn't want it, then he says, "I got a party that wants to sell one."

"For how much?"

"Forty dollars."

"Why don't you say forty million?" I say, and I start walking again. I don't know where I'm going. Blubber wants to know. I say, "No place," and he tags along. We don't talk now. We pass a bar. Maybe my old man is in there. I don't look, don't want to. The hell with him and everything else. I wish I had that pistol.

"Hey, man, where we going?" Blubber finally says.

"No place," I tell him. "You better go back."

"Maybe you don't want company."

"I don't want nothing," I say, figuring he'll walk. But he don't. He stays close. Got something on his mind.

Finally he says, "How about inhaling some weed?"

"You got some?" .

"Not much. One for you, one for me. Good stuff."

"I'll take it."

It was good stuff. We moved over to the park and smoked it. It put a head on me, made me feel real light, like I got no body at all.

Then Blubber says, "I'm feeling fine for a job. There's pickings around here tonight."

Me, I'm ready for anything now and I nod my head. Got a crazy feeling in my hands, like I can do anything, beat anybody.

4.

Blubber spots this guy. He's coming along the path, walking alone. A real character. We let him pass and say nothing. Then Blubber gets up. Me too. It's routine. We follow the guy. I'm thinking crazy now, about the gun and my old man and Moms and Jess. Maybe this guy has a real bankroll. If he has, I got that pistol in my pocket already. We're up on the guy's back now, in a dark spot under trees. Nobody around. Blubber moves fast. Real fast, but this guy must have known. Anyway, he got his arm up when Blubber clamped for his neck. Then he hollered. Jesus, I didn't think a man could holler like that. It made my hair stand. Blubber's still holding but can't shut him. I come around front and bust him in the gut. No good. He still hollers. I give him the knee where it does the most good.

That does it. He's shut. Blubber drops him and he goes down like a hunk of lead. There ain't no noise now but that guy hollered real loud. Next thing, I hear steps. Somebody coming. Maybe a flatfoot. We bust away fast. Got to. We split. I hit for some big bushes. Bam, I go through, my shirt gets torn, my face scratched.

I hear that guy holler again. That's all. I'm through the bushes, running across the dark. Blubber's gone. Maybe they got him. I hit bushes again. Bam, I go through and hit the deck. It's like nothing ain't there. Just twigs and stones, the lousy smell of rotten old leaves. I want to stay because I hit my knee going down and I got no wind. I can't run no more.

Yeah, not much. I hear somebody hit them bushes like a wild horse and I'm running again. I got me a new knee and new wind. Got to get out of here. Patrol cars be cruising around soon. I ain't thinking of Blubber now and nobody else. Can't. I got to get me over that fence.

I made it okay. Hell, I could have made the Empire State building the way I was going. It was safe enough to walk then. Nobody sees me come over the fence. Hell, I'm all in now. My legs are shaking and my heart's like a fist punching in my chest. All of a sudden I'm tired. My knee hurts. Didn't feel it much before but now I got to pull up my pants. Blood's running down my leg. I got a good gash.

But that's better than being caught. I wondered what happened to Blubber. Anyway, I know he won't talk if they got him. They couldn't beat it out of him with lead pipes.

There was no place to go so I headed back to the house. My knee was stiff by the time I got there. Little kids running around the street. A fire hydrant open. I don't feature that any more but I'm hot, greasy with sweat. I felt like laying down in the gutter under that water. I went on to the house.

There's Blubber sitting on the step and smoking a cigarette.

"Man, I thought they had you in the precinct by now, beating you with a hose," he said.

"Not me, I flew."

"You fall? You're limping, boy."

"I near to busted my neck running through bushes."

Blubber shook his head and said, "Man, we messed that one bad. I thought I had him and I didn't. He hollered like a hyena."

"Anyway, he's got a sore belly. I got him good below the belt. He went down."

"Yeah, but we got nothing for our trouble."

"Don't talk about that."

"Anyway, the night is young yet. There's much picking." Blubber said.

I shook my head.

"What's wrong, man?" he said. "You miss the meat and catch the gravy, that's all."

"Not tonight," I said, and he's got an ugly look in his eye now. I know what he's thinking, that I'm punking out. He don't say nothing though, and that's worse, so I show him my knee.

"That's a bad cut," he says. "And there's always another night."

We didn't seem to have no more to say then. I didn't feel like talking. It was like I wanted to throw up after all that running. Got a funny weakness in my body. After a while I told him I had to blow upstairs.

"Yeah, I'll see you," he said, and he walked away.

I watched him shuffle off down the block. Then I went in the house, but I was lying about going upstairs. That was the last place in the world I wanted to be. If Moms was alone, she'd only jump all over me. If Pops was home, they'd be fighting like wildcats.

I hiked up to the roof but first I stopped by my door. No sound there. Too early for Pops to be in. He's still belting that pay-check. I went up to the roof thinking of that and I'm mad again. I hate his guts when he's drinking. He's not the same. It's like some evil inside him and he don't even know you. Look at him wrong and he'll knock your head off. When he's not drinking, he's different, but it seems like he's always drinking.

The hell with him. I don't like to think of none of it. Thinking only makes it worse. It don't fix nothing. I lit a cigarette on the roof. It was nice there, almost cool. A little wind blowing. Nobody around. That was the best part of it. I stretched out and looked up at the sky. It was good but it scared me—all them stars up there and all that dark. I closed my eyes. I could hear traffic licking up the avenue, the little kids down in the street, and that water pushing out of the hydrant. That seemed to get louder and louder, like it's roaring in my head, then soft. Soon I don't hear nothing.

It seemed like maybe a minute later when I opened my eyes and I get a funny feeling. Everything's quiet as hell, weird up there. A cool wind on my face. I went to the edge of the roof and looked down and nobody's there, the little kids gone, the stoops empty. Real quiet, like a crazy street in a dream. Nobody there. Just a light on each corner and one in the middle of the block. Nothing else. That don't scare me, it's something else, like it's pushing me, telling me to jump. I shut my eyes, step back, cross the roof fast and go down the back fire-escape.

Soon as I climb in my window I know everybody's asleep. That feeling is in the house. Pops is home. Moms is asleep. I hit the bed without taking my clothes off, but now I can't sleep. I'm wide awake in the dark, thinking crazy things, itchy, hot now. The whole world is goofed up, that's all I know. I kept rolling around till the sky started getting light. Bam, I hear the big trucks starting to roll, moving down the avenue. Then there's nothing again.

6.

When I wake up the room is full of sunlight, it's hot and I'm sweating like a pig. Nobody's home. Pops is gone. Moms is out. I lam out of the house quick with my shine box and hit for my special spot.

There's a guy there ahead of me. But he don't know no better. One, two and I kicked him out of there.

A lot good that done. Business is bad. It's like nobody's wearing shoes no more. Everything is bugged up. Man, I know I ain't going to be a billionaire. Ain't even collecting enough to buy a cap pistol, much less the real thing.

Talk about the heat. The asphalt is melting by eleven. Must be everybody is sitting in the bathtub. A raggity wino came up and buzzed me for a quarter. I felt like kicking him in the face. It was too hot. I told him to breeze. He did. He crossed the street, tripped on the curb and laid out.

There's no business at all now, my tongue is out like a rag so I walked into the place on the corner and bought an orange drink and a frank. My shine box is outside. I don't have to worry cause no punk will touch it while I'm around.

Another orange drink and I think of my girl. Maybe she's home. I leg it to her house, tap on the door. She opens and gives me a big hello, then a funny look cause I'm dripping like a horse.

"It's not that hot, is it?" she says.

"Hotter," I say and I walk in. Nobody's ever home in the day so I'm King. My shine box is under the stairway where she won't see it. I take a drink in the kitchen and flop on the couch, my club jacket on and my zip-gun in my pocket.

May comes in. She went to the bathroom to fix her face. "If you're so hot, why are you wearing that jacket?" she asks.

"Because it looks good on me."

"It does, but it's hot. You weren't around last night."

"Club meeting," I say, and she gives me a funny look. Maybe she knows which way the wind's blowing but she don't say nothing.

"You know, I'm hungry," I say. That's all, and she gives me a big smile and moves toward the kitchen.

"What would you like to have?" she says from there.

"You got ham and eggs?"

"Yeah, Dusty."

"Then beat it out." Sweet Gal, I say to myself, feeling good now. Damn, all of a sudden I got everything, like I'm married and all. May's in the kitchen, making me stuff and singing to herself. I get up and put some records on the player, light me a cigarette, hang my jacket on a knob and move to the bathroom to wash up.

Coming out, I'm whistling and when I get back to the living room I see May. She's holding my zip-gun like it's going to bite and she says, "What's this?"

I seen red and couldn't stop myself. I took the zip with one hand and whipped her silly with the other till she was laying on the couch crying.

"Next time you'll know better than go in my pockets," I tell her. I would have left but I can smell that ham and eggs, so I snatch a plate in the kitchen and have me some.

May followed me in. She can't look at me, her eyes is wet. I give her a pat and that does it. She smiles. Beat 'em first and they like it. She was all over me then, got me beer from the icebox and wanted to make more ham and eggs. I had to stop her.

The last record went off the player and she went in to change the discs. I followed and caught her hand, pulled her around. That's all there was to it. She didn't say nothing, like she's shy, but she ain't.

7.

Later, I put my jacket on, ready to go. May slips her arms around me and feels the zip-gun.

"That bothring you?" I say.

"Not really, Dusty, but that's a bad thing."

"That ain't nothing. Wait till you see the real pistol I'm getting."

"Yeah?" She gives me a funny look and says, "That's nothing. I already got one."

"Sure. Yeah."

"Have it your way."

"You mean you got a little old pistol? Where is it?"

"Oh, I got it."

She gives me that same funny look and then she gets it and brings it to me. Damn, it's the real thing, a cool cannon. I look it over, put it in my pocket and say, "Thanks, I'll take care of this because you're liable to get hurt with it."

That's when she blows her lid and starts blubbering. It ain't hers but her old man's.

"Too bad," I say, "because he shouldn't have it, if it is his. Anyway, you ain't getting it."

But that don't go down. She has to get nasty, so I belt her, knock her down and tell her she'd get worse if she didn't shut.

"What'll I tell my father?" she says.

"Tell him nothing," I say, and I walk out.

I go down the stairs, behind the cellar door. I got to look at that pistol again. Can't resist. I yank it out, look at it and the cellar door busts open and here's this character, his eyes popping, a nasty-looking guy with yellow in his eyes. I shove the pistol in my shine box but he seen it. He don't say nothing, though. He just looks at me funny-like, and I take out for the sidewalk.

With the pistol in the shine box it feels like it's full of bricks and I got the shakes now. I cut straight for home. Man, that seemed far.

I feel like I'm walking across Siberia and my house ain't but two blocks away. It's the longest walk in the world and that box is like a ton of bricks.

I'm thinking of that guy that popped out of the cellar and the second block I'm almost running. Got the jitters. When I hit the stoop I race up the steps. Inside the hall it's like dark after the sun light, cool, and a naturally nasty smell but that's most welcome now. Nobody in the hall. I could hear a radio upstairs. Nothing else. Then I know something's wrong. Soon as I put my foot on the first step I hear the door open behind me and I know it's got to do with the pistol. I can't even turn. A hand grabs me and this guy's got me by the collar. He yanked me around.

I'm looking into a real nasty face now. It's the guy from the cellar.

"Let's have it, cute-boy," he says.

I know what he means but I say, "Have what? Take your punky paw off me."

"When I have what's in the box," he says, and he ain't letting go.

"There ain't nothing but polish and rags," I say, but I know he's got me. There ain't no way out so I swing the box up fast. He ain't expecting nothing like that. Bam, I bust him in the face with it and he lets go. Then I'm hitting the steps, flying. I'm on the second flight when I hear him coming up.

I hit the roof and fly down the fire-escape. There ain't no fence in the back. I lick it across the yard to the house across the way. I'm in and out of that basement like a rabbit. But there ain't no stopping now. A truck is coming by. I hop the back of it and ride three blocks before I jump off.

It still ain't safe, but I got that pistol. Can't go home, though. That guy is like to be waiting around for a long time.

Can't hang around here, either. That guy wants my head. I dumped my shine box and hit for a movie.

8.

Didn't get home till late and then I sneaked in from the back street, hid the pistol down the cellar and went upstairs. Moms is home, Pops ain't. Cooling his tongue again. There's a bad air in the house like the walls is going to start busting down. Nothing on the table. I don't say nothing, don't look at Moms.

Finally I mouse into my room. It's dark outside. I go down the fire-escape, pick up the pistol, and everything is nuts again. I'm mad inside, like I hate everybody, the whole world.

When I hit the meeting place the mob is there. Beer cans is all over the place, clouds of smoke. I see Jess. He takes the butt out of his mouth and grins, wise-like.

"Cool it, men," he says, "here's that big bad cat again."

"Yeah, without his shine box."

That's all I had to hear. In the next second I got that pistol on them and they all start flipping and diving. "Cool this," I say.

Then I hear Blubber laugh. "Yeah, he done it. I told you that kitty was real stuff."

The others relax. Jess comes over and hands me a can of beer. "That's a sweet-looking iron," he says. "Where'd you snatch it?"

"From Little Red Riding Hood."

"Cool. Real cool. We'll be using that against the Cobras."

"When is that?"

"Any night now. Maybe Saturday. I hear them boys is running a dance."

"Let's bust into that dance. I feel like practicing targets on hide," I say.

Everybody was for it. Everybody starts talking at once, how we going to hit that other club, what we going to do to them. Yeah, somebody's like to be killed but who cares?

It'll hit the papers next day and everybody'll read about it.

Hit and Run

Richard Deming

December 1954

A t one o'clock in the morning the taverns along Sixth Street are usually full. But there aren't many people on the street. With only a half hour left until curfew, most people don't want to waste drinking time walking from one bar to another.

When I stepped out of the *Happy Hollow*, the only other person in sight was an elderly and rather shabbily-dressed man who was just starting to cross the street. And the only moving vehicle in sight was the green Buick convertible which came streaking along Sixth just in time to catch the elderly man with its left front fender as he stepped from between two parked cars. The car was driving on the left side of the street because Sixth is one-way at that point and either lane is legal.

The old man flew back between the cars he had just walked between to land in a heap on the sidewalk. With a screech of brakes the green convertible swerved right clear across the street and sideswiped two parked cars.

The crash was more terrific than the damage. Metal screamed in agony as a front fender was torn from the first parked car and a rear fender half ripped from the body of the second. The convertible caromed to the center of the street, hesitated for a moment, then gunned off like a scared rabbit.

But not before I had seen all I needed to see. That section of Sixth is a solid bank of taverns and clubs, and neon signs make it as bright as day. With the convertible's top down, I could see the occupants clearly.

The driver was a woman, hatless and with raven black hair to her shoulders. I could see her only in profile, but I got an impression of evenly molded features and suntanned complexion. The man next to her I saw full face, for as the car shot away he stared back over his shoulder at the motionless figure on the sidewalk. He too was hatless, a blond, handsome man with a hairline mustache. I recognized him instantly.

He was Harry Cushman, twice-married and twice-divorced café society playboy whose romantic entanglements regularly got him in the local gossip columns.

Automatically I noted the license number of the Buick convertible was X-42-209-30.

The crash brought people pouring from doorways all along the block. A yell of rage from across the street, followed by a steady stream of swearing, told me at least one of the damaged cars' owners had arrived on the scene.

"Anybody see it?" I heard someone near me ask.

Then somebody discovered the man lying on the sidewalk. As a crowd began to gather around him, I crossed the street to look at the two damaged cars. Beyond a ruined fender on each, neither seemed particularly harmed. One was a Dodge and one a Ford, and I tried to file the license number of each in my mind along with the Buick's.

Apparently someone in the crowd had thought to call an ambulance and the police, for a few moments later they arrived simultaneously. I stood at the edge of the crowd as the police cleared a path for the City Hospital intern who had come with the ambulance and the intern bent over the injured man.

The man wasn't dead, for I could hear the intern asking him questions and the old man answering in a weak voice. I couldn't hear what they said, but after a few moments the intern rose and spoke in a louder voice to one of the cops.

"He may have a fractured hip. Can't tell for sure without X-rays. I don't think anything else is broken."

Then, under the intern's instructions, two attendants got the old man on a stretcher and put him in the ambulance.

"I didn't get the guy's name," the cop complained.

"John Lischer," the intern said. "You can get his address later. His temporary address for a while will be City Hospital."

By now it was twenty after one.

I re-entered the *Happy Hollow* for a nightcap, and while I was sipping it I wrote down on an envelope I found in my pocket the three license numbers and the name John Lischer.

2.

The private detective business isn't particularly good in St. Louis. In New York State a private cop can pick up a lot of business gathering divorce evidence, because up there the only grounds for divorce is adultery. But in Missouri you can get a divorce for cruelty, desertion, non-support, alcoholism, if your spouse commits a felony, impotency, if your wife is pregnant at marriage, indignities, or if the husband is a vagrant. So why hire a private cop to prove adultery?

I have to pick up nickels wherever I can find them.

By noon the next day I'd learned horn the Bureau of Motor Vehicle records that license X-42-209-30 was registered to Mrs. Lawrence Powers at a Lindell address across the street from Forest Park. The address gave me a lift, because there aren't any merely well-off people in that section. Most of them are millionaires.

I also checked the licenses of the Dodge and the Ford, learning their owners were respectively a James Talmadge on South Jefferson and a Henry Taft on Skinker Boulevard. Then I called City Hospital and asked about the condition of John Lischer.

The switchboard operator informed me it was listed as fair.

I waited another twenty-four hours before calling on Mrs. Lawrence Powers. I picked two p.m. as the best time to arrive.

The Powers's home was a huge rose granite affair of at least fourteen rooms, surrounded by fifty-feet of perfect lawn in all four directions. A colored maid came to the door.

"Mrs. Powers, please," I said, handing the maid one of my cards reading: *Bernard Calhoun, Confidential Investigations.*

She let me into a small foyer, left me standing there while she went off with the card. In a few minutes she came back with a dubious expression on her face.

"Mrs. Powers is right filled up with appointments this afternoon, Mr. Calhoun. She wants to know have you got some particular business?"

I said, "Tell her it's about an auto accident."

The colored girl disappeared again, but returned almost immediately. "Just follow me please, sir," she said.

She led me through a living room about thirty feet long whose furnishings alone probably cost a year of my income, through an equally expensive dining room and onto a large sun-flooded sun porch at the side of the house. Mrs. Lawrence Powers reclined at full length in a canvas deck chair, wearing brief red shorts and a similarly-colored scarf. She wore nothing else, not even shoes, and obviously had been sun bathing when I interrupted her.

The maid left us alone and I examined Mrs. Powers at the same time she was studying me. She was the same woman I had seen at the wheel of the Buick convertible. She was about thirty, I judged, a couple of years younger than me, and she had a body which started my heart hammering the moment I saw her. Not only was it perfectly contoured, her flesh was a creamy tan so satiny in texture, I had to control an impulse to reach out and test if it were real. She was beautiful clear from the tip of her delicately-shaped little nose to the tips of her small toes. Even her feet were lovely.

But her face didn't have any more expression than a billiard ball.

After a moment she calmly rose from her deck chair, turned her back to me and said, "Tie me up, please." Her voice was pleasantly husky, but there was a curious flatness to it.

She had folded the scarf into a triangle and now held the two ends behind her for me to tie together. Taking them, I crossed them in the middle of her back. The touch of my knuckles against her bare flesh sent a tremor up my arms and I had an idiotic impulse to lean down and press my mouth against the smooth shoulder immediately in front of me.

Killing the impulse, I asked, "Tight enough?"

"It'll do."

I tied a square knot.

She turned around right where she was, which put her face an inch in front of mine and about six inches below. She was a tall woman, about five feet eight, because I stand six feet two.

Looking up at me without expression, she said in a toneless voice, "You're a big man, Mr. Calhoun."

For several moments I stood staring down at her, not even thinking. I'm not used to having scantily-clad women push themselves so close to me on first meeting, and I wasn't sure how to take her. Then I got my brain functioning again and decided she probably wasn't used to having strange men walk into her house, take one look at her and then grab her and kiss her. Probably, despite her seeming provocation she'd scream for her maid.

I said, "Two-ten in my bare skin," backed away and took a deck chair similar to hers. Gracefully Mrs. Powers sank back into her own.

"You're a private detective, Mr. Calhoun?" she asked.

"Yes."

"And you wanted to see me about some accident?"

"The one night before last. Involving a green Buick convertible with license X-42-209-30, a parked Dodge belonging to a man named James Talmadge, a parked Ford belonging to a man named Henry Taft, and a pedestrian named John Lischer who's currently at City Hospital in fair condition. A hit-and-run accident."

She was silent for a moment. Then she merely said, "I see."

"I happened to be coming out of *Happy Hollow* just as it took place," I said. "I was the only person on the street aside from John Lischer, and I'm sure I was the only witness. I got a good look at both the driver of the Buick and the passenger. Good enough to recognize both. You were the driver and Harry Cushman was the passenger."

Again she said, "I see." Then, after studying me without expression, she asked, "What do you want?"

"Have you reported the accident?"

When she looked thoughtful, I said, "I can easily check at headquarters. I haven't yet because I didn't want to be questioned."

"I see. No. I haven't reported it."

"What does your husband do, Mrs. Powers?"

A fleeting frown marred the smoothness of her brow, but it was gone almost instantly.

"He's president of Haver National Bank."

"Then you haven't told your husband about the accident either."

I made it a statement instead of a question.

She regarded me thoughtfully. "Why do you assume that?"

"Because I don't think the president of Haver National Bank would let an accident his wife was involved in go unreported for thirty-seven hours. Particularly where no one was seriously hurt, you undoubtedly have liability insurance, and the worst you could expect if you turned yourself in voluntarily would be a fine and temporary suspension of your driver's license. He'd know the charge against you would be much more serious if the police have to track you down than if you turned yourself in on your own even at this late date."

Her face remained deadpan. "So?"

"So I think the reason you didn't stop, and the reason you don't intend to report the accident, isn't because you lost your head. You don't impress me as the panicky type. I think the reason you didn't stop was because you couldn't afford to let your husband find out you were out with Harry Cushman at one in the morning."

When she said nothing at all, I asked, "Have you tried to have your car fixed yet?"

She shook her head.

"Where is it?"

"In the garage out back."

"How come your husband hasn't noticed the damage?"

"It's all on the right side," she said tonelessly. "A smashed front fender, bent bumper and dented door. Nothing was knocked loose. We have a three-car garage and my stall is the far right one. I parked it close to the wall so no one could walk around on that side. The station wagon's between my car and my husband's Packard, so there isn't much likelihood of him noticing the damage."

"You say nothing was knocked loose? Was your headlight broken?"

"No. I don't believe I left any clues at the scene of the crime."

I leaned back and put the tips of my fingers together. In a conversational tone I said, "You must have left some green paint on the two cars you hit. By now the police have alerted every repair garage within a fifty-mile radius to watch for a green car. Have you thought of that?"

"Yes."

"How you plan to get around it?"

"I haven't yet solved the problem."

"Would you be interested in some advice?"

"What advice?" she asked.

"Hire a private detective to get you out of your jam," I said.

3.

For a long time she looked at me, her expression completely blank. When she spoke there was the slightest touch of mockery in her voice.

"I was frightened when Alice said you wanted to see me about an auto accident, Mr. Calhoun. But almost from the moment you walked through the door I knew you hadn't come to investigate me on behalf of that old man or either of the two car owners. I'm a pretty good judge of character. Out of the four people involved, how did you happen to pick me as your potential client?"

"I doubt that any of the others could stand my fee."

Her face grew thoughtful again. "I see. What kind of service do you offer?"

"I offer to arrange a quiet payment of damages to the owners of the other two cars, so you don't have to worry about eventual suits if they ever find out who side-swiped them. With a bonus tossed in to keep them from telling the cops there'd been a contact. And to make the same kind of arrangement with John Lischer. I warn you in advance that part will cost plenty, because on top of whatever I can get him to agree to for damages, he'll have to be paid to keep it from the cops that there's been a settlement. I'll also take care of having your car repaired safely."

"Why can't you do just the last part?" she asked. "If no one ever discovers it was my car, why should we risk contacting the other people?"

"I'm thinking of your interest," I said. "Once there's a settlement, even a secret one, none of the other parties will press charges in the event the police ever catch up with you. Because I'll get quitclaim agreements from all of them. Then if you do get caught, the probability is the cops won't press charges on their own. And even if they do, proof that you made cash settlements with all the injured parties will be an extenuating circumstance. I doubt that any judge would give you more than a token fine and suspend your driver's license for six months. But without settling, you're in for a jail sentence if you ever get caught."

"I see." Her brow puckered in a slight frown. "And you say you can get my car repaired safely?"

"Safely," I assured her.

"How? I wouldn't care to have some shady repairman work on it. All he'd have to do is check the license plate like you did, and be all set for a little blackmail."

"I said safely. Does your husband ever go out of town?"

"He flies to New York this coming Monday. A banker's convention. He'll be gone a full week."

"What time's he leave?"

"Six p.m. from the airport."

"Fine," I said. "As soon as it's dark Monday night, I'll pick up the car and drive it to Kansas City. I'll switch plates and take it to a garage where I can get fast service. By the time your husband gets back from New York, your car will be back in the garage as good as new. Meantime, between now and Monday, I'll arrange settlements with John Lischer and the other two car owners."

She thought it over. Finally she said, "What is your fee?"

"Five thousand dollars," I said.

She didn't even blink. "I see. You're a rather expensive man, Mr. Calhoun."

I shrugged.

"And if I refuse to engage you?"

I said, "I have my duty as a citizen."

"How would you explain to the police keeping silent thirty-seven hours?"

"I'd phone and ask why they haven't acknowledged my letter," I said blandly. "I was quite drunk that night. Too drunk for it to occur to me I ought to tell the police at the scene I had seen your license number. But the very next morning I wrote them a letter. Letters can get lost in the mail."

She nodded slightly. "I guess you're in a pretty good bargaining position, Mr. Calhoun. But I have one more question. Suppose this John Lischer insists on as much as a five-thousand-dollar settlement? With your fee, that would run the amount up to ten thousand. Where do you suggest I get that much money?"

I looked at her in surprise. "With this home and with three cars in the garage, I assume you're not exactly a pauper."

"No," she admitted. "My husband is quite wealthy. And I can have all the money I want for any purpose I want just by asking. The only catch is I have to tell what it's for. I haven't a cent of my own except a checking account which currently contains about five hundred dollars. I could get the money by telling my husband what it's for, but if I did that I wouldn't need your services. I'm not afraid of the police. The sole reason I'm willing to engage you is to prevent my husband from finding out I wasn't home in bed at the time of the accident."

"Think up some other excuse. A charity donation, for instance."

She shook her head. "My husband handles all our charity donations personally. There simply isn't any excuse I could give him. If I told him I wanted a ten-thousand-dollar launch, he'd tell me to order it and have the company bill him. He wouldn't give me the money for it. I've never in my life asked him for more than a couple of hundred dollars in cash."

I said, "Then hit your boyfriend. Harry Cushman's got a couple of odd million lying around, last I heard, and nothing to spend it on except alimony and nightclubbing."

She looked thoughtful. "Yes, I suppose that would work. Harry wouldn't want publicity any more than I would. Shall I ask him for a check?"

"Cash," I said.

"I'll phone him as soon as you leave. Suppose you come back about this same time tomorrow?"

"Fine," I said. It sounded like a dismissal, so I got to my feet.

She gave me an impersonal nod of good-by. She was leaning forward and reaching behind her back to untie my square knot when I walked out of the room.

4.

The next day was Thursday. At noon I phoned City Hospital and learned John Lischer's condition was charted as unchanged. Two hours later the colored maid Alice again let me into the foyer of the Powers home.

This time, instead of making me wait while she checked with her mistress, she merely said, "Mrs. Powers is expecting you, sir," walked off and let me find my own way to the sun porch.

Thick carpeting in the big living room and dining room muffled my footsteps so that Mrs. Powers couldn't hear me coming. I stopped at the open door of the sun porch.

Perhaps Mrs. Powers was expecting me, but apparently she had also expected the maid at least to announce my arrival, because she wasn't exactly dressed for company. As yesterday, she was stretched out in one of the deck chairs with sun flooding her body, tier eyes were closed, though she didn't seem to be asleep, and she wore nothing but a bra and a pair of yellow shorts as brief as the red ones she had worn the previous day.

A man can stand only so much temptation. When she looked up at me with no expression whatever on her face, I dropped a hand on each of her smooth shoulders, pulled her against my chest and kissed her.

She made no resistance, but she made no response either. She just stood there, her lips soft but unmoving, and her eyes wide open. After a moment I pushed her away.

"Was your mother frightened by an ice cube?" I growled at her.

"Maybe you're just not the man to melt the ice, Mr. Calhoun."

Turning, she padded across the enclosed porch on bare feet to a small table. A brightly-colored straw bag lay on the table, and she removed a banded sheaf of currency from it.

"Your fee," she said, returning and handing me the money. "One hundred fifties."

"How about the settlement?"

"We don't know what that's going to amount to, do we?" she said. "Harry wants to see the agreements releasing me from further claims in writing before he pays any more money. When you bring me those, I'll see that you get whatever money the agreements call for."

"Harry is smarter than I thought he was," I remarked.

I riffled through the bills enough to make sure they were all fifties, then stuffed them in a pocket without counting them. "I'll pay my personal expenses and the car repairs out of this, and you can pay me back when it's all over."

Without comment she returned to her deck chair.

"I'll try to have all three agreements drawn up by tomorrow," I said. "Is it all right if I take them directly to Cushman for approval instead of bringing them here?"

"Why?" she asked.

"Because I'd like to get that part of it settled before I take off with the car. So I won't be in quite so much of a jam in case I get picked up driving it. By the time I deliver the agreements to you, you relay them on to Cushman and I call to get them back again, it will already be Monday."

After reflecting she said, "I suppose that will be all right. I'll phone Harry to expect you sometime tomorrow."

"I'll pick up the car about eight thirty Monday night. Leave the garage unlocked and the keys in the car."

"Hadn't I better phone you first?" she asked. "Suppose Lawrence changed his mind at the last minute and didn't go?"

"Yeah," I said after a moment's thought. "Maybe you better." I gave her my home number.

5.

My plan was to contact the injured John Lischer before I got in touch with either of the other two men as there would be no point in trying to settle with the others at all if Lischer refused to co-operate. But before even doing that, I decided it would be smart to find out just how much of an interest the police were taking in the case.

In St. Louis the Homicide Squad investigates all hit-and-runs in which there's personal injury, even if the injury isn't serious. This procedure is based on the sound theory that if unexpected complications happen to develop and the accident victim dies, Homicide has been on the case from the beginning and doesn't have to pick up a cold trail.

So I dropped in on Lieutenant Ben Simmons, head of the St. Louis Homicide Squad.

I found him alone in Room 405, morosely going over a stack of case records. Ben Simmons is a big man, nearly as big as I am, with an air of restrained energy about him. He hates desk work, which makes up a good part of his job, and usually's glad of any excuse to postpone it. While we're friendly enough, we've never been intimate pals, but because my arrival gave him an excuse to push his case records aside, he looked up at me almost with relief.

"Hi, Barney," he said. "Pull up a cigarette and sit down. I was just getting ready to take a break." Sliding a chair over to one side of his desk, I produced a pack, offered him a cigarette and flipped another in my own mouth. He furnished the fire.

Simmons leaned back in his chair and blew an appreciative shaft of smoke across the desk. "If you came in to report a corpse, walk right out again. I'm up to my neck now."

"Just killing time," I said. "Thought maybe I could dig up a client from among your unsolved cases. I haven't had a job in five weeks."

The lieutenant laughed. Regular cops always seem to get a kick out of hearing a private cop isn't doing so well.

"You should have stayed on the force," he said. "Probably you'd have been a sergeant by now."

"Probably I'd still be pounding a beat. Anything interesting stirring?"

"In unsolveds? A stickup killing and a hit-and-run is all. Unless you want to look up some of the old ones from years back."

"What's the hit-and-run?" I asked. "Any insurance companies involved?"

"Not for the dead guy. He didn't have any insurance. There was a little property damage covered by insurance, but not enough to pay the insurance company to hire a private eye to track down the hit-and-runner."

Apparently he was talking about a different case, I thought, since John Lischer hadn't either been dead or in any immediate danger of dying when I'd last checked City Hospital at noon that day.

I said, "You've only got one unsolved hit-and-run?"

"At the moment. And this one I was hoping I could turn over. The thing happened about one a.m. Tuesday morning, and the guy's condition was listed as fair up until one p.m. today. Then he suddenly conked out. I just got the call an hour ago."

I felt my insides turn cold. Forcing my tone to remain only politely interested, I asked, "Who was he?"

"Old fellow named John Lischer. All he had was a fractured hip, but he was pushing eighty and I guess he couldn't stand the shock. His heart gave out."

I went on calmly puffing my cigarette, but my mind was racing. Up to this moment my actions in the case hadn't been exactly ethical, but the most I'd been risking was my license. Once I had succeeded in arriving at settlements with the three injured parties, there wasn't much likelihood I'd get into serious trouble for not reporting what I knew to the police, even if the whole story eventually came out.

But the unexpected death of John Lischer changed the whole picture. Suddenly, instead of merely being guilty of somewhat unethical practice, I was an accessory to homicide. For in Missouri hit-and-run driving resulting in death is manslaughter, and carries a penalty of from three months to ten years.

I asked casually, "Got any leads on the case?"

"A little green paint and a bumper guard. Enough to identify the car as a green Buick."

That did it, I thought. So much for Mrs. Powers's assurance that she'd left no clues at the scene of the crime. With the case now a homicide instead of merely a hit-and-run, there'd be a statewide alert for a damaged green Buick. Even Kansas City wouldn't be safe.

Somehow I managed to get through another five minutes of idle conversation with Ben Simmons. Then I pushed myself erect with simulated laziness.

"I guess I won't pick up any nickels here," I said. "See you around."

"Sure," the lieutenant said. "Drop in any time."

It was four o'clock when I left Headquarters. I debated returning to the Powers home at once, then decided it was too close to the time Mr. Powers would be getting home from the bank. Instead I phoned from a pay station.

The colored maid Alice answered the phone, but Mrs. Powers came on almost immediately.

"Barney Calhoun," I said. "There's been a development. I have to see both you and Cushman at once."

"Now?" she asked. "I expect my husband home within an hour."

"Arrange some excuse with Alice. I wouldn't ask if it wasn't urgent. Can you get in touch with Cushman?"

"I suppose."

"Then both of you be at my place by a quarter of five. It's on Twentieth between Locust and Olive. West side of the street, just right of the alley. Lower right flat. Got it?"

"That isn't a very nice neighborhood," she said with a slight sniff.

"I'm not a very nice person," I told her, and hung up.

6.

Harry Cushman arrived first, coming in a taxi.

When I opened the door, he asked, "You're Calhoun?"

"Yeah," I said. "Come on in."

He didn't offer his hand. Following me into my small and not particularly well-furnished front room, he looked around superciliously, finally chose a straight-backed chair as the least likely piece of furniture to be contaminated.

"Helena said it was urgent," he said. "I hope you can make it fast. I have a five-thirty cocktail date."

It was the first time I had heard Mrs. Powers's first name. Helena Powers. Somehow it seemed to suit her calm and expressionless beauty.

I said, "Depends on how fast Helena gets here. What I have to say won't take long."

The buzzer sounded at that moment and I went to let Helena Powers in. Glancing past her at the curb, I saw she had come in the station wagon.

Harry Cushman rose when she came into the room, crossed and bent to kiss her. She turned her cheek, then moved away from him and took my easy chair with the broken spring. She was wearing a bright sun dress which left her shoulders bare, open-toed pumps and no stockings. Her jet-black hair was tied back with a red ribbon and she looked about sixteen years old.

Cushman returned to his chair.

Without preliminary I said, "John Lischer's dead."

Cushman stared at me with his mouth open. As usual Helena's face showed no expression.

"But you told Helena you'd been checking the hospital and his condition was listed as fair," Cushman said stupidly.

"His heart gave out. All he had was a fractured hip, but he was nearly eighty." Helena asked in a calm voice, "How does this affect our arrangements?"

"It changes the whole picture," I told her. "You can't settle with a corpse. If you get caught now, you'll be charged with manslaughter. You'll be charged even if you turn yourself in."

Harry Cushman's face was gray. "Listen, I can't afford to be accessory to a manslaughter."

"You already are," I informed him. "You were in the car that killed Lischer. If you didn't want to be an accessory, you should have reported to the cops at once." I let a little contempt creep into my voice. "Of course if you go to them right now, they'll probably let you off the hook because they'll be more interested in the driver. Mrs. Powers will take the rap . . . probably five years . . . and all you'll get is a little bad publicity."

He licked his lips and flicked his eyes at Helena, who stared back at him expressionlessly.

"Naturally we have to protect Helena," Cushman said with an effort to sound protective. "What's your suggestion?"

"They know it was a green Buick." I looked at Helena. "Your belief that you hadn't knocked anything loose was a little wrong. You left a bumper guard at the accident scene." I turned my attention back to Cushman. "Now that it's classified as a homicide instead of just a hit-and-run, every repair garage in the state and halfway across Illinois will be alerted. The risk of getting the car fixed has at least tripled. And so has my fee. I want another ten thousand dollars."

"Ten thousand!" Cushman squeaked. "You agreed to five!"

"Not to help cover a homicide, I didn't. Make up your mind fast. Either it's fifteen grand or nothing. If you don't want to play, I'll hand back your five right now and call the police."

Both of them stared at me, Cushman with petulant belligerence and Helena with mild curiosity, as she might have examined an interesting bug on a flower.

Finally Helena's husky voice said, "I don't see what there is to argue about, Harry. Mr. Calhoun seems to be in a perfect bargaining position. He always seems to be in a perfect bargaining position."

Cushman sputtered and fumed for a few minutes more, but finally he agreed to deliver me ten thousand more in cash at noon the next day. The money didn't mean anything to him, of course, because he'd been left more millions than he could possibly spend in a lifetime, but I think he was beginning to wish he'd never heard of the beautiful Helena Powers. I could tell by the way he looked at her she held a terrific fascination for him, but I suspect he was beginning to wonder if she was worth the complications she was bringing into his life.

I didn't care what he thought so long as he came up with an additional ten thousand dollars.

7.

Hit-and-run deaths don't create much newspaper stir in a city the size of St. Louis, particularly where the victim isn't important from a news point of view. The Friday papers carried a brief account of John Lischer's death and the statement that the police were searching for a green Buick damaged on the right side. The original report of the accident had been only a paragraph back in the stock market sections, but this appeared on the second page of both the *Post* and the *Globe*. Apparently there was a dearth of other news.

At noon Cushman brought me two more sheafs of fifty-dollar bills. I took them and the original packet down to my safe deposit vault, first transferring a thousand dollars to my wallet.

Then I relaxed for the weekend, resting up in the expectation of not getting any sleep at all Monday night.

At seven o'clock Monday evening Helena Powers phoned me to say her husband had caught his plane and the way was clear for me to pick up the Buick.

"The keys in the car?" I asked.

"No. Stop at the house for them. Alice isn't here and I'm all alone. No one will see you."

At eight-thirty, just as it was beginning to get dark, she opened the front door to my ring. She was wearing a plain street dress and a pert little straw hat, and she carried a light jacket over her arm. Silently she locked the door behind me, then led me back to the kitchen, switching off lights as we passed through each room. On the kitchen table stood a small suitcase.

"You going somewhere?" I asked.

"With you," she said, giving me a deadpan look.

Setting down my own bag, I looked at her in astonishment. "Why?"

"Because I want to."

"I'll be gone nearly a week."

"I've made arrangements with Alice," she said. "She thinks I'm driving up to my sister's in Columbia. I gave her a week off."

"Suppose your husband tries to phone long distance and doesn't get any answer?"

"He never phones. He just writes a card every day when he's gone. And I never write back."

I shrugged. "It's your car. I guess you can ride in it if you want." I picked up her bag and my own, waited while she flicked out the lights and opened the back door for me. Then I waited again while she locked the door behind us.

In the garage I set down the bags and asked her for the car keys. Silently she handed me a leather key case.

"Which is the trunk key?" I asked.

She pointed to one.

I slid it into the lock, but it wouldn't turn. I tried it upside down, but it wouldn't go in.

"The lock's jammed," I said.

Helena tried it with no more success than I had. Finally she said, "I'm sure it's the right key," and looked puzzled.

"The devil with it," I said. "We haven't got that much luggage anyway."

I tossed our bags on the floor of the small back seat. The top of the convertible was still down, as it had been on the night of the accident, but I put it up before we started.

Apparently the only damage the car had suffered was body damage, because it drove perfectly. I noted with satisfaction the gas tank registered nearly three-fourths full, which should take us better than two hundred miles before we'd have to worry about refueling.

I didn't figure there was much risk of us being stopped even in St. Louis by some cruising patrol car, because it was now six days since the accident and four days since John Lischer had died. I knew a routine order would have been issued to all cars to look for a damaged green Buick, but I had also ridden patrol enough back in my police days to know that by now this order would be filed 'way at the back of most cruising cops' minds. They wouldn't actually be searching for the hit-and-run car to the extent of carefully looking over every green automobile they saw. Even if we ran into a cop and he noticed the damage, there was a good chance it wouldn't register on him immediately that our car was green or that it was a Buick.

It also helped that it was now dark and that the damage was all on the right side. Simply by keeping in the right-hand lane I could prevent any cars passing us in the same direction we were going from noticing it. The only real danger was in meeting a squad car coming from the opposite direction, for the front bumper was badly bent and the front right fender was crushed all out of shape.

To increase our odds, I skirted the congested part of town. My destination was Illinois, but instead of turning east, I took Lindell west to Skinker Boulevard, circled Washington University campus to Big Bend Road, turned right and drove north to the edge of town. Then I cut across to North Eighth, turned right again and headed toward McKinley Bridge.

Puzzled by this maneuvering, Helena said, "I thought we were going to Kansas City."

"That was before I was accessory to a homicide," I said. "We're going to Chicago."

"Chicago! That's three hundred miles!"

"K. C is two fifty," I told her. "K. C garages will be looking for a bent Buick. Chicago garages won't. We'll be there by morning."

At that moment we had a bad break. Up to now we hadn't seen a single radio car, but now, only five blocks from McKinley Bridge and relative safety, one suddenly appeared coming toward us. As it cruised by, it blinked on its highway lights, then lowered them again.

With my heart in my mouth I wondered if the two patrolmen in the car had noticed our damaged right front. In the rear-view mirror I saw them swing in a U-turn and start back toward us. I had been traveling at twenty-five, but I risked increasing the speed to thirty.

A siren ground out a summons to halt.

For a wild moment I contemplated pushing the accelerator to the floor and running it out. Then I realized there wasn't any safe place to run. If I tried to dash over McKinley Bridge to Illinois, the cops would simply use the phone at this end of the bridge and we'd run into a block at the far toll gate. They'd have all the time in the world to set one up, because the Mississippi is nearly a mile wide at that point. And if I kept straight ahead instead of crossing the bridge, Eighth Street would shoot us into the most congested part of town.

I pulled over to the curb and stopped.

When the police car pulled next to us, neither cop got out. The one on the right said, "Haven't you got any dimmers on that thing, mister?

At first his words failed to penetrate, because I was expecting some question about our smashed fender. Then I flicked my eyes at the dashboard and saw the small red light which indicated my highway lights were on. My left foot felt for the floor switch and pressed it down.

"Sorry," I said. "I didn't notice I had the brights on."

The cop nodded peremptorily and the car swung left in another U-turn to go back the way it had been going. With shaking fingers I lighted a cigarette before starting on.

8.

We had no trouble at the bridge. If the toll collector had been instructed to watch for a damaged green Buick, he wasn't watching very carefully, because he didn't even glance at our right front fender. Of course he approached the car from my side, but even then he couldn't have failed to notice the damage if he'd looked across the hood.

Then we were in Venice, Illinois.

I took 66, driving along at a steady fifty-five so as not to risk getting picked up for speeding. We hit Springfield about eleven-thirty and I drove aimlessly up and down side streets for a few minutes.

"What are you doing now?" Helena asked.

"We need gas."

"We passed a station right in the center of town."

"I know," I said. "But we're not going to leave any record of a banged-up green Buick with Missouri plates stopping anywhere for gas. The alert won't reach as far as Chicago for a mere hit-and-run homicide, but it's sure to have gone this far."

Finally I found what I wanted. A car parked on a side street where all the houses in the block were dark. Pulling up next to it on the wrong side of the street, I got out, reached in back for my bag, opened it and drew out a length of hose.

Helena watched silently as I siphoned gas from the parked car into the Buick's tank.

When we were on the way again she remarked, "I'd never have thought of that. I'm beginning to think you earn your money, Mr. Calhoun."

"Why so formal?" I asked. "My name's Barney."

In the darkness I could see her looking at me sidewise. "All right, Barney," she said after a moment.

We stopped for gas once more in Bloomington, getting it by the same method. Then we didn't stop again until we hit the outskirts of Chicago at seven a.m.

As I began to slow down with the intention of turning in at a truck stop, Helena said, "What do we want here?"

"Breakfast," I said.

"Shouldn't we rent a couple of cabins before we do anything else?"

"No," I said. "We've got several more important things to do first."

By the time we had finished breakfast at the truck stop it was eight, and by the time we got far enough into town to begin to run into small neighborhood businesses, barber shops were open. I accomplished the second of the more important things we had to do by getting a shave.

"Couldn't that have waited?" Helena complained when I rejoined her.

"I have to look respectable for my next stop," I told her.

Heading in the general direction of the Loop, I drove until I spotted a sign reading "Car Rentals." I parked half a block beyond it.

"Just wait here," I instructed Helena. "When I come by in another car, follow me."

As usual she showed no surprise. As I got out of the car she slid over into the driver's seat.

The car rental place didn't have exactly what I wanted, but it was close enough. I would have preferred a Buick coupe or convertible the same color as Helena's, but the man didn't have any Buicks. I settled for a Dodge coupe a shade darker green than the convertible. The rate was five dollars a day plus eight cents a mile, and I told the man I wanted it for a week. I gave him the name Henry Graves, a Detroit address and left a seventy-five dollar deposit.

Only ten minutes after I had left her I pulled up alongside Helena in the Dodge, honked the horn and pulled away again. In the rear-view mirror I could see her pull out to follow me.

I led her back to the southwest edge of town, found a street which seemed relatively deserted and parked. Helena parked behind me.

In the trunk of the rented car I found a screwdriver and a pair of pliers. Helena watched with her customary lack of expression as I switched plates on the two cars.

Then she said, "I don't think I understand."

"Probably an unnecessary precaution, because I'm sure repair garages this far from St. Louis won't be watching for a green Buick. But up here a Missouri plate stands out more than an Illinois one. Now when I take this thing in to be fixed, it'll just be another local car. And on the off chance there's ever a check to find out who it belonged to, the license won't lead anywhere except to a car rental outfit and a non-existent guy named Henry Graves of Detroit."

Her lip corners quirked ever so slightly. "You think of everything, don't you, Barney?"

"I try to," I told her. "I'll drive the Buick now, and you follow me in the Dodge. Next stop is a repair garage."

She remained where she was. In her husky but slightly flat voice she said, "Let's get settled in cabins first. I want a bath and a change of clothes."

"It won't take an hour to locate a garage and make arrangements," I argued.

She shook her head. "We've been here over two hours now. I wanted a cabin at seven, but I waited while you fed yourself, got a shave, rented a car and changed plates. I'm not waiting another minute." She looked at me serenely and added, "Besides, they take your license number at tourist courts. We'll have to drive in with the Buick."

She was right, I realized on reflection. We should have signed in somewhere before I changed the plates, as I didn't want the Missouri plates which were now on the Dodge listed even on a tourist court's records. Disconsolately I considered the prospect of having to change the plates back again, then decided it wasn't necessary. There wasn't much danger in letting some tourist court proprietor see the damaged Buick so long as it didn't have its own plates on it.

"You win," I said. "Follow me again."

Helena shook her head again. "You follow me this time. I saw just the court I want when we came in on 66. Maybe you're smart on some things, but I prefer to trust my own judgment on a place to sleep."

Shrugging, I climbed back in the Dodge and waited for her to start the procession.

Helena drove nearly ten miles out of town on 66, passing a half dozen motels which looked adequate to me before pulling off to the side of the road suddenly and parking. I parked behind her.

"Lock it up," she called back to me.

Winding the windows shut, I got out and locked the Dodge. When I slid into the Buick next to her, she pointed through the windshield toward a large tourist court about a hundred yards ahead on the opposite side of the road.

"That's the one. Isn't it nice?"

It didn't look any different to me than the half dozen others we'd passed, except that this one had open front stalls for automobiles.

"It's lovely," I growled. "Let's get it over with."

9.

The place was called the Starview Motor Court and advertised hot baths and steam heat. Since the temperature hovered around eighty, neither seemed like much of an inducement to me.

Though it was probably an unnecessary precaution, I had Helena swing the car so that the left side was toward the office. With dozens of different automobiles driving in and out of the court daily, it wasn't likely the proprietor would notice our green Buick convertible had changed to a green Dodge coupe a few hours after we checked in, but there wasn't any point in deliberately calling attention to our smashed fender. Just possibly it would catch his notice enough to make it register on him.

The proprietor was a sad-faced man in his fifties who had an equally sad-faced wife. They occupied quarters behind the small office. For some reason both of them went along to show us cabins.

They were nice modern cabins, clean and airy and walled with knotty pine. The baths were large instead of the usual tiny affairs you find at most tourist courts, and contained combination bathtubs and showers.

"We'll take two," I told the proprietor. "We'll be here a week, so I'll pay the full week now. How much?"

He said the normal rate was nine dollars a day, but as a weekly rate we could have them for fifty-six dollars each. "With another fifty cent a day knocked off if you do your own cleaning instead of having maid service," he added.

Helena surprised me by saying she preferred to do the cleaning herself, which caused the proprietor's wife to give her a pleased smile. Apparently the wife constituted the maid service.

Helena stayed outside when I went back to the office to resister.

I signed as Howard Bliss and sister, Benton, Illinois, and listed the Illinois license number registered to the Dodge. Then I paid him a hundred and five dollars.

Our cabins were numbers six and seven. When I got outside again, I discovered Helena had backed the Buick into the car port between them while I was registering.

"You could have left it in front of the cabins," I said to her. "We aren't going to be here long."

"We'll be here at least a half hour. I told you I'm going to take a bath."

"Several times," I said wearily. "Which cabin do you want?"

She looked at both speculatively. The one on the right went with the car port we were using, because a door near the rear wall of the port led into the cabin.

Helena said, "I'll take the right one."

Getting her bag from the car, I carried it into the right-hand cabin via the car port door and set it on her bed. Then I got my own bag from the car and went into my own cabin.

Inasmuch as I was going to have to kill a half hour anyway, I decided to take a cold shower myself. I took my time under the water, letting its coldness knock the tiredness out of my muscles and wash some of the sleepiness from my eyes. Twenty-five minutes later, refreshed and in clean clothes, I knocked at the next cabin door.

"Just a minute," Helena called. "I'm still dressing."

It was closer to ten minutes before she appeared, and meantime I stood out in the sun letting the heat wilt my collar and undo all the good a cold shower had done me. When she finally appeared she was dressed in a white sun dress, low-heeled sandals which exposed bare, red-tipped toes, and no hat. Her long hair was pulled up in a pony tail.

Carefully she locked her cabin door behind her and dropped the key in a straw purse.

This time I drove the Buick.

When we pulled up alongside the parked Dodge, I handed her the keys to it.

"Instead of following you, suppose we arrange to meet somewhere?" Helena suggested. "I'd like to do a little shopping."

"You know Chicago?" I asked.

She shook her head.

"Then we'll make it somewhere simple." I looked at my watch, noting it was nearly ten a.m. "The Statler Cocktail Lounge at two p.m.?"

"All right."

"Be careful you don't get picked up for anything," I cautioned. "Even a parking ticket would put us in the soup with that Missouri plate on the Dodge."

"I'll be careful."

I drove off while she was unlocking the coupe door.

I didn't have any trouble arranging for the car to be fixed. I stopped at the first Buick service garage I saw.

The chief repairman, a cheerful middle-aged man, carefully looked over the damage. "What's the other guy look like?" he asked.

"There wasn't any other guy," I told him. "My wife mistook a tree next to our drive for the garage."

He told me he could do the whole job, including a check of wheel alignment, in three days for approximately a hundred dollars.

"That's a rough estimate, you understand," he said. "May vary a few bucks one way or the other."

I gave him the name George Seward and a South Chicago address a couple of miles from the repair garage. When he asked for my phone number, I said I didn't have a phone and just to hold the car when it was finished until I picked it up.

My business was all completed by noon and suddenly I was exhausted from lack of sleep and the strain of driving three hundred miles at night. I began to wish I had arranged to meet Helena at twelve-thirty instead of at two.

There was nothing to do but kill two hours, however. I took a taxi to the Statler, had lunch and then slowly sipped four highballs in the cocktail lounge while I waited for her. She showed up at ten after two.

"Want a drink?" I asked. "Or shall we go back to the court and collapse? I'm ready to fall on my face."

She looked me over consideringly. "You do look tired," she said. "We'll pick up a couple of bottles of bourbon and some soda on the way and I'll have my drink at the court. Maybe we can get some ice from the proprietor."

My four drinks had relaxed me just enough so that I had difficulty keeping my eyes open. I let Helena drive.

I was just beginning to drift off to sleep sitting up when the car braked to a stop, then backed into a parking place at the curb. I opened my eyes to see we were in front of a liquor store.

Reluctantly I climbed out of the car. "You say bourbon?" I asked Helena.

When she merely nodded, I went on into the store. I bought two quarts of bourbon and a six-bottle carry-pack of soda.

When I raised the Dodge's trunk lid to stow away my purchases. I was surprised to find the floor of the trunk was soaking wet. There hadn't been any water on it when I had searched the trunk for tools to change license plates.

But I was too sleepy to wonder about it much. Slamming the lid shut, I climbed back in the car and let myself sink into a semi-coma again. Helena had to shake me awake when we got back to the tourist court.

I slept straight through until eight o'clock that night. Presumably Helena did the same, for when I finally looked outside to peer next door, her cabin was dark and the Dodge was still in its car port. She must have awakened about the same time I did, though, because she knocked at my door just as I finished dressing.

She was carrying the two bottles of bourbon and the carry-pack of soda.

"I thought we'd have a drink before we went out for dinner," she said.

I found two glasses in the bathroom, but the prospect of warm bourbon and soda didn't appeal to me.

"I'll see it I can get some ice at the office," I said.

But the proprietor told me he was sorry, they had only enough ice for their personal needs. When I returned to the cabin, I suggested we have our before-dinner drink at the same place we picked to eat.

"Maybe I can get some ice from him," Helena said.

A drink didn't mean that much to me, but since she seemed so set on one, I didn't argue. From my open door I watched as she moved toward the office. The movement walking gave to her body would have made a corpse sit up in his casket. It occurred to me the motel proprietor would have to be made of ice himself to refuse her.

In a few moments she reappeared carrying a china water pitcher.

She stopped at her own cabin door, said to me, "I'll be with you in a minute, Barney," unlocked the door and went inside.

What she was going into her cabin for, I couldn't decide, because when she reappeared a few moments later, she still carried nothing but the pitcher. Carefully she locked the door behind her and came over to my door. When she handed me the pitcher I saw it was full of cracked ice instead of cubes.

"What's he have, an old-fashioned icebox?" I asked in surprise.

"I didn't inquire," Helena said. "I just asked for ice."

We had two highballs each before going out to hunt a place for dinner.

10.

We dined at a place called the *White Swan*, a roadhouse about a half mile from the tourist court on route 66. The place had an orchestra and after dinner we alternately danced and sat at the bar until two a.m. And every time I took her in my arms, my temperature went up another degree.

I got the impression the closeness of our bodies on the dance floor was beginning to have an effect on her too. Not from anything she said, for we did remarkably little talking during the evening, but each time we danced she seemed to move more compliantly into my arms and her eyes seemed to develop a warmer shine.

When I finally drove the Dodge back into the car port, I was on the verge of suggesting she come into my cabin for a nightcap, but before I could open my mouth Helena jumped out of the car and entered her cabin by means of the car port door without saying a word to me.

Then, as I sat there foolishly looking at her closed door, I experienced a terrific letdown. I was tempted to get angry, but on reflection I realized she hadn't actually said or done anything to make me think she had been sharing my own cozy thoughts. Maybe she just realized the direction my thoughts were taking, and wanted to leave no doubts in my mind that our relationship was strictly a business one.

Shrugging, I locked the Dodge and went into my own cabin.

Five minutes later, just as I finished pulling on my pajamas, there was a knock at the door. I put on a robe and opened it to find Helena standing there with her suitcase in her hand.

When I had stared at her expressionless face without saying anything for nearly a minute, she asked, "Aren't you going to let me in?"

"Sure," I said, recovering my wits enough to step aside.

Walking past me, she set the suitcase on a chair, opened it and drew out a nearly transparent nylon nightgown. Then she turned and, holding the nightgown out in front of her, examined it critically.

Her husky but flat voice said, "I'm frightened all alone over there. Am I welcome here?"

I didn't answer because I was afraid my voice would shake. I merely closed the door, which up till then I had been too stupefied to shut, locked it and unsteadily poured out two substantial shots of bourbon.

The ice in the pitcher had all melted by now, but I needed mine straight anyway.

11.

The next three days were like a honeymoon. We didn't have a thing to do but wait for the Buick to be repaired, so we simply relaxed and enjoyed ourselves. With Helena doing the housework, which consisted only of making the bed, emptying ash trays and washing our whisky glasses, we weren't even disturbed by the proprietor's wife coming in to clean. Daily we slept till noon, then showered, had a leisurely lunch and spent the rest of the day at the beach.

Evenings we spent dancing and drinking at the *White Swan*.

In looking back I can see that Helena's attraction for me was almost entirely physical, because except for her beauty and an unexpected fiery passion, she wasn't a very stimulating companion. We had almost no conversation aside from routine discussions of our plans for each day, and aside from such physical pleasures as sunbathing, dancing, drinking and love making, I don't believe she had a single interest.

Two things about her puzzled me. One was her disappearance for a short time every morning. I would awaken about eight a.m. to find myself alone, drift back to sleep and a short time later be awakened again by her climbing back in bed. Her explanation was that she had to have breakfast coffee but didn't want to disturb me, so she dressed and drove down the road to a diner alone.

The other thing that puzzled me was her ability to get ice from the motel proprietor. Both Wednesday and Thursday noon as soon as she was dressed, she left the cabin carrying the china water pitcher and returned with it full of cracked ice. But when on Friday I happened to get dressed first and took the pitcher to the office while Helena was still under the shower, the proprietor gave me an irritated look and told me he'd already informed me once he didn't supply ice for guests.

When I returned empty handed, Helena took the pitcher and came back with it full five minutes later.

Friday afternoon I had Helena drive me to the Buick repair garage and discovered the convertible was all ready. The bill was a hundred and fifteen dollars.

"I had to put on a new bumper bracket," the chief repairman said. "Could have straightened the other, but it would have left it weak. I put the old one in your trunk."

"How'd you manage that?" I asked. "The lock was jammed last I tried it."

"Ain't now." He demonstrated by walking behind the car, inserting a key and turning it. The lid raised without difficulty. He locked it again and handed me the keys.

I tried the trunk key myself and it worked perfectly.

When I drove out of the service garage Helena was waiting for me in the Dodge a half block away. Again I led the way to a quiet side street, where we stopped long enough for me to switch plates back to the right cars. Then I took the Dodge and Helena followed in the Buick while I drove to the car rental lot.

I had thirty-four dollars coming back from the seventy-five I'd deposited.

As we drove back toward the tourist court I said, "We may as well start back tonight. We can have the car back in your garage by tomorrow morning."

Helena didn't say anything at the moment. She waited until we were back in my cabin and I had mixed a couple of drinks.

Then she said, "There's one other little job we have to do before we go back to St. Louis, Barney."

"What's that?" I asked.

"Drink your drink first, then I'll show you."

"Show me?" I asked, puzzled. "Why can't you just tell me?"

"Drink your drink," she repeated.

She sounded as though she meant I might need it. I looked at her dubiously for a minute, then drained my glass.

"All right," I said. "I drank my drink. Now show me."

Setting down her own drink unfinished, she took my hand and led me to the door. Still holding my hand, she led me to her own cabin door, unlocked it and drew me inside. Then she released her grip on me and locked the door behind us.

"It's in the bathroom," she said.

Now completely puzzled, I followed her. In the bathroom the shower curtains were drawn around the bathtub and a glittering new icepick lay on the edge of the washbowl. Without comment Helena drew the shower curtains wide.

Three damp burlap bags were spread over something bulky in the bathtub.

For a few moments I simply stared at the bags, the hair at the base of my neck prickling in anticipation of shock. Then I pushed Helena aside and lifted one of the pieces of burlap.

Underneath, cozily packed in what must have been more than a hundred pounds of cracked ice, was the naked body of a man. He lay on his side, his knees drawn up to his chest and his back to me. The back of his head was oddly flattened and was matted with dried blood.

Letting the burlap fall back into place, I staggered out of the room and collapsed in a chair in the bedroom. Helena followed as far as the bathroom door, then stood watching me with curiously bright eyes as I stared at her in stupefaction.

Finally I managed to whisper, "Who is it?"

"Lawrence," she said without emotion. "My husband."

I closed my eyes and tried to make some sense out of the nightmarish discovery that Lawrence Powers, who was supposed to be at a banker's convention in New York City, was actually lying dead in an improvised icebox not a dozen feet away. Surprisingly it did make sense. Like the tumblers of a lock falling into place, various oddities in Helena's behavior which had been vaguely puzzling me ever since we started the trip began to develop meaning.

Opening my eyes, I said in a dazed voice, "He was in the trunk all the way from St. Louis, wasn't he? That's why the key wouldn't work. You substituted some other key so I couldn't open the trunk, then put the right one back on the ring after you got his body out of the trunk and into your cabin."

"It was the key to the trunk of Lawrence's Packard you tried in the lock that first time," she said calmly. "I had the Buick trunk key in my purse."

"And that's why you insisted on this particular tourist court," I went on. "You wanted one with car ports, so you could get him out of the trunk and into your cabin without being seen. You dragged him in through the car port door while I was taking a shower."

She shrugged. "He wasn't very heavy. A hundred and forty. I weigh one twenty-five myself."

Leaning forward, I put my head in my hands and mumbled, "Tell me the rest of it."

Without a trace of emotion in her voice she said, "While you were arranging for the Buick to be fixed I located an ice house only two miles from here. I thought of ice because I knew he'd begin to smell after a few days if he wasn't preserved. I had the man put four twenty-five pound pieces of ice in the trunk of the Dodge. He also sold me an icepick. Then I came back here and carried the pieces in one at a time.

"I left the plug out of the bathtub so the melted ice would run away, and I've been adding fifty pounds a day. I got it while you were still in bed and thought I was out after coffee." She paused, then added, "The burlap bags were in our garage at home. I put them on the floor of the trunk in case he bled any."

I thought of something. "Good God!" I said. "All you borrowed from the motel proprietor was an empty pitcher. The ice for our drinks has been coming out of that bathtub!"

When her lip corners quirked upward in the suggestion of a smile, I got to my feet, reeled into the bathroom and threw up.

When I returned to the bedroom Helena had seated herself on the bed and was serenely smoking a cigarette.

"Tell me how it happened," I suggested dully.

"He was going to call the police," she said. "It was all because he insisted on getting everywhere early. His plane didn't leave until six, and I planned to start driving him to the airport at five. But he was all packed and ready to go before four. I intended taking the station wagon, figuring I'd make some excuse if he asked why I wasn't driving the Buick. But Lawrence tried to be helpful. Without my knowing what he intended doing, he went out to the garage at four o'clock and backed the convertible out for me."

She paused to crush out her cigarette and light another. "When I heard the car start up, I rushed out back to stop him. I did get him to drive it back in the garage, but it was too late. He'd already noticed the damage. And he guessed at once what had caused it. He used to read every inch of both papers, so he knew the police were looking for a green Buick. He didn't even ask me. He just looked at me in a horrified way and said, 'Helena, you killed that old man.'"

She blew twin streams of smoke from her nostrils, creating a curious mental impression on me. With her immobile face and motionless body, the smoke issuing from her nostrils made her look like a carved oriental idol.

Tonelessly she went on, "There wasn't any reasoning with him, Barney. He was the most self-righteous man who ever lived. It didn't mean a thing to him that I might go to jail for months or years if I was discovered. I actually pleaded with him, but he was determined to phone the police. We have five phone extensions and one of them is in the garage. He marched over to it like an avenging angel and was dialing 0 when I picked up a wrench and hit him over the back of the head."

I said huskily, "Why'd you wait until now to mention all this? Why not before we started for Chicago?"

"Because I wanted to make sure you'd help me get rid of the body," she said serenely. "I wouldn't have the faintest idea how to dispose of it myself. And you might have backed out of the whole deal if you'd known about Lawrence."

"What makes you think I won't anyway?" I asked. "I'm not an accessory to this yet. Suppose I just walk out?"

Helena yawned slightly. "Then I suppose I'd be caught. But I doubt that the police would believe you knew nothing about it. I'd tell them it was you who killed Lawrence, of course. And even if they didn't believe me, they'd certainly never accept your story that you had nothing at all to do with it. Particularly after the motel proprietor identified you as the man who'd been with me."

She was right, I knew. No cop would ever believe I'd transported a body three hundred miles without knowing it, or that the woman I was traveling with had kept it on ice in her bathtub for three days without my knowledge. I had to save Helena in order to save myself.

If it was possible to save either of us.

I didn't waste any time upbraiding her. In the first place it wouldn't have accomplished anything, and in the second place I didn't think it would bother her in the least.

"Let's go over to my cabin where I can think," I said wearily.

I spent the next twenty minutes thinking, pacing up and down and chain smoking while Helena calmly watched me and sipped a highball. I had one straight shot myself. I would have preferred a highball, but I refused to use any more of Helena's ice.

Finally I stopped pacing and faced her. "Look," I said. "I think I've figured out how to get rid of him, but before we even discuss that, we've got to plan a story to cover you. When your husband doesn't show up Monday, you're going to have to act as a normal wife would. First phone his bank to ask if they've heard from him. Then on Tuesday wire convention headquarters in New York. They'll wire back that he never showed, of course. Soon as you get that wire, you'll have to phone the police and put on a worried wife act. Think you can manage all that?"

She nodded indifferently.

"Then the hard part will start. First the police will discover he never caught that plane, so they'll know he disappeared in St. Louis . . ."

"I thought of that two minutes after I killed him," Helena interrupted. "He'll be listed on the flight."

I stared at her. "How?"

"It was only four when all this happened," she said. "By four twenty I had Lawrence stripped, his clothes hidden in the garage and his body in the car trunk. Then I went back inside, told Alice I wouldn't be home for dinner after I took Mr. Powers to the airport, and she could go home. I also told her I intended driving up to my sister's in Columbia the next morning, so she could take the week off. I had her out of the house by four thirty."

"How'd that get your husband listed on the plane flight he was supposed to take?" I asked.

"I haven't finished. As soon as Alice left I phoned Harry Cushman. He took a taxi to the house, picked up Lawrence's ticket and plane reservation and went straight to the airport. He flew to New York under Lawrence's name and took another plane back under a different name as soon as he arrived. When the police start looking for Lawrence, they'll start looking in New York."

12.

For a long time I looked at her in wonderment. Finally I asked, "How'd you ever talk Cushman into doing a silly thing like that?"

"Silly?"

"Naturally the police will question the airline personnel," I said patiently. "The minute they get Cushman's description from the stewardess, they'll know somebody substituted on the flight for your husband."

She shook her head. "In the first place, neither Lawrence nor Harry is known on the New York run. Lawrence often flies to Washington, but almost never to New York. I know he hasn't made the trip in three years. And Harry never flies anywhere. In the second place, though Harry is ten years younger than Lawrence was and twenty pounds heavier, a rough description of either would fit the other. Both have light hair, neither is grey, both have lean builds and both wear small mustaches. In the third place the police won't question the stewardess too closely. Just enough to satisfy themselves Lawrence was on the plane."

"What makes you think that?"

"Because they won't suspect murder. The first thing the police do when a banker disappears is request an audit of bank funds."

She was right again, I realized. The probability was the first premise the police would work on was that Lawrence Powers had disappeared voluntarily. And by the time a bank audit disclosed he hadn't absconded with any funds, the trail would be too cold to pick up.

I said, "I still don't understand how you talked Cushman into sticking his neck out."

"He's in love with me," she said complacently.

I studied her broodingly, not satisfied with the answer. "Look, Helena, if I'm going to help cover up your murders, I want the whole story. Maybe Cushman's in love with you, but he was in a blue funk over being accessory to mere manslaughter. I don't think he'd stick his neck out for first degree homicide even for you."

She shrugged. "Of course Harry doesn't know Lawrence is dead." Again I studied her broodingly Finally I asked in an exasperated tone, "What in the devil story *did* you tell him?"

"You don't have to shout," she said. "I told him Lawrence had discovered the damage to the car and guessed what caused it. I said he had threatened to call the police, but I explained to him I'd already hired a private detective to try to arrange a quiet settlement of damages, and I talked him into holding off calling the police at least until he'd discussed it with you. I said Lawrence and I went to see you at your flat, and you and Lawrence had a fight. You knocked him out and tied him up. I told Harry this was the opportunity to accomplish everything we'd planned together. For me to obtain grounds for divorce against Lawrence and marry him."

"How did that follow?" I asked, fascinated.

"I told Harry you had agreed to hold Lawrence captive until we could get the car fixed. Then, after it was back in the garage, you'd transport Lawrence to New York in a private plane owned by a friend of yours and turn him loose in the city unshaven and in dirty clothes. When Lawrence took his story to the police, they'd think he was crazy. The flight list would show he'd flown to New York as scheduled, and when he walked into a New York police station, he'd look like he'd been on a several-day drunk. When the police came to check my car, they'd find it undamaged. Then I'd announce my husband had been suffering delusions about me for some time, I thought he was insane, and I'd file for a divorce on the ground that he constantly made me suffer indignity."

I was conscious that my mouth had drooped open as she was speaking. "And Cushman believed that fantastic yarn?" I asked in amazement.

"Why not? He knew I've wanted a divorce for some time and would jump at any grounds for one. It was the divorce idea that sold him. He wants me to marry him. I don't think he'd have agreed to take Lawrence's place on the plane if I hadn't included that, because he was scared silly." She added reflectively. "Then too, Harry isn't very bright. He's got so much money, he's never had to do any thinking."

He must not be bright, I thought. But it was just as well for our chances that he wasn't. Having taken that plane to New York under Lawrence Powers's name, he was an accessory to murder clear up to his neck, because he'd never be able to convince the police he didn't know Powers was dead at the time. It occurred to me that pointing that fact out to him when we got back to St. Louis ought to silence any urge he might ever develop to tell his story.

Then it also occurred to me that Helena Powers had a remarkable talent for placing her aides in positions where they had to protect her in order to protect themselves. For she had me in the identical position she had Harry Cushman. We all three had to hang together, or hang separately.

Helena broke into my thoughts by inquiring, "How do you plan to get rid of Lawrence?"

Glancing at my watch, I saw it was seven p.m. "I don't tonight. He'll keep in his icebox another day. But we've got some scouting to do. Better put on a jacket, because it may be chilly along the lake."

I drove the car on our scouting trip. Our tourist court was not far from Berwyn Summit, and I cut straight east to the University of Chicago. Then I turned south along Lake Michigan until we began to run into beach areas.

At eight-thirty Helena said, "Shouldn't we be thinking about dinner soon?"

"No," I said shortly. Ever since I'd lifted that burlap bag I hadn't been able to think of anything but the iced corpse beneath it, and the thought didn't induce much appetite.

I drove as slowly as the traffic would let me, checking signs on the left side of the road. Finally, about nine o'clock, I spotted one which looked promising. It was on a wooden arch over an unpaved road and read: "Crestwood Beach, Private Road."

We were past it before I spotted it, however. I had to drive on another mile before I could turn around.

Crestwood Beach proved as promising as it had looked. The beach itself was but a narrow strip of sand, and clustered along its edge were some two dozen modest summer cottages. I noted with satisfaction lights showed in not more than a half dozen.

Parking next to one of the dark cottages, I examined it carefully before getting out of the car. Apparently its owner's summer vacation had not started yet, for the windows were still boarded up. The cottages either side of it, each a good fifty yards away, were dark also.

I climbed out of the car and told Helena to get out also.

Together we walked the scant fifty feet down to the water. As I had hoped, each of the cottages had its own small boat dock. Nothing much, merely a series of planks laid across embedded steel rods, but adequate for an outboard boat.

"Think you can find this same place alone tomorrow night?" I asked Helena.

"If I have to."

I pointed out over the calm, moonlit water. "I'll be out there somewhere in an outboard. I won't be able to tell one beach from another in the dark, so you're going to have to signal me with the car lights. We'll set a time for the first signal, and you blink them twice. Just on and off fast, because we don't want any of the other cottagers out here to come investigating. Then regularly every five minutes blink them again. Got it?"

"Yes."

We went back to the car and I drove back under the wooden arch to the main road again. A mile and a half northwest of Crestwood Beach I stopped once more, this time at a sign which read: "Boats for rent." This sign too was at the entrance to an unpaved road. I followed the road only about fifty yards before coming to the boat livery.

The proprietor was a grizzled old man in his seventies who chewed tobacco. He sat on the screened porch of a small cottage reading a Bible by the light of a Coleman gasoline lantern.

"They're all taken tonight, mister," he said as soon as I put my feet on the steps. He shot a stream of tobacco juice at a cuspidor halfway across the porch. "Everybody heard the large-mouths is biting."

Then he let out a cackle. "Don't know who starts them rumors. Look at that lake. Calm as glass. They'll come in with a mess of six-inch perch." He spat again.

"You booked up for tomorrow night?" I asked through the screen-door.

"Nope." He got up and opened the door for me.

Walking onto the porch, I said, "Then I'd like to reserve a boat. When's best to go out?"

"Ain't much point till it gets dark. If you mean to use live bait, that is. Eight-thirty, nine o'clock."

I told him I'd be there at nine and paid in advance. The price of a boat and a fifteen-horsepower motor was six dollars, a Coleman lantern fifty cents extra, and I gave him a dollar for a can of night crawlers.

When I got back to the car, Helena asked, "May we eat now?"

I stopped at a roadside eatery and let her have some dinner while I drank two cups of coffee. I hadn't eaten since noon, but I still couldn't develop any appetite.

13.

By ten the next morning we were downtown at the largest branch of Sears Roebuck. Why criminals ever buy their necessary equipment anywhere else, I can't imagine. Police records are full of cases where kidnappers were trapped because the paper of the ransom note was traced to some exclusive stationery shop, or murderers were caught because a hammer was traced to some neighborhood hardware store where every customer is remembered. At a place like Sears you are only one of thousands of faces seen by the clerk waiting on you, and even if by some unlikely chance the item you buy is traced back to that particular clerk, the chance of his remembering anything at all about the person who bought it is remote. The chance of its being traced that far is even more remote, since identical items are sold across Sears counters all over the country every day.

In the men's clothing department I bought the cheapest fishing jacket I could find.

In the sporting department I bought a cheap glass casting rod, a three-dollar-and-ninety-five-cent metal and plastic reel, fifty yards of nylon line, a cheap bait box and an assortment of leaders, sinkers, hooks and lures to fill up the bait box. I didn't intend to use any of it, but it might have excited comment at the boat livery if I had showed up to go fishing without any gear.

I also bought two eight-pound rowboat anchors. I intended to use them.

In the hardware department I bought fifty feet of sash cord. Also to use.

I stowed all of my purchases in the trunk of the convertible.

The rest of the day we simply waited.

At seven thirty in the evening we started the job of disposing of Lawrence Powers's body. First I transferred my fishing gear, the anchors and the sash cord from the car trunk to the rear seat of the car. The fishing jacket I put on. Then I carefully covered the floor of the trunk with the three burlap bags.

We hadn't added any ice to the tub since Helena showed me the body, and it had melted away to no more than about twenty-five pounds. I managed to lift the dead man out without spilling ice all over the floor.

The body was stiffened in its prenatal position, the ice apparently having caused it to retain rigor mortis longer than it normally would have. I made no attempt to straighten it out because I would only have had to fold the knees up to the chest again in order to get it into the trunk.

There was little danger of anyone seeing me carry it the one or two steps from the car port door to the trunk, inasmuch as the car itself blocked the view from outside, but I had Helena stand in front of the stall anyway as a lookout.

The body was cold and slippery against my arms and chest as I staggered through the door with it and shoved it into the trunk. When I locked the trunk, I found I was drenched with sweat.

I let Helena drive. It was just nine o'clock when we pulled up across the road from the boat livery. I had Helena co-ordinate her watch with mine.

"I'll give you a half hour," I said. "Blink your lights exactly at nine thirty, and then again every five minutes after that until I dock. O.K.?"

"I understand," she said.

Collecting my fishing gear from the back seat, but leaving the anchors and sash cord, I got out of the car. Helena drove off without a word.

The boat the old man gave me was a flat-bottomed scow about ten feet long. In addition to the motor it contained a pair of oars and a gas can with an extra gallon of gas. The Coleman lantern he furnished had a bolt welded to its bottom which fitted into one of the oarlocks.

I had to wait while he picked two dozen night crawlers from a large box of moss. I didn't have a use in the world for them, but it would have looked peculiar to go fishing without bait.

When I was settled in the boat, the old man said, "Looks like a good night for bass."

I looked out over the water, which was as smooth and moonlit as it had been the previous night.

"Yeah," I said sarcastically. "Just a little choppy."

He let out a cackle. "Them little six-inch perch is good eating anyway, even if they ain't much sport. You ought to catch a bushel."

I started the motor and pulled away while he was still cackling at his own humor.

14.

For about a quarter mile I set a course straight out from shore, then swung right and followed the shoreline for what I judged to be about a mile. The water was dotted with lights of other night fishermen, some farther out and some between me and the shore.

At twenty-five minutes past nine I picked a spot several hundred yards from the nearest fisherman's light, cut the motor and let the boat drift. There was a slight inshore current, but I figured I would maintain the same relative position to the other boats because I assumed they would take advantage of the current for drift trolling instead of anchoring and doing still fishing.

At nine twenty-nine by my watch I began studying the shoreline, concentrating on the point I judged Crestwood Beach would be. Minutes passed and nothing happened.

With my eyes straining at the shoreline, dotted here and there by cottage lights and silhouetted by the lights of moving traffic on the highway beyond it, I sat motionless for minutes more. Finally I risked lowering my gaze long enough to glance at the time, and was shocked to see it was twenty minutes to ten. By then Helena should have flashed her lights three times.

Just as I raised my eyes again, a pair of headlights blinked twice off to my right, a good quarter mile from where I had been searching for them. I only caught them from the corner of my eye, and they blinked on and off too fast for me to take a fix. There was nothing to do but wait another five minutes with my gaze centered in that direction.

Eventually they blinked twice again.

Starting the motor, I headed at full throttle toward the point where I had seen the lights. But running a boat in the dark is confusing. I was fifty yards offshore, had turned out my Coleman lantern and was heading confidently toward a narrow dock I could see protruding out over the water when the lights blinked again a hundred yards to my left.

Changing course, I cut the throttle way down and slowly chugged up to the small dock Helena and I had stood on the night before. As I tied up I could make out the dim shadow of the convertible next to the dark and boarded-up cottage.

Helena greeted me with a calm, "Hello, Barney."

"Any trouble?" I asked.

"Not since I got here. I missed the turn and was a few minutes late. But no one from the other cottages has come out to ask why I was blinking my lights."

Looking in both directions, I could see no one. The cottages both sides of us were still dark. Going behind the car, I lifted the trunk lid and took the dead body of Lawrence Powers in my arms.

As I lurched past the front seat with my burden, I said, "Bring the gunny sacks."

I'm a fairly strong man, but it's quite a chore even for a strong man to carry an inanimate hundred and forty pounds over uneven ground in the dark. Once I stumbled and nearly dropped the body, and as I started to lower it into the boat, it slipped from my grip and nearly tumbled into the water before bouncing off the gunwale and settling just where I wanted it on the bottom of the boat.

Again I found myself drenched with sweat.

When I finished wiping my face with a handkerchief, I found Helena standing on the dock beside me, the three burlap bags in her hands. Carefully I covered her husband's body with them.

Then I returned to the car for the two anchors and the sash cord.

When I was finally reseated in the boat and ready to start, Helena still stood on the dock.

"Can't I go along and help?" she asked.

"I'd never find this place again in the dark," I told her. I looked at my watch, noting it was five of ten. "Pick me up at the boat livery at ten thirty."

When she didn't say anything, I glanced up at her. Maybe it was only an effect of the moonlight, but I imagined there was a look of disappointment on her usually expressionless face, as though I had refused her some pleasure she particularly wanted to enjoy.

"Ten thirty," I repeated.

She merely nodded, and I started the motor and pulled away.

I headed straight out from shore at quarter speed for about fifty yards, then stopped long enough to light my lantern. I didn't care to have the Naval Reserve pick me up for running without lights.

When I started up again, I opened to full throttle and held it until I was even with the farthest boats from shore, approximately two miles out. I didn't want to risk calling attention to myself by going out beyond them.

There weren't many boats out that far, perhaps a half dozen spaced several hundred yards apart. I cut my motor halfway between two.

There was no risk working under the bright glare of the Coleman lantern for since I could see nothing of the other boats except their lights, I knew it was impossible for them to see what was going on in mine. Working rapidly. I uncovered the body, cut a length of sash cord and tied one of the anchors around Lawrence Powers's neck. The other I tied firmly to his feet after lashing his ankles together.

I was standing up in the boat and just getting ready to heave him over the side when a voice said almost in my ear, "Any luck?"

Starting violently, I lost my balance, made a wild grab for the side of the boat and sat down with a thump on the body. I took one wild look over my shoulder, expecting to see someone within feet of me, then drew a deep sigh of relief. There was a boat light slowly coming toward me, but it was still a good twenty yards away. I realized it was only the acoustic effect of sound traveling across water which had made the voice seem so near.

Since the two figures in the other boat were only faceless shapes to me, I realized they couldn't see into my boat any clearer than I could see into theirs. Quickly I pulled the burlap sacks over the body and pushed myself up onto the rear seat next to the motor.

The Best of *Manhunt*

Only then did it occur to me I hadn't even answered the other boat's hail. Belatedly I called back in as calm a voice as I could muster, "Couple of small perch is all."

The boat was now within ten yards, and I could make out the two men in it. The one in front was in his early twenties and the man operating the motor was middle-aged. The motor was barely turning over, which was the reason I hadn't heard their approach. But they hadn't been trying to sneak up on me, I realized when I saw a line stretching back from either side of the boat. They were moving at that slow speed because they were trolling.

They passed within three yards of me. As they went by, the middle-aged man said, "We ain't having any luck either. We're about ready to go in."

Then they were past. Neither had glanced at the burlap-covered mound in the bottom of my boat.

I waited until I could see nothing of them but their light, then uncovered the body again, lifted it in my arms and heaved it into the water. It landed on its back, the sightless eyes peering straight up at me for a final second before it disappeared in a gurgle of bubbles.

I tossed the burlap bags overboard after it. Then, with shaking fingers, I lit a cigarette and drew a deep and relieved drag.

15.

I was halfway back to shore before it occurred to me the old man at the boat livery might think it odd if he noticed my line wasn't wet. Cutting the motor, I tied a yellow and red flatfish to my line and made a long cast out over the water. I knew the chance of getting a strike on an artificial lure at night was remote, but all I was interested in was getting the line wet.

My usual fisherman's luck held. If I had been fishing seriously, I could have sat there all night without a single strike. But because the last thing in the world I wanted at that moment was a fish, I nailed a northern pike which must have weighed close to five pounds. It took me nearly ten minutes to land it.

Then I had another thought. I didn't have an Illinois fishing license. And it would be just my luck to step out of the boat into the arms of a game warden.

So I unhooked one of the nicest northerns I ever boated and tossed it back in the water.

When I pulled in at the boat livery dock, the old man asked me, "Any luck?"

"A five pound northern," I said. "But I tossed it back in."

He cackled. I knew he wouldn't believe me.

Helena had parked the car just off the highway on the dirt road leading down to the boat livery. She was sitting on the right side of the seat, so after tossing my fishing gear in the back, I slid under the wheel.

"Everything go all right?"

"O.K. I even caught a fish on the way in."

"Oh? Do you like fishing?"

"Under ordinary circumstances," I said. "It's my favorite sport."

"Then why didn't you stay out a while?" she asked seriously. "I wouldn't have minded waiting."

The question solidified an opinion I had already formed. Beneath her beautiful exterior Helena was almost psychotically callous. The casual way in which she had borrowed ice for our drinks from the tub containing the corpse of her husband had convinced me of that. Her suggestion that I might have enjoyed a little fishing immediately after dumping the same corpse in Lake Michigan only confirmed my judgment.

I didn't try to explain it to her. I just said, "I wasn't particularly in the mood for fishing tonight."

Back at the tourist court we had one more job. I set Helena to work scrubbing out the tub which had been her husband's bier for five days.

Then I informed her there wasn't any reason, now that her cabin was corpseless, that she couldn't sleep in her own bed that night. She gave me a mildly surprised look, but she made no objection.

I didn't think it necessary to explain that musing on her homicidal tendencies had begun to give me the feeling it might not be too safe to go to sleep in the same room she was in.

I locked my cabin door that night.

My last thought before going to sleep was speculation as to what Helena's feelings would be when she stepped into that tub for a shower the next morning. Then I stopped speculating, because I knew it wouldn't bother her in the slightest.

16.

The trip back to St. Louis on Sunday was uneventful. Enroute I briefed Helena again on how she must behave on Monday in order to keep suspicion from herself. I elaborated a little on my original instructions and made her repeat them back to me.

"I'm to meet the plane Lawrence intended to come back on just as though I expected him to be on it," she said tonelessly. "After it lands and everyone is off, I'm to check with the flight office and pretend to be upset because he wasn't listed on the flight. Then I'm to wire Lawrence in care of convention headquarters in New York. When word comes back that the telegram isn't deliverable, I'm to wire an inquiry to convention headquarters itself." She paused, then asked, "But will anybody be there if the convention is over?"

"Conventions are always headed up by local people in the town where the convention's held," I told her. "Usual procedure is for the chairman to rent a temporary post office box under the convention's name, then inform Western Union wires addressed to convention headquarters are to be delivered either to his office or home. He'll have the same office and home after the convention."

"I see. Well, when the wire comes back from convention headquarters saying Lawrence never reported in. I'm to phone the police and report him missing."

"You've got it pretty well," I said, satisfied that she could carry it off. "There's only one more thing. You've got to get it across to Harry Cushman that if he mentions his part in this, he's an accessory to first-degree murder. He's going to have to know Lawrence is dead, because otherwise he may get rattled enough at his continued disappearance to take his story to the police. Don't give him any details. Just give it to him cold that Lawrence is dead and he'd better keep his mouth shut if he wants to stay out of jail. Also tell him to stay completely away from you for the present. I don't want the cops accidentally stumbling over him, because while I'm sure he'll keep his mouth shut if he's left alone, I think he'd break pretty easily under questioning. If he keeps away from you, there isn't any reason for the cops to find out you even know him."

"I understand," she said. "I can handle Harry."

We took Mac Arthur Bridge back into St. Louis. I drove straight to my flat, then turned the car over to Helena. I didn't invite her in.

Standing on the sidewalk with my bag in one hand and my new fishing gear in the other, I said, "I've kept a list of expenses. But I'll wait until the police lose interest in your husband and you get your affairs straightened out before I bill you. I imagine your money will be tied up for some time if everything was in Lawrence's name."

"Are you adding an additional fee for disposing of Lawrence?" she asked.

"That was on the house. Just don't give me any more little jobs like that."

"Will I see you again, Barney? I mean aside from when you submit your expense account."

I shook my head definitely. "You're a lovely woman, and except for the third party you rang in on our trip, I enjoyed the week thoroughly. But this is the end. When things quiet down, you divorce Lawrence for desertion and marry some nice millionaire. Harry Cushman, maybe, if he isn't too scared to come near you again."

I thought for a moment her expressionless face looked a little wistful, but it may have been imagination. Her voice was as totally lacking in emotion as usual when she spoke.

"Good-by, Barney."

"Good-by, Helena," I said.

She drove away.

17.

I had hoped that was the end of it, but at nine Monday evening Helena phoned me at home.

"Everything went smoothly, Barney," she announced the moment I picked up the phone. "It worked out just as you said. The police were just here for a picture of Lawrence to teletype to New York. They weren't in the least suspicious, and about all they asked me was if he'd said anything about financial troubles recently."

Her call upset me. "Listen," I said. "Did it occur to you your phone might be tapped?"

She was silent for a moment. Then she asked, "Could it be?"

"No," I snapped. "They wouldn't tap a phone on a routine missing person case. But don't call me again. It's an unnecessary risk."

"I'm sorry, Barney. I thought you'd want to know."

"Just let me know if something goes wrong," I said. "If I don't hear from you, I'll assume you're doing fine."

But she phoned me again at nine Tuesday night.

As soon as I recognized her voice, I said bitterly, "I told you not to phone!"

"You said I should if something went wrong. Well, something has."

I felt a cold chill run along my spine. "What?"

"You'll have to come out here, Barney. Right away."

"Why?"

"I can't tell you over the phone. But you must come. Immediately."

"As soon as I can get a taxi," I said, and hung up.

All the way out to Helena's home in the cab I wondered what possibly could have gone wrong. There wasn't anything that *could* have gone wrong, I kept assuring myself. If ever a perfect murder had been pulled, Lawrence Powers's was it. Not only was the body beyond recovery, the police didn't even suspect there had been a murder, and probably never would.

The only thing I could think of was that Harry Cushman had gone to the police. But that seemed inconceivable to me. If I had evaluated him right, he'd stay as far away from both the police and Helena as he could get from the minute he realized he could be charged as an accessory to first-degree homicide.

My thoughts hadn't accomplished anything but to get me all upset by the time we arrived at Helena's home.

Helena met me at the front door. She wore a red off-the-shoulder hostess gown, and she looked as calm and unruffled as ever.

"Alice isn't here," she greeted me. "I sent her home at six because I expected Harry at seven."

So it was Harry Cushman after all who was causing whatever the trouble was, I thought.

I asked, "He still here?"

Instead of answering, she led me into the front room. "Would you like a drink before we talk?"

"No, I wouldn't like a drink before we talk," I said, exasperated. "Just tell me what's wrong."

"I'd rather show you."

The words raised the hair at the base of my neck. The last time she'd used similar words, she led me to her husband's iced corpse. Now she took my hand, just as she had that previous time, and led me into the dining room. I followed numbly, almost knowing what to expect.

The light was off in the dining room, but the switch was by the door and Helena flicked it on as we entered. Then she dropped my hand and looked at me expectantly.

The dining room was large and had a fireplace on the outside wall. Against the wall closest to us was a sideboard containing a tray of bottles and glasses and a bowl of ice cubes.

Lying face down in front of the sideboard was Harry Cushman, the entire back of his head a pulpy and bloody mass from some terrific blow. His left hand clutched a glass from which the liquid had spilled, and near his outstretched right hand lay a siphon bottle on its side. Next to him lay a pair of brass fire tongs with blood on them.

The shock was not as great as you might expect, because I had anticipated something on this order from the moment Helena said she would rather "show" me. Glancing about the room, I saw the drapes were drawn so that we were safe from outside observation.

I said coldly, "It looks like you hit him from behind while he was mixing a drink. Right?"

She merely nodded.

"Why?"

"Because I was afraid he might give us away. He was in a panic when I told him Lawrence was dead."

"Did he threaten to go to the police?"

She shook her head.

"What *did* he say?"

Helena shrugged slightly. "Nothing, really, except that I hadn't any right to involve him in murder. It was the way he acted. He shook like a leaf."

For a long time I looked at her. "Let me get this straight," I said finally. "He didn't threaten to expose us. He wasn't going to the police. But just because he seemed to you like a bad security risk, you murdered him."

She frowned slightly. "You make it sound worse than it was."

"Then make it sound better."

She made an impatient gesture. "What difference does it make now? It's done. And we have to dispose of the body."

Again she looked at me expectantly, a curious brightness in her eyes. And suddenly I realized something I had been aware of subconsciously for some time, but hadn't brought to the front of my mind for examination.

Helena enjoyed watching me solve the problems brought on by murder.

It was a game to her, I knew with abrupt understanding, for the first time really knowing what went on under that expressionless face.

I said, "What do you mean, *we* have to dispose of the body? I haven't killed anybody."

Her lip corners curved upward in a barely discernible smile. "I'm sure you wouldn't want me caught, Barney. You can only be executed for one murder. So there wouldn't be any point in not telling the police about Lawrence if I got caught for this one. Including how cleverly you got rid of the body."

With a feeling of horror I looked off into the future, seeing myself disposing of corpse after corpse as Helena repeatedly indulged her newly discovered thrill.

With only one result. Nobody gets away with murder forever.

I knew what I had to do then.

For a moment I examined her moodily. Then I shrugged. "All right, Helena. We may as well start now. Get some rags."

Obediently she went into the kitchen, returning in a few moments with several large rags. Taking one from her, I picked up the tongs.

"Lift his head a little," I said. "So I can spread a rag under it."

Turning her back to me, she put both hands under the dead man's shoulders and tugged upward. I swung the brass fire tongs down on top of her head with all my force.

It isn't much harder to dispose of two bodies than it is to dispose of one. Not with a river as deep as the Mississippi so close by.

The Killer

John D. Macdonald

January 1955

W e certainly got sick of John Lash. A lot of the guys stopped coming after he started to attend every meeting. It's a skin diving club—you know, just a few guys who like to swim under water in masks and all, shoot fish with those spear guns, all that. We started originally with six guys and we called ourselves The Deep Six. Even when it got up to about fifteen, we kept the name.

When it started we just had masks and fins and crude rigs. We live and work on the Florida Keys. I work in a garage in Marathon. Dusty has a bait and boat rental business in Craig. Lew manages a motel down on Ramrod. That's just to give you an idea of the kind of jokers we are. Just guys who got bitten by this skin diving bug. We tried to meet once a week. Dusty had an old tub that's ideal for it. We meet and pick a spot and head for it and anchor and go down and see what's there. You never know what you'll find. There are holes down there that are crawling with fish.

Once the bug gets you, you're hooked. There are a lot of little clubs like ours. Guys that get along. Guys who like to slant down through that green country, kicking yourself along with your fins, hunting those big fish right down in their own backyard.

We got better equipment as we went along. We bought snorkel tubes when those came out. But the Aqua-lungs were beyond our price range. I think it was Lew who had the idea of everybody chipping in, and of putting in the money we got from selling the catches. When we had enough we bought a lung and two tanks, and then another. In between meetings somebody would run the four tanks up and get them refilled. There was enough time on the tanks so that during a full day everybody got a crack at using one of the lungs.

It was fine there for quite a while. We'd usually get ten or twelve, and some of the wives would come along. We'd have food and beer out there in the sun on that old tub and we had some excitement, some danger, and a lot of fish.

Croy Danton was about the best. A little guy with big shoulders, who didn't have much to say. Not a gloomy guy. He just didn't talk much. His wife, Betty, would usually come along when she could. They've got some rental units at Marathon. He did a lot of the building himself, with the help of a G.I. loan. Betty is what I would call a beautiful girl. She's a blonde and almost the same height as Croy, and you can look at her all day without finding anything wrong with her. She dives a little.

Like I said, it was fine there for a while, until Lew brought this John Lash along one day. Afterward Lew said he was sorry, that Lash had seemed like a nice guy. In all fairness to Lew, I will admit that the first time John Lash joined us he seemed okay. We let him pay his dues. He was new to the Keys. He said he was looking around, and he had a temporary job tending bar.

One thing about him, he was certainly built. One of those guys who looks as if he was fat when you see him in clothes. But in his swimming trunks he looked like one of those advertisements. He had a sort of smallish round head and round face and not much neck. He was blonde and beginning to go a little bald. The head didn't seem to fit the rest of him, all that tough brown bulge of muscle. He looked as if a meat axe would bounce right off him. He'd come over from California and he had belonged to a couple of clubs out there and had two West Coast records. He said he had those records and we didn't check, but I guess he did. He certainly knew his way around in the water.

This part is hard to explain. Maybe you have had it happen to you. Like at a party. You're having a good time, a lot of laughs, and then somebody joins the party and it changes everything. You still laugh, but it isn't the same kind of laugh. Everything is different. Like one of those days when the sun is out and then before you know it there is a little haze across the sun and everything looks sort of funny. The water looks oily and the colors are different. That is what John Lash did to The Deep Six. It makes you wonder what happened to a guy like that when he was a kid. It isn't exactly a competitive instinct. They seem to be able to guess just how to rub everybody the wrong way. But you can't put your finger on it. Any of us could tell Dusty his old tub needed a paint job and the bottom scraped and Dusty would say we should come around and help if we were so particular. But John Lash could say it in such a way that it would make Dusty feel ashamed and make the rest of us feel ashamed, as though we were all second rate, and John Lash was used to things being first rate.

When he kidded you he rubbed you raw. When he talked about himself it wasn't bragging because he could always follow it up. He liked horseplay. He was always roughing somebody around, laughing to show it was all in fun, but you had the feeling he was right on the edge of going crazy mad and trying to kill you. We had been a close group, but after he joined we started to give each other a bad time, too. There were arguments and quarrels that John Lash wasn't even in. But they happened because he was there. It was spoiling the way it used to be, and there just wasn't anything we could do about it because it wasn't the sort of club where you can vote people out.

Without the lung, with just the mask, he could stay downstairs longer than anybody. Longer than Croy Danton even, and Croy had been the best until John Lash showed up. We had all tried to outdo Croy, but it had been sort of a gag competition. When we tried to outdo John Lash some of the guys stayed down so long that they were pretty sick when they came back up. But nobody beat him.

Another thing about him I didn't like. Suppose we'd try a place and find nothing worth shooting. For John Lash there wasn't anything that wasn't worth shooting. He had to come up with a fish. I've seen him down there, waving the shiny barb slowly back and forth. The fish come up to take a look at it. A thing like that attracts them. An angel fish or a parrot fish or a lookdown would come up and hang right in front of the barb, studying this strange shiny thing. Then John Lash would pull the trigger. There would be a big gout of bubbles and sometimes the spear would go completely through the fish so that it was threaded on the line like a big bright bead. He'd come up grinning and pull it off and toss it over the side and say, "Let's try another spot, children."

The group shrunk until we were practically down to the original six. Some of the other guys were going out on their own, just to stay away from John Lash. Croy Danton kept coming, and most of the time he would bring Betty. John Lash never horsed around with Croy. Croy, being so quiet, never gave anybody much of an opening. John Lash never paid any special attention to Betty. But I saw it happen. Betty wasn't going to dive after fish. She was just going to take a dip to cool off. John Lash had just taken a can of beer out of the ice chest. He had opened it and it was a little bit warm. I saw him glance up to the bow where Betty was poised to dive. She stood there and then dived off cleanly. John Lash sat there without moving, just staring at the place where she had been. And the too-warm beer foamed out of the can and ran down his fingers and dropped onto his thigh, darkening and matting the coarse blonde hair that had been sundried since his last dive. I saw him drain the can and saw him close his big hand on it, crumpling it, before throwing it over the side. And I saw him watch Betty climb back aboard, sleek and wet, smiling at Croy, her hair waterpasted down across one eye so that as soon as she stood up in the boat, she thumbed it back behind her ear.

I saw all that and it gave me a funny feeling in my stomach. It made me think of the way he would lure the lookdowns close to the barb, and it made me think of the way blood spreads in the water.

After that, John Lash began to move in on Betty with all the grace and tact of a bulldozer. He tried to dab at her with a towel when she came out of the water. If she brought anything up, he had to bustle over to take it off her spear. He found reasons to touch her. Imaginary bugs. Helping her in or out of the boat. Things like that. And all the time his eyes burning in his head.

At first you could see that Croy and Betty had talked about it between meetings, and they had agreed, I guess, to think of it as being sort of amusing. At least they exchanged quick smiles when John Lash was around her. But a thing like that cannot stay amusing very long when the guy on the make keeps going just a little bit further each time. It got pretty tense and, after the worst day, Croy started leaving Betty home. He left her home for two weeks in a row.

Croy left her home the third week and John Lash didn't show up either. We sat on the dock waiting for latecomers. We waited longer than usual. Dusty said, "I saw Lash at the bar yesterday and he said today he was off."

There were only five of us. The smallest in a long, long time. We waited. Croy finally said, "Well, let's go." As we took the boat out I saw Croy watching the receding dock, no expression on his face. It was a funny strained day. I guess we were all thinking the same thing. We had good luck, but it didn't seem to matter. We left earlier than usual. Croy sat in the bow all the way back, as if in that way he'd be nearer shore, and the first one home.

2.

Croy came around to see me at the garage the next morning. I was trying to find a short in an old Willys. When I turned around he was standing there behind me with a funny look on his face. Like a man who's just heard a funny sound in the distance and can't figure out just what it was. He looked right over my left shoulder, and said, "You can tell him for me, Dobey, that I'm going to kill him."

"What do you mean?"

"He came around yesterday. He was a little drunk. He scared Betty. He knew I wouldn't be there. He came around and he scared her. The Sandersons were there. She got loose of him and went over where they were. He kept hanging around. She had to stay with them most of the day. He's got her nervous now. You tell him for me if he makes one more little bit of a move toward her at any time, I'll sure kill him stone dead." He turned around and walked out with that funny look still on his face. It was the most I ever heard him say all at one time.

At noon I went over to the bar where John Lash was working. He'd just come on. I got a beer and he rung it up and slapped my change down. He seemed a little nervous.

"Get anything yesterday?"

"Lew got a big 'cuda. Croy got some nice grouper. Where were you?"

"Oh, I had things to do."

"You better not have any more things like that to do."

He looked at me and put his big hands on the bar and put his face closer to mine. "What kind of a crack is that?"

"Don't try to get tough with me. You messed around Betty Danton yesterday. You scared her. She told Croy. Croy came in this morning and gave me a message to give you. He says you bother her in any other kind of way at any time and he's going to kill you." It sounded funny to say it like that. As if I was in a movie.

John Lash just stared at me out of those little hot eyes of his. "What kind of talk is that? Kill me? With all the come-on that blonde of his has been giving me? Why don't he come here and tell me that? You know damn well why he didn't come here. By God, I'd have thrown him halfway out to the road."

"He told me to tell you. It sounded like he meant it."

"I'm scared to death. Look at me shake."

I finished my beer and put the glass down. "See you," I said.

"I'll be along the next time."

I walked out. One thing about that Lash, he didn't scare worth a damn. I would have been scared. One of those fellows who do a lot of talking wouldn't scare me much. But the quiet ones, like Croy, they bottle things up.

It was nearly three o'clock when Betty came into the garage. She had on a white dress and when she stood there it made the old garage with all the grease and dirt look darker than ever before. She is a girl who looks right at you. Her eyes were worried. I wiped my hands and lit a cigarette and went over to her.

"Dobey, did Croy talk to you?"

"He was in."

"What did he say?"

"Wouldn't he tell you what he said?"

"He just said he gave you a message for John Lash. What was it, Dobey? He won't tell me. He acts so funny. I'm scared, Dobey."

"He told me to tell Lash if he messed around you he was going to kill him. He said Lash scared you."

"Well, he did scare me, sort of. Because he was drunk. But the Sandersons were there. So it was all right. Croy says I have to come along with you next time. What did Lash say?"

"What do you think he said? You can't scare him off that way. I don't think anybody ought to go out next time, Betty. I think we ought to call it off. I think it's going to be a mess."

"Croy says we're going. He's acting funny. We'll have to go. You've got to come along too, Dobey. Please."

3.

That's the way it was. It was something you couldn't stop. Like one of those runaway trains in the old movie serials. Picking up speed as it went. I had time during the week to get hold of the other guys and tell them what was up. I don't know now why we didn't form a sort of delegation and go see John Lash and tell him to move along, off the Keys. There would have been enough of us. But there was something about Lash. Something wild and close to the surface. You could have done all that to a normal guy, but he wasn't normal. I'm not saying he was crazy.

Anyway, I loaded the little Jap automatic I had brought back from Saipan and put it in the paper sack with my lunch. That's the way I felt about the day.

Dusty and Lew and I were the first ones to arrive. We put the gear in the old tub. Lew had gotten his new Arbalete gun with the double sling and we hefted it and admired it and then we talked about maybe getting our own compressor some time for the two double-tank lungs. I crushed a damp cigarette and rubbed the glass on my face mask. Two more of the regulars arrived. There was the feel of trouble in that day. A different shimmer in the water. A different blue in the sky. A car door slammed and pretty soon Croy and Betty came around the corner of the fish house and down to the dock, laden with gear. For a time I guess we were all hoping that John Lash wouldn't show. It would have been a good day then, like the days before he came along and joined us.

But as hope grew stronger and Dusty started to fool with the old engine, John Lash came down to the dock, walking cat-light, carrying his sack of gear and lunch and beer, his personal Saetta gun in his other hand, looking slimmer and frailer than it was because it was John Lash who carried it, walking toward us, sun picking sweat-lights off his brown shoulders.

I expected it right then and there. I saw Betty hunch herself a little closer to Croy and start to put her hand on his arm and then change her mind. But John Lash came aboard, saying a lot of loud hellos, banging his gear down, opening the ice chest to pile his cans of beer in there.

He didn't seem to pay any special attention to Betty, or Croy either. He sat on the rail back near Dusty at the wheel while we headed out and down the coast. It was enough to make you want to relax, but you couldn't. The water had a greased look. We had agreed to try Gilman's Reef. There is good coral there, and rock holes. I don't know whether we were trying to keep a lid on trouble, but the other five of us did more talking than usual, more kidding around. But laughter had a flat sound across the water. Lew checked the Aqualungs. I had me a beer.

When we got close I went up and stood on the bow and had Dusty bring it up to a place that looked right. I let the anchor line slide through my hands. It hit bottom in twenty-five feet, which was about right. We drifted back and it caught and we swung and steadied there, about twenty feet off the reef shallows. No trouble had started and it didn't look like there would be any. Croy and Lew went down first, Lew with a lung and Croy with a mask only, just to take a look around. I noticed that when Croy lowered himself easily into the water he glanced at Betty and then back to where John Lash was working his feet into the fins. He ducked under and one fin swirled the water as he went down.

John Lash got his fins on and flapped forward to where Betty sat on the rail. He laughed out loud and wrapped a big brown fist in that blonde hair of hers and turned her face upward and kissed her hard on the mouth. She struggled and clawed at him and fell to her hands and knees when he released her.

"Hard to get, aren't you, blondie?" he asked.

Dusty said, "Cut it out, Lash. Cut it out!"

"This is nothing to you, Dusty. Keep out of it! This is me and Betty."

"Get away from me," she said. Her eyes were funny and her mouth had a broken look. I picked up the paper sack and put my hand inside and got hold of the automatic. I couldn't tell what he was going to try to do. He stood spread-legged on the deck watching the water. Betty moved away from him toward the stern, beyond me and Dusty.

Croy broke water and shoved his mask up. He was a dozen feet from the boat.

John Lash stood there and laughed down at him and said, "I just kissed your woman, Danton. I understand you got ideas of making something out of it. I got a message from you."

Croy took one glance at Betty. He brought the Arbalete spear gun up almost off-hand and fired it directly at John Lash's middle. I heard the zing and slap of the rubber slings, heard Betty's scream, heard John Lash's hard grunt of surprise as he threw himself violently to one side. I don't know how he got away from it. But he did. The spear hit the end of the nylon and fell to the water on the far side of the boat. John Lash recovered his balance. He stared at Croy as though he were shocked. He roared then and went off the side in a long flat dive, hurling himself at Croy. There was a splash of water, a flash of brown arms and then they were both gone. I got a glimpse of them under the water as they sank out of sight. Betty screamed again, not as loud.

4.

Nobody was set to go down. We all started grabbing gear at once. I went off the side about the same moment as Dusty, and at the last moment I had snatched up John Lash's Saetta gun. It was cocked and I don't know what I expected to do with it but I took it. I went down through the deepening shades of green, looking for them. I saw movement and cut over toward it, but it was Lew wearing the lung. He saw me and spread his arms in a gesture that meant he hadn't spotted anything worth shooting. He didn't know what was going on. I motioned him to go up. I guess I looked as though I meant it. He shrugged and headed up.

I looked hard, but I couldn't find them and I could tell by the way my chest felt that it was nearly time to head up. I took it as long as I could. I thought I saw movement below me and to the right but I was close to blacking out and I went up. Dusty was hanging on the side of the boat. Betty stood staring down into the water. I knew from her face that they hadn't come up. I took deep breaths and turned and went down again and got part way down when I saw them. John Lash with a look of agony on his face, was working his way up, kicking hard, one hand holding Croy by the waistband of his trunks. Croy was loose in the water. I went over and got hold of Croy by the wrist. I fired the spear off to the side so the gun would float up. Lash was having a hard time of it. I got Croy up and we got him over the side and put him face down on the bottom and Lew, who had the lung and tanks off, began to work on him. Somebody behind me helped John Lash aboard. Dusty had to grab Betty and pull her away from Croy so Les could use the artificial respiration without her getting in his way.

She turned against Dusty and she was crying. Those were the sounds. The small noises she made, and John Lash's labored breathing, and the rhythmic slap and creak of the respiration.

"Tried . . . to kill me," Lash said. "You . . . you saw it. Then . . . tried to drown me. Tried to hold me even . . . after he'd passed out."

Nobody answered him. The boat moved in the offshore swell. Loose gear rattled. Croy retched and coughed. Les continued until Croy began to struggle weakly. Les moved back then and Croy rolled over, closing his eyes against the sun.

Betty dropped to her knees beside him saying words that did not make sentences. Croy raised his head. He looked at her and then pushed her aside, gently. He got to his knees. I tried to help him up but he refused the help. He got to his feet with an enormous effort. He stood unsteadily and looked around until he saw John Lash. As soon as he saw Lash he bent and picked up a loose spear. He held it by the middle, the muscles of his arm bunching.

John Lash moved quickly. He got, up and said, "Wait! Hold it! Croy, wait . . ." Dusty tried to grab Croy but he moved quickly. The spear tip gashed John Lash's arm as he tried to fend it off, and as Croy drew back to thrust again, John Lash hit him flush in the face with one of those big brown fists. Croy bounced back and hit the engine hatch and rebounded to fall heavily and awkwardly, unconscious.

Betty reached him and turned him and sat, his head in her lap, arm curled protectively around his head, murmuring to him. Lew wet the end of a towel and gave it to her. She wiped the blood from his mouth and looked at John Lash and then the rest of us with cold hate. "Why didn't you stop him? Why are you letting him do this to Croy?"

"I had to hit him!" John Lash said, his voice a half-octave higher than usual. "You saw what he was trying to do. Why didn't you guys stop him?"

Croy's mouth puffed rapidly. He mumbled something. Dusty started the engine. "We better get back. You want to get the anchor up, Dobey?"

I broke it free and hauled it in, coiling the line. When I moved back I saw that Croy was sitting up. Betty was holding onto his arm. She was saying, with a gradually increasing edge in her voice, "No, darling. No. No please, darling."

But Croy was looking beyond her, looking at John Lash. Lash was trying to grin. It wasn't a grin as much as it was just a sort of twist he was wearing on his mouth. He'd look at Croy and then look away. Croy got up then with Betty holding onto him. He lurched over toward the rail and grabbed one of the gaffs. Lash came back up onto his feet quickly and said, "Grab him!"

Croy shook Betty loose. Lew and I grabbed Croy. It was like grabbing hard rubber. He lowered his head and butted Lew over the rail. Dusty swung the boat to keep the prop clear of Lew. It made me lose my balance. As I staggered Croy rapped me across my shins with the handle end of the gaff and hot stars went off behind my eyes from the sudden pain of it. When I could see again I saw him going for Lash with the gaff. They were poised for a moment, muscles like they were cut out of stone, both holding onto the long gaff. Then John Lash, with his greater strength, hurled Croy back toward the stern again. Croy fell, harder than before, but he hadn't been hit.

"Keep him off me!" Lash yelled. "Keep him off me!"

Croy got slowly and clumsily back to his feet and started back toward Lash. I was set to take another grab at Croy. Lew was climbing aboard. The other two guys were having no part of it. They were plain scared. Just as I was about to grab Croy he put his weight on his left foot and went down. I could see the ankle puffing visibly. He never took his eyes off John Lash. He had fallen near his gear. He fumbled and came out with a fish knife with a cork handle. Holding it in his hand he began to crawl toward the bow, toward John Lash again, the handle thumping against the cockpit boards every time he put his right hand down. I fell on his arm. I could hear Lash yelling. I couldn't make out what he was saying. I got Croy's wrist and managed to twist the knife out of his hand. Lew had him around the middle. We hauled him over and tried to sit on him. He kept struggling with stubborn, single-minded strength. Once he broke free and started crawling again toward Lash, puffed lips pulled back from bloody teeth, but we got him again.

Dusty helped that time and one of the other guys and we held him and tried to talk sense into him, but he kept on struggling. We finally got heavy nylon line around his wrists and tied his arms behind him. We thought that was going to be enough, but even with his hands like that he managed to get on his feet and, limping badly, try to get at Lash. Dusty put a length of the anchor line around the engine hatch and we tied him there around his chest, sitting on the litter of gear and water and smashed sandwiches and cans of beer, staring at John Lash and fighting the heavy line constantly.

5.

Once he was tied up, Betty kneeling beside him, trying to soothe him, John Lash lighted a cigarette. His hands shook. He grinned. "He get like that often?" he asked "Look at him. He still wants to get at me."

Croy's shoulders bulged as he fought the rope. Lash kept glancing at him. We were all breathing hard. Dusty examined skinned knuckles. "I never see him like that, not that bad. Old Croy he gets an idea in his head, you can't get it out. No sir."

"He'll get over this, won't he? When he cools off."

"He's not going to cool off at all," Dusty said. "Not one little bit. Tomorrow, the next day, it'll be just the same."

"What am I supposed to do then?" Lash asked.

"I don't know. I really don't know," Dusty said. "You got to either kill him or he's got it in his mind he's going to kill you. Known him twenty years and he's never gone back on his word one time. Or his daddy before him."

Lash licked his lips. I watched him. I saw him sitting there, nervous. It was something he'd never run into. It was something I guess few men ever run into in their lifetime. I could see him wishing he'd never made any sort of a pass at Betty.

Croy fought the rope, doggedly, constantly, sweat running down his face.

John Lash lighted another cigarette. "He'll get over it," he said unconvincingly.

"I wouldn't want to bet much on that," I said.

There was that big John Lash sitting there in the sun, a whole head and forty-fifty pounds bigger than little Croy Danton. And without the faintest idea in the world as to what to do about it. Either way, there didn't seem to be any kind of an out for John Lash.

"He's nuts. You people are all nuts down here." Lash said.

I sensed what was forming in his mind. I said, "When we dock we'll see if we can hold him right here for about an hour. You ought to pack up and take off."

"Run from a character like him?" Lash said.

Croy's arms came free suddenly and he tried to shove the line up off his chest. His wrists were bloody where the nylon had punished them. Three of us jumped him and got his wrists tied again. He didn't make a sound. But he fought hard. Betty kept trying to quiet him down, talking gentle, her lips close to his ear. But you could see that for Croy there were two people left in the world. Him and John Lash.

It took about forty minutes to get back in. Nobody talked. I didn't like to watch Croy. It was a sort of thing I have seen in Havana at the cock fights. I hear it is like that, too, at the bull fights. A distillation, I guess you would call it, of violence. The will to kill. Something that comes from a sort of crazy pride, a primitive pride, and once you have started it, you can't turn it off.

It was easy to see that John Lash didn't want to look at him either. But he had to keep glancing at him to make sure he wasn't getting loose. During that forty minutes John Lash slowly unraveled. He came apart way down in the middle of himself where it counted. I don't think any of us would say he was a coward. He wasn't yellow. But this was something he couldn't understand. He'd never faced it before and few men ever face it in their lifetime. To Lash I guess Croy wasn't a man any more. He was a thing that wanted to kill him. A thing that lusted to kill him so badly that even defenseless it would still keep coming at him.

By the time we got in, John Lash wasn't even able to edge by Croy to pick up his gear. We had to get it and pass it up to him where he stood on the dock. John

Lash looked down and he looked older in the face. Maybe it was the first time he had seriously thought about his own death. It shrunk him a little.

"Hold him for an hour. I'll go away," he said. He didn't say goodbye. There wasn't any room in him to think of things like that. He walked away quickly and a bit unsteadily. He went around the corner of the fish house. We've never seen him since.

Croy kept watching the place where John Lash had disappeared. Betty kept whispering to him. But in about ten minutes Croy stopped struggling.

"There, baby. There," I heard Betty whisper.

He gave a big convulsive shudder and looked around, first at her and then at the rest of us, frowning a little as if he had forgotten something.

"Sorry," he said huskily. "Real sorry." And that is all he ever said about it. He promised that he was all right. I carried his stuff to their car. Betty bound his ankle with a strip of towel. He leaned heavily on her to the car.

6.

That's almost all, except the part I don't understand. The Deep Six is back up to about fifteen again. We have a compressor now, and new spots to go, and we did fine in the inter-club competitions this year. We're easy with each other, and have some laughs.

But Croy never came back. He and Betty, they go out by themselves in a kicker boat when the weather is right. I don't see any reason why he didn't come back. He says hello when we see him around. Maybe he's ashamed we saw him like that, saw that wildness.

One morning not long ago I went out alone on the Gulf side. I got out there early and mist hung heavy on the water. I tilted my old outboard up and rowed silently. It was kind of eerie there in the mist in the early morning. All of a sudden I began to hear voices. It was hard to tell direction but they kept getting louder. There was a deep voice, a man's voice, talking and talking and talking, and every so often a woman would say one or two words, soft and soothing.

All of a sudden I recognized the voices as Croy's and Betty's. I couldn't catch any of the words. I rested on the oars. It made me feel strange. I figured I could get closer and find out what in the world Croy could talk about for so long.

But then understanding came to me suddenly, and it wasn't necessary to listen. I understood suddenly that there was only one subject on which a quiet guy like Croy could talk and talk and talk, and that the situation wasn't over and maybe would never be over. And I realized that embarrassment was only part of the reason Croy didn't come skin-diving with us any more; the rest of the reason was that the sight of us reminded him too strongly of John Lash. I turned the dinghy and headed off the other way until their voices faded and were gone.

Later in the morning after the sun had burned the mist off, I was spin casting with a dude and monofilament line over a weed bed when they went by, heading in, their big outboard roaring, the bow wave breaking the glassy look of the morning Gulf.

Croy was at the motor, Betty up in the bow.

Betty waved at me and Croy gave me a sort of little nod as they went by. I waved back. Their swell rocked me and then they were gone in the distance.

She is the most beautiful woman I have ever seen. You could look at her all day and not find anything wrong.

The Day It Began Again
Fletcher Flora

April 1955

I went up in the elevator to the top floor and out into a long, light corridor of
smooth stone. I told a guard there who I was, and he took me down the corridor
and let me through a gate of steel bars into a large room, and I went over and sat
down on a straight chair facing a steel screen.

It was light in the room, just as it had been in the corridor, and it was very
clean and up so high that the surrounding buildings did not shut off the sunlight,
and the sunlight slanted down in long shafts through the high windows that had
heavy steel screen on the outside that was just like the screen I sat facing. I thought
that it wasn't much like what you'd expect a municipal prison to be, not dark and
gloomy and damp, and I thought that it would really have been better if it *had* been
like that, like you'd expect it to be, because the way it was, it looked like someone
was trying to make it cheerful, and it was a kind of perversion and only made it
worse.

I sat and watched the shafts of sunlight and smelled the faint institutional
odor, and after a while a door opened and closed on the other side of the screen,
and Carlos came down and sat in a chair facing me, but he didn't look at me. He
looked at his hands. He folded them on the narrow table-like ledge that ran in front
of him and sat there staring at them.

His golden hair was as thick and curly as it had ever been, and his skin had a
kind of glowing transparency, and in spite of the drawn muscles of his face and the
heavy shadows under his eyes, he looked very young, no more than a boy, as if the
years had not passed and the events of the years had never happened.

"Hello, Carlos," I said.

He lifted his eyes for a second, and they widened a little at the sound of my
voice in the shape of his name, but he lowered them again without speaking and
looked at his folded hands.

"How are you, Carlos?" I said.

But he didn't answer, only nodding his head a little, and I could see the extent
of his withdrawal, what an incalculable distance away he was, and I began talking
quietly about things related to the two of us, little things that had happened a long
time ago and a short time ago, but whatever they were, or whenever, it made no
difference at all, and it was no use trying. I couldn't bring him back.

After a while a guard came up to him on the other side of the screen, and it
was time to leave so I stood up and said good-by and started away, and then he
spoke for the first time, using my name as if it were something he'd recalled
suddenly after severe mental effort.

"Jake," he said.

I turned and looked at him through the screen, and he lifted a hand in a
gesture of supplication, and I could see the luminous terror in his big eyes.

"Don't let them kill me, Jake," he said. "Don't let them."

The Best of *Manhunt*

Then the guard jerked his arm and led him away, and I went out and down in the elevator and walked about ten blocks to a park and sat on a bench in the sun. The sunlight was thin and didn't have much warmth in it at first, but it kept getting a little warmer as the sun climbed in the sky, and I sat there for a long, long time thinking and watching the things that happened around me in the park.

About ten-thirty the kids began coming into the park from the apartment buildings near by, and the women who came to watch them play, the mothers or nurses or whatever they were, sat on benches and looked at magazines and books and lifted their eyes now and then to see where the kids were and what they were doing and to yell at them if they were someplace they shouldn't have been or were doing something they shouldn't have been doing. One of the women sat on the same bench I was on, but she didn't speak to me or even look at me, and I didn't speak to her, either, although I looked at her long enough to see that she was short and too heavy and not at all pretty. She was reading a book and was almost half finished with it, and her voice when she yelled at the two kids she'd brought was harsh and querulous, and it was evident that she didn't like to have her reading interrupted.

I kept thinking about Carlos in the old days and how it had been then. I didn't make an effort to remember anything in particular or in any particular sequence but just let things come and go in my mind however they would, and one of the things I remembered was the day he'd moved with his mother and father into the house next door to ours, and how he had come out in the afternoon and sat under a tree in the yard and had begun to play with some sticks he picked up off the ground. What he did was lay the sticks out in all the different shapes he could think of, all sorts of geometrical figures, and when he'd used up all the sticks, he gathered them up and started all over again and made different figures, and he kept doing it over and over until his mother finally came out onto the porch and called him into the house.

It seemed to me at the time a pretty dull way to spend an afternoon in the yard, and maybe that's why I remembered it and never forgot it, because it seemed such an odd thing to do, but what I remembered best was how beautiful he was. I watched him from my side of the hedge, and the sun filtered through the leaves of the branches above him and touched his hair with a kind of pale fire, and his hair was golden, really golden, and curled in silken ringlets all over his head like in the pictures of young Greek boys in ancient times that you saw in Bulfinch's Mythology. He had a face as delicately molded as a pretty girl's, and it gave me a kind of pain in the chest to see him there, and a kind of angry resentment, too, because it didn't seem right for a boy to be so beautiful and make another boy feel so ugly, but after a while I began to feel that resentment of beauty like that was utterly futile, even a sort of sacrilege, and the resentment passed and never returned.

I grew to love him. I loved him very much, and he loved me, I'm sure, and it wasn't the kind of love you might have thought it would be between two boys, and later two men, but it was clean and sweet like the love between Jonathan and David, I think it was, and it was always the best thing in my life after it started, and probably it was the best thing in his life, too, though I can't really be certain of that, not knowing what it may have made him think or do or keep from doing.

Anyhow, it lasted. It was natural, and we didn't have to work at it to keep it alive, and it went on and on from year to year. He wasn't sickly or anything like that but was just delicately built, with small bones and all, and I did a lot of fighting for him, because there are always guys wanting to beat up another guy if he's too good-looking, and it wasn't that he was a coward, either, and afraid to do his own fighting, but just that he was delicately built this way and not good at rough stuff, and I wanted to do it for him.

Another thing, he was a genius. What they call a psychological genius. It means he came out very high on tests and was able to learn easily a lot of things many guys can never learn at all. Things like physics and trigonometry and calculus and such. He used to help me a lot and never consciously made me feel inferior, just like he never consciously made me feel ugly, and he'd have felt very bad if he'd known I'd ever felt that way, which I did for a little while, like I said.

I guess the strangest thing about him was his shyness. What I mean, a boy so beautiful and so brilliant might have been arrogant and vain because of it, and you couldn't have blamed him much if he'd been like that, but it wasn't so with Carlos, and the simple truth is, he wasn't *enough* that way. His shyness was so intense that it sometimes made him unhappy, and he had periods of depression that you couldn't see any reason for, but they were very real just the same, and his mind, in spite of being so sharp and all, or maybe because of it rather than in spite of it, seemed to be sort of delicate, like his bone structure, and not able to stand up to as much as a common sort of mind like mine, for instance.

The girls were wild about him, of course. You'd have expected that. On the other hand, though, he never showed much interest in the girls, and that was something you *wouldn't* have expected. Oh, he went out with them now and then as we grew older, and laughed and talked with them sometimes, and even took some of them to one of the popular places for cokes or something, but he never really got involved with any of them, except this one girl named Nelly, who was very pretty and not a bad kid, but the thing she did to him was bad, and it almost ruined him.

She was wild about him, like the others, and she wouldn't let him alone, and she finally got him in a mess. There was a legal technicality about it, and it looked for a while like her old man, who was vindictive and mean as the devil about it, would have Carlos sent to reform school or prison or whichever it would have been in his case. What I said at the time and always afterward was that it wasn't Carlos's fault, and you had to consider that he was subjected to a lot more temptation and *pressure* about things like that than the average fellow, the girls losing their heads and throwing themselves at him as they did, and if the average fellow had that pressure on him, he'd be in trouble all the time. It didn't seem fair to hold him responsible. That's what this girl named Nelly thought, too, and she had the guts to say it, that it had been her fault and she'd pressured him into it, and that was what saved him in the end.

But he never got over it, and he never had anything more to do with girls, or women as he grew older. Like I said, he was sensitive about such things. He started seeing all of them as a menace, a terrible kind of menace that threatened his security and even his life and made him seem a monster or something in his own eyes, and they filled him, I think, with fear and anger, and those that must have appealed to him, that he must have desired in spite of everything, he feared and hated most of all.

I sat there on the bench in the park a very long time thinking about these things, and the woman on my bench stood up with a snap of her book and called the two kids and took them away, and gradually all the other women and kids went away, too, and the sun climbed the sky and started down the other side. It got to be time to eat, and past time, but I wasn't hungry, so I continued to sit on the bench, and after a while my mind got stuck on the last thing that had happened between Carlos and me, on the sight of him behind the steel screen with the luminous terror in his eyes and on the sound of his voice when he asked me not to let them kill him. It was a bad thing to think about, a disturbing thing, and I was glad when it was time for me to go. I left the park and walked through the streets to the Professional Building and went up in the elevator to the seventh floor. Down the hall from the elevator was a door with a pane of frosted glass that had *Wallace King, Attorney-at-Law*, printed across it in chaste gold letters. I went through this door into a reception room, and because I'd been there before, the receptionist recognized me and spoke to me by name.

"Do you wish to see Mr. King?" she said.

I said I did, and she said, "He's busy with a client at the moment, but I'm sure he'll be able to see you. Will you sit down?"

I sat down and picked up a magazine and leafed through it without seeing it. I put the magazine down and sat looking over the receptionist's head to the closed door of Wallace King's office, and I tried to arrange in my mind the words that I wanted to say to him, but I wasn't at all sure what the words were, or even what I wanted precisely to say, so it wasn't much use. After a short while the door opened, and a woman came out and crossed the reception room and went past me into the hall, and the receptionist snapped a switch on a box and said something and listened to something and then looked at me and nodded, and I got up and went into the office.

Wallace King stood up and offered me a dry hand and sat down again, and I thought that he looked old and tired in the light that came through the bank of windows behind him.

His face was deeply creased and had the gray, dry look of dust, and his hair was thin and also gray and was brushed across his wide skull from a low side part. He looked a little like pictures of Clarence Darrow, and I had a feeling that he probably knew it and cultivated the resemblance.

"I've been to see Carlos," I said.

He closed his eyes and sighed and opened them again. "Yes? How was he?"

"Not good. He's very frightened, and he seems to be losing contact."

"I know. It's a kind of defense mechanism, that withdrawal. Perhaps in the end it will serve a good purpose."

"How do you mean?"

"In case of an insanity plea."

"The plea is not guilty."

"I've been wanting to discuss that with you."

"You mean you want to change it?"

"Yes."

"Why?"

He closed his eyes again and kept them closed for a long time, and when he opened them at last they were full of his age and his weariness. "Because he's guilty. Because the prosecutor will convince a jury without any difficulty at all."

I moved and felt the anger move within me. "No. He's not guilty. I believe that, and if you're going to defend him, you must believe it, too."

"Listen to me." He leaned across his desk and measured his words. "They have a witness who will identify him as the person seen running from the scene of the last crime. They have the clerk who remembers selling him a dozen pairs of thirty-six-inch shoestrings. How many men buy thirty-six-inch shoestrings? And Carlos is a person easy to remember, you know. They have other witnesses to testify to seeing him near the scenes of two of the other crimes about the time they were committed. Very convincing. Against this, we have nothing. No alibi for even one of the crimes. You lived with him. You lived in the same apartment for several years, and even you have nothing to offer. You say yourself that he wasn't at home any one of the nights when the crimes occurred."

"I could testify otherwise in court."

"A lie? Perjury?" He shook his head and was not shocked or angry but only tired and sad. He said softly, *"Are you sure that you want Carlos to go free?"*

"He's innocent," I said. "I want him free."

"Then you'll see him executed instead. He's guilty, but he's certainly also mad, and that's our only hope of saving him. We can support an insanity plea with convincing evidence. Remember his traumatic experience with the girl years ago. Remember the effect of that experience to which you and others could testify. Remember that he was forced to leave college for one year to receive treatment in a sanitarium for a serious mental breakdown. Remember that we can present professional opinions to support our plea."

"An institution for the criminally insane is no substitute for freedom."

"It's a fair substitute for death."

I stood up, the anger within me stirring and growing and making me sick, and he leaned back in his chair and looked up at me and then down at his desk quickly, as if the sight of me was something he couldn't bear any longer.

"How long has Carlos been confined?" he said.

"You know as well as I. Over a month. Almost five weeks."

"And how many women have been strangled in that time?"

"None."

"Exactly. But before that there had been one a week for six straight weeks. A pattern of method. A pattern of time. Don't you see? The discontinuance of the murders is the most damning evidence of all. The simple fact that they've stopped is pretty definitive."

There was nothing more to say, nothing at all, so I turned and went out of the office and out of the building and started walking back toward the apartment I'd shared with Carlos. It was a long way and took me over an hour to get there, and the sun descended the sky behind me, and its light thinned again and lost the little warmth it had gained. I reached the apartment and went inside and sat in a chair in the living room, and after a while the silence was more than I could stand.

There's only one chance lift to save him, I thought. *Only one way.*

I got up and went into the bedroom and got one of the thirty-six-inch shoestrings that I had found in Carlos's things and hidden before the police came. I put the shoe string in my pocket and went out into the dark street.

Moonshine
Gil Brewer

March 1955

She wouldn't be expecting me home from work this early. I'd planned on that. I parked the coupé four houses down, got my lunch pail off the seat, and started along the sidewalk. It looked all right down there. Our five-year-old twins, Denise and Danny, were playing around a palm tree with young Gregory from next door.

I began walking on the grass, watching the front bedroom window; the Venetian blinds. Luckily the kids didn't see me, and then the blinds flicked open and shut. I walked a little faster around the side of the house, by the Australian pine hedge. I didn't want to run.

The back door slammed and I heard him running like hell for the alley. I came around the side of the house and saw a flash of yellow sweater. The alley gate was still swinging. A car door whammed shut, and he gunned it down the alley, out of sight in a rattling shower of gravel.

He figured he'd made it again. Well, I stood there and it all washed around inside me like a kind of filthy sludge. For too long, I'd asked myself what I was supposed to do. Now I knew this had happened once too often.

I went inside. Supper wasn't on yet, and she was in there parked on the couch, knitting. She sure could knit.

"Oh," she said. "You home already, honey?"

I carefully set my lunch pail on the shelf in the kitchen and went over to the sink. For a moment I just stood there, hanging onto the edge of the sink, staring down at the drain, remembering all those things you try so hard to forget. Finally, I washed my hands, dried them, combed my hair and walked into the living room.

She was humming and knitting. She glanced up and smiled. The guilt was all through her. You could smell it. Her lipstick was on a bit cockeyed. She was barefoot and I knew she didn't have a stitch on under that red skirt. I always wondered how she kept her smooth blonde hair combed at times like this; maybe they had it worked so she could put her head in a box, or something.

"You surprised me," she said.

I sat down and looked at her.

"Supper isn't ready," she said. "I'll get right at it. How come you're early?"

"Never mind supper just yet."

She laid down her knitting, smiling and humming, not looking at me.

"You see the children?" she said.

"No. Where are they? They weren't around the house."

She jumped up, a little frantic, but not really showing it. Most of the time she had everything under control. But I had studied her for a long while. She was easy to read. She went over by one of the front windows, then turned grinning.

"You kidder," she said. "They're right out there."

"Oh, are they?"

She walked past me, breezing the way they do, humming again. I watched her hips sway back and forth under that red skirt. I knew what I had to do, but I wondered whether it should be him or her?

"Where's the car?" she called from the kitchen. "Didn't hear you drive in, Jim."

"I parked it down the block."

There was a long silence and she rattled some pans. She was troubled. "Why ever did you do that?"

"It was heated up."

She came bouncing back into the living room, holding her hair flat against her head with both hands. She was wearing one of my T-shirts.

"I clean forgot!" she said. She ran over and slipped onto my lap. Her lipstick was very neat now. "You were going to trade it in today. That's why you're home so early. You didn't go yet?"

Hell, I thought. She wants to call him back. So, right then I made up my mind.

"No," I said. "I'm just going. Can you hold supper?"

"Sure."

Her body was really hot under her clothes.

"It'll be swell for the kids," she said, "having a larger car. Things are so tight in the coupé."

"Maybe we should keep both cars," I said.

She went for that. She kissed me and hugged me. She was thrilled. I thought about how much better back seats were and said, "I could use the coupé for work and leave the other one home, so you could run errands and stuff."

She got carried away. I shoved her off my lap. You'd think she'd be a little tired because she didn't eat much.

I went into the bedroom and got out my key and unlocked my foot locker. It hadn't been tampered with. I just looked at my .45 automatic there, for a minute, kind of holding my breath. Then I picked it up. It was loaded. I stuck it in my jacket pocket, closed the foot locker and went into the living room.

"Did you want something?" she said.

"No. I'll run along."

She was practically dancing, standing still. She wanted to make contact with him again, so I'd have to hurry like hell.

Out front, I ran for the car, got in and drove away thinking about the kids. I headed fast for this gin mill over on Tangerine. He was there every day at this hour. I found him at the bar, alone, working on some port wine. When he saw me come in, he choked, turned red, and you could see him think of the back door. Then he pulled the nonchalant act.

"Hi," I said. "How you doing?"

"Oh, great!"

"Give me a beer," I said to the barman. "Draft. You have another?" I said to him, turning and looking straight into those baby blue eyes. I honest to God could smell her on him.

"Well, no," he said. "I gotta be running."

"Stick around, have a drink." I made it imperative, bending it a little tight and banking on his character.

"Well, O. K.," he said. He laughed, looked at the barman and wiped a long finger of black hair out of his eyes. "Yeah, gimme another port." He turned to me, tight dungarees, tight yellow sweater over his broad shoulders, white teeth and all. "How's it going?" He was breathing hard.

"All right."

For a minute I thought *he* was going to hum.

We got our drinks. He had stubby fingered hands and they were shaky. He was sweating a lot, but it was a cool early evening. Twilight marched down Tangerine.

"I'll have to be going right after this," he said.

"Stick around. What's there to do?"

He grinned. "Yeah," he said. "This town's real dead."

"All how you look at it."

We sat there a while and I kept thinking about Denise and Danny, remembering how they looked playing in the front yard. The barman was picking his teeth, staring out the window, waiting for the after-supper crowd.

"Everybody's eating," he said. "Guess I should ought to go eat." He stretched and yawned, turned around on his bar stool.

"No supper for me tonight."

"No?" He held it, sticking to the bar stool. "How come?" He yawned. He was forcing a lot of yawns.

"Fight with the wife," I said. "Think I'll run over to Tampa. Change my luck. I know a good place."

He thought that over.

He laughed, nudged my arm. "Not going home and smooth it over, eh?"

"The hell with that," I said.

There was a good long silence. I ordered another beer and another wine for him before he could do anything. I decided to bank on his character all the way.

"I should really get going," he said.

I'll bet, I thought. She's called him and he doesn't know what in hell to do. She figured she's got maybe an hour. There were some blonde hairs sticking to his yellow sweater, and he had the short sleeves of the sweater rolled up tight against his shoulders. There was a red smear of lipstick on his left shoulder, and in my mind's eye I could see her lips putting it there. He was some filthy character, all right.

But you could tell he really didn't want to go. He wanted to sit right here and drink with me. Can you beat that? We were like brothers, I suppose; something, anyway. He couldn't help himself now. He had to stay with me. Maybe he was just nuts, I couldn't tell.

"You remember my wife," I said. "You met her when you worked in that gas station, remember?"

"Oh, yeah. Sure—now I remember. Blonde, nice-looking blonde." He drank some of his wine, turned and grinned. The black hair was in his eyes again. Everything was rosy now. He was sure I knew nothing. This was going to be a hot one to tell the boys, all right. "Hell," he said. "It's silly, you wanting to stay away from *her*."

I shrugged. "Wait'll you're married."

"I suppose so. I suppose you can even get tired of your wife."

You louse, I thought. You dirty louse, you're talking too much.

I swallowed. "Sure," I said. "I know a couple good ones over in Tampa. Real nice, full of fun. Full of everything." I forced a laugh and drank some beer. "Say," I said. "Why don't you come along? This blonde I know of, she goes for guys like you. Black hair. We could make a night of it."

"Yeah?"

"Sure," I said. "She'll make your toenails curl up."

"Well, I don't know."

I looked at the clock over the bar. "We can get going early."

"I'm broke."

"Hell, I just got paid."

"I can't use your money."

"I'm going to spend it anyway," I said, thinking about his wonderful ethics and then how he didn't have to worry about money at all. "You want something that'll dry out your eyeballs, let's get going."

I knew he was thinking, This is a hell of a one. Wait'll I tell her about this.

"I already called the one I plan to meet," I told him. "She said something about her girl friend not having a date, so it's a cinch." I winked at him. "Date, hell," I said. "Your nose won't run for a week."

"What'll we do," he said. "Take both cars?"

"No. We'll take my car."

"I got a sedan."

"They know my car. Besides, we won't be in a car."

After we were on Fourth Street, heading out toward Gandy Bridge, he got a little quiet. The wine was wearing off and he was leaving his stamping grounds. He was conscious of being with the husband of the woman he was sleeping with at least once a day.

"Maybe I ought to stop off home," he said. "These clothes. I ought to put on some clean clothes."

"Where you're going, you won't need clothes," I said. "You won't wear any clothes."

I grinned at him but he didn't say anything.

We came along past all the bright-colored motels and trailer parks, the beer joints and the alligator farms. After a while, we were nearing the bridge. I turned the car off on a dirt road that slanted through some jungle toward the bay. I could feel the sweat beginning under my shirt and my palms were slippery on the wheel.

He went along with it, but he was scared, right off.

Finally, he said, "Where we going?" He tried to make it nonchalant.

"A fishing camp, down here. I just want to stop for a minute. I told a friend of mine I'd go out with him tomorrow morning. Have to put it off."

"Oh, hell, yes. You won't want to fish."

I didn't say anything. It was as if everything were ordered and there was nothing I could do about it. It wasn't too good. You feel as if you might burst, yet you feel numb, and dark around the eyes.

The road began to peter out in the jungle. It was a noisy stretch through here, bull frogs, crickets, birds screeching. It was night now and the headlights cut a bright swath in darkness and then the road quit altogether.

"He's right up through here," I said. "We'll have to walk the rest of the way."

"I'll just wait for you."

"No. Come on along. I'll introduce you to him. Fix it so you can get a free boat—any time you want to go fishing."

He said he didn't fish. He cleared his throat. "I'll just wait here."

I went around and opened the door on his side.

"Come on," I said. "We can get a drink. He always has a drink handy. Moonshine. It's terrific stuff."

"Yeah?"

"Hell, yes. Come on, now."

He couldn't very well do anything else, because I was going to stand right there and argue with him till he came. He sensed that. I give him that much credit. He got out and I slammed the door.

"Watch your step," I said. "Snakes, you know."

"Oh, yeah—snakes."

We came along a path in the jungle. You could smell the sulphur from the bay. The crickets were so loud the noise got in your ears. We came along until there was a break in some mangroves.

"Right through here," I said. "Just down a ways."

"How in hell does anybody find his place?"

I didn't even answer now. The hell with it. We came out onto the beach. The crabs streamed away from us on the stinking gray sands, like waves of dry leaves. It was as though even the crabs knew what was going on and didn't want any part of me. You could hear the water licking at the shore.

"Well," I said, "brother. How you like the moonshine?"

He stared at me. The moon was big and white and bright on his face and his mouth was open. The moon was in my throat. I took out the .45 and watched the fear grow in him until it winked in his eyes.

"What are you doing!" he said. His voice went shrill and it was like his eyes screamed too.

I shot him twice in the face. He fell down. I stood there looking at the gun in my hand, listening to the echo of the explosions rattle out across the bay. The crickets had ceased. Then one by one they picked up their song again and the water gurgled on the sands. I flipped the safety on and put the gun in my jacket pocket, thinking about her back there at the house and of how it had once been, and now this.

I stripped naked and hauled him out in the bay. I swam as far as I could. He was a heavy load. Finally I could feel the tide. There's a really strong tide by Gandy Bridge. With any luck he'd sail right out into the Gulf—but it didn't really matter.

I came back and dressed and got the car and drove toward town. Maybe there was a chance, now. Maybe she would be all right, and the kids would be all right. We would be together and everything would be all right—the way we should be.

When I reached the gin mill on Tangerine Avenue, there were two or three guys at the bar.

"Say," I said to the barman. "You seen that bird I was drinking with a little while ago? He went home, said he'd meet me here. He come back?"

"He didn't come back," the barman said.

"Well, he comes back, you tell him it's all off for tonight. I got to get on home. O. K.?"

I went on out and drove home and parked the car in the carport. She came running out into the living room as I entered the front door.

"Oh," she said. "It's you."

The kids were playing at the far end of the living room. I went over there and grabbed them up, one in each arm, holding them as tight as I could. It went all through me.

"Hi, Daddy!" Denise said. She gave me a big wet kiss.

"Everything's fine," I said to the kids, putting them down again. "You hear?"

My wife said, "The—uh, did you get the car?"

I turned and looked at her, then walked over to where she was standing.

"No. I figured you should come along, too."

"Oh," she said. "That's nice. Yes. Sure." She swatted her hips back and forth beneath that red skirt, just standing there. Then she breezed by me toward the kitchen, paused, turned and looked back at me. She was some woman, all right.

I wondered what in hell was the matter with her. She looked troubled.

"Supper ready?" I said.

"I thought I ought to wait for you," she said. "I didn't know when you'd get back."

"All right."

I started for the bedroom. She took two quick steps toward me, then stopped, one hand up, grinning.

"Something the matter?"

"No, I was just going to ask you what you wanted for supper." She swallowed, watching me.

"Anything," I told her. "Anything at all."

She kept on watching me. Hell. I went into the bedroom. It was dark and the moonlight came through the Venetian blinds in ribbons of bright white. I went over to the closet and stood there, taking off my jacket. I got it off, took the gun out of the pocket and reached in and hung the jacket on a man's face.

He busted out of there and rammed into me. He turned toward the wrong side of the room, heading for the window. I shot him in the back. He fell over against the bed and drooped there, dying. I went over and looked at him. He sprawled onto the floor, dead. One of his heels kept scraping as his leg straightened out. His face was in the moonlight. It was a guy who lived two blocks down from our house. I remembered seeing him talking to my wife in the front yard once. He didn't have a car. I kept looking at him, knowing everything was gone now—everything.

"Jim!" my wife said. "Jim!"

She was in the doorway and the kids were trying to push past her.

"Get out of here," I said. I herded them into the living room. The kids kept trying to run back into the bedroom. I had the gun in my hand and I had done the other one for my kids and now things were getting out of hand. They kept trying to get past me into the bedroom.

She looked at me, her face white as the moonlight, her mouth torn with fright.

The kids were laughing. They thought it was a game. They kept trying to rush past me into the bedroom.

"I took care of the other one, too," I said. "The one that was the gas station attendant? He was here this afternoon?" I hesitated. "I didn't know what to do about this one."

She began to cry, standing there with her hands stiff along her sides, the tears busting out of her face.

"I did it for the kids," I said.

She sobbed and went on crying, standing stiff and straight, with my T-shirt on and the red skirt mussed and wrinkled and the lipstick smeared and sweat on her upper lip and her forehead. Her hair was mussed a little, too. Not much, though.

"It's got out of hand," I said.

She kept on crying, standing there and she began to tremble all through her body.

"Can't you see?" I said, trying to explain something that I could never explain to her. "It's hopeless, it's all gone. The kids and all, and us. All gone to hell. You had too many of them, ramming through here, all the time." My voice got hoarse and I knew I wasn't reaching her. "I couldn't stand it. You see?"

Her head began to bob up and down.

She whirled and ran for the kitchen. I went after her, caught her arm, turned her around. I let go of her and she began to get real wild.

"Please!" she cried. "Jim—I'll do anything!"

Now, just what the hell could she do? She'd done it all, there wasn't anything left. I shot her. She started to scream but it changed into a kind of hot bubbling. She fell down.

The kids went quiet. They walked over by me and stood there looking at her on the floor.

"Daddy," Denise whispered. "Why did you do that?"

I couldn't speak. I couldn't even think right. I checked the clip in the gun and my hand was trembling, and then it was real steady. I didn't dare look at the kids. I went into the bedroom and stepped over him and got into the footlocker. I loaded the clip and socked one into the breech.

"Daddy," Denise said. "What you doing?"

I began to talk wild and crazy. I got down there on the floor and held my kids and I could hear my voice spilling all kinds of crazy stuff. I kept sweating and talking and trying to tell them that everything was all right.

"Is Mommy sick?" Danny said.

"Daddy," Denise said, squirming in my arms. "What's the matter with Herbie?"

"What?" I said. "What? Who's Herbie?"

"There, on the floor," Denise said. "That's Herbie. We ain't s'posed to tell. Is Mommy sick?"

I stood up and looked at my kids. It was all gone and there wasn't any use.

I was shaking just a little bit, light and easy, and when I spoke, the shaking was in my voice.

"Here," I said. I went over and sat on the bed. I looked at them and they looked at me. You could hear the crickets outside in the grass. "You two kids stand there by the dresser. That's it, right there. Now, stand still. We'll all be together in a minute."

I lifted the gun. Moonlight was bright on their faces.

Rat Hater

Harlan Ellison®

I had them bring Chuckling Harry Kroenfeld to me in the old Steel Pier warehouse.

Most people don't remember that warehouse, but back in the Twenties it was one of the best in the city. Handled cargo, month in and month out, with no slack season. It was a good warehouse far off where a scream couldn't be heard, and dirty . . . very dirty; that was important.

I remembered the old Steel Pier warehouse. It was a bit of memory to me. It was the jump-off place for my sister. Well, she didn't actually jump; she was pushed. But it didn't make very much difference after it was done.

Harry wouldn't like being brought by two cheap hoods, but then, he was in no position to complain. Twenty-five years ago he might have been able to do something about it, but that was twenty-five years ago. Harry and the mob had fallen out a long while back. He was lucky they had let him live after the break. But again, that doesn't matter now.

Neither of the pistoleros who brought Harry to me knew the story. It wouldn't have done any good to tell them, either. They were being paid and they didn't care why I was going to kill an old, fat man. Money was money, and as Chuckling Harry used to point out to me—before he'd had my sister shot, weighted, and put in the harbor—business is undeniably business.

He was right, in a way. But revenge is revenge, too.

When they opened the seamed metal door and pushed Harry through, I was surprised at how much he'd changed. I just stared at him for a moment, hearing with another part of my senses the two hired thugs bolting the door from the outside.

That didn't worry me, of course. I had a key I could use to get out—afterward. But right now, we were locked in together. The only thing that kept us apart—and it was a very real barrier, I assure you—was the .45 I held oh, so steady in my left hand.

"Hello, Harry," I said.

He was lying against the metal wall, the back of one fat hand scrunched to his mouth. I'd never seen eyes quite that large before. Or skin quite that pasty-looking. But then, I'd never actually killed a man before. Harry'd never died before, either, which rather evened things.

"Lew. L-Lew Greenberg. Hi, Lew. How long's it been?" Chuckling Harry had always been a lousy bluff. He was stuttering and sweating; I expected him to slip and slide in his own wet in another minute.

"Well, Harry," I said, considering—the .45 up to my lips in thought—"it's been about eighteen years. Right after the Christmas jobs in '57. Oh, I'm sure you remember, Harry."

The Best of *Manhunt*

I sat down on a packing crate that creaked under me, though I don't weigh much, and crossed my legs.

"Oh, yeah, sure—sure! Now I remember, Lew. It's good—good to—uh—*see* you, Lew." He put the *strangest* inflection on the word "*see.*"

There was only one light in the warehouse. Right in the center of the space I'd cleared of garbage and boxes; it cast a disc of yellow brilliance. All the rest of the place was shadowy dark. I'd fixed it up just for this. Even so, it was difficult telling whether Chuckling Harry was more frightened of the gun or me.

I was disappointed a bit. I'd expected more shock on his part. But I consoled myself with knowing it would come in time.

Chuckling Harry made as if to rise, watching me carefully to see if I'd stop him. I didn't, and he got up, brushing off his suit.

"That isn't a very expensive suit, Harry."

He looked down at it, stretched over his paunch, as though seeing it for the very first time. "Oh, well . . . You know how it is, Lew. Wanted a suit in a hurry . . ."

"Did you go to one of the fat men's stores, Harry?"

He grew red, the blossoming of it making his dead white face all the whiter. He'd never liked being reminded he was an obese hulk.

"Fat man's store, hell! I got this uptown! Bought it at . . ." He started to continue, caught another short look at the automatic in my lap, and fell silent, licking his droopy lower lip with a pink tip of tongue.

"Bet that only ran about seventy bucks, Harry. Cheap. I remember the days you used to have thirty suits, all tailor made, all over three hundred bucks each. Remember those days, Harry?"

He waved his blocky hands inadequately. "You know how things are, Lew. Times change. Why, in the old days, I was . . ." He ran down of his own accord, licking his lips again.

"Come on over and take a chair," I said, motioning to the lone straight-backed chair in the center of the circle of light. He moved toward it slowly, looking around as if to make certain no one else was in the warehouse with us.

"No one else, Harry," I said quietly.

He sat down in the chair, sliding forward a bit, allowing for his bulk. The round, saggy columns of his legs were placed far apart, supporting him. His buttocks drooped over the sides of the seat. I knew he was wondering what was going on.

He was still Chuckling Harry. He was still fat—I don't think anything could change that. Except, perhaps, death. But Chuckling Harry Kroenfeld had altered much since the day eighteen years before, when I'd told him I had to quit the mob and find steadier employment to support my mother. Then he had been dynamic, powerful. Now he was tired and beaten. He was washed-up and washed-out. Harry was an old man at last.

He still had an almost monk-like circlet of white hair ringing his bald head; his eyes were still that fishy, watery blue; his face was still puffy and drooping with lard. Looking at him there in the chair I could almost imagine the rosebud-pink lips forming the words they'd formed when he'd said goodbye.

So long, Lew. Here's a couple hundred, just to keep you going. No hard feelings about Sheila, of course!

Of course. He'd chuckled then, and handed me the two crisp hundred dollar bills, which I'd taken. Of course.

He wasn't chuckling now. He looked tired and unhappy, and getting more frightened as the seconds passed.

"Wh-what are you doing these days, Lew?" he asked, toying with a pinkie ring on his right hand.

"I have a string of supermarkets, Harry," I answered, amiably.

"Oh, yeah, yeah," he said, waving a pudgy hand in slow remembrance. "We heard about it around. Heard you were doing real well. Real well." He chuckled and licked his lips again, looking around, as though expecting someone else to add to the conversation.

The conversation was threatened by lag, and I certainly didn't want that to happen. "Do you see those ropes attached to the chair, Harry?" I pointed the muzzle of the .45 at the thick cords.

A tic leaped in his right cheek, but he bent from the hips, looking at them. He didn't answer.

"I dislike asking you to do it, Harry," I said, politely, "but would you mind tying your feet securely?"

"Say! What is this!" Harry shouted, almost leaping up. This time I waggled the gun, indicating it would be wisest if he sat where he was. I ran a hand through my thinning hair, smiling broadly at Chuckling Harry Kroenfeld.

"I'd appreciate it if you'd tie your feet, Harry. It would facilitate matters a great deal." I half-rose, the gun leveling as I did.

He looked at me once, quickly, seeing the big smile on my face and the big hole in the front of the automatic. He bent once more and began wrapping the thick ropes about his ankles. "Up higher, and tie them to the legs of the chair." I directed him, seeking the most secure job.

By the time he was finished, perspiration had beaded his forehead, some of it running crookedly down his face, into the neck of his shirt.

He'd done a good job, though. I've got to give Harry that. I was going to give him more, of course, but I gave him that first. I don't forget old times.

He straightened, wiping at his florid cheeks. "Say, look, Lew, I don't know what this is all about, but I've got to get home. I don't know why you had those two guys grab me when I closed the shop, but I've got a kid waiting, and my wife holding dinner for me, and I've got to get back . . ."

"Yes." I cut him off. "It was rather neat the way the boys checked what time you closed, wasn't it, Harry?" I continued to smile. My nose itched, so I rubbed it slowly.

"You don't understand, Lew; I don't have time for fun tonight. The wife and kid are waiting and maybe some other time, if you give me a call, we can get together . . ."

It was pleasant cutting him off, so I did it again. In the old days, nobody cut off Chuckling Harry Kroenfeld. "Still the same wife, Harry?"

"Yeah, yeah," he answered, nervously, "still Helen. We got a kid now. Robert." He bit his lip, looking pained, and I could tell his eyes were saying, *I'm an old man now! Please leave me alone!* Yes, he was old, but some people hadn't gotten the chance to grow old.

"How old's your son, Harry?" I inquired conversationally. I was interested, truly.

"Seven." He answered me reluctantly, and I could tell he had lost his sense of hospitality. He wouldn't be much of a conversationalist from here on out. But of course it didn't matter.

I stood up. "Would you mind wrapping your arms around the back of the chair, Harry, I'd like to—"

"Goddamit, what the hell is this? What do you want from me, Greenberg! No, I *won't* wrap—"

I'm afraid I lost my temper a bit. I grated the words really fine throwing them at him: "Get your lousy, stinking hands around the back of that chair, Harry, before I blow your guts out through your stinking fat back!"

However, I must admit it was the kind of talk Harry had always understood best, and he slowly slid his jelly-roll fat arms around the back, joining the fingers.

I picked up the coil of rope from behind the crate and walked over to him. Then I cooled down, and became rather ashamed of myself. "I'm sorry, Harry," I said, tightening the ropes around his hands, tying his arms securely to the chair. I was surprised how much like a baby's his hands were. "It's been a long time since I've lost my temper. Forgive me, Harry?"

He didn't answer. I put the barrel of the gun at his ear. "Forgive me?" I asked again, most sincerely.

He bobbed his head, his sagging jowls bobbing humorously. "Yeah, yeah, I forgive you, Lew." I finished tying him.

I went back to the packing crate, sucking on my lower lip in thought. "So your son's seven now, is he?" I nodded my head in admiration. "Bet he's a cute little boy. Just like his pop," I said, smiling toward Chuckling Harry but keeping the gun on him.

"How old would Sheila be now, Harry?" I asked, interested, though I knew, of course.

I could tell he knew what this was all about, suddenly. If I'd thought he was white before, now he became chalky. He shook, and the chair clattered a bit on the cement floor.

"Look . . . Lew . . . that's all in the past . . . you wouldn't . . . I'm an honest guy now, Lew, I broke with the mob years ago . . . I've been going straight . . . I'm sorry, Lew . . . she just found out a few things, and I couldn't chance having her around! She was too dangerous . . . you understand, *don't you, Lew?*"

He was bubbling, froth starting to ooze from a corner of his mouth. I didn't feel sorry for him.

"Do you still hate rats, Harry?" I asked, looking back over my shoulder at the dimness of the warehouse.

His head came up sharply; his nostrils quivered; the tic came once more. "R-rats?"

"Why, yes, Harry. Rats. I know how much you hated them."

I remembered how he'd almost killed one of the guys in the gang who'd wrapped a rat as a birthday present gag. How he'd taken special pains to live near the top of all buildings, so the chance of getting rodents would be smaller. The time he'd jellied into a heap, until three of the boys had killed a rat that ran across his path.

"Rats, Harry," I repeated, savoring the word.

"W-why? Why do you ask? Yeah, I suppose I still don't like 'em. So what?" He didn't know whether to answer or not. He was squinting at me, licking his lips, really nervous.

"Do you have your wife clean real good, so the rats don't get into the cupboards, Harry? Do you call in the exterminators every year at the store, whether you need them or not? I'll bet you smack your kid if he laughs at a Mickey Mouse cartoon. Is that right, Harry, do you?" I'd spoken softly, but steadily.

"Why do you wanta know? *Why?*" The sweat glistened like bubbles on his face.

"I just thought I'd inquire, Harry. You see, this entire place is filled with them. See them?"

Some men fear death, some fear closed places, some water. Chuckling Harry Kroenfeld feared rats. With an almost pathological fear. I wasn't going to just kill Harry—please credit me with more ingenuity than that—I was going to *kill* him!

"Rats, Harry! Large, black, crawling rats, with thin, wiry whiskers and little, pointed snouts, sniffing. They're all over the place, Harry! See them? See them, Harry?"

I had been talking quietly, but his head began snapping back and forth on his neck, as though he were on scent, as though he wanted away from there desperately. He probably did.

"No! There aren't any . . . I don't see any . . . Lew, look, you got to—uh—let me go home now! Helen's waiting for me, Lew!" He was getting frantic, his voice was rising. But that didn't matter. The old Steel Pier warehouse is way down away from everything. No one would hear.

"Certainly I'll let you go, Harry. After the rats have eaten away your pants cuffs, and started on the bones in your fat legs. Do you have bones in there, Harry? They'll find them! How long do you think it will take them to eat through all that fat, Harry?"

"*Lew!*" he screamed, straining at his bonds. The chair clattered toward me, but I motioned him off with the gun. I could tell it hadn't completely sunk in yet. He still didn't believe I'd do it. Chuckling Harry has been known to be wrong.

"I wouldn't worry too much, Harry, because it'll take them at least three hours to finish you. They're pretty messy eaters."

I smiled in a friendly way, then I shot him.

The .45 erupted, Harry screamed once at the pain, then spun around—still tied to the chair—and fell onto his back. There was a neat, round hole in his pant leg, and it was becoming stained dark very quickly. Blood was streaming out of his left leg. "It could have been a bit higher," I mused, "I'd always thought there was more blood higher up the leg. Oh well . . ."

I walked over and looked down at Harry. He'd fainted. Or perhaps it was just a state of shock. Either way, he was lying there, eyes shut, mouth half-open, tic in his cheek jumping. I shoved the gun into my pocket, bent down.

I lifted Harry and the chair. It was quite a job; a big man, and in that half-conscious shock state he was dead weight. Well, not exactly *dead*, but soon—soon.

I tipped the chair up, set it back on its legs, and brushed off my hands. That warehouse was filthy. They really should have taken better care of it.

I held the gun steady on Chuckling Harry while I fished the knife out of my pocket. I had to open the blade with my teeth.

Harry's head was tipped back on his shoulders, the tongue protruding from his gummy lips just a bit. He was still in shock. I laid the automatic down, taking the fabric of his pant leg in my hand. I carefully slit it up past the thigh, letting the fabric fall away from the leg. The bullet had gone through the bone, just below the kneecap. It was a messy wound—I was willing to bet it would hurt Harry plenty when he woke up.

I brushed off my hands again, and my knees. The place was deep in garbage-leavings from winos who had camped in there. That was good.

Just as I was going back to my packing crate, Harry began moaning; then he came to. His eyes snapped open and whipped back and forth around the warehouse. I knew all he could see were the dark corners; the shimmering, hanging cobwebs; the .45 and me.

"You've waited eighteen years for this, haven't you, Greenberg?" His eyes were glazed, but a sort of sanity seemed to come over him for a moment.

"For what, Harry? For the rats to eat your intestines out? That's very true; I have. It'll be fun. I'm not a vengeful man, as you know, but Sheila just wouldn't rest easily if I didn't make some sort of gesture in her behalf—"

He winced and moaned as the pain from his leg hit him. Harry licked his lips, turned his head from side to side. I've got to admit—he suffered. Then I took his mind off the leg; I said, "Rats, Harry? What do you think happens when they smell all that rich Kroenfeld blood?"

Harry began straining his eyes into the gloom, trying to see the rats. "They're back there," I reassured him, pointing to a hollow scraping behind some crates. He drew back against the chair, struggling with the ropes that bound him.

"They're tight, Harry: You and I tied them, and we were old buddies, weren't we, Harry? Harry? Are you listening? Hear them scrabbling on the floor?"

I could tell he heard them. His face was a white balloon dotted with sick sweat. I knew *he* could hear them, because *I* could hear them. I felt for the plastic sack in my pocket.

The noise from the darkness was beginning to mount. Tight, tiny squeals came from all around us. Occasionally a gray shadow leaped from one patch of black to another. They'd smelled the blood.

"They want *you*, Harry! Remember the days when we'd come down here to the waterfront, for collections, and you'd stay in the car till we brought you the take? You didn't like them, did you, Harry?"

I knew he was picturing the wharf rodents, fresh from the tramp steamers, tumbling over one another as they ripped apart a dead fish. Their clicking, vicious teeth leaving nothing of a bleeding gutter-mutt. The stench of them rooting in the grain bins and garbage piles.

He watched, fascinated, as I drew the plastic sack from my side pocket. I looked up, and caught him staring at me. "You know what this is, Harry?" His eyes were dull, lifeless. The leg wound was pumping shiny rivulets of blood into his sock and shoe.

I ripped the tape from the mouth of the bag, getting up. I drew out a wet, dripping piece of bread. It was brown and soggy. The smell overpowered me for a moment. I almost gagged. "Bread, Harry. Just bread. Dipped in chicken blood. My butcher was really surprised when I asked him to make some of this up. You should have seen his face!"

I moved around the warehouse, dropping the blood-soaked pieces of bread in dim corners, kicking the stuff into the darkness. One piece slid out of sight beneath a pile of broken timbers and an instant later I could hear them tearing at it.

"Lew! My God, Lew!" I turned around, where I stood in the darkness, looked at Harry in the center of the yellow circle. Suddenly he leaned forward, sweating like the pig he resembled.

"Lew, I've—I've saved some money from the old days! I—I can give you ten thousand if you'll let me go! I'll f-forget this whole thing, Lew! I'm an honest shopkeeper now! Please, Lew, forgive me!"

I'd never seen a man struggle so, sweat so, bite his lips so often. He had become a parody of himself. He did the same things over and over again. It was really something to watch.

I walked over to him. Looked down into the horror that stared from his eyes.

"Money, Harry? No, money doesn't mean anything to me now. I have a great deal of it. A fine home, a wife, two children—everything I missed when I was a kid, Harry. But I've got something more—something *you* don't have. I have a big hate, Harry. One that I've been nursing for eighteen years. One that I—oh! What's that? There's a rat, over there, behind that stack of bricks, isn't there, Harry?"

He was staring up at me, terror swimming freely in his eyes. So I went on. "A *big* hate, Harry. I overheard a conversation a long time ago; you were talking to one of the boys, telling him how Sheila had bled more than you thought one woman had any right to bleed. I heard you say she was still kicking when they dumped her. Right off the loading dock of this warehouse, wasn't it, Harry? Eighteen years ago, wasn't it, Harry?"

His eyes rolled up and for a second I thought he was going to have a seizure, robbing me of the climax. I brought my fist back and cracked him across the mouth. His head snapped around and his eyes slid back down. They were small, small, compared to the white that surrounded them.

"Getting weak, Harry?"

He was so pale, it was amazing he was still conscious after the shot. I'd counted on fear keeping him awake. This was the big moment I'd waited eighteen years to enjoy.

"Wait till they come after you, Harry. Just wait. Rats, Harry, rats! Think of all that warm, bristly fur; think of all the fleas and death they're carrying. First they'll go for that bleeding leg, Harry; they'll get a whiff of all that gore and come running! Then the ripping starts! And after a while the pain will be so big you won't have to worry about the bullet in your leg. That'll be nice, won't it, Harry?"

I was going to continue, but the scream I'd seen building as I'd begun—broke.

He opened his cavernous mouth wide, saliva drooling, and screamed. Oh, my God! So loud I thought the dust would fly off everything and roar around the room!

He began kicking out, his feet still tied together, and making little mewling noises at the same time. His feet would get just a bit away from the chair, before the ropes stopped their movement. He seemed to be kicking at the rats, though they hadn't ventured into the light yet.

But they would. Meals are too far apart on the wharves for them to pass up as juicy a feast as Chuckling Harry Kroenfeld.

He screamed again. This one was a loud, bubbling thing that started deep in his stomach and rattled up.

"Oh, stop, stop, Harry," I begged him. "You don't want to frighten them off, do you?"

He didn't stop. In fact, he screamed louder. Now I could see the fingers of his bound hands clutching at the back of the chair. He was straining his quaking fat toward me, leaning forward as far as the ropes would allow. His legs writhed, his knees heaved, his body trembled.

He was looking past me in grotesque agony. I turned to see what he was staring at.

Then I saw the first one.

It was a little monster, with protruding teeth I knew were as sharp as a guillotine blade. Beady, hateful red eyes glared out of the darkness. The tentative piping of its voice reached toward us.

"They're coming, Harry," I said, risking a closer look into the dark. They were back there—straining toward the fat in the chair. All I had to do was remove that source of fear—the light—and they'd be on him.

I started walking toward the seamed metal door. "They've smelled and eaten all that bloody bread, and they're hot now. They're stirred up, Harry. They're hot and hungry and they smell a good meal."

"Lew! Please, dear God in heaven, don't let him do this to me, don't let him, don't—"

It was interesting to listen to the changes in tone as his cries climbed higher and higher. I took the key from my pocket. He was bouncing on the chair, scraping and clattering in a very small circle. I moved out of the circle of light that held him; moved from its edges toward the door.

They were coming now—coming in full force. I could hear their claws scratching the stone floor. There must have been a thousand of them. More than I'd counted on. Harry could hear them.

I tried not to listen to his ravings from behind me, as I started to unlock the door. I turned once to look at him—for the last time.

"*Lew!*" he answered. "*Lew! I didn't mean to do it! I didn't mean to hurt Sheila—I didn't mean it, Lew, so help me God!*"

I tried to believe him. Right then I wanted to believe him very much. I tried to think of her, as I stood there, just one year younger than me, and so pretty, so grown-up, all the fellows in the block beat each other up just to get a date with her. I tried to think how Harry had seen her one night when I'd brought her to a party he'd thrown. I tried to think how nice it would have been if Harry had married Sheila, even though Harry *was* a bit fat and a bit older than her. It would have been nice, even at that.

I tried to think of her blonde hair, and her tiny pixie figure, and her high, giggly laugh, and the way Harry had said her mouth was open when they'd dumped her with the tire chains around her slim ankles. How she'd taken in water at the mouth and nose, and sunk, eighteen years ago, before they'd even gotten a chance to hear her call out for her brother Lew.

I'd been hearing that call for eighteen years.

I tried to think of those things, but Harry's screams kept interrupting.

"*Lew, Lew, help me, Lew, don't let them at me!*"

"Sorry, Harry," I mumbled over my shoulder as I unlocked the door, "I can't deprive them of their pleasure. We all get our kicks one way or another. You had yours eighteen years ago—the rats get theirs today."

I took a final look at his dead-fish face before I clicked the lights off. He was on the verge of madness. The darkness fell in and was complete.

"Goodbye, Harry."

I stepped over the sill, slammed and locked the door. I leaned up against it, found myself panting. My back was cold, perspiring. It hadn't been easy. I'd had to steel myself for years to do this. It hadn't been easy; in the instant before I'd shut the door, I'd seen them racing across the dirty floor, making for him.

I could hear his screams from inside the warehouse. They tore at me. The boys would have a real clean-up job when they came two days later.

I turned away and walked up the pier to my car. I could have stayed and watched through a window, I suppose. But I didn't really want to. That warehouse was filthy.

And I hate rats.

The Last Spin
Evan Hunter

September 1956

T he boy sitting opposite him was his enemy.
The boy sitting opposite him was called Tigo, and he wore a green silk jacket with an orange stripe on each sleeve. The jacket told Dave that Tigo was his enemy. The jacket shrieked, "Enemy, enemy!"

"This is a good piece," Tigo said, indicating the gun on the table. "This runs you close to forty-five bucks, you try to buy it in a store. That's a lot of money."

The gun on the table was a Smith & Wesson .38 Police Special.

It rested exactly in the center of the table, its sawed-off, two-inch barrel abruptly terminating the otherwise lethal grace of the weapon. There was a checked walnut stock on the gun, and the gun was finished in a flat blue. Alongside the gun were three .38 Special cartridges.

Dave looked at the gun disinterestedly. He was nervous and apprehensive, but he kept tight control of his face. He could not show Tigo what he was feeling. Tigo was the enemy, and so he presented a mask to the enemy, cocking one eyebrow and saying, "I seen pieces before. There's nothing special about this one."

"Except what we got to do with it," Tigo said.

Tigo was studying him with large brown eyes. The eyes were moist-looking. He was not a bad-looking kid, Tigo, with thick black hair and maybe a nose that was too long, but his mouth and chin were good. You could usually tell a cat by his mouth and his chin. Tigo would not turkey out of this particular rumble. Of that, Dave was sure.

"Why don't we start?" Dave asked. He wet his lips and looked across at Tigo.

"You understand," Tigo said, "I got no bad blood for you."

"I understand."

"This is what the club said. This is how the club said we should settle it. Without a big street diddlebop, you dig? But I want you to know I don't know you from a hole in the wall—except you wear a blue and gold jacket."

"And you wear a green and orange one," Dave said, "and that's enough for me."

"Sure, but what I was tryin' to say . . ."

"We going to sit and talk all night, or we going to get this thing rolling?" Dave asked.

"What I'm tryin' to say . . ." Tigo went on, "is that I just happened to be picked for this, you know? Like to settle this thing that's between the two clubs. I mean, you got to admit your boys shouldn't have come in our territory last night."

"I got to admit nothing," Dave said flatly.

"Well, anyway, they shot at the candy store. That wasn't right. There's supposed to be a truce on."

"Okay, okay," Dave said.

The Last Spin

299

"So like . . . like this is the way we agreed to settle it. I mean, one of us and . . . and one of you. Fair and square. Without any street boppin', and without any law trouble."

"Let's get on with it," Dave said.

"I'm tryin' to say, I never even seen you on the street before this. So, this ain't nothin' personal with me. Whichever way it turns out, like . . ."

"I never seen you neither," Dave said.

Tigo stared at him for a long time. "That's 'cause you're new around here. Where you from originally?"

"My people come down from the Bronx."

"You got a big family?"

"A sister and two brothers, that's all."

"Yeah, I only got a sister." Tigo shrugged. "Well." He sighed. "So." He sighed again. "Let's make it, huh?"

"I'm waitin'," Dave said.

Tigo picked up the gun, and then he took one of the cartridges from the tabletop. He broke open the gun, slid the cartridge into the cylinder, and then snapped the gun shut and twirled the cylinder.

"Round and round she goes," he said, "and where she stops, nobody knows. There's six chambers in the cylinder and only one cartridge. That makes the odds five-to-one that the cartridge won't be in firing position when the cylinder stops whirling. You dig?"

"I dig."

"I'll go first," Tigo said.

Dave looked at him suspiciously.

"Why?"

"You want to go first?"

"I don't know."

"I'm giving you a break." Tigo grinned. "I may blow my head off first time out."

"Why you giving me a break?" Dave asked.

Tigo shrugged. "What the hell's the difference?" He gave the cylinder a fast twirl.

"The Russians invented this, huh?" Dave asked.

"Yeah."

"I always said they was crazy bastards."

"Yeah, I always . . ."

Tigo stopped talking. The cylinder was stopped now. He took a deep breath, put the barrel of the .38 to his temple, and then squeezed the trigger. The firing pin clicked on an empty chamber.

"Well, that was easy, wasn't it?" he asked. He shoved the gun across the table. "Your turn, Dave."

Dave reached for the gun. It was cold in the basement room, but he was sweating now. He pulled the gun toward him, then left it on the table while he dried his palms on his trousers. He picked up the gun then and stared at it.

The Best of *Manhunt*

"It's a nifty piece," Tigo said. "I like a good piece."

"Yeah, I do, too," Dave said. "You can tell a good piece just by the way it feels in your hand."

Tigo looked surprised. "I mentioned that to one of the guys yesterday, and he thought I was nuts."

"Lots of guys don't know about pieces," Dave said, shrugging.

"I was thinking," Tigo said, "when I get old enough, I'll join the Army, you know? I'd like to work around pieces."

"I thought of that, too. I'd join now, only my old lady won't give me permission. She's got to sign if I join now."

"Yeah, they're all the same," Tigo said, smiling. "Your old lady born here or the old country?"

"The old country," Dave said.

"Yeah, well you know they got these old-fashioned ideas."

"I better spin," Dave said.

"Yeah," Tigo agreed.

Dave slapped the cylinder with his left hand. The cylinder whirled, whirled, and then stopped. Slowly, Dave put the gun to his head. He wanted to close his eyes, but he didn't dare. Tigo, the enemy, was watching him. He returned Tigo's stare, and then he squeezed the trigger. His heart skipped a beat, and then over the roar of his blood he heard the empty click. Hastily he put the gun down on the table.

"Makes you sweat, don't it?" Tigo said.

Dave nodded, saying nothing. He watched Tigo. Tigo was looking at the gun.

"Me now, huh?" Tigo said. He took a deep breath, then picked up the .38. He twirled the cylinder, waited for it to stop, and then put the gun to his head.

"Bang!" Tigo said, and then he squeezed the trigger. Again the firing pin clicked on an empty chamber. Tigo let out his breath and put the gun down.

"I thought I was dead that time," he said.

"I could hear the harps," Dave said.

"This is a good way to lose weight, you know that?" Tigo laughed nervously, and then his laugh became honest when he saw Dave was laughing with him.

"Ain't it the truth? You could lose ten pounds this way."

"My old lady's like a house," Dave said laughing. "She ought to try this kind of a diet." He laughed at his own humor, pleased when Tigo joined him.

"That's the trouble," Tigo said. "You see a nice deb in the street, you think it's crazy, you know? Then they get to be our people's age, and they turn to fat." He shook his head.

"You got a chick?" Dave asked.

"Yeah, I got one."

"What's her name?"

"Aw, you don't know her."

"Maybe I do," Dave said.

"Her name is Juana." Tigo watched him. "She's about five-two, got these brown eyes . . ."

"I think I know her," Dave said. He nodded. "Yeah, I think I know her."

"She's nice, ain't she?" Tigo asked. He leaned forward, as if Dave's answer was of great importance to him.

"Yeah, she's nice," Dave said.

"The guys rib me about her. You know, all they're after-well, you know—they don't understand something like Juana."

"I got a chick, too," Dave said.

"Yeah? Hey, maybe sometime we could . . ." Tigo cut himself short. He looked down at the gun, and his sudden enthusiasm seemed to ebb completely. "It's your turn," he said.

"Here goes nothing," Dave said. He twirled the cylinder, sucked in his breath, and then fired.

The empty click was loud in the stillness of the room.

"Man!" Dave said.

"We're pretty lucky, you know?" Tigo said.

"So far."

"We better lower the odds. The boys won't like it if we . . ." He stopped himself again, and then reached for one of the cartridges on the table. He broke open the gun again, and slipped the second cartridge into the cylinder. "Now we got two cartridges in here," he said. "Two cartridges, six chambers. That's four-to-two. Divide it, and you get two-to-one." He paused. "You game?"

"That's . . . that's what we're here for, ain't it?"

"Sure."

"Okay then."

"Gone," Tigo said, nodding his head. "You got courage, Dave."

"You're the one needs the courage," Dave said gently. "It's your spin."

Tigo lifted the gun. Idly, he began spinning the cylinder.

"You live on the next block, don't you?" Dave asked.

"Yeah." Tigo kept slapping the cylinder. It spun with a gently whirring sound.

"That's how come we never crossed paths, I guess. Also, I'm new on the scene."

"Yeah, well you know, you get hooked up with one club, that's the way it is."

"You like the guys in your club?" Dave asked, wondering why he was asking such a stupid question, listening to the whirring of the cylinder at the same time.

"They're okay." Tigo shrugged. "None of them really send me, but that's the club on my block, so what're you gonna do, huh?" His hand left the cylinder. It stopped spinning. He put the gun to his head.

"Wait!" Dave said.

Tigo looked puzzled. "What's the matter?"

"Nothin. I just wanted to say . . . I mean . . ." Dave frowned. "I don't dig too many of the guys in my club, either."

Tigo nodded. For a moment, their eyes locked. Then Tigo shrugged, and fired. The empty click filled the basement room.

"Phew," Tigo said.

"Man, you can say that again."

Tigo slid the gun across the table. Dave hesitated an instant. He did not want to pick up the gun. He felt sure that this time the firing pin would strike the percussion cap of one of the cartridges. He was sure that this time he would shoot himself.

"Sometimes I think I'm turkey," he said to Tigo, surprised that his thoughts had found voice.

"I feel that way sometimes, too," Tigo said.

"I never told that to nobody," Dave said. "The guys in my club would laugh at me, I ever told them that."

"Some things you got to keep to yourself. There ain't nobody you can trust in this world."

"There should be somebody you can trust," Dave said. "Hell, you can't tell nothing to your people. They don't understand."

Tigo laughed. "That's an old story. But that's the way things are. What're you gonna do?"

"Yeah. Still, sometimes I think I'm turkey."

"Sure, sure," Tigo said. "But it ain't only that, though. Like sometimes . . . well, don't you wonder what you're doing stomping some guy in the street? Like . . . you know what I mean? Like . . . who's the guy to you? What you got to beat him up for? 'Cause he messed with somebody else's girl?" Tigo shook his head. "It gets complicated sometimes."

"Yeah, but . . ." Dave frowned again. "You got to stick with the club. Don't you?"

"Sure, sure . . . no question."

Again, their eyes locked.

"Well, here goes," Dave said. He lifted the gun. "It's just . . ." He shook his head, and then twirled the cylinder. The cylinder spun, and then stopped. He studied the gun, wondering if one of the cartridges would roar from the barrel when he squeezed the trigger.

Then he fired.

Click

"I didn't think you was going through with it," Tigo said.

"I didn't neither."

"You got heart, Dave," Tigo said. He looked at the gun. He picked it up and broke it open.

"What you doing?" Dave asked.

"Another cartridge," Tigo said. "Six chambers, three cartridges. That makes it even money. You game?"

"You?"

"The boys said . . ." Tigo stopped talking. "Yeah, I'm game," he added, his voice curiously low.

"It's your turn, you know."

"I know."

Dave watched as Tigo picked up the gun.

"You ever been rowboating on the lake?"

Tigo looked across the table at Dave, his eyes wide. "Once," he said. "I went with Juana."

"Is it . . . is it any kicks?"

"Yeah. Yeah, it's grand kicks. You mean you never been?"

"No," Dave said.

"Hey, you got to try it, man," Tigo said excitedly. "You'll like it. Hey, you try it."

"Yeah, I was thinking maybe this Sunday I'd . . ." He did not complete the sentence.

"My spin," Tigo said wearily. He twirled the cylinder. "Here goes a good man," he said, and he put the revolver to his head and squeezed the trigger.

Click.

Dave smiled nervously. "No rest for the weary," he said. "But, Jesus, you got heart, I don't know if I can go through with it."

"Sure, you can," Tigo assured him. "Listen, what's there to be afraid of?" He slid the gun across the table.

"We keep this up all night?" Dave asked.

"They said . . . you know . . ."

"Well, it ain't so bad. I mean, hell, we didn't have this operation, we wouldn'ta got a chance to talk, huh?" He grinned feebly.

"Yeah," Tigo said, his face splitting in a wide grin. "It ain't been so bad, huh?"

"No . . . it's been . . . well . . . you know, these guys in the club, who can talk to them?"

He picked up the gun.

"We could . . ." Tigo started.

"What?"

"We could say . . . well . . . like we kept shootin' an' nothin happened, so . . ." Tigo shrugged. "What the hell! We can't do this all night, can we?"

"I don't know."

"Let's make this the last spin. Listen, they don't like it, they can take a flying leap, you know?"

"I don't think they'll like it. We supposed to settle this for the clubs."

"Screw the clubs!" Tigo said vehemently. "Can't we pick our own . . ." The word was hard coming. When it came, he said it softly, and his eyes did not leave Dave's face, " . . . friends?"

"Sure we can," Dave said fervently "Sure we can! Why not?"

"The last spin," Tigo said "Come on, the last spin."

"Gone," Dave said. "Hey you know, I'm glad they got this idea. You know that? I'm actually glad!" He twirled the cylinder. "Look, you want to go on the lake this Sunday? I mean with your girl and mine? We could get two boats. Or even one if you want."

"Yeah, one boat," Tigo said. "Hey, your girl'll like Juana, I mean it. She's a swell chick."

The cylinder stopped. Dave put the gun to his head quickly.

"Here's to Sunday," he said. He grinned at Tigo, and Tigo grinned back, and then Dave fired.

The explosion rocked the small basement room, ripping away half of Dave's head, shattering his face. A small cry escaped Tigo's throat, and a look of incredulous shock knifed his eyes. Then he put his head on the table and began weeping.

Night of Crisis
Harry Whittington

October 1956

He spent three hours going through the picture files before he tapped one of the photographs and said, "This is it. This is the guy, all right."

The detective took the photo, turned it over. "Arn Cowley." He said. "Three-time loser."

The assistant D. A. said, "I thought Cowley was in the pen. Last time I heard of him he was in the pen."

"They parole them, Tom," the detective said. "They parole them even faster than we send them back up there." He turned and stared at Jim. "You ever know Cowley before?"

Jim caught his breath, hating the way the detective looked at him. "I told you I never had. If I'd known him why would I need to spend all this time going through the files?"

"Why don't you let me ask the questions?" the detective said. "We'll get through quicker that way. We'll save a lot of time."

Jim looked up, met the detective's gaze, held it.

"Where do you work, Cooper?" the assistant D. A. said.

"At Dodge Tobacco Wholesale. I'm a salesman."

"How old are you, Cooper?"

"Twenty-nine. What's the point in all this? Why do you treat me like I'm the criminal. I came to you people. I—"

"You married, Cooper?"

"Yes. I'm married. I have a child. I'm buying my house. It's a G. I. loan. I'm paying for my car. It's a Plymouth and almost two years old. But then I'm still paying for my child and he's almost two years old, too."

"Pretty deep in debt, aren't you, Cooper?"

Jim moved up on the edge of the chair. He felt a muscle work in his jaw. He told himself it wouldn't buy him anything to let them tee him off.

"Nothing I can't handle," he said. Anger made his voice quaver. He took a deep breath trying to calm himself. "What's the point in all this?"

"We don't know," the assistant D. A. said. With a pencil, be made short backward strokes across a pad. "I'm just kicking this around for what it's worth."

"How long you known Arn Cowley, Cooper?" The detective leaned forward, bracing himself against the desk.

Jim Cooper turned in the chair as though the detective had struck him. This cop was big, six-three anyway, with prematurely grey hair chopped in a crew cut, a thick featured stupid face.

Jim started up from the chair, face white. His hands gripped the chair until his fingers ached. He caught himself, sank back, shook his head.

He sat back in the chair, all the way back. He reached into his pocket for a cigarette. There was only one left in the pack. He shook it out, placed it between his lips, held his lighter to it. His hands shook.

"You want to run through it again?" the assistant D. A. said.

"All right. I was in this bar. I stopped in for a beer on my way home. There was only this man at the bar. This Arn Cowley—"

"How did you know it was Cowley?" the detective said.

"I didn't. Not then. You just told me his name. You remember? I went into the men's room. I was in there maybe two or three minutes. When I opened the door to come out, I saw Dutch—that's the fellow owns this bar—had his hands up. When Dutch saw me, he started to say something, maybe yell at me, I don't know. This man—I didn't know his name—turned to look toward me and Dutch jumped him. He turned back around, fired at Dutch point-blank. I stood there and he turned around again. I saw he was going to take a shot at me so I ducked back into the men's room. This guy fired anyhow. There was a lock on the door, and I threw it. All I could think was, I'd seen him rob Dutch and shoot him. I was sure he wasn't going to let me live. There was a window in the room, but it was one of those long narrow things like they have in men's johns. No chance to get out of it. I waited in there, but the guy must have been afraid the sound of the two shots would bring people. He ran by the door of the men's room. He fired once through the door facing and then ran out the alley."

"And what did you do?"

"Just what I've already told you three times I did. I came out, went in the pay booth and called you people. I spent a lousy dime doing it. For the first time in my life I regret it."

"You've just begun to regret it," the detective said. "Wait until we're through with you."

Jim stood up now. He held his hands clenched at his sides. He couldn't understand this. He had seen Dutch Obermeyer shot and killed. He had gotten a look at the man who shot Dutch, and had then taken a shot at him. He had called the police, come down here to find the killer in the files if he could, and ever since he had walked into this office these two men had treated him as though he were the criminal.

"No wonder nobody wants to cooperate with you people," he said. "No wonder you can't get witnesses. I've told you the truth."

The detective said, "Look, friend. Thirteen years. I been in this thirteen years. Seen it all. Your gimmick leaves me cold. You went in this caper with Cowley. You checked the men's room. Cowley got anxious. You get yourself trapped in the joint when he went out shooting and so you try to play the honest citizen. I'm not buying."

Jim stared at the flat stupid features of the detective. He tried to find some human understanding in the man's face. There was none. He turned slowly, looked at the assistant D. A.

Tom Donnelly was a little better. He was a stout man with short stubby hands and harried eyes. He looked as though he didn't know what to believe, as though he'd found out it wasn't smart to believe anything.

"That's the way it happened," Jim said.

"It's not going to be easy proving it happened that way," Tom said. "You've already admitted you're over your head in debt——"

"I never admitted anything. I told you of my own free will that I owed some money. Doesn't everybody? Don't you?"

"Maybe he does," the detective said. "Only difference is, he didn't witness no robbery-killing—and live to tell about it. And you did."

"God," Cooper whispered, feeling the helplessness crawling through him. "If I'd gotten killed, you'd have believed me?"

"If you'd gotten scratched," the detective said.

"He shot at me."

"That's what you told us."

"Lay off, Hank," Tom said. "Any way you look at it, Mr. Cooper, it looks like you're in trouble."

Jim sat down because his legs would no longer support him.

"Now what are you talking about?" he asked.

Tom Donnelly scratched some more marks on the pad. He wrinkled his nose as though he smelled something disagreeable. He said, "You want to tell him about it, Dackrich?"

The detective nodded. "Sure. Why not? We're going to have to arrest you, Cooper."

"Arrest me? Why?" Jim didn't bother looking at the detective. He stared, eyes wide, at Donnelly.

Hank Dackrich answered him. "As a material witness. As a protective move."

"For your protection," Donnelly said.

Jim swallowed the sickness that had boiled up in his throat. He moved his head, staring at them. "My protection?"

Dackrich shrugged. "Suppose you're telling the truth, Cooper. And we let you go. Don't you think that guy Cowley is out there right now somewhere, thinking about you? You saw him kill Obermeyer. You're the only one who did. You're the one man who can put him in the electric chair. How long can he afford to let you live?"

Jim didn't move.

"He'll find you," Dackrich's voice pounded at him. "He'll follow you home. No, Cooper, whether you're lying to us or not, there's just one safe place for you. That's in jail, until we can pick up Cowley."

"I haven't done anything. You can't arrest me."

Tom Donnelly drew some more marks, pushed the pad from him. He spread his stubby fingers and stared at the backs of them.

"You love your wife, Cooper? Your baby?"

Jim scrubbed his hand across his face, trying to obliterate the nightmare. "Yes. Yes. What has this got to do with them?"

"Suppose Crowley finds out you identified him?" Dackrich said. "We can't keep that out of the papers. Suppose Crowley decided he could stop you through your wife and kid?"

Jim stood up. "I'm going home," he said.

"Sit down," Dackrich told him.

"You go to hell. You arrest me and I'll sue. I swear I will. False arrest."

"We can hold you twenty-four hours, fella, and not even book you."

Jim stared about the room, the rows of brown backed law books, the leather-covered chairs, and back to the flat face of Dackrich.

"You arrest me," he said. His voice was hoarse. "You arrest me, and if anything happens to my wife—or my baby, so help me God, I'll kill you."

Dackrich just looked at him. Nothing moved him in anyway any more. He had heard everything, seen everything. All the edges were dulled, all the meaning gone.

"What'll that get you?" he said.

Jim stared at him. "Why don't you ask yourself what it will get you? They're all I've got. I did one wrong thing. I called you people when I should have walked out of there and kept my mouth shut. If anything happens to my wife—or my baby— you won't be able to hide well enough. There aren't enough cops to stand between us. Because when I—"

"You want to change your story?" Donnelly said.

"No. Why should I? I've told you the truth. I'm going home. Arrest me, and anything that happen is on you." He stood there, waiting, looking at them.

Donnelly stood up behind his desk. His ruddy face was taut. He looked from Jim to Dackrich and back again. "I don't like to be threatened, Cooper, not at all."

Jim didn't speak. He picked up his hat, held it in his hand. Donnelly glanced again at Dackrich.

The detective shrugged. "Let him go. He's got no use for cops. We can watch him. He can't go anywhere. And when Cowley crawls out from under his rock to kill him, we can nab Cowley. If we don't get him in time—why that'll be tough."

They stood there looking at Jim. He placed his hat on his head and walked to the door. He opened it and stepped outside.

He walked down the steps, getting colder with apprehension by the minute. It was late. He should have telephoned Mary from the bar. Instead of playing honest citizen, he should have called Mary and told her not to worry.

He walked out of the police station. Something nagged at him, a chill moved to the nape of his neck.

He felt as though somebody were watching him. He looked both ways along the sidewalk. The street was deserted. A few cars lined the curb, but appeared empty.

He remembered he had ridden from Dutch's bar down to the police nation in Dackrich's cruiser. He recalled suddenly the icy way Dackrich had acted from the first. He hadn't noticed then, too upset about the death, too busy trying to help them find the killer.

They didn't want the killer. They wanted somebody who couldn't prove his innocence. Anybody. Take a young average guy named Jim Cooper and call him guilty.

He wanted to run. He kept walking until he got to the corner. He got into a cab and gave the address of Dutch's Bar.

It was far out on Park. When they got there, a crowd had gathered outside Dutch's Bar. The door was closed, but people were staring, talking.

Jim walked through them, went along the walk to his car. He wondered if Arn Cowley would be watching this car? Why should he? Cowley didn't know him or his car.

He got in, fumbled the key into the switch. He had to press three times to get the engine going. He drove away from the curb, anxious to be out of this neighborhood.

It was less than three blocks to his small five-room cottage. It sat back in a grass plotted yard. One light burned in the living room. Mary would be wearing a mad because he was so late. He didn't care. Let her scold. He'd be thankful just to get inside that house and lock the door.

He drove the car into the garage, pulled down the door. He walked down the drive, stared along the street. It was quiet, a slight wind in the elms, light in the windows.

The paper was in the yard. He scowled, thinking this was odd. He picked up the paper, went to the front door. He opened the door, called, "Mary."

There was no answer. His voice died in the empty house. He felt the impact of panic, sharp and strong.

"Mary."

He slammed the front door behind him. He strode into the front room. The TV set was pale and lifeless. The playpen was set in the middle of the room, toys strewn outside it, the way Skip liked them.

He went into the kitchen, telling himself to calm down. The stove was cold. There was a kettle on one burner, no other sign that Mary had started supper.

He walked into the bedroom, trying to search back through his harried mind. Had Mary planned to spend the day away from home? He could not remember her mentioning it, but maybe she had.

The nursery looked pretty messy, as though she had not had time to straighten it. Their bedroom was in good shape. It looked chilled, as though nobody had even been in it for an hour.

He wanted to sit down, he wanted to fall down, but knew he had to keep moving. He could not surrender either to panic or to the fear that was slowly paralyzing him.

He walked through the house again, searching for a note. There was none. At the telephone, he dialed Mary's mother. "Mrs. Brazey?" he said. "Is Mary still there? Was I supposed to drop by and pick her up?"

"Mary isn't here, Jim."

"Hasn't she been at your place?"

"No. She hasn't phoned all day. You sure she was supposed to be here?"

"Oh. No." He swallowed, forcing his voice to remain flat "I remember now. She was spending the day with Joanie. Sorry to worry you."

"Have you been drinking, Jim?"

"Yeah. Had a couple. Just a little fuzzy. Forgive me?" He hung up quickly.

He dialed Joan Fortson and Don answered. He asked if they had seen Mary, knowing they hadn't ... Don said no, sounding pretty stuffy about a wife's unexplained absence at 11 P.M.

Jim replaced the receiver, sat down on a straight chair. He stared at the playpen, at the toys. Why not face it? He had stopped in Dutch's at a little after five. It was now after eleven. That gave Arn Cowley five hours.

Could Cowley have seen him in the bar before? Was it a fact that thieves cased a place pretty thoroughly before they held it up? Had Dutch yelled his name, just before Cowley shot him? How could Cowley have found out where Jim Cooper lived? It was crazy to think he could have. It didn't make sense. Yet, what did make sense? The way the cops had treated him, how much sense had that made?

Five hours. That gave Mary time to build a real mad, take the baby and—and—What? Go to a movie? Skip wouldn't sit still for that. Go to a neighbor? Mary wouldn't. When she got angry, she didn't want to make small talk. Besides, he couldn't run around asking if the neighbors had seen his wife.

What could he do? He had to do something. He suddenly wished he had seen just some of the things that Dackrich had seen in his thirteen years as a cop. Dackrich would know what to do. Dackrich had a callous where his soul should be, but Dackrich wouldn't sit helpless, sweating and paralyzed like this.

He picked up the telephone, dialed police headquarters. He asked for Sergeant Dackrich, and after a moment he recognized the expressionless voice. "Dackrich speaking."

"This is Jim Cooper, Sergeant. My wife—and baby—they're not here."

Nothing surprised Dackrich. "All right, fella. You sit right there. You ready to play it smart now and let us handle it, we'll see what we can do?"

"I've got to find my wife."

"You've got to keep your shirt on. You want to get her killed, you fool around with this thing." The thud in his ear meant Dackrich had slammed down the receiver.

Jim felt tears sting his eyes. He held the receiver a moment, staring at it. Then he replaced it on its cradle.

Before he could lift his hand, the bell shrilled. The sound jarred him and he trembled.

He told himself it was Mary. She was all right; she had called to tell him she was all right.

He lifted the receiver. "Hello."

There was a pause. He heard the vibrant hum across the wires. Panic flooded through him. His voice cracked. "Hello. Hello."

"Cooper? Jim Cooper?"

"Yes. This is Jim Cooper. Who is this? What do you want?"

"Cooper. This is a friend of yours. I got to have a word with you. I ain't got much time. So you want to listen?"

"What is it?"

"Cooper. I got your wife and kid with me. Now if they mean anything to you, you'll be real cagey, and do like I say."

"All right."

"Don't go to the police, Cooper. I'm telling you. Don't."

Cooper choked back the sob. He did not speak.

"Tomorrow morning's paper comes out, and there is nothing in it about you identifying me, good. Fine. You just forget you were in that bar, and everything is all right. Your wife, your kid, they'll be back home okay. But—cross me—and I'll send them back to you, Cooper—a little bit at a time. Now you got that? Don't think I'm kidding you. I'm a three-time loser, Cooper, and whatever I do now won't change what the law will do to me. Your wife's a cute little dish, Cooper, when she stops crying, she is. So you play it cagey for her and your kid. Don't try to be no hero. You leave that to the cops."

Cooper could not speak.

"Cooper. You there?"

"I'm here."

"All right. One last thing. You better pray them cops don't come looking for me, Cooper. Because if they do, I'll know you been to 'em. They might get me, but when they do, I'm going to be alone."

Jim pressed his fist against his throat. He wanted to speak. He had to ask if Mary was all right, if Skip was. There was a click in his ear and the line went dead.

He sat there with the receiver in his fist. He did not replace it.

He heard a car come into the drive, its tires screaming. He stood up, and then realized he was still holding the receiver. He dropped it in its cradle and walked toward the front door.

When he opened it, Dackrich and another plainclothes detective stood there. Dackrich had his thumb out, ready to jamb the bell button.

"Come in," Jim said. He did not recognize his own voice.

The two men came into the house. The smaller detective weighed over two hundred, was under medium height, and there was a scar under his right eye. He kept his hat on.

Dackrich said, "Heard from your wife yet?"

Jim shook his head. He looked from Dackrich to the fat detective. "No. But there's something I've got to tell you."

"Okay," Dackrich said. He was watching Jim closely. He sat down on the edge of the divan, a big man, his elbows on his knees. "Sit down, Grant. Go ahead, Cooper."

Jim stood in the center of the room. He stared at the toys beside the playpen. The two men sat on the edge of the divan, watching him. He scrubbed the back of his hand across his mouth. He heard the drip of a faucet from the kitchen.

"About that story," he said, speaking slowly, his throat aching, "that I told you about the bar—about what happened."

"Yeah? What about it?"

"Well, I lied to you."

Jim watched Dackrich's face. The detective's eyes narrowed slightly, that was the only change in his expression

"I was in on the job," Jim said. "Like you and the assistant D. A. thought, I got in debt. I thought I could go in on a job like that, and get enough money—to pay off some of it."

Dackrich's mouth twisted. "Go on."

"I didn't shoot Dutch. But like you said, I went in the men's room to be sure there was nobody else in there. And I lied about something else, too—"

"Did you?"

"Yes. It wasn't Arn Cowley. I—just happened to pick him out."

"Pretty good picking. He's got a record a yard long on bar and grocer jobs like this one."

Jim's voice got urgent, full of panic. "I can't help it. I just picked him out. It just happened."

"Why'd you pick him?"

"What difference does it make? You already said I was in on it, and I just pulled this story trying to get away with it. And—that's right. We—planned it that way—"

"You and Cowley?"

"No. I never heard of him. This—guy I met in the bar. I was to go to the police station, identify some punk, and you people would look for him, and that would take the heat off my—my friend—and I'd get paid off and that would end it."

Dackrich stood up suddenly. His expression did not alter. He stepped forward, grabbed Jim's lapels, twisting. "Listen to me, Cooper. What kind of fool do you think I am? Don't you think I know what happened? You came home, your wife was gone, you called me, and before I got here, Cowley called you, warning you off. He found out where you lived, came here and lured your wife out on some lie about you being in trouble. Now he's scaring you into calling off the hunt. It won't work. Cowley killed a man. We're going to get him."

"It's my wife," Jims said. He grabbed Dackrich's hand, thrust it down. "He'll kill my wife and my baby."

"Not if we find him in time."

"But he told me, if the morning paper has the story that I've been to you, he'll kill my wife and kid. You've got to stop that story. You've got to call it off. Just until he lets my wife go. Then you can get him."

Dackrich checked his watch, shook his head. "It's too late, Cooper. We can't stop the papers, most of them are probably folded by now and ready for delivery. There's a pick-up out on Cowley. We've got to find him before that paper comes out."

"He'll kill them."

"All right. You've got to stop lying to us, and start trying to help. We've got a slim chance to save your wife, but not unless you start playing right along with us."

Jim nodded. "I'll do anything. Only for God's sake don't—don't let him hurt them."

Dackrich shook his head. "It's a big town, Cooper. We got maybe five hours before those papers come out. He's out there somewhere. We'll do what we can."

Jim caught Dackrich's arm. "But he warned me. If you—try to take him—he'll know I identified him—he'll kill them. He knows he's a three-time loser, with one murder already."

Dackrich's mouth twisted. "I told you, we'd handle it, Cooper. Now you better make up your mind to let us handle it."

Dackrich jerked his head toward Grant and the fat man got to his feet. They walked toward the door.

Jim ran after them. "Where are you going?"

"We can't stay here and hold your head, Cooper. We got a killer to find. Now here's one thing. You hear from Cowley, or anybody, you get in touch with headquarters. And fast."

Jim nodded. He saw Dackrich nod at Grant, not knowing what that nod meant, not caring, too sick to care.

He watched them leave. After a moment he heard the car back down the drive. He felt alone and helpless. The world was black and empty and full of terror.

He closed the door, went back into the front room. He could not sit down. He prowled through the house, hearing the drip of the kitchen faucet, the tick of the bedroom clock. A car passed on the street. The telephone rang.

He sprang at the phone. His hands trembled so badly he had difficulty grabbing it up. "Hello. Hello."

There was the waiting again, the tension, the killer letting his nerves draw fine. "What do you want?" Jim said.

"Just called to tell you goodbye, Cooper. For your wife and kid. I told you to stay away from them cops. You wouldn't listen—"

"How—?" Jim stopped, biting down hard on his underlip. He glanced at his watch, his heart slugging. No newspapers were on the streets yet, wouldn't be for hours. How could Cowley know the cops had been here?

Jim's hands trembled. There were just two ways. Cowley knew the cops were looking for him. Or Cowley had seen Dackrich and Grant come into the yard, and seen them leave.

Sweat stood like cold marbles on his forehead. His lips were dry. He licked his tongue across them. If Cowley had seen them leave, then that meant he was somewhere near where he could watch.

"I told you not to play hero, Cooper."

"Those weren't cops," Jim said.

He held his breath, feeling his face muscles grow rigid. "They were friends of mine. They dropped in."

"Don't lie, Cowley. Cops I can smell a mile. They were cops."

For a moment Jim felt his heart stop, then it hammered crazily against his ribs.

Cowley's voice raised. "Just wanted to tell you, Cooper, you can't play smart with me. Now it's too late for you to do anything." The receiver was slammed down, hard.

Jim replaced the receiver. He mopped his hand across his forehead. Arn Cowley was somewhere in this neighborhood. He had to be. It made sense. It was the first thing in this nightmarish day that did.

He stood there, trying to know what to do. He had to call Dackrich. Dackrich was tough and callous, but he was a cop and knew what to do. But what could he do? Call in his police officers and let them search the neighborhood? Cowley would not let Mary and Skip live through that.

If he tried to find them alone, and failed . . .

He doused that thought from his mind. If Arn Cowley were in this neighborhood, that meant he was holed up in a house where he could watch this place. What made better sense? Where was the last place anybody would look for Arn Cowley? In this quiet residential neighborhood.

He glanced at the telephone, thinking he had to call Dackrich.

He stared at it, and there was the answer. Joan and Don Fortson. The odd way Don had talked over the phone. Don hadn't been stuffy. Don had been scared. Deep in his guts, he'd been scared.

Jim went into his bedroom. He got the Luger from his souvenir drawer. There were no shells for it. Once he'd had shells, but Mary had been afraid with Skip toddling around. She'd said that either the gun went or the shells.

He left the light burning in the bedroom.

He walked into the kitchen with the Luger at his side. He started out the back door, turned and closed the door between the front of the house and the kitchen.

He stepped out into the night. He walked slowly around the side of the house, stood staring at Don Fortson's place at an angle across the street.

He heard a sudden obscure noise in the darkness. He stopped, frozen, waiting. There was no movement. He told himself it was a cat or the wind in a hedge.

Most of the houses were dark now, people in bed or watching the late TV movies. There were lights in Don's house. The only odd note about it was the way the Venetian blinds were tightly drawn in the lighted windows.

He stepped back into the shadows. In one of those darkened rooms, Arn Cowley sat with a gun in his fist, watching this street, this house.

He went out into the alley, and then, putting the Luger in his pocket, he ran to the corner. He did not know how little time he had, only that if there were the sound of a gun from Don Fortson's, his world would end.

He reached the alley behind the Fortson house and then walked along it, holding his breath, his hand clenching the Luger.

He walked across the backyard. There was a light in the kitchen. He moved close, but could not see in because the blind was closed.

He looked around, trying to be sure of what he was about to do. At the rear corner of the house, adjoining the back porch, there was a darkened window.

He went up the porch steps, listened a moment at the back door. There was silence, as though breathing were suspended inside the house.

Quietly he moved to the darkened window. From his pocket he took a pen knife, sliced the screen above the hook. He discarded his shoes. Cat-like, he let himself in. He must think well, and fast, when the time came. Urgency, necessity made him shrewd.

He slipped across the floor of the room, listened at the door that led to Don's front room. There was a heavy silence in there, the silence of people. He had to know exactly where Cowley was before he could make his move. Spot Cowley. Then fling the door open, throw the gun at him simultaneous with the charge. If Cowley shot him—well, all of it should take enough time for Don to be able to jump in. It might work. It had to. There was nothing else.

He lay down but could not see into the room through the bottom of the transom. He would have to risk opening the door, ever so slightly. There was no other way.

Gun ready in his right hand, Jim reached up with his left and slowly—very slowly—turned the knob. He heard the baby rattle bounce on the other side and knew Cowley had placed it lightly on the door knob as a warning signal.

He stopped breathing; panic coursed through him. He didn't mind dying, even foolishly, if it would save the others. But to die without making their lives safe—to cause their death—

He heard someone gritting an order in a low tone. Footsteps came across to Jim. He felt the sweat running down his forehead.

"It's me, Mrs. Cooper," he heard his wife's voice say as she opened the door. She stood there silhouetted by the light from the living room. Past her ankles he could see no one.

Then she saw him, and his name escaped her lips, "Jim-*no!*"

Even in so desperate a situation, he felt like an ass lying there on the floor, powerless.

"Come out, smart guy," the gritty voice ordered. "And don't try nothin' funny. I'm holding your kid right in front of me. If you've got a gun or anything else toss it out here, or so help me I'll wipe out the room."

He tossed the gun out, rose slowly.

"Come in here!" Cowley ordered. "Hands on your head. And no tricks."

He went in with Mary, silently cursing himself that Cowley should have out-thought him.

"Keep those hands on your head," Cowley told him, jabbing the gun hard into his ribs. "I'll tell you when to put them down, smart guy." Cowley's left hand patted Jim in a quick, expert frisking operation.

"That's all then," he said. "This." He looked at the Luger and laughed. "An empty gun. Turn around, smart guy."

Jim turned and Cowley cracked the Luger across his face. The room spun and wheeled on a red pin. Jim crumpled to his knees. He felt the blood running out of his torn cheek.

He pressed his hands against his face, trying to make the room stop spinning. He heard Mary moan, "Oh," as though the pain were hers. That was the only sound.

Still on his knees, Jim raised his head. He felt a line of blood ooze along his jaw and his neck but did not wipe It away.

"So now you know how I feel about smart guys," Cowley said. "Now you won't be smart no more."

Jim looked at Mary. Her face was bloodless and her eyes red-rimmed, but her jaw was set now as though nobody could make her cry again. She held the baby, which Cowley had returned to her, against her shoulder and kept her gaze fixed on Cowley. Her face showed her sick hatred.

Joan Fortson was sitting in a big chair under a reading lamp. Her face muscles were rigid, and she pushed herself back into the chair as though she wanted to sink into it, become part of it. Don sat on the edge of the divan. He stared at the floor. There was a dark welt across his forehead. His eyes were dead, and the life was gone out of him. The way he sat said whatever move he had made, he was not going to make again.

"Get up," Cowley ordered Jim. "Sit in a chair where I can watch you. Keep your mouth shut."

Cowley looked at the Luger again, mouth twisting. He dropped it in his packet. "Had to be a hero, eh, Cooper? Had to go to the cops."

Jim licked his tongue across his lips. He looked at Mary a moment, moved his gaze back to Cowley. Cowley was scowling, deep in thought.

"I went to the cops," Jim said. "You can't stay here. But you can still get away."

"Shut up. I told you to keep your mouth shut."

"There's a car out there in the garage," Jim said. "You can get away. You won't gain anything by staying here. Not now. Soon the cops'll come to this neighborhood because they know you would be looking for me. Then you won't get away."

Cowley stared at him. "Yeah." He thought this over. His mind was going over all the angles. Watching Cowley, Jim felt even more helpless. You'd have to be trained, somebody like Dackrich, to know even some of the angles Cowley was considering.

"You don't think I'm going to let you live to put the finger on me in court?" Cowley said.

Jim swallowed. "They've already got my sworn statement. You kill me maybe it won't he heard. You kill all of us, all those shot—they'd be heard. You'd have no chance."

Cowley thought that over. "Maybe you've come up with a good idea, smart boy," he said at last. "Right now, I don't see nothing wrong with it. Give me whatever money you got, Cooper." He glanced toward Don. "Same for you."

Don moved like a robot. He removed his wallet from his pocket, tossed it at Cowley's feet.

Cowley jerked his head toward Jim. Jim tossed his wallet beside Don's. Cowley smiled, knelt and picked up the two wallets. He removed the bills, dropped the wallets. He thumbed through the money. "You two boys ain't exactly big money men, are you?" he said, his voice bitter. He stepped toward Don. "On your feet."

Don stood up. Jim tensed, waiting for Cowley to turn his back. Cowley laughed, as though reading Jim's thoughts. He turned so he could watch both of them. "You. Let's go out the back way. You back your car out, turn it around, back in so it's headed out. Leave the door open and the motor running. Then you come back in here."

Jim held his breath, hoping Don would see this was a chance to get help.

The baby whimpered. Cowley jerked his head around. "I told you to keep the brat quiet."

Mary held the baby tighter, whispering to it.

Cowley spoke to Joan. "Okay, blondie, you come over here and stand right in front of me. We're going to be here watching you, Don. Only blondie ain't going to like it with this gun against her head."

Jim stared at the gun pressed against Joan's head.

Don said, "I'm going to do what you tell me. You don't have to threaten her with that gun."

"Sure, I don't But I'm going to. Because I don't ever take no chances. This way you'll hurry."

Don nodded. He stumbled, going down the steps. Jim sat on the edge of the chair, hearing the car start, hearing it go down the drive and turn around in the street. After a moment, Don backed it into the garage.

Jim tried to think what Cowley would do next. Cowley had to get away, and the quieter he went, the better. Jim felt numb. He knew he could never outthink Cowley.

Don came back in. He did not look at any of them.

Cowley removed the gun from Joan's head. She sagged against the door jamb, her mouth quivering.

Cowley moved his gaze around the room. He strode across, took the baby from Mary's arms. She cried out, one stark sound of agony.

Cowley moved toward the door. "You better not get in touch with the cops, Cooper. They try to stop me, you got a dead kid."

Cowley turned and backed toward the kitchen door. He watched Jim, as he kept the gun fixed on him. Jim did not take his gaze from the baby as he walked after Cowley, taking slow, long steps.

Cowley's mouth worked. "You stay where you are, Cooper. Don't make me shoot you. Don't make me shoot the kid."

"Put down my baby."

Cowley moved to the door, went through it. Jim kept walking forward, knowing it was an empty threat.

Swiftly, Cowley backed the short distance to where Don had parked the car. Watching Don and the others who were behind Don, the gun ready, he slid the baby across the seat, slid under the wheel.

Jim tensed for a quick spring forward, feeling maybe he could risk it now. He heard the baby wail. Then he held himself back, even held his expression rigid as he saw Dackrich rising from the rear floor of Don's car and with a single sharp motion crack his gun hard against the back of Cowley's head. Cowley sagged forward onto the steering wheel.

Jim felt overwhelmingly tired, weak. As he walked around to get the baby, knowing Dackrich had done what he was trained to do, without flashy heroics but by plain common-sense police shadowing, he still felt a trace of hatred for the way Dackrich had treated him.

Jim lifted the baby and it stopped crying. Mary came to him as Dackrich's partner came from out of the nearby hedge. Without asking, Jim knew they had heard him talk with Cowley before Cowley had taken him inside.

Mary pressed hard against him. He felt a sudden sense of release. He handed the baby over to her. The whole thing had been a nightmare, and it was over.

Dackrich seemed to read his thoughts. Dackrich's voice remained flat. "Cops. Eh, fella?"

Jim met his gaze, did not speak.

Dackrich shrugged. A bitter amusement flickered in his eyes. "We do our best, Cooper. Sometimes we're wrong. Why don't you look at it that way?"

Pigeon in an Iron Lung
Talmage Powell

November 1956

I lay in the iron lung listening for some sound of her. The lung chuffed softly with that steady rhythm that meant breath and life for me.

The door of the room opened and I saw her in the tilted, curved mirror that was attached to the lung over my face. She stood motionless for a moment, lithe, tanned, tall, beautiful in white shorts and halter, a yachting cap cocked to one side on her close-cut blonde hair.

I caught the dark thing in her face and eyes. It was there only a moment. Then she was crossing the room, smiling, as only she could smile, with her full red lips and perfect white teeth.

"How do you feel, darling?" she asked. She had a soft, liquid southern accent that made you think of lazy water in the depths of a hot, mysterious bayou.

"Fine," I said. "Going out?"

"I thought I would go sailing with Arnold."

"Arnold again?" I said with a laugh.

She kissed the tip of her forefinger and pressed it to my lips. "Don't fret, Dave. I have little enough to do here."

"I won't fret, Cindy. I'm just a trifle narrow-minded."

For a moment, it was almost naked in her face. Her distaste of anything sick and helpless. Her boredom. Her realization that she could do anything she pleased and that I couldn't do a damn thing about it.

I felt tired and drained. I closed my eyes. "Will you be back for dinner?"

"I think so."

I was hungry for companionship, for talk. I hated myself, but I said, "Why not bring Arnold?"

"You mean that, Dave?"

"Certainly. If he's your friend, why shouldn't he be mine?"

"I'll see if it can be arranged," she said. She turned and went out.

I lay there thinking about my wife, about us. The road I'd travelled had started in the slums of Chicago. A tough kid with a lot of ambition and money hunger. And a yen to be respectable. I had fought my way to the top of a labor organization and put a couple of politicians in my back pocket. I had a sharp instinct for putting money in the right investments. As a consequence, I had made a mint. It wasn't enough. I had hit Florida at the beginning of the post war housing boom. The money had doubled, tripled, quadrupled. State senators asked my opinion on pending legislation that would affect real estate. I even had my own lawyer in the capital.

No doubt about it, I was at last respectable.

But it was not quite enough.

Cindy had been the house guest of a wealthy Miami Beach developer when I'd met her. She came from an old southern family that could trace its lineage back to revolutionary times. The pages of southern history were dotted with the names of her forebears. But time had decayed the glory of her family and dissipated its money. Cindy was the end of the line.

She spent her time drifting from Miami to Charleston to Bar Harbor. From friend to friend. She was beautiful and decorative and that social background still brought her in contact with people eager to have her as a guest.

She accepted their gifts and favors as a matter of course. Just as she accepted my proposal to marry her. She looked up at me with her lazy green eyes. "Even if I don't love you, Dave?"

"You're what I've been looking for," I said. "I think we'll make a team. I'll reach you in time."

Her eyes had flashed briefly. "Are you sure anyone will ever reach me, Dave? I warn you, I like myself. I like myself very much."

"I don't exactly hate myself, Cindy. I'm glad we understand each other."

For a wedding present, I gave her the long, sweeping house on Indian Shores Beach. It overlooked a thousand feet of private beach, a boat dock where a cruiser bobbed at anchor, and the limitless stretches of the Gulf of Mexico.

The first few months were O.K. by me. The terrace and long living room, that gave you the feeling you were living out of doors, was the scene of gay parties where smart people moved and talked.

We danced, swam, fished from the cruiser. Cindy never talked a great deal and the remoteness never completely left her green eyes. One night on the cruiser deck when I was kissing her, I raised my head to find her staring abstractedly at the distant stars.

Then one morning I woke with fever and nausea. I was in my physical prime. But a few days later, I couldn't move. The polio virus had done what the slums had never been able to do. It had put Dave Ramey on his back.

Lying there, with the lung sucking life into me, I tried to clear my mind of its train of thought. I wanted to quit thinking of the way in which Cindy had changed her life after my illness. But I couldn't stop thinking.

Now there was Arnold Barrett. He was the sort, dark and tall, that some women would call a dreamboat. He and Cindy had met a week ago. He lived in a cottage down the beach. They were seeing each other constantly, and a foreboding of disaster grew stronger in me each day. Arnold had nothing, except his good looks. While Cindy had a helpless hulk of a husband who was kept alive by mechanical means.

"Miss Collins!"

The short, stout, middle-aged woman who was my private nurse came in from the adjoining room. "Yes, Mr. Ramey?"

"I'd like to go out on the terrace, please."

She turned the lung on its big rubber casters and rolled me out on the long, screened terrace.

"Turn me so I can see the water, Miss Collins."

She turned the lung and adjusted the mirror. "Anything else, Mr. Ramey?"

"No, that'll be all."

"Yes, sir. By the way, Mr. Ramey, Mrs. Ramey said I might have the evening off."

"Oh?"

"Yes. She said she would be here with you. Of course, if you prefer—"

"No," I said. "That's all right, Miss Collins."

"Thank you, sir."

She settled on a chaise longue at the far side of the terrace, picked up a book, and started reading.

I lay on my back, looking into the mirror. Its curvature gave me a broad view. The Gulf was beautiful today, green as an emerald. A light breeze, right for pleasant sailing, rippled little mare's tails across the water.

I saw the rented sailboat as it hove into view. Arnold was at the helm and Cindy was forward. Distance made them smaller than doll creatures in the mirror. But imagination could magnify them. Could bring to life the lazy ripple of water against the boat. The stir of the semi-tropical breeze with its tang of salt and its heat. The image of her standing on the prow, a tall, golden figurehead. Especially desirable, because she lingered just beyond reach.

Lips parted, she gazed into the reaches of open sky and water. Undoubtedly thinking of the sickening wreck who had once been her husband, but who now was nothing more than an obstacle between her and freedom.

The signs were there. I had observed them for days now. But I had to know. I had to make sure. I must be positive that the sickness of my body was not now becoming a sickness of the mind as well.

Arnold tried to tack, lost headway. The sails flapped. She went back to help him, moving along the boat with feline grace.

The boat got underway and moved beyond the view line of the mirror.

"Miss Collins."

"Yes, Mr. Ramey?"

"Bring me a phone, please."

The nurse got up, with a rustle of her crisp nylon uniform. She left the terrace and returned with a phone. She plugged it in, set its special cradle on the small platform beside my head, and put the phone on the cradle. By turning my head, I had the phone in position.

She dialed a delicatessen for me and I ordered a dinner to be delivered that night. Roast chicken, oyster dressing, a good selection of relishes and wine. Miss Collins took the phone away and I slept.

When I awoke, I knew I had been having a nightmare. I couldn't remember the dream, but its effects lingered. I was sweating, my mind upset with the turbulence of anxiety.

It was late afternoon and Miss Collins still sat near me, reading. I became calmer and asked her for a cigarette.

I had finished the cigarette when I heard their voices. Cindy's and Arnold's. He was laughing at something she had said. He had a big, deep, easy laugh. It fitted his dark good looks. It caressed a woman with the right shade of intimacy.

They came onto the terrace, warmed by the sun, healthy, alive. They came walking into the soft chug-chug of the lung and Arnold wasn't laughing.

"Hello, Dave."

"How was the sail, Arnold?"

"Oh, fine. Your missus—she really knows boats."

"She knows a lot about a lot of things, Arnold."

Cindy glanced at me. "Yes, don't I, darling?"

I gave her a smile. "I understand you told Collins she could take the evening off."

For an instant, it was there between them. She returned my smile coolly. Arnold let his head swing around, his gaze search the Gulfs expanse.

"You don't mind, do you, Dave?" Cindy said.

"Of course not. You're familiar with the workings of the lung. It won't be the first time Collins has had a few hours to herself."

"That's right. She's only been off twice in the past two weeks, hasn't she? She really deserves it."

"Why not let her go on now?" I asked. "I've already arranged to have dinner sent from Max's. Arnold will stay, of course."

They couldn't keep from flicking a brief glance at each other. I was playing into their hands and I could sense that it was working even better than Cindy'd hoped.

"Well, I was supposed to—" Arnold began. Then he reached a decision. "I'd enjoy staying, Dave."

"Good. Why don't you mix a drink while Collins gets ready to go? Then you could drop her at the bus stop, if she's planning to spend the evening in town."

"Where else would I plan an evening?" Miss Collins said.

She left the terrace. Arnold made drinks. Cindy brought mine to me, put the bent glass straw between my lips. I took a sip. Arnold mixed a very good martini.

Miss Collins was ready to go in a few minutes. I heard the car leaving the driveway. My car. Arnold driving it. What was he thinking as he drove? That it was a nice handling job?

Cindy was on her third drink. I watched her in the mirror.

"I hope it will be painless," I said. "Painless?"

"The killing," I said.

She moved around until she was standing just to one side and over me, looking down into my face. There was no emotion in her eyes. But in the soft gold column of her throat a tiny pulse beat. Another pulse showed in the soft hollow of tanned flesh below the white halter.

"What are you talking about, Dave?" she said softly.

"All my life I've dealt with people, Cindy. I know them pretty well. You don't have to draw me a map. It was O.K. for awhile, wasn't it?"

She stood for a long time without speaking. The surf murmured in the near distance and the lung beat softly. Like a heart that would never stop. I knew she was listening to it.

"Yes, Dave, it was fine when you were on your feet."

"But everything is different now."

"You're more dead than alive," she said without inflection. "I've wondered—knowing you—don't you want to die?"

"No, Cindy. And that shows how little you really know me. Life in the lung isn't too bad. With assistance I read, play cards. I do a certain amount of business by telephone. I watch television—secondhand from the mirror. I enjoy the breeze on the terrace here and I like the feeling that I started with nothing and built this house. What man has more, Cindy?"

"Except a wife, Dave."

"I've never had you."

"Yes, you did. For awhile. As much of me as I was able to give."

"Now I have none of you."

"That's the hard, cold fact of life, Dave. You have to accept these things."

"Without shame, remorse, guilt, any feeling?"

She shrugged. "You started this conversation. What are those things?"

"You wouldn't know, would you, Cindy?"

"I didn't want to talk about it, remember."

"But I do. Now there is Arnold. There is freedom, just over the horizon, and barrels of money. Nothing at all in your way, except a man more dead than alive. Did you plan it for tonight?"

"Do you really want to know?" she said. A faint glow had come to her eyes. She looked more alive now than she had in days.

"I guess not. How will it happen? A little accident, a cotter pin or some little something going wrong with the lung?"

"No one could ever blame me, Dave."

"They might suspect."

"Who cares? Suspecting and proving are two different things."

"I might tell someone what you're planning."

"But there's no one here but us, darling."

"There's the phone."

"And who's to plug it in for you? I'm afraid, Dave, there's another hard, cold fact you'll have to face up to. There's nothing you can do. You can't move; you can't even breathe without that thing doing it for you. You're helpless, Dave, completely at my mercy."

"I see," I said. "One thing I insist on—that the killing be painless."

"I'm really sorry, Dave, that you had to come down with this thing. I liked you—as a whole man. I saw your courage when this thing struck. Now I see how deep that courage really is."

She drained her glass, looked at me over the rim of it and smiled. "I'll always remember how brave you were, darling."

She fed me that evening, sitting close to me, arranging my after dinner coffee so I could sip it with a straw. Arnold was silent during most of the meal.

When dinner was over, I caught his eye. "This has been pretty drab, I'm afraid. Why don't you two go for a swim?"

"Well, I—" Arnold said.

"I insist," I said. "Turn on the television for me and enjoy yourselves. Later, we'll have drinks."

"Why not?" Cindy said. "It's still early. I feel like rolling in the surf. I want to feel the pull and tug of the tide. Come on, Arnold. Dave will be right here when we get back."

"That's a certain bet," I said. "Arnold, you can borrow a pair of my trunks. Cindy'll get them for you."

I heard them leave the room. Alone now. The lung and I. The metal casing that served for a body. The cell that made me helpless.

I pictured them walking into the surf together. Arnold big and handsome and she lithe and slim. The plunge into the water. His laughter. The roll of their bodies as they swam together in the moonlight. I wouldn't think beyond their swimming together.

An hour passed.

I heard the door open and close. Arnold entered the room alone. He walked over and turned down the sound on the television set.

"It's all over, Dave. It'll look like an accident. They'll find her body with the early change of tide tomorrow. I checked the currents the way you instructed."

"You were always a good strong-arm man, Arnold."

"Thanks," he said. "Just like old times in Chicago, eh, Dave?"

"Just like old times. I'm glad you came down when you got my call. The money'll reach you by special messenger after you get back to Chi, Arnold, and the whole thing dies down. Fifty grand for it."

"Fair enough," Arnold said. "Now I think I'll have a drink."

He turned toward the liquor cabinet across the romp. He was an efficient man in his job. I knew he had made it as painless for her as possible. I was glad she hadn't suffered. I had insisted the killing be as painless as Arnold could make it. Only a brute would have wanted her to suffer needlessly.

Cop for a Day
Henry Slesar

January 1957

They had eighteen thousand dollars, they couldn't spend a nickel. Davy Wyatt spread the money on the kitchen table, in neat piles, according to their various denominations, and just sat there, looking. After awhile this got on Phil Pennick's nerves.

"Cut it out, kid," the older man said. "You're just eatin' your heart out."

"Don't I know it."

Davy sighed, and swept the bills back into the neat leather briefcase. He tossed it carelessly onto his bunk, and joined it there a minute later, lying down with his fingers locked behind his head.

"I'm goin' out," Phil said suddenly.

"Where to?"

"Pick up some sandwiches, maybe a newspaper. Take a little walk."

The kid's face paled. "Think it's a good idea?"

"You got a better one? Listen, we can rot in this crummy joint." Phil looked around the one-room flat that had been their prison for two days, and made a noise that didn't nearly show his full disgust. Then he grabbed for his jacket and put it on.

"It's your neck," the kid said. "Don't blame me if you get picked up. With that dame playin' footsie with the cops—"

"Shut up! If they get me, they'll have your neck in the chopper ten minutes later. So don't wish me any bad luck, pal."

Davy sat up quickly. "Hey, no kidding. Think you ought to take the chance?"

The older man smiled. The smile did nothing for the grim set of his features, merely shifted the frozen blankness, which was the result of three prison terms. He put a soft fedora on his gray head and adjusted it carefully.

"We took our chance already," he said as he opened the door. "And as far as the dame goes—you leave that up to me."

He hoisted the .38 out of his shoulder holster, checked the cartridges, and slipped it back. The gesture was so casual, so relaxed, that the kid realized once again that he was working with a pro.

Davy swallowed hard, and said, "Sure, Phil. I'll leave it up to you."

The street was full of children. Phil Pennick liked children, especially around a hideout. They discouraged rash action by the police. He walked along like a man out to get the morning paper, or a pack of cigarettes, or to shoot a game of pool. Nobody looked at him twice, even though his clothes were a shade better than anybody else's in that slum area.

Davy's last words were stuck in his thoughts. *"I'll leave it up to you . . ."* It was easy enough to reassure the kid that the old pro would work them out of trouble. Only this time, the old pro wasn't so sure.

They had planned a pretty sound caper. Something simple, without elaborate preparations. It involved one small bank messenger, from a little colonial-style bank in Brooklyn, the kind of messenger who never seemed to tote more than a few grand around. Only they had been doubly surprised. The bank messenger had turned out to be a scrapper, and the loot had turned out to be bigger than they had ever dreamed. Now they had the money, and the little bonded errand boy had two bullets in his chest. Was he dead or alive? Phil didn't know, and hardly cared. One more arrest and conviction, and he was as good as dead anyway. He wasn't made to be a lifer; he'd rather be a corpse.

But they had the money. That was the important thing. In twenty years of trying, Phil Pennick had never come up with the big one. It would have been a truly great triumph, if the cops hadn't found their witness. They hadn't seen the woman until it was too late. She was standing in a doorway of the side street where they had made their play. She was a honey blonde, with a figure out of 52nd Street, and a pair of sharp eyes. Her face didn't change a bit when Phil spotted her. She just looked back, coldly, and watched the bank messenger sink to the sidewalk with his hands trying to block the blood. Then she had slammed the front door behind her.

The kid had wanted to go in after her, but Phil said no. The shots had been loud, and he wasn't going to take any more chances. They had rushed into the waiting auto, and headed for the pre-arranged hideout.

Phil stopped by a newsstand. He bought some cigarettes, a couple of candy bars, and the Journal. He was reading the headlines as he walked into the tiny delicatessen adjoining. The holdup story was boxed at the bottom of the page. It didn't tell him anything he didn't already know. The honey blonde had talked all right. And she was ready to identify the two men who had shot and killed the bank's errand boy. *Shot and killed* . . . Phil shook his head. The poor slob, he thought.

In the delicatessen, he bought four roast beef sandwiches and a half dozen cans of cold beer. Then he walked back to the apartment, thinking hard.

As soon as he came in, the kid grabbed for the newspaper. He found the story and read it avidly. When he looked up, his round young face was frightened.

"What'll we do, Phil? This dame can hang us!"

"Take it easy." He opened a beer.

"Are you kidding? Listen, one of the first things the cops'll do is go looking for you. I mean—let's face it, Phil—this is your kind of caper."

The older man frowned. "So what?"

"So what? So they'll parade you in front of this dame, and she'll scream bloody murder. Then what happens to me?"

Phil took his gun out and began cleaning it. "I'll stop her," he promised.

"How? They probably got a million cops surrounding her. They won't take any chances. Hell no. So how can you stop her?"

"I got a plan," Phil said. "You're just going to have to trust me, kid. Okay?"

"Yeah, but—"

"I said trust me. Don't forget, Davy." He looked at his partner hard. "This wouldn't have happened at all—if you didn't have a jerky trigger finger."

They ate the sandwiches, drank the beer, and then the older man went to the leather brief case and opened it. He lifted out a thin packet of bills and put it into his wallet.

"Hey," Davy said.

"Don't get in an uproar. I'm goin' to need a few bucks, for what I've got in mind. Until I come back, I'll trust you to take care of the rest." Phil put on his jacket again. "Don't get wild ideas, kid. Remember, you don't leave the room until I get back. And if we have any visitors—watch that itchy finger."

"Sure, Phil," the kid said.

Phil had a hard time getting a taxi. When he did, he gave the driver the Manhattan address of a garment house on lower Seventh Avenue.

There was a girl behind the frosted glass cage on the fifth floor, and she was pretty snippy.

"I want to see Marty Hirsch," Phil said.

"I'm sorry, Mr. Hirsch is in conference—"

"Don't give me that conference junk. Just pick up your little phone and tell him a good friend from Brooklyn Heights is here. He'll know who it is."

The girl's nose tilted up, but she made the call.

The man who hurried out to see Phil was short and paunchy. He was in shirtsleeves, and his sunset-colored tie was hanging loosely around his neck.

"Er, hello," he said nervously, looking towards the switchboard. "Look, Phil, suppose we can talk in the hallway? I got a customer inside."

"What's the matter, Marty? Ashamed of your friends?"

"Please, Phil!"

In the hallway, the garment man said: "Look, I told you never to come here." He wiped sweat from his face. "It doesn't look good, for both of us. We should do all our business by phone."

"You don't understand," Phil said. "I ain't got nothin' hot for you to buy. I'm out of that business, Marty."

"Oh? So what is it then?"

"I just want a little favor, Marty. For an old pal."

The small eyes narrowed. "What kind of favor?"

"You got a big uniform department. Right?"

"Yeah. So what? Army and Navy stuff. Things like that. So what do you want?"

"A uniform," Phil said easily. "That's all. A cop uniform. Only it's gotta be good."

"Now look, Phil—"

"Don't give me a hard time, Marty. We got too long a friendship. I want to play a joke on a friend of mine. You can fix me up with something, can't you?"

The garment man frowned. "I'll tell you what. I got here some stock models. Only they're not so new, and they ain't got no badges. And no gun, you understand."

"Don't worry about that. I got the potsy. Will this uniform pass? I mean, if another cop saw it?"

"Yeah, yeah, sure. It'll pass. I'm telling you."

"Swell. Then trot it out, Marty." The man looked doubtful, so Phil added: "For the sake of a friend, huh?"

Phil walked out into the street with the large flat box under his arm, feeling that he was getting somewhere. Then he waved a cab up to the curb, and gave him the cross streets where Davy Wyatt had killed the bank messenger.

It was chancey, but worth it. He didn't know whether the blonde was cooling her high heels in a police station, or just knee-deep in cops guarding her at her own apartment house.

He knew the answer the minute he stepped out of the cab. There was a police car parked at the opposite curb, and two uniformed patrolmen were gabbing near the front entrance of the blonde's residence.

He looked up and down the street until he found what he was looking for. There was a small restaurant with a red-striped awning. He walked up to it briskly, and saw it was called: ANGIE'S. He glanced at the menu pasted to the window, then pushed the door open.

He surveyed the room, and it looked good. The men's john was in a hallway out of the main dining room, and there was a side exit that would come in handy when he made the switch in clothing.

There weren't many customers. Phil took a table near the hall, and placed his package on the opposite chair. A bored waiter took his order. After being served, Phil chewed patiently on a dish of tired spaghetti. Then he paid his check and went into the john.

He changed swiftly, in a booth. Then he put the clothes he'd taken off inside the box and tied the string tight. He pinned the badge to his shirt, and dropped the .38 into the police holster.

Leaving by the side door, he dropped the box into one of the trash cans near the exit.

Then he crossed the street nonchalantly, headed straight for the apartment house.

"Hi," he said, to the two cops out front. "You guys seen Weber?" Weber was a precinct lieutenant that Phil knew only too well.

"Weber? Hell, no. Was he supposed to be here?"

"I thought so. I'm from the Fourth Precinct. We got a call from him awhile ago. We picked up somebody last night, on a B and E; might be one of the guys you're looking for."

"Search me," one of the cops said. "What do you want us to do about it?"

Phil swore. "I don't know what to do myself. Sendin' me on a wild goose chase. He was supposed to be here by now."

"Can't help you, pal." The other cop yawned widely.

"Dame in her apartment?" Phil asked casually.

"Yeah," the second cop answered. "Lying down." He snickered. "I wouldn't mind sharing the bunk."

"Maybe I better talk to her. I got the guy's picture. Maybe she can tell me something."

"I donno." The first cop scratched his cheek. "We ain't heard nothing about that."

"What the hell," the second one said. He turned to Phil. "She's in Four E."

"Okay," Phil said. He started into the house. "If Weber shows up, you tell him I'm upstairs. Right?"

"Right."

He shut the door behind him, stood there long enough to let out a relieved sigh. Then he stepped into the automatic elevator, punched the button marked Four.

On the fourth floor, he rapped gently on the door marked E. "Yeah?" The woman's voice sounded tired, but not scared. "Who is it?"

"Police," Phil said crisply. "Got a picture for you lady."

"What kind of a picture?" Her voice was close to the doorframe.

"Guy we picked up last night. Maybe the one we're lookin' for."

He could hear the chain being lifted; the door was opened. Close up, the blonde wasn't as young or as lush as he had imagined. She was wearing a faded housecoat of some shiny material, clutching it around her waist without too much concern for the white flesh that was still revealed.

Phil stepped inside and took off his cap. "This won't take long, lady." He closed the door.

She turned her back on him and walked into the room. He unbuttoned the holster without hurry, and lifted the gun out. When she turned around, the gun was pointed dead center. She opened her mouth, but not a sound came out.

"One word and I shoot," Phil said evenly. He backed her against a sofa, and shot a look towards the other room. "What's in there?"

"Bedroom," she said.

"Move."

She cooperated nicely. She stretched out on the bed at his command—and smiled coyly. She must have figured he wanted something else besides her death. Then he picked up a pillow and shoved it into her stomach.

"Hold that," he said.

She held it. Then he shoved the gun up against it and squeezed the trigger. She looked surprised and angry and deceived, and then she was dead.

The sound had been well muffled, but Phil wanted to be sure. He went to the window that faced the street and looked down. The two cops were still out front, chewing the fat complacently. He smiled, slipped the gun into the holster, and went out.

The cops looked at him without too much interest.

"Well?" the first one said.

"Dames," Phil grinned. "Says she knows from nothing. Weber's gonna be awfully disappointed." He waved his hand. "I'm goin' back to the precinct. So long, guys."

They said, "So long," and resumed their gabbing.

Phil rounded the corner. There was a cab at the hack stand. He climbed into the back.

"What's up, officer?" the hackie grinned. "Lost your prowl car?"

"Don't be a wise guy." He gave him the address and settled back into a contented silence, thinking about the money.

It was dusk by the time he reached the neighborhood. He got off some four blocks from the tenement, and walked the rest of the distance. Some of the kids on the block hooted at him because of the uniform, and he grinned.

He went up the stairs feeling good. When he pushed open the door, Davy shot him once in the stomach. Phil didn't have time to make him realize the mistake he was making before the second bullet struck him in the center of his forehead.

Somebody's Going to Die
Talmage Powell

I'm afraid to go home tonight.

I'll go, of course. To a modern, lovely house on Coquina Beach overlooking the Gulf of Mexico. The beach is not the habitat of paupers.

A singularly beautiful and devoted woman waits for me there. Doreen. My wife.

We are ringleaders in a smart cocktail set. We get special service whenever we go into a beach restaurant. Everything has worked perfectly. No one on the beach suspects how we came into our money.

To an outsider I might well be a person to envy. Yet I would give five years of my life if I could escape going home tonight.

Doreen was unaware of the jam I was in when we went on that hunting trip together six months back. We had been married only a few weeks at the time, after getting acquainted during a business trip I took to Atlanta.

She was still pretty much of a stranger to me, and she was such an intense person I didn't know how she would take the news.

We'd had a wonderful time on the trip. Few women would have taken the dark, tangled swamp, the south Georgia heat as Doreen had. Snakes, alligators, they didn't faze her. Neither had the panther.

We were in Okeefanokee hunting deer. I'd struck the panther's spoor in late afternoon. I'd wanted Doreen to turn back, but she'd looked at me strangely.

"Enos," she said, "I never suspected you'd be afraid of anything. You're big, ugly, direct, blunt, hardheaded, cruel—or is that only a front?" She finished with a short laugh, but there was a seriousness beneath her words.

"I'm not afraid for myself," I said.

"Then never be afraid for me," she said excitedly. "Come on, Enos, I want to see you get this cat."

I jumped the cat twenty minutes later. As it came out of a clump of palmetto and saw grass I put a 30-30 slug in her. My aim was a trifle high. The panther screamed, pinwheeled in the air, and came at me, a crazed mass of fury and hatred.

Doreen stood her ground and waited for me to shoot the cat. When the beast lay still and prone, it was I who had to wipe sweat from my face.

Doreen walked to the cat slowly. Blood on the animal's hide was already beginning to draw flies and gnats.

"See, Enos," Doreen said, "some of it is still pumping out of her, the hot, red life. Wasn't she beautiful in death?"

I shivered. "Yeah," I said. "Yeah. Let's get back to camp."

We returned to camp and Doreen cooked our supper. Rabbit on a wooden spit and sourdough biscuits.

When we had eaten, we retired to our tent behind mosquito netting. Around us the swamp was coming to life. Its music was a symphony with tones ranging from the shrill of crickets to the basso of the frogs. The swamp rustled and sighed and screamed occasionally.

Doreen slipped into my arms. "You were wonderful with the cat today, Enos."

Thinking of it, her breath quickened and I could feel her heart beating against me.

"I've shot 'em before," I said.

She pulled my chin around with her thumb and forefinger. "I don't interest you a bit at the moment, Enos," she stated. "What's bothering you?"

"A business detail. Nothing for you to worry about."

"I'm your wife," she said. "Tell me."

"All right," I said looking directly into her eyes. They were large and dark. In the dim light of the lantern her pupils were dilated and as black as the glossy midnight color of her hair.

"I'm in trouble," I added after a moment. "Serious trouble. I might even be yanked into prison."

"Why?"

"I've taken some money that doesn't belong to me."

"From whom?"

"Sam Fickens."

"Your business partner," she said.

"That's right. You know we've been spending at a heavy clip, Doreen. The house was costly. A good buy, you don't find many old colonials on an estate any more. But costly."

"You're sorry, Enos?"

"I'm not sorry for a thing," I said. "Except that money ran short. Sam and I had this deal with the Birmingham company coming up. My share would cover the shortage. But the deal blew up. And Sam discovered the shortage the day before you and I left on this trip. He told me to go ahead and take the trip—and use it to figure out whether I want to make him sole owner of the company or spend a few years in prison."

"Why, the dirty snake," Doreen said, not without a degree of admiration in her voice. "It's nothing short of blackmail."

"True."

"You're not going to let him get away with it, are you?"

"What can I do?"

She looked at me oddly. "You're asking me. You, a man, asking a woman?"

I colored a little. "I told you not to worry your head with it. I'll figure something out."

She lay back on her cot. I smoked a cigarette. I was lighting a second from it when she said, "Enos?"

"Yes?"

"If anything happened to Sam what would happen to the business?"

"I'd get his share. It's not an unusual partnership arrangement."

"Well, you didn't hesitate when that cat was coming after you this afternoon, did you?"

I went cold under the muggy sweat on my body. "You mean kill Sam."

"You've killed before, haven't you?"

"That was war."

"This is too. What's the difference? A stranger with a yellow skin is out to kill you in a jungle. You kill him first. Everybody says wonderful, good guy, well done. Now a man is hunting you in a jungle of sorts—and with dirty weapons. You owe it to both of us to protect yourself."

"The difference is in a little thing called the law, Doreen."

She threw back her head and laughed, raised on her elbows and sat looking at me until I glanced away.

Then she turned on her side away from me. "I really thought I'd married a man with guts, Enos." She sounded genuinely hurt, disappointed. And I'd been afraid of how she would react to the news that I'd embezzled some money.

I turned in, but I didn't sleep. I lay there listening to the swamp, aware of her an arm's length away.

Finally I said, "How would you go about it?"

"How'd you know I wasn't asleep, Enos?"

"I could tell. I asked you a question."

"Well, I'd do it with witnesses. Then I'd call the law, hand over the gun, and stand trial. That way, when you walk out of the courtroom, a free man, there can never be any kickbacks."

"Just like that, huh? I'm going to confess to a murder and get off scot free?"

She sat up and turned to face me. Her face had changed. It was as if the angles and bones had shifted to form new shadows. She laughed, soft and low.

"Who said anything about murder, Enos? You know your people here in south Georgia. You know their code, the way they live, their outlook. Do you think a jury of such men will condemn another man for protecting the sanctity of his home?"

I wanted to tell her to stop talking right now. I didn't want to think about killing Sam. He was a hard, greedy cookie without much mercy in his makeup, but he . . . Well, he had me in a corner.

He would use any weapon at hand. He'd proved that.

I'd worked hard. My part of the business was worth plenty. Sam was a swine, grabbing his chance to take it all.

It was really his fault. He was leaving me no out. He knew I wouldn't face prison.

He'd asked for it. . . .

He wasn't in the office the day I got back to Mulberry. It was four o'clock before he came in. I heard him in the outer office talking to Miss Sims, our secretary, and then the door of our private office opened to admit him.

"Hello, Enos. Sims said you were back."

He was a big, florid, meaty man. Meaty lips, hands, nose. His brows and hair were pale red. Sims had said he'd been out to the turpentine fields all day inspecting a new lease.

"How does the lease look?" I asked.

He gave me a smug grin. "You think the lease really concerns you, Enos?"

I studied his face. All I could see was a man gloating. "I'd hoped you'd softened your attitude, Sam."

His laugh was his reply.

"You know I can make that few thousand up in a matter of weeks, Sam. We've been in business . . ."

"And business is business, Enos." A sneer came into his eyes. "You should have thought of that. I needed a partner when we started this company."

"And you don't now?"

"Not a stinking crook. No, I don't need that kind of partner." He sat down behind his desk. "What'll it be, Enos? Sign the papers? Or go to jail?"

"I don't hanker to be locked up, Sam."

"No," he said acidly. "I was sure you wouldn't. You're too great a lover of life for that, too much the gladhanded popularity guy."

It struck me that he hated me, had always hated me. To him, in this case, business was going to be a pleasure.

"I'll make one last appeal, Sam . . ."

"Save it. I've said all I'm going to."

"But I'll say it anyhow. You know what my portion of the company is worth. Many times the few thousand I borrowed . . ."

"Stole, Enos, that's the word."

I drew in a breath while he sat and watched me and enjoyed himself.

"Well," I said. "Surely you could pay a few thousand more . . ."

"You've had every dime you're going to get for your share, Enos. That's it. Now make up your mind. We either have the papers signed before noon tomorrow or I'm swearing out a warrant."

I sat and looked at him for a minute. But I didn't need to make a decision. It had been made all ready. It was seething in my blood and flashing hotly across my brain.

"Have you mentioned any of this to another living soul?" I asked.

"No."

"If I make this sacrifice," I said, "I'll be doing it to keep my name absolutely clean."

"I know that," he said. "I know it's my lever, my weapon, Enos. Made up your mind?"

I stood and nodded. "Come out to the house tonight. About eight. I have an errand to do, but Doreen will be there. You can chin with her if I'm late. Have a drink, if you like. I guess we might as well settle this with as little rancor as possible."

"That's sensible talk, Enos. I'm glad you're taking it this well."

"What can I do?"

"Not a damn thing," he said in huge enjoyment. "Don't worry. I'll be there. Waiting for you."

Early that evening I drove over to Macon to see a cousin who had been ill for some time. He was surprised and glad to see me. We made small talk for an hour or so. Business. My marriage. The weather. I left with a promise that I'd bring

Doreen and we'd have a real old-fashioned Georgia watermelon cutting sometime soon.

I was back in Mulberry by nine-thirty. Driving through the elm and maple-lined back streets in the darkness I felt tension building in me. There was a thickness in my throat and a tingling in the tips of my fingers. The large, old houses, set beyond wide lawns, were peaceful, serene.

At the edge of town I turned left, picked up the sideroad that ran to The Willows, the fine old place I'd bought for Doreen.

I drove down the dark tunnel with weeping willows on either side. Then my headlights picked up the house, the wide veranda, the white columns. A portion of the downstairs was lighted.

I parked in the driveway beside the house, cut the lights, opened the glove compartment, and transferred the .38 revolver to the side pocket of my coat.

I found Sam and Doreen in the front parlor of the house. A pig about everything, Sam had partaken well of the brandy from the bottle on the sideboard.

His eyes were heavy-lidded, his face reddish purple with blood. He looked up at me and grinned. "You took long enough, Enos."

"But I'm here now," I said. "Everything all set, I suppose." Doreen had risen to stand behind Sam. She nodded. Sam said everything was set. His words meant nothing. Her nod was what interested me.

Only minutes of life remained to Sam now. I tried to keep from thinking about it. My knees were weak, and my mouth was so dry I wondered if I could get the next words out.

"Okay," I said. "Come on and we'll get it over with."

Doreen started from the room. Her eyes were glinting as if sheened with satin.

Sam sat a moment, shrugged, and got up.

We went down a corridor. Doreen opened a door on a dark room.

We entered and I heeled the door closed. I palmed the gun and pulled it out of my pocket.

Doreen switched on the light.

Sam started. "Hell, this isn't an office or a den—it's a bedroom!"

I heard Doreen breathing. "That's right, Sam," she said softly.

He turned to look at her, and I let him have it. Another five seconds and the last of my nerve would have been gone. I had to do it then.

The bullet hit him in the left temple, ranged upward, and left a hole the size of a half dollar when it came out of his skull.

And yet he didn't die immediately. He lived for perhaps five seconds. He twitched, the breath rattled in his throat. He half-turned himself on the carpet where he lay. Then he was dead.

Doreen had watched every bit of it. She was half-kneeling, to watch the final flick of light fade from his face. She rose, and in her face and eyes was a rapt expression.

I felt like shaking at her, yelling at her.

She turned her face toward me, her eyes trying to focus through the fever in them. She didn't seem to know where she was for a moment. Then she started laughing, low and soft.

"Cut it out!" I said. "Doreen—stop it!"

She brushed her glossy hair away from her temples with both hands. "Hello, Enos. Dear Enos. I feel higher than the proverbial Georgia pine right now. Did you see it, the way death came creeping over him? He fought, Enos. Every cell of him wanted to live. But we had that power over him, didn't we? The power to smash the life out of him . . ."

This was the worst moment yet. I felt sweat running down the sides of my face.

I grabbed her by the shoulder and slapped her across the cheek. She didn't seem to feel the blow, but her eyes cleared a little.

"There's still a lot to be done," I said. "We haven't much time."

I ripped her blouse across the shoulder and struck her again so that my finger marks were on her cheek. Doreen said nothing.

"I've got to make the phone call now," I said. "Sure you're okay?"

She nodded. "Give me a cigarette."

I gave her a cigarette. "Come on," I said.

She was still looking at Sam over her shoulder as I pulled her from the room.

In the front parlor, I steadied myself and dialed Dolph Crowder's number.

The sheriff answered on the second ring.

"Dolph," I said, "this is Enos Mavery. I think you better come out to The Willows right away."

"What's the trouble, Enos?"

"I've just shot and killed Sam Fickens."

I heard him take an explosive breath. Then he said in a tight but quiet tone, "I'll be there in five minutes."

He was as good as his word. In five minutes he was pounding on the front door. I had used the time to burn and flush into non-existence the papers Sam had brought with him tonight, the papers giving him full control of the company.

I gave Doreen a glance. Her eyes were clear now, her face composed.

I opened the front door just as Dolph started to knock again. He was a thin, long-faced man. Ice blue eyes. Long, sharp nose, razor keen jaw.

"Where is he, Enos?"

"In my wife's bedroom," I said. "Here's the gun."

I handed him the revolver. He looked at it, sniffed at it, dropped it in his pocket and stepped into the hallway. He nodded a greeting to Doreen, not missing the finger marks on her face, the tear in her blouse.

"Which way?" he asked.

"I'll show you," I said. Doreen started with us. "You stay here," I told her.

"Enos, I . . ."

"Stay here!" I didn't know exactly why. But I didn't want her to look at the dead man again. More precisely, I feared, for some reason, having Dolph see her if she should look at him.

Dolph and I went back to the bedroom.

Dolph stood looking down at Sam for several seconds. "You did one hell of a complete and messy job, Enos."

"I meant to—at the time. When I came in here and saw what he was trying to do I didn't think of but one thing, Dolph. The same thing you and any other man around here would think of."

"I see," he said softly. "Better tell me the rest of it."

"There isn't much to tell," I said. "Sam knew I was going to Macon tonight. He came here in my absence on a pretext he wanted to talk to me about business. He was already pretty well boiled. My wife let him in—after all, he was my business partner. He had a brandy in the front parlor, she told me. Then he began to want to get cozy. When she ordered him out, he got pretty vile and coarse with his talk. To escape him, she came back here. She couldn't get the door locked, he was too close behind her, telling her what a fool she was for marrying a homely mug like me, how much more he could do for her, how many nights he'd lain awake just thinking about her."

I paused for breath. Dolph waited patiently.

"You ought to be able to piece the rest of it together," I said. "I heard her scream. She was trying to get away from Sam when I came in the room. I tell you, Dolph, I didn't know what the hell I was doing. I heard him laughing at her, telling her to be nice, to be sweet to him . . . that kind of stuff."

"I went for him. To tell you the truth, I meant to strangle him. He shoved me to one side. I was off balance and stumbled against the bureau. I don't remember getting the gun . . . it was in the bureau drawer. I don't even remember shooting him, but I did. One minute he was there; then he was on the floor and I was standing over him cussing him for everything I could lay my tongue to. Then I saw he was dead and that knocked me back into kilter. I phoned you—and that's it."

"You have any trouble with Sam before this?" Dolph Crowder asked.

"No. I never liked him much as a person. But who did?"

Dolph nodded. "The town thought of him as a pig. A greedy one at that. A sort of smug, self-sufficient man who figured anything he wanted was his just because he was Sam Fickens."

"I know all that, Dolph. But I never let him get under my skin before. We had a growing company. We were making money. I didn't care too much what he was like."

"He ever come around here before when you were gone?"

"Once or twice," I said. "Doreen told me. She didn't like him. Said he gave her the willies."

"How about when you were here?"

"Come to think of it, he's been a lot more sociable since I got married . . . But I don't think he'd have pulled this act tonight if he hadn't been drunk. I swear, Dolph, I'm sorry now I did it. I should have just beat him up and thrown him out. But for a few seconds there I didn't know what I was doing . . . coming home . . . hearing her scream . . . walking in to see him . . . ."

"Don't dwell on it," Dolph said. "I'll have to take you into town."

"Yeah, I guess so."

"Your wife will have to make a statement, of course."

"I know you're just doing your job, Dolph."

I had a private cell in the local pokey that night. Dolph's wife brought me a fine breakfast next morning, country ham, redeye gravy, grits swimming in butter, eggs, hot biscuits, steaming coffee.

That breakfast did more than fill my stomach. It fed my mental state. It told me the whole town was buzzing—with the talk in my favor.

I was charged with manslaughter and out on bail before noon. Folks in town did their best to talk and act as if I had no charge hanging over me. Doreen was relaxed, in good spirits, contented as a cat that's had a big bowl of warm milk.

I went on trial in circuit court the fifth day of the following month. When the trial opened, I had my lawyer ask the judge if I could make a statement to the court. The request was granted.

I got to my feet, conscious of the packed courtroom. I walked quietly to the stand, the same Enos Mavery they'd known all my life, the Enos who paused to crack a joke or a fruit jar of corn. The Enos who could talk to a dirt farmer as well as a fellow member of our country club.

I was sworn in and sat down in the witness chair.

"Folks," I said, "I don't see much point in dragging this thing out. We're all taxpayers and every hour this court sits costs us money.

"Clay Rogers is a fine prosecutor. I ought to know. I went to school with him. He's going to tell you that I shot Sam Fickens. Now old Clay ain't givin' to lying, and I don't deny it. I sure did shoot him—and I guess I might do it again under the same circumstances. I came home that night and found the dirty skunk using his brute strength on my wife. I went as crazy as a loon, got my hands on a gun, and pulled the trigger. I didn't try to hide a thing, and I'm not trying to now. I got Dolph Crowder on the phone soon as I saw what I had done, and I'm here now to tell you I did it. The man entered my home under a pretext, followed my wife when she tried to get away, forced himself into the bedroom—and I'm just thankful I got there when I did. If that makes me a criminal, then justice in the state of Georgia ain't what I've always thought it to be . . . I thank you."

There was more testimony. From Dolph, Doc Joyner, who is coroner in his spare time, from several people who had known Sam. And from Doreen. She simply backed up what I had said. She was dressed as always, attractively, making no pretense that she wasn't a beautiful woman.

The jury was out for an hour.

I walked out of the courtroom a free and rich man.

Doreen and I sold out a few weeks later. She was restless, and I had no real desire to live in Mulberry longer.

We toured Florida and decided on the Coquina Beach place. For awhile it appeared life might settle to normal, but when we were through the decorating, the hundred and one things in establishing a new residence that kept us busy, Doreen became restless again.

I tried everything. Cocktail parties—they were too vapid. Another hunting trip—but a bleeding animal held no more interest for her.

Doreen hired a yard man last week and fixed up quarters over the garage for him. But we don't really need a full-time yard man. I looked into his background. A bum. From the downtown waterfront and wino jungles. Comes from nowhere.

But I suspect where he is going. It's been building in Doreen for quite awhile now. And I don't know what to do. If I warned the yard man, somebody else would be marked.

Somebody's going to die—to provide a thrill for Doreen. Nothing less will calm that mounting restlessness.

I certainly am afraid to go home tonight.

Stranger in the House
Theodore Pratt

January 1957

H er regular cleaning woman had not appeared that morning, and by the time
Mrs. Belding decided she was not coming, and had called the employment
agency to send over another to her apartment, it was nearly ten o'clock.

The woman the agency sent was a big creature. She was so tall that she stooped,
giving her broad, harsh face a rather ridiculous look as it peered out from under a
crazy, flopping little hat set on a mass of straggly gray hair. Her blood-shot gray
eyes lighted up, blazing, upon seeing Mrs. Belding, as if in fierce anticipation at
working for so lovely a lady.

She was so formidable in appearance that Mrs. Belding was a little disturbed
at the idea of having her in the apartment all day. She had heard stories of how
strange servants had robbed their employers. She hesitated as she looked at the
woman. But when she thought of the reputation of the employment agency and saw
again the woman's funny hat, she asked the woman if she were willing, considering
how late she had come, to work until six instead of five.

The woman boomed out readily, in a deep and husky voice, "Sure, Ma'm, sure
am." She didn't smile, but seemed deathly serious, as if sincerity might be a passion
with her. Her name, she said, was Hattie.

Mrs. Belding regretted her decision a little when Hattie had prepared herself
for work by simply setting her hat on a chair in the hall. Without her crazy hat
perched on her frizzly head, the woman no longer seemed amusing. She was now
almost threatening. But when Mrs. Belding explained what was to be done, and
Hattie had started, attacking the tasks with a surprising willingness and speed, Mrs.
Belding decided that her fears were groundless.

At the same time, it occurred to her, for the first time, that she would have to
stay in the apartment all day. It wouldn't do to leave it in charge of an unknown
cleaning woman. Mrs. Belding had meant to shop for some new stockings to go
with the evening dress she would wear that night when she dined out with friends.
She considered doing her shopping anyway, wondering if she could trust Hattie.

She thought of calling up the employment agency and asking about Hattie.
But agencies couldn't know everything about the people they sent, and besides she
couldn't very well make the inquiry with Hattie listening. She saw Hattie moving
the piano to clean in back of it, thrusting the heavy instrument aside as if it were
little more than a heavy chair. She decided that the old stockings, mended, would
have to do.

Mrs. Belding watched Hattie closely, but the only thing she saw was the
woman's strength. She had difficulty composing herself, or finding a comfortable
place to sit, as Hattie bustled about, doing work in a few minutes that ordinarily
took the better part of an hour to accomplish. It rather alarmed Mrs. Belding. It
made her feel nervous. But she reflected that ability, speed, willingness, and
strength were no qualities to complain about in a cleaning woman. She had been

accustomed to laziness and sometimes downright shirking—such as the regular woman not coming at all today and sending no message.

She felt angry with the regular woman, and friendly toward Hattie, resolving to keep Hattie permanently if she turned out to be all right in other respects. She examined the work that had already been done, and was pleased.

If Mrs. Belding watched Hattie, and contrived to stay much in the same room with her, Hattie followed the same tactics herself. She didn't seem to mind being supervised at all, but appeared to like having Mrs. Belding with her, and several times followed her about. She kept looking at Mrs. Belding, as if in deep admiration, but this did not interfere with her work. She went steadily about it all that morning, almost grimly, and silently—except when an especially energetic outburst made her pant a little.

At noon, when Mrs. Belding began preparing lunch, Hattie suggested, "You let me fix it, Mrs. Belding." And when she was told she could do so if she wished, she said with serious gratitude, "Yes, Ma'm."

Hattie's meal was dainty and delicious. She served it to Mrs. Belding as if she had been long a retainer in the household. She was highly solicitous, several times interrupting her own lunch, which she was having in the kitchen, to come in and inquire if everything were satisfactory. She hovered about anxiously wanting to please. Mrs. Belding had never before experienced such attention and devotion in the short course of a meal.

Hattie was almost loving in her service. Mrs. Belding complimented her and the woman replied, from a voice choked with emotion, "Sure, Ma'm."

By this time Mrs. Belding was assured that Hattie did not mean to rob her. If the woman meant to, she would certainly have attempted it before this, instead of working so hard and efficiently all the time. She looked at Hattie's face and found it drawn. Trying to make a good impression and overdoing the effort, thought Mrs. Belding. Poor thing.

Mrs. Belding did not object when, in the afternoon, Hattie slowed down considerably and became talkative. The woman had started on the closets. And when she came to the one in Mrs. Belding's bedroom, she spent some time in it. She busied herself at examining the clothes there, sometimes touching them, as with envious hands.

"You got fine clothes, Mrs. Belding," she announced.

Her voice went through the room, through the whole apartment, resounding against the walls. "All women's clothes, too. No man's clothes here. You don't have a man, Mrs. Belding?"

Mrs. Belding smiled at this inquisitiveness that had been so long in coming out, and replied, "No, Hattie."

A little later, Hattie observed the things that had been laid out on the bed and said, "You got your evening dress ready. I'll bet you got a man coming to call for you tonight, ain't you, Mrs. Belding?" And Hattie touched the dress softly.

"No, I . . ."

Something in the way Hattie asked this made Mrs. Belding check herself. This was no business of Hattie's. Even if Hattie seemed all right, possibly it was not a good plan to admit that there was no man about the place. She tried to cover up her admission. "Yes," she said, "there is a gentleman calling for me later."

Hattie laughed. It was a long, throaty laugh, full and unrestrained. Caressing the clothes with big, affectionate hands, and stooping over them, she said, "I like to imagine how you'll look in that dress, Mrs. Belding. I sure like to work for a beautiful woman like you, Mrs. Belding."

Hattie's laugh remained in the room, echoing, for minutes after she left it.

Mrs. Belding had been disturbed by the whole thing. But she, finally, decided that Hattie's comments on the clothes had simply been in the nature of a hint that she be given some old clothes, either those of a woman, or of a man. Cleaning women were always wanting clothes, and asking for them by admiring those of the people for whom they worked. That was the way they obtained much of their clothing.

Mrs. Belding laughed herself when she pictured Hattie in any of her cast-off things; they wouldn't cover half the woman. But then, maybe she wanted them for a sister—or a friend.

Late in the afternoon, Mrs. Belding was sitting on the stool before her dressing-table mending a run in the top of one of the stockings she was to wear that evening. She had not heard Hattie at her work for some time. She listened, and when a number of minutes went by and there was still no noise, she rose and went out to see what Hattie was doing.

Hattie was not in the living room. She was not in the hall nor in the kitchen. Mystified, Mrs. Belding glanced at the closed bathroom door. The woman must be there. She called her name.

From behind the door, muffled, but still booming, came Hattie's voice. "Yes, Ma'm, you want me, Mrs. Belding?"

"I didn't know where you were," Mrs. Belding said, speaking in the direction of the bathroom.

"I'll be ready in a minute, Mrs. Belding," Hattie said from behind the door.

Mrs. Belding went back to her bedroom. Something about Hattie's reply bothered her, but she didn't know what it was. She thought Hattie had finished in the bathroom, but evidently she hadn't.

Mrs. Belding took up the mending of her stocking again. She listened for Hattie, but heard nothing. When a longer time than before went by without any noise being made, she called out as she had before, but this time from where she sat.

There was no answer. She called again. Still there was no reply. She wondered what Hattie could be doing. Whatever it was, she was taking a long time about it. Mrs. Belding wanted her to get through, for she meant to take a bath in a few minutes. Surely the woman must have heard her. She put down her mending, got up, and went out into the hall.

"Hattie!" she called. There was no reply. "Hattie!" Her call was nearly a cry this time. But no answer came from the bathroom. Nor was there any sound of movement.

What had happened to the woman? She must still be in the bathroom. Or had she sneaked out, perhaps to let someone else in the apartment?

Mrs. Belding turned quickly about, looking. There was no one to be seen. There was no sound in the apartment.

She took a step toward the bathroom door, then stopped, cautiously. It was indeed strange.

"Hattie!" she called again.

Only silence answered her.

Mrs. Belding stood there, her heart beating fast. The thought came to her that Hattie had left without saying anything, without collecting her wages. While trying to figure out why the woman would do such a thing, she looked for Hattie's hat.

The crazy little thing was still on the chair. Hattie was still in the apartment.

Mrs. Belding wanted to call in a neighbor, or the building superintendent, or a policeman, to help her investigate. But she hesitated at the prospect of raising a hue and cry over what might be nothing.

In her irresolution at deciding what to do, another thought, a more logical solution, came to her. She remembered the drawn look on Hattie's face, and how Hattie had slowed down at the work, as though tired. The woman had probably gone beyond the capacity of her strength and fainted in the bathroom. That was it, of course. That was why she hadn't answered.

Concerned, and a little irritated, Mrs. Belding went to the door and opened it. Hattie was not to be seen. Mrs. Belding stepped into the bathroom.

As soon as she was well into the room, the door swung closed behind her, snapping shut with a sharp click. There was a movement there, and she whirled around quickly to see what it was.

An utterly naked man, who looked gigantic, stood against the door.

In the confusion and shock of her first horror, Mrs. Belding looked about for Hattie. All that was to be seen of her were a heap of clothing and a wig of straggly gray hair lying on the floor. Other than that, there was only the man standing there starkly nude, exposed and horribly ready, staring down at her from his blood-shot eyes which were now wide and burning.

Mrs. Belding's lips parted to emit a scream that her terror had so far denied her, but, before she could get it out a firm, large hot hand was placed over her mouth, twisting her about so that the back of her head was pressed against a hard sweaty chest that was breathing fast, and another hand began to tear viciously at the clothing on her shoulder.

Enough Rope for Two
Clark Howard

February 1957

The Greyhound bus pulled into the Los Angeles main terminal at noon. Joe Kedzie got off and walked out into the sunlight of a city he had not seen in ten years. Instinctively, he headed for Main Street. He walked slowly, recalling how the stores and clothes and cars had all changed. No more double-breasted suits. Very few black cars—mostly red and yellow and pink and chartreuse now. The stores were all modern, larger, with a lot of glass. And the skirts—a little longer maybe, but tight in the right places. He pushed the thought of women from his mind. There would be time for them later. After he had his hundred grand.

At Main he turned the corner and began to pass the cheap bars and honky tonks he had known so well. He remembered the shooting gallery, the penny arcade, the strip joints, the café where the pushers made—and probably still make—their headquarters. This part of the world will never change, he thought. If I was sent up for another ten years, it would still be the same when I got back again.

Between a bar and a Chinese hand laundry was the entrance to the Main Line Hotel. Kedzie opened the door and walked up the six steps to the lobby. A young, pimply-faced man was behind the desk. He held a racing form and studied it sleepily. Kedzie stood at the desk until it became apparent that the youth was ignoring him; he then reached across the counter and yanked the racing form out of his hand. The clerk jumped up, his face flushing.

"What's the idea!" he demanded.

"Just want a little service," said Kedzie calmly, laying the paper on the desk. "Does Madge Griffin still live here?"

The desk clerk tried to act tough. "Who wants to know?"

"Don't play games with me, punk," said Kedzie harshly, "or I'll break your arm! Does Madge Griffin live here or doesn't she?"

"She lives here," said the clerk, scared now. "Room two-twelve."

Kedzie nodded. He left the desk and walked across the lobby and up a flight of stairs. Two-twelve was the last room at the end of the dingy hallway. He stood before the door and lighted a cigarette, then rapped softly. Madge's voice came through the door.

"Who is it?"

"Errol Flynn. Open up."

He heard her walk across the room; then the door opened. She stood framed in the doorway, her eyes widening, plainly startled.

"Joe!"

"Hello, Madge."

She moved aside, as he moved forward, to let him enter. The room was small, not as crummy as he had expected, but still crummy enough. He walked to a chair and sat down. She watched him curiously for a moment, then closed the door and leaned back against it.

"How've you been, Madge?" he asked in his matter-of-fact tone, as if he had seen her a month ago instead of ten years ago.

"I've been getting along, Joe. How have you been?"

He grunted, but did not answer. He looked her over, taking his time. Ten years older, but she still had it, and just enough of it wherever it belonged. He decided that she was just a little heavier in the hips than when she had been his girl. Still—and this thought amused him—she wasn't then, and still wasn't now, the kind you would want if you had a hundred grand.

"How'd you know where to find me, Joe?" she asked suddenly.

"Just a guess. I figured you'd come back here. It's just about your speed."

"What's that supposed to mean?" she demanded, her eyes flashing angrily.

"Forget it, baby," he said easily, and to change the subject added, "have you got a drink?"

She walked over to the closet and took a nearly full bottle of gin from the shelf. "There's nothing to mix it with," she said. "Want it straight?"

He shook his head. "It would probably knock me out. Forget it."

She put the bottle back on the shelf. Kedzie crushed out his cigarette and lighted a fresh one. It figured, he thought. A bottle of gin in the closet. Madge never could stand the stuff. But gin was always Maxie's drink. He's not far away. Just wait and be patient. He'll show up.

Madge walked over to the bed and sat down. They began to talk, idly, pleasantly. Two people have a lot to talk about after ten years.

Kedzie waited for her to mention Maxie, but she did not. That convinced him that she knew where he was. And the minute she left the room and got to a telephone, Maxie would know that he, Kedzie, was back in town.

They talked until five o'clock. Finally she asked, "What are you going to do now, Joe?"

He decided to play it straight. "What do you mean?"

"I mean, have you got a place to stay tonight?"

"No, not yet. I'm so used to having my bunk waiting for me, I guess I forgot that I have to take care of those things myself now." The bait had been dropped. He waited for her to snap at it. After a moment's hesitation, she did.

"Why don't you let me get you a room here, Joe? Then you won't have to bother looking for a place."

"Well, I don't know, Madge. I don't—"

"Look, I'll tell you what—I'll go down to the desk and get you a room, and then go down the street to Jasi's and get a pizza and some cold beer. You can lie down and rest while I'm gone; then when I get back, we can eat right here in the room. You looked tired, Joe. Why don't you take off your coat and lie down for a while."

"Well, I am pretty tired. First bus ride in ten years, you know."

"You just rest, Joe." She picked up her purse quickly. "I'll only be a couple minutes."

When she was gone, he took off his coat and stretched out on the bed. It won't be long now, he thought. Five minutes from now she'll be in a phone booth. Maxie should be here by eight o'clock.

Madge returned an hour later with the food. Kedzie pulled a small writing desk up to the bed and put the pizza on it. He sat down on the side of the bed and began to eat. Madge opened two cans of beer and brought them to the table. She drew up a chair opposite him and sat down.

Kedzie ate sparingly and left half the beer in the can. He was not accustomed to highly seasoned food, much less alcohol. Later, when he had his money, he would eat only the best.

It was nearly seven when they finished eating. Kedzie lighted a cigarette and walked over to the open window and the lights of Main Street.

Madge walked over and stood beside him. "What are you thinking about, Joe?" she asked.

"Just the lights, down there—how many times I dreamed about them while I was in the joint."

"Was it really bad, Joe—all those years?" Her voice was gentle, sincere. It was a tone that Joe Kedzie did not accept coming from her.

"No," he said sarcastically, "it was a hell of a lot of fun. I wanted to stay, but they wouldn't let me. Said you had to leave when your time was up."

Once again he saw the anger flash in her eyes. He didn't care. She had served her purpose as far as he was concerned, for she had told Maxie where to find him.

"You always were like that, Joe!" she said hotly. "Always crawling into your shell, always keeping everything to yourself, never trusting anybody. You haven't changed a bit in ten years!"

He looked at her coldly, feeling the urge to slam his fist into her face. He wanted to tell her he hadn't grown stupid in ten years, that he wasn't so blind he hadn't figured out she and Maxie had caused him to fall after the payroll job. He wanted to scream out to her that he had thought about that possibility even before the job. He wanted to let her know the reason they hadn't pulled off their little double-cross completely was because he had figured out another hiding place for the money beforehand, had put it in a place only he knew about.

Kedzie was at the point of cursing her, when a knock sounded at the door. A moment's hesitation, apprehension, and Madge walked over to the door, opening it.

For the second time that day, Joe Kedzie looked upon a face he had not seen in ten years. Maxie had not changed much. He still looked like what he was—a sharpie. You can spot a guy like him anywhere, thought Kedzie. Handsome, always smiling, shifty-eyed, overdressed. The kind that's always on the make for a fast buck.

"Hello, Joe-boy," said Maxie, with a false air of friendliness.

"Hello, Maxie." You son of a bitch, thought Kedzie, you took ten years away from me!

Maxie stepped in and closed the door. He walked casually to the bed and sat down. Madge moved to a chair in the corner, away from both men. Kedzie dropped his cigarette out the window and sat back against the sill.

"Heard you were out, Joe-boy," said Maxie. "Thought I better look you up before you left town."

"What makes you think I'm leaving town?" asked Kedzie calmly.

Maxie flashed the wide smile that was his trademark. He leaned back on his elbows. "Just thought you might be heading back toward El Paso. Thought maybe you might have left something around there someplace."

"The only thing I left in El Paso was a day of glory for the local cops."

"Nothing else?"

"Nothing that you've got any interest in, buddy."

Maxie sat up quickly. His jaw tightened and both hands closed into fists. "Look, Joe," he said harshly, "I've waited for that dough as long as you have! I've got a right to my share!"

Kedzie remained calm. He casually lighted another cigarette. "The only difference is, Maxie," he said easily, "is that you waited outside while I waited inside."

"That's the breaks, Joe." Maxie stood up. His face was serious, challenging. "The money's still only half yours."

Kedzie looked down at the floor. There was a hundred thousand dollars riding on this play. There was no sense in risking it all with Maxie at this late date. He thought of the tail that had followed him from prison, that had expected to be taken right to the dough; the trouble he'd had throwing the tail clear off the track. After all that, it made sense to play it easy for a while longer.

"I'll lay it on the line for you, Maxie," he said. "I figure I'm entitled to that dough more than you. I figure I've earned it by taking the rap for the job. So I don't intend to split that package with you or anybody else."

Anger showed plainly on Maxie's face. Got to make it good, thought Kedzie. If this doesn't work I'll have to kill him right now, right here. He continued talking.

"The only thing that's holding me back is that I need a stake to get to the dough. I need some cash-a couple of hundred at least—and a car. I want some clothes, so I can get out of this burlap I'm wearing."

Maxie's anger had clearly changed from anger to curiosity. It's working, thought Kedzie.

"I'll make a deal with you," Kedzie went on. "You get me a car, a couple of hundred bucks, and some decent clothes, and I'll cut you in for a quarter of the dough. You'll get twenty-five grand, no strings attached. How about it?"

Maxie looked thoughtfully at Kedzie, thinking that it wouldn't be easy to force Kedzie to tell him where the money was hidden.

"I'll go along with that, Joe-boy," he said, and added quickly, "—but only on one condition."

"Name it," said Kedzie.

"I stay with you every minute from here on out, and we go for the money together."

"How about the car," asked Kedzie, "and the other things?"

"I'll fix it so Madge can get everything you want. You and me will stay right here in this room until we're ready to go for the money."

"It's a deal," said Kedzie. "And if you can get what I need tonight, we'll leave in the morning."

"The sooner the better," grinned Maxie eagerly. "Madge can go out and rent a car tonight. On the way back she can stop at my place and pick up clothes for you."

"How about the two hundred?"

Maxie smiled. "I've got three bills in my pocket right now. A long shot came in at Hollywood Park today. So we're all set, Joe-boy. Two days from now we can be in El Paso."

It was Joe Kedzie's turn to smile. "We're not going to El Paso, partner," he said slyly. "Surprised?"

Maxie's grin vanished and suspicion shadowed his face. "What do you mean?" he asked quickly.

"The dough isn't in El Paso. It's in New Mexico—right out in the middle of nowhere."

Suddenly Maxie began to laugh, somewhat hysterically. He laughed long and loud. He was thinking of all the hours and days he had spent asking questions in El Paso, trying to follow every move Joe Kedzie had made, trying to trace where Kedzie had hidden the money.

Joe Kedzie also began to laugh, but he was not thinking about the past, only the future.

At ten minutes before eight the next morning, Joe Kedzie and Maxie walked out of the Main Line Hotel onto Main Street. Kedzie had shed the rough grey suit the prison had discharged him in, and now wore slacks and a short-sleeved sport shirt. On his arm he held one of Maxie's sport coats. Maxie, following him, carried a small tan suitcase with their extra clothes.

They walked down the block to a green Ford sedan Madge had rented for them. Maxie unlocked the car and tossed the suitcase on the back seat.

"You drive," said Kedzie. "I don't have a license." Maxie nodded and slid behind the wheel. He turned the ignition on and started the motor. Before he could shift into gear Kedzie spoke again. "How about the two hundred, Maxie?"

Maxie looked at him oddly. "I've got it," he said flatly.

"Give it to me," said Kedzie.

Maxie shook his head in anger and disgust, but he drew a wallet from his inside coat pocket and counted out two hundred dollars in tens and twenties. He tossed the bills, with a display of anger, on the seat between them. Kedzie gathered them up, folded them neatly in half, and put them in his shirt pocket.

They drove out to Sunset Boulevard, then swung onto the Ramona Freeway. Kedzie sat back and relaxed, feeling fresh and invigorated on his first free morning in ten years. He ignored Maxie completely and interested himself in looking out the window at the stores and the cars and the girls.

The car sped along, through Monterey Park, Covina, past Pomona, and on into San Bernardino. By eleven o'clock they had reached Indio. They stopped for gas and Kedzie got out and picked up a roadmap. They left Indio on Route 99, heading south.

At one o'clock they pulled into El Centro. Maxie stopped at the first highway restaurant outside town and they went in and ordered lunch. Kedzie borrowed a pencil from the waitress and spread the roadmap out on the table . . . He began to figure their mileage. When he was finished, he said, "It's a little over three hundred to Tucson. If we drive straight through, we should make it by nine tonight."

"How far do we have to go past Tucson?" asked Maxie irritably.

"Not far," said Kedzie.

"Getting anxious, Maxie?" Joe Kedzie asked, smiling.

Maxie cursed as he got up from the table. He went over to a pinball machine and dropped a coin into it. Kedzie watched him, thinking, If you'd spent the last ten years where I did, rat, you'd have more patience.

They pulled into Tucson, tired and dirty, at nine-fifteen that night. All along the highway they saw NO VACANCY signs lighting their path. Finally, five miles past the eastern city limits, they found a motel room.

Maxie registered at the office and they dropped the suitcase off at the room. Then they drove back into Tucson for something to eat. It was nearly midnight when they returned to the motel and went to bed.

By eight o'clock the next morning, they were on the road again. Kedzie decided he'd take a chance and drive; he was tired of just sitting. Fifty miles southeast of Tucson they turned off onto Route 666 and headed north. The highway made a wide, sweeping arc around the Dos Cabezas mountain range, then swung south again. Shortly before eleven o'clock they crossed the State Line into New Mexico. The first roadsign they saw said: Lordsburg 20 Miles.

"We're about there," said Kedzie casually. "It's about an hour's drive after we pass Lordsburg." Maxie grunted. "We'll have to stop in Lordsburg," continued Kedzie. "There's some things I have to buy."

Maxie glanced at him suspiciously. "Like what, for instance?" he asked irritably.

"Like a long piece of rope, for instance."

"What the hell do we need a rope for?" demanded Maxie.

"You want the money, don't you? Well, we'll need a rope to get it. The package is at the bottom of a forty-foot well that must've gone dry a long time ago."

Maxie's mouth dropped open. "Well, I'll be damned!"

"We'll need some other things, too—a flashlight, maybe a small shovel in case we have to do some digging. I guess a couple of feet of sand could have blown down that well in all this time."

In Lordsburg they stopped at the first large General Store they came to. Inside, Kedzie asked the clerk for sixty feet of strong rope. The clerk led him into the storeroom and showed him several large bolts of rope. Kedzie picked out the sturdiest he could find and the clerk began to measure off sixty feet. Kedzie walked back out into the store and picked up a small hand shovel from a display rack. He handed it to Maxie. When the clerk brought the heavy roll of rope out, Kedzie took this, too, and handed it to Maxie.

"Put this stuff in the car," he said easily. "I'll get a flashlight and be right out."

Maxie turned and carried the things out of the store. After Kedzie had picked out a flashlight and batteries, he walked across the room to a glass showcase. He appeared casual as he looked over the merchandise. When the clerk approached him, he said, "Let's see one of those target pistols."

The clerk opened the case and took out a medium-sized, black automatic pistol. "This is the Sports Standard," he said, going into his sales pitch. "One of the best made. Only weighs half a pound. Shoots .22 shorts or longs. A real accurate piece for targets or small game."

"How much for this one?" asked Kedzie.

"That's the six-and-three-quarter barrel. It'll run you forty-four fifty plus tax."

"Okay," said Kedzie quickly, glancing toward the front door. "Give me a box of shells too, and then figure up the whole bill."

Outside, Maxie closed the door of the car and walked back to the store to see what was keeping Kedzie. When he looked through the window, he saw Kedzie forcing bullets into a magazine. A new target pistol lay on the counter before him. Maxie's face turned white and his hands began to tremble. He watched Kedzie shove the loaded magazine into the grip of the weapon and tuck the gun in his belt, and under his shirt.

Maxie turned and walked back to the car, feeling sick. He opened the door and slid under the wheel. He looked at the dashboard. Kedzie had done all the driving that morning; he had the car keys. He knows, thought Maxie helplessly. He knows I fingered him after the payroll job and now he's going to kill me for it. He never meant to give me a split of the dough. The whole deal was a trick to get me out here so he could kill me!

Suddenly a thought occurred to Maxie, a possible way out.

He turned in the seat and looked back at the rope and shovel lying on the floorboard. Quickly he reached back and opened the suitcase. He fumbled through the soiled clothing and drew out his shaving kit. His hands shook as he unzipped the case.

When Kedzie got back to the car, he found Maxie sitting calmly behind the wheel. He got in and handed Maxie the car keys. "Take Route 80," he said, "south out of town and keep going until I tell you where to turn."

The highway ran in an almost straight line past Lordsburg. It was a thin grey streak surrounded on either side by dry, flat land. The brilliant sun overhead moved up to a point directly in the center of the sky as the noon hour approached. It cast its heat down onto the sands of the Hidalgo country and made all living creatures look for shade. By twelve o'clock the temperature had risen to a hundred and one.

Inside the car, Joe Kedzie sat sideways with one hand inside his shirt and against the cold metal of the gun. Maxie kept his eyes straight ahead, squinting against the sun. They moved along in silence, passing no other traffic. Kedzie had also taken this into account in his plan. It was common in the desert for people to avoid being out in the noonday heat. Kedzie had counted on having the desert all to themselves.

A half-hour later, they passed a wide place in the road called Separ. Kedzie had remembered that name for ten years—had kept it in his mind by spelling it backwards; what it spelled backwards made it easier to remember.

"You'll come to a turn in the road up ahead," he said. "About three miles past that is where we turn off. First road on the right."

Maxie didn't answer. He had not spoken a word since Lordsburg. When they came to the road Kedzie had indicated, he turned off the highway. The blacktop was pitted, rough. Maxie looked at Kedzie for instructions. "Just keep going," said Kedzie. "It's not far now."

They bumped along for eight miles. The terrain around them began to rise slightly in places, forming low knolls and finally small hills. Kedzie watched the mileage dial intently, glancing ahead from time to time for familiar landmarks. Finally he saw the old dirt road cutting off at an angle from the black top. "Turn there," he said, pointing ahead.

Maxie turned off. The dirt road was smoother than the blacktop had been and the car settled down to a level ride again. The road curved down into a washed-out gulley that had once been excavated for mining. Kedzie watched through the rear window until the black-top passed from sight. Then he turned to Maxie and said, "Pull over, partner."

When the car stopped, Kedzie got out quickly. Maxie stepped out on the driver's side. The two men faced each other across the hood of the car.

"You know, don't you, Joe?" said Maxie simply.

"Yeah, Maxie, I know." Kedzie drew the automatic from beneath his shirt and held it loosely.

"I don't know what made me do it, Joe," began Maxie. "I just—"

"I'll tell you why you did it, rat," interrupted Kedzie harshly. "Two things— Madge and a hundred grand!"

"I don't know what came over me, Joe," continued Maxie desperately. "I just didn't realize—"

"Never mind!" snapped Kedzie. He waved the gun toward the car. "Get that rope and shovel out."

Maxie dragged the heavy rope out, threw it over his shoulder, and picked up the shovel. Kedzie directed him down a narrow path, following a few feet behind. The path ended at the entrance to a mine shaft which was near the gulley bottom. Twenty feet off to one side was the dry well. It had once been surrounded by a three-foot brick and clay wall, but most of the wall had deteriorated and fallen. Only one beam remained of a pair that once had held a small roof over the then precious supply of water. The wheel that had raised and lowered a bucket now lay broken and rotted in the dust.

"There it is, Judas," said Kedzie sardonically. "That's Joe Kedzie's private bank."

Maxie stopped and half turned when Kedzie spoke. "Keep walking," warned Kedzie, raising the gun. Maxie resumed his pace. Kedzie lowered the gun again.

When Maxie got to the edge of the well, he dropped the rope to the ground. For a moment he stood staring down into the deep hole; his right hand gripped the small shovel tightly. Suddenly he whirled and hurled the shovel at Joe Kedzie's face.

Kedzie stepped easily aside and the shovel slammed into the wall of the mine shaft. He laughed and said, "Nice try, rat." Then he leveled the target pistol and pulled the trigger.

The bullet struck Maxie in his stomach. He stumbled back, grasping the wound with both hands, but did not fall. Kedzie fired a second time, and a third. Both bullets smashed into Maxie's chest. He fell backwards, dropping head first into the well.

Kedzie stuck the gun in his belt and walked slowly to the edge of the well. He calmly lighted a cigarette, then took out the flashlight and directed its beam into the dark pit. The well was so deep that the beam failed to reach the bottom.

When he had finished his cigarette, Kedzie bent down and picked up the rope. He dragged one end to a large boulder, around which he wrapped it securely, tying it. Then he walked back to the well and dropped the rest of the rope into the blackness. He heard a thud as it struck bottom.

Carefully, he sat down on the well's edge and began to lower himself into the hole. He braced his feet flat against the wall, arching his body, descending one cautious step at a time. Soon the darkness of the well surrounded him. He edged farther and farther below the surface.

The rope snapped just before his feet reached the halfway mark. Kedzie screamed; the darkness rushed up past him for a fleeting second; then he slammed into the hard ground at the bottom.

He rolled over, dazed, his head spinning. He reached out in the darkness and felt the wall. His body ached all over and his head was beating wildly. The rope had fallen on top of him and was tangled around him. He pulled it away from his body and forced himself up into a sitting position. As he leaned back against the wall of the well, he felt very sick. For a moment he thought he was going to faint. He sat very still and sucked in deep breaths of air to calm himself.

It's all right, he thought over and over again, it's all right. I can get back up without the rope. The well isn't too wide. I can brace my feet against one side and my back against the other and I can work my way back up. It'll be hard and it'll take a while, but I can do it. I can make it back up without a rope. I can make it.

He rested for a moment until the nausea passed, then fumbled in his pocket for the flashlight. He felt pain, too, but the excitement of his fall and of his predicament did not allow him to dwell on it. He was relieved when he switched on the flashlight and saw that the fall had not damaged it. He found the piece of rope that had fallen with him, gathered it up until he had the broken end. He was puzzled that such a strong rope would break under so little weight. He examined the end carefully under the light. Only a few strands, he saw, had been torn apart. The rest had been neatly and evenly cut-and on an angle so that it could not be easily noticed.

Enough Rope for Two

Maxie was the only other person who had handled the rope. He must have cut it while he had been in the car alone!

Kedzie flashed the light around until it shined on Maxie's face. He cursed the dead man aloud. Then he laughed. It won't work, Maxie, he thought. I can still make it. I can still get out—rope or no rope!

Kedzie pushed himself to his feet. Excruciating pain shot up through his right leg and he fell back to the ground moaning. He tried again, staggered, and fell a second time. He groaned in agony. The pain in his leg was unbearable. Desperately he twisted into a sitting position again and drew up his trouser leg. He shined the light on his leg and saw that the flesh between his knee and ankle was split apart and that a jagged bone protruded through the opening.

He leaned back against the wall, feeling fear well up in his body and overshadow the pain. His hand dropped to the ground beside him and he felt a hard, square object. He shined the flashlight down on it and saw the plastic-wrapped package he had dreamed of for ten years. Tears ran down his face and he began to tremble. Suddenly he grabbed up the package, swore. To hell with his broken leg. Maxie hadn't beat him yet out of that hundred grand. He had one good leg; he'd make it out of there.

Clutching the package, Kedzie worked his back up the wall in an attempt to get upright. He made it, panting hard, sweating. Now he had to shift his weight onto his broken leg. He waited a moment before trying, waiting for his breathing to still.

Terrific pain knifed through him, the instant he tried to place a little bit of his weight on his broken leg. He fell to the ground in pain and despair. He still held to the package, but the flashlight had fallen from his hand, its beam of light unextinguished and directed straight along the ground to Maxie's face.

The way it looked to Kedzie, the dead man was smiling at him.

Body on a White Carpet
Al James

April 1957

Mac couldn't remember when he first noticed the broad. It might have been after the fifth shot of rot gut or when the muted juke box in the corner of the gin palace started playing something dreamy that made him think of his mother. Only she didn't look like his mother. At least not as he remembered his mother slobbering over a hot stove with five kids pulling at her skirt tails.

Mac dawdled over the colored fire in the shot glass and eyed the broad down at the other end of the wood. Even in the dim light of the bar she looked like the real thing. He shifted his bulk on the bar stool so that it rode easier and he could get a better look. Most of what he could see was white. He saw a white creamy face punctuated by very juicy lips sucking in an ultra sophisticated manner at the frost covered glass she clutched in her gloved hand. And even at the distance of six bar stools he could see plenty of her breasts as she stooped low over the bar. Mac moistened his lips with the tip of his tongue. Jeez, he thought, what a handful.

He drained his glass and dropped another fin on the bar as a hint to the barkeep to get going on another drink. Then he mentally calculated the dough he had left from the last job. Enough, he decided, to show the broad a good time and perhaps purchase a room for the night befitting her royal manner.

Then he made his move. Nothing subtle. He picked up his drink and change and moved to the other end of the bar just in time to snap a light to her unlighted cigarette. He returned the gold lighter, he'd kept out of the jewelry store loot, to his pocket and smiled.

She smiled back.

"Another drink?" He indicated her empty glass.

She continued to smile and nodded yes.

Mac snapped his fingers and the barkeep came quickly, like a well trained police dog, and refilled her glass.

She tilted the two ounces and drained it.

Mac smiled and pushed his long, black hair out of his eyes. Sliding easily off the tall bar stool, he ambled toward the multi-colored mechanical marvel that hid the cracked plaster in one corner of the bar room. He slid two bits worth of nickels in its giant maw and flicked his brown eyes over the choice of selections. Habit forced his finger to something soothing by Elvis Presley, but at the last minute he decided on some concert stuff. Over his shoulder, he noticed the broad looking interestedly at him. A high class dish like her would dig upper story music. He hated it, but figured it was a small sacrifice if it would help him make time with her.

He shuffled back over the sawdust covered floor and remounted his stool, giving her the eye as he settled into place. Close up she was all cream, ready to be lapped up. Every strand of the blonde hair hung in its proper place, the whole mop sweeping luxuriantly down across her naked shoulders. Mac wet his lips again because the low cut dress didn't cover much, just kept her inside the law.

She poised the cigarette in mid-air and again flashed her teeth in a smile. Mac tingled a little in the lower regions as he wondered what it would feel like to squash her lips with his. He snapped his fingers and soon two new drinks appeared.

"If I may be so bold," he began, swinging his eyes over the length of the crummy bar, "what is a dish like you doing in a joint like this down on South State Street?"

The gold headed broad put the rot gut right on top of the other in her gorgeous stomach and held her smile. "You might say I was looking for someone." Her voice purred like a caddy engine at low throttle. She shifted her shape so that her left breast ended up nudging Mac's arm leaning on the bar. He pressed and she didn't move by a hair's breadth.

"Have you found the joker yet?" he asked, trying to be casual and trying not to spill the drink halfway to his lips.

She pressed closer until he could smell the perfumed fragrance of her and that left breast threatened to burn a hole in the sleeve of his coat. "I don't know," she purred. "Have I?"

Mac needed air. He guzzled his glass and lit a cigarette. There was no doubt about it, he thought, that this doll was the champagne type and he was way out in deep water with her. But hell, it was about time he quit running around with chorus floozies and climbed a little. He thought of Mabel and felt a little guilty. He'd just come into the bar to down a few while she finished her last strip across the street. But gals like Mabel were ten for a dollar and the price of a room. It would be a novelty to down a broad with five dollar panties. Maybe a little of her class would rub onto him.

The blonde broke the long silence by pointing a long, well manicured finger nail at her empty glass. "May I have another?" she said sweetly.

Mac snapped his fingers and the barkeep raced down to the end of the bar and slopped the glasses full.

Mac noticed the glare of her diamond incrusted hand. "It looks as if you've found your boy," he said.

"It could very well be," she agreed. Her sullen blue eyes turned up to full candle power and hit Mac dead center. "What I want is a favor," she went on. Then added, "A very small favor."

Mac placed a calculated hand on her knee. "Sure," he said. "You name it. I'll do it." He slid his hand upwards over her skirt, feeling the heat of her leg. "What's the reward?" he chuckled.

The juicy blonde leaned toward Mac until he caught the scent of her lipstick. With her left hand she snuffed out her cigarette, with the right she pulled his hand in a massaging motion over her torso. Mac's temperature shot up to the danger mark.

He found his voice after awhile. "Good enough," he said huskily, descending from the bar stool. He held out his arm and the blonde, flashing teeth, eased down to the floor.

He and the girl side-slipped out of the bar onto State street. And before Mac could determine the direction he wanted to go, Brogan, the local cop, strolled up to the couple. His eyes were chipped stone as they mentally frisked Mac.

"Well if it isn't the boy delinquent," he sneered, his eyes moving to the girl and over her. "You're out of your class tonight. What, no jewelry stores available?"

Mac sniffed in contempt for the man in blue. The truth was he'd had a place cased and ready to push over, but other interests had come along. The cop didn't know how lucky he really was.

Mac flagged down a cab and pulled the girl into it before the cop could make any more observations.

She crossed her legs, flashing the white of her thighs. Mac put his arm around her bare shoulders. She leaned against him. "Well?" he asked. "Where to?" He was feeling like one of the big number boys with this girl at his side. It was about time he was getting up in the world, he thought. Instead of a fast heist, maybe next time he'd do a bank job. Another year and he'd be pushing twenty two. A man had to improve himself. This blonde was a good omen.

"I'd like to have you do the favor first," she said sweetly, rattling her silver arm bracelet as she fumbled for a cigarette.

"Okay," Mac said. "Anything you want." He lit her cigarette for her and lit one of his own. "Where to?"

She snuggled closer. "Come to my place."

Mac choked on his cigarette. It was going to be quite an evening.

The cab played football through the loop, place kicking a few pedestrians and then scoring a touchdown as it slid over the Michigan Avenue bridge, finally, making the extra point by skidding up to the address the girl had given the driver.

They got out and the yellow roared back into the game, leaving Mac and the girl at the bottom of a building with clouds for a top floor. Mac whistled and followed the broad. This was grade 'A' class, having an apartment in a section like this. She punched a button in the glistening, marble lobby and they slid through the door that obeyed the command of her finger. She punched another and the elevator hummed up and up and up.

"I appreciate this," the blonde purred, moving in on the sweating Mac. He came to life and put his palms on the small of her back and started drawing her nearer. She beat him to it, plastering her size nine figure to his body and closing in on his mouth. But her lips touched his only briefly, tantalizingly. Then she pulled away and turned her back to him. "Unfasten my blouse," she said.

Mac hoped his rib cage would manage to hold his pounding heart. He dried his hands down the sides of his pants. "Hadn't we better wait until we're in your apartment?" he asked, a little surprised at his sudden timidness. The doll was a little fast for him. He liked speed but . . . The rest of the thought dropped to the floor.

"Silly," she smiled. "This *is* the apartment. It's my private elevator to the penthouse."

"Oh how stupid of me," Mac chuckled. He wiped his hands again and unfastened the four buttons that held the back of the blouse together. He wondered how many thousand feet the elevator had traveled.

The blonde slipped out of the thin piece of black and let it fall to the floor. And what Mac saw sent his heat up again. The tiny net brassier didn't cover anything.

He wiped the sweat from his forehead, while she whipped off the remaining covering.

He was about to go for her when the elevator doors slid open.

Mac followed the blonde as she waltzed into the dimly lighted, plush living room. The girl, calmly oblivious of the naked front she was exhibiting, plucked a pastel colored cigarette from the gold case on the ebony black coffee table and struck a silver lighter to it. She offered Mac one, but he refused. He didn't go for green cigarettes. Instead, he stuffed a white one in his dry mouth and shakily succeeded in lighting it. Then, once again, he started for her.

"Not yet," she told him. "You promised to do me a favor."

Mac wet his lips with the tip of his tongue and slipped back into first gear. "Yeah," he said. "I did. Well let's go to it so we can begin the party. What have you got?" He glanced around at the lush layout. "A leaky faucet?"

She smiled at his joke and led the way down a long carpeted hall to a door with a silver plated door knob. Reaching inside, she flicked on the light. "In here," she said.

Mac slipped by her and stopped cold, his scalp trying to crawl off his head.

If the man wasn't dead, he was giving a mighty convincing performance. The naked corpse was spread like an eagle in flight on the white carpet and a small red hole neatly punctuated his forehead. Next to him, a small caliber, ivory-handled gun was almost lost in the deep nap of the rug.

With an effort, Mac started breathing again and about faced. "Ugh, ugh, baby. This is my stop. I think I heard my mother calling."

The girl pouted, "But you said you'd do me a favor."

Mac wiped the sweat from his dripping forehead. "Look, honey. A leaking faucet is one thing but . . ." He waved helplessly in the direction of the corpse.

The blonde walked into the lighted room and sat on the bed. Mac couldn't keep his eyes off of her. She smiled and flicked the zipper on her skirt, tossing it and her half slip into the corner of the room, followed by her spiked shoes. She stood up and dropped her jewelry on the bed and slowly retraced her steps toward the perspiring Mac. She encircled him with her arms and pressed her open mouth to his, breathing, "I've a lot to offer as a reward."

And the poor fish was hooked. Mac wanted her bad. She was class and that was what he was after. When he came up for air, he asked, "Friend of yours?"

She drew away and a frown crossed her face. "No," she said shortly. "He was blackmailing me."

"For what?"

"Something I did a long time before I met my husband," she said.

Again Mac approached the girl, but she drew back. "After you've dumped him." She pointed to the body as if it were a hunk of something that had spoiled.

Mac sighed and ripped the sheet off the bed and wrapped the body in it. "Where are his clothes?" he asked.

She jerked them off the chair and he stuffed them in the sheet. Then he hoisted the bundle on his shoulder and headed for the elevator. He turned before he entered the cage. "By the way. Where is your husband?"

The girl laughed a musical tinkle. "He won't be here when you get back for your reward, don't worry."

Mac didn't miss an alley in East Chicago. He staggered through the darkness with his heavy load trying to figure out the best place to get rid of it. He finally wound up in Lincoln Park amongst the shrubbery, as good a place as any, for his burden, he decided. Mac folded up the sheet and checked the man's pockets for any loose change. Nothing. Tucking the sheet under his arm, he ambled back to the apartment house, planning just how he would make love to the blonde.

Whistling, he punched the elevator button and was lifted towards his evening of love. It hadn't been hard at all, he thought. Just getting rid of a body for a chance in bed with a dish like the blonde. He nearly drowned in his own saliva, before the doors opened again.

The girl was sitting on the couch, fully dressed in a high necked blouse, when he strode into the velvet-lined love nest. She looked up from her magazine as he approached. "May I ask what the big idea is, barging in here at this time of night?" she demanded haughtily.

Mac stopped like he'd hit a brick wall. "We have a date," he said when he'd recovered his voice.

The blonde put down the magazine and stood up. "A date?" She said it like she'd just discovered a cockroach in her perfume. "I'm afraid you are mistaken whoever you are."

Mac stood frozen to the small square of rug. The blonde continued staring through him as though he were window glass. He shook his head to clear away the fog. "Yeah," he said. "A date. I dumped a body for you in the park less than half hour ago. When I left here you was ready to trot when I got back."

The blonde reached for the small white phone. "You're drunk," she accused. "If you don't leave here this minute, I'll call the police."

"I get it," Mac said. He wasn't quite sure of what he'd got, but he had one hell of a good idea. "You needed someone and I was the holder of the short straw." He laughed mirthlessly and retreated to the elevator as she picked up the phone and began dialing. On the way down he grew hotter with every floor. By the time he hit ground, steam all but streamed from his ears. With determination he began walking.

The apartment was dark when the elevator doors opened. Mac sweated through the blackness and felt his way down the long hall, opening the doorway at one end and feeling around for the light.

The sudden glow flowed over the girl in bed. She opened her eyes and sat bolt upright, staring at Mac and opening her mouth to scream.

"Ugh, ugh, baby," Mac warned. "I wouldn't do that if I was you. We got company." He tugged his bundle over to the bed and spilled it out onto the floor. The body rolled a few feet and lay face up on the carpet. "You better get dressed, doll," Mac said, "and go hunt up another sucker."

Mac turned then and went quickly out the door, slamming it after him.

A Piece of Ground
Helen Nielsen

July 1957

They called him the farmer. He had a name the same as any man; but it was seldom spoken. Names weren't important in the city. A number on a badge, a number on a time card, a number on the front of a rooming house—that's all anyone needed. Names were for people who got into the newspapers; and, down around the warehouses that backed up against the river, a man didn't get into the newspapers unless he was found with his throat cut or his head bashed in. Even then he rarely had a name. He was just another unidentified body.

He was a tall man. He stooped when he went through doorways, out of habit. He had long arms with big hands stuck on the ends of them—calloused and splinter-cut from handling the rough pine crates of produce; and he had large feet that hurt from walking and standing all the time on cement and not ever feeling the earth under them any more. He had a large-boned face and sad eyes, and he never laughed and seldom smiled unless he was alone, to himself, and thinking of something remembered. He worked hard and took his pay to the bank, except for the few dollars he needed for the landlady at the rooming house, the little food he ate, and some pipe tobacco. He never spent money for liquor or women. It was a joke all along the river-front.

"The farmer ain't give up yet. He's saving to buy out the corporation that took over his farm."

It was a big joke, but it wasn't true. Not quite. Once a week he wrote home:

> Well, I put another thirty dollars in the bank this week. It's beginning to add up. I hope Uncle Matt don't get tired of having you and the kids around the place. You make them help out now. We don't want to be beholding to anybody. It looks like I might get in some overtime next week and that will sure help. Don't forget to keep an eye open for any small farms put up for sale. It shouldn't take me long to get enough for a down payment, and I know if we can get a little piece of ground somewhere everything will work out this time. We just had some bad luck before.
>
> I am fine and hope you are the same,
> Your loving husband

The letters were pretty much the same every week, and the answers were pretty much the same, too, because he and Amy had never had to write letters to one another before and didn't really know how. If he missed her, and he did, he couldn't put it down on paper without feeling foolish; and if he hated every minute in the city, and he did, he didn't want her to know it and worry. It was just one of the hard things that happened in life, like the kids getting whooping cough or the hail stripping the corn when it was ready to tassel. It was just one of the things that had to be endured.

The winter months were bad, but, when the last of the snows had melted and the first rains came, it was harder than ever. Spring was planting time. Even in a back room of the rooming house he could smell the earth around him. He took to walking out nights, smoking his pipe and looking for a plot of grass at his feet, or for a star in the strip of sky showing above the rooftops. The city wasn't quite so ugly at night. The dirt didn't show in the shadows. He walked slowly, and he never spoke to anyone until the night he met Blanche.

It was a Saturday night and warm. Spring came early along the river. There had been a shower earlier, and pools of water still stood in the street. When he came to the corner, he looked down and saw a star reflected in the puddle. It seemed strange. He'd looked for stars in the sky and never found them, and here was a star at his feet. He hesitated a moment thinking about it, and while he stood there a woman came and stood beside him. He knew it was a woman by the smell of her powder and perfume.

"It sure is warm tonight," she said.

He didn't answer or look around. The neighborhood was full of women of her kind, and he didn't like to look at them. He hadn't had any woman but Amy for the seventeen years of their marriage, and he missed her too much to dare look at a woman now.

But she didn't go away.

"Lose something in the puddle?" she asked.

"The star—"

The words slipped out. He didn't want to talk to her about anything, but especially not the star. That was crazy. Only she didn't think so.

"Oh, I see it! It's pretty, ain't it?" She crowded closer to him. He could feel her body next to his. "You don't see many stars in the city," she added. "It's because of all the lights, I guess."

Her voice wasn't the way he expected it to be. It had a kind of wonder— something almost childish in it. He looked at her then and was surprised at what he saw. She was young, not much more than a schoolgirl. She did wear powder, but not very much, and she had a soft look about her. She was small and dark and wore a plain blue sweater over a cotton dress.

"Are you—" He struggled with words. He hadn't used them much for many months. "—from the country?"

She nodded. "A long time ago—when I was a little girl. I was born on a farm on the other side of the river."

"Now that's funny," he said. "I was born on a farm, too, only I come from the other way—back towards Jefferson City. I only been here a few months."

"Alone?" she asked.

"Yes, alone. That is, I got a wife and two girls, but they didn't come. I didn't think this was any place—" He caught back the words. He'd started to say that he didn't think this was any place to bring up his girls, but he didn't want to insult her. "I just came to make a little money and go back," he explained.

It was hard to be sure with her face ducked down and only the street lamp to see by, but she seemed to be smiling. Not a happy Smile, but a kind of twisted one. Then she looked up, and for a moment he looked straight into her eyes and saw that they weren't young at all.

But it was a warm spring night, and he hadn't talked to a woman for a long time.

"I was just going down to the corner for a beer," she said. "Maybe you were going the same place. We could walk together."

He wasn't; but he did. Some of the faces that peered at them as they walked past the bar to the booths in the rear were familiar. He could see the grins and the heads wagging. The farmer had a woman. The farmer was going to spend some money. By this time he wished he hadn't come; but the woman sat down in the last booth and he sat down across from her. They ordered two beers and he put a fifty-cent piece on the table.

"I didn't mean that you had to pay for mine," she said.

She didn't seem at all like what he knew she was; and he did know. There was never any doubt about that. They talked a little more about the country, and about the weather, and then one of the men who had been drinking at the bar—one he didn't recognize from the warehouse—came back to the booth and stood looking down at them. He was a little man compared to the farmer; but his suit had wide shoulders, and he wore his roll-brimmed hat at a cocky angle as if he were the biggest man on the river-front.

"Well, if Blanche ain't got herself a new friend!" he said.

"Knock it off, Morrell," she answered.

Her voice had turned hard; but Morrell didn't go away. Instead, he sat down beside her in the booth. He looked straight at the farmer.

"I heard about you," he said, after studying him for a few seconds. "You're the one they call 'the farmer'—the one who saves all his money."

"I got a reason," the farmer said.

"Who needs a reason? You think I'm like those stupid bums over at the bar? You think I make fun of a guy who saves his money? Look at me, I got a few put away myself. Only trouble is, Blanche don't seem to like the color of my money. How do you figure that, farmer?"

"I said knock it off," Blanche repeated.

"I guess there just ain't no accounting for tastes," Morrell added. "I guess a woman can have it for one guy and not for another."

Morrell grinned at Blanche, but she didn't even look at him. It was hard to know what to do or what to say. Maybe there was something between these two, and the farmer didn't want to get mixed up in anything. He finished his beer and came to his feet.

"Leaving so soon?" Blanche looked disappointed.

"I've got to get back to my room," he said. "I've got to write a letter."

"But it's early."

Morrell laughed.

"Leave him alone, Blanche, Can't you see he don't want any? Leave him be smart and save his money. It's a good thing somebody has sense. Go ahead, farmer. I'll buy Blanche another beer. Go write your letter."

He didn't like to go then. He didn't like the way Blanche looked up at him, or the way she edged away from Morrell. But he still didn't want to get mixed up in anything. He walked out, trying to not to hear the laughter behind him, and went back to the rooming house to write the longest letter he'd ever written.

It was a full week before he went out for a walk again. He didn't pay any attention to the cracks made around the warehouse about him buying a beer for Blanche, and he tried not to listen to the things they said about her. He just made up his mind not to be so foolish again. When Saturday night came, he sat down and started his letter:

Dear Amy,
Well, I got in that overtime like I said, and put forty dollars in the bank this week. It's adding up, and it can't add up too soon . . .

It was hot in the room. A bunch of kids were playing handball in the alley, and their screaming was in his ears until he could hardly think. He started to write again.

. . . I sure don't like the city. It's noisy and hot, and there isn't anybody to talk to. It's not like back home. You can't hardly meet anybody . . .

He put down his pencil and looked at the words. They were true. Everything was different in the city, but people were still people. They still got lonely and knew hunger. If a starving man stole a loaf of bread it wasn't the same as stealing for profit. Everything was different in the city.

The ball kept bouncing against the wall, and now it was as if it were bouncing against his head. He wrinkled up the letter and threw it on the floor. It was too hot to write. He couldn't sit in a hot room forever . . .

He met Blanche about three houses down the street. He never asked, but she might have been waiting for him.

"I'm going down to the corner for a beer," he said, "Maybe you'd like to come with me."

She wasn't wearing the blue sweater. It was too warm for that. Spring and summer had a way of running together this time of year. She wore the cotton dress and that soft look that came sometimes when the shadows were kind.

"A friend of mine got generous and gave me a whole case of beer," she answered. "Why don't we go to my place? I don't like the corner much any more."

Her words were as good as any. He went along with her for a couple of blocks to a rooming house the duplicate of his own. She lived on the second floor. He stooped when he went through the doorway.

"You're big," she said, closing the door behind them. "Golly, you're big—you know?" Then she ran her hand up his back and around his shoulders. "But you're so skinny I can feel the bones through your shirt. I bet you don't eat half enough."

"I don't like restaurant cooking," he said.

"I don't either! I tell you what you should do. I've got a hot plate, see?"

He saw. He saw a room no larger than his own, but with a hot plate and a sink and a yellowed enamel refrigerator in one corner. He looked for a chair, but the only one he could find had laundry on it. He sat down on the edge of the bed. By this time, she'd taken the beer out of the refrigerator, opened the cans, and handed one to him. All the time she kept talking.

"I do most of my own cooking, so if there's something you'd like—something you're hungry for—you just buy it and bring it here. Those restaurants can kill you."

She took a couple of pulls at the beer.

"God, it's hot!" she said. She pulled off her dress. She didn't wear anything underneath except a slip as thin as a silk curtain. She was thin, too, her thighs, her stomach, her small breasts poking at the slip. She finished her beer and tossed the can into the sink, and then reached down for the hem of her slip. Then she looked at the window. The shade was rolled up to let in the night breeze in case one ever came, so she turned out the light.

Afterwards, he lay with her a while, staring at the ceiling and listening to his heart beat. Finally he spoke.

"That man at the bar last week—Morrell. Is he the friend who gave you the beer?"

It wasn't that he had to make conversation. It was that he felt guilty and wanted to be reassured that it was nothing to her.

"What of it?" she answered. "I work for him sometimes. I entertain his customers."

"He's got some kind of business, then?"

"Morrell? He's got all kinds of business."

"I guess some people know how to make money. I wish I knew."

"Morrell knows, all right. That's one thing he knows."

Blanche sounded sleepy. He waited a while, thinking she might speak again; but she didn't and he left her that way. He wasn't sure what to do, so he left two dollars on the refrigerator.

He didn't intend to go back; but he did, of course. After a few more Saturdays it didn't bother him. He'd give her a few dollars for groceries, and she'd have supper waiting when he got off work. The rest of his pay went into the bank the same as before, and he wrote home every week as usual. One night Blanche wanted to go out, so they went back to the bar on the corner and had a couple of beers and listened to the music in the record machine. Then Morrell came back to their booth.

"Well, it's been a long time," he said. "You don't come around much any more, Blanche. What's the matter? Got somebody keeping you busy?"

He had an obscene smile. He sat down beside Blanche again, and she edged over toward the wall.

"Still saving your money, farmer? Still going to buy back that farm?"

He shook his head. "I don't aim to buy back anything," he said. "All I want is a few acres for a truck garden and a house. Just a little piece of ground."

Morrell nodded, still smiling,

"That's what I like to hear—a man with ambition. But the trouble is, farmer, you're going to be an old man before you get that piece of ground doing it the hard way."

Morrell's teeth were like pearls, and a diamond ring on his finger shot fire. The farmer listened.

"Is there an easy way?" he asked.

"Look at me," Morrell said. "Six years ago I was broke—hoisting crates at the warehouse the same as you. But I got smart, I saved my dough, too, and then I did what the big boys do. I invested my dough."

"In a business?"

"In the market, chum. Ain't you ever heard?"

"But I don't know anything about the market."

"So who knows? I got me a broker—one of those young sharpies out of college. He studies all the time—tells me what to buy and when to sell. Not this six and seven percent old lady stuff, but the sweet stuff. You got to gamble to get anywhere in this world."

Blanche was restless. She shoved her half-finished beer away from her.

"You talk big, Morrell," she said, "but talk don't do the farmer any good."

"So why should I do the farmer good?"

"Why should you blow your mouth off?"

The farmer didn't want any part of the argument. He would just as soon have dropped the subject; but Blanche's taunt only made Morrell talk more.

"You think I talk big and that's all?" he said. "You think I'm bluffing? Okay. I'll show you how I'm bluffing. You want me to cut you in, farmer? It happens I've got a sweet thing going right now. Give me a hundred dollars and I'll double it for you. Go ahead, try me and see."

The farmer hesitated. He looked at Blanche and caught a glimpse of that twisted smile again.

"My money's in the bank," he said.

"Okay, so the bank opens Monday morning, don't it? One hundred dollars, that's all I'll cut you in for. I know you've got it. You've got plenty."

One hundred dollars. Monday noon he went to the bank on his lunch hour, and Monday night he gave the money to Morrell. He knew that he was a fool and never expected to see the money again; but Blanche had set it up for him and he didn't want to back out.

It was exactly three weeks later that Morrell gave him two hundred dollars.

"You got lucky," Blanche said.

"Luck?" Morrell laughed. "Using your head ain't luck, honey. Anv time you want to get smart again, farmer, let me know. Any time . . ."

It nagged at his mind. For the next few weeks everything went on as usual. He still went to Blanche every Saturday, and he still wrote home; but now the time seemed to pass more slowly because in the back of his mind he carried Morrell's words. Only one thing about them bothered him.

And then one week the letter from Amy had news:

> . . . *It's just a little place, but it has water on it and the house could be fixed up nice. Uncle Matt thinks we could get it for two thousand down, and he'll go our note for the rest* . . .

He read the letter over several times, and each time he could see the place more clearly and almost smell the earth and the water. Finally, he went to see Morrell.

"There's just one thing I want to know," he told him. "Why did you cut me in, and why did you say 'any time'? You ain't a man to give anything away."

Morrell grinned.

"That's right, farmer. You're smart enough to think of that, but how come you ain't smart enough to think of the answer? Don't you know what I want? I want you to get that little piece of ground and clear the hell out of here!"

"Because of Blanche?"

"What do you think?"

"But she's nothing to me."

"It ain't what she is to you that bothers me, farmer. It's what she is to me—or could be with you out of the way. Now, what's on your mind?"

"I need two thousand dollars," he said.

"How much have you got to invest?"

He handed Morrell his bank book. All the months of saving had gone into it—the winter, the spring, the summer, and autumn on the way; but it was still only a little over a thousand dollars,

"Okay," Morrell said. "I'll meet you at the bank tomorrow—no, better make it tomorrow night at my office. You know where that is?"

The farmer nodded. He passed it every day going down to the warehouse.

"Make it about nine o'clock. That'll give me time to see my broker and have him find something good for you. And don't tell anybody what I'm doing. I'll have every bum on the river-front trying to cut in."

The next day at noon, he went to the bank and drew out everything. He kept it in an envelope pinned to the inside of his shirt until he was through work. After work he was too nervous to eat. He sat alone in his room until it was time to put the envelope in his pocket and start for Morrell's office. Out on the street, he met Blanche. She was looking for him.

"I thought you might come over tonight," she said. "I bought some pork chops."

She clung to his arm, leaning against him. He pulled away.

"Maybe later," he said. "I've got to see somebody first."

"Morrell?"

"Just somebody. I'll tell you about it later."

He was lying. He walked off down the street knowing that he'd never go to Blanche again. That kind of life was over. He was going to go home and get clean.

After a time, he came to Morrell's office. He opened the door and saw no one, but the door banged shut behind him and Morrell laughed once as he stepped forward. The farmer felt a gun cold against the back of his neck.

Even then he didn't know what had happened or what had gone wrong; he wasn't thinking at all. He felt terror and panic creep slowly up his body, but he made no move, not even when the door opened again and Blanche came in and walked past him.

"Has he got it with him?" Morrell asked from behind him.

"He's got it," Blanche said. "I felt it in his pocket."

"Good. I'll be up later with your cut. In the meantime, you don't have to stay here. You might look around for another farmer who's saving his money. You've got a real technique with the country boys, and there's plenty of them around."

Now the farmer knew that it was all over. He was finished. Fear remained, but the panic was gone; there was nothing for him to do. He felt only sick, and dirty, and he waited for Morrell to fire the gun and cleanse him. "At least he'll get what he wanted," Blanche said, far away in the distance. "At least he'll get a little piece of ground."

Say a Prayer for the Guy
Nelson Algren

June 1958

That game began as it always began, the drinkers drank what they always drank. The talkers said what they always said, "Keep a seat open for Joe."

Frank, John, Pete, and I, each thinking tonight might be the night he'd win back all he'd lost last week to Joe. Yes, and perhaps a little more.

Joe, poor old Joe, all his joys but three have been taken away. To count his money, play stud poker, then secretly to count it once more—and the last count always the best—that there is more there than before is no secret.

Joe, old Joe, with his wallet fat as sausage and his money green as leaves. Who needs sports, cats, them like that? That call for mixed drinks and blame God if they've mixed too much? Who needs heavy spenders, loudmouth hollerers, them like *that?* Drinking is to make the head heavy, not the tongue loose. Drinking is for when nobody shows up to play poker. You want to make the feet light? Go dancing. Dance all night.

"Here come Joe," Phil, the bartender, told us, and sure enough, here he came. With his wallet full.

"Joe, you don't look so good," John told him as soon as he sat down, "you look so *peckid.*"

"I don't feel so good," the old man told us, "I *feel* peckid."

"You feel peckid, take it easy," advised Frank.

I put a dime in the juke, all on Perry Como. I don't care what Perry sings, so long as he sings. The box coughed once and gave me back my dime. It doesn't like Perry. Well, it was my dime. I put it right back. *I* like Perry.

This time it didn't cough. It picked Elvis Presley singing *All Shook Up.* I got nothing against Elvis. It was just that it was my dime.

But that Frank began humming and shaking along with the song as if it had been his money.

Then the game went as it always went, the drinkers drank what they always drank, the talkers said what they always said, "Looks like Joe's night again."

Yet, just as Joe reached for the deck, as the juke cried out *I Need Your Love,* everything went strange.

The juke coughed on a note, and went on coughing, how it does when someone leans against it. I saw Joe's hands shuffling, but he shuffled too slow. A red deuce twisted out of the deck and dropped to the floor like a splash of blood. Joe fell forward onto the table, without a gasp, without a sound.

Up jumped Frank, the first to realize. "Joe! Wake up!" He seized Joe's wrists and began massaging them. I opened the old man's collar and his head flopped like a rooster's. O, I didn't like the looks of things in the least. Now I wanted the juke to play *anything.*

"*Please* wake up," Frank pleaded. "Old friend! My one true friend!"

But his one true friend didn't hear.

So we lifted Joe, old Joe, onto the long glass of the shuffleboard. We lay him down gently under the lights that say GAME COMPLETED. Frank began to massage his heart.

"I saw something wrong the second he sat down," John boasted. "I told him."

"Now you look a little peckid yourself," I told him. He didn't like that.

"You typewriter pounder," he told me, "how some day *you* look," and drew back his lips in a grin almost as bad as Joe's.

"How *you* look, too, someday, old dummy John," little Pete suddenly took my part, and stretched his mouth back and made a horrible face, so that he looked even worse than Joe. Then he ducked under the table to gather the cards.

"Give up," I told Frank, "if he comes to now, he'd be an idiot the rest of his days. When the breath stops the brain starts to melt, right that same second." It was something I'd read somewhere.

"That would be all right," Pete said from under the table, "maybe that way we'd win some of our money back."

"He was my one friend, my *only* friend," Frank reminded us, and went right on massaging. Yet more in sorrow than in hope of winning back his friend. He didn't give up till the pulmotor squad arrived. How they found out I still don't know. I think they just stopped in for a drink on the way home from some job and found another.

They tossed a coin, and the one who lost hauled the inhalator over to the shuffleboard.

"One side, buddy," he told Frank, but our Frank stood his ground. After all, he's from this neighborhood.

"Let him try, too, Frank," I told him. "We stand for fair play." Actually it wasn't fair play I wanted to see so much. It was just that it had been some time now since anyone raised anyone from the dead and I wanted to be on hand if it happened again.

But that Frank, he wouldn't give up. He went to the other side of the shuffleboard, yet he kept his hand on the old man's heart. I figured he figured that, if the old man did come around, he'd get at least half the credit. If he had we would have given him all of it. After all, he's from this neighborhood.

"If you'd stop blowing cigar smoke in his face," the fireman told me, "he'd stand a better chance."

"Where does it say NO SMOKING?" I asked him to show me. Why should I take stuff off *him?*

After a time, the fireman took the head-piece off Joe's big blue nose and motioned to his friend at the bar. It was all over.

It took them a long time to get through the mob of kids in the door. It was a Spring night, and the kids wanted to see, but were afraid to come all the way in because it was a tavern.

But they made a path for some sort of serious little fellow with a black moustache. "I'm the doctor," he told us as if there were only one in the whole precinct.

Still, he must really have been a doctor at that, because he had a gold watch and didn't in the least mind showing it off. He listened to Joe's right wrist, gave it a bit of a shake, glanced at the watch, gave the left wrist a shake and looked at the watch again. He shook his head.

It isn't true what they say about pennies holding down a dead man's eyes, because they didn't hold down Joe's. Maybe he's got heavy eyes, I don't know, but the pennies kept rolling off. He tried half a dozen, but they'd slip and roll down the floor. Every time one passed the table I saw Pete's hand come out—there was one penny the doctor wouldn't see again.

"Try a dime," I told him to see if he would think that was heavier, and he did. When he lost that one I said, "Try a quarter."

"Give me two nickels," he told me, and two was just what I had. But I didn't get a dime for them. "The dime is under the table," he told me.

I wouldn't bend for it. I knew it was no use.

When he got the old man's lids closed under the nickels he wrote something in a little book, and left. "The boys will pick him up shortly," he told us.

What boys? The boys from the Royal Barons S. A. C.? They've buried a couple parties, but not officially.

"He meant the ambulance boys," Phil, the bartender, guessed. "You can't die in a public place unless you're a pauper. You got to go to a hospital to make it official."

"I think he meant the boys from Racine Street Station," Pete spoke up, and that sounded closest. "Anyhow, say a prayer for the guy," Frank asked us, giving up his work at last. And began one himself— "Our Father who art in Heaven"—then the whiskey hit him and he couldn't remember the rest.

"Hollowed be Thy name," I remembered, and that was as far as *I* could go.

"Let's wait for the priest," I told Frank.

The kids in the doorway stood aside to let Father Francis through. He didn't look our way but we took off our caps all the same. He went right to the shuffleboard and did as fast and neat a job of extreme unction as if that old man were lying in bed. Someone brought an army blanket and covered the poor old stiff with that.

Father F. didn't look our way till he'd made the sign of the cross and pulled the blanket up. Then he came to where we waited.

"Oh, *Father,*" Frank shouted like the priest had come just in time to save *him.* "I *forgot* the Lord's Prayer, Father."

"Remembering it isn't your trade," Father F. told Frank, "that's mine. Has the family been notified?"

Nobody had thought of that. But right away everyone wanted to be the first. John wanted to run straight to Joe's house, Sam said he'd phone. But Phil said, since it happened in his place, it was his job.

Then, it turned out, nobody knew where the old man lived or even what his full name was. Nobody had called him anything but *Joe* for years. Some said it was Wroblewski, some said it was Makisch, another said it was Orlov.

"Try looking in his wallet," somebody said from under the table.

Nobody had thought of that, either. "Bring it to me, Frank," Father F. said.

"He was my one friend, let someone else," Frank declined.

Father F. went over and turned the blanket down and reached in and brought back Joe's wallet.

Joe's wallet, fat as leaves. But when he laid it on the bar it just lay there, so thin, so flat, so gone, it looked like it must have had some sort of little stroke of its own. When Father F. reached in, all there was one thin single, nothing more.

Everybody pushed to see.

"What was he doing when he went?" Father wanted to know.

"Playing poker, Father," we told him.

"Penny ante?"

"Two-dollar limit."

"Put on Perry Como," I told one of the kids, because I didn't care how I spent just then.

Perry came on singing *Whither Thou Goest I Shall Go*. Oh, he sang it so easy, he sang it so free. And while he sang Phil poured a shot for John and a shot for me. He poured a shot for Father F. and a shot for Sam and a shot for Al and a shot for Frank. Then he poured a shot for himself and lifted his glass.

"To Joe, old Joe," he made a kind of toast.

"Oh, Frank," I heard a whisper from under the table. "How you massage! So *good!* How God is going to punish!"

An Empty Threat
Donald E. Westlake

February 1960

Ah, the South Seas. Maugham heroes and the young native girls, buxom and burgeoning at eighteen, so warm, so soft, so simple and oh, so willing. Ah, the South Seas and simple youth and the soothing, sun-tanned sirens of Samoa. Ah, for romance with the charming native girls, who never never never, it seems, give birth.

And ah, the daydreams in the cold, cold winter air. With all the car windows closed, Frederick Leary shriveled in the dry warm air spewed from the heater beside his knees, and the windshield misted over. With a window open, the cold air outside reached thin freezing fingers in to icily tweak his thin nose, and the vulnerable virgins of the South Pacific receded, waving, undulating, growing small and indistinct and far, far out of reach.

And Frederick Leary was only Frederick Leary after all. Manager of the local branch of the Bonham Bookstore chain. Well-read, through accretion. A husband, but not a father. Thirty-two, but not wealthy. College-trained, and distantly liked by his employees.

Irritated, annoyed, obscurely cheated, Frederick Leary turned into his driveway, and the car that had been following him pulled to the curb three houses away. Frederick pushed open the car door, which squeaked and cracked, and plodded through the snow to push up the garage door, an overhead, put in at great expense and a damned nuisance for all the cost. And the car that had been following him disgorged its occupant, a pale and indecisive youth, who shrunk inside his overcoat, who stood hatless in the gentle fall of snow, who chewed viciously upon a filter-tip cigarette and fondled the gun in his pocket, wondering if he had the nerve.

Returning to his car, Frederick drove it into the garage. Armed with a brown paper sack containing bread and milk, he left car and garage, pulled down the damned overhead behind him, and slogged through the new-fallen snow toward the back porch. And the youth threw away the soggy butt and shuffled away, to walk around the block, kicking at the drifts of snow, building up his courage for the act.

The back porch was screened, and the slamming of the screen door made an odd contrast to the snow collapsing from the sky. Frederick maneuvered the brown paper bag from hand to hand as he removed his overshoes, then pushed open the back door and walked into a blast of heat and bright yellow. The kitchen.

Louise had her back to him. She was doing something to a vegetable with a knife, and she didn't bother to turn around. She already knew who it was. She said, "You're home late."

"Late shoppers," Frederick told her, as he put the milk in the refrigerator and the bread in the bread-box. "You know Saturday. Particularly before Christmas. People buy books and give them to each other and nobody ever reads them. Didn't get to close the store till twenty after six."

"Supper in ten minutes," Louise told him, still with her back to him, and brushed the chopped vegetable into a bowl.

Frederick walked through the house to the stairs and the foyer and the front door. He put his coat and hat in the closet and trotted upstairs to wash his hands, noticing for the thousandth time the places where the stair treads were coming loose. From his angle of vision, it seemed at times as though everything in the world were coming loose. Overhead doors, screen doors, stair treads. And the cold water faucet. He left the bathroom, refusing to listen to the measured drip of cold water behind him.

And outside, the youth completed his circuit of the block. He paused before the Leary house, looking this way and that, and a phrase came to him, from somewhere, from a conversation or television. "Calculated risk." That's what it was, and if he played it smart he could bring it off. He hurried along the driveway to the back of the house. He could feel his heart beating, and he touched the gun in his pocket for assurance. A calculated risk. He could do it.

On Saturday and Sunday, Frederick and Louise dined in the dining room, using the good silver, the good dishes and the good tablecloth. It was a habit that had once been an adventure. In silence they sat facing one another, in silence they fed, both aware that the good dishes were mostly chipped, the good silverware was just slightly tarnished. In pouring gravy on his boiled potatoes, Frederick spotted the tablecloth again. He looked guiltily at his wife, but she ate stolidly and silently, looking at the spot of gravy but not speaking. In the silence, the cold water dripped in the sink far away upstairs, and the tarnished silver clinked against the chipped dishes.

Stealthily, slowly, silently, the youth pushed open the screen door, sidled through, and gently closed it once again. He crept to the back door, his long thin fingers curled around the knob, soundlessly he opened the door and gained entrance to the house.

Louise looked up. "I feel a chill."

Frederick said, "I feel fine."

Louise said, "It's gone now," and looked back at her plate.

In the yellow warmth of the kitchen, the youth stood and dripped quietly upon the floor. He opened his overcoat, allowing warmth to spread closer against his body. The uncertainty crowded in on him, but he fought it away. He took the pistol from his overcoat pocket, feeling the metal cold against the skin of his hand. He stood there, tightly holding the gun until the metal grew warmer, until he was sure again, then slid forward through the hall to the dining room.

He stood in the doorway, looking at them, watching them eat, and neither looked up. He held the pistol aimed at the table, midway between the two of them, and when he was sure he could do it, he said, "Don't move."

Louise dropped her fork and pressed her palm against her mouth. Instinctively, she knew that it would be dangerous, perhaps fatal, for her to scream, and she held the scream back in her mouth with a taut and quivering hand.

Frederick pushed his chair back and half-rose, saying, "What—?" But then he saw the gun, and he subsided, flopping back into the chair with his mouth open and soundless.

Now that he had committed himself, the youth felt suddenly at ease. It was a risk, a calculated risk. They were afraid of him, he could see it in their eyes, and now he was strong. "Just sit there," he ordered. "Don't make any noise. Do like I tell you, and you'll be all right."

Frederick closed his mouth and swallowed. He said, "What do you want?"

The youth pointed the pistol at Frederick. "I'm gonna send you on a little trip," he said. "You're gonna go back to that bookstore of yours, and you're gonna open the safe and take out the money that's in it. You got Friday night's receipts in there and you got today's receipts, all in there, maybe five or six grand. You're gonna take the money out of the safe and put it in a paper bag. And then you're gonna bring it right back here to me. I'll be waiting right here for you. With your wife." He looked at his watch. "It's just about seven o'clock. I'll give you till eight o'clock to get back here with the money from the store. If you don't come back, I'll kill your wife. If you call the cops and they come around, I'll kill her for that, too."

They stared at him, and he stared back at them. He looked at Frederick, and he said, "Do you believe me?"

"What?" Frederick started, as though he'd been asleep.

"Do you believe me? If you don't do what I tell you, I'll kill your wife."

Frederick looked at the hard bright eyes of the youth, and he nodded. "I believe you."

Now the youth was sure. It had worked, it was going to pay off. "You better get started," he said. "You only got till eight o'clock."

Frederick got slowly to his feet. Then he stopped. "What if I do what you tell me?" he asked. "Maybe you'll kill the both of us anyway."

The youth stiffened. This was the tough part. He knew that might occur to them, that he couldn't let them live, that they could identify him, and he had to get over it, he had to make them believe a lie. "That's the chance you got to take," he said. He remembered his own thoughts, out in front of the house, and he smiled. "It's what they call a calculated risk. Only I wouldn't worry. I don't think I'd kill anybody who did what I told them and who gave me five or six grand."

"I'm not sure there's that much there."

"For your sake," said the youth softly, "I hope there is."

Frederick glanced at Louise. She was still staring at the youth, and her hand was still pressed against her mouth. He looked back at the youth again. "I'll get my coat."

The youth relaxed. It was done, the guy had gone for it. "You only got till eight o'clock," he said. "You better hurry."

"Hurry," said Frederick. He turned and walked to the hallway closet and put on his coat and hat. He came back, paused to say to his wife, "I'll be right back," but the sentence sounded inane, said before the boy with the gun. "I'll hurry back," he said, but Louise still stared at the youth, and her arm was still bent and tense as she tightly gripped her mouth.

Frederick moved quickly through the house and out the back door. Automatically, he put on his overshoes, wet and cold against his ankles. He pushed open the screen door and hurried over to the garage. He had trouble opening the overhead door. He scraped between the side of the car and the concrete block wall of the garage, squeezed behind the wheel, backed the car out of the garage. Still automatically, he got out of the car and closed the overhead door again. And then the enormity of it hit him. Inside there was Louise, with a killer. A youth who would murder her, if Frederick didn't get back in time.

He scurried back to the car, backed out to the street, turned and fled down the dark and silent, snow-covered street.

Hurry. He had to hurry. The windshield misted and he wiped impatiently at it, opened the window a bit and a touch of frost brushed his ear. The car was cold, but soon the heater was working full-strength, pumping warm dry air into the car.

His mind raced on, in a thousand directions at once, far ahead of the car. Way in the back of his mind, the Samoan virgins swayed and danced, motioning to him, beckoning to him. At the front of his mind loomed the face of the youth and the functional terror of the pistol. He would kill Louise, he really would.

He might kill her anyway. He might kill them both. Should he call the police? Should he stop and call the police? What was it the youth had said? Calculated risk. Calculated risk.

He turned right, turned left, skidded as he pressed too hard on the accelerator, barely missed a parked car and hurried on. His heart pounded, now because of the narrow escape from an accident. He could kill himself in the car, without any youths with pistols and sharp bitter faces.

Nonsense. Even at thirty miles an hour, bundled up in an overcoat the way he was, hitting a parked car wouldn't kill him. It might knock him out, shake him up, but it wouldn't kill him.

But it would kill Louise, because he wouldn't get back in time.

Calculated risk. He slowed, thought of a life without Louise. The snow collapsed from the sky, and he thought of Samoa. What if he didn't go back?

What if he didn't go back?

But the boy might not kill her after all. And he would return, tomorrow or the next day, and she would be waiting for him, and she would know why he hadn't come back. She would know that he had hoped the boy would kill her.

But what if he *couldn't* go back?

Calculated risk. With sudden decision he accelerated, tearing down the empty residential street. He jammed his foot on the brakes, the tires slid on ice, he twisted the wheel, and the car hurtled into a telephone pole. The car crumpled against the pole with a squealing, jarring crash, but Frederick was lulled to unconsciousness by the sweet, sweet songs of the islands.

Frozen Stiff
Lawrence Block

June 1962

A t ten minutes to five the Mexican kid finished sweeping the floor. He stood by the counter, leaning on his broom and looking at the big white-faced clock.

"Go on home," Brad told him. "Nobody's going to want any lamb chops delivered anymore. You're through, go get some rest."

The kid flashed teeth in a smile. He took off his apron and hung it on a peg, put on a poplin windbreaker.

"Take it easy," Brad said.

"You stayin' here?"

"For a few minutes," Brad said. "I got a few things to see to." The kid walked to the door, then turned at the last moment. "You watch out for the freezer, Mr. Malden. You get in there, man, nobody can get you out."

"I'll be careful."

"I'll see you, Mr. Malden."

"Yeah," Brad said. "Sure."

The kid walked out. Brad watched the door close after him, then walked behind the meat counter and leaned over it, his weight propped up on his elbows. He was a big man, heavy with muscle, broad-faced and barrel-chested. He was forty-six, and he looked years younger until you saw the furrowed forehead and the drawn, anxious lines at the corners of his mouth. Then he looked fifty.

He took a deep breath and let it out slowly. He picked a heavy cleaver from a hook behind him, lifted it high overhead, and brought it down upon a wooden chopping block. The blade sank four inches into the block.

Strong, he thought. Like an ox.

He left the cleaver in the block. The freezer was in the back, and he walked through a sawdust-covered hallway to it. He opened the door and looked inside. Slabs of beef hung from the ceiling. Other cuts and sections of meat were piled on the floor. There were cleavers and hooks on pegs in the walls. The room was very cold.

He looked at the inside of the door. There was a safety latch there, installed so that the door could be opened from the inside if a person managed to lock himself in.

Two days ago he had smashed the safety latch. He broke it neatly and deliberately with a single blow of the cleaver, and then he told the Mexican kid what had happened.

"Watch yourself in the cold bin," he had told the kid. "I busted the goddamn latch. That door shuts on you and you're in trouble. The room's soundproof. Nobody can hear you if you yell. So make damn sure the door's open when you're in there."

He told Vicki about it that same night. "I did a real smart thing today," he said. "Broke the damn safety latch on the cold bin door."

"So what?" she said.

"So I got to watch it," he said. "The door shuts when I'm in there and there's no way out. A guy could freeze to death."

"You should have it fixed."

"Well," he had said, shrugging, "one of these days."

He stood looking into the cold bin for a few more moments now. Then he turned slowly and walked back to the front of the store. He closed the door, latched it. He turned off the lights. Then he went back to the cold bin.

He opened the door. This time he walked inside, stopping the door with a small wooden wedge. The wedge left the door open an inch or so. He took a deep breath, filling his lungs with icy air.

He looked at his watch. Five-fifteen, it read. He took another breath and smiled slowly, gently, to himself.

By eight or nine he would be dead.

It started with a little pain in the chest. Just a twinge, really. It hurt him when he took a deep breath, and sometimes it made him cough. A little pain—you get to expect them now and then when you pass forty. The body starts to go to hell in one way or the other and you get a little pain from time to time.

He didn't go to the doctor. What the hell, a big guy like Brad Malden, he should go to the doctor like a kid every time he gets a little pain? He didn't go to the doctor. Then the pain got worse, and he started getting other pains in his stomach and legs, and he had a six-letter idea what it was all about.

He was right. By the time he went to a doctor, finally, it was inoperable. "You should have come in earlier," the doctor told him. "Cancer's curable, you know. We could have taken out a lung—"

Sure, he thought. And I could breathe with my liver. Sure.

"I want to get you to the hospital right away," the doctor had said.

And he asked, reasonably, "What the hell for?"

"Radium treatments. Radical surgery. We can help you, make the pain easier, delay the progress of the disease—"

Make me live longer, he had thought. Make it last longer, and hurt longer, and cost more.

"Forget it," he said.

"Mr. Malden—"

"Forget it. Forget I came to you, understand? I never came here, I never saw you, period. Got it?"

The doctor did not like it that way. Brad didn't care whether he liked it or not. He didn't have to like it. It wasn't his life.

He took a deep breath again and the pain was like a knife in his chest. Like a cleaver. Not for me, he thought. No lying in bed for a year dying by inches. No wasting away from two hundred pounds to eighty pounds. No pain. No dribbling away the money on doctors and hospitals until he was gone and there was nothing left for Vicki but a pile of bills that the insurance would barely cover. Thanks, doc. But no thanks. Not for me.

He looked again at his watch. Five-twenty. Go ahead, he told himself angrily. Get rid of the wedge, shut the door, lie down, and go to sleep. It was cold, and you closed your eyes and relaxed, and bit by bit you got numb all over. Go ahead, shut the door and die.

But he left the wedge where it was. No rush, he thought. There was plenty of time for dying.

He walked to the wall, leaned against it. This was the better way. In the morning they would find him frozen to death, and they would figure logically enough that the wedge had slipped and he had frozen to death. Vicki would cry over him and bury him, and the insurance policy would pay her a hundred thousand dollars. He had fifty thousand dollars of straight life insurance with a double indemnity clause for accidental death, and this could only be interpreted as an accident. With that kind of money Vicki could get a decent income for life. She was young and pretty, they didn't have any kids, in a few years she could remarry and start anew.

Fine.

The pain came, and this time it was sharp. He doubled over, clutching at his chest. God, he hoped the doctor would keep his mouth shut. Though it would still go as accidental death. It had to. No one committed suicide by locking himself in a cold bin. They jumped out of windows, they slashed their wrists, they took poison, they left the gas jets on. They didn't freeze themselves like a leg of lamb. Even if they suspected suicide, they had to pay the claim. They were stuck with it.

When the next stab of pain came he couldn't stand any longer. It had been hell trying not to wince, trying to conceal the pain from Vicki. Now he was alone; he didn't have to hide it. He hugged both hands to his chest and sank slowly to the floor. He sat on a slab of bacon, then moved the slab aside and sat on the floor. The floor was very cold. Hell, he thought, it was funny to sit in the cold bin. He'd never spent much time there before, just walked in to get some meat or to hang some up. It was a funny feeling, sitting on the floor.

How cold was it? He wasn't sure exactly. The thermostat was outside by the door; otherwise the suicide wouldn't have been possible, since he could have turned up the temperature. The damn place was a natural, he thought. A death trap.

He put his hand to his forehead. Getting cold already, he thought. It shouldn't take too long, not at this rate. And he didn't even have the door closed. He should close the door now. It would go a little faster with the door closed.

Could he smoke a cigarette? Sure, he thought. Why not?

He considered it. If they found the cigarette they would know he'd had a smoke before he froze to death. So? Even if it were an accident, a guy would smoke, wouldn't he? Besides, he'd make damn sure they'd think he tried to get out. Flail at the door with the cleaver, throw some meat around, things like that. They wouldn't make a federal case out of a goddamn cigarette.

He took one out, put it between his lips, scratched a match and lighted it. He smoked thoughtfully, wincing slightly when the pain gripped his chest like a vise. A year of this? No, not for him. The quick death was better.

Better for him. Better for Vicki, too. God, he loved that woman! Too much, maybe. Sometimes he got the feeling that he loved her too hard, that he cared more for her than she did for him. Well, it was only natural. He was a fatheaded butcher, not too bright, not much to look at. She was twenty-six and beautiful and there were times when he couldn't understand why she had married him in the first place. Couldn't understand, but remained eternally grateful.

The cigarette warmed his fingers slightly. They were growing cold now, and their tips were becoming numb. All he had to do was flip the wedge out. It wouldn't take long.

He finished the cigarette, put it out. He was on his way to get rid of the wedge when he heard the front door open.

It could only be Vicki, he thought. No one else had a key. He heard her footsteps, and he smiled quickly to himself. Then he heard her voice and he frowned.

"He must be here," she was saying. Her voice was a whisper. "In the back."

"Let's go."

A man's voice, that one. He walked to the cold bin door and put his face to the one-inch opening. When they came into view he stiffened. She was with a man, a young man. He had a gun in one hand. She went into his arms and he kissed her hard.

Vicki, he thought! God!

They were coming back now. He moved away, moved back into the cold bin, waiting. The door opened and the man was pointing a gun at him and he shivered. The pain came, like a sword, and he was shaking. Vicki mistook it for fear and grinned at him.

She said, "Wait, Jay."

The gun was still pointing at him. Vicki had her hand on the man's arm. She was smiling. Evil, Brad thought. Evil.

"Don't shoot him," she was saying. "It was a lousy idea anyway. Killed in a robbery—who the hell robs a butcher shop? You know how much dough he takes in during a day? Next to nothing."

"You got a better way, Vicki?"

"Yes," she said. "A much better way."

And she was pulling Jay back, leading him away from the door. And then she was kicking the wooden wedge aside, and laughing, and shutting the door. He heard her laughter, and he heard the terribly final sound the door made when it clicked shut, and then he did not hear anything at all. They were leaving the shop, undoubtedly making all sorts of sounds. The cold bin was soundproof. He heard nothing.

He took a deep, deep breath, and the pain in his chest knocked him to his knees.

You should have waited, he thought. One more minute, Vicki, and I could have done it myself. Your hands would be clean, Vicki. I could have died happy, Vicki. I could have died not knowing.

You're a bitch, Vicki.

The Best of *Manhunt*

Now lie down, he told himself. Now go to sleep, just the way you planned it yourself. Nothing's different. And you can't get out, because you planned it this way. You're through.

Double indemnity. The bitch was going to collect double indemnity!

No, he thought. No.

It took him fifteen minutes to think of it. He had to find a way, and it wasn't easy. If they thought about murder they would have her, of course. She'd left prints all over the cold-bin door. But they would not be looking for prints, not the way things stood. They'd call it an accident and that would be that. Which was the trouble with setting things up so perfectly.

He could make it look like suicide. That might cheat her out of the insurance. He could slash his wrists or something, or—

No.

He could cheat her out of more than the insurance.

It took awhile, but he worked it out neatly. First he scooped up his cigarette butt and stuck it in his pants pocket. Then he scattered the ashes around. Step one.

Next he walked to the rear of the cold bin and took a meat cleaver from the peg on the wall. He set the cleaver on top of a hanging side of beef, gave the meat a push. The cleaver toppled over and plummeted to the floor. It landed on the handle and bounced.

He tried again with another slab of meat. He tried time after time, until he found the piece that was just the right distance from the floor and found just the spot to set the cleaver. When he nudged the meat, the cleaver came down, turned over once, and landed blade-down in the floor.

He tried it four times to make sure it would work. It never missed. Then he picked the cleaver from the floor, wiped his prints from the blade and handle with his apron, and placed the cleaver in position on top of the hunk of meat. It was a leg of lamb, the meat blood-red, the fat sickly white. He sat down on the floor, then stretched out on his back looking up at the leg of lamb. Good meat, he thought. Prime.

He smiled, tensed with pain from his chest and stomach, relaxed and smiled again. Not quite like going to sleep this way, he thought. Not painless, like freezing. But faster.

He lifted a leg, touched his foot to the leg of lamb. He gave it a gentle little push, and the cleaver sliced through the air and found his throat.

Afterword: The Graveyard Rats
Barry N. Malzberg

January 2019

Lawrence Block's Foreword to this anthology gives furious focus, *rallentando* if you will, to the experience of a first sale and also of the modest, elegant corruption and self-service of the Scott Meredith Literary Agency which ran the magazine from its offices and used it as a receptacle for their clients' manuscripts while simultaneously representing the magazine as an open market. There were other examples of such double-dealing in the Agency's history; a minor science fiction magazine, *Cosmos* was run from their offices, used as a dump market for its clients and edited by Larry Harris (later Laurence Janifer), who was all of 19. These two magazines were minor examples of the Agency's practice; in half-decade from the end of the 1950's to the mid-1960's the Agency was the exclusive supplier of manuscripts to a West Coast publisher, collecting 2K per manuscript and paying out $1250 to the authors which they also commissioned down to $1125. It was a merry business for the Agency and a pretty good one in fact for many of the writers, some would become (or already were) well known and one of them noted later "I was making 50K a year at the age of 25 before I was being told by veteran editors and publishers that it was impossible to embark upon a writing career and become—immediately—not only successful but rich."

Manhunt was one of a number of mystery digest magazines of the 50's, successor to the pre-television 30's and 40's pulps, which was generally regarded as close to the best of them if hardly the best-paying: Larry Block's three cents a word was in fact (because he was an Agency employee) at the top of the scale, the going rate was two cents a word and a look at the table of contents of this celebratory anthology indicates how many accomplished crime writers were willing to write for that. (Of course two cents a word in the mid-50's was effectively twenty cents a word today and by that standard the writers were making $500-$1000 in 2019 dollars for work which a practiced hand could write in an afternoon.) It was all about the money, it was in fact always about the money throughout the entire range of commercial fiction (quick definition: fiction written for money as opposed to fiction written for tenure or what the sf fans would call "egoboo," *i.e., ego boost*). The most prestigious literary quarterlies in the 1950's, *Sewanee Review, Hudson Review*, the new *Paris Review* were paying less than *Manhunt* let alone *Galaxy* or *Astounding Science Fiction*. It is a past which is easy to sentimentalize and essays like Larry Block's or my own made that an almost irresistible trap.

But a *trap* it was if the writers' ambition went much beyond relatively fast money and the commendation of peers; it was a trap because in terms of the ongoing cultural life of the planet or at least this fragment of the planet, the contents of *Manhunt* or *Astounding Science Fiction, Ellery Queen's Mystery Magazine* or *Alfred Hitchcock's Magazine* were effectively invisible. The two major annual anthologies of the short story, *O. Henry Prize Stories* and Martha Foley'd *Best American Short Stories* ignored the entire range of the commercial (or alternatively defined "genre") markets. No story from *Manhunt, Alfred Hitchcock, Astounding, Galaxy, Guilty, Pursuit,* was ever reprinted in either of those anthologies; none from these markets was ever listed in Foley's rather taunting "Roll of Honor," Ultimately, and over two decades, three stories from *Ellery Queen* and two from *The Magazine of Fantasy & Science Fiction* were reprinted in the Foley anthologies. An aggregate of maybe ten other stories might have been listed in Foley's taunting "Roll of Honor." A range, an age, a ferocious accumulation of narrative force and ferocity might in the view of those custodians not have existed at all.

In other venues I have written of my own ambition to write of "the buried life of the Continent", the enormous, steaming and not subterranean convulsions, the diet of obsession, racial hatred, self-hatred, self-enamorment turned to dreadful purposes, all of this which has emerged in every aspect of our political life but whose sources remain less examined in the "official", the "approved literature". You can get stray examples in the works of Flannery O'Connor or "The Five Forty-Eight" by Cheever, maybe in the gentility of Updike's "A Gift from the City", but if you really wanted to know (we science fiction people would mumble that the purpose of mainstream literature was to satisfy the needs of those who did *not* want to know) the real news was to be heard in the tormentings of Chuck Berry or Ray Charles. Rock and Roll was here to stay and so in the 50's for a while was *Manhunt* and its competitors who were trying to get the real story out in time to save us, to congeal somehow, material toward an understanding that we were fated to enact a Secret History which Martha Foley would never tell us.

Spillane had the news and, however crudely, he brought it to every precinct that would not lock him out; in the mid-fifties half of the copies of any paperback novel sold were by him, in very little time and with a kind of desperation born of greed, greed born of desperation, *Judged* and *Guilty* and the rest piled on and until television and the destruction of the American News Corporation, the major magazine distributor did them in, they had a splendid run. "Spillane and His Bloody Hammer," Christopher LaFarge called these magazines in one of his hi-falutin' essays for a hi-falutin' journal in 1954 and the fear of invasion which ran all through this essay ran through the popular and the "high" culture as well. With a tilted historian's perspective we can now see foreshadowed November 22, 1963 and all that it meant and didn't mean; the dreadful procession of our time is compacted in these magazines, this magazine, these stories. They are radiant with knowledge. They are riven with pain. *True Story* was hardly the only magazine that had the true story.